FIRED BY DEFIANT DREAMS, THEY LIVED A LEGEND OF COURAGE AND DESIRE. . . .

CONSTANCE—Passionate and headstrong, she denied her birthright for the fever of love.

ELIZABETH—Defying tradition to follow her heart, she demanded a price unbearable to pay.

TIERNEY—Endowed with the rare gifts of the ancient bards, still he would risk everything for Ireland—even the woman he adored.

SEANEEN—Firebrand and revolutionary, he raised a storm he couldn't quell.

TAHG AND WINSTON—Sons of devoted sisters, they were dangerous rivals and deadly enemies.

"A LUSHLY WRITTEN SAGA OF LOVE AND REBELLION AND CIVIL WAR."   —*Washington Post Book World*

"LARGER THAN LIFE"   —*The Boston Irish Echo*

"A CAST OF RICH CHARACTERS THAT DO HONOR TO [THE NOVEL'S] RICH MATERIAL."
                              —*Daily News* (Los Angeles)

Other books by Cathy Cash Spellman

Notes To My Daughters
So Many Partings
Paint the Wind

An Excess of Love

Cathy Cash Spellman

A DELL BOOK

Published by
Dell Publishing
a division of
Bantam Doubleday Dell Publishing Group, Inc.
666 Fifth Avenue
New York, New York 10103

This novel is a work of fiction. It includes historical characters as background for the story I wish to tell. Except for individuals well-known from the accounts of these times, the characters in these pages are the product of my imagination, and any resemblance to real individuals is unintended and entirely coincidental.

Grateful acknowledgment is made to the following for permission to use 9 lines from "Easter 1916" and 4 lines from "When You Are Old" by W. B. Yeats: Macmillan Publishing Company, from *The Poems of W. B. Yeats*, edited by Richard J. Finneran, copyright 1912 by Macmillan Publishing Co., Inc., renewed 1952 by Bertha Georgie Yeats. Michael B. Yeats and Macmillan London, Ltd. from *Collected Poems of W. B. Yeats*.

The trademark Dell® is registered in the U.S. Patent and Trademark Office.

ISBN: 0-440-12394-1

Reprinted by arrangement with Delacorte Press, New York, New York

Printed in the United States of America

Published simultaneously in Canada

August 1986

10 9 8 7 6 5 4 3

RAD

To my sister Conny:

For the comfort of your hand across
    the uneven years . . .
For always, always coming through,
    and the odds be damned—
For all the trust and love and laughter . . .
With all my heart, this book is yours.

Acknowledgments

A few very special people have lovingly helped to transform *An Excess of Love* from a story in my mind to a finished book. My heartfelt thanks to:

Carole Baron, my editor and friend, who, in working her intuitive and powerful magic with my books, has done more than anyone else to make my dreams come true.

Edith Heal Berrien, who helped me in so many ways, not least of which was by encouragement.

Richard Brown, who unselfishly shared his vast and affectionate knowledge of Michael Collins with me.

Marion R. Casey, whose extraordinary efforts and lovely insights made the journey from 1897 to 1923 accurate, fruitful, and, best of all, a pleasure.

Harry Cash, my father, who lovingly took so many burdens off my shoulders so I could write in peace . . . just as he has forever made my life infinitely better than it might have been.

Michael Collins of the Irish Consulate, who was kind enough to go out of his way to help me with my research whenever I asked.

Meryl Earl, who loves her sister as I do mine, and who took *An Excess of Love* under her wing in a very special way.

Jackie Farber, whose cheerful, warm, and encouraging words really made my day.

Isabel Geffner, whose enthusiasm, support, and friendship helped make the adventure of publishing joyous.

Bea Hurwitz, who kindly sought permission for me to use all those lovely quotes that Irishmen cannot live without.

Mort Janklow, who not only *believed* from the very beginning, but who generously transformed a wish into reality.

Johanna Lee, my forever friend, who lovingly kept my errant characters on the right path, just as she always does me.

Jean McClatchey Lenton, who arrived as an "angel unawares" and stayed long enough to become my friend.

Tommy Makem, to whom I am indebted for the story Tommy McGowan tells about O'Brien—and whose music has brought me more joy over the years than I could possibly recount.

Professor John McCarthy, who was kind enough to use his great knowledge of Irish history to keep me from going too far astray about the momentous events of this time period.

Karen Pinkman, who so lovingly kept me going through the bleak times. Had she not called me relentlessly every time my courage flagged, with both wisdom and encouragement, I would probably still be on page 164.

Caroline Shookhoff, Diane Moriarity, Cindy Rouff, and *Jennifer Lynch,* who typed heroically and organized against all odds.

Anne Sibbald, who, from the very beginning, added the beautiful spirit of friendship to the business of being published.

Bronwyn Spellman, who read, critiqued, and cheered me as only a loving daughter could and who did so much to encourage me to "keep on keeping on."

Cee Cee Spellman, who really came through when it counted, and who made the summer joyous with her humor, help, and love.

Charles Spicer, whose perception, advice, and kindness made the experience of being edited a rare pleasure.

To all the generous-spirited readers who wrote me so affectionately about *So Many Partings:* I'd like you to know that your kindness added something very special to my life.

A great many years ago my mother, *Catherine Gibbons Cash,* told me about Easter Week. She sang me the songs, recited the poetry, stirred me with the rhetoric. Had that seed never been planted, *An Excess of Love* might never have been written.

For that, as for all the other loving gifts she's given me, I'm more heartily grateful than I could ever say.

For my own dear husband, *Joe Spellman,* who held my hand so tightly through the dark times and laughed with me in the light, who understood when the world didn't, and never, ever stopped believing . . . there are no words adequate to express what's in my heart. I love you, Joe . . . more than everything.

And what if excess of love
Bewildered them till they died?
I write it out in a verse—
MacDonagh and MacBride
And Connolly and Pearse
Now and in time to be,
Wherever green is worn,
Are changed, changed utterly:
A terrible beauty is born.

William Butler Yeats
"Easter 1916"

PROLOGUE

∽ I always loved my sister. More than siblings are wont to do . . . more perhaps than the world could ever understand . . . but not more than she deserved.

Looking back now it's easy to see that everything about her tended to inspire superlatives . . . the *most* passionate, the *most* headstrong, the *most* loyal. She was the rarest soul I've ever known and, in the end, the gentlest of us all.

Constance FitzGibbon, she was born—with her high heart and her spirit deep as the bog and wild as the sea that lapped the strand beyond our childhood home. She was the best of us. Perhaps she was the best we mortals can ever be.

It isn't easy for me now—even after all the years that separate us—this telling of her story, considering my love for her, and the fact that her life has become the stuff of legend. How could she have become entangled in wilder schemes than I could ever dream? In schemes that some thought foolish and others glorious? I've asked myself that question countless times through all the long years—I am seventy-five years of age as I begin this memoir and have had ample time to ponder—but in truth I know the answer, for all the schemes she lived were honorable and courageous. My sister, you see, had always, even as a little girl, been both.

She was my junior by four years; thus, when she was born, I was already old enough to fancy myself her mother. Our own mother had died within three days of my sister's birth, so although both Constance and I had a governess, I took to the role of surrogate mother with immense enthusiasm and all the dignity of which a four-year-old is capable.

My mama had been frail as long as I could remember her, a slender wisp of a creature, not small, but so vulnerable as to seem transparent. My father loved her very much, but he was possessed of such a robust life force that my mother's frailty seemed by comparison all the more pronounced, and where I thought him perfect, I found her less so.

My father was a gargantuan presence, regally mustached as befitted a gentleman of his rank, with the stamp of the regiment in his posture and the unmistakable aura of aristocracy in his bearing. To say that I worshiped the man would be a grievous understatement. Worshiped more than loved, mind you, for his was too autocratic a presence to be truly loved.

I could understand, even as a child, why my mother adored Papa—his strength and feats of horsemanship and intellect were quite famous in his time, and he was handsome as a matinee idol. It seemed to me more difficult to understand his love for my mother—timid, tender blossom that she was. I'm ashamed to say she struck me as too sad and soft and bloodless; although I admired her grace and dignity, I longed for a mother who would provide a more monumental match for my peerless Papa. A Juno to his Jupiter would have seemed to me more appropriate, and in this heroic comparison I found her sadly wanting.

How unfair are the judgments of children. Later, when I was grown, I happened on my mother's diaries, and reading them through, I found her (to my sorrow, in having misjudged) a loving and courageous woman, doomed at the age of twenty-eight by an incurable illness. It was an outgrowth of the consumption she had contracted as a child in India, where her father had gone for a tour of duty, and the Irish climate had not acted felicitously on her condition. Never strong, she had nonetheless taken on the rigors of childrearing and the manifold duties of a large household—we had forty servants (if you counted the nine gardeners) in those days—because of her devotion to my father.

She seemed, in her diaries, an intrepid, warm and sturdy soul, entrapped in a porous vessel from which her life's strength drained relentlessly away. What I had mistaken for bloodlessness was no more than resignation to a fate that could not be outrun.

The doctor, it seems, had told her that the birth of another child would be her doom, but she had kept the news conscientiously from my father; whether out of wifely duty or optimism I do not know. Whatever the motivation—perhaps it was as simple as love—she conceived. And so into the world that twenty-first day of March 1879 my sister and dearest friend Constance FitzGibbon was born. I loved my older brother Desmond dearly, but the bond between me and my sister was, from the first, of sterner stuff.

She was my treasure from the moment I saw her in Nurse's sturdy arms, a tiny red-faced mite with a fringe of silken hair. Nurse placed her in my lap, a squiggling buntingful of life; the miraculous fingers curled around my own with an astounding strength and I somehow knew that she was mine. Not my mother's and father's, mind you; they were merely the instruments of her physical construction. But the life-force, the spirit, the perfect, glorious little person I held in my arms was mine.

People later said I doted on my newborn sister because of the trauma of losing my mama, and I let them think that, for they allowed me more latitude with the baby because they pitied me. But in truth my mother's death had nothing whatsoever to do with my devotion.

Con was a wondrous child. Headstrong, funny and with a lightning wit; an old/young creature with a passionate nature and a sunny disposition; a combination not at all contradictory, despite the picture one has of people of high passions being brooding and contemplative.

She was anything but that. She could ride like the child of centaurs from the moment she could walk. She took chances that sent the grooms into agonies of apprehension for her safety, yet she seemed protected by angels, for never in her life was she so much as bruised in the effort of horsemanship.

My father was enthralled by her *joie de vivre,* her robust, hearty spirit, her horsemanship, her love of hunting and all outdoor sports—rare qualities in a little girl in those times.

Now, looking back across the years, I cannot help but wonder if all the fatherly camaraderie, which seemed so good for the child in its time, was in reality what set her on the briar path she was to tread. Had he never taught her to shoot, might it be that I would never have seen her as she was that fearful Easter Friday morning at the barricade, commanding a troop of ragtag and bobtail rebels in the last desperate days of the Uprising? Despite the more than thirty years that have passed by since, I can see her clearly now, as she was then, tall and spare, in her soldier's motley, a blood-soaked bandage wound unnoticed around her ribs, a rifle at her shoulder, carried with the casual pride of one who knows full well how to use it. An ancient warrior queen like Maeve, she seemed to me that day; and yet she cried as we embraced, fearing never again to see each other on this side of eternity.

Had she not been taught by my father to compete and to fancy herself any man's equal, could she have had the courage to defy an empire? Or is it simply that all our fates are in God's hidden place and my sister, like the rest of us, merely went about the business of fulfilling her destiny, with never a choice possible but to do so. Perhaps the why of it doesn't matter now. . . .

But, I get ahead of myself. What matter the "why" of her growing up to be the wild swan that she was? In truth, there is only one need that matters—that I tell her story.

And so to begin . . . the tale of her life and of mine, of all those whom I have loved, living and dead—and, of course, of that strange fated place, or state of mind, that wove the threads to the tangled skein of all our destinies—Ireland.

Our childhood was a strange one, Con's, Desmond's and mine. Our mother dead too young, our father so busy with the practice of the law and the running of a great estate that he had little time for us. For the most part, we were at the disposal of nannies and servants so that our very upper-class childhood was spent in the company of the lower classes; we learned a comfort with them that remained with us always.

We were tutored from eight until noon each day and free from the noon meal on. As the kitchen was the hub of the household, that is where we gravitated. There we shared all the tidbits of gossip that servants thrive on . . . there we learned about the Irish. We heard of flowers that must be strewn on the doorsteps on the first of May to keep out the fairies, and of the need to tell the cows when someone dies. We learned of banshees who foretell death and of the wee folk who live in the hollow hills. We heard the lyrical cadence of the Irish speakers and discovered the terrors of hellfire and damnation that seem to beset Catholics so much more than other folk.

My father was a barrister of great renown who knew nothing of such things. From him we learned what was to be expected of children of our social class. He favored order in all matters, including those of his household, and ran every aspect of his life with the precision of a Swiss timepiece. Thus, at my mother's death he had employed a precise woman to manage his household precisely; but as she preferred management of accounts and servants to management of children, we soon found that by behaving ourselves modestly and obeying the rules, we three could more or less govern ourselves for the afternoons, a freedom Desmond and I had not enjoyed when our mother was alive.

Neither Con nor I had much difficulty with the regulations of the household, but Desmond, being male, tended to impetuous behavior, so he bore the brunt of Mrs. McGinty's "management" on a regular basis.

Father supervised our education, which was rigorous, and included both Greek and Latin. Contrary to the custom of the time, he insisted that Con and I be educated identically with Desmond. People said it was easier for him to do that than to employ a separate tutor for us, but I believe it was conviction, not convenience, that prompted this educational largesse.

Father also undertook our education in upper-class pursuits like riding and the hunt. Desmond was good, but Con was better, and I, who had no great talent in either area, was left to my own devices while my siblings went off to ride with Papa several times a week.

To even up the tally of hours he spent with each of us, Papa would set aside time on these same evenings to read aloud with me, my very favorite pastime. If it cannot be said that I had other noticeable talents, I could read aloud quite competently. Since Con and Desmond found such recitation tedious, I had my precious private moments with my father. In short, we each received from him a special part of himself, and since we thought him so remarkable, we were grateful for the gift.

Desmond's life was far harder than Con's or mine, for men like my father make monumental demands of a son that they don't of a daughter. And, too, Des's temperament—explosive, adventurous, irreverent—was so different from Father's judiciousness that they were volatile as flint and tinder.

Nonetheless, we had happy childhoods for the most part . . . childhoods in which our love for each other was very strong indeed. Con, Des and I were the family universe, with our father an imposing, God-like person on its periphery. In retrospect that perception of "we three against the world" figured strongly in our later destinies.

There's little more that I need tell you of our childhood, except to say that I was by far the least interesting of the three of us. I was docile and bookish, I had no great desire toward rebellion, I liked life and I worshiped my sister and brother. I fully intended to grow up doing everything that was expected of me. My plan, if you could call it that, was to marry a man my father approved of, to govern a large household, produce lovely docile children and somewhere along the line to write novels and poetry. If there was any passion in me in those days, it was a passion for the written word.

My sister and brother, on the other hand, made plans by the hour for adventures they would seek. Des would join the Foreign Legion or a pirate crew; he would visit the Suleiman Empire and trade with the Sultan of Baghdad. He would follow the Nile to its source and hunt polar bears at the Arctic Circle. His dreams were irrepressible and feisty and his swashbuckling personality, even in childhood, made it all seem plausible.

Con would lead the Sligo Harriers and compose grand opera. She would ride astride, instead of sidesaddle; live in Paris and practice free love; have illegitimate children and call them all her nieces and nephews. Kings would vie for her favors and she would die rich, on an island in the South Seas where the natives would bury her body in a sacred volcano.

Even I thought I was a bore by comparison.

So we grew up clannish and steeped in the juices of our own imaginations. When Des went off to school, Con and I were disconsolate. Father spent far less time with us once we'd left childhood behind—whether because he felt we were "finished" and no longer needed tutelage, or because he felt a certain discomfort with us once we'd grown to womanhood, I could never be sure. Whatever the reason, my sister and I were very much left to ourselves during our teenage years and, as a result, we developed a certain independence of spirit that played a part in what I wish to tell you.

How can I adequately describe the closeness between Con and me? We were not alike, she fiery, I passive; she reaching beyond our world, I content with it. Yet we were inseparable in spirit. A Gypsy tinker told us once that we had been together in a thousand lifetimes and we never doubted it. We understood each other, not with intellectual effort, but with inner knowledge, for the bond we shared was of the spirit. The world somehow consisted of the two of us—and then all the rest of humanity. We were the observers together and the arbiters; we looked at life through a special set of lenses that only we possessed. We were scrupulously honest with each other, which made for an abiding trust. If Con needed, I gave; if I needed, she did. There was nothing we couldn't say and nothing we wouldn't share.

I loved my brother Desmond dearly, as did Con. But he was male and, as such, a mysterious being, full of hard-edged rules of manhood that could not be transgressed. Con and I had no such rules to restrict our love for each other. One of my favorite childhood poems to read aloud was one by R. L. Stevenson that ended with the lines:

> O Lord, Behold our family here assembled,
> Give us peace, gaiety and the quiet mind
> That we may be brave in peril,
> Constant in all changes of fortune,
> And that down to the gates of death
> We may be loyal and love one another.

It was our motto, you might say. Something pledged in childhood and remembered in age. It was also prophetic, of course, but in youth we had no way of knowing it would be Con's epitaph as well.

I sometimes think everything started on a certain day in the year 1897. . . . I was at the time newly married to Lord Edmond Manningham, Earl of Sligo, who was our neighbor to the east at Manningham Castle; as befit a twenty-two-year-old girl in such circumstances, I thought I was in love. My husband was considerably older than I (thirty-eight to my twenty-two, to be precise) and he held an old and distinguished Anglo-Irish title that went back to the time when the English had first set foot in our lovely land.

It is an extraordinary story, that of how the English came to be in Ireland, and I must digress for just a moment to tell you a bit of it so that you may understand the history of my husband's clan.

In the year 1169 there were four provinces in Ireland, just as there are today. But in those times they had kings, one each for Ulster, Munster, Leinster and Connacht. One of these provincial rulers sought the aid of Henry II of England in a local dispute and offered him vassalage in return. In light of what has happened since, I expect I needn't tell you the outcome of inviting the English into Ireland, where they have managed to remain for the ensuing seven centuries. Curiously all this tale had begun right there in County Sligo, at Breffni Castle, a place quite well preserved to this day, despite the tragedy of seven hundred years' duration that began there.

At any rate, I've digressed into history only to explain how the Manninghams, my in-laws, came to receive their Irish land grant from the King of England. For, you see, once Ireland had been made subject to England in a mad extension of that original vassalage, England felt the need to keep the Irish natives subjugated. Thus, generous grants of land and titles were handed out to those Englishmen who had distinguished themselves in battle or in some other service to the Crown, and the Ascendency Class of Anglo-Irish came to be. Rich, powerful, Anglo-educated and Anglo-inclined they were, but transplanted forever to Ireland as landlords to the very people whose property they had usurped.

The Manninghams were of the Ascendency Class I've just described. So, indeed, were my brother, sister and I, although in our family (as later events proved beyond doubt) the Anglicanization seemed not to have taken proper hold.

FitzGibbon Hall, where Con and I were born, was the seat of the landlord for a considerable acreage around and my family was well thought of in the county. There was a family legend that Red Henry FitzGibbon, the ancestor who had been deeded the land by the Crown had been given the right to as much territory as his prize hawk could fly over. If that was the case of it, the hawk had been a hardy bird, indeed. Dozens of tiny farms paid rents or bartered produce for the right to work the land, and Merrion FitzGibbon, my father, was a decent landlord to his tenants, by the standards of the area.

Being good-natured by inclination, my family had shown considerable restraint during the Famine and after, a time when most of the owners of the "great houses" had ousted the poor farmers for missed rent payments owing to the failure of the potato crop. My great-grandfather had shown a largesse and leniency which had inspired the locals to name him Good Fitz-Gibbon, a fact which stood the family in excellent stead through my own generation.

My husband's family, the Manninghams, had been less obliging and were considerably less revered. Edmond's grandfather, Lord George Manningham—having torn the poor farmers from their meager homes and personally supervised the sordid proceedings while his overseer crashed down their pathetic dwellings with a battering ram—went to his eternal reward with the knowledge that he had been personally responsible for reducing a great many families to wandering and starvation. And he went to his reward early as a result.

Lord George's ill-placed enthusiasm for cruelty had earned him a well-placed bullet from the rebels who rode boldly up to the french doors of his dining room one night shouting, "Thus always to tyrants," in Gaelic, and shot him through the heart as he carved his roast at the head of the table.

Needless to say, the Manninghams were not supporters of Fenianism or of any other attempt on the part of the Irish to oust the English from their soil.

At the time of our marriage, I believe my husband was quite content with the match he had made in me. Both my sister and I were considered prize catches in Sligo, and, for that matter, in Ireland. We were pretty and refined—I had had one novella published thanks to the help of a school chum of Desmond's who was the scion of a Dublin publishing family. While my book had sold an infinitesimal number of copies, it had been kindly received by the critics, so I fancied myself a writer. My sister was a noted horsewoman and musician—to say nothing of the fact that although our brother, Desmond, would inherit the family castle and the bulk of the money, we were, nonetheless, rich.

Edmond Manningham was a charming, erudite and proper gentleman, or so he seemed to me in those days. He had courted me tenderly and promised me a lovely life as mistress of a great estate and mother of well-bred children who would inherit a considerable fortune. Looking back, it was hardly enough to constitute the basis of a marriage, but girls knew little in those days of what marriage meant. So in my usual docile fashion I had married and was feeling quite smug about my newfound connubial knowledge.

Con and I still managed to spend time together, and on that day when everything changed we had planned an outing. . . .

It was a rare silver afternoon. The rain whispered softly before the rising storm; the trees at the edge of Sligo Bay stood listeningly still, as if all the world awaited an imminent event of great importance.

We had been walking on the strand together, dipping our youthful feet into the icy waters, just for the joy of the lowering day and the sensual pleasure of the sand between our toes; our ruffled petticoats hung damp from the waves' assault and tiny sand crystals clung to the fabric's eyelit rim.

Con was eighteen on that day that changed our lives. The rain that was the catalyst, sweet as it was, sent us scampering for shelter; the haven which fate provided was a cottage on the edge of the wild sea. It was perched with one foot on the crest of a small rocky promontory and one, it seemed, on the damp strand itself.

It was, like all Irish cottages of its ilk, made of whitewashed stone and mud-wall, with a pleasant thatch and a chimneyful of fine turf smoke that suggested both warmth and safe harbor. So in we went, with all the aplomb of the gentry, who assume they are welcome anywhere that chance finds them.

The cottage was occupied by a young man and a woman of middle age, although, like all the poor, the woman seemed fully twenty years older than her age must have been. Her husband was a fisherman, she said, off at his boat—and this was their son, Tierney O'Connor, a fine strapping lad who helped his father at his chores when he wasn't off dreaming of going to Dublin to be a poet. On and on she babbled in the merry jargon of the West, besprinkled as it is with the Gaelic that makes it so different in cadence and meter from any English spoken elsewhere on earth.

But by that time I was no longer listening to her words, for rather was I watching the two young people in the dim firelit room, who seemed to need no light to see each other. There beside me in that dirt-floored hovel stood my glorious gazelle-like sister in her Ascendency finery—the price of the half of which could have fed this family for a year—and the handsomest young man I had ever seen. A fact which apparently wasn't lost upon Constance.

He was wonderfully tall, and broad as a Druid oak. Dark, wild curls, I could almost call them, fell in profusion over his forehead and the collar of his shirt; his eyes were the color of the calm sea after a storm, and there was an inner beauty about him that hounds me to this day. The beauty of character and integrity and courage, I could call it now, from the vantage point of the years; but on that day nearly a half century ago, it simply seemed the beauty of a soul born out of its proper time and place. For surely this was a nobleman like the Whistling Gypsy, who had hidden his royal heritage in order to woo fair maid on his own merits before revealing his aristocracy.

Constance and Tierney stood in an embrace of eyes as if the rest of us had been swallowed by a feary cairn. The vision of them—she looking up entranced into those fair, brooding eyes, and he looking down from his fine rugged height, as enraptured as if Athena herself had entered the place—will be with me forever. So perfectly beautiful they seemed, and so strangely in tune from the first moment.

I, too, was young, and thought myself in love, so I was able to recognize the symptoms, when they manifested themselves in the cottage that rainy afternoon.

What am I saying? None but the blind, deaf and dumb could have missed the lighting of that conflagration. Con and Tierney finally managed to remember there were others in the world (at least as much as they ever would again) and we all sat down for tea.

If you've never been in an Irish mud-walled cottage, perhaps I'd best explain that tea there should not be confused with tea at Buckingham Palace.

All over Sligo these cottages were the same: dirt-floored,

thick-walled against the ocean's worst, a tiny window cut here or there (too many would let in danger and the cold), a huge stone hearth that sent billows of turf smoke into the atmosphere of the badly ventilated space and on up to blacken the thatch that held out the sky. Such thatching also tended to harbor as many field creatures as could seek comfort there, so that their squeaking and rustling added another animated dimension to the cottage's persona.

Whatever paltry sticks of furniture there were—a chair or two, a table, a bed and nightstand in the wealthiest of such households—would have been constructed by the tenant himself, according to his skills. Often there would be a pile of straw in the hearth corner for the chickens and the pigs to lie in—if the folk were lucky enough to have them. I saw no such wealth of livestock here.

Mrs. O'Connor made tea on the hob, pouring it into crockery mugs of ancient date and apologizing profusely over the fact that there was no cow anymore, so there was none but bull's milk (the clabber to be gleaned from skimming oatmeal in the pot) in the house.

"You'll not apologize for being poor, Mammy," said Tierney in a deep voice, full of character. "Our poverty is honest and I'll not apologize to an Englishwoman for it." The articulate resonance and conviction with which it was said thrilled me, in a way. Con, too.

She said, "We aren't English at all, Mr. O'Connor. My sister and I are FitzGibbons and have only Irish blood in our veins."

"But not Fenian blood I suspect, Miss FitzGibbon," he responded, a little less belligerently, I thought.

"I don't know very much about the Fenians, Mr. O'Connor . . ." said my sister, who knew full well about them, at least from the gentry's point of view.

"That could be remedied . . ." said our gallant host, who began at that very moment our education about Ireland.

My God, but he was eloquent—and passionate and full of knowledge. We finally emigrated from the cottage, having thanked Tierney's mother for her hospitality. We walked the remainder of the afternoon away upon the damp sand of the bay, listening, listening . . . to a tale that changes you if you hear it aright, that changes you utterly.

I was somewhat less vulnerable to it all than Con—or was it simply that I was less courageous? I was well on my way to a settled life that would leave all thought of revolution far behind. Or so I thought. So much for man's plans versus God's. ∽

PART ONE

Con and Tierney

How many loved your moments of glad grace,
And loved your beauty with love false or true,
But one man loved the pilgrim soul in you,
And loved the sorrows of your changing face.

WILLIAM BUTLER YEATS

1 Con left the house directly after breakfast. She tended to think of it as *her* house, although she would not inherit, for she of all the children loved it best.

FitzGibbon Hall was a rambling affair of ancient crenellated battlements and Georgian graces. The west wing was the old keep, tenanted in the late 1800s only by mice and ravens and any other wild things intrepid enough to brave the intransigent ivy. The north wing was comprised of a still habitable long hall, replete with antique arms, colorful heraldry and the staggeringly massive heads of two monstrous Irish elk, a breed long extinct.

This long hall was a sort of bridge between the ancient and the modern parts of the house, for the remainder of the Hall was a Palladian structure begun in the late 1700s and furbished relentlessly with all the skilled labor money could buy for the better part of a century. It was a grand old house and Constance loved it with a special fervor.

For as long as she could remember, she and Beth had sat together in the Hall's morning room every day after breakfast. The room had been their sanctuary. A place in which to enjoy each other's company, or that of the other young ladies who came to call on visiting days. In truth, no one's company ever pleased them as much as each other's.

The morning room was drenched perpetually in sunlight, a feat of some accomplishment in the dour climate of Ireland. Great french windows faceted the octagonal room from floor to ceiling, so that one could see a vast expanse of lawn and formal garden blanketing its way to Sligo Bay; and one could hear, for the better part of the year, the chatter of a dozen species of birds that nested in the trees outside. Trees whose ancient foliage draped the windows in such a fashion that light filtered through them in lacy filigrees to dance playful patterns upon the polished floors and the whitened walls within.

The room had seemed sadly silent and lonely to Con since her sister's marriage. They had been so uncommonly close in thought and deed, despite their differences in temperament, that the first weeks after the wedding had been blighted with loneliness and a worrisome sense of final loss.

Constance wrapped her cloak about her shoulders, grateful that this day seemed to promise fair weather. She was tall and slim, but with an athletic exuberance about her; she never walked, but rather strode ahead, as if, by her very verve, to challenge nature and the accepted mode.

Her light brown hair was long and electric; she wore its abundant waves pulled back from her face and casually clipped at the temples as if she had no time for feminine frills, nor need of them either.

She had a face that matched her body in strength, square-jawed and determined, but with a surprising softness and beauty about it that echoed the contradictions of her personality.

She hesitated for a moment, inhibited by a sudden sense of the madness of what she intended, then she shook off the unwelcome feeling and set out toward the sea. She had decided to walk the pleasant mile to the strand, to give herself time for the internal debate.

Con had been at war with herself for the three days since she and Beth had stumbled on the cottage and its inhabitants. It was insane, of course, to go back . . . to seek out that handsome young man; but he had filled her mind from the first moment with enticing question marks.

Con covered the verdant ground between the Hall and the edge of the meadow rapidly; then, turning right at the bottom of the hill, she left sight of the Big House and headed toward the Bay, her mind and body restless with anticipation. She had wakened this morning knowing unequivocally that she would see him today.

Tierney O'Connor sat at the water's edge knotting the nets his father relied on to bring in the fish from the cold waters of Sligo Bay. This was the last day he could afford to linger over the task, for he was needed on his father's boat. He had been hoping the girl from the Hall would return to the strand. In fact, from the moment he had first seen her in the cabin he had thought of little else.

It was ridiculous, of course. For a fisherman to dream of friendship with such a lady was the height of absurdity—but nonetheless she had piqued both his desire and his curiosity. She was intriguing in a different way from the girls he knew, the diffident, well-meaning, ignorant girls, unschooled in any of the graces he had always dreamed possible. That was it: she was someone out of his indefinable dreams. The dreams that made him write poetry, that made him long for things that had no place in a fisherman's life; the dreams that had caused him to join the Irish Republican Brotherhood.

"Mr. O'Connor!" Con's voice carried over the sounds of the water and startled him from his daydream. "Mr. O'Connor, is that you? I'd so hoped to find you here!"

Tierney scrambled up from the entangling web of damp nets and, wiping his hand self-consciously on his trousers, he moved toward the elegant young woman. He was tall and muscular, his body the product of large forebears and a lifetime of physical labor. She saw that he moved with a certain comfort with his environment that could easily be mistaken for grace.

"Be careful there, Miss FitzGibbon," he called to her with concern. " 'Tis slippery on those rocks. The seaweed catches in them and you'll lose your footing if you're not careful."

She reached out to the man, to maintain her balance. His rough hand closed on hers and she felt the strength of him spread through her like laudanum. His features were less regular than she remembered, more rugged, less handsome. But there was a maleness about him that was palpable and unutterably attractive.

"Why aren't you out to sea, Mr. O'Connor?" she managed, as he helped her find her footing.

"If you want the truth of it, lass, I've been waiting for you to return." The same interesting smile she had seen in the cabin played at his lips and she thought again that she had never seen a man so arresting.

Con threw back her head and laughed aloud at the unexpected honesty of the reply, a lovely merry sound against the sea. There was no shyness in her bearing, he noted, no undue forwardness either. Just a lovely confidence. But then she had everything to be confident about.

Tierney noticed the golden glints in her hair, which hung long and loose from the clasps that held it. He saw in her face an evenness of feature that made her, if not quite beautiful, lovely and memorable. But there was pugnacity, too. And an amused determination.

"I've come to hear about your Fenian," said Constance, as she watched the man push the nets aside to make a seat for her.

He looked up hastily from the task and said, "Ah now, isn't that a shame, then. I had hoped you would come to see *me.*" Constance FitzGibbon, used to the casual flatteries of the gallant young men who came to court her, was startled enough to respond with honesty.

"I did come to see *you,* Mr. O'Connor. I've intended to come back here since we left you three days ago."

He nodded, as if he had expected the answer, and looked out toward the sea. "When I was a lad, I used to come here with my da, to mend the nets and patch the sails and such. But I was a daydreamer, and like as not he'd find me sitting with the work in my lap and my mind a thousand miles away, over the seas or under them. My head filled with words struggling to fashion themselves into poetry." Tierney looked up at her as if to see if she was interested. He motioned her to sit beside him, and holding back her long skirt to keep the worst of the wet sand from it, she did so.

He laughed ruefully. "You can imagine how happy it made my da to think that he'd sired, not a fine burly boyo to help haul in the wee fishes, but some changeling who was filled with dreams to the point of incompetency."

He leaned back on one elbow and looked into the girl's face, which gave her a chance to study his. "I told him once I wanted to go to Dublin to be a poet. 'God help us,' he said. 'I'll have your mother pray you get over such a daft notion before anyone hears of it.'" Tierney chuckled a little. "He didn't quite mean it, of course. But almost."

"What kinds of things do you write about, Mr. O'Connor?" she asked curiously. He had a good face, she'd decided. Rougher hewn than the ones she was used to. But a good face nonetheless.

"Irish things, mostly. Wild things. Patriotic ramblings and

stories of the ancient myths. Tales of Celtic gods and goddesses, of heroes and saints and sinners . . . all the usual things that stir an Irishman." He seemed brooding and good-humored simultaneously, an oddly provocative combination.

"Will you tell me these stories?" she asked.

"I shall tell you the stories and anything else you'd like to know," he said, looking at her again with that same disturbing intensity. It didn't seem flirtation, but something else that was in his gaze. "I was born with a caul, you see," he said quickly, as if to explain, "and my mother says I've always been able to see things others can't." Con couldn't tell for sure if he was just being forward, yet he seemed earnest enough.

Tierney was quiet for a moment, watching her closely, as if deciding if it were wise to say what he felt. Then he said quite seriously, "Wouldn't it be grand, Miss FitzGibbon, if we never told each other anything but the truth? For all our lives, only the truth."

"Are we planning to know each other so long a time then, Mr. O'Connor?" she asked, surprised by the intimacy of the statement.

"Didn't you feel that we would from the first of it?" he asked, oddly. "As if we'd always known each other and always would?"

She laughed again, nervously, disconcerted by the question, and shook her head wonderingly. "As a matter of fact I did, Mr. O'Connor. If we must always tell the truth of things to each other, I must admit to you that I did feel precisely that."

"Whether 'tis so or not, Constance FitzGibbon," he continued, before she had time to respond, "I have the feeling you and I are meant to be friends to one another. Absurd as that may sound," he added and laughed self-effacingly.

With that Tierney got up from the rocks he'd been seated on and, running his fingers through his thick hair in a gesture she had thought winsome when she first saw it in the cabin, he offered her his hand. "Forgive me if I seem forward in what I've said." He spoke quietly. "It wasn't my intention to offend you."

"And you have not done so," she replied.

"Will you walk with me, then, and let me tell you of the ancient heroes?"

"I will, indeed, Mr. O'Connor."

He smiled a little at the immediate reply.

"And will you call me Tierney, so we needn't be so formal in our wanderings together?"

She laughed at the gentle freedom of the man. "My name is Constance," she answered him. "I'll call you Tierney, if you'll call me by my Christian name as well."

He stood back and regarded her with a quizzical eye. "I think not, lass," he said at length. " 'Tis too Saxon a name for so fair a lady. You shall be Con to me, from this day forward. 'Tis the look of a Fenian warrior you have, and not a Protestant. Conn the Hundred-Fighter or Connla, the son of Cuchulain—the old names suit you more." His eyes were merry when he spoke. "Or perhaps I'll call you Beauty. 'Twould be the most accurate."

She tilted her head to one side, her eyes narrowing quizzically. Surely no one could mistake the flirtatiousness of *that* statement.

He smiled at her when she didn't answer him. Then, picking up a smooth pebble, he skipped it lightly out over the water. "Do you not know of Cuchulain's battle with Connla at all then?" he asked suddenly.

She shook her head to say no. She felt confused, tipped off balance by this man; she was unused to the feeling.

"Ah, then I must tell you the tale, for it's one of my favorites." Tierney closed his eyes as he began the storytelling, his deep voice warm as the sun on the sand. It seemed to Con a curiously vulnerable gesture, as if he, too, had to collect himself after their interchange.

"Cuchulain," he began, "was the mightiest of the great warriors of the Red Branch Knights, in the time of Conchubar the King. He had a wife named Emer, whom he left behind so that he might roam over the world's rim with his knightly companions; and he left her with a fine young son whose name was Connla."

They began to walk while Tierney spoke, as if the momentum of the story propelled them somehow into motion.

"Now Emer was jealous of Cuchulain, for she'd heard that he'd taken another woman to his bed. So Emer planned that Connla would avenge her. As soon as the lad was full grown, she sent him to restore her honor by challenging his father to single combat."

Tierney's voice in storytelling seemed more musical than in ordinary speech, and Con saw that he was caught up in the old tale. As the story grew more animated, he reached out for her hand and held it briefly in his own. She felt the momentary warmth and strength of him in the clasp, before he dropped her hand self-consciously and went on with the story.

"You see, Con, both Cuchulain and his son were bound by the same Druid gaesa . . . a spell was on them so that neither could tell his own name to the man he challenged in battle. Thus, when Connla provoked Cuchulain to a duel, the man had no way to know he fought his only son.

"Your face reminds me of someone I once loved," said Cuchulain to the boy as the battle wore on, and he asked the lad to yield. But Connla continued the fight until Cuchulain struck him a fatal blow.

"The old warrior was strangely moved by the boy's courage and daring. He loosened the lad's tunic, and found on his breast an amulet that he, himself, had given Connla at his birth. Only then did the great warrior recognize his son, too late to save him."

Con listened in fascination to the emotion in Tierney's voice as he told the tale. There was something very special about a man who could be affected so by a story. Such sensitivity seemed so at odds with his appearance that the puzzle of the man deepened for her as he continued.

"Cuchulain, realizing what he had done, went mad with grief!

"And Conchubar, fearing Cuchulain might, in his rage, slay them all, had his Druids cast a spell on the weeping giant.

"For three days the Druids chanted runes into the agonized warrior's ear, and on the morning of the fourth day, Cuchulain rose in an enchantment. He heard his own name called amidst the sounds of battle, and, in his delirium fought the unrelenting sea."

Con heard the unmistakable poetry in Tierney's voice and, warmed by it, she turned to face him. He looked down from his height at her upturned face with such intensity in his gaze that, hardly knowing she intended to do so, she lifted her chin toward him, expecting to be kissed.

But instead Tierney reached his large callused hand to her face and lifted back the windblown strands from her cheek with astounding gentleness. He said in a low husky voice, "I'll not be taking liberties with you, Con FitzGibbon."

"I would not have thought it a liberty, man, had you kissed me," she replied, stung by his refusal and her own desire. "I myself have chosen to be alone here with you, and I myself made it clear to you that I wanted to be kissed." She could hear the petulance in her own voice and was embarrassed by it.

He looked troubled by her annoyance and after a moment of thought said, "When I kiss you, Con FitzGibbon, and kiss you I will, it must be because I have something more to offer you than a fisherman's cottage!" He reached for her hand unexpectedly and, pressing her fingers to his lips as if they were sacred things, he smiled at her.

Con shook her head wonderingly at the curious behavior, her own, as much as his. What kind of strange conversation was this? What kind of man was this fisherman-poet who seemed able to unbalance her so effortlessly? There was an earthiness about him that was unnerving and damnably attractive. His hands were work-worn, his clothes shabby, but there was nothing shabby about his mind. What was wrong with her that he seemed infinitely more attractive than the polished perfection of the other men she knew? The men who called on her were all cut from the same cloth, well-educated, well-bred, dandified and arrogant in their male superiority. This man was simply a *man* . . . what an intriguing idea!

Con walked with Tierney to the edge of the beach and then as far into her family's demesne as she thought it safe for him to go, lest any of the farmhands see and tattle to her father.

She went back to the manor house in a turmoil of curiosity and anticipation. She told herself that a friendship with a penniless fisherman was utterly unthinkable—knowing that the fact didn't matter to her in the least.

⌁ Constance began to rendezvous with Tierney whenever he could sneak away to be with her. He worked hard at the fishing with his father and brothers and there was little time for leisure; yet they managed to find time for each other.

There was a great change in my sister as the summer progressed. She began to study Irish history, earnestly scouring our library for material, dragging home badly written rebellious propaganda from God knows where, talking late and early of the injustices she was uncovering.

She fussed about her appearance in a new way, too. Always

pretty, she had worried little about her looks; now I caught her at the mirror whenever we were together, fussing over her clothes and pinching her already rosy cheeks to make them glow.

God, but she was happy, and Tierney was the cause of it. She had found in him both friend and confidant, it seemed . . . and more, she had found a cause into which she could throw her passionate nature, for his love for Ireland was intense and she was caught up in it from the first.

I paid it all relatively little mind in the beginning, for I was newly busy with the duties of wifehood, but as the warm months wore on it became apparent that this was no infatuation that would be easily dispelled and I began to worry about where it would lead them. And, too, the closer she grew to Tierney, the less she confided in me. She had a right to her privacy, of course, but I rankled at the exclusion. I told myself it was simple fear for her safety that upset me. In truth, I felt left out for the first time.

I was relieved when my brother Desmond came home from Trinity near the summer's end, for I wanted to seek his advice about what was happening. I was determined that we three spend time together, despite his busy social schedule. Des was finishing his last year of university and was being sought after by every mother with a marriageable daughter in the county round. He had been besieged with party invitations and was glad to escape with us for a day of riding and a picnic.

My brother Desmond was two years my senior, and as handsome a figure of a man as you'd want to see. He was dark-haired and blue-eyed and he sported an elegant mustache. An obvious product of the Armada that had sunk off the Sligo coast, or so we used to tease him. Only a dalliance on the part of some distant ancestress with a wild Spanish grandee, we asserted, could have produced that arresting combination of Castilian and Hibernian good looks that had set hearts aflutter in every county between ours and Dublin.

My brother's only fault that I can recall was a certain impulsiveness and arrogance, which I think went hand in hand with his station. The arrogance of privilege, power, money, and position gives to a young man of a certain temperament a daredevil quality. It's an attitude which says, "I can dare anything and win, for the gods are on my side." It was this very impetuosity

—to say nothing of his better qualities like courage, honor and a desire for justice—which later propelled Desmond into the cause of Irish freedom. Although, when he arrived home that summer, we had no way of knowing what the future would hold.

We stopped to rest and sat down on the ground under a shady arbutus tree, all three of us in high spirits.

"Have you met Con's fisherman?" I asked my brother, knowing he had and anxious for a male appraisal.

"Aye, I've met him indeed," said Des soberly. "And others like him in Dublin, since I've been there."

"What do you mean by that?" asked Con sharply. There was *no one* in the world like Tierney as far as she was concerned.

"Don't misunderstand me, Constance," he said hastily. "I know how enticing they are to women, these rebels. And to be honest, I liked the man. But the fact remains that he's an unsuitable match for you and nothing either of you can do will change that in the least."

Con looked angry, hurt, or both, but she said nothing, and Des went on. "Playing with fire there, Constance, dear. The way you two look at each other . . . why, there's no place for such a flirtation to lead except disaster." He sounded very brotherly and concerned. Des tended to speak in fragments of sentences when he was unsettled.

"He's a lovely man, Des," Con said finally in response, trying to control her temper. "He's more honest . . . less bogged down by pretensions and rules and regulations than anyone I know. I like everything about him."

"And he's also considerably less bogged down by breeding and money, Constance! And quite unsuitable because of it. If you were a man you could just have an affair, and be done with your little flirtation. But you're a woman . . ." He let the thought trail off.

"What *do* you intend, Con?" I asked, genuinely hoping she'd have a sensible answer, glad it was at last being spoken of.

"I don't know, exactly, Beth," she replied. "I like the strength of him and the lack of pretensions, I suppose. And I'm intrigued by what he tells me about Ireland. I've never seen anyone so caught up in a Cause . . ."

"Are you absolutely certain you aren't just intrigued because

he's such forbidden fruit?" asked Des. It was a question on both
our minds, but I would never have voiced it.

"And what if that *is* part of it?" Con retorted testily. "You
know I can't picture myself living life always by the rules, Des.
I want so much *more* than that. More than a husband like all
the men we know, and a gaggle of children, and a thousand
years of balls and garden parties and riding to hounds!"

"What *do* you want, then?" I asked, a little hurt that she'd so
easily denigrated all my ambitions in one sentence.

"Life!" she replied in an instant. "Adventure . . . excitement . . . love. Oh lord! Beth, I don't even know what I want!
All I know is that I want more than I'm going to get around
here. And Tierney is the first man I've ever met who makes me
believe I can have what I'm after."

"Well for God's sake, be careful, Constance," Des responded.
"Play out this little adventure then . . . if you must. . . . Be
sure you know what you're doing. . . . Damned attractive
man for all his poverty. Get yourself into mischief, you could."

"Good heavens, Des," I said, horrified by his implication.
"Surely you don't think Constance would do anything foolish?"

Con looked at Des and then at me for a long moment, then
said, "But that's exactly what he's thinking, Bethy . . . and
what's more, he may be right!"

With that she got up from the ground, grabbed her horse's
halter and in a defiant gesture leaped up onto his back and was
off in a clatter of hoofbeats, hair flying wildly behind her as she
went.

Des and I stood up, too, in consternation. He seemed about
to speak but, changing his mind, said nothing. Then he too
mounted and there didn't seem much else for me to do but
follow suit.

But the conversation stayed with me for days after.

My sister was always a force to be reckoned with. Even as a
small child she had known her own mind, and often as not it
was in opposition to the norm. I suppose it had been naive of
me to think Con would choose to live her life as I did, but I
could conceive of no other viable way then. And besides, I
thought her such a splendid person that it didn't seem too much
to hope that the world would always bend to her will.

Nonetheless, it seemed to me that she was heading toward

deep water and, powerful swimmer or not, I feared the current might pull her beyond safety or, worse, beyond my reach. ✍

Con dressed hurriedly and rode to the strand. It was a ritual now, this meeting Tierney every day that he was able to steal from his work. . . .

She saw Tierney standing by the sea wall, the strange amorphous mists of morning at the seaside encircling him, so that he seemed only partially visible. She called to him from the distance, but her voice was lost in the soft blanket of fog and wind that caressed the beach.

Con watched the man for a moment, assessing him. There *was* something otherworldly about him; there was some elusive quality that made him seem to belong in another setting. She thought of a story he had told her of the ancient hero Oisín, who, having lived three hundred years in the Land of Faery, came back to Ireland only to find his giant friends long gone and the race of men there shrunk to mortal size, so that his heroic stature was sadly out of place. Tierney was like that somehow.

He turned as if aware of Con's scrutiny and waved to her, smiling broadly. She urged the horse forward, the same sense of well-being filling her that she always found with him.

"Grand day to you, Beauty," he called to her as she pulled alongside him. He reached up, gripping her around the waist, and lifted her from the saddle easily. She felt his hands tighten around her, felt the warmth of his body as he pressed her close to him for an instant before setting her down. She wished he would never let her go.

"And to your own fine self," she replied, laughing to hide the nervous flutter she always felt when near him.

"We've a Druid sky this morning, Con," Tierney said, sensing her nervousness. "I saw you watching the mists from across the strand."

"I was watching *you,*" she replied.

"Were you now? And wouldn't the Druids approve of that, too?"

"And why is that?"

"Because they were a lusty lot in those days, my girl. Before Christianity gelded us, we Irish were a fierce and lusty race."

Con smiled at the laughter in his voice and told herself to be patient with the man, for surely he too felt as she did.

"What was it like in those times, Tierney? Tell me," she prompted, knowing how he loved to weave stories for her pleasure. She insinuated her hand into his, which he clasped gratefully, and they began to walk at the water's edge, the slick sand trailing footprints behind them.

"In those days, Con, there were high kings who were great warriors . . ." he began, and she smiled to herself at his willingness to please her.

"I love to hear you tell me stories, Tierney," she said suddenly. "They touch some part of me I never knew existed before you." She reached her hand to touch his cheek and he caught it with his hand and lips together, kissing her fingertips; but he seemed self-conscious in doing so. She thought surely he would take her in his arms and kiss her then; instead he let go her hand hastily and continued his story. Yet she could see that he was troubled by their having touched.

What holds him back? she wondered. What keeps his body distant, when his heart and mind seem to fold me closer and closer every time we meet? "Nothing to offer but a fisherman's cottage," he had said. That was it, of course. That had to be the reason.

"The Druids were also the judges in those times, Beauty," she heard him continue. "All justice was in their hands. Even the succession to the throne was theirs to decide."

"I think you would have made a lovely king, Mr. O'Connor," she replied earnestly.

He laughed aloud at that. "Four or five hundred years ago there were O'Connors who were kings, lass—one of them tried to drive the Normans out of Ireland. But it seems unlikely that we'll be having any more of them in the family these days."

"It's the principle of the thing I had in mind, my love," she said, laughing too.

"Am I that, then?" he asked, suddenly serious.

"Are you what?"

"Am I your love?"

The two stood quite still for a moment and the strange soft sounds of the sea were rivaled by the thudding of their hearts.

"Yes," Con said simply. She felt his arms close around her

questioningly, but there was more doubt than happiness in his gesture.

"Beauty, I'm afraid . . ." he said softly, and the husky sound of his voice sent shivers through her. She moved closer, willing him to hold her. She could feel a terrible reticence and a fierce desire in the arms that encircled her. Instinctively, unthinkingly, she reached her hand around his neck, grateful for the touch of warm skin beneath her fingers; with the other hand she sought to wend her way beneath the sweater that he wore. She felt wanton in taking the lead; then, as if an unseen barrier had been breached, she felt him respond to her need for him, suddenly crushing her to him.

Con felt the beating of her own heart rising in her throat as Tierney's hands and arms enmeshed themselves in her being; they seemed to caress her consciousness beyond her body, so that nothing mattered but their entwining, caressing strength and the relief of knowing she was wanted by him as she'd longed to be.

Hungrily, he sought her mouth, her own hunger welling up in an urgency that frightened her. She felt his hands, strong rough hands, on her back and in her hair, pressing her into his own hard body until she realized through the welter of agitated feelings that a strange hardness was pressing into her belly, hardness she hadn't felt before. Just as she realized what she was feeling, Con felt the man pull roughly away from her. They stood facing each other, the first wildness still pounding in their bodies; he knowing well enough what should happen next, she not knowing, but wanting to know as she had never before wanted anything in the world.

Tierney collected himself with an obvious effort of will; he seemed very shaken. Taking Con's face in both his hands, he said so low she could barely hear, "And what are we to do about this love of ours, my heart's own? Where are we to go with it, do you suppose? Me, a poor fisherman and you a great lady, as you are?" She could hear in the painful question the echo of his having asked it of himself a hundred times before.

"We must go wherever it takes us," she replied, wondering if he could hear her over the sounds of her own heart.

"That could be costly, Beauty," he said, his voice strained and sad.

"Whatever it costs, wouldn't it be worth it?"

"To me it would, my Con," he replied. "But you have more to lose."

"Nothing that I wouldn't give," she said, meaning it, and he knew somehow that she was telling the truth. But that didn't change in the least the impossibility of the situation.

The little lady's maid who had served both FitzGibbon sisters until Beth's marriage carefully examined Con's discarded garments for imperfections and, finding none, hung the dress and cloak in the huge Jacobean armoire and carefully gathered the underclothes for laundering. Con had seen the girl perform these simple tasks for so long, she scarcely noticed her efforts. Tonight she had other things on her mind.

The maid bade her mistress good night and tiptoed from the room, sensing the young woman's need for solitude. Con, grateful to be alone, sat before the mirrored dressing table and undid the plaiting of her hair. The wavy cascade that fell about her shoulders seemed as undulant as her emotions had been all afternoon and evening. She brushed her hair languorously, staring intently at her reflection as she did so, as if to find a hidden answer in her mirrored self. Tierney's question burned in her mind. "Where are we to go with this love of ours . . . ?" he had asked. How *could* they go anywhere with it, at all? she asked her mirror image. She needed the answer with a terrible need. Her body and brain had ached for Tierney ever since she'd left the strand.

God, but she *wanted* him. This strange, virile man who filled her with longings too overwhelming to tolerate. Wanted his callused hands on her body, his questing mouth, his mysterious eyes, his hard muscular strength that promised knowledge as old as the world.

What would it be like to be a woman, finally . . . a girl no longer? She had seen horses mate, despite the grooms' attempts to keep her ignorant. She'd seen the wild, fierce vigor of the stallion as he pierced the mare and pinned her with his bulk and strength. Yet never, never before today had she been able to imagine the same process between man and woman. Now she understood and needed, needed.

The chill night air raised tiny bumps all over Con's body. She ran her hands lingeringly over her cooling skin, imagining *his* hands. Blessed God, what must it be like to feel yourself naked

in the arms of one you love? To lie forever in an embrace powerful enough to hold the world at bay? The world and *conscience;*
the word crept stealthily into her head. It was not easy to keep
conscience silent when people could be hurt by the taking on of
the knowledge you longed for.

Her father who loved her so, who prided himself on his flamboyant daughter—he would be humiliated in front of his peers.
Her sister and brother? No. They would learn to know Tierney;
they would see the strength of him, the love . . . and they
would understand. Des might be difficult at first, but he would
come around. Surely she, herself, would be the one to suffer
most. Losing the opulent comforts she'd taken for granted all
her life. In Tierney's world there were no maids to hang your
clothes at night or choose them in the morning. No cooks and
grooms and butlers whose only job it was to cosset and to serve.

She thought of the hurt of leaving FitzGibbon Hall forever
. . . this great stone fortress that she loved like a living thing
. . . whose every cranny she'd explored in childhood, whose
every ancient staircase and tower, crenellated battlement and
gracious paneled room was *hers.* Her domain . . . her heritage
. . . her children's birthright.

Con folded her arms across her breasts and squeezed herself
tightly, as if to reestablish the mysterious dream that had been
banished by such dismal thoughts, but the moment had ended.
Suddenly chilled, she resolutely walked to the armoire and removed a long white cotton gown with tiny white stitches in
rosebud patterns from the cupboard; she slipped it on. Then,
standing at the darkened window, she plaited her long loose
hair into one thick braid and fastened it with a tiny red ribbon,
a rebellious touch.

"I love you, Tierney O'Connor," she said suddenly to the
silent dark outside the window. "And poor or rich I'll be your
wife. By God, I will!"

Then, smiling inwardly at her own foolishness, she blew out
the candle and crept between the bedclothes that had been
warmed and readied by a servant, thinking only of the man
whose bed she longed to share.

2   Seaneen O'Sullivan, the Fenian organizer from Dublin, stood on the little makeshift platform and raised his hand for quiet. It was large and scored like tooled leather. The men shifted noisily in their chairs at his gesture, as if settling in for the long haul.

"I'm here tonight to talk about the subject of freedom," O'Sullivan began in his deep resonant voice. "A heady subject for a bunch of ignorant peasants like ourselves, wouldn't you say?" The question was greeted with a titter of easy laughter. Tierney looked around at the burly fishermen and farmers who comprised the eager group and wondered how many other such small cells of incipient rebellion this Dublin revolutionary had raised to dreams of action.

"You know," Seaneen said amiably, "my father used to tell me when I was a lad that there were three things not to be trusted—a bull's horn, a horse's hoof and a Saxon's smile. I can't say that the observations of a lifetime have proved him wrong." The men once more responded with laughter and the man continued, sure of his audience. "I thought perhaps we'd start tonight with a small history of how well our English patrons have governed this little island of ours for the past few hundred years, and what better place to begin than in 1845. Is there any among you who has personal knowledge of the famine years?"

Heads turned to right and left.

"I have!" An old man with white hair and a blackthorn stick pulled himself out of his chair with difficulty. "John Molloy is me name."

"John, is it?" asked Seaneen, squinting toward the man. "Will you tell us what you remember, then?"

"Aye, that I will," the old man said with conviction. "In 18 and 45 I was a lad of fourteen years. Me father and mother had a wee farm in Mayo. Not enough land to put in your hat, mind you, but enough to feed us our eight or nine pounds of praties every day, with a lick of cabbage and enough lamb to grease the pot of a Sunday.

"Me da had built our cottage with his own hands and me mammy, two sisters and three brothers lived as best we could in it." Tierney heard the emotion in the old man's voice and knew that fifty years hadn't dulled the pain of the memories it carried.

"But this August of '45 came and we pulled the praties from the lazy beds as usual, just as plump and fine as ever they could be. But two days later they turned rotten and black as swill, with a smell that must have sickened God Himself. The whole lot of them worthless.

"Without the praties we couldn't pay our rent, so the landlord said he'd tumble our cottage and burn us out—the bloody bastard Earl of Mayo it was. Me mammy was in childbed the day they pulled our cottage down around her. Me da begged the landlord to wait until she could travel, but the hard-hearted son of a bitch laughed at his begging." The old man passed his hand quickly over his eyes to hide the moisture there, and his voice cracked with emotion.

"Me da went mad with the pain of it—he attacked the bastard." He paused for a moment to gain control of himself. "They shot him in the head in front of us and me mother died before the day was over." He pulled a tattered handkerchief from his pocket and blew his nose audibly before continuing.

"We took to the roads, the whole lot of us that was left. The winter was coming on and none of our neighbors could help us, for the law said once a tenant was evicted, those who took him in would have their cottage battered, too. Famine fever took me sister, and a terrible death it was, God rest her. And the two youngest lads went right after her. Me older brother sailed for America on a bloody Famine boat and me uncle passed over in a food riot in Liverpool, where we'd gone to find work. I got this game leg of mine that day in the very same fight." He tapped his crippled leg with his blackthorn stick for emphasis.

It was easy to see on Seaneen's face that he was touched by the old man's distress.

Tierney watched the Dubliner with intense concentration. The man was in command, easily, knowledgeably, as if there was no question of his leadership.

O'Sullivan was just shy of six feet and so broad as to seem almost muscle-bound. His neck was like the thickset branch of a tree, his hands huge and callused from day labor in prison stone quarries.

His hair was black where it wasn't gray, and his eyes were dark and fierce under bushy black brows. His face was a roadway of crevices, tanned like cowhide—a difficult achievement in Ireland's climate. His face was old and world-weary, but his powerful body seemed younger. It was impossible to guess his age.

Every man in the little room knew that Seaneen was something of a legend among Fenians. Imprisoned on six separate occasions, he had spent a considerable amount of time at the Queen's expense. When in solitary confinement, he'd endured the silent loneliness by reciting Fenian ballads and poetry to his guards. Forced to live with hands and feet shackled, eating like a dog from the floor with hands bound behind him, he had infuriated his jailers by sending his compliments to the chef. Tortured for information about his friends, his bull-like body withstood the worst they could devise, although legend had it that after he had been released from Brixton it had taken six months of nursing to snatch him back from death, so severe were his wounds of body and spirit. The diminutive "Seaneen" was unquestionably one of affection and not diminution. O'Sullivan was considerably larger than life-size.

Now he stood easy in his power and authority, holding the audience gently in his grasp.

"As you know," he said, after all the Famine tales had been retold. He spoke in a commanding brogue that men and women alike found winsome. "We've a long way to go before we're finally free . . ."

In the next three hours Seaneen began to reweave the old dream . . . telling them what could happen and how they could participate.

When the speechmaking was done Tierney made his way to the platform to speak with the Dubliner. The time was coming when he'd have to make his own choices about the future. Perhaps Seaneen was the one who would be the catalyst.

Tierney walked the long way home from the meeting alone. His head ached with fatigue, but the elation of what he'd heard was breathtaking. O'Sullivan had touched him with the possibilities. Irish freedom! he had said. The dream that had inspired the risings in '98 and '67. But this time planned on such a scale and with such fervor that only victory could crown their efforts. An Irish Ireland! he'd said. The Sassanach at long last routed and Ireland free. By God, the thought was as heady as a jolt of poteen from O'Shaughnessy's still.

Dublin it was for him, then. He'd always known it, of course. But ever since the advent of Con FitzGibbon in his life he'd tried to push the thought far back into insignificance. Fiery, laughing Con. Impossible match, Con. Dear God, but she filled him with fierce needs. He felt his own urgency at the thought of her, angry at himself that he had nothing to offer her.

And wherever did a woman fit in with what he'd heard to-night of revolution anyway? And what kind of a life could he provide for Con if he followed his dream?

"You're an idiot, Tierney O'Connor!" he shouted to the echo-ing water and the darkened rocks and shore. And to himself for being such a fool as to think he could have her.

Tierney pulled his jacket tighter around his chest, as if to ward off the internal chill; how could he ever declare himself, ever ask her to be his, ever hold her in the long nights as he dreamed of doing? No matter what she'd said about the future, how could he ever ask her to be his own? Con naked in his arms. Con in his bed. Con with no thought but their own plea-sure. What would she be like? he wondered. As wild and free as she was in the rest of her life? As passionate and as full of laughter?

Tierney smiled to himself in the dark at the loveliness of the image he saw in his imaginings and the words of a poem began to form themselves unbidden in his mind. He hurried his steps along the strand, the thought of rebellion suddenly blurred by the rhythm of the words that were struggling to fashion them-selves into poetry.

Constance reined her horse in sharply and waited for Tierney's mount to catch up. The ride along the deserted beach was exhilarating and she felt breathless from exercise and high spirits. She wore a riding costume of deep green velvet and she had a curious habit of leaning into the wind, over her horse's neck, as she rode, whispering encouragements into his ear. It made her seem eager to leap into the future, and there was a careless confidence in the way she sat the horse that would have seemed recklessness in a poorer rider. In Constance's case, the perfect beauty of her horsemanship had made her the envy of men and women all over the county. She would, without question, be Mistress of the Sligo Hunt when her age permitted, riding with others of her class in studied dignity. But today she had no thought but to ride with Tierney.

"You ride like a woman of the Shee," he shouted to her over the wind's resistance; comparing her to the fairies put laughter in his voice. "I'm green with envy."

"And a perfect color it is for you, too, my Fenian friend," she laughed back.

They dismounted as if by mutual consent in an unspoken communication, a little way down the strand. She watched Tierney leading the fine roan stallion she'd taken from her father's stable. His shoulders were broad and he carried himself well, she thought—not like the men she knew who were schooled to mannered grace—but rather it was a quiet connection to the world in which he moved that made his motions fluid.

"And what is it you see, Beauty?" he asked suddenly. "Watching me closely as you are?"

"I was simply speculating on the kind of man you are," she replied easily.

"Ah now, surely that would depend on whether you choose to think of me as the fisherman I am or the poet I wish to be." He smiled at her as he said it.

"And what exactly is the difference between the two?" she asked.

"Well now, my Beauty, let me see. I'd say that fishermen are men of action, and poets are men of peace . . . for the most part, at least. Although in times gone by poets were sometimes warriors, too. Like the Minstrel Boy. Do you know the tune at all?" She shook her head no, and without warning he began to sing, with only the barest touch of self-consciousness in doing so, the haunting melody of "The Minstrel Boy." He sang the lyric carefully, as if the words had special meaning for him:

"The Minstrel Boy to the War is gone,
    In the ranks of death you'll find him.
His father's sword he hath girded on
    And his wild harp slung behind him.

" 'Land of song,' sang the warrior bard,
  'Though all the world betray thee,
One sword at least thy rights shall guard
One faithful harp shall praise thee.'

"The minstrel fell!—but the foeman's chains
  Could not bring his proud soul under.
The harp he loved never spoke again
  For he tore its chords asunder;

"And said, 'No chain shall sully thee,
  Harp of love and bravery!
Thy songs were made for the pure and free,
  They shall never sound in slavery.' "

He finished the melody, then leaned down suddenly and kissed her hair. The song produced in him an obvious emotion.

"When I was a lad," he said as if to explain his actions, "I used to sing that song and think about the minstrel and his wild harp. He seemed to me exactly what I wanted to be one day, a minstrel and a warrior. One who uses his poetry to proclaim a cause, or to rally men round it; one who isn't afraid to do battle for what he believes in.

"What astonishing courage must it take? I would ask myself, for one such as that to rend the strings from his own harp, as a gesture. To silence his own muse to declare that his jailers could imprison his body, but they could never subjugate his soul." The notion seemed to excite the man.

"But wasn't that self-defeating on the part of your minstrel, my love?" Con asked, interestedly. "Wouldn't it have been better for him to keep right on singing and proclaiming, even in captivity?"

Tierney smiled his strange half-smile at that and said, "Ah, but that, Con, my Beauty, is indeed the question, as only a practical woman could put it. Is it better to make the grand gesture that spits in the eye of the tyrant or to keep on working, one song at a time if need be, against him? I hadn't the answer as a lad, and I haven't it now, if the truth be known.

"But this I do know, Con FitzGibbon. In our own time we will need to make the choice. The great explosive gesture, or the drop of water on the stone of the Empire."

"I'm afraid I'd be more inclined toward the drop of water," she said.

He regarded her carefully, as if evaluating what she had said in the light of some inner knowledge. Finally he spoke. "Would you now, my warrior queen? I have my doubts of it."

Tierney tethered the horses to a piece of silvered wood that had once been a tree. He wondered absently as he did so where the tree had been in its tidal journey, far, farther than he had ever been from home. He glanced at Con, who seemed to be watching him again, as if she were seeking the answer to a question she hadn't voiced.

Con and Tierney spread a blanket on the damp sand; they sat down comfortably in the hazy early autumn sun. They didn't speak for a quiet while, each lost in long thoughts, for the passing of the summer had been on both their minds of late.

They had been together every minute possible through the soft months, although it seemed to them to have been little enough time, when he could escape obligations and she her family. Yet their emotions had progressed far beyond the bonds of simple friendship, and each was troubled by the need to take the next step.

Never, after the one day when he had kissed her so wildly and said that he loved her, had Tierney made any real sexual advances beyond an occasional kiss. Instead, he spent his energies educating her about the cause of Irish freedom.

Even when they kissed, their loveplay always ended abruptly . . . reluctantly. How could he stop at that? she wondered each time it happened; she wanted so much more. Wanted his hands, and mouth; wanted his arms around her. Blessed God, she didn't even know *what* it was she wanted, but she wanted it nonetheless! Surely he must feel her wanting, she told herself. Every day it seemed to grow greater. But only his eyes, which held hers in their grasp, gave indication that he understood and wanted, too. For the rest, he seemed almost shy with her. She knew that the difference in their stations was, for him, almost insurmountable. . . .

Oh, to be a man! she thought, frustrated. To be able to make the first move. To touch when you wanted to touch, to reach out and take what was needed. Not always to have to play the reticent lady, too demure to demand or even desire.

"Do you love me, Tierney?" asked the girl, suddenly, turning to look the man in the face. She had been brooding on the question for so long that it was a relief to give it voice.

"Aye, lass, as well you know." Tierney seemed startled by the question.

"Then why don't you try to take more liberties with me, man? Why don't you ever try to make love to me? It's driving me wild that you don't."

The vehemence of the question made Tierney roar with laughter.

"Well, now, don't you be sounding the experienced lady? To be asking a man to make love to you!"

"Damn you, Tierney, you know exactly what I mean, and you mustn't tease me about it! I love you and you love me, yet we've barely touched each other since that one day. If you won't talk of it, then surely I must!"

As suddenly as it had come, the laughter died. Tierney looked angry when he replied.

"Damn you, Constánce FitzGibbon! And don't you think that I dream of nothing more than to have the right to make love to you? To hold you naked in my arms, so I could make you forget your Ascendency world, and your riches and all the fine trappings of that gilded cage that keeps you from me? Don't you think it's driving me mad that I've no right to ask anything of you? No right at all!"

There was a hurt in his voice that she'd never heard there; the man stood up angrily and strode off down the beach before she had a chance to reply.

Constance jumped up in consternation and ran after him, the damp sand sticking to the velvet of her riding clothes. When she caught him he turned on her, anger in his eyes.

"Do you think I could take you," he shouted at her against the wind, "knowing there's no future in it but a mud-walled cottage full of fisherman's children and the fine art of poverty? Do you think I want you worn out as my mother is worn in twenty years' time? Why in God's name do you think I haven't touched you since that day? Don't you understand, Constance? I can't trust myself to ever let you go again!" He turned his face from her, but as he did it was the sorrow beneath the anger that she could see most clearly.

"So he does love me as I hoped," she breathed the relief of the thought into herself before replying.

"Now you must listen to me, Tierney O'Connor," she shouted back at him. "Do you really think you suffer this alone? Do you think I lie alone in my bed at night and think about my fine clothes and my fine heritage? I do not! I think about you and what we might have if we were together." She saw the uncertainty in his eyes, so she continued.

"You may as well know it now, Tierney—I have no intention of living my life without you, man. So if we cannot live it in my world, then we must live it in yours and be glad that it's there for us. And if you won't have me for your wife, then, by God, I swear I'll . . . I'll seduce you anyway!" She looked so defiant with her hands on her hips and her velvet riding skirt blowing in the damp breeze that the man felt amusement stir beneath his anger.

"If there's any seducing to be done, my girl," he said gently, "I'll be doing it myself, if you don't mind."

"Will you really?" she asked, knowing the answer.

There was an electric tension between them, a current that wasn't anger anymore, but something stronger, more primal, less easily eluded.

"I will, Beauty," said Tierney with a catch in his voice. "You must know I've thought of little else since first I held you in my arms." He put his hands on her shoulders and she felt a tremor pass through her. He was asking her something with his eyes and she was answering, answering. He moved his arms around her suddenly, pulling her to him; he kissed her anxious mouth and eyes and hair, and it was the same as before but different from before.

Constance felt herself swept along by a wildness beyond any she had ever known, caught up in feelings that were older than the world. An agony of need opened inside her, and she felt if it were not filled, nothing else in her life would ever matter again.

Never had she felt what a man's mouth or hands could evoke; nor dreamt that her body knew more than her mind knew of love. Never had she imagined that being out of control could be so right, so inordinately, anciently necessary. She felt herself carried along as on a rising tide, going somewhere she needed desperately to go, knowing suddenly how to get there, although she hadn't known only a moment before.

Then, as if the very urgency of the act had brought him back to his senses, Tierney pushed her away from him as he had on that other day. Straightening himself, he said deliberately, "No, Con. No! This is *not* how it should be for us. What we feel for each other should not be sullied so." Constance stared at the man she loved, her heart pounding in her chest so loudly she could barely hear. She would not let him make that choice a second time.

"I love you, Tierney," she said clearly. "Nothing that we ever do together could sully us."

But he shook his dark head. "Don't you see, Beauty?" he said in a terrible whisper. "You can still change your mind and go back to your world with no loss behind you—and you must do it! For I warn you, love of my heart, if I once take you in my arms, I'll never, ever let you go."

"If you were never to take me in your arms again, nothing else would ever matter to me," she said, on the verge of tears.

"I want to marry you, Con, if we can find a way."

"And I you, love, but who will marry us here in Sligo, do you suppose? Who but you and me. The priest will have none of us and the minister would have my father's wrath down on us before he opened his prayer book. We must leave here, Tierney."

He nodded assent; there was no way for them to be married anywhere in this county.

"You could go back to your own world and forget me . . ." he whispered, but he knew even as he said it that the words were meaningless.

She reached up to touch his lips, keeping him from finishing the foolish thought. The feel of his mouth beneath her fingers answered all the questions. Constance raised herself up on tiptoe and kissed the man she loved, twining her arms around his neck and pushing the soft roundness of her body against the resistant strength of his.

"There's no need to fight me, Tierney," she whispered into his ear as she felt him stiffen against her approach. "You know we're meant to love each other, whatever the world says. You've always known it."

He grasped both her shoulders in his hands and held her away from him for a moment, his eyes searching hers as if to find salvation there. Finally, deliberately, he spoke, the urgency of his voice almost frightening.

"Then I pledge myself to you, Constance FitzGibbon. Now,

before God, as surely as if we were in a church, I pledge you my love and my honor and my life, as much as if we were wed before a priest. I'll have you no other way."

"And I pledge myself to you, Tierney O'Connor. Before God and man, for better or worse, richer or poorer, in sickness and health . . ." She said the words, feeling the ancient power of the ritual connect them.

". . . until death do us part, then—" he finished the pledge and with infinite tenderness he began to loose the buttons of the dress that kept her from him.

3 ∽ "I'm getting all caught up in this Ireland business, Bethy," Con told me as she and I sat in the drawing room at Manningham, waiting for Dermot to bring us tea that afternoon in early October. "I've a terrible desire to meet all the people I'm hearing and reading about . . . O'Leary and the other Fenians."

"That should put Papa into a fine temper," I replied, trying to sound more amused than concerned. I knew she had something very important to say to me. I had felt it in the air around us for days.

She looked up sharply at me and said, "My dear, the time has come for you to take me very seriously about all this." She looked troubled and concerned.

"Are you having an affair with Tierney, Constance dear?" I asked directly, feeling very daring even to have suggested such a thing. Wanting above all to be able to talk it through . . . to eliminate the secrecy that I had felt surrounding Con's inmost thoughts.

"Worse than that. I intend to marry him," she said steadily.

"Do you love him that much, then?" I asked gently, unnerved by hearing it said aloud at last. It was a foolish question, of course. No one who had ever seen them together could have doubted their love.

"I *love* him, Beth!" she said as if the word were a sacrament. "So wildly that it frightens me a little. And I love what he's teaching me about Ireland; you'll get caught up in it too, you'll see. It's all so unjust, Bethy. So cruel and unjust. I'd like to do something about it."

I reached over to grasp my sister's hand. She was so animated . . . seemed so sure . . . yet what she was saying was so unthinkable.

"I'm *in love* with him, Bethy," Con repeated. "Truly in love with him!" She stood up agitatedly and began to pace up and down.

I ran to the door to close it.

"You must keep your voice down," I warned her. "The servants will gossip if they hear. You know I'll try to help you, love," I said. "But I feel I'm supposed to warn you of the folly in this! Have you thought what you'll lose if you go off with him?" A sudden vision of my sister in the O'Connor hovel rose in my mind.

She stopped pacing and turned to me. "What will I lose, Bethy? That's exactly what I've been asking myself. Money and comforts, without question. But I've never cared all that much about them."

"How can you know that when you've never been a day without them?" I asked concernedly. She ignored my question.

"What of FitzGibbon Hall?" I suggested, knowing how she loved it, wondering why I even bothered to say these things. It was all so inevitable.

"The Hall will never be mine anyway, Bethy. You know it will all belong to Desmond, and I'd be the last to begrudge it to him."

"Your place in society?" I was grasping at straws in an effort to be dutiful, so half hearted in my argument, no one could have taken me seriously—least of all Con.

"You know I've never cared one whit for society! That's the last thing that would hold me."

"Has he asked you to marry him, dear Con?" I asked, articulating the thought for the first time.

"I asked him," she said with a small secret smile.

"Constance! You didn't."

"Oh yes, I did. He was always so damnably circumspect and careful not to overstep his bounds."

I sat down in one of the chintz wing chairs that flanked the windows, defeated. My sister was headstrong, I'd always known

that. But what she was contemplating quite defied imagination.
And the worst of it was that I could understand perfectly well
why she was doing it.

I had been with them often enough in those few months to
see how it was for them. In my heart I knew how much she
loved him and, to be honest, I knew why, too.

In a way I think I envied Con at that moment. Tierney was
so special a man; so full of life and honor; so very much in love
with her, that the rest of the world had subsided into insignificance. I, too, could feel the love and lust they shared; the wild
passion that seemed to flare between them whenever they laid
eyes on each other was exciting and seductive.

I loved my stately, imperious husband, and he loved me—or
so I thought. But we loved dependably, appropriately, ex-
pectedly. No fierce burning passion set our bed ablaze; no Troys
would be burned because our love had lit the spark.

But they had *that* . . . that extraordinary burning-coal-in-
the-breast splendor about their love from the very first. I can't
even say that I was angry with myself for envying. It was right
to do so, for it was love of the kind few mortals ever see and its
very intensity demanded something in return.

I've sometimes wondered if—had I paid closer attention to
what was happening, early on—I might have cautioned them to
be more conservative. But I think not. Our destinies are set in
motion by another hand than ours. And, too, I would not, in
retrospect, begrudge them one moment of each other's love.

"The most awful part of it," I said finally, groping for the
right words, "is that I understand entirely why you love him." I
must have sounded so upset by the whole puzzle that Con burst
into laughter; it was infectious and soon we were both laughing.
She came and sat on the floor at my feet, her pretty organdy
skirt spread out around her like a flower. "He is *wonderful,* isn't
he?" she asked me, hopefully.

"Of course he's wonderful," I replied, loving her happiness.
"And handsome, and forbidden and all sorts of heavenly things.
But have you given any thought at all to living in a cottage like
the one where we first met him? It's unthinkable."

"But we wouldn't live in a cottage, Bethy. We're going to
Dublin."

My heart sank at the thought of her leaving and she saw it in
my face.

"Oh, my dear Bethy," she said, squeezing my hand, "the only thing at all about this that saddens me is leaving you. We have shared *everything* all our lives . . . but now that we'll both be married, our worlds will be separate. For the first time. It's so dreadful to think about."

I nodded, unable to speak. I'd always known she was meant for a bigger world than mine, but I hadn't known it would come so soon.

"I love you, Con," I said, my eyes filling. "Nothing will ever really separate us."

She nodded, but we both knew it was untrue.

"You must promise me you won't do anything foolish," I managed to say, although my voice was constricted by a terrible sense of loss, for I knew as I said it that the die was already cast.

"I can't promise you that, my dearest sister," she said quietly. "For that may be the only way to get what I want." ∾

4 "Mrs. O'Connor." Con spoke the words softly, for the woman she addressed was seated by the fire, struggling to read from a prayer book in the inadequate light. She looked up at first startled, then, recognizing her guest, got up hurriedly, straightening her apron and brushing her gray hair back from her face in an effort at tidiness.

"May I speak with you for a moment?" Con asked. "I've been hoping to talk with you alone, Mrs. O'Connor. Do you remember me from the day my sister and I . . . ."

The woman interrupted. "I know who you are, Miss FitzGibbon. Surely you must know that Tierney speaks of naught else but you, since you two met."

The woman's voice seemed infinitely weary and strained, a marked difference from the cheerfulness of their other visit.

"That's why I've come, Mrs. O'Connor," Con replied. "Your son has asked me to marry him." She said it tentatively, unsure of the emotions she read in the older woman's eyes. "I'd like your blessing."

Mrs. O'Connor stood very still, as if gathering words or

strength for what she meant to say. Then she motioned Constance to a chair by the hearth and, moving the teakettle into place on the hob, she herself sat down.

"All mothers love their sons, Miss FitzGibbon . . ." she began slowly. "I no less than any other. Each of my boys is special in his way—Liam with his fine broad back and his skill with hurling and the nets . . . Seamus with his music . . . Donal with his wild ways. But Tierney . . . Tierney is the light of my heart, Miss FitzGibbon. Never was there a better son, nor one more loved." She paused as if to see if this alien young woman understood at all what she was saying.

"If the truth were known, I've begrudged him all his life to anyone or anything that could ensnare him from me. I've grudged him his Fenians that could lure him to danger . . . I've grudged him the girls who've followed him about since boyhood. Oh, not that I've not wished to see him happy and loved, nor that I haven't wanted his children to hold to my heart, mind you. But he's a rare one, miss. Too rare for a fisherman's world, and I suppose I've always known that because of it, he'd be taken far from me. And I begrudged the day when he'd vanish forever."

"I don't mean to take him from you, Mrs. O'Connor," Con responded softly, moved by the woman's honesty.

"But you will, Miss FitzGibbon. Nonetheless, you will. And 'tis only as it should be, I know. The lad is meant for larger things than are here in our village. I've always known it would be so." She paused, to gather words, and then said, more vehemently than before, "I'm sorry to say this to you, miss, but I fear you are wrong for my son. He should stay with one of our own girls . . . one who can love and understand him. What can you possibly know of a man like Tierney, Miss FitzGibbon?" Her voice had turned hard.

"And what can you possibly know of the suffering and privation that life brings to the likes of us? Can you even imagine going to bed hungry or seeing your child die because there's no money for doctors and medicines? Can you, in your wildest nightmares, know what it's like to have no rights under the law, with the memory of famine and losses in your head and the hurt of them in your heart? My own grandfather and grandmother died in the Great Hunger, and though 'tis more than fifty years ago and before I was born, the knowledge of it's in my own soul!

"And it's in Tierney's, too, miss. The history of all we've suffered and all we've lost is as strong in him as if he'd seen it all with his own eyes. It can *never* be in you, miss. Not if you loved my son more than life itself could you ever know what he carries within him!"

"But he's teaching me, Mrs. O'Connor," said Con desperately. "I know all the stories now."

"Aye . . . and stories is all they are to you. But it's life itself to Tierney, miss. Life itself and no less."

Con stood perplexed and shaken under the woman's gaze. What could one say to refute such simple truth. The mother, watching her discomfiture, continued, "I fear for you, *both,* you see, miss. You don't know how to be poor, and he'll not know how to be humbled by your people's hatred. Tierney's a proud man like his father and he'll not know how to fare, despised by your kind.

"And you, miss, do you love my son enough to bear his children in a cottage like this one that is his heritage—you who was born to the manor house and its comforts? Do you love him enough to let him risk himself for the Cause that means everything to him without trying to distract him from his purpose—a purpose you cannot share? Do you love him enough never once to remind him of what you've given up to follow him?"

"I love him enough to breach hell itself for him, Mrs. O'Connor!" Con replied, and the words carried a fierce conviction in the still cabin. "It's no more my fault I was born rich than Tierney's he was born poor, ma'am. I'll make your son a good wife and I'll bear him fine strong children. And as to throwing up to him what I'm giving up—surely you, of all people, should know how much I'm gaining in the exchange!" Her breath came hard and fast with the words. She felt hurt and angry— but not righteous, for she knew the woman spoke only the truth.

Mrs. O'Connor watched Con for a long moment before she spoke again.

"There's fire in you, miss," she said unexpectedly. "My Tierney's a gentle sort, but there's fire in him, too."

The older woman sighed as she reached for the boiling teakettle. "I can see that what he's said of you is no more than true, miss." The older woman looked into Con's eyes, as if reaching for something there, before she spoke.

"You mustn't think that I'm so old I've forgotten what love is. My husband's a good man and I've loved him as long as I can remember. It's just that life is so much harder than anyone knows at your age, so we old ones try to warn our children of the pitfalls and the thorns. It's no use, of course. No one young can know what life will take from you. No one can know." She was still for a minute; Con said nothing.

"There's no stopping love, miss, once it's begun. Not for those that are loyal and true. I'm old enough to know that now. Once the flame of it is lit there's no argument in the world can put out the fire. The Church would say nae to that, I'd wager, and perhaps even my own husband . . . but if Tierney's given you his heart, miss, then you two will surely do as you must, and the world nor I will have a say in it."

She looked up then, as if her verbal musing had led to a conclusion. "You'll hoe a hard row, miss, you and my son," she said. "Maybe it will be worth it." She nodded her head as if to emphasize the last enigmatic statement, then resolutely poured tea from the pot and handed it to Constance, who was surprised to see the woman smile at her as she did so.

"Now, child," she said, as if having made a decision. "You must tell me of yourself and of your love for each other, for that will sustain me when you're gone, as gone I know you soon must be. And I'll tell you all the little things about my son that none but a mother knows."

Con, startled by the change in the woman's attitude, clasped the older hand in her own and was surprised by the strength she found there. And by the tears that she noticed running down her own cheeks.

Desmond FitzGibbon reined in his horse and waited for the second rider to catch up. He had seen his father ride this furiously only two or three times in his life and, having glimpsed the older man from the crest of the hill, there was nothing to do but wait for him to pull astride.

His father's face looked apoplectic as he neared. "Thank God I've caught you!" the man shouted to his son breathlessly. "Your sister Constance has run off with some peasant Lothario,

Desmond. We must go after her immediately and bring the child back before some irreparable harm is done her."

Desmond smiled inwardly at his father's circumlocution of his sister's virginity. "Father, I'm afraid we're going to have to talk about this. Constance isn't a child and it isn't as simple as all that."

"Not as simple!" roared the father. "By God it's as simple as a fortune hunter and an innocent girl."

"No!" Desmond shouted the word to cut short the expected diatribe. "Forgive me, Father, for contradicting you, but neither of those premises is true. If you'll let me explain, I'll tell you what I know of it."

"What you know of it!" shouted the enraged father. "You'd best not let me learn that you know anything at all about this!"

Desmond stood his ground, trying to keep his own temper in check; he knew his father's would dissipate and the man would become rational again. He had had ample opportunity to study his father's wrath over the years. He reached out to touch the older man's mount to steady it, the black gelding he rode twitching nervously under him. But his father yanked at the reins harshly; the horse reared back and then was still.

"She's in love with the man, Father, and O'Connor's not a fortune hunter. Truth is, except for his poverty, he's an all-around first-class fellow. His family holds one of our fishing leases and he's a writer of poetry and such."

"Dear God!" expostulated the pained father, and Desmond was moved by the despondency in his cry. "She could have told me . . ."

"Had she told you, Father, you would have felt duty bound to keep her from doing this. Beth and I both warned her of the dangers—"

"Beth, too?" Merrion FitzGibbon barely breathed the question.

"There was no dissuading her, Father. She's so much in love with the man, and he with her, they had no choice but to go." Des watched the sorrow and anger struggle for first place in his father's distinguished face.

The older man nodded, finally, as if the unwanted truth had found its mark.

"She'll not set foot in my home again," he said, his voice a harsh whisper.

"Don't say that, Father! O'Connor's a good man—he'll care for her—"

"Then let him do so . . . for by heaven, she'll never see a farthing from her father." With that he pulled fiercely on the reins, his horse's head jerking up at the unaccustomed savagery. The large animal reared and then plunged past Desmond's mount to gallop wildly across the meadow, his rider's crop stinging his flanks.

How like him, thought Desmond angrily; it would never occur to him to listen or to try to understand. He watched the dust cloud fade into the silvery distance.

"Poor Con," he said aloud as he turned his horse toward home, "like as not he'll keep his word."

∾ Merrion FitzGibbon tossed the horse's reins to the groom with unaccustomed rudeness. He pushed past the startled man and trudged to the house at double time, nearly knocking down the manservant who answered his ring.

What insanity had taken hold of his children? His precious, marvelous Constance throwing away her bounty on a man of no account. Her brother and sister witlessly approving of her folly.

Why had he not listened to his sister Jennifer's advice and sent the girl to England to be educated? "She's headstrong, Merrion," the woman had sagely warned him. "That girl will go her own way if some of that sassiness isn't purged from her." And how he had scoffed at the notion! Why, the child loved him, he'd said; she'd never dream of going against his wishes on anything of consequence. Besides, he would have missed her laughter and her verve; missed the glowing pride he felt when she rode to hounds, fearless and patrician on the heels of the howling pack.

How could one he loved so much hurt him this viscerally? he wondered, heartsick. How could she cast away the civilities of her class to live with a loutish peasant whose home was a dirt-floored cottage, with no prospect of ever having better? What dangers of poverty and ignorance would she face without the protection of her class and family?

With trembling fingers he poured himself a whiskey, then set it down on the table beside his chair and, holding his head in his hands, sat for a moment trying to compose himself.

"Father?" My whisper intruded on his painful silence. "I've come to talk with you about Constance," I said trepidatiously.

He nodded briefly, and I saw him pass his hand over his moist eyes self-consciously. He looked up into my face and I saw the lines of weariness crisscrossing his forehead.

"She loves you, Father."

"That is not apparent at the moment."

"She wanted to come to you before leaving, but she knew you would stop her if she did. Constance left me a letter for you, Papa—it's a kind of explanation I think . . . and more than that. She needs you to know how very much she loves you."

"Has she no notion of what she is giving up, Elizabeth? Has she no sense of loyalty to her family whatsoever? Can this man have bewitched her so much that no glimmer of common sense can be appealed to?"

The agonized queries sounded so heartbroken that I leaned down and put my arms around him before answering.

"She has found what we all seek, Papa," I said. "A great love . . . a rare and special love." He pulled away from me roughly.

"Would you have me believe that such is possible with a fisherman?"

I pulled back, thinking, how does one explain this? How does one describe a Tierney O'Connor to a man like my father? Pulling the letter from the pocket of my dress, I handed it to him, aching for what he must be feeling.

"Perhaps Con can best tell you in her own words, Papa," I said. "She is very like you, you know. You must not hate her now for the independence of spirit that you've always loved in her. Constance is who she is . . . fearless, optimistic and free. You have never wished her to be anything less." I think he must have heard the concern in my voice for he took the letter from my hand and shook his head helplessly, unable to respond. I touched his shoulder, wanting to say something more, but did not, and left him alone with the letter. I saw him weigh it in his hand before opening it, as I left the room. I knew the contents, for Constance had shown it to me before leaving.

My dearest Papa,
      How angry you must be . . . and how hurt by my departure. I would seek your forgiveness, needless to say —but far more even than that, I would beg your under-

standing. So I shall try, within the limits of my powers, to explain to you what has precipitated what must appear to you to be the rashest of acts. Would that I had Beth's eloquence with the written word! Lacking that, I can only hope that your knowledge of the love I bear you will help to overcome my failings of articulation. So I will try to speak to your heart.

I have met a man. So unlike the men I have known that even the words I must use to describe him seem to me inadequate. He is a poet. And a fisherman. And a visionary. He *feels* with a different fervor . . . thinks with a sharper clarity . . . loves with a higher passion than anyone I have ever known. ("The ravings of an infatuated child," I hear you mumbling as you read—but not so, my dear Papa! For surely you know me to be, above all other things, a realist.)

He loves me! Oh, would that you could know the bliss those words impart to me. ("But other men would love you—men of your own class." I can hear the thought take form in your mind.) But not like this, dear Papa! Not wildly, madly, freely, passionately, permanently . . . as I need to be loved. It is simply not the way of our class to love without encumbrance or mitigation.

What would you wish to know of his character? He is honorable, forthright, gentle, generous and noble-spirited. Hardworking and conscientious. He will take care of me and whatever children we may be blessed with to the best of his ability. Unreservedly. Totally. And he will count himself lucky to have us every day of his life. Can you think of any of our friends who could be party to such a commitment?

As to his prospects (You see, I try to interview him as you would have done had the circumstances been different):

If he can get his poetry and plays to the attention of the right persons in Dublin, I believe that even those of our class will come to know of his gifts. If not, he is tall and strong and good and willing and will find, I'm sure, enough work to support us.

There is more that I would say to you, Papa, so very much more. But it has to do with you and me rather than with Tierney. You see, all my life I've been an independent sort. I've done much as I pleased; not in an arrogant fashion, I think, and not merely to kick over the traces as an empty gesture. But rather because I see things in a different—heartier—way than the women of my class. Truth be told, I'm more like you than Beth or Mama. I would have made an excellent son. And isn't that part of why you love me, my dear Papa? I have always thought so.

I say this not to share the burden of blame for my defection, but merely to remind you that never have you had in me a docile daughter, nor one who promised to live life by the rules. If you are honest at the last of it, Papa, my decision must not seem to you entirely out of character—but rather merely headstrong and, perhaps, foolish.

If you can find it in your heart to forgive me, Beth and Desmond will have my address in Dublin. Tierney and I would welcome you to our home with open arms and more love than you can imagine. If you cannot bring yourself to come to us, I pray that at least you may recall always the love I bear you. I revere you as the best of fathers. I remember you as the best of comrades. And I shall hope each day of my life that this breach between us will be of short duration.

Your loving daughter,
Constance

Merrion FitzGibbon held the letter in his hand for a long while, the tears in his eyes making it nearly impossible to focus on the forthright handwriting. Then he walked to the satinwood desk in the center of the room and, taking a small key from his watch chain, opened the lock of a tiny drawer in the left-hand corner of the huge piece of furniture. In it were two bundles of old letters, each tied with a faded satin ribbon. He stared for a moment at the gently cursive writing of his dead wife in the one pile and his own strong, scratchy script in the other. Then he laid his daughter's letter atop the two small bundles, closed and locked the drawer and left the room. ✍

5 ∽ My life with Edmond seemed to deteriorate sharply after Con's departure. I missed her terribly and felt alone in an unaccustomed way. At least while she was there I could pretend that my old happiness continued—and, too, there was joy in being around Con and Tierney, as there always is in the presence of great love.

Once she had gone I had only Edmond. How can I explain the disillusionment of marriage without admitting how unrealistic my expectations had been? I expected courtship to continue . . . expected romance and intimacy and the kind of connection I had sensed years before between my parents. But Edmond was cold and correct, distant and self-contained. He had his butler to run his household, his peers for conversation and his politics for intellectual stimulation. It is even conceivable that he had a mistress for sexual diversion, although at the time I was too naive to consider such a possibility. My role, it seemed, was to be that of broodmare. To that end my husband bent considerable effort until I was safely pregnant.

At first I thought his sexual ardor a sign of love; although our lovemaking was perfunctory on his part, it was frequent. I was woefully lacking in knowledge, but I meant well. I tried to be coquettish . . . he seemed amused. I tried to be wanton . . . he was appalled. I asked questions that seemed to shock him, and then, when my pregnancy became apparent, his attentions ceased altogether.

I ventured to invite him to my bed one night, a week or so after I had announced my condition.

"I hardly think that would be for the best," he said enigmatically.

"Why not?" I asked, to his discomfort.

"Why, my dear, it is no longer necessary," he said, as if speaking to a slow-witted child.

So I was lonely in more ways than one. And I was puzzled. Why had no one ever told me what marriage would mean? Why had Desmond not warned me? I asked him.

"To what end, Bethy?" he replied, looking concerned and somewhat embarrassed. "It's just the way life is, I'm afraid, dear girl. Women of our class are supposed to be fulfilled by having children and taking care of their homes . . . entertaining and such. Security in all that, don't you see? Why, you'll always be taken care of by Edmond."

"But he doesn't seem to love me, Des."

"Not possible, my girl," he said emphatically. "Couldn't help but love you. It's just that Edmond's a great deal older. Set in his ways. We men aren't used to compromise."

"But why did he marry me?"

"Wanted a family, I expect."

"Why didn't you tell me, if you knew all this?"

"Thought you understood what it was all about, I suppose." He had the grace to look sheepish.

"After all, not many choices for you. Good as any, Edmond. Better than most. Honorable chap." His speaking in fragments let me know how unnerved he was.

"Damned sorry you're unhappy, though," he said, meaning it, and put his hand over both of mine in my lap. "Anything I can do?"

I shook my head ruefully, wondering if there was anything anyone could do. Also wondering why what was acceptable to all other women didn't seem so to me. I'd always been so accepting of things.

"Could it be this, er . . . baby business that's making you restless, d'you suppose?" he asked hopefully.

"I don't know, love," I replied. "I rather hope that's all it is, but I expect not."

We parted company after a while. I sat for a long time thinking about what he'd said. Con was pregnant, too, she'd written to say so, sounding elated and filled with a sense of adventure. Not in the least bogged down in it as I was. I took her letter from my pocket and reread it for the third time, trying to absorb something inexplicable from it:

Marlborough Street
Dublin
2 December 1897

My darling Bethy,
    Dublin is extraordinary. There's revolution on every

other tongue. The Socialists are fomenting the workers, the literati are turning out masterpieces. The intellectuals are trying to *do* something instead of just talking the battle. I feel that I've never really seen the city clearly before.

There is a curious gray-green quality to the light here —as if it has been filtered through rain clouds before being allowed to enter. I'm told this is because of the large buildings that block the sun, but there's more to it than that, I think, an almost metaphysical silvering that alters the look of life here.

And there is *life* here, Beth. Life in the pubs at night, where revolution is talked of in shouts or whispers; where songs and stories remind one of more heroic times. The young men boast of their willingness to fight the English over a pint of bitters or Guinness dark stout, and become quiet as church mice when the Regimentals enter. It is all very new to me.

You were right about poverty, by the way. It is ghastly beyond comprehension. I hadn't an idea of what life is like without comforts. Learning that what you and I think of as the barest necessities are regarded by others as unattainable luxuries is a terrible shock to one's sensibilities.

Remember our visits to Dublin with Papa and Des when we were small? Remember the gracious squares and parks that marked the domains of the rich? Now I am learning of the parts that we never knew existed—the slums and the crowded alleyways. It is inconceivable that the fine Georgian houses that ring St. Stephen's Green and Merrion Square, with their gracious fan windows and brass-plaqued doors, inhabit the same world with the poor of this city. There are beggars everywhere to break your heart.

We have lodgings now on Marlborough Street, a room in a house whose windows face the Liffey—I try not to see the sewage in the river, but it is impossible not to long for the sight of the sea. Not even the servants live in such austerity at home—yet somehow I am content as I have never been.

Our room is small—I think you could lose the whole of

the boardinghouse in the dining gallery at the Hall—you would be either amused or appalled by it, I think. But it is *ours*—and love does seem to conquer all, so you must not worry for me. Curiously, the fact that everyone around us is similarly poor seems to make our circumstances acceptable in some odd way. However, I will need whatever of my clothes you can gather and send to me, my dear, for I have a feeling I may be wearing them for a good many years to come. But enough of the dreary part. . . .

We are married, of course, and no great problém it proved here in this anonymous place. And! Brace yourself, dear sister—I am with child. Several months so, in fact. I hope you will forgive me for keeping the fact of it from you while at home, but you were so worried about me that I couldn't bear to make your worry worse with knowledge of my condition.

It is the oddest feeling, this—I have felt slowed to a snail's pace, although my kindly neighbor, who has borne nine lovely children, assures me that the robust strength of the middle months will more than compensate. I worry about bringing a child into such comfortless surroundings, but all around me youngsters seem to live and prosper and surely life will change for the better financially once Tierney's plays and poems are seen by the proper persons.

I am overjoyed that you, too, are with child, Bethy—of course I shall be with you for your lying-in, and fully understand that you cannot be here for mine. I've asked Tierney to come home with me, despite Father's protests, but my husband is such a proud man, I don't know if he'll do more than just deposit me and come to fetch me home. He must see his first niece or nephew, of course. Ah well, much can happen in all those months between now and the babies, so we mustn't fret.

Dearest sister, isn't it splendid to be alive? I thank whichever ancient deity it was who gave me the courage to run off with my husband (it couldn't have been *our* deity, of course—the older gods were so much lustier than the new!). Tierney has opened a world to me that is incredibly vital! Whyever, I wonder, don't those of our class know how to be so alive? Is it bred out of us—or trained out by nannies? The people here seem so full of plans and futures—perhaps because their "present" leaves so much to be desired. I can't remember ever feeling that people at home worried about futures at all. Perhaps when futures are assured one needn't speculate, whereas here, nothing, not even the next meal, is assured.

Forgive me, if I seem to be demeaning what goes on at home, it's just that I'm bursting to tell you *everything* and to share the newness of it all. I miss you more than you can know. Tierney and I are great friends as well as lovers, but I miss never having to explain things, as was always the case with you and me. And men, God knows, are mysterious creatures when all is said and done.

But enough of such wild ramblings. I am urging Tierney to see the people at the theater about his work . . . I'll write to let you know if they are responsive.

Save all your news for your next letters . . . it is very hard to be so far away from you now. Give my love to Des and do encourage Papa to forgive . . .

> All my love, as ever,
> Your sister Constance

I put down the paper with a curious feeling of regret. It sounded so much like Con—the exuberance, the perceptiveness, the breathless wonderful life force of her. I felt bereft and terribly lonely.

Could it be that I envied my sister her new life? Or did I simply miss her? Miss desperately the connection and the shared past, the thoughts that needed no verbal expression to be understood. I shook my head to clear it and put down the letter . . . I hadn't been feeling well of late. The baby seemed to be draining me of energy and married life was not turning out to be at all as I had hoped. ✑

6   "So you've come, have you?" Seaneen O'Sullivan looked up at Tierney from under his black brows. Putting his hands firmly on the table he used as a desk, he pushed back his chair.

"I've come," replied Tierney.

"And you've brought a wife with you, I hear."

"That, too."

"And what exactly do you plan to do in Dublin?" The voice seemed emotionless, weary but interested.

Tierney looked at the man, knowing he was being measured by him.

"I've been doing day labor and looking for a job that's more permanent. I'm trained as a fisherman and I'm big. I'll find something." He hesitated a moment, then went on. "I write as well."

Seaneen's eyebrows went up quizzically. Tierney replied as if the question had been voiced.

"Poetry. Plays. I don't know if they're any good, but I'm going to show them around and see if I can sell any."

Seaneen nodded noncommittally; he had the chair tipped back against the wall, a casual gesture. But there was nothing casual about O'Sullivan. He seemed a man always on the alert, always braced for danger. He was guarded as a virgin, but infinitely more experienced.

"And what do you want from the Brotherhood?"

"To be put to use."

"I don't like having married men in the group. They're too vulnerable to attack. And too prone to spill their secrets over dinner."

"What can I say to that?" replied Tierney steadily. "I am who I am, and married is part of it. I'll keep what secrets I need to and I'll work my hardest any way you choose to let me. But my wife's my own business."

Seaneen's eyebrows went up again, this time with a glint of amusement in the dark eyes beneath them.

"So you've a bit of a temper, too, eh, O'Connor, and you'd like to put me on notice that your private life's your own?

"Well, let me tell you what a crock of horseshit that is! You'll have *no* private life in the Brotherhood. And I'll have no man with mixed loyalties at my back. Oh, you may do your job for us and you may plod along for years before the time comes when we need you. But by God, when that time comes, O'Connor, there must be no choice for you to suffer over. Ireland! O'Connor. She must be your wife and mistress and child and friend. Are you capable of that kind of selfless loyalty? I wonder. Neither of us knows right now if you are." He tipped the chair back into its normal position, as if to signal a decision made.

"But I like you well enough, lad, from what I can see of you. So I'll take you in and we'll see what you're made of. We'll both see."

Tierney felt the awesome power of the older man as he spoke and tried to name it for himself. Was it the power of conscience-lessness . . . or power drawn from knowledge of things no man should ever know?

Something about him said *Beware* . . . something said this man of flesh and bone is a rock that cannot be moved.

Tierney realized they had been staring at each other for some time. "I accept your terms," he said.

Seaneen nodded curtly, as if in dismissal. "You'll hear from me, then," he said, and turned his attention back to his work.

Tierney walked down the rickety stairs with a prickling sensation at the back of his neck and a sense that revolution was a seedier business than ever it had seemed in the heroic stories he'd been weaned on.

It was too late to search for work today. He'd use the time to go to the library. A few hours among the books there always changed his view of life, renewed his possibilities. He could go home, of course, to Con . . . but it was hard to know exactly what to say to her just now. He felt a terrible uneasiness about the life he'd brought her to. Hard, poor, comfortless. She had not complained at any of it, but the horrified look on her face when she'd seen the boardinghouse he'd brought her to had remained with him.

God, but he loved her! And she seemed to love him wholly. It was her nature, of course, to give totally, once committed. Even

Ireland seemed to consume her now . . . this Cause she'd ab-
sorbed by osmosis from his songs and stories. And the child
that was coming . . . he, too, would absorb the full scope of
her attention. Tierney smiled ruefully to himself at how quickly
responsibility follows passion. He didn't mind, really. Didn't
mind anything that meant they were together . . . they and
the child to come.

The thought of the baby momentarily tightened his gut.
Work was what he needed—steady, secure, everyday work to
support them when the baby came. The shock of it was why he
felt so glum. He wanted the baby, but it was a bit frightening to
know it would come so soon.

Tierney fought down a momentary guilt as he entered the
library. His dream of writing seemed so selfish now, so futile, so
self-indulgent. "Better a good fisherman than a lousy poet," his
brother had once said to him. "Ah, but better a good poet than
a lousy fisherman," he had replied. So he would try for today,
at least, to be a good poet.

Tierney pulled his cap from his head and stuffed it into his
pocket. Con would understand if he spent these hours in the
library trying to be a good poet.

He headed for his favorite corner and, pulling a notebook and
pencil from his pocket, he left the library behind and entered
into his own mind, far from the world around him.

"Do you still love me, laddie, now that I'm round as a grape
with this great child of yours?" Con asked it as she lay beside
her husband in their bed. The cold starlight, visible through
their window, scattered tiny pinpoints of light on the black
blanket of night sky.

Tierney placed his hand on his wife's linen nightdress and ran
it tenderly over her belly by way of reply. "I love you more than
the world, Mrs. O'Connor. I love the shape of you and the feel
of you and this great mound of belly that houses our son."

"A son is it?" She smiled contentedly at him. "And exactly
how would you be knowing it's a son?"

"The same way I knew you'd marry me, my Beauty." Tierney smiled at her, his own special smile. Con laughed softly at
the pride in his voice. It was so evidently filled with happiness
that she belonged to him.

"I love you, Tierney," she said through her laughter. "And

what's more, I *want* you all the time." Her voice was mischievous.

He smiled at the childish delight she seemed to be feeling, and ran his hand up over her body to her breasts. The scratchiness of the calluses on his palm ran shivers of pleasure through her.

"Make love to me, Tierney," she said softly. "I'm never so happy as when we make love."

"Have I told you lately what a wanton piece of baggage you've become, Mrs. O'Connor?" He sounded amused as he said it. Tierney bent his head to hers and she met his kiss with a fervor that excited him.

"Teach me everything, Tierney," Con whispered to him, elated by the sheer joy of intimacy. She felt his mouth respond to hers and his hands fold around her with a strength that was curiously gentle.

"You'll be teaching *me* in a month, lass," he whispered back, the sound of his voice lost in the muffling of her soft skin.

She buried one hand in his thick black hair and wound the other around his back. She could sense his trying to restrain himself because of the baby, but she wanted him fiercely, wildly tonight—thrusting into her world, blotting out everything but the oneness of their love.

When their love dance was over, Tierney cradled his wife in his arms. They lay quietly for a moment, but she could sense that there was something he wanted to say. She waited expectantly, contentedly, for him to voice what was on his mind. Finally he spoke.

"I've been to see O'Sullivan, the organizer I told you about in Sligo. I've asked him to put me to work for the Irish Republican Brotherhood." The silence with which Con greeted his statement made it seem she was disturbed by the news of the secret society but unwilling to say so.

"I must know what's to be needed of me by the Brotherhood before I can make other plans," he said gently.

"It isn't fair, you know," she replied. "You're a fine poet, Tierney. If it weren't for Ireland, you'd have no such fanatical demands to keep you from your writing."

"And if it weren't for Ireland, I'd have nothing of consequence to write about, either. You know my poetry is just the other side of the Fenian coin to me. It all springs from the same source. Ireland first, Ireland free . . . that's the beginning and the end of everything for me."

"And where do we fit into your everything, the baby and me?"

"If you don't know that, Con my love, I could never explain it to you." His voice sounded troubled. He was silent for a moment in the darkness; she couldn't tell if he was angry or merely unsettled by her question. Finally, he spoke, his voice low and serious.

"When I asked you to marry me, Con, I told you our life would never be as other people's . . . that was the truth. Some things I know before they happen, that's one of them. I also told you that if you came with me I would protect you from all harm to the very limits of myself. That's also truth. The answer to your question is that I love you more than myself, more than Ireland, more than life . . . but I cannot tell you that there will never come a time when I might have to do something that endangers us, because I've been ordered to do so."

She felt disturbed by the honesty of his reply and wished she hadn't asked the question.

"But I will do my best for you, Con. That I swear to you. I'll do the best I can for you and the lad."

She wanted to say something to reassure him that she understood, but the words stuck in her throat. If his honor demanded that he die and leave them alone, he would do it. She knew that now . . . perhaps she had always known it. She felt suddenly powerless and lonely and afraid.

Con moved her hand beneath the covers, stroking his warm skin intimately. "Make love to me again, Tierney," she whispered.

"You're insatiable, Mrs. O'Connor," he whispered back in the quiet dark, but he knew as he took her in his arms that she had only made the request out of fear for the future.

"Repose sits on you like the mantle of a queen." Tierney said it and there was tenderness in his voice. He had been watching Con as she sewed for the baby. She moved with the awkwardness of late pregnancy, her belly a great ball under the embroidered white linen gown she had brought with her from home. There was a knitted sea-green shawl, just the color of her eyes, thrown carelessly around her shoulders; she had been humming as she worked.

Con looked up, immensely pleased by the compliment. "I have nothing to do with my time *but* be in repose," she laughed good-humoredly. "Besides, I'm learning all your songs, my love; as I stitch, I sing them to myself and it makes me feel close to you." She had a voice that everyone found pleasing and she had always taken pride in singing.

"As if I'd ever let you get far from me."

"Oh, you have your meetings and your secrets and your work. But I just sit here contented as a Kerry cow, struggling to do needlework—which has never been my long suit—and wondering what it is you're up to."

"I'm not up to anything as important as you are, you may be sure of that." He smiled as he reached out and patted her swollen abdomen, and she grasped his hand as he did so. Pressing it hard against the smooth roundness, she said, "Do you feel him, Tierney? What a mighty fellow he is, with his kicks and thumps. There's not much sleep for him these days, it seems."

"Nor for his father either," the man said with a laugh. "I miss making love to my wife, you know."

She frowned momentarily at that, annoyed that the midwife had told them that lovemaking was a danger in the last month of pregnancy. Con reached out and tousled his thick dark hair and, grabbing a handful, pulled his face close to her own. "Not as much as I miss you, you may be sure," she laughed ruefully. "The day after this great broth of a lad enters the world, I intend to seduce you."

"Would God you have so easy a time of it that you can," he said, suddenly serious.

"Are you worried about the birth, Tierney?" she asked, startled.

"Of course I'm worried."

"Well, don't be. I've been watching horses foal for a lifetime and I don't intend to have any more trouble with it than they do. I'm young and healthy and athletic and I shall make short shrift of this childbirth business so I can get back to living."

"There's a brave lass." He smiled at her. "We could use you in the Brotherhood."

"Indeed you could, and that's something else I intend to do

when this interminable pregnancy's over. I intend to wheedle your secrets out of you so I can be part of it all."

Tierney shook his head and chuckled at his wife. She was exactly as he'd hoped she'd be; or perhaps better than he'd dared to hope. He prayed that they'd be granted the years together they'd need to build a life and wished fervently that his gift for knowing things others did not might give him a clearer glimpse of their future. But so far he had seen only fragments that he couldn't make sense of—and the problems of the present were more than enough to occupy his mind. There was much that was unsettling and uncertain. He'd feel better if he had a steady job—any steady job—before the baby came.

Con busied herself about the little flat, humming as she cleaned. She was feeling better this morning, despite having slept fitfully. If only the nagging pain in her lower back would lessen, all would be well.

The baby she carried seemed to have grown so large that it crowded out the possibility of a deep breath, or a good night's sleep. She tried to straighten up from her task of cleaning the kitchen table, but the effort seemed immense.

She wondered what time it might be, wishing she had brought a clock with her from Sligo. There would probably be hours and hours to wait until Tierney got home. She always missed him when he left, especially now that she had such difficulty in walking that she had to stay close to their room.

She untied the kerchief she had used to keep her hair back and realized that her face was damp with sweat from the small effort she had made.

Then she felt the first pain creep around from back to belly, encircling her for a moment, then receding. What an ancient sense of recognition it carried with it, she realized.

Con made her way to the door, grateful that her next-door neighbor was both kind and knowledgeable about childbirth. She had a feeling that before the day was over she herself would know things she didn't know now.

By the time Tierney returned from work, Con had been long in labor and she looked worn from it. The midwife had been fetched and she smiled at the man as she neared his wife's side.

"She's sore pressed," she said to him, "but she's a good strong lass and she's doing well. It shouldn't be long now."

Tierney held Con's hand as long as the midwife let him stay. Toward the end she sent him to the hall to wait and he sat miserably on the landing of the staircase listening to the groans and cries from within. Finally, one long piercing cry . . . then silence. He heard the midwife shout his name, her voice imperative, worried.

"What's wrong?" he whispered urgently to the woman as he entered the room.

"Get me a blanket and olive oil," she said breathlessly, her concentration riveted on the child in her arms. It was unmoving. "We must hurry!"

Tierney did as he was told; he realized, stricken, that the child had uttered no cry. The woman wrapped the infant in the receiving blanket and moved her hushed little burden to the hearth.

Silently she spread the blanket and laid the still baby in its center. First blessing herself, then dipping into the bowl of olive oil, she began to knead the unmoving body rhythmically. First the chest with its untried lungs and fluttering heart, then the abdomen, arms, legs in turn; then the chest again. Tierney ran to the bed, where Con struggled to see what was happening to their child. She looked ravaged by her ordeal, hair matted with sweat, her face blotched with pain and effort.

"Water, please, Mr. O'Connor," the woman said once as she worked, and when Tierney brought it, she took one hand from her rhythmic kneading and poured a few drops on the doll-like head. Tierney saw that the boy was large and perfectly formed; it seemed uncanny that he had not breathed.

"I baptize thee in the name of the Father, Son and Holy Ghost," the woman murmured, her hands already back at work searching for the barest spark of life to fan into a flame. She offered no explanation, but the intensity of her actions seemed to say that she was willing life into the baby.

And then it moved, the tiniest flutter of a movement that was the baby's own and not the midwife's. And it made a sound. No hearty, lusty cry as other babies make at birth, but a fragile gasp as life came to it . . . a whispering in of the air that was life itself and a small sound of protest.

"Thanks be to God," breathed the woman who had fanned

the spark, crossing herself, as the gasp became a cry and the small lungs could be seen to fill and rise and fall in the well-formed chest. Arms and legs began to flail, as babies' arms and legs must do. The small cry became a louder one, a robust, healthy birth-cry, a protest at being forced from the warmth and safety of his mother's womb into the cold of the world.

The midwife sat back for a moment watching the movement gratefully; an immense sigh of relief escaped her. "I've seen it before," she said softly and reverently. "The baptism sometimes brings them back from the gate of the grave. But only when God has plans for the child. He's been saved for some great purpose, this lad of yours. You mark my words, Mr. O'Connor. He'll not have an ordinary life."

Con and Tierney held each other, tears of gratitude on their faces.

"At least he'll have a chance at life, thanks to you," said Tierney, and Con could hear the terrible strain in his voice.

The midwife wrapped the child carefully and handed him to Con. She took the now-animate bundle gingerly, as the woman held it out to her. She must put the awful thought of what had nearly happened away, she told herself as she touched the perfect little face with awe and wonder.

Their baby! Alive and real, warm and wriggling in her arms. Their own miracle. A sweet pink face, with eyes squinted closed, was moving in the blanket. Hands, so small they seemed impossible in their perfection, made little fists and pushed hard at the covers.

"He'll not have an ordinary life," the midwife's words echoed in her ears. What would this newborn's destiny be? she wondered. Was it possible that predetermined pathways already yawned before him? "God's plans," the woman had said. "He's been saved for some great purpose." Could that really be, or was it only a midwife's superstition? She was too tired to wonder or worry . . . too happy of his salvation to question.

"And will you look at the size of him?" she heard the midwife say to Tierney. "He's torn her up a bit. You must take good care of your wife now, Mr. O'Connor. Ah, but I can well enough see by the look on your face that you'll do your best."

Con watched the woman bustle about collecting her things, grateful that she would soon be gone and they could be alone.

Tahg Mor O'Connor they named him; the Gaelic word

"mor" or big, seemed appropriate enough, for the midwife had said he was nine or ten pounds and looked like a month-old child.

"Do you think he's beautiful enough to be a child of our love?" Con murmured to her husband, her voice muffled by the exhaustion that was so overwhelming now that the danger was past.

"Aye, lass, he's wonderful enough . . ." replied her husband, "but you're the beauty in this family."

She smiled gratefully at the love in his voice and drifted off to sleep, wondering why no one had ever told her how very hard it is to give the gift of life.

A strange communion with her mother washed through her. As she had struggled with the birth pains, Con had imagined her, the gentle creature of the painting in her father's study. How terrible a way to die, she had thought, sending her love and sympathy to her mother through all the years, thanking her for the gift of life so dearly paid for. "Saved for some great purpose," her mother's voice that she had never heard, now seemed to echo the midwife's . . . or perhaps it was the sound of her own heart. She was tired . . . so very tired and so very very glad that it was over.

Con and Tierney lay in their bed; the baby nursed hungrily at Con's breast; small sucking, slurping sounds filled the space between them in the quiet night.

Tierney, propped against a pillow, watched his wife and son with love and tenderness. He raised his head up, resting it on his hand, elbow left on the pillow, and watched the maternal picture, drinking in the primal loveliness, thinking that no poem could convey the perfection the moment held.

Con looked up at him from her concentrated effort of feeding their son, and smiled.

"I'd like to give you something splendid in return for what you've given me," he said. "But nothing seems to measure up."

"There is something you could give me," she answered after thinking for a moment. "Something very special."

"Anything that's in my power," he replied.

"Take your work to someone in the theater, Tierney," she said deliberately. "Let someone look at it and tell you that it has merit."

He frowned at the thought; he'd known for a while that it was time for him to do just that. He had amassed a substantial number of poems since coming to Dublin and had gotten a good start on the play that had been growing within him, almost as the baby had grown within Con. But something had always held him back. Fear of rejection? Or fear of acceptance? He wasn't sure which was worse, for by now he knew where Seaneen O'Sullivan stood on the matter of his writing. "Divided loyalties," the commandant had said contemptuously, when the subject had come up. "Ireland first or not at all, O'Connor," the tone of his voice leaving no room to mistake his meaning.

"You're right, Con," he said, answering his wife's request. "It's time." And he leaned over their suckling son to touch the soft silkiness of her breast above the baby's hungry mouth. He felt the skin stretched taut over its milky fullness; saw his son's small fists pushing rhythmically at the swollen flesh; felt the intense connection of these two that he loved most in life.

"I love you," he said softly. "I love you both more than everything." He wondered as he said it how Seaneen would respond if he knew how much competition there was, in Tierney's soul, for Ireland.

7   The Mechanics Institute Theatre was dark and echoing as Tierney entered it. He tried not to think that the future hinged on what would happen here—at least whatever part of his future would have to do with writing. Dock work and day labor paid little enough, but probably more than writing ever would. He hardly dared know what to hope about the outcome of this day. Perhaps, if they hated what he'd written, he could at last put it away—at last purge this terrible need from his heart and get on about the business of living. If they *liked* what he'd written—impossible dream—then there would be the problem of Seaneen to deal with.

Ah well, he'd worry about it all once he knew what they had to say about his work.

A small scattering of people occupied seats in the first four rows. The stage was half lit and a woman stood at its center. She was unusually tall and very beautiful; her throaty voice sounded musical in the near-empty auditorium. She was reciting some lines by William Butler Yeats; Tierney, clutching his manuscript, stopped to listen.

Halfway through the quatrain, the actress suddenly raised her script to heaven in a gesture of mock despair and said to a thin angular man in the third row, "Really, Willy, this is too ghastly . . ."

"The poor workman quarrels with his tools, dear," someone in the second row threw back at her acidly and she made a disdainful face at him.

The angular man stood up with the awkwardness of the very tall. "No, no, Dan. If Maudie says it's ghastly, it may very well be ghastly. You know I'm never certain of these words until I hear them spoken."

So, that was Willy Yeats and the woman Maud Gonne! Tierney's original nervousness gave way to awe; he hadn't imagined that two such famous people would be in attendance. On the other hand, perhaps it was a rare bit of luck that would solve his problem for him. If Miss Gonne felt free to excoriate the work of Ireland's greatest poet, she'd hardly take pains to be kind to the likes of him.

Yeats had moved to the stage to confer with the actress about the questionable lines. As he turned to retrieve his seat, he noticed Tierney standing in the aisle. The handsome young man caught his eye and he beckoned him closer.

"Are you an actor, sir?" he called out to him. "Auditions are on Thursdays. Come back then, if you will; we must have a place in something for a lad who looks like he might have fought for Conchubar."

Several heads turned toward Tierney at that, and Miss Gonne moved past the footlights to peer into the audience at him.

"I'm not an actor, sir," replied Tierney with a smile in his voice. "I'm afraid I'm something far less desirable than that. I write poetry, you see."

"Dear me, with a face like that it seems a terrible waste," said the poet. But he smiled as he said it and motioned Tierney to take the seat beside him. "Come along then; when we've finished here I'll have a look at your work. I suppose that's what you want of me?"

"Good lord, yes, if you would, Mr. Yeats," Tierney managed to reply, surprised by the man's easy kindness.

But Yeats had already fastened his concentration back on the script in his hand and paid him no further attention for the moment.

"He said what?" Con leaned forward over the baby held in her lap and touched his face with both her hands. "Tell me everything!"

"Mr. Yeats liked my work. 'Quite extraordinary,' he said. As a matter of fact, he said it twice. 'Incendiary as brimstone, lad, but damned good work!' Can you believe it? Can you believe any of it?" He looked so pleased and excited, Con threw her arms around him and kissed him.

"Of course I can believe it! You're a bloody genius, as I've told you myself on numerous occasions. Mr. Yeats is merely confirming my opinion." She laughed aloud at the incredible good fortune of it, knowing that it seemed less a miracle to her than to her husband, whose life had been, until that moment, circumscribed by poverty and hopes. By God, it was all going to happen just as she'd dreamed it.

"Now tell me *exactly* what he said you are to do."

"He said I'm to gather as much of my work as I can carry and bring it to his house tomorrow." Tierney fumbled in his pocket for the address. "He said he was certain we'd find something there that they could use. Can you imagine that, Con? They might actually produce something of mine."

"Of course I can imagine it. I've imagined nothing but that for months." She shifted the baby in her lap so she could grasp his hand in her own.

"Don't you know how I believe in you? Why, in a year or two everyone in Dublin will know of Tierney O'Connor and young playwrights will be coming to *you* seeking advice."

Tierney knelt beside her chair and laid his dark head in her lap, beside his sleeping son.

"It's been such a dream, Con, this writing thing. A wistful, hopeful, hopeless, dream. Something I couldn't help but do, yet I never ever wanted to let myself believe anything would come of it." He didn't mention the Brotherhood's opposition; the excitement of the moment was too lush to spoil. He would worry about Seaneen later.

"Nothing come of it?" Con said incredulously. "Is this the same man who told me that we humans are made of naught but dreams and bones? And if you thought nothing would come of it, exactly how did you intend to support me and your son now that you've lured us away from the comforts of Sligo and . . ."

She laughingly took his head in both her hands and kissed him soundly, being careful not to wake the baby. What incredible good fortune it would be if Yeats really liked his work. Perhaps then Tierney would begin to believe in himself as she believed in him.

The sound of Tierney's voice died slowly. The strains of the old ballad had moved even the men, and Seaneen O'Sullivan looked around the quiet room full of Gaelic Leaguers, men and women devoted to the knowledge of Irish mythical history as well as the use of the Irish language.

If we can harness the power the lad has to move people, we've a potent weapon in that one, he thought. For whatever reason, people took to Tierney; whether he sang or he spoke, men and women alike were entranced by his gifts and the warmth of him. Seaneen had watched people's reaction to his new recruit on several occasions now and had been brooding on how best to make use of him.

Applause drowned out the thought as the listeners began to shout for more. The small stringed instrument Tierney played was a minstrel's harp, devised centuries before to be small enough for a bard to carry into battle. It wasn't the only instrument he played, merely his favorite. He ran his hands over the strings and laughingly called out to the audience, "I'll sing again if you do!" The applause that greeted the suggestion showed its wisdom. " 'Roddy McCorly,' then," he said, as he strummed the opening chords.

Tierney had been singing to them for over an hour; now all their voices rose in the familiar martyr's tale. Martyrs are what we do best in Ireland, Seaneen thought, suddenly angry. Our mightiest weapon, our greatest tragedy of all.

One song ended and another began. Voices—young, old, strong, wavering, melodic and not—filled the room with the mythology of triumph. How remarkable it is, thought Seaneen sadly, all our songs are of defeated revolutions and yet they fill us with such a sense of victory. What a strange race we are—sad love songs, merry wars—and always, always the belief that we can win.

When the singing had finally quieted and the last stragglers had left the old forge on the outskirts of Dublin, Seaneen stood beside Tierney, who was sipping at a whiskey to soothe his song-scratched throat. "You know," he said, "I knew a wise man once who believed if a man were permitted to make all the ballads, he needn't give a damn who made the laws."

"I thought we'd be here till morning singing the old songs," the young man replied laughingly.

"Aye. Now that we've found a place out of earshot of town, they're in rare voice. They've been starved for it."

"We've a long history of being starved for our own music and poetry," replied Tierney, referring to the fact that Irish songs and poems had been banned under pain of death during the hundred years of the Penal Code.

"We're all bloody good at talking and singing a great battle," O'Sullivan said acidly.

"They'll fight with more than that when the time comes, Seaneen."

"Aye. We'd better hope they will," said the older man, seemingly in a strange mood; then he changed the subject. "I've had an idea of singular brilliance tonight, laddie. Under the inspiration of the fine voice God gave you." The mischief came back into his dark eyes as he spoke.

"And would you be sharing the brilliance with me, then?"

"I would. If we could use your talent to get you a job in a pub —say as bartender and occasional entertainer—you'd be in a grand position to glean information. And maybe to pass it on as well."

"A bartender, you say. Well now, it couldn't be worse than hod carrying, could it? Have you a place in mind, Seaneen? I know a fair amount about drinking the stuff, but not enough to put in a gnat's eye about serving it."

" 'Our doubts are traitors,' " quoted Seaneen with a smile, " 'and make us lose the good we oft might win, by fearing to attempt.' "

Tierney chuckled at the literate chiding. He knew that the

copy of Shakespeare Seaneen had carried with him into solitary confinement had kept the man sane.

"Which means I'll have to learn, is all," he responded.

"Get one of those bloody books from the library you spend all your spare time at," said Seaneen. "You get yourself ready and I'll find the pub." He poured another drink into Tierney's glass as he spoke.

"Meanwhile, throw that across your chest before we venture out in the heavy dew." The steady drizzle had gone on since nightfall and it would be a long walk home in the cold and wet.

Tierney smiled as he took the whiskey from the man and downed it. O'Sullivan seemed in a strange mood tonight. He'd meant to broach the subject of his talk with Yeats to the man, but Seaneen's mood had precluded it. He felt a growing friendship for Scaneen, a growing sense of the full stature of the man. He wasn't one you'd like to let down and still call yourself a man, he thought, watching him closing up the forge. Everything about him demanded of you that you be the best you could be.

Tierney reached the pub early in the morning, as Seaneen had told him to. Tommy McGowan rose early, unlike most tavern-keepers. He could do so because he was a teetotaller, said Seaneen; not a drop of the "water of life" ever crossed his lips. Tierney smiled at the thought of a nondrinking pub-keeper; the fellow had probably seen more than his share of what the drink could do to a man, perhaps it was no wonder he disdained it.

McGowan was not in the IRB, but his son Rob was. So, according to Seaneen, he was willing to cooperate. Tierney pulled his cap squarely onto his head, ducked a little at the low doorway and entered the semidarkness. This was probably the one time of the day when the pub's customers were still in their beds, for it was barely dawn.

"You're O'Connor," a thick Belfast brogue greeted Tierney as he tried to accustom himself to the gloom.

"Aye. You must be McGowan."

"I am."

"Seaneen said . . ."

"I know exactly what Seaneen had to say, lad. By God, the man could talk the devil out of sinful souls with the mouth on him, or I never would of had you in here at all." Suddenly a hand shot out; Tierney took it gratefully. There'd be problems if he couldn't get along with McGowan or if the man didn't accept him and the IRB.

"But seeing as I've said yes and here you stand, fine strapping lad that you are, let's get down to it. Tell me what the boys need of you, and I'll tell you what I'll be needing as well and we'll see if the two needs are at all compatible." The man had a mischievous twinkle in his eye, but his demeanor was otherwise serious.

They sat at a wooden table and Tierney looked closer at Tommy. He was an inch or so under six feet and fiftyish. His hair was a soft brown with ample white mixed in and his expression was both quizzical and intelligent. His eyes were alert and they moved constantly, as if to take in everything, digesting it quickly, discarding the unimportant, then making judgments. "He's doing that now," thought Tierney as he watched the man watching him. "He's deciding."

"I've a need to see and to hear . . ." explained Tierney. "Gossip, news from the Castle, whatever I can glean. I'll need to act as an intermediary at certain times and as a courier at others. It shouldn't interfere much with what goes on here."

"Bullshit, it won't!" shot back the man with equanimity. "If you do your job right, it'll interfere plenty with my peaceful little business. But I'm not hiring you because of your bartending capability, lad. It's because of Rob I'm doing it, to help his Cause and his friends. Let's have that straight from the first of it. But in for a penny, in for a pound!"

Tierney nodded.

"I'm told you've a voice on you."

"I can sing a bit."

"Well now, that's in your favor. I'm the entertainment here most nights and I could use you to spell me if you're any good. Do you play an instrument?"

"Some. The minstrel's harp, guitar, squeeze box, the penny whistle . . . banjo in a pinch."

The other man's expressive eyebrows went up approvingly. "Well, then. That's it, isn't it? You'll tend bar while I sing and I'll do the same with you. You'll clean the place and I'll keep it stocked up and we'll work out the other details as we go along." He looked at Tierney inquiringly to see if he agreed. Then they shook hands. Tierney noticed that the man's cheeks became round apples when he smiled, which he seemed to do often, and that his eyes were bright and expressive as a child's.

"You'll work four in the afternoon until she closes. I'm getting on in years and I'd welcome a bit more shut-eye if I had someone here I could trust. Rob says you're that. Do you drink, young fella?"

"A bit. Not as much as some."

"Hmm. Well then, let me give you a bit of advice to go with it. The pub-keeper that drinks is a dunderhead! It's the curse of our race in this godforsaken climate, the drink is. I'd be the last to try to keep a man from a wee drop to warm him, mind you, but a drunk is no good to any man, least of all himself, and you'll need your wits about you to handle others in their cups. Do you understand me?"

Tierney nodded.

"The fact you're as big as you are will help a mite. There's few men like to tangle with a bigger . . . but nonetheless, when they tuck in enough of John Barleycorn you'd best be ready for anything."

"I'll do the best I can for you, Mr. McGowan . . . as well as for the lads."

"I've not a doubt of it . . . and you'll be calling me Tommy."

The man moved abruptly from the table to the corner of the room where two chairs stood alone and a small accordion with them. He tossed it to Tierney.

"Let's hear what you can do with that, laddie, and then you can be on your way until tonight."

Tierney caught the small instrument and, testing a few notes, began to play. He could see the delight on Tommy's face as he listened to the sweet strains of the music in the echoing room. Then he started to sing.

"Well now, you've got the golden tonsils, haven't you?" McGowan said with great glee when it was finished. "Well, thanks be to God for that. There's no one will wonder at my taking on a lad with a voice like yours!"

Tierney left the pub elated. He liked McGowan and the thought of steady work was a blessing in itself.

The IRB, thought Tommy McGowan as he watched Tierney stride happily down the street, that's a spoon you'll sup sorrow with. He shook his head sadly at the thought. Another fine brave lad for the gallant Cause—too long had he lived not to know how many such had gone down already. How many such lovely lads had been sacrificed to an old dream.

Ah well, it would be good to have the boy about. It was a lonely life now that Rob was on his keeping. On the run, he was; safe one day, endangered the next, he supposed. Like his brother Liam before him. His brother who lay to rest in Belfast Cemetery these eight long years, beside his mother.

Tommy shook the sad thoughts from his mind and absently picked up the guitar from beside the chair where he'd laid it. He strummed a few soft chords in keeping with his mood. Lord, how his Eileen had loved the music. " 'Tis the soul of the world in sound," she'd told him once, enraptured by the beauty he could command with his fingertips. She'd always looked at him with such love and admiration in her eye. God, how he missed her still.

Their marriage had been an uncommonly good one, it had seemed to him at the time. He knew men who remembered their dead wives with an affection they'd never lavished on them in life, but such had not been the case with himself and Eileen.

They had known each other from childhood. Tiny farms, side by next, had been their homes, and many's the day they'd followed their fathers into the fields for the haying, or the plucking of potatoes from the lazybeds, or the cutting of the turf . . . and somehow they had always known they'd be together. Not that they weren't the butt of a good deal of ribbing about it from their friends as they grew up, but they'd managed good-naturedly enough.

So they'd married when they were the right age and Eileen had given birth to two sons that they'd managed to raise and two daughters that they didn't. They'd had little enough money all the years, but as none of their neighbors had more, it didn't matter much.

Then their son Liam had joined the IRB and been shot in the back for his pains. And Eileen had pined for him. "I've lost a part of meself," she had told him when they buried the boy, and the truth was she'd never been the same after. Then Robbie, their youngest, had joined up, and a terrible melancholia had taken hold of the woman and a daft religiosity.

"Only through prayer and sacrifice can you petition God to

save your son Rob," the local priest, Father Flynn, had told her. And weekly it seemed he suggested new sacrifices she might add to her burden in order to beg God's mercy.

"It's a damned pagan ritual you're about!" Tommy had shouted at her, he who had never raised his voice to his wife in twenty-five years of marriage. "All these sacrifices and fasts and fears will be the death of you!"

"But the priest says . . ." She would recite the man's words like holy writ and Tommy would subside, defeated. She lived on her knees then, his little wife. She fasted away her sweet plumpness, and the bloom that middle age had not been able to banish left her cheeks.

Even in their bed things had begun to change, for she feared that any small pleasure she experienced would weigh against her rosary of sacrifices so laboriously collected to lay before the throne of God in return for Robbie's life.

So she had waxed frailer and frailer until the first bad influenza epidemic had taken her from him. Christ, how he'd hated the IRB then, and the Church and Ireland and all the forces that had contrived to destroy his happy life.

He had sold his farm and come to Dublin, a great need on him to flee from the memories and the sadness. So he had opened a public house where people came to be merry and self-indulgent . . . where he could sing and play his music and try to forget.

But of course there was no forgetting. There were the infrequent visits from Rob, and now there was this new recruit of the IRB. If only his feelings about them and their Cause were less complicated! He was proud of his sons. Nothing would keep him from helping Rob if he could. They were all good, brave lads. This new one, too, looked honest and stalwart. But it was damned hard to see them all go out to break their strength in a losing battle. Damned hard.

Tommy began to sing to his own accompaniment. There was solace in song. Eileen had been right about it being the soul of the world.

Tommy laid the guitar down, feeling better. It was right to help the lads. Little enough were they asking of him, and it would be good to have someone around to talk to. He tied an apron around his clothes and headed for the bar, where there were always glasses to be washed and put away.

8 "Your work is most substantial, Mr. O'Connor. Most provocative and substantial." William Butler Yeats at thirty-four was not in the habit of tossing idle compliments to every aspiring poet who passed his way. There were too many of them for that and it was too important that a standard of excellence be developed in Irish letters.

He laid the heap of handwritten papers down thoughtfully and leaned forward in his chair. His straight brown forelock fell down over his eye as he did so, and he reached up self-consciously to push it back into place.

"May I offer some suggestions?" he asked, and Tierney looked up sharply, amused by the idea that the finest poet in Ireland, perhaps in Europe, should be asking his permission for anything.

"I'd welcome your suggestions, Mr. Yeats. It means a great deal to me that you've taken the time to even read my work."

Yeats brushed away the modesty with a gesture of the hand. "Your work, sir, is more than worthy of my attention. You have no need to think this charity. You're a damned good poet." He paused, as if considering the rest of what he wished to say.

"But I do have a criticism, if you will . . ." He seemed to be considering his words carefully. "You touch things that stir me, Mr. O'Connor . . . and then you let their elusive magic slip away unexplored. Take me on the journey, sir! Don't leave me groping on a lesser plane!

"There's *power* in what you're pursuing here. Ancient mysteries . . . older than the world. You're tapping into a reserve I've been seeking for a lifetime. If you have the gift, for God's sake, O'Connor, have the courage to follow where it leads!"

He looked away for a moment, as if embarrassed by his own passion, then asked, "Have you ever studied spiritualism?"

"No," Tierney replied, surprised by the question. "I've had no chance for that. Séances, spirit rapping and such. Why do you ask?"

"Because I've believed for some time that there is a psychic dynamism in this island of ours. A reserve of psychical power that once enabled the Druids to command the focus of nature.

"It's a bit difficult to discuss, because most people think one barmy, but I've come to believe that if we could tap into this source of power, we might be able to use it to free Ireland."

He laughed a little at his own enthusiasm. "You must think me quite mad."

Tierney looked a bit startled at the unorthodox idea, but replied slowly, "I don't think you're mad, Mr. Yeats. Far from it. I've had a few bouts with psychic things myself, though I seldom speak of them. I was born with a caul, you see—the farmers and fisherfolk believe that gives one 'the sight.' I can sometimes see the future . . . just glimpses, mind you, but the future nonetheless. And I can sometimes see the past. Not the past of books and history, but something more ancient and primal."

Yeats clapped his thin hands with excitement. "That's what I sensed in your writing, then! What you touch upon that eludes you."

Tierney nodded. "A doorway opens and I can see amazing things . . . glimpse the heart of the world for a moment or two. And then the door shuts and the best I can do is try to write it down before it fades forever." He hesitated, then said, "Of course it may all be no more than a foolish imagination."

Yeats watched Tierney thoughtfully. He felt a twinge of jealousy that this man should possess without effort the gift he had so long sought by laborious means. He fought the twinge back and continued.

"I know a man who may be able to help you explore this gift of yours," he said finally.

Tierney looked at him quizzically.

"Yes," said the poet, as if coming to a conclusion. "You must come with me to a metaphysical group I've been working with. Perhaps together we may find what you seek."

Abruptly, he changed his tack. "Your poetry has passion and wit. Your cadence is your own, and unschooled, I take it?" Tierney nodded affirmatively,. fascinated by Yeats's evident mood shifts.

"It's quite novel and interesting—don't change it. Don't emulate those better educated and less gifted.

"Take this play of yours very seriously, Mr. O'Connor. It

could stir people. It could make you enemies. It bears the seeds of a great talent and a terrible discontent. I wonder if you understand the consequences of trying to bring such as this to fruition."

"I don't think I understand what you're saying to me, Mr. Yeats," said Tierney evenly.

" 'Of those to whom much is given, much is expected,' " Yeats quoted enigmatically.

"It's hard for a fisherman to think that he has been given much," Tierney replied with a wry laugh.

"You've been given everything!" Yeats said quickly and emphatically. "Nothing matters but the intellect and the spirit. Nothing!

"You will suffer for what you've been given, Mr. O'Connor. Make no mistake about it. Do you recall the folk tale of the mermaid who exchanged her fins for legs to marry her prince? But every step she trod was bloody agony? So it is with poets. We have exchanged our ordinary sensibilities for those of the gods, and we must bleed for it."

There was nothing to be said in reply. It would be dizzying to keep pace with such a moody intellect, but what an awesome adventure it would be to try.

"I've enjoyed talking with you, Mr. O'Connor," said Yeats as Tierney took his leave of him. "Keep at it. You can contribute something to us all."

Such simple words, thought Tierney. But with the power to change a life in an instant. Contribute something. . . . It was too heady to imagine what that something might be.

Tierney wanted to dance for joy . . . to run . . . to leap . . . to laugh, sing, shout. Most of all, he wanted to tell Con.

Tierney thought about the play he was nearly finished with. He'd been so exhilarated by Yeats's praise, yet it seemed his depression about writing had deepened since his visit to the poet.

He pushed the papers farther away on the tiny table and put down the pen disgustedly. The small puddle of lamplight ringed the pages in a warmth he didn't feel about them. Both elbows resting on the table, he bent his head into his hands and sat immobile, wondering, wondering.

Why was he doing this? Why striving to accomplish something people far more educated than he shied from? What business did a fisherman have trying to be a poet? His metaphors were homegrown things . . . shabby, unschooled, bound by the world he knew of farmers and fishermen, mothers and children, men like his father, who struggled and lived and died without ever going more than ten miles from where they were born.

Yet epics raged in his head. Mighty sagas, heroes of a stature that defied simple humanity. Wild, lusty stories that somehow had to find expression in these homely farmers and fishermen that he gave birth to.

Why would anyone want to read what he'd written? It wasn't high-minded and glittering with intellect as was Yeats's work. Nor fanciful as James Stephens's. Nor whimsical as Dunsany's. What in God's name was it, anyway? And where had it come from within him?

Its outer wrappings were easy to trace; externally it was no more than a reworking of the life he'd always known. But underneath that, such a passionate painful conviction raged. Would anything other than outrage be provoked by it?

He picked up the pen and forced himself to write another line. Perhaps, if he simply kept on writing . . . if he could push back the fear of what people would think when they read it . . . perhaps whatever it was inside him would finally wrench itself free and leave him in peace.

It was worth a try, at least.

Seaneen O'Sullivan supervised Tierney's education over the following year; he'd grown fond of the serious lad with the great gifts. He gave Tierney jobs of increasing usefulness and introduced him to the men on whose courage and daring Ireland's future would depend. A curious mixed bag they were—tall and short, educated and unschooled, farmers and college professors. They met at pubs and meeting houses. They gathered in each other's rooms and flats. They went to poetry readings and free concerts and recognized each other without acknowledgment on the street. It was a strange and vital time in Dublin.

To the unskilled eye, the city glittered with the elegance of an imperial capital. In the parks the band of the Royal Hussars paraded resplendently and filled the air with the music of a martial Empire. British military heroes were immortalized all over the city of Dublin in statuary, and cavalry squadrons in military splendor galloped prettily through the parks and streets as if they owned them.

At night the lovely squares were lit by candlelight spilling from crystal chandeliers in the ballrooms of the rich. "I have been told," wrote a socialite of some renown, "that for magnificence and brilliance, only the Indian vice-regal court with its mingling colors of East and West can compare with the Dublin Castle Season." It was a particularly apt comparison since Ireland at the time was garrisoned with more British forces than the entire subcontinent of India.

Waltz music wafted through the courtyards, and dressmakers like Mrs. Simms, "the Worth of Dublin," were kept in a constant state of lucrative exhaustion by the young ladies who came to the city to be presented to the Viceroy, the Queen's representative in Ireland.

The social life that centered around Dublin Castle was, of course, a far cry from that of the poor, whose slums rivaled any in Europe. This poverty and its incumbent foment of the working class had led to the beginnings of unions, and men like Jim Larken and James Connolly were becoming recognized names among the workers.

Somewhere between the two extremes, but with a foot in each camp, were the members of the incipient literary renaissance.

In the course of a single day you might see William Butler Yeats escorting Maud Gonne through the streets, or Oliver St. John Gogarty, crotchety in his rose-pink waistcoat, or James Joyce and a group of his fellow students laughing heartily at the expense of the Empire.

In all it was a roisterous, fertile moment, a time when each night of the week belonged to someone. Yeats had his salon on Monday, the poet AE on Sunday and George Moore on Wednesday. Stephen MacKenna held court on Tuesday, but at his house only Greek or Gaelic were spoken.

As Tierney and Con were not privy to any of this literate high living, they owned all their own nights, which they happily shared in the tiny flat on Capel Street they had moved to after Tahg's birth.

All life seemed better to Tierney since he worked at Tommy's pub. There was a great sense of relief in steady work; it cleared his mind for other things. And having an assured income had given them the courage to move. Although Con had refused the money her brother and sister had tried to give them, she had sold some of her jewelry to buy furnishings. The tiny flat seemed more a home than the rented room had been.

Tierney's writing was progressing. Yeats's urging had encouraged him to pursue in himself the knowledge that had eluded him; it had begun to seep through his conscious efforts and the results were gratifying. If only he could let go and let it happen, he chided himself. But the battle between conscious effort and subconscious reality plagued him. He had noticed, too, that "the Sight" had again begun to manifest itself. Twice lately he had seen flashes of the future. Nothing concrete and nothing fixed firmly enough in time to be really prophetic. But glimpses nonetheless, one of himself and Con embracing at some happy unknown future moment. The other disturbing—a battle in the Dublin streets, people running, shooting, dying. Somehow both visions had been disquieting because they had pointed up how very much could be lost if the revolution really came to pass.

Yet, despite these visions, all of life was better now. Con content and happy with their son. Con proud of her regained slimness and new motherhood. He himself pleased with his progress in the Brotherhood and his friendship with both Tommy and O'Sullivan.

There was one serpent in the garden, of course: Seaneen's disapproval of his writing. "A bloody distraction" he'd called it.

"And what the fuck do you think you'll do with fame and fortune, laddie, when it comes to you? When your plays are famous and you're hobnobbing with the gentry? Where will the Brotherhood come then in your priorities? It's already behind Con and Tahg. Next it'll be behind comfort and fame. Then it won't be on the list at all!" He had left no doubt about the strength of his opinion on the subject.

" 'It is easier for a camel to pass through the eye of a needle than for a rich man to enter the kingdom of heaven,' says the Bible. Well, I'll give you one from O'Sullivan's bible, laddie. 'It is easier for a fucking Englishman to fight for Ireland, than for a rich and famous Irishman to do the same!' "

They'd stayed with him, the words that Seaneen had thrown at him. It's easy indeed to be rebellious when you're poor and without anything to risk in the game. But what if the tables turn? What if you're given everything you've ever dreamed of? What conflicts of the heart would tear at you then?

Tierney tried to put the disquieting thoughts from his mind but they remained, for he knew them to be the simple truth.

Ah, but it was good to feel safe and secure. So seductive was the safety of steady work and the happiness of his family. So enticing was the company of Yeats and Maud Gonne and the others he had met through them. Others who had been legendary names to him before Dublin. So seductive was the love he felt for his wife and child, so strong the need for their safety and protection.

And then there was Ireland.

And his belief in the need to serve at her bloody sacrificial altar.

Where did it all fit into the puzzle of life? Where the priorities; where the right?

Every time he tried to sort it through the overwhelming confusions engulfed him. Maybe it was simply not time for him to know the answers, he finally concluded—maybe one day it would all be clear.

And for now he would taste the pleasures he had dreamed of. If only for a little while.

Tierney watched with immense amusement from behind the bar as McGowan wrapped the audience around his fingers. The man had so many gifts; he could make people laugh with his stories and cry with his ballads. He could gauge an audience within seconds of beginning to perform and could tailor-make his act to what they wanted to hear. And his repertoire was astounding. Rollicking sea chanteys and passionate love songs, bawdy music-hall limericks and a repertoire of songs of rebellion that dated back three hundred years.

The man was a fine musician and something of a bard as well, for the songs he wrote were as stirring as anything he'd heard or gathered.

"Now, have I told you about my friend O'Brien who lived next door to me?" he heard McGowan call to the enthusiastic audience. "O'Brien with the eighteen children?" They laughed back a "No."

"He was the one, you know, whose wife sewed up his pajamas after she'd had nine children, for she'd heard a stitch in time saves nine!"

The men with the mugs of beer or Guinness in their rough hands roared at that. They'd all heard about O'Brien's wife for years now. What a relief it was to poke fun at someone else's life after all.

Tierney had grown fond of Tommy since he'd worked for him. He was a fair man with a big heart and a robust sense of humor who managed to find something to laugh at in most all of life's vicissitudes.

The audience roared and clapped and stamped their feet at that and Tommy picked up the banjo and began to sing the rollicking strains of "The Old Orange Flute."

Tommy was halfway through the song when a contingent of uniformed soldiers came through the door and seated themselves noisily at the long table near the room's center. Tierney could see the immediate change in the pub's atmosphere as people shifted their chairs to right or left to give the Royal Hussars room. There wasn't any open hostility these days with the men at the Castle but they weren't loved either.

Nellie, the barmaid, threw a knowing glance at Tierney as she moved toward the table to take their drink order; Tierney laid down the towel on the bar, nerves alert and on edge. They seldom had any trouble from the Regimentals who occasionally came there from the barracks at the Castle—but it was Saturday night and you never could tell.

"I say, sir!" called one of the soldiers to Tommy as he finished his song. "Let's have a few choruses of 'God Save the Queen,' shall we?" He laughed and so did his companions.

Tommy glanced at Tierney before he spoke and then answered the man genially.

"I'm afraid you're a little late, gentlemen, for the entertainment. This set is just finished and we won't have another for an hour or two. But if you'd care to stay with us a bit . . ." He left the thought uncompleted.

"I said I'd care to hear you sing 'God Save the Queen!'" repeated the soldier, more belligerently than before.

Tierney removed his apron and walked from behind the bar into the room near the uniformed men. "Now, gentlemen," he said with forced affability, "my tonsils are a wee bit less tired than Mr. McGowan's here. And it just so happens I know your

regimental tune. Perhaps you'd like to sing along with me?"
Without waiting for a reply, Tierney signaled Tommy to pass
him the squeeze box and he began to sing.

Several tentative voices in the room took up the chorus and
finally, reluctantly, the five men in regimental uniform joined in
as well.

Without waiting for another request, Tierney segued into one
bawdy barrack-room ballad after another. Eventually, the men
finished their beers and left.

"Thanks, lad," said Tommy when they'd departed. "I want
no trouble here if I can avoid it, but I'll be damned if I'll sing
'God Save the Queen' while I've still a bit of life in the old
bones."

"It was easy to see they were more after mischief than music," replied Tierney. "We're lucky they backed off as they did."

"Aye, but it reminds me to tell you what I've been thinking
about since you've been here, laddie."

Tierney looked quizzically at his employer.

"I've been thinking it's time for me to take a bit more active
part in this rebellion of yours. I've a mind to join the IRB
meself. It seems to me if there were two of us listening to the
gossip around here, we might hear twice as much. What would
you think of that now?"

"Nothing in the world would please me more, Tommy," replied Tierney, wondering what had brought on the change of
heart. "But are you sure of what you're saying?"

"Aye, lad. Truth is, I've watched you for a while now—and
you've made me feel guilty. I've decided I could be more help to
you if I knew what you were about. So, I'm your new recruit."
He smiled affably as he said it, but Tierney knew what the
decision must have cost him.

"You're a good man, Tommy," Tierney said, meaning it.
"And a damned good friend." He paused for a moment. "I just
hope I'll not be leading you into something that'll harm you."

"Nae, lad. The whole idea is to harm *them* buggers. Not the
other way around!" Both men laughed at that and went back to
their chores.

9 Maud Gonne was the most magnificent creature Willy Yeats had ever laid eyes on . . . or ever would. He thought the old thought once again as he sat with her in MacGregor Mathers's house in Dublin and waited for the ritual to begin.

Knowing she was worshiped was so much a part of Maud's daily life that she'd had to rise beyond it, into her work of politics and of bringing aid to the beleaguered peasants. She was six feet tall with an aureole of Titian hair piled upon her stately head that made her appear even taller. She had a square jaw that would have seemed pugnacious in a less arresting face, but in Maud's case it simply seemed to evince an appropriate strength for the rest of her passions. She smiled at Willy's adoring gaze and hoped he wouldn't ask her to marry him again tonight.

If all went well, this would be an informative evening for them both—the young man and woman they'd brought along as guests were interesting. She sensed strong stuff in both the O'Connors. The woman was gently bred, that was apparent . . . and he . . . he was of earthier material, but no less intriguing for that. And he was very handsome.

Maud settled back to watch her host. MacGregor Mathers was the talk of literary Dublin. Like most of those who frequented the Castle circuit, he had no need of employment. But he did have an occupation. Both MacGregor and his wife were occultists. They divined the future, read tarot cards, and instructed devotees in the arts of astrology, numerology and spiritualism. Most intriguing of all, they practiced ritual magic.

A little black boy dressed in the gaudy costume of the East came through the double doors swinging an incense-filled censer. Behind him, in a richly embroidered brocade robe came a man of medium height, with dark, luminous eyes and long, straight black hair. He had the look of a priest of some ancient cult, as indeed he was. MacGregor Mathers was a magus.

He swept into the room, followed by his wife, who was wearing a robe sewn with crescent moons and astrological glyphs; her feet were not visible beneath the gown and she somehow seemed to glide behind her husband, which prompted Yeats to lean toward the entranced Maud and whisper, "Do you suppose she travels on wheels, or is she merely wafted along like that by fairies?"

"Are you amused by the servants of the ancient gods, Mr. Yeats?" Mathers's voice thundered the question, startling all in the room.

"Certainly not!" replied the poet with dignity. "I'm merely feeling in high spirits this evening, Mr. Mathers."

Maud looked at her friend reproachfully and rose to give Mathers her hand. When she was standing, the magus and his wife were both dwarfed by her six-foot stature. It occurred to Willy that Maud had not been called the most beautiful young woman in Europe without reason.

Yeats introduced Con, Tierney and the other guests he had brought with him, and Mathers acknowledged them before beginning to speak.

"The study of ritual magic," said Mathers portentously, "requires a great commitment from those who seek its knowledge and power. To learn the secrets of the universe . . . to learn to travel on the astral airwaves . . . one must become an initiate in a secret order of Hermetic rites. The training is arduous and there are dangers on its path."

Con and Tierney looked at each other, and Tierney squeezed his wife's hand. It seemed this would be an entertaining night, if nothing else.

Mathers leaned back in his chair, eyeing the gathering shrewdly. He placed the palms of his slender hands together in a meditative pyramid, and watched his audience calculatingly. Then he spoke.

"Ladies and gentlemen," he said. "Tonight we shall speak of that most fearsome of all human terrors . . . death."

At the word "death" Maud made a startled sound—her child had died at the age of three, and thoughts of him still haunted her. "And what exactly does a metaphysician believe of death, Mr. Mathers?" she asked warily, hopefully.

"We know death to be a simple change of consciousness, Miss Gonne," replied Mathers smoothly. "The soul journeys through many lifetimes in its quest for knowledge."

"Is there, then, no hell nor heaven?" asked Tierney.

"The soul passes through many stages after death, Mr. O'Connor"—he smiled—"that it may gain an understanding of the events of one's life. If one has done much evil, seeing it reenacted could be hellish. If one has done good, the experience may be quite heavenly. There is a period of tranquility between lifetimes—we call it 'the Other Side,' perhaps your churchmen call it 'heaven.' "

"And where does one spend that time of tranquility, Mr. Mathers?" asked Con.

" 'The Other Side' is a realm of spirit, not matter, Mrs. O'Connor. One can construct it to suit oneself. Many people use the metaphor of crossing a great river and coming to rest in a gentle meadow." He looked at her speculatively.

"How is it, Mr. Mathers," interrupted Tierney, "that a body of knowledge as profound as what you suggest could exist in the world and most people not even know of it?"

"Only according to your gifts and your willingness can you learn the secrets of the universe, Mr. O'Connor," he replied, smiling as if possessed of an important secret.

"You, for example, are gifted with 'the Sight.' You use it constantly in your writing and yet you are, for the most part, not even aware that you are drawing on knowledge from other realms."

Tierney looked startled. "I've never mentioned 'the Sight' to you," he said.

"There was no need for you to mention it, Mr. O'Connor. Even Mr. Yeats recognized the gift of vision in your work."

"See here, Mathers!" interjected Yeats. "I've never once discussed that with you."

The magus smiled at everyone's evident discomfiture.

"Your Shakespeare said it very well, Mr. Yeats. 'There are more things in heaven and earth than are dreamt of in your philosophy.' "

When no one spoke, Mathers smiled enigmatically and clapped his hands once. Instantly, the little black boy appeared at his side, his turban bobbing as he bowed low before his master. "Bring us tea, Achmed. We have work to do in the library." And turning suddenly, he led them all imperiously into the next room to continue their education.

* * *

"Do you think he knows what he's talking about, Willy?" Maud asked after the lecture as she drew her fur-trimmed cloak about her; the fiery fox trim of the hood blended with her own auburn tresses to give her a majestic, animal-like appearance.

"I think that he *thinks* he does, at least, Maudie. He's quite sincere about it, in my opinion. And you know what a skeptic I am about these fellows." Maud smiled at that, for she knew that Willy would travel any arcane avenue to pursue his poetic vision. Yeats pulled his own hat down on his forehead against the wet snow that had begun to fall while they were indoors. "I'd like to give it all a try," he said.

"This Hermetic rites business?"

"That and the astral travel he spoke of. Damned fine way to get about if it works, you know." There was the hint of amusement in his voice as he gave the young woman his arm and led her toward the waiting carriage.

She laughed, a hearty honest laugh; unlike the coquetry of most young women, Maud tended always to express exactly what she thought. Damned hard to deal with that, Yeats had often mused, but vastly better than all the silly, fluffy fakery of most women. Not that it wouldn't be nice to have Maud just a little less unconventional, just a little more willing to settle down to home and hearth. But she was who she was.

He rather liked the O'Connor couple now that he'd had a chance to see them together. So much in love they seemed—and intelligent, both. And Tierney had real talent . . . an exceedingly Irish talent at that, and well worth cultivating. If the man really had "the Sight," it could be an extraordinary adjunct to his own explorations of the ancient religion. Ah well, there'd be time enough to find all that out.

Con and Tierney made their way back from the spiritualist meeting through the frosty night. The wintry wind nipped at their faces and Con felt Tierney's arm go automatically around her to ward off the chill. She thought once again that loving him made all the deprivations of their life seem bearable.

"What do you really think of it all?" Con asked her husband companionably as they walked along. She didn't entirely like Mathers and his wife, but she was fascinated by much of what he'd had to say.

"I'm comfortable with unseen things, I suppose," he answered thoughtfully, "especially since I seem to be having flashes of 'the Sight' again. I know there's more to this world than the realists think. And I'm more than willing to believe that Mathers has gifts and knowledge the rest of us can barely imagine. Perhaps we all have gifts, but we don't know how to develop them."

"I like the way they look at death," said Con thoughtfully, holding closely to his arm. "It's so very gentle and hopeful."

Her husband smiled at her upturned face and hugged her closer in the darkness.

"Aye, Beauty. It seems only sensible to have more than one lifetime in which to put what we've learned to use, doesn't it? What kind of a just God would make men as unequal as they are, and then judge them with the same measure? It makes life seem *fairer* to me to think of being rich in one life and poor in another."

"It certainly makes more sense than to think of some poor wretch born with nothing, dying with nothing, with never the chance for more," replied Con. "And then having just as much expected of him at the Judgment Seat as someone with all the privileges this world can offer!"

"You sound like a socialist, not a spiritualist, my love." A smile tugged at the corners of Tierney's mouth as he said it. "Maybe we should bring James Connolly to meet them, eh?" He knew she admired Connolly's writing on socialism and that she wanted to meet the man.

Con laughed in the silent street, her laughter echoing on the crisp air. "I've an idea," she said suddenly. "Let's make a plan about where we'll meet on 'the Other Side,' so we'll be sure to find each other."

"We're not going to be there for a long while yet, are we?" He smiled at her enthusiasm.

"No, no, of course not. But we should still make a plan, just in case we get separated en route. If it's as Mathers said, and we can make a clear image for ourselves, let's make it the loveliest place we can think of!"

"With weather a little warmer than tonight's," he responded.

"Yes, and green grass on a lovely hillside with an enormous shade tree . . ."

"On the banks of a lazy river. Remember, they did say we must cross a great river."

"Good idea not to have our spot too far from the river, though," she bantered. "No sense making it easy to lose each other."

"As if there were any chance of that! You know, you've made 'the Other Side' sound a bit like your father's estate."

"I've always thought heaven would have much in common with Sligo, now that you mention it." She laughed softly as she said it, and her husband squeezed her shoulders affectionately.

"Do you miss home, then? I wouldn't blame you for that."

"Home is where you are, Tierney. You and Tahg. If we could go there together it would be a different story. That's why I like the idea of our green hill with the shade tree."

"I like it, too. Now we just have to hope we don't get there too soon."

She looked up at him and saw the corners of his mouth turn down a fraction, as they always did when he smiled.

He too was changed, she thought, by all that had happened to them. No longer simply the young poet longing for rebellious adventure in a grand cause, he was now a man whose personal plans encompassed more than Ireland. She wondered for a moment how all the learnings they'd been party to would finally mesh. Rebellion, poetry, spiritualism, country, family, love . . . were they all just pieces of the same great puzzle, some sort of master plan of life as Mathers claimed? Or were they warring elements in a battle where one day some must win and some must lose?

They climbed the stairs to their flat, grateful to be home. Con dropped her small purse on the table and, turning, hugged her husband unexpectedly.

"I think that either the spiritualist meeting or the snowy air has made me want you very much," she whispered to him.

"Then we should go to as many meetings as possible this winter . . ." he said as he gathered her into his arms. She felt the encouraging strength of him as he held her, and thought that not even death would seem frightening if they were together . . . not even death.

Beth and Edmond

10   My husband, Edmond Manningham, was lean and athletic at nearly forty years of age. He had a disposition well suited to his role as a country gentleman and seemed always to be smugly comfortable with his lot in life. He was intelligent and exceedingly articulate; he prided himself on being both a student of human nature and an excellent judge of character. He believed wholeheartedly in the systems that surrounded his life . . . the system of government that had brought the civilizing influence of England to his island home . . . the system of primogeniture that had given him a three-hundred-year-old domain and its income . . . the system of chivalry that had provided him a suitable wife. In those early days of our marriage I thought him an enviably happy man.

Edmond's father had been a stern and unyielding fellow who had given little to his son but a firm sense of discipline and a staunch integrity. He had been violently opposed to Irish Home Rule and had never quite gotten over the fact of his father's assassination by the rebels.

Edmond's feelings about the Irish were less vehement than his father's, but certainly no less oppositional. He had respected his grandfather, but had not loved him, so the old man's assassination by the rebels had not affected his assessment of the situation appreciably. And while he took his own father's opinions into account, he was not unduly influenced by the man's prejudices. The Irish were a rough and unschooled force of childlike peasants, it seemed to my husband. They were incapable of governing themselves and incapable of intellectual process. Beyond that, they were useful as brawny workers; their dispositions were relatively cheerful, their music vulgar but pleasant, and their comings and goings were of no great matter to him.

Edmond Manningham suspected my family of having some

sort of unwholesome sympathy for the Republicans. After all, Con had committed the unpardonable sin in running off with her fisherman and Desmond had implied that he approved the appalling match. Edmond actually told me once that he sensed a definite weakness in my family strain that allowed us to be seduced by Ireland. He hoped no such weakness would present itself in our children. I did not seem to display any Fenian tendencies, he assured me—unless you considered my stubborn insistence that I understood Constance's insane behavior as a sign of weakness.

He said that women made their judgments based upon emotion and it was obvious that this handsome young rogue had bewitched both Con and me with his good looks and his ghastly Fenian ballads. But that was only to be expected. I was brighter than most of the flibbertigibbet women he'd had his pick of at balls and hunts and socials over the years, but I was a woman, nonetheless, and women's hearts ruled their heads and that was that.

I had begun writing again—but whereas during courtship Edmond had feigned interest in my ability, now he disdained it. I had been published as a social kindness by a family friend, he told me. I would be foolish to imagine that the world waited breathlessly for my next work. If, on the other hand, it pleased me to dabble in such girlish entertainment as keeping a journal, he could see no harm in that. Provided, of course, that it didn't interfere with my wifely duties. It was an unsettling conversation for me, as you might imagine. As, indeed, most everything I was learning about my husband's attitude toward me was unsettling.

Perhaps it was the difference in our ages that made Edmond contemptuous of my abilities, I told myself, and, as if to prove myself a capable wife, I cast about in my mind for some gesture that would force Edmond to accept me as an equal. Finally I hit on the idea of planning a dinner party, which would enable me to show off my skills as both wife and hostess. If the party were successful, I reasoned, others would express their admiration and Edmond would see me in a different light. How naive I was. But at the time I could come up with no better plan.

The day before the party I finished dressing hurriedly and pulled the bell cord sharply twice, as a signal to Dermot, the butler. As this was to be my first big party as hostess in my new home, the responsibilities were enormous. I struggled to push the fact of my pregnancy from my consciousness. That was simply one of the consequences of being a grown-up woman, I told myself. Odds were I'd spend the better part of the next twenty years pregnant, so I'd better begin to be used to it! I had no intention of letting pregnancy make me an invalid, as it had my mother.

I stood by the window for a brief moment looking out over the lush hills where Con and Des and I had played together as children. How simple life had been then . . . and how pre-ordained.

"You rang, ma'am?" Dermot's voice jarred me from my thoughts.

"Yes. Yes, I did, Dermot. I thought we'd best go over the seating arrangements again. I just realized that I've put old Sir Mallory next to my brother Desmond. If Desmond gets his dander up, Sir Mallory will be putting it about that we're a bunch of Republicans and it would do my reputation as a hoot ess no good to have one of my guests die of apoplexy at my first party." I babbled on, knowing one should not be so familiar with a servant . . . but I was lonely.

The butler's eyes twinkled at my obvious nervousness, but he, at least, seemed to approve of me and I felt comforted by his acceptance.

"I've not a doubt in me mind, ma'am, but 'twould do Sir Mallory a world of good to meet a Republican face to face, now."

I smiled at the wizened old man; he took more liberties in his speech than one should allow, but I liked him and it amused me to see that despite all Edmond's proper authority this funny old man ruled the roost at Manningham Castle.

"You wouldn't be having a bit of a tendency toward rebellion yourself, would you now, Dermot?" I asked mischievously.

"Ah, mum, with me whole heart and soul, I'm for Ireland."

I regarded him quietly for a moment, unsure of whether it was safe to be so open with a servant. I wanted to say that I felt much the same way, but propriety made me hold back.

"I think that very laudable, Dermot," I finally said.

His face crinkled into an ancient smile. "God bless the good day you'd be telling me a darlin' thing like that, Yer Ladyship!"

he said with genuine approval, something I needed rather badly just then.

"Now, shall we switch Sir Mallory's seat, in deference to my husband's digestion?" I asked, to change the subject.

"Indeed we shall, mum," said the old man with a chuckle. "Indeed we shall. For two apoplectics would be too much entirely for the staff to handle."

In a way I think that conversation was the beginning of my friendship with Dermot, a friendship that was later to prove of some consequence in my life.

I had wanted to ask Con and Tierney to the party. They couldn't have come, of course, but I felt hurt that Edmond had greeted my suggestion with such distaste.

"Really, my dear," he had said in his maddeningly genteel manner. "We don't entertain *fishermen* at Manningham Castle," and I had bitten back the quick reply that came to my lips and said nothing. In my short span of married life I had learned how little was to be gained for a woman by direct confrontation with a man. I longed for the comfort of Con's sensible advice. . . . I felt insecure and terribly alone.

It was a curious powerlessness that had begun to envelop me. My husband's decisions, my husband's successes, my husband's needs and desires would henceforth circumscribe my world. And I must find a way to let this happen gracefully, as other women did. I hadn't the courage that Con had; it was not in my nature to make waves. Yet I lay awake often in my first year of marriage puzzling out how to assert myself. How to find a way to truly be mistress in my own home.

I was determined to be a good wife . . . and I was filled with a sense of purpose. I had married "the right kind of man," I reasoned; I had fulfilled my destiny; there had to be a way to make it work. If not, there must be some shortcoming in myself that was at fault. Edmond was certainly "the right kind of man"—he was civilized and sensible, a peer of the realm, an intelligent, articulate person with all the right credentials for husbandhood.

But as the months of marriage wore on, my first heresy occurred to me: that there were many qualities he did not possess and that they too would have been important credentials for marriage.

He was cold and silent much of the time. There was an imposing austerity to his demeanor that in the beginning I'd hoped to break through. But he rejected my attempts at cajolery or intimacy as if they were an unwanted invasion of his privacy.

I offered him advice; he treated it contemptuously. I attempted to learn of his work, so that I might participate. He said that ladies did not meddle in men's affairs.

I attempted to seduce him with coquetry and womanly wiles. He seemed more amused by my efforts at sensuality than enticed.

I found that the more disappointments I endured, the stronger my need to write became. I began to commit to paper my sorrows and confusions, my angers and frustrations, my fading dreams.

It was a puzzling and disappointing time for me, this first year of wifehood. I, who had felt so smugly safe in my marital cocoon, began to see long years of proper imprisonment stretching before me. So I consigned my sorrows to paper and pinned my hopes on the party. Surely my performance as hostess would prove my worth.

The long hall at Manningham Castle was ablaze with light. The massive crystal chandelier, which had to be secured within the ceiling by special iron beams, glittered with the flame of scores of candles. The sconces that adorned the wainscoted walls echoed their glimmering light with candles of their own.

The gardeners had festooned the banisters of the mezzanine above the hall with flowers from the greenhouses, and with holly and gorse in profusion. Streamers fluttered from white satin bows and furbelows, which in turn had been sewn with silver beadings to catch the light and reflect it back like captured fireflies.

I had marshaled the servants into nearly military precision, with the help of Dermot. There wasn't a speck of dust or an ornament out of place anywhere in the huge house and I could see by the pride shining in Edmond's eyes as he greeted his guests that he approved of my efforts.

Music from three separate rooms wafted cheerily through the echoing space. I'd engaged a string quartet and a chamber-music orchestra to entertain and to provide for our guests' dancing after dinner. As a special surprise I'd employed a local harpist of some renown to play Irish airs during the meal, and had even had a special dress made for the girl to wear, as she had no appropriate garment of her own. The harpist would appear during dinner all in white chambray with a wreath of white freesia in her flowing hair, an angelic presence to add just the perfect touch to the dinner, which would be served in the huge dining gallery. I was very pleased with myself for having thought of it.

Carriages from all over the county had been arriving through the afternoon and Manningham Castle's long unused scores of bedrooms had once again been primped for company. I felt a breathless elation at the festivities, a glorious womanly sense of myself as mistress of a great house. I wished Con could be there to share it with me.

What must my sister's life be like? I wondered, considering the confusions of my own. What must it be like to love so wildly that all "having" is insignificant by comparison?

I heard my name called and saw that Edmond was beckoning to me. His lean face was shining with pleasure; I knew that the success of this dinner could only do him good in his aspiration toward politics.

"My dear," he said amiably as I drew near, "may I present Sir Horace Courtney and his delightful wife, Lady Alison."

I reached out my hand, curtsying. "Sir Horace, Lady Alison," I said, "you are most welcome to our home."

"You've done wonders with this old mausoleum, child," bubbled the portly middle-aged woman vivaciously. "One can see your deft touch at every turn." She beamed approval on me and took my arm proprietarily. "You simply must take me on a tour so that I may see what you've been up to, my dear. I knew your husband's mother, don't you know, and I must say, since her untimely death, this old place had nearly gone to pot! All stuffy and filled with hunting trophies and the like at every door post. Damned grisly, those decapitated heads our darling husbands insist on dragging home at the slightest provocation, eh?" She was as round as a partridge and her many chins wobbled when she spoke.

I swept along beside the funny woman, amused by the torrent of verbiage, flattered to be showing off the results of my decorating efforts, relieved to be thought a success, at last.

By the time we'd returned from touring the refurbished areas of the house, the hall was already filled with guests. The men were resplendent in their morning coats and the women looked like a bouquet of giant flowers in ballgowns of every color and fabric. I could see a group of substantial-looking gentlemen surrounding Edmond. My brother Desmond was by far the youngest of the men.

"But gentlemen, gentlemen"—I could hear Des saying— "even ex-Prime Minister Gladstone was in favor of Home Rule for this little island of ours. Surely that must be deemed important. 'Go to the length and breadth of the world,' he said, 'ransack the literature of all countries and find if you can a single voice which says that England's conduct toward Ireland is anywhere treated but with contempt and condemnation.' "

"By heaven, Desmond, it's a sorry day indeed when our young men have taken to memorizing rebellious poppycock!" Sir Horace glowered at Des from under his imperious eyebrows.

"I'm simply playing devil's advocate, sir." Des smiled at the number of suddenly jutted-out chins that told the response of his audience to his sentiments. "I'm simply reminding you that this Home Rule we all fear so much could very well become a fact of life for us in this decade."

"We'd damned well better hope it does not!" interjected Sir Bertie Ambrose, entering the fray for the first time. "We've a tidy little life here thanks to our gracious government. Without England's international trade and England's market for our produce and England's civilizing influence—"

"And England's occupying army?" Desmond slipped in the jibe with a sardonic smile that was at once insulting and well-bred.

"Damned right, and grateful for it! We need her army to hold these cocksure peasants at bay *now*, young man. Just what do you suppose would keep these louts from murdering us all in our beds if there were no army in residence? Why, we'd never sleep a night!"

"I wonder we can sleep at night as it is, sir, knowing we've bludgeoned them into hating us that vengefully."

Edmond, seeing the hostile expression on the men's faces, signaled with his eyes to me to rescue him.

"Gentlemen, gentlemen," I cooed as smoothly as I could, "you have left us ladies alone for entirely too long with all your terribly important politics and conversation. Now, I intend to spirit you all to the gallery, where dinner is about to be served.

Surely you can tear yourselves away from politics long enough to give us ladies the pleasure of your company for an hour or two?"

"My dear Lady Manningham," answered Sir Horace, instantly the gentleman, "you've graciously provided us with such a splendid evening, we shall be most delighted to save our conversation for a more appropriate moment. You're quite right to chide us for our bad manners." He deftly took my arm and led the parade gallantly to the table, his tall, patrician body as graceful at sixty-five years of age as if he were a dancing master.

The seventy-foot dining hall was really quite breathtaking, thanks to Dermot's efforts and my own. The women oohed and aahed pleasantly as they were seated. The gilded Manningham porcelain lay in magnificent contrast to the Irish-linen cloth beneath. The vermeil service for one hundred that had filled the cupboards in the huge butler's pantry was resplendent in the glow of the candles that lit the long table at four-foot intervals. Flowers in tiny Waterford crystal vases graced every place, a nuance I'd seen in London on my wedding trip. Liveried footmen, twenty on each side of the immense table, waited patiently at attention while the guests were seated and the succession of courses it would be their place to serve would be brought from the kitchen. Dermot stood quietly behind my chair, his gnarled old fingers gloved in white. When I gave the signal to begin, a veritable ballet of service commenced, and I breathed a sigh of relief and pride.

At the end of the second course, as everyone had settled with varying degrees of contentment into appropriate dinner conversation with the partner to his right, I signaled to Dermot that the Irish harpist was to enter. The slender redheaded girl walked gracefully into the room in her unaccustomed finery; her eyes lingered for a moment on the table that held enough food for the village and half the neighboring county. Then she walked deliberately to her instrument and, seating herself, she passed her hands tenderly over the golden strings and persuaded a sound as sweet as celestial music from the ancient harp.

As the poignant strains of the music began to insinuate themselves into the atmosphere, conversation slowed and the audience paid closer attention to the girl's performance.

"I say, what a splendid musician, my dear," said Sir Horace, seated to my right. "Wherever did you find her?"

"A local talent," I answered, delighted by his enthusiasm. "My butler, Dermot, told me about her and she auditioned for me just a week ago."

"And where did she study?" he asked.

"She told me that her mother taught her the basic chords of the instrument and she taught herself the rest."

"Charming little air she's playing; don't suppose she sings, too?"

"I don't really know, Sir Horace," I said truthfully, "but Dermot would."

I signaled to the butler, who moved soundlessly to my side. "Does Maire sing as well as play, Dermot?" I whispered to him.

"Like an angel, Yer Ladyship."

"Sir Horace is charmed by the air she's performing; he wondered if perhaps it has lyrics?"

"It does, ma'am."

"Would you then ask the girl to sing them for us?"

"If you wish, ma'am," replied Dermot deferentially as he moved away from the table.

I thought curiously that the old man's eyes had looked surprisingly troubled as he'd responded to my question, but I felt far too buoyant about the way the evening was going to be concerned. He moved to the girl's side, spoke softly to her and a moment later her young sweet voice filled the echoing hall with the sounds of the minor-keyed melody.

"I sat within the valley green;
I sat me with my true love;
My sad heart strove the two between,
The old love and the new love;
The old for her, the new that made
Me think of Ireland dearly,
While soft the wind blew down the glade,
And shook the golden barley.

" 'Twas hard the woeful words to frame
To break the ties that bound us;
But harder still to bear the shame
Of foreign chains around us.

> And so I said, 'The mountain glen
> I'll seek at morning early,
> And join the brave United Men.'
> While soft winds shake the barley."

It took me two full stanzas to recognize the direction of the inflammatory lyrics; having her mention the secret revolutionary group that had wreaked such havoc in Ireland in the late eighteenth century seemed a dreadful breach of taste!

"See here!" broke in Edmond, reality dawning on him at the same moment. "We'll hear none of that kind of thing!"

"Let her sing, Edmond," interposed Desmond diabolically. "It'll do us all good to hear what the Irish think of us." I looked at my brother with all the reproach I could muster, but he persisted. "Besides, she sings like the muse herself," he added, smiling engagingly at me.

Seeing my stricken face, the courtly Sir Horace squinted his huge brows together in a formidable scowl and pursed his lips judgmentally.

"I quite agree with Desmond . . . for once." He added the last pointedly and several men chuckled. "Have we sunk so low that we cannot hear this gifted young lady's song without a row developing over it? Surely we can muster a bit more civility than that, eh?"

"You're very kind, Sir Horace," I breathed, meaning every word of it. "I'm terribly embarrassed."

"No need for that, my dear. Charming girl. Let her continue, by all means."

I nodded acquiescence miserably, not daring to let more of a scene develop, and the girl took up her interrupted song:

> "While sad I kissed away her tears
> My fond arms round her flinging,
> The foeman's shot burst on our ears,
> From out the wildwood ringing;
> The bullet pierced my true love's side,
> In life's young spring so early,
> And on my breast in blood she died,
> While soft winds shook the barley.
>
> "But 'blood for blood without remorse'
> I've taken out Oulart Hollow;

I've placed my true love's clay-cold corpse
Where I full soon will follow;
And round her grave I wander drear,
Noon, night, and morning early,
With breaking heart when e'er I hear
The wind that shakes the barley!"

The haunting melody died away and the harpist continued her repertoire without lyrics, but the uncomfortable faces at the table made it clear that the message had been received. I saw my father scowl at me from the far end of the room and felt my heart sink to its lowest ebb.

We ladies retired to refresh ourselves and Lady Alison made a point of trying to console me, but I was disconsolate. I had all I could do to get through the remainder of the evening without dissolving into tears.

Edmond was in a fury by the time the last guest had been bedded down for the night and we had reached our bedroom.

"You stupid girl!" he hissed at me. Fear of being overheard kept him from shouting, not fondness for me. "You've ruined everything!"

I sat exhausted and crestfallen on the bed, all my lovely plans for redeeming myself in his eyes in ruins.

"You've made us both appear proper fools in front of the entire county by bringing that horrid girl here. This fiasco will be gossiped about by every old crone in Sligo for the next half year!"

"Edmond"—I tried to defend myself miserably—"I'm dreadfully sorry about what happened tonight—you must know that —but it was an accident, after all. There was no way I could have known about that song; and it wasn't I who asked her to sing that awful lyric."

"Whatever excuses you make for yourself, Elizabeth," he said very archly, "you have dealt my public image a great blow. Never before have I been a laughingstock.

"I realize that you are inexperienced at the business of being an adult, but I hardly thought you had the same capacity for disastrous behavior as the rest of your ridiculous family!"

I recoiled as if he'd slapped me. Everything seemed to crystallize for me in that moment. I missed my family! I missed being in the company of people who loved and appreciated me. Here at Manningham I was nothing more than an alien in my husband's home.

I no longer felt penitent, but very, very angry. A great desire took hold of me to do something that would really be worthy of Edmond's misplaced wrath. I went to sleep that night lonely and miserable, but for the first time determined that I'd find a way to fight back. I cast about in my mind for some potential weapon against him and the one that occurred to me was Ireland. Con and Tierney and Des were sympathetic to the Irish; I would learn about them, too!

Why choose Ireland as my weapon? It gave me a perverse pleasure to do something forbidden behind Edmond's back, of course, but it was more than that. The Irish Cause made me feel a communion with my family that I longed for and, too, I had learned to feel an empathy for the downtrodden that I'd never felt before. I, too, was without recourse if wronged, and that very vulnerability made me sympathetic to the Irish.

I felt secretly triumphant about everyone's lavish praise as they left us the next day, but it was only a bittersweet compensation.

Edmond was niggardly with his speech and aloof, making certain I knew that he had not forgiven me for the indiscretion of the harpist, but neither of us spoke of it again.

Two days later, Desmond called at Manningham on an errand of horse breeding, a subject of some importance to both estates. He greeted me merrily and with high compliments about my success as a hostess.

I was thrilled to see him, and clung to him like a lonely child when he embraced me. I longed so much for the effervescent warmth of my own family—Des seemed the last link to a happier past. I seated him in the drawing room and we talked animatedly while we awaited Edmond.

My brother planned a trip to Dublin on his way to the Continent, where he had business, and he would stop to see Constance, so I must give him a letter to take along. We chatted happily for ten minutes or so, and then Edmond entered the room and frowned to see me there.

We continued to talk for a moment, all three; then Des

brought up the question of the horses and I enthusiastically gave my opinion.

"Really, my dear," said Edmond coolly in the middle of my sentence, "we have no further need of you in this discussion."

I was startled as a struck child.

"Beth and Constance have always been involved with the horses . . ." Des interjected, but Edmond cut him short.

"I have absolutely no intention, Desmond, of seeking advice from my wife on matters that are of concern only to men. It is time for you to run along, Elizabeth."

As simply as that; I was dismissed. I felt my cheeks burning with embarrassment and dared not look into Des's eyes. But as I rose to go, I caught sight of his angry face and, fearing his rash temper, kissed him quickly and fled the room. As I rushed through the door, I heard Edmond say, "Your father, I fear, was far too lenient with his daughters. And see what he has wrought in them. One who defies him to run off with a bounder and another who barely knows her place." I couldn't hear Desmond's reply but the tone of his voice sounded fierce, indeed, and I knew he was defending me.

Where do loves and marriages end? I've asked myself since. Most often not in a single conflagration . . . but rather in a thousand drops of water on a single stone.

I left the room planning my first major disobedience.

When I asked Dermot to take me to visit the people on our estate, I can't say he was surprised. He was a canny old man and I grew fond of him as he and I pursued our visits around the countryside. Good lord, but I learned so much of what Tierney had alluded to the previous summer. I met women old before their time and children barely able to speak who already knew whom to hate and how to do so. I met men whose lives were circumscribed by the hated gombeen-man who did His Lordship's bidding in collecting rents and assessing taxes. I met many memorable people in those times, but none I loved like Terrance Kiernan, a tenant farmer on my husband's estate.

He was old as the Hill in Archaim—his teeth were few and far between; the ancient stubble on his chin had once been a beard, but "I outgrew the damned thing," he told me, and by the time I met him, stubble it was and no more.

He had been tall and broad in his youth, and occasionally

some story that he told me would cause him to rouse himself to a shadow of that former stature. But for the most part he was stooped and crippled with arthritis and with the marks of the torture he had endured at the hands of prison guards in Brixton.

He had the eyes of a fanatic or a saint . . . sharp, burning eyes that stabbed questions at you one minute or smiled compassionate balm the next. He was a man who had seen things mortals shouldn't of man's inhumanity to man, and all that knowledge was hidden in those passionate eyes.

He was like living history. His father had been with Wolfe Tone in '98 and he himself had lived through the Famine to fight with the Irish Republican Brotherhood in the Rising of '67.

Terrance was no saintly martyr to the Cause, mind you. He cursed (always apologizing to "Yer Ladyship") and swore and blasphemed ("Them hypocritical bastards in the Church would sell their surplices to Satan for the right price and a commendation from the Queen!").

He could be as courtly as a peer of the realm or as earthy as a dockworker, but he was Ireland. Blood and sinew, bone and brain, he was what stirred poets and patriots. He was a paean to individuality and the kind of courageous endurance that sets men apart from the lower life forms.

I loved the man. He was old enough to be my grandfather and he was of a class I was never even to have met, but I loved him and admired his indomitable endurance. I spent the better part of a lonely fall and winter listening to him and learning history and rebellion.

Terrance lived alone on the tiniest of farms. His wife had died fifty years before and he held her memory sacred enough that he had never remarried. Did he have a picture of her? I asked once, hearing him wax eloquent about her beauty—forgetting that a portrait or a photograph would be so far beyond this man's means as to be unthinkable.

"Sure and what need have I for a picture of the lass," he responded incredulously, "when the beauty of her proud face is engraved on my own heart so I see it every night when I close my eyes, and every morning when I wake?" Dermot told me that Sarah Kiernan and all of their five children had died of famine fever. She had been twenty-four years of age at the time.

I hoped that the "beauty of her proud face" that he remembered was as it must have been before the blight and I, too, tried to see her in my mind's eye, young and fair and in love with her handsome, tall husband.

At any rate, I'd been meeting with Terrance for several months and was very far along in my pregnancy when one night, in my enthusiasm for the old man, I ventured to tell Edmond about him at dinner. It was an ingenuous thing to do, I suppose, but it seemed to me that a member of the House of Lords should know at least something of the people of his carldom and, too, Edmond and I had so little to talk about that I was always casting about for some tidbit of innocent conversation. I babbled on to my husband about this fascinating character and praised him in glowing terms.

Edmond listened without much real response, and, disappointed, I put the conversation from my mind until two days later when I was passing Edmond's study and heard the name Kiernan on the lips of Edmond's gombeen-man, MacClay. It was not my habit to eavesdrop, but I stopped to listen.

"He's to be consolidated, then?" asked MacClay.

"I think it would be for the best," said Edmond.

"The land is small potatoes, My Lord, but it's well placed near the river. If we consolidate the Mackelhennys and the O'Tooles as well, we'll have a tidy little parcel."

"Then do so," said my husband, dispensing with people's livelihoods and homes as if he were God Almighty.

"When I pack him off to the workhouse, sir, what shall I say if he protests?"

"Tell him I'll have no peasant dissident filling the Countess' head with seditious nonsense. Tell him he's lucky I'm not bringing charges against him for spreading treasonable gossip."

Can a human heart really break? I think mine did in that moment. At least I was sure it had ceased to function. I stood riveted in the hallway, tears of rage and horror in my eyes. What in God's name had I done? Who was this callous, coldhearted bastard I was struggling so hard to be a wife to? How could I undo this terrible deed?

I burst in on Edmond, trying desperately to stay in control of myself. By the sheepish look on his face I could see he knew I had overheard the conversation.

"You mustn't do this, Edmond!" I said with so much emotion in my voice that I fancied he would be his better self and respond.

"The man had no right to attempt to subvert you to his way of thinking, Elizabeth. And he had less right than that to be on such intimate terms with my wife!"

"Intimate terms? Are you mad? The man is eighty years of age!"

"An age when he should know better how to control his actions."

"I beg of you, Edmond, for the sake of our marriage, don't do this thing. Don't use my own well-meaning act against me to hurt an old man who can do you no harm."

"That old man you speak of so lovingly is a felon and a murderer. I've checked into his background and I'll not have such a reprehensible character in contact with my wife."

I stood back from the vehemence of what he was saying and in that instant I saw him clearly. When the scales fall away from one's eyes there is no replacing them.

"If you will not save this man from the ignominy of the workhouse, Edmond, for the sake of human decency—then I will ask you to save him as a kindness to me, for I don't think I can live with such a terrible consequence of an action of mine."

That stopped him for a moment and I think he might have relented had it not been for the presence of MacClay. Had I been older or wiser, perhaps I would have known to wait until my husband was alone before appealing to him.

He glanced from me to the gombeen-man, then cleared his throat and without looking me in the eye he said, "I'm afraid, my dear, that the land the man occupies is an important part of our consolidation efforts . . . this is not merely a whim, but a necessity."

He was actually capable of doing this . . . my own husband, the man to whom I had entrusted my life and my unborn child's.

"I beg of you, Edmond . . . this man is my friend!"

"All the more reason for my resolve, Elizabeth." His voice was hard and deadly.

I ran to Dermot. We must warn Terrance of what was afoot! We must find him a place to stay. I had no money of my own but there were some pieces of jewelry of my mother's that I could give the man. Dear God, there had to be a way to save him!

I saddled up my horse and, having gathered my jewelry into a sack, I galloped to the old man's cottage—despite the doctor's warning that I shouldn't ride while pregnant—but MacClay was there already. I stood by in horror as I watched Terrance pack his few possessions.

"Is he not even to have time to say good-bye to his neighbors?" I screamed at MacClay and his henchmen like a fishwife. *"You may not do this thing!"* I ranted. They all ignored me as if I did not exist. I tried to speak to Terrance but we knew not what to say to each other. He tried to show me that he understood, but his heart was too heavy to speak. I stood there dumbstruck, and watched the courageous old man leave his home for the last time.

" 'Tis all right, Yer Ladyship," he told me as he passed me by. "I've been on me keeping most all me life. 'Tis no different now. Yer not to blame yerself for the Manningham rot."

I watched wordlessly as he marched down the road, the gombeen man riding behind him. His step was high and his posture straighter than I had ever seen it. Too proud he was to let them see him bested.

When Terrance and his persecutors were out of sight, I screamed to heaven at the outrage in my heart. Screamed and cursed and kicked at the tumbledown door of his cottage in futile, impotent rage at *powerlessness*. Never before that moment had I understood the uses of power. That kindly, defiant old man was powerless and I was powerless. I, Elizabeth FitzGibbon Manningham, Countess of Sligo, was as powerless as he.

My husband and all of his arrogant breed had *power* . . . power to allow life or to take it away, power to decide the future, power to disallow justice.

Terrance was a victim because he was Irish and poor and old. I was a victim, despite my gilded trappings, because I was a woman. I could not save one old man and I could not save myself.

I was filled with self-loathing. Filled with knowledge that life could never be for me as I had dreamed. How could I have been so stupid that I'd lived a lifetime without understanding the condition of women? We were pampered children if rich, and willing slaves if poor. We were allowed our modest needs only so long as they did not disagree with those of our husbands. We were good enough for bed and board and breeding, but not for the simplest decisions of life.

But Con had known! Dear God, she had tried to tell me to rebel a thousand times in her own way and I had smiled sweetly, thinking her obstreperous, thinking that she fussed overmuch at lawful authority. "To win one's point gently, by subterfuge or sweetness, is a womanly art," I had said to her, stupidly. "What does it cost a woman to allow her man this latitude?" And she had stared at me in disbelief of the question. "Everything!" she had replied, and I had not understood.

Sweet Jesus, but I understood it now! Standing in the dirt of an Irish roadside, in the mire of a dirty deed, I learned about human rights and women's rights in a single afternoon from an old man named Terrance Kiernan.

After brooding over poor Terrance half the night, I went to Edmond and asked him for a divorce.

"I can't live with you any longer," I told him dully. "You are cruel and callous and not the man I thought I had married."

I could see that he was deeply hurt by my speech, but he responded by withdrawing himself from me, not by reaching out. His voice and aspect were cold and authoritative when he replied.

"Whatever you may think of me, Elizabeth," he said, "you have absolutely no choice but to stay married to me. I won't hear of divorce and without my consent your case would be hopeless from a legal point of view. You have no money of your own and you are about to bear a child. In short, my dear, you have absolutely no choice but to remain my wife."

He stopped for a moment, then said as an afterthought, "And if you take it into your head to disdain my bed, I must tell you that there are a great many willing women in the world with whom I can attend to my needs—so if you imagine *that* a weapon, you should disabuse yourself of the idea."

His tone was so flat and matter-of-fact that it defeated me.

"Is there nothing of love or kindness that you feel for me, Edmond?" I asked, overwhelmed by the realization of all that had been sucked from my life.

"You, who wish to divorce me, would have me love you at

the same moment?" he said derisively. "That really is a bit cruel and callous of *you,* isn't it, Elizabeth?

"You are my wife and the mother of my unborn child. I require of you that you perform the duties of those two roles publicly and that you treat me with civility in private. Beyond that, our marriage will be as you choose to make it.

"If you insist on letting a dissident old man destroy our lives, so be it. I, myself, believe that you should reconsider."

The olive branch then, however paltry and spavined, was being offered. He was right, of course, about my legal status. I had none. Chattel I was, like every other woman.

What was to be gained by my fighting him as I wished to? Nothing. Less than nothing. It was all so clear to me in a moment. The way to win was not by confrontation, but by becoming strong. Had I not been pregnant I might have had the courage to go to Father or to Des for help, but what help could there be for a breeding woman in those times?

My biological defeat added to the emotional one, and I felt as if the whole topsy-turvy world had come crashing in on me. I would be forced to continue my marriage. There would be no choices for me. We would go on and share a life. Yet I knew as I stood there that I would never forgive him for what he had done. Even knowing that he was no better nor worse than others of his sex and time, I would never forgive him.

I made my way blindly toward my room—desperate, weary, hurt and hurting. Before I'd made it up the stairs to the second landing I realized that the hurt I felt was no longer merely an emotional one.

Strange angry pains were shooting through my back and legs. I felt light headed enough so that as I reached the landing I cried out for Dermot. Then a cold frightening blackness settled over me and I never felt myself fall to the bottom of the staircase.

When I began to again focus on what was happening, I was already in my bed, dressed in a nightgown. I had no recollection of being brought there.

The most terrible pains tore at me . . . red searing pains, low strangling pains, inhuman pains, so that I felt like a trapped animal unable to free myself long enough to be dignified or coherent.

I awakened at the end of a scream and realized only when it was done that I had been the screamer.

The local doctor stood by the side of the bed peering through his rimless spectacles at me. It seemed impossible that I had been unconscious long enough for him to have been fetched from town.

Winston Manningham was born two dreadful days later. He was small and wizened, I'm told, and with a cranky disposition from the first. I cannot tell firsthand because I hovered between life and death for more than a week after his arrival. So serious did the doctor deem my condition that Edmond was forced to send for my family. Des in turn sent for Con, who came from Dublin to be with me, despite Edmond's protests. ✑

11 ✑ Lying in bed, weaker than my newborn son, I listened to Con tell me about life. She had been with me constantly since the birth, cheering, chattering, giving me advice about motherhood. I knew from Dermot that both she and Tierney had their problems with Edmond, but I knew that my brother Des had somehow bullied Edmond into allowing them entry into Manningham, although they lodged with Tierney's family at their cottage. I was so grateful for their presence that I questioned nothing.

My sister had that extraordinary capacity to devote herself so totally to those she loved that nothing else was permitted to interfere. All our lives, when anything threatened those closest to her, she girded her loins and went out to do battle. In truth, none of us ever thought she could be brought down. There was such strength to Con, such strength and fearlessness. And an indomitable will that brooked no interference with its plans. I drank in that strength and it sustained me.

So she talked when I was too weak to. And she bossed the nurses and servants unmercifully and banished any with a long face or a sad tale so that I had no choice but to recover.

While I lay there listening, I studied her. Whether she knew I did, I'll never know. Con had always been formidable—headstrong, willful, high-spirited and smart. But there was more to her now. A competency about life that was astonishing. It was as if wifehood and motherhood had caused her to grow into her own full stature.

The household I had struggled to learn to run, she ran effortlessly. The servants didn't love her, as they did me, but their respect was apparent. It amused me to see the competency with which she handled the vast entourage, while never letting any of it interfere even slightly with her constant vigil at my bedside.

I also watched her with Tahg, a great rosy robust boy of several months who suckled with the enthusiasm of a baby bull. She took all motherhood in stride, cuffing her son lovingly like a tigress with an unruly cub. Curiously, she handled my tiny Winston with great delicacy, as if afraid he might break if manhandled. Yet her own boy she treated to an offhand, laughing camaraderie such as I had never before witnessed between mother and son.

Tierney, on the other hand, treated Tahg as if he were ten years of age. He took the boy with him on long walks, carrying him in his arms, chattering gaily to him in English or Gaelic or both. I could see them off over the hills from my window, great father and small son in his arms, off to see the world.

Winston's nurse had offered to see to both children but Tierney had said no. If Con was busy with me, he'd see to the boy—and so he did. He had somehow managed a few weeks' leave from his employment so that he could accompany Con.

If you have ever come close to dying, you know that uncommon insights are part of the experience. One sees things with a different clarity from the edge of eternity. And on the return journey new knowledge crowds one's senses and halos everyday events with a radiant glow.

The simple act of breathing becomes a miracle. Freedom from pain, a blessing beyond price. That Con was with me while I metamorphosed back into health was a joy I shall always remember with gratitude. I drank in her life and her optimism. Her ability to shed the unimportant. And her laughter. Not since she'd left the house had I dissolved into gales of giggles as we two had been wont to do for a lifetime.

When, finally, she deemed me well enough so that she could leave, I felt bereft, as if a part of me had gone with her back to Dublin.

The time after Con and Tierney left Manningham is blurred in my vision now, after all the years.

I was a woman at last. My life had irrevocably changed. Weak and lonely for my sister's strength, disconnected from my husband not only by the ugliness of what had happened between us, but because I now feared the inevitability of facing childbirth yet again.

And, of course, I was a mother. Winston managed to thrive beyond his scrawny beginnings, and by the time I was well and whole again he was a robust four months of age and as active as such an age must dictate.

He was a strange child, cool and self-sufficient from the first. In those days I worried that his aloofness was a reflection on my motherhood, a proof of some terrible failure on my part that made him unresponsive. Later I had reason to feel otherwise.

I remember through the hazy reveries of that time some crystalline moments when my newfound insights and maturity tinged life with a very special tincture. I practiced the art of motherhood as best I could, knowing little or nothing about how to do so, and when strong enough I began to write again.

I also made great sweeping resolutions about changing my life; since I had so much time on my hands for self-examination, the list was endless. I had not forgiven Edmond for what had happened before Win's birth, but I was so grateful to be alive that nothing else seemed important by comparison. He had suggested taking me back to his bed after my recovery with the same lukewarm affection as before, but I put off intimacies as long as possible, using my illness as an excuse. When the doctor suggested a change of scene to speed my recovery, I leapt at the chance and I begged leave of Edmond to visit Dublin.

Lady Mallory had written me to say that she and her husband intended to spend two months on the Continent, a happenstance that would leave their town house in Dublin free during September and October, and would I care to convalesce there?

I was thrilled by the idea of being nearer Con and Tierney for a time, and equally happy to escape my husband. I accepted with great pleasure, telling myself that I'd deal with my failed marriage when I returned.

* * *

Dublin is a lovely place, tenderly appointed with wide boulevards and exquisite architecture. The gray Liffey adds a dimension of spaciousness and a dollop of largesse to the landscape, for it seems to wind its unhurried way through the city without urgency, as if meant only for decoration.

The Dublin I found on my arrival was, of course, a different sort from that of my sister's day-to-day life there, although I then had no real knowledge of how Con and Tierney lived. All I knew was that the silver salver in the entrance foyer of my borrowed home was spilling over with invitations which I, who had languished through the months of illness, was overjoyed to receive.

Dublin in those days was a small community of the rich, and I knew that life would be good and full of fun for the likes of me in this new city. I looked forward to the balls and parties and glittering dinners that awaited me—it seemed a blessed escape from the boredom of my marriage and the fear that childbirth had engendered.

If this makes me seem to you a shallow woman, I can only say by way of explanation that the class one grows up in seems the proper class, and I had only begun to know better. To be popular and young and rich and pretty; to be the wife of a peer and the mother of the next Earl of Sligo; to be welcomed into the Castle society of Dublin as if it were my due—these things were normal expectations—and I looked forward to each new pleasure as a means of banishing the unhappiness of the previous months.

I wanted desperately to *live* again. I do not mean to excuse myself; I know now that my needs then were foolish ones, but perhaps at twenty-three one is permitted some shortcomings. Life itself soon manages to temper us into stronger steel no matter what our social station. Perhaps the careless frivolity God allows us in youth is meant to sustain us later, when life denies us much and gives us only wisdom in compensation.

The journey from home had taken its toll on my strength and I was therefore confined to resting for the first week. I sent word to Con and Tierney that I was in Dublin, and much to my surprise, I received a letter back instead of a visit. I've kept it all the years, as even then I sensed it to be the beginning of my education.

17 Capel Street
Dublin
20 November 1898

My darling sister,

. . . that you are well enough to be in Dublin is a great joy to me. There is more life here on a street corner than in all of Sligo, and it will set you on your feet again, I have no doubt.

You may think this strange, but I want you to visit *us,* not the other way round. Being at Manningham Castle during your illness I was so struck by the cotton wool in which you and I were coddled all our lives that, in a bizarre reversal of snobbery, I found myself longing to escape the patrician womb and return to Dublin.

Not that I cherish being poor, mind you! Till the day I die, the very notion of poverty will chill me bone deep. But I cherish the knowledge of the world that Tierney has given me *and that world is here.* The knowledge of how *most* of humanity lives and breeds and loves and strives and dies is a revelation so important . . . so staggering in its impact on all intellectual and emotional considerations . . . that I would share it with you, as I have shared everything of consequence for a lifetime.

You may not like the gift at first. I daresay in the beginning you will be repelled as I was by the tawdriness and the vulgarity of it; the ugliness of the struggles people face, that turns them ugly in its wake, is hard on one's sensibilities. (Can you believe that when I got here I thought all Dubliners grotesque in their rags and hand-me-downs, with their unwashed hair and bodies and the patches on all parts of their lives . . . and now I deem them beautiful?) You do not understand yet, my sister, but you shall. You shall! And one day you will bless me for the gift I seek to give you.

Your writing will change, your relationships will change. You will have an opportunity for expansion that you cannot yet imagine.

Come to see us, Beth, when you are able. All things will become clear when you do so.

I miss and love you,
Your sister Constance

Need I recount the curious emotions raised by this unexpected communication? I resolved to go round to their flat the very next day.

She was right of course. It was the beginning of everything.

I can't describe the excitement I felt as Con and Tierney walked with me to the first Gaelic League meeting I was to attend. It seemed illicit, which was exciting, and rebellious, which I longed to be, although I hadn't yet admitted such to myself.

I was in high spirits and so were they. So very much in love, they seemed to be; so lustily, vibrantly, wonderfully in tune with each other. And there was a mysterious sexuality about them—as if they shared the best secret in the world. It made me envious at the same time that I adored them.

The room where the League met that night was a dreary attic over a shop building. There were no refreshments, which I thought a great oversight—but there were twenty or so people, such as I had never met before.

A relatively unwashed lot they were, and I was surprised to see my sister greet them each by name, amid much comradely banter. My clothes, of course, made me seem ludicrously out of place and I found myself wanting to apologize for my dressmaker's handiwork.

I listened, totally entranced. From the moment Seaneen O'Sullivan took the floor I was riveted by his presence. He wasn't eloquent in the poetic way that Tierney was, but the power of the man reached me like a physical blow. I felt held in my seat by it, pushed and battered by his voice and his stories. It was exhausting and exhilarating and several things I couldn't quite catalog.

He was large and powerful and very, very male. From that day to this, although I've seen many handsomer, I've never seen a man I thought more attractive.

He looked like a blacksmith, which he had been in his youth, or a longshoreman, which he had been often since then. There was a bull-like quality to the man that one could not help but respond to. An overpowering maleness that must have somehow pleased both sexes, for Con had said that the men followed him almost worshipfully. My sister told me she had bristled at first at being left out of the men's councils until Seaneen had taken her aside one night and said to her, "You have a great desire to be privy to our plans, have you not?" She'd nodded her head in a puzzled affirmation.

"Then you must know that your husband is under direct orders from his commanding officer, my own fine self, to stay silent. Not because we don't trust you, lass—we do and implicitly. But it would weaken your husband were he to have to worry about you and the wane any more than he already does.

"Informers are the bane of our existence, child. The eyes and ears of the Crown are everywhere. If it were deemed that you had information, it is not beyond them to try to take it from you.

"It may have become apparent to you that none of the other men who are trusted with the most delicate matters are married. That's not an accident.

"A man who loves a woman is twice vulnerable." He'd said the last with an odd catch in his deep voice and none of his usual bantering humor and she had somehow known enough not to argue before he walked away.

A man who had been standing near enough to overhear had come closer then. "He loved a girl once, too, Con," he'd said conspiratorially to her. "She was his wife of a year when the constabulary grabbed her. He was on the run, on his keeping, as they say, and they tried to make her tell them where he and the men were hiding. They tied her up and questioned her for hours.

"Well, the girl—her name was Maired—was pregnant, you see, although I doubt the men who left her unable to help herself knew that. Four or five months she was, and the strain of the questioning made her miscarry. By the time Seaneen doubled back to the farm, she was dead. A ghastly bloody horror it must have been to find the woman you loved like that. The man went mad, they say. He went after the bastards and killed the whole bloody lot of them. Nobody could ever prove he did it, of course, but the people knew. So the next time they caught him for some minor raid or other, they stuck him into solitary and tortured him, so they say. He's a strong man, our Seaneen."

Con repeated the story to me exactly as it had been told to her. It seemed full of honor and dignity and strength; I was deeply moved. Never had I met a man in the least like Seaneen. The meeting ended and we were introduced, but I found myself tongue-tied as a schoolgirl.

I felt his brooding eyes exploring mine with the odd sensation that he had uncovered my soul. Some men undress you with their eyes. Seaneen's investigations went deeper than simple nakedness.

"Welcome, My Lady," he said very quietly and deliberately —and somehow it wasn't a title but an endearment. My heart beat so violently I could barely hear.

"I so very much enjoyed listening to you," I stammered, thinking how inadequately that expressed what I had felt.

"You must come here with Con and Tierney often, while you are in Dublin."

I nodded assent and caught an amused and knowing look pass between my sister and her husband. It embarrassed me and I made a hasty retreat from this unsettling man.

"I've never seen him so courtly," said Con vehemently as we left. "Have you?"

"No indeed," replied Tierney. "I think he was quite smitten with you, Beth. I've never seen him show the least interest in any woman at our meetings before."

"Has he not married again?"

"No. He keeps pretty much to himself," volunteered Tierney. "The Brotherhood is his mistress. And like most of the leaders, he's convinced that a close relationship with a woman makes a man too vulnerable to attack."

"What a lonely life," I said nervously, trying to sort out my burdensome response to this surprising man.

"Aye. That it must be," said Tierney solemnly. "He's a good man, though, Beth. I know none better."

Con and I sat up late that night and spoke of many things. We were both concerned for Des. He had been engaged to a neighbor of ours, Evelyn FitzMaurice, but she had been taken ill and died quite unexpectedly the month before, and our brother had been quite inconsolable ever since. I'd been so starved for the pleasure of talking things through with Con, and there was so much to occupy our thoughts that it was very late before I brought the conversation around to asking her what she knew of Seaneen. I tried, of course, to sound disinterested.

"Be careful about him," she replied, seeing through me. "Rebellion is all he has in his life, love. It could devour you." Direct and insightful as always, she swept away all possibility of subterfuge. Of course she knew how attracted to him I had been; of course she knew the disappointment of my marriage. I was still of a class that lived by subterfuge—she had crossed over into honesty.

"I'll be careful, Con," I replied, trying to sound offhand. "I've no intention of being unfaithful to Edmond."

She eyed me, a cynical look on her face, then said unexpectedly, "Edmond is a lout, my dear sister, for all his superior breeding—and I've no doubt he's as much of a bore in bed as out."

Women in those days were woefully reticent to speak of such things, even among intimates, and I was startled by what she said. She looked at me with consternation, as if she had much more to say but wondered about the wisdom of saying it.

"I would give anything in this world," she said finally, "for you to have in your life what Tierney and I have—in bed as much as elsewhere. We women are bred to know so little of what we should seek in a man, Bethy. It infuriates me that we go into lifetime commitments with no knowledge to support us in our choices. We are virgins in many more ways than one, love! It's part of the way they keep us subjugated." I waited for the end of it—I could always tell when Con had more to say.

"It's my belief that if you had an affair with Seaneen, my dear sister, it would open such a hunger in you that you might not survive it." She looked terribly distressed by what she was saying.

"You are too loyal and honorable and tender to live a double life, Bethy. And, I fear, too tied to the life you *must* live at Manningham. I'd push you into Seaneen's bed myself if I thought you could bear it. I'd even advise you to live with the guilt of it in return for the beauty. But to have to go back to a man like Edmond after having tasted of a man like Seaneen? Christ! I think you'd spend the rest of your life in agony."

I was shocked beyond words by the speech. Not by the fact that she'd said it, but by the truth it laid bare. Better to live numb in a loveless limbo than to *feel* love and then knowledgeable, to be left without.

"I love you, Bethy," she said sadly. "I'm so very sorry."

We went to bed soon after, but I lay awake much of the night trying to reestablish control of myself. It was madness for me to be attracted to this man . . . or to any man. I was a married woman for better or for worse and I *would* keep my bargain. I struggled with myself half the night, but by morning, somehow, I knew that I could meet with Seaneen again, without tumbling into the abyss. I had such a strong sense of commitment then and had been bred to a severe sense of discipline. Besides which, my vision of myself did not include the picture of an unfaithful wife.

So we returned to the Gaelic League and I learned . . . oh, so many things. I adored Seaneen and had to keep myself carefully under control when I was with him. But not for a very long time did he truly complicate my life.

How can I tell you now with the proper degree of exhilaration the story of the people I met and the juxtaposition of light and darkness in my life while I stayed in Dublin? You see, one night I would dine with the Vice Regent, and the next I would be taken to meet Tierney's friends. One night Mrs. Sims would outfit me in shimmering satin for a ball at Dublin Castle and the next I would meet with Seaneen O'Sullivan and hear of revolution in the company of unwashed farmers and shopkeepers. It was a time of consummate revelation for me. Con was right. Never had I felt or been more alive.

I must admit I experienced great trepidation at the prospect of going home, but as the happy weeks wore on I realized that I couldn't live like this forever. I was a married woman, and I had a son who should know his father. I also had a powerful set of confusions about my own growing desire for independence, about the emotions Seaneen seemed capable of provoking in me, about my connection to the cause of Irish freedom. Confusions or none, the Mallorys returned from Europe and I resigned myself to going home. ✍

12 ✍ I arrived back at Manningham a different person from the one who'd left—the beginnings of an independent woman had been forged. To understand how

enormous a statement that is, you must have knowledge of the times in which I lived.

You see, to be born female in 1875 was to be born under someone else's control. First, your father's, then your husband's, finally your son's, if you lived long enough. It was assumed that as a woman you needed guardianship because you were congenitally incapable of self-government.

You could not own property . . . you could not have custody of your children . . . you could not sign a will or legal document . . . you could not vote. You could not support yourself outside the home except by menial labor . . . you could not divorce without your husband's consent. Your husband could consign you to an asylum for the insane if he so chose . . . you could not do the same to him.

If you left an unhappy marriage, you could not take your children with you. And where would you go, unskilled in any but household tasks?

It was assumed that from your birth, home, church and family would comprise your needs. You had no sexuality, except that permitted by your husband . . . you had no rights under the law and no legal status.

And you were so bred to docility . . . to selflessness . . . to subservience . . . that it took a very long while before you realized that being totally in someone else's power was dangerous, if that someone meant you ill—and unfree, even if he cared for you.

When I got back from Dublin I began to read about the cause of women's suffrage: having been free of Edmond for a matter of months, I had learned that I was a quite competent human being. And, too, the lovelessness of my marriage had made me restless. I enlisted Con's and Desmond's aid in getting books and pamphlets, for Edmond had forbidden me such things. I continued to write assiduously, as an outlet for my frustrations, but in truth, for the next five unhappy years, most of my time was spent in bearing and caring for a suitable number of children.

Winston, my eldest, had grown to be the image of his father. No one would ever mistake him for other than an aristocrat. Dear God, but I believe that arrogant carriage is bred in the bone, like the shape of one's nose or the length of one's fingers.

The child frustrated me. I wanted so much to coddle and touch and cosset, as Con did Tahg, but Winston would have none of it.

"Quite the little man he is, madam," said Nanny, by way of explanation when I questioned his behavior. I thought that cold disdain was hardly a charming attribute of manliness, if indeed one had to do with the other at all.

He was intelligent and articulate, he spoke early and well, as if even then he would brook no imperfection. He could be adorable in his precocity, but one was always aware of a great manipulative brain at work. I had the feeling that we had somehow trapped an adult in a boy's body, much to everyone's discomfort but Edmond's.

Soon after my return from Dublin I had again found myself pregnant. It seemed a significant irony, as Edmond made his way to my bed so seldom that I'd deemed myself out of danger. But such was not the case. What a bizarre jest of nature's it was to make me so damnably fertile, with a disinterested husband, while Con and Tierney, who longed for more children, were denied that comfort.

The winter when Win was a year and a half old I bore a pair of twins. A bouncing boy and girl they were, she dark, he fair, and both beautiful.

Somehow I had imagined each child would be born a clean white blotter, ready to soak up each ink stain of learning I would impart. I had no understanding then that each child enters the world a finished product, filled with his own needs and strengths and weaknesses. There are theories now, of course, that a child's environment shapes him, but theories are one thing and life is another. I'm an old woman who has lived to see three generations of my line and can declare with absolute certainty that each child brings his own joys and griefs with him when he enters the world. The Hamartia, the Greeks called it—the fatal flaw—is there from birth—and, too, the strength to win the battle over it, if one chooses.

Jamie, my second son, was as far a cry from his brother as night is from day. He was gentle and generous, even his erudition was a gift he sought to share. What relief I found in that loving boy.

Merry was his twin—the most aptly named of all my brood. We called her Merrion after Papa, but she was never called anything but Merry because of her sunshine disposition. She was a round little dumpling of a child, full of dimples and laughter. She had the pale Irish skin, dark, dark hair and blue-velvet eyes of my brother Desmond—the most arresting combination. I never once saw anyone look into her eyes who wasn't captivated by their specialness.

After Merry, I gave birth to my delicate daughter Bethany, and lastly came beautiful Angelica. I named her that because I thought she looked like a cherub in a Raphael painting . . . but her story I will tell you in its proper time.

Bethany was frail from birth. Dermot called her "sofa-sick" . . . which meant that she spent a large portion of her life propped up on the sofa by the bay window outside her bedroom. It wasn't a specific ailment that made her ill, but rather a lack of strength that kept her from the robust health the others enjoyed.

Win was five and a half, the twins were four, Bethany three and Angelica two when everything changed abruptly.

I had rebelled against Edmond whenever I could—small rebellions but important acts of independence. I visited the people of our estate; got to know their woes and their children. I encouraged them in their constant struggle against the gombeenmen. I wrote letters for them and read to the illiterate ones. In these small efforts toward freeing them, I freed myself. But it was still perfunctory. I was still the unhappy wife, dabbling in small rebellions. Until the turning point:

I was well known among the tenants—despite the fact that Edmond disapproved violently of my friendship with them. I had been to tea with a Mrs. O'Shaughnessy on Wednesday and had played with her children, two bright lads of three and four. Jamie and Merry had been with me at their cottage.

On Sunday, Dermot brought me the news that the two O'Shaughnessy children had been stricken with typhoid fever and that many of the neighboring children were similarly afflicted.

I felt fingers of fear tighten around my stomach as he spoke the terrible words. Typhoid was a highly contagious disease and there was no cure. Suddenly in my mind I saw my darling Jamie drinking from the same cup as the O'Shaughnessy boy, Merry playing with his toys.

I ran to the nursery to see the children. They were fine, said their Nanny, not a sign of illness was on them. Thank God. I said nothing to Edmond but went to sleep in a frenzy of apprehension.

The specter of my own disobedience hounded me. If I had not been running around the country against my husband's wishes, my children wouldn't be in danger. No! That was nonsensical Calvinistic thinking. I'd done a perfectly Christian charitable act in visiting that family, surely God could not be cruel enough to punish me for that.

Forty-eight hours later I was awakened in the night by Nanny. Bethany was already ill, Jamie and Merry feverish, she said. Win and Angelica were curiously unaffected. I ran to the nursery in my nightgown and wrapper, praying it would be no more than a cold . . . knowing that was not the case.

Little Bethany was fiery red and restless. She cried intermittently and gave us to know that her throat hurt dreadfully. She was a darling child, sweet-natured and dear despite her frailty, but it was evident from the first that she had been badly stricken by the disease.

The doctor was summoned, already exhausted from the spreading epidemic. He pronounced all three children sick with typhoid, gave us instructions for their care and left.

"We have no cure for the disease, madam," he told me. "Their temperatures will rise for seven to ten days, then hold steady but high for the same length of time. There will be red spots, violent diarrhea and delirium in some. Intestinal hemorrhage or perforation is the surest sign of death to follow. If you can get them past the third week living—the crisis will be past."

I listened to the list of symptoms in a state of panic, but I barely heard them. *Typhoid,* I kept saying over and over in my head. *Typhoid* kills people. I must not let it kill my children.

The following days were a nightmare of escalating horrors. Bethany cried, it seemed, night and day; how she had the strength for it in that little body I'll never know. She alternated chills and fever, kicking off the blankets one minute, teeth chattering the next. She could take no nourishment at all and grew thinner and weaker by the day, as if the fever was draining all life from her but pain and suffering.

Merry and Jamie clung to each other in their illness. Old enough to fear death, they lay in a kind of terrified malaise for days. Their little sweat-soaked bodies looked so frail to me when I changed their bedclothes that each day I feared I saw them slipping further toward death.

It is bizarre that only certain images stay with you from such a time, but I can see those little trusting faces staring up at me, eyes seeming bigger every day in their sunken faces. "I'm very sick, Mama," they seemed to say. "Why don't you fix me?"

Great eyes staring upward, hot little hands clutching mine, wasting bodies with ribs visible, helpless sobs when they see that you cannot help to ease their suffering.

I could not bring myself to leave the nursery. Edmond tried to persuade me to leave the children to Nurse, but I was like a madwoman when he suggested it. The doctor came daily and tried to convince me that my own health would suffer and that the disease would run its course with or without me—but I could not look at those pleading eyes and leave them.

I think the most awful part of seeing your children in a terrible illness is the unnatural quiet of it. To see a child who normally runs you ragged with his unfailing energy lying stilled beneath the covers, asking for help you cannot give, is beyond bearing.

I nursed them endlessly, hoping to expiate my sin of having placed them in danger by sheer self-sacrifice.

After the first fortnight it became apparent that the twins were far less ill than Bethany. I had moved their two beds together and they held each other's hands or slept in each other's arms; that seemed to comfort them. There is a bond between twins that other mortals cannot know.

On the nineteenth day, Bethany's hemorrhaging began. Can you even imagine the hopelessness of it? That tiny emaciated body had no blood to lose. I stood beside the bed and saw the fatal signs.

To my everlasting shame, I collapsed when I saw the inevitable signal of death. I remember staring at my child, the awful knowledge flooding me with despair, then blackness. When I awoke I was in my own room. Edmond, a doctor and a nurse were with me.

"You are endangering yourself too greatly by nursing that child, Elizabeth," he said. "There is no way to save her now. She is already in a coma. You have other children to think of. I won't permit you to be so foolish as to return to the nursery."

I looked at my husband disbelieving. It wasn't possible that anyone would try to separate a mother from her dying child. It simply wasn't possible.

"I can't leave her," I cried, struggling to get out of bed.

"I'm afraid you have no choice," said Edmond coldly. It was obvious that he blamed me for the children's contagion, but I didn't think of that then.

"What do you mean?" I asked, struggling to my feet.

"I've employed a woman to stay with Bethany. For your own good you must get some rest. I shall insist on it."

"I don't want any rest."

"I'm afraid you must do as you are told or you will be ill."

"No."

"I'm your husband, Elizabeth—you *will* do as I bid you."

"No!"

I tried to get past them. I screamed, fought, kicked, bit like an animal to get free. Finally they locked me in my room. I ranted, pounded on the door, cursed, screamed . . . and finally begged to be let out so I could go to my child.

Frustration so overwhelming engulfed me that could I have killed Edmond I would have done so, if I hanged for it.

Finally, I fell into an exhausted slumber. How long I slept, I don't know, but it was dark when I awakened to see Edmond standing by my bed.

"She's gone," he said in a hollow voice. "There's nothing that you could have done that wasn't done." How he must have hated me to punish me thus.

"Bastard!" I breathed, so hoarse from crying that my voice was a whisper. "I will never forgive you for this."

"Me?" he said with a sardonic laugh. "Me? *You* are the one who brought the disease into this house. You with your confounded peasants. Do you see what your disobedience has brought you? You've killed our child."

He turned and left and I remained on the bed for a long while, trying desperately to decide if he was right.

And so she died . . . this tiny, frail life that I had nurtured and tried to strengthen was laid in the Manningham plot, much against my will. I had begged to have her buried near my gentle mother at FitzGibbon Hall, but Edmond blamed me for her death and ignored my pleas. Christ, how I hated him.

He had kept me from my child as she lay dying. Now she was

gone and nothing . . . nothing he would ever do would make me forgive him.

There is an irrevocable loneliness that comes with the death of your child, as if a part of you has been emptied that can never be refilled. On the day of the funeral I stood tearless by Bethany's grave until long after the other mourners had left. Edmond tried to shame me into seeing to the guests who had come for the funeral, but I turned on him so viciously that, fearing I had gone mad with grief, and wanting to avoid a scene, he left me with the gravedigger and the small coffin.

When it was dark and the coffin lay covered with the sifting of earth that would house it forever, I became aware of my surroundings once again, for I had been traveling in my mind to some far place with my child, the world around me lost. Finally, pulling my cloak about me, I turned toward home.

Behind me on the grass sat Des and Con. They must have been there through all the hours since the funeral. Wordlessly, they rose and each took my hand. Together we returned to the house.

Edmond met us in the hallway, a disdainful look on his face; one could see he had been weeping. He started to speak, then seeing the warning look on Desmond's face, he thought better of it and let me pass.

Three days later I started to write about the plight of women, the book that made me famous. I called it *Woman Alone;* it was a novel about a woman forced by circumstance to fight for the right to independence. Into my heroine I poured all the anger and anguish of my life.

To his eternal credit, Desmond not only encouraged me in my writing during this ghastly time but it was he who was ultimately responsible for seeing that my manuscript reached a publisher.

I remember quite vividly my brother's face when he finished reading what I had written. He looked at me as if seeing me clearly for the first time, his expression redolent of both admiration and sorrow.

"You've been hurt so very much, my Bethy," he said gently as he handed me back the pages. I thought I saw moisture in his eyes. "We men are so often fools. You've laid us bare here. It will anger men to see themselves unmasked."

"Do you think, then, that it is unpublishable?" I asked, hope fading.

"Far from it," he replied, shaking his head emphatically. "I think it's more than publishable. Provided, of course, that we can find someone who isn't afraid of controversy." Des smiled at me, a bit ruefully, and added, "This is hardly the stuff of your novella, Bethy. I doubt seriously that your former publisher would wish to be party to such heresy as you've written here. Might be better off out of Ireland, entirely," he said, his sentence structure deteriorating.

"I've heard that publishers in Edinburgh are more adventurous than those in Dublin at the moment . . . more open to new ideas." He paused for a moment, and then said emphatically, "Edinburgh is considerably farther away from Edmond's sphere of influence as well . . . good thing, that. Can't imagine he won't try to stop you from publishing this." I nodded, miserably, knowing I'd have to face a confrontation with Edmond before too long.

I had told my husband some time before that I was writing another book, but he had showed little interest in the announcement. I'd even offered to have him read it, but he'd said he was far too busy to do so—and for once I'd been delighted by his indifference.

Reading my troubled expression, Des said quickly, "Don't worry, Bethy. I'll take this to Scotland for you. Don't know how other men will respond to what you've written, but it damned well deserves to be seen."

True to his word, my brother took my manuscript to Edinburgh, where he found a publisher willing to take a chance on my story.

Needless to say, when Edmond finally read *Woman Alone,* he was enraged.

When he called me to his study for the confrontation, his usual composure was visibly shaken. Edmond held a copy of my offending manuscript in his hand and waved it at me, as if it were contaminated.

"You can't be serious, Elizabeth," he exploded at me as I entered the room. "This manuscript is not only offensive, it's outrageous!"

I tried to remain calm—he still had the capacity to frighten me—but I was armed with the knowledge that my book had been accepted for publication, so I stood my ground.

"It expresses my feelings, Edmond," I replied as evenly as I could.

"I don't care in the least about your feelings . . ." he began.

"Perhaps that's why I've written as I have," I replied.

Edmond looked as if he might strike me—but instead he gained control of his temper with obvious effort and started again in a quieter voice. "As your husband and as a man, Elizabeth, I'm utterly horrified by what you've written. But you must see that however unpleasant the situation between us, you cannot publish this. Surely it is not your intention to make laughingstocks of us both."

"No," I said, trying to keep my voice from betraying my nervousness, "that isn't my intention."

"What is your intention, then?" he asked thunderously.

"To write the best that I'm capable of, with what small talent I've been given," I responded and heard the tremor in my own voice as I did so. "I never hid from you my desire to write, Edmond," I finished, hoping he didn't realize how much I feared him.

"Nor did you ever hint that you would write such vitriol," he shot back.

"I had no need for vitriol when first we met," I replied miserably. "Don't you see, Edmond, my book is as much your creation as it is mine." He seemed genuinely struck by that, but he managed to recover himself.

Edmond tossed the pages onto the Queen Anne table that separated us. "This discussion is fruitless, I'm afraid. You'll never find a publisher for drivel like this."

"I've already found a publisher," I said quickly, striving to keep my courage up.

"How dare you do such a thing behind my back, Elizabeth? Have you no conscience at all?"

"Your back is very nearly the only part of you I ever see, Edmond," I responded, anger surfacing through my fear.

"I will not permit you to do this, Elizabeth. I simply will not permit it. I am not without influence in Dublin."

"My publisher is not in Ireland, Edmond, and I don't believe he will be influenced by your threats. He seems quite taken with my work and he strikes me in his letters as one who wouldn't respond well to intimidation."

"I'll make you regret this." Edmond spat the words at me in impotent fury.

"Oh, Edmond," I whispered with all the pent-up frustration of my life in my words. "What can you possibly take from me that you haven't already taken?"

He began to reply, thought better of it and, turning abruptly, walked from the room, leaving me standing alone, trying to control the awful pounding in my chest.

I had won, but what a poignant victory it seemed to me. Had I been able to win what I truly craved from Edmond—love and approval—*Woman Alone* would never have been written.

My story must have struck some universal chord for women in the suffrage movement and out of it. Within six months of the publication of my book, my name was both famous and synonymous with the cause of women's rights: a singular irony, since I felt I had so few.

Terrance Kiernan . . . Bethany Manningham . . . what wrongs must we endure before we begin to seek our rights. ∽

The Wild Harp

The stranger shall hear thy lament on his plains;
The sight of thy harp shall be sent o'er the deep,
Till thy masters themselves, as they rivet thy chains,
Shall pause at the song of their captive and weep!

THOMAS MOORE

13 ❧ During the period of time that I've just chronicled, much had happened to Con and Tierney in Dublin, so I must bring you up to date on the events that marked their lives during my years of domesticity.

I should tell you, too, that my father died soon after Bethany, and my brother inherited FitzGibbon Hall. Because his fiancée's unfortunate death had left him melancholy and restless, he chose to live abroad for quite a number of years. Desmond loved Paris, and as a bachelor with no real family ties, it must have seemed to him the perfect place to work out his grief and disappointment. He dabbled a bit in the foreign service and in whatever romantic adventures he could find, but as his life was so far removed from ours, Con and I followed his exploits only in his letters for over a decade.

Con's letters during this time were long, news-filled and always, always full of Tierney. Tierney's plays, Tierney's poems, Tierney's work with the Brotherhood.

Yet I began to sense a new note in them as time wore on. A discontent—not just with the injustice that she was witnessing —but also with the fact of her exclusion from the Brotherhood that ruled Tierney's time.

"I didn't come to Dublin to stand outside with my nose against the glass," she wrote to me, and I understood perfectly. Fate had denied them more children and she was restless to share in Tierney's struggles, both as a commitment and a way to occupy her considerable energies.

And she hated poverty. The more she learned of it, the angrier she got. I expect that her later connection to James Connolly, the socialist, was somehow tangled up in those early days of learning the inequity of poverty. She wrote me that her neighbor, a sweet young woman with three children, had proudly taken her by the hand into her own apartment and Con had felt appalled by her own anger at the shabby surroundings that were shown with such touching pride.

She wrote of learning to conserve fuel in the little coal stove so that there would be warmth in the flat when Tierney arrived home at night. She learned to cook things that provided leftovers for another day, thinking always of the largesse of our father's home where three cooks labored daily to keep the family fed in opulent abundance. And the waste of that great Fitz-Gibbon kitchen! She must have hypothesized how many families in their little tenement could be fed on a day's waste from our father's house.

I sensed a growing restlessness and anger in my volatile sister and I wondered how she would resolve it. I was fighting my own chains at that point and I knew that she was far more explosive than I.

Con had begun to fill her time by amassing information about Fenianism—her letters brimmed with it. I knew there must be a growing tension between her and Tierney about her exclusion from the Brotherhood, and I was sure she intended to cause a showdown. I think the only thing that stayed her was her awe of his writing, which always seemed to her a sacred trust. She would ramble on and on in her letters about this verse or that, or about the play he labored over. Somehow she had convinced herself that once he was published, their lives would change for the better. . . . Willy Yeats would be of help and all would work out for the best.

I wondered how long that dream would keep her restless spirit at bay—it couldn't be forever. ✑

Con watched her little son with pride and affection. He was a strapping lad, bigger than the other boys, taller and broader; yet he never seemed to use his size to get his way. A curious trait in a little boy, she thought, but very like his father.

He had Tierney's dark curls and sea-gray eyes as well, although she could detect a trace of Desmond in the shape of his head and in the firm, yet playful, set of his mouth. And he was quieter than either, and somehow more mysterious.

What a miracle he is, she thought as she sat on a bench in Stephen's Green and watched Tahg and the other youngsters playing wildly in the grass. He's like a puzzle put together from pieces of us all. Grandfather's ears, and Beth's dimple when he laughs, and Tierney's stance, so funny to see in a little boy's body.

In some ways life felt safer now that Tierney worked in Tommy McGowan's Public House. Life was not safe in reality, she knew, but it felt so, nonetheless. Perhaps she had just grown used to the danger, or perhaps it was the knowledge that at least during working hours her husband was safe and snug in the warmth of the pub. Tending bar and singing ballads was a far better living than the docks or the road gangs and construction crews. Best of all, he was less exhausted by it and his writing was beginning to be voluminous.

If it were not for the incursions of the Brotherhood into their lives and for her feeling of restlessness, they could be perfectly happy. But the IRB was all too much a reality—and so was her exclusion from it.

She felt it eroding at her—a deep inevitable gnawing; like the Spartan boy with the fox in his shirt, she carried it with her. Why did Tierney not see that his passionate devotion to something she could not share left her feeling useless and alone? She didn't begrudge him the Cause he believed in; she merely needed to share it.

Con felt Tahg's eyes on her as she picked him out of the little crowd of scrambling boys easily. He smiled his father's smile at her and waved his hand gaily. She waved back.

She thought, sometimes, of what her life would have been like if she had married among her own kind, into the life she'd been raised for. Filled with the largesse of having; the comforts of a rich man's home. All fine and good, she thought, for others, but wrong, wrong it would have been for her. She knew that now. She'd known forever that she wasn't destined to live by the rules of the game. Too predictable and too inflexible they were; too constraining and lacking in individuality. Tierney was not the only rebel in the family, she thought emphatically. Then looking at her son, a small pang struck her. What seeds of rebellion did he carry within him? What iconoclastic bits of each of them might be implanted in his heart and mind? And where might such implantations lead him in this strange land of lost rebellions?

She shook the unsettling thought from her and, pulling her shawl closer about her shoulders, beckoned her son from the screaming tangle of little-boy arms and legs that tumbled on the ground before her. She had a sudden urge to hold him close to her body.

Tierney was nearly finished with his play. Nearly at the point where he would show it to Willy Yeats and hope that the man would produce it. When that happened their whole lives would expand in a different way.

Tierney would receive the accolades she dreamed of for his writing; she was sure of it. He might even be able to work full-time with the theater people. And surely, surely such success would make the excitement of the IRB fade at least a little in his mind.

Even as she formed the thought, something deep within her knew it was a lie. For better or worse, she was wedded to Ireland as much as to Tierney. For Ireland was in his blood and bone; neither success nor failure would alter that.

"Why can I not be in the Brotherhood?" Con asked, once again, with annoyance.

"Because Seaneen won't hear of it," replied her husband.

"It makes no sense, Tierney," she pursued. "I can contribute . . . somehow. I've learned everything there is to learn about Ireland. I've read every journal, every pamphlet, every speech, every bloody word. I'm as incensed by it all as you are. Sometimes I think I'm more angry about all this injustice than you!"

Tierney looked at her, his patience tried sorely. "Everything you're saying is true, Con. Every word. But it's also true that you've a son to take care of and, if we're lucky, there'll be other children . . ."

"I can have children and still do *something*, Tierney. Oh, love, don't you see? I can't bear being on the outside of your secrets. I can't bear not knowing what you're worrying about."

"There's too much danger in your knowing, Con. You must see that. I can't let you be in danger."

"And just how safe do you think I am with a husband who's in the Brotherhood? Do you think I'm such a fool that I don't worry each time you leave this house? We're all in danger from your involvement in this thing, Tierney. And if we're to be in danger, at least I should share the knowledge of what's going on with you."

"It's impossible to argue with you!" he said unhappily.

"Because you know I'm right!"

"Even if I thought you were right I could do nothing about it! It's Seaneen's decision, not mine." He looked up from his papers to see if that had won his point. She was standing with her back to him, but he thought he saw a lessening of tension in her shoulders.

He got up from the desk and went to her. He said, "I hate it when we argue."

"I do, too," she quietly replied. "But you must know, Tierney, I *need* to get involved in this. I'm too active to remain nothing more than a Dublin housewife. It just won't work for me. I need more."

He put his arms around her. "It's my own fault for marrying such a rebellious woman," he said, hoping to cheer her.

"I am, you know," she said seriously. "I am exactly that."

And holding her in his arms, he knew that she was speaking only the truth. Not more than a week ago he had seen her in a vision—dressed in a soldier's uniform and holding a rifle in her hand. There had been terrible danger all around her and he had been badly shaken by the picture in his mind. Did such a vision presage an inevitable event? he wondered. Or could Fate's hand be stayed by keeping her out of the IRB? And how in God's name could they resolve this anger that was gnawing at her?

"Funny," he said to her, uncertainty in his words. "I used to worry that poverty and privation would come between us. It never occurred to me it would be Ireland."

"It isn't Ireland that's the problem, love. It's my need not to be a bystander."

"Aye," he said thoughtfully. "That is the problem, indeed."

Con let the last piece of paper drop from her hands to her lap with tears in her eyes.

It was a masterpiece. A wildly evocative rendering of life. So like his poetry. And yet with another quality. Fiery, tender, insightful and so very Irish. She smiled as she fingered the pages that seemed to her almost living things.

What a profound change in life these little words, these

The Wild Harp   151

pages, these thoughts would produce. She knew as she sat there holding them that this play had the power to alter everything. Just as she'd dreamed it would. *Now* Tierney would have the fame he deserved. *Now* their fortune would be made and she would be vindicated in the eyes of those who had derided her choice of husband. *Now* the whole world would understand who Tierney O'Connor was born to be!

She settled back into the chair and let the bliss of it fill her with contentment. No one could read *this* play and not feel the presence of genius.

She felt, more than heard, her husband come up behind her.

"What do you think of it?" he asked shyly.

"I think it's everything we ever dreamed you would write." She smiled up at his anxious face and he could see the intensity of love in her eyes.

"Then you think they'll want to produce it?"

"Unless they've turned to stone."

"It's the first thing I've written that I believe in, Con," he said with a shy enthusiasm. "The first thing I think is good. It's the strangest feeling. As if some primal part of me is on that page for all the world to see. Some intimate part that I'm not sure should be uncovered.

"Writing is a fearful calling, Con. If you write from the head, the words are safe, but they're not what you want to say. If you write from the heart, they're what you want to say, but you worry about saying it in public." He laughed softly.

"It's a beautiful, wonderful, important play, Tierney. It will change your life."

"Aye, lass. Words have the power to do that, to be sure. I'll take the manuscript to Mr. Yeats and to Seaneen . . ."

"Why Seaneen?"

"I've given him my word that I would, when I finished it."

Con started to speak, then thought better of it. This was not the moment for an argument. This was the moment for perfect happiness and pride and joy. She would not spoil this shining moment for him with an argument about his secret life. Soon, soon he would have to listen to what was in her heart about it. But not this glorious proud moment.

"Produce it?" Willy Yeats smiled. "Of course I shall produce it! This is the finest piece of work that's come into my hands in years. It was well worth waiting for.

"I'll send it to Maud this very afternoon. The lead will fit her like the paper on the wall. And Ireland! Tierney. It will fit old Ireland in the very same way, lad!

"By God you've got something here that will make people sit up and take notice of their heritage."

So it would happen then. . . . Tierney breathed the relief and joy of it into every fiber of himself as he left the brownstone at 5 Woburn Buildings. All the dreams really could come true after all. The dreams of being a writer . . . the dreams of leaving behind some tiny essence of himself . . . the dreams of helping stir people about Ireland.

He held the manuscript tightly under his arm as he walked rapidly down the street. How wonderful to think that Con hadn't believed in him in vain.

"You can't do it, lad." Seaneen O'Sullivan looked sad but determined as he said the devastating words.

Stricken, Tierney said nothing and waited for an explanation.

"You'll have to make up your mind now, I'm afraid. The writing or the IRB."

Anger blazed behind Tierney's eyes.

"That's a fine fucking arbitrary judgment, O'Sullivan! Just like that you destroy everything I've hoped for."

"Nothing of the kind. You can write if you want. It's brilliant stuff, no doubt of it. But you can't do both."

"Why not?"

"Because it'll consume you, is why! Because you'll be famous and applauded and maybe rich, but you'll never be the same hungry man who stood before me and said he wanted to give his all for Ireland!"

Seaneen's eyes, too, were angry, and his fists on the table were clenched and hard.

"You may as well make your decision now, O'Connor. 'Delays have dangerous ends.' It won't get any easier from here on in. I like you and I want you in the Brotherhood. But I'll not have you with divided loyalties, and I'll not have you parading your patriotism under the nose of Dublin Castle so that they start to watch you night and day. A fine lot of good you'd be to me then."

His voice sounded softer when he said, "My advice to you is to take your play home to your wife and tell her the good news of your success. And then I'd enjoy it for all it's worth, lad. You've a great gift. I'd use it if I were you and thank God for the chance. And I'd forget the IRB and this fucking island that sucks the lifeblood from a man's gut."

Tierney watched O'Sullivan, uncomprehending.

"*Why* must I choose, Seaneen?" he demanded, his voice strained with emotion.

"You know the answer to that as well as I do!" Seaneen responded, his voice harsh and strong.

"It'll break Con's heart," said Tierney, a great sorrow in his words. "All her hopes are tied up in this play being produced. You don't *own* me, O'Sullivan. I came to you of my own volition."

"Aye. And when you did you swore on oath to follow orders."

"You can't expect me to do this to Con."

"I don't expect it. I told you what you should do."

O'Sullivan's voice was firm and powerful in the small room. It was the voice of the man in charge, not of a friend.

Tierney nodded finally, unable to speak. The man was right of course; there was no room in the IRB for divided loyalties. It was time for a choice. This was the agony that had lurked at the back of his consciousness for so long, unspoken. It was the reason he had taken so long to finish the play. He had always known that he couldn't have both. God curse the day he'd started writing! God curse the day he'd pledged himself to Ireland! God curse the day he'd been born!

He picked up the manuscript roughly and walked out the door without saying good-bye.

Seaneen watched the man's departure thoughtfully. He liked Tierney and counted him a friend, as much as any man could permit himself a friend in this imperfect world. He liked his erudition and his passionate love of Ireland. He admired his glorious gift of words, a gift he himself had once longed for, and he was warmed by the love he saw between the man and his wife. He even trusted him—as much as he trusted any man. But there were terrible conflicts in the lad.

He loved his wife, that was a problem; he had great gifts and ambitions of a personal nature, that was a problem, too. There is no room for personal plans in a soldier—no room for anything that could interfere with the following of orders. Tierney was too sensitive and too intuitive; too smart to follow orders blindly. Assessment was always going on behind those quiet eyes. Assessment of what he'd been asked to do, assessment of the leadership. Bad, bad traits in a soldier.

"Ah, but good traits in a man!" Seaneen answered himself with a sad smile. "Damned good traits in a man."

Tierney covered the sixteen blocks to the pub with little enthusiasm. He felt as if the world had come to an abrupt and unexpected end. What tangled dreams they were—Ireland, writing, Con, Tahg. Most times they'd all seemed one to him. All the future, all the hopes.

All destroyed in an afternoon.

He pushed in the door of the pub and laid the offending manuscript on the nearest table. How could something that had possessed such joyous magic just a few hours before have turned to dross? He felt like crying out against the unfairness of life. But what a fool he had been to think it could be otherwise.

And Con. Dear, patient, expectant Con. How could he shatter her dreams with this unwanted knowledge?

"Sure and you look like a wet fortnight," said Tommy as he walked into the room.

"I feel worse," replied Tierney.

"What's up?"

"My play. I finished it and Yeats wants to produce it. But Seaneen has ordered me not to do it. He says I must choose between the IRB and fame and fortune for my future. I can't have it both ways."

Tommy's rubbery face crinkled itself into a frown. "Like as not he's right, God blast him," he said. "I'm heart sorry, lad. I know you and Con had a power of hope wrapped up in it."

He motioned Tierney to sit down and, walking behind the bar, opened a Guinness and poured it into a pint jar. He handed the drink to Tierney, who took it gratefully, knowing the kindness behind the gesture.

"What can I say to her, Tommy? She who was born to so much and gave it all up to come with me. The only thing she's ever asked of me was that I be a writer. To her it's always been the dream . . . the way out of poverty and the way to be *some-one*."

Tommy listened thoughtfully, then said, "Nae, lad. Sometimes I think you didn't turn up when good sense was being distributed. You're wrong about the lass. There's more to the dream she had, I'm thinking. The writing, the poetry . . . she loves them because they're the expression of the man she loves in you. If money was what she'd needed, she could have stayed home for that."

Tierney looked up, unconvinced. He took a long swallow of the stout, and said nothing.

"There's no doubt she'd like to see you famous and rich, mind you, and who wouldn't? No doubt she'd like to be able to spit in the eye of those as said she married poorly. But I think you're missing the point of what's ailing her lately, laddie. She mistrusts the Brotherhood because it takes you away from her, not because she doesn't love the Cause. She fears your rebel nature because it could get you killed. And your rebel friends with their almighty secrets take you from her. She's talked to me about it—you know we're as tight as a Protestant's lips, your wife and I." He smiled and his apple cheeks bobbed up. He and Con had indeed struck up a friendship, and a good one. He weighed his words now, trying to judge the best way to help them both, her and Tierney.

"Your poetry and your plays, lad . . . there she shares your soul with you, and she knows it. She's a woman and she loves you. Maybe she needs you to keep on writing because that's the part of your life she can best share with you. But you must handle this gently, Tierney. She's too much woman to be trifled with and this play means the world to her."

Tierney put the glass down on the table and nodded at his friend's sagacity. "You know, Tommy, all my life I've dreamed of doing something for Ireland. From the time I was a wee lad it's meant everything to me. The songs I learned to sing were of rebellion, the poetry I wrote, the stories I told . . . all Ireland. As if Ireland and the songs and the stories were all one and the same. As if Cathleen ni Houlihan, Ireland's eternal metaphor, was my own personal muse, mind you.

"And then, today, when Seaneen said to me that I couldn't produce the play, couldn't do as I'd always hoped . . . all I could think of was Con. Not my ambitions—and I've got them, man, believe me! I'd like to be *somebody* instead of a fisherman, you may be sure of it. But none of that mattered to me. Con mattered. Her hopes, her dreams mattered. Our life together mattered.''

Tommy cocked his head to one side and the fine lines at the sides of his eyes crinkled up as they did when he was full of thought, and he said softly, "Did you ever think, lad, that Ireland might be a boy's dream and your writing and your family that of a man? Maybe the only way to escape the pull of it is to leave here and be done with the damned thing. You know what they say in Belfast? What's all the world to a man when his wife is a widow?" He waited for Tierney to smile at that, but he didn't.

"Could you get out of the movement with your life, do you suppose?" Tommy asked earnestly, for they both knew that secret societies were not pleased by defectors.

"I don't know the answer to that," Tierney replied. "I'm privy to a lot of their plans. But Seaneen said I could go. The terrible thing is, Tommy, I don't know for sure if I can walk away and still live with myself."

Tommy heard the depth of misery in Tierney's voice and knitted his unruly brows together thoughtfully as he watched him. "So, maybe the truth of it is that whether they'd let you out or not, it's stuck inside you, lad. Is that it?"

"I don't know, Tommy. Today, after this . . ." He waved his hand over the manuscript. "I just don't know."

Tommy watched the young man knowingly. There was no question what his choice would be. It was interesting that the outcome seemed unclear to Tierney, inevitable as it was.

"I don't envy you having to tell the lass," he replied, making a grimace that said he'd been through such confrontations on occasion himself.

Tierney shook his head and laughed a little, sadly. "Aye. I'm not looking forward to this conversation much."

Standing up, he shrugged himself into his pea coat and pulled on his cap. "Thanks for the Guinness, Tommy," he said as he picked up the sheaf of papers. "And the good-hearted wisdom."

"It's welcome you are to both, lad. A friend's eye is a good mirror."

Tierney nodded, then walked to the door, stood a moment to

blink himself into familiarity with the light . . . then he was gone.

"You're stuck with Ireland, O'Connor," said Tommy to the empty street when Tierney had gone. "You may not know it yet, but there's no going back from that particular seduction."

"But you can't be serious!" The incredulity and derision in Con's voice cut deeply at Tierney. "Not after everything we've hoped for!"

"I haven't a choice, Con! You've always known that I'm bound by oath to the IRB." He couldn't believe that he sounded so convinced, when the question marks were still so large in his mind.

"And what of the oath you swore to me that first day?" She spat the words maliciously at him, fury and hurt evident in every contour of her body. "And all the oaths since. They were meaningless, I suppose?"

"They were *not* meaningless, and well you know it! Nothing between us has ever been meaningless. I know how disappointed you are, Con, and so am I—but Seaneen has his own reasons for what he's asking. You must believe me." He looked in despair at his wife, wondering how in God's name he could make her accept what he himself resented so.

"Seaneen has his reasons, has he?" she replied, close to tears. "Well, I've some reasons of my own, Tierney O'Connor, and a few dreams too that you seem so willing to destroy. I'm telling you right now that if you let them keep your play from being shown . . . if you persist in putting the Brotherhood ahead of Tahg and me . . . I'll leave you!"

The words stunned the man into silence. Never, never would he have thought her capable of saying such to him.

"You don't mean that!" he whispered hoarsely, his heart pounding, but her flashing angry eyes said otherwise.

"By God, I do mean it! Don't you think I'm sick to death of your IRB? Sick of these eternal secrets that come between us; sick of the fear that sucks at my gut every time you let yourself out that door. Sick of playing second fiddle to a phantom that I can't even see or touch. It's tearing at me, Tierney! Tearing at us, at our love for each other. The IRB *needs,* the IRB *wants,* the IRB *expects!* God blast the IRB, I say!"

Stunned, he watched as she turned unexpectedly to the table

where a group of Republican pamphlets lay; grabbing a handful, she tore at them furiously; tearing the pages to pieces, she threw them at him, her rage overcoming all her restraint. He had never seen her in such a frenzy of anger, never, never out of control. He saw the depth of her torment with a sickening realization. What a fool I've been, he thought in the split second before she grabbed at the manuscript that lay on the table.

"I might as well tear this to shreds, too, while I'm at it!" she sobbed, wrenching at it, but unable to bring herself to harm the precious pages, she let the manuscript drop to the floor. Shaking with frustration, she watched the pages flutter uselessly about the room.

"I hate your goddamned Brotherhood!" she screamed to Tierney and to the world at large. She cast about with her eyes for something, anything on which to vent her anger, and finally in an explosion of pent-up fury she threw herself at her husband, flailing with her fists against his broad chest. Tierney, shocked beyond movement by her actions, caught her by the wrists, and although she struggled fiercely to free herself, he held them in his hands wordlessly, holding her at bay. Horrified, not knowing what to do to calm her, he pressed her arms to her sides and, as he did so, struggled to envelop her in his own arms. But she fought her way free of him. . . . Moving away from him, she stood defiantly, her eyes so fierce that they seemed almost black, her hair tangled from their struggle, her whole aspect tense with fury.

"I've given up everything for you, Tierney," she said in a harsh whisper. "I lived with you in poverty and counted myself lucky every day because you were mine.

"And I've never complained about any of it. Not about the cold, nor the rats in the alley, nor the food that sickens me, nor the hand-me-down clothes, nor the look on people's faces in the tenements when I open my mouth to speak and they think I'm putting on airs.

"But this one thing I asked of you . . . that you let me keep the dream! If it had taken you a thousand years to write the play, or if no one had ever loved it or wanted it, I could have borne with that and kept the dream alive.

"But to take it and trample it beneath your feet . . ." Her voice held such infinite sorrow under the anger that he stood rooted, unable to answer her. "You threw our future away and you never even *asked* me. Ah, Tierney. How could you do it to me?"

With that she snatched up the shawl from the hook near the door and, not waiting for a reply, fled into the hallway and down the stairs into the street.

Tierney started to go after her, then realizing that he didn't know what more to say, stood clutching the banister and looking down helplessly at the empty stairwell where she had been.

"And you never even asked me . . ." she had said, so desperately. It was true, of course. *He* had made the decision. *He* had decided for both of them.

Tierney walked back inside the flat and, closing the door, he sat down heavily at the kitchen table and put his head in his hands and wept.

Con heard her own running footsteps on the pavement. The street was nearly deserted and the darkness made her feel disoriented. She was never out alone after dark and the alleyways seemed strangely unfamiliar through her tears.

She heard the river before she saw it and, making her way in its direction, she leaned against the stone stanchion that supported the bridge and cried and cried.

It was over now. All the possibilities were gone. Only the reality remained. She struggled to find a handkerchief in her pocket and, drawing out a scrap of linen, blew her nose and tried to gain control of herself.

Oh hurt, hurt self that felt so betrayed. Disappointed self that would never have the chance to say "I told you so" to the scoffers.

She stared down into the ugly green depth of water below her and tried to clear her mind, but her heart kept getting in the way.

"Do you love him enough to let him risk himself for the Cause that means everything to him without trying to distract him from his purpose . . . ?" Tierney's mother had asked her a thousand years ago, and she had answered with the glib stupidity of youth. "Do you love him enough never once to remind him what you've given up to follow him?"

That was the real question, wasn't it, when all the confusions were swept away?

Con watched the endless dark eddies of the current flowing

under the bridge for a long while before she was sure enough of
the answer to go home.

Con opened the door tentatively and saw Tierney sitting dis-
consolately at the kitchen table, his dark head in his hands. The
sound of the door made him look up.

Seeing her, he rose quickly and moved toward her. "Thank
God, you're back!" he breathed, all the worry of the past hour
in his voice.

"I'm so frightened, Tierney," she said as she felt his arms go
around her; she could hear the despair in her own voice. "I'm
so desperately disappointed. We must talk about this." She said
it wondering if there were enough words in all the world to
make any difference.

"Aye," he replied, letting her go. "I wish I knew how to
begin . . ."

She held up her hand to stop him. "No. Let me start," she
said quickly. "Let me say what I must." Walking to the side of
the bed, she sat down, but Tierney noted that she still clutched
the shawl about her shoulders.

"I was so angry and so hurt," she said softly, "that I said
things I wish I could unsay. I never meant to complain to you
about our life together . . . about being poor. I knew when I
left my father's house that we'd not be rich. I had no way of
knowing what that really meant, of course . . . but nonetheless I made the choice and I've never regretted it." She sighed
deeply, as if she were reaching far down inside herself to draw
out what she meant to say.

"But tonight . . . I felt betrayed. And I struck back. I'm
sorry, Tierney, for what I said of our life." He saw that she had
caught her bottom lip with her teeth as she finished speaking—
it was a little-girl gesture he'd noted in her when there was
something she could not bring herself to say.

"I've done it all wrong, Con," he said quickly, filling the
silence. "I've been a fool."

She reached out and took his hand, and they sat, side by side,
wordlessly on the bed. But she couldn't bring herself to look
into his face.

"I never thought there'd be anything of consequence we'd
disagree on," she started lamely. "Never anything that would

tear us apart." He nodded miserably, then spoke in a hoarse voice.

"While you were gone, I tried to find the words to explain to you why I'd made the decision I did—and why I did it without you.

"You must believe me, Con, that I didn't do it maliciously—my own confusion and heartache were so great that it seemed I had to struggle through it alone . . . had to decide . . . had to search within myself for answers to unanswerable questions. Everything about the Brotherhood has been a secret that I wanted to share with you but couldn't. This seemed the same to me. A man's decision, a man's sacrifice.

"It was as if I couldn't be true to you, Con, unless I were true to myself. Does that make any sense at all to you?" Tierney seemed so stricken by what he was trying to articulate that Con felt moved by his pain—yet her own kept her from forgiving.

When she didn't answer, he continued. "When I left Seaneen, I was angry. What right had he to take something so precious from us? I asked myself. What right to demand such a sacrifice? Then it dawned on me that the reason I was so angry with him was that I knew in my gut he was right!" He turned to face her on the bed, forcing her to look at him.

"Con, my dear love, you cannot serve two masters! You cannot let yourself be seduced by fame and money and comfort and still be a revolutionary. If I couldn't make this sacrifice now, how could I be expected to make the others, later? If we had all we'd ever dreamed of, could we still be angry enough at the plight of others not so lucky as we, that we'd sacrifice for *them?*

"Sacrifice, Con! The ability to lay down your life for Ireland is something I've been bred to since the day I was born. Most people lay down their lives because a bullet or a hangman's noose brings it all to an end. I'm being asked to lay down my life and go on living.

"Don't you see, Con? We're all the Minstrel Boy. Every last one of us who's ever dreamed of freedom for Ireland must sacrifice to attain it. I didn't know until today if I had the strength to do what would be asked of me."

He stopped and took a deep breath before going on.

"What I had no right to do was to sacrifice *you* without your consent, my own love. I'm heart sorry, Con, that I didn't know how not to do that."

There was no doubting the sincerity in what he said, or the anguish.

Finally, she understood the metaphor. Tierney, the minstrel, had rent the strings of his harp as a gesture. How unbearably, inevitably Irish an act it was. How Catholic to believe there could be no victory except through sacrifice. She wondered, staring at him, if Tierney really understood the enormity of what he had just said to her.

"I know," she whispered finally. "Perhaps I've always known enough to fear this." Even as she said the words she wondered where the truth lay. Do we ever really know the person we are marrying? Do we sense in them their breadth and depth of soul and character, yet never give it name or substance . . . until some crisis forces us to name it. Or do we simply love because we love . . . irrationally, inexplicably, unreasonably, inevitably.

He is who he is, she thought, defeated by her love for him. It is the same poetry and mysticism, the same sense of honor that made me fall in love with him that has brought us to this inescapable moment.

"I love you," she said very simply, pushing the bitterness back with the words. "But if I, too, am to make the sacrifice, I, too, must share the secrets."

"I know that," he answered. "I've been a goddamned fool to think it could be otherwise. There can be no secrets between us. They're poisoning us—making you doubt me. It's been tearing at me, this knowledge, under the surface where I couldn't get at it; it's been tearing at me and at you."

Con turned her whole body toward him, willing the hurt and anger to dissipate. Looking once into his eyes as if to find salvation there, she put her arms around her husband and felt his own encircle her body, uncertainly, as if he weren't sure that she would welcome him. The very uncertainty of it opened the floodgates within her and she began to cry. For all that she had lost, and all that she had learned, and all that would never be.

"Hush, love," he whispered to her, patting her sobbing body as if she were a child. "Hush now, my heart's own; I know what's wrong. I'll find a way to fix it for us. You'll see. I'll find a way."

She felt his hands touching, caressing the pain from her. She sought his mouth, hungry for the strength of him. Hungry for a means of blotting out the hurt. She felt him caress her as if she were a stranger . . . someone he was unsure of . . . and she wanted to cry for the undermining of their love.

"I've been such a fool," she heard him say again, the words muffled by the closeness of her body as he enfolded her.

"And I," she whispered back, loving him, overcome by her love for him.

She felt the strange power of it as their bodies took over from minds too tired by anger to think. Finally, she reveled in the *feeling* of him. The strong, hot hardness and the passionate tangling of arms and legs that could keep the world away, if only for a little while.

Oh, the sweetness of that rare place that they could reach together, only together. Wasn't it worth giving up the world for that sweetness? Sunlit darkness, moonlit eternity. Wasn't all the rest an illusion? No words. No words. No words. Only the magic of them in their love for each other. Only the magic remained as they drifted into an exhausted slumber—the hurt, the fears, the sorrows banished for a time by something more profound.

"You've made your decision?" Seaneen stated more than asked.

"I have," replied Tierney, very deliberately. "But there's more to it than that."

Seaneen cocked an inquisitive eye at the lad; there was always more to him than you expected. He had known that Tierney would choose Ireland over the writing. It was obvious in the writing itself that his love of Ireland went far beyond rational choice. But now there was something more. Always a little something more with this one than you bargained for.

"Well?" he prompted.

"I'll give up the idea of having the play produced, but I won't give up the writing," Tierney began seriously.

Seaneen nodded. "Fair enough," he said.

"And I want Con in on what we're up to."

"You know how I feel about women."

"That's your problem, Seaneen. Con is mine. The secrecy is eating at her. And the exclusion. If she's to give up what she wanted most to serve Ireland, she deserves to be one of us."

"A cogent argument," replied Seaneen unexpectedly. "I'll take it into account."

Tierney started to reply, thought better of it and moved to go. When he reached the door, he turned back.

"They're my terms, Seaneen," he said. "Let me know tomorrow if you'll take them or leave them." Then he was gone.

Seaneen smiled enigmatically as the door closed. Always a little more to the lad than there needed to be, he mused thoughtfully. Always just a little bit more.

"Damned fool boy!" Willy Yeats said contemptuously to Maud as he recounted the absurd conversation between himself and Tierney.

"Afraid of succeeding, that's the only explanation. He must be terrified of what success would bring him. Perhaps even embarrassed about hobnobbing with his betters. Who can say?" He was furious that the attentions he'd wasted on the man would go unrewarded after all.

Maud looked amused at his flustering, but she felt a bit irked by his noblesse oblige, too.

"I thought you told me he didn't have many 'betters'—at least where poetry was concerned," she said, baiting him.

It was Willy's turn to look annoyed. "There must have been more peasant in him than I cared to acknowledge," he said grandly. "There is simply no other explanation for his throwing away an opportunity like this. It won't come again, I'll tell you that!"

"I thought you said he wasn't planning to give up writing, only the notion of having the play produced just now."

"That's what he said, but what utter nonsense!" Yeats replied animatedly. "Scared to death of success, that's my diagnosis. Why the gods would bother to bestow gifts of that magnitude on a coward is really something we must take up with Mathers."

"Now, Willy, that is really too much!" said Maud. "I'm utterly appalled by your lack of intuition about this. Have you even bothered to consider that it may be the very opposite of cowardice that's involved here? It may have taken courage of an extraordinary stripe for that man to have walked away from what you offered him."

"And what exactly do you mean by that?"

"He could give you no explanation for his sudden change of heart, could he? Does that not strike you as odd? He has never struck me as lacking in articulation." She looked at him shrewdly. "Has it not occurred to you that he may be under some sort of orders that are constraining him? Why, you've only to read his work to know how devoted he is to Ireland. I smell the IRB in this, Willy. By God I do."

"Poppycock! Maudie, you sense revolution under every tea-cup! You're always up to your glorious nose in Republicanism and I believe it has quite tainted your vision of the world. I might add it is the *only* thing about you that I find irritating."

"Quite right, my dear Willy," she rejoined amiably. "And it is precisely because I am up to my nose in the movement that I can sniff out a patriot when there's one about. That boy is under orders, make no mistake of it."

Willy contemplated that for a moment, then said, "Damned waste of real talent and insight, if it's so." He thought again.

"Interesting concept though, now that you mention it, Maudie. Handsome young patriot giving up his selfish dreams to serve Ireland. Might be something in that to write about . . ."

"Really, Willy," she beamed at him. "You are the very limit. Is there anything in life that you don't consider poetic?"

"Indeed there is, now you've mentioned it. I think it very unpoetic for you to be contemplating this political trip to the West. Stumping about on rickety platforms, inciting peasants to riot, getting tossed into country jails . . . not poetic and not ladylike, either." He sounded miffed by the very thought of what she planned.

"My poor Willy," said Maud, unexpectedly serious. "It's a rum lot for you being in love with the likes of me, isn't it? You'd be so much better off with some gently bred lady who'd see to your tea and slippers, and simply adore you properly. You know you really are the most *adorable* man and I'm the last woman on earth you should be tinkering with."

She seemed genuinely concerned, and Yeats wanted to hold her, touch her, comfort her, be comforted, but his sense of propriety stayed him. Under the kind words was the usual message . . . the unwanted message . . . I am not going to marry you.

14 What a strange turn life has taken, thought Con after Tierney had left for the pub. The loss of the dream of Tierney's writing seemed an old loss to her now. Like a childhood fantasy or a first infatuation. Whatever flash flood of understanding that had passed between them on that terrible day of reckoning had washed away the bitterness and left instead a closer bond. He had, at the awful moment when all could have been lost, understood. Not just an intellectual understanding, but a thing of the soul. And she had known beyond questioning that he had understood.

So he had put it all on the line for her, he had risked his Cause to force Seaneen to let her in. And he had won. Miraculously he had won. Now must come the second step. Now *she* must make a place for herself in the IRB. Now she must do something worthwhile so that Tierney's sacrifice—no, both their sacrifices—would not have been in vain.

His writing would come later, she told herself, unable to abandon it even in thought. He would keep on writing and she would guard the words as a sacred trust—and one day when the world was sane again, when there was no further need for rebellion, it would all be published. Meanwhile, they would work together to help such a sane world come to birth.

Suddenly determined, she threw her coat about her, lured Tahg from the corner where he sat practicing his letters and took him to the next flat where she knocked hopefully at the door.

"Mrs. Healy?" she called through the door as she heard footsteps on the other side, "it's Constance O'Connor."

A thin consumptive-looking woman opened the door a bit and smiled when she saw Con and Tahg.

"Could I leave him with you for an hour, Sally?" Con asked eagerly. "I've an errand to run."

"Oh, yes, dearie," said the woman, reaching a hand out to Tahg, "you know how I love the lad to visit." The boy went eagerly enough to the woman, and Con breathed a sigh of relief and made her way down the stairs.

She tried hard not to think about the rickety condition of the old building they lived in; it was hard enough to accustom herself to the shabbiness of everything without dwelling on specifics. She remembered a conversation with Beth about what she would be giving up in running off with Tierney; Christ, it seemed a thousand years ago.

Con made her way to the theater on Abbey Street; she hoped she would find Maud Gonne there. She wasn't entirely sure what she would say to her once she found her, but it seemed terribly important that she try.

Maud Gonne had somehow managed to do something important, despite being female. She was both an actress *and* an effective agitator for Ireland. She collected large sums of money for the Cause, and her gender didn't seem a hindrance. Perhaps she would be of help.

Con made her way to the stage door nervously. An old man answered her knock and let her in, leading her through the darkened backstage area to a dressing room with "Miss Gonne" printed in bold block letters on the door. There he left her wordlessly and padded back to his post at the rear of the theater.

Con knocked self-consciously and a strong, mellifluous voice called out, *"Entrez!"* As she entered, she saw herself reflected in the huge mirror in front of which the actress was seated, and was startled to see how very like the other Dublin women she had become. Drab clothes, drab coloring, unfashionable hair. It was a revelation.

"Good heavens!" said Maud as she recognized the visitor. "Constance O'Connor—whatever brings you here?" She turned from the mirror with a smile, but did not rise.

"The need for advice," Con answered determinedly. "I was hoping you'd take the time to talk to me. What with Tierney at odds with Mr. Yeats about what to do with his play . . . I wasn't at all sure when or if I'd be seeing you again."

Maud cocked her head to one side; her every gesture seemed calculated to make one aware of her great beauty, thought Con. Or perhaps she simply couldn't help but appear beautiful.

"I did hear there was some question about what your husband wanted done with his work," she said noncommittally. "If you don't mind my continuing to get ready for dress rehearsal, I'd be happy to listen to what's on your mind." She looked quizzically at Con, then turned her gaze again to the mirror and, tying back her mass of auburn hair, began to do her makeup.

"I know this may be presuming on our short acquaintance, Miss Gonne," said Con, "but I tend to be rather direct and I know you do, too, so perhaps I'd best get right to the point."

She paused for breath and saw the actress watching her amusedly in the mirror; she realized that she must seem very flustered.

"You see, I've rather a difficult dilemma. I want to do *something* for Ireland, but I'm not certain how to begin.

"I've got brains and an education and I'll be damned if I'm going to sit around Dublin for a lifetime being a mother and wife when there's so much else to be done . . . but I don't know quite how to get started. I'm hoping you might advise me."

"You come from a wealthy family, obviously," replied Maud. "Where?"

"In Sligo."

"Which means, of course, that you know what the situation there is like for the farmers. You might come along with me on my next lecture tour, you know. I intend to cover the western province." She made it sound more a question than an answer.

"I have a little boy," Con replied. "I don't know if I could travel while Tahg is still so young. Is there nothing I could do here?"

"Oh, there's plenty to do here, but to do it you must pass muster with the old guard first, I'm afraid."

"How would one do that?"

"I'd start with Arthur Griffith, if I were you. He's into everything of any importance. Do you write by any chance? He's a newspaperman, you know. Runs the *United Irishman.*"

"My sister's a writer. Perhaps you know of her novel—it's called *Woman Alone?*"

Maud smiled and waved her hand in an elegant gesture of acknowledgment, as if to say, "Is there any woman in the British Isles who doesn't know of it?"

"And my husband is a writer, of course," Con continued, watching her. "I suppose I could try my hand at it."

"If you could manage some patriotic piece of prose for the *United Irishman* it would at least get your foot in the door. Mr. Griffith is quite fond of me, I'm sure he'd see you if I suggest it. Beyond that, think about the travel. There's so much to be done, all over Ireland." She put a finishing touch on her makeup and turned from the mirror to Con.

"My view of it, Mrs. O'Connor," she said earnestly, "is that it doesn't matter a tinker's dam if you're a woman, as long as you're willing to be treated like a man. You may be beaten, put into prison, even killed, I suppose—although I've never really felt in danger of that. But if you can get the attention of the people . . . make them understand that there's hope if they're willing to fight back . . . why, you can do your part as well as any man. Better, perhaps." She looked shrewdly at Con as if assessing her.

"But don't be surprised if people loathe you for your pains, my dear. It seems to incense men to have us women working beside them, no matter how gallant the cause. There's plenty of opposition you'll face, even from your own, if you choose this fight. Perhaps, even your husband may disapprove?"

Con nodded her head slowly. "He'll try to support me in this, Miss Gonne. He knows how important it is to me."

Maud smiled, her perfect, even teeth a dazzlement in the strong patrician face. "If your husband can sanction your involvement in all this, he's a better man than most, Mrs. O'Connor. I've never known one who could bear to see his woman a rebel. Not that there aren't those who give it lip service, mind you. But deep down *they* want to be the adventurers . . . *they* want to be the heroes. You'll see."

Con smiled. "I've always been the family rebel. I'm afraid I've years of practice at making people aghast at my behavior. I might just as well put all those years of rebellion to use for someone's good!"

Maud Gonne laughed winningly at that and Con rose to thank her.

"Give me a week or two to see about the writing and I'll be ready to meet your Mr. Griffith. You've given me hope, you know."

"And you've given me an idea," responded Maud. "Have you met the Countess Markievicz?"

"Not yet. But I've heard of her of course."

"Perfect! Then she'll be next on the list of people you must know. She's from Sligo, too. You may have much in common." Con watched the graceful way in which the regal woman moved; it's no wonder every man who meets her is mad for her, Con thought idly. Thanking Maud for the advice and encouragement, she started home, feeling lighter-hearted than she had in months.

Con paused before the ornate brass door knocker and caught herself envying its solid beauty. Oh Lord, she thought, I remember when appointments such as these were so much a part of my life that I never stopped to admire their loveliness.

She glanced down at her dress; it was adequate, if not quite in fashion any longer, one of those she had brought with her from home reworked in an effort to keep it stylish. But it would do.

A servant opened the door and told her that Madame Markievicz was expecting her. Con followed him into the cool and paneled interior of the house, relieved at once again being in a proper dwelling.

Maud Gonne, already seated in the drawing room with a handsome woman of about the same age as the actress, rose to greet Con as she entered.

"You don't know me, Mrs. O'Connor, but I have seen you ride. Several years ago at the Sligo Harriers I was standing next to a certain Bertie Ambrose, who spent the day delivering encomia on your elegant seat." The woman smiled amiably as she held out her hand to Con, who responded with a warm smile of her own.

"Dear old Bertie," she said mirthfully. "It seems a thousand years since I've seen him . . . or been on a horse for that matter."

"What a terrible waste, my dear," said Madame Markievicz. "You really were quite splendid, you know. And coming from someone like myself, brought up in a county where eight-bar fences are not uncommon, you may be sure that is a compliment of some magnitude. You were very, very good."

"Well, now she's choosing to be good at something more important, Con," interjected Maud. Since that first meeting the women were on a first-name basis. "And by the way, it's going to be quite confusing for us all, since you both have the same first name!" She laughed merrily as she said it. "Or perhaps we should simply call you 'Madame,' as does everyone else in Dublin."

Con seated herself between the two women, liking them immensely.

"Con Markievicz," Maud continued, "is as involved in Ireland as I am. And she's had a hard time being accepted by the men in the Brotherhood, too—so I've decided to enlist her aid in our conspiracy."

"Damned glad you want to be part of it!" said Markievicz, slapping the sofa cushion for emphasis. "Need more women of substance in all this."

"You'll have to get used to Madame's salty tongue, Con." Maud smiled. "She can't see any reason why women's speech shouldn't have the same freedom as men's."

"Damned right!" said the Countess, pouring tea from the silver service in front of her and dropping in two cubes of sugar, as if for emphasis.

"As a matter of fact, there's precious little reason I can think of why we shouldn't have *all* the same freedoms as they!"

"Here, here," said Con, delighted by the woman's candor. "But precisely how do you get the men to agree with you about that?"

"Oh, but I don't, you see! Not that it's ever deterred me in the least from doing what I want to do, of course."

"What would you do if you were in my shoes?" Con asked.

"Precisely what Maudie has suggested, my dear. Why, Griffith's absolutely mad about her, as is every other man in Dublin, of course." Markievicz smiled broadly at her friend, as if she thought Maud's popularity no more than her due. "If she asks him to take an interest in you, he will do so . . . unquestionably. I think writing's just the ticket. Writing is so blissfully genderless. Once there's something good down on paper, no one will give a damn whether it was written by a woman or a man."

Con left the two women after an hour or two with a new determination. She still had to puzzle out what exactly she had to offer. But at least she had allies now: Tierney, in his rebellion against Seaneen for her sake, and these two remarkable women.

Now, all that remained to be seen was whether or not she could live up to their confidence.

THE PRICE OF FREEDOM—AN ESSAY

"What will you give me for the right to be free?" the old woman in the black shawl wheedled, singsong.

"I'll give you my money and my time," said the younger one, pulling her children closer to her skirt, for she sensed danger and felt fear. "I'll give you my sweat and toil and my righteous anger," she added, for there was power in this old woman and knowledge. She wasn't to be taken lightly.

"You'll give me your sons and your husbands, your pride and your dignity. And your lifeblood, too, before I'm through with you," the old woman cackled madly, and the young one shuddered. "And small payment it'll be when all's said and done. . . ."

Con's pen ran furiously over the paper, words she had thought would be an effort tumbling out with a startling momentum.

Con finished the first essay and, without stopping to read it through, she began the next. So much injustice, so much poverty, so many injuries to the human spirit. There was enough material in her head for a thousand essays. It was as if every impression she had collected in all the time she'd been with Tierney had coalesced into language—torrential, activist language.

Con let herself be swept along in the tidal excitement of the words and was startled, when she heard Tierney's heavy step on the stair, to realize that it was nearly 3 A.M. Hastily she gathered up the sheaf of papers that had collected and tucked them into the drawer in the kitchen table. There would be time enough to show them to Tierney if Arthur Griffith thought they had any merit.

"And whose work is this, might I ask?" Griffith's voice thundered over the sounds of the printing press in the storefront office on Nassau Street. He waved a sheaf of notes in his hand and his face was animated. He was a smallish man with a strong, stern jaw, and Con noted that he walked with an odd rolling gait, like that of a seaman. He was an unremarkable fellow except for his notable blue eyes, which were alive with intelligent energy and fervor.

"They're mine, Mr. Griffith," answered Con quickly. "Miss Gonne thought you should have a look at them." She knew that Maud had spoken to him about her.

"A look at them, my girl! I'd have to hold them with pincers to keep from burning my hands on the likes of these. There's enough fire and brimstone in here to raise blisters on an evangelist!"

Constance laughed at what she knew was uncommon praise from Griffith.

"I've more of them back at the flat, Mr. Griffith. If you think they're publishable, I'll bring them here."

Griffith turned his bright blue eyes thoughtfully on the handsome young woman before him.

"Publishable they are indeed, Mrs. O'Connor. But if we print them under your own name you'll have the Castle down on you in no time flat and your husband will relieve me of my hide an inch at a time in thanks for that, I'd wager. I've met him, you know," he added with a kindly twinkle in his eye.

"I've thought about needing a new name for protection," answered Con, excited by Griffith's enthusiasm. "A pen name like Mr. Wilde's 'Speranza' or George Russell's 'A.E.' It might add a touch of mystery if the writing comes from an unidentified source, don't you think?"

"You've a name in mind, I take it?" he asked.

"I do. It seems it should have some significance from the old days. I thought to take the notion of the Wild Harp from 'The Minstrel Boy.' It was the first rebel song Tierney ever sang to me."

She was an interesting one, this aristocrat turned would-be patriot, thought Griffith, amused by her excitement, warmed by the quality of her writing. And by Maud's recommendation.

"The Wild Harp, is it?"

"What do you think?"

"The perfect sobriquet for a warrior bard, my girl. Let's hope there's no occasion for 'its chords to be torn asunder.' "

Con smiled, immensely relieved that Griffith had liked the essays. Although the *United Irishman* paid a pittance to its contributors, each penny meant something in their household. She still felt confused by the fact that the ideas for the essays had come so easily to her. And it would give her a tiny foothold in Tierney's world. A foothold that might be a step toward showing him his belief in her hadn't been in vain.

As she left the office of the *United Irishman* the strange thought struck her: if Tierney was the Minstrel Boy, she, herself, was the Wild Harp "slung behind him."

> 17 Capel Street
> Dublin
> 15 January 1905

My darling sister,

I can't tell you how our lives have changed for the better since Tierney made it clear to Seaneen that I must be privy to the Brotherhood's plans. I don't know how he convinced Seaneen, but now we are in this together and I'm learning, learning. I would not trust this letter to the mails and could not say this much except for its being hand-delivered by Desmond, who is back from Europe for a brief visit and looking grand. I must caution you to burn it when you have finished reading, however, for such information could be dangerous if traced.

The most extraordinary things are happening here. We have all survived King Edward's visit to Dublin and Arthur Griffith has organized something called the National Council to provide us separatists a forum. Constance and Eva Gore-Booth from Lissadell are both involved, Constance far more actively. Do you remember ever meeting them? Constance is now the Countess Markievicz—she married a Polish nobleman—and she is in the thick of all this. . . . I'm rather proud of the fact that she, Maud Gonne and I are the only women who are treated as comrades by our small revolutionary group.

At any rate, the possibilities are immense, if we can actually get a political party into action. We women are also determined to make women's rights an important issue (as you might imagine!) and I've finally gotten to the point in life when I have the right outlet for my energies. I have even joined Maud Gonne's new organization Inghinidhe na hEireann. We are calling ourselves "militant nationalists" lest any mistake our motives!

Strange as it sounds, my dear sister, I think I'm better at all this than is Tierney. What heresy! eh? But you know what a fighter I am at heart and you know I'm never better than when I have some passionate cause to consume my imagination. And more important still, now that the terrible wall of secrecy that was destroying me has been rent, I am filled with an enormous energy that I can put to good use for Ireland.

Tierney, on the other hand, does not thrive on intrigue. He is impatient with the leaders and their petty squabbles. In short, I fear my husband has too poetic a nature for this kind of life, over the long haul. But, of course, I cannot say that to him, for it is what he has chosen—and at great sacrifice.

One incident happened a week or two ago that you will laugh about I'm sure:

We IRB women were told by Seaneen that we ought to learn marksmanship in order to protect ourselves if and when the Rising should come. Pat O'Reilly was supposed to teach us to shoot and we all, along with Seaneen, drove to a spot outside the city for our target practice. I'd told them that I knew something of guns from my hunting days with Papa, but O'Reilly was rather patronizing (it is so very hard for men to accept our expertise in anything, isn't it, Bethy dear?). So I let him rattle on about how to hold a rifle and pistol and so forth. I suppose I don't need to tell you that I beat him on the target range. And so did Constance Markievicz!

I must say Pat wasn't in the least amused, but Seaneen and the others nearly split their sides with laughter. And I do think there has been a less grudging camaraderie from them all, ever since.

Truth is, they're a lovely bunch and I'm proud to be a part of them. The more I learn of Ireland, the more I see of the poor, the more I understand what it is like to be the oppressed . . . the prouder I am of Tierney and his Cause.

And, my darling sister, I might add that, much to my amazement, the Wild Harp is becoming quite famous (or, perhaps, infamous would be the word chosen by the Castle). Would that the fame was not anonymous, but nonetheless it is quite thrilling to see how people rally round the sentiments of the Harper. One can pass people standing on street corners reading the column on each Saturday when the *United Irishman* is published.

And the Crown has become just as interested as the people, I am told. Griffith has been harassed by the police on two occasions now, trying to ascertain the identity of the Harper, as everyone calls me now. Best of all, I'm happier than I've ever been.

I'm feeling marvelously healthy and, except for being in the last month of pregnancy, I'd be spending all my spare time working for the Brotherhood.

Isn't it strange that growth can come out of loss and sorrow? I was so racked by Tierney's decision not to publish, and yet out of that has come my involvement in Ireland's future. I feel fulfilled and uplifted by all this in a way that is quite indescribable—it is as if by becoming the Harper, I am becoming more myself. Does that sound mad or arrogant or foolish? I do hope not—I would so much like you to share the happiness of what I feel.

Write to me when you can, my darling Bethy, but be careful of what you say if you send the letter by post. By the way, your suffrage issue looms large here now. Isn't it marvelous that your book has become the rallying cry for women everywhere—I'm very proud of you! Come to Dublin after the baby is born and we will fight for the right together!

> All my love, as ever,
> Your sister Con

ᑫ I had been so thrilled to hear of Con's second pregnancy and of all the new excitements in her life that I decided to go to Dublin to visit her after her baby's birth. Fortunately it would be summer when I arrived and the children's schooling wouldn't keep me from traveling.

Edmond and I had settled into a loveless conventionality in our life together. We were civil to each other and we shared both history and the nurturing of our children. Even loveless connections can be strong ones, as time goes on.

My novel, conceived as it was out of my own misfortunes and frustrations, had, indeed, as Con suggested, become a rallying cry for women. It was also, of course, the catalyst for changing the parameters of my own world. I was invited to lecture and to attend conferences. I was asked to write articles for the feminist publications that were springing up in Dublin, London and Edinburgh. Women began to correspond with me.

I, the least iconoclastic of women, found myself touted as a champion of women's rights. I, who hadn't the courage to save myself, was a symbol to other women of the possibility of salvation.

I began to act independently of Edmond . . . making my own plans, traveling, lecturing, writing . . . and much to my amazement he did little to stop me.

I was excited about my first real visit to Dublin after such a long absence. I looked forward to meeting Madame Markievicz, Con's friend who was the leading light in the suffrage movement there. And, of course, I was elated at the prospect of having time to spend with my sister.

I had no way of knowing as I set out to visit Con that there would be trouble when I arrived. ✧

15   Con watched at little Eamon's bedside with increasing concern. His breathing was beginning to come harder and the two-month-old body seemed to be struggling beyond its endurance. He had come into the world easier than Tahg and had seemed healthy enough until a few days before.

She wished that Tierney were there, but when he'd left for the pub earlier in the evening the baby had seemed only to have a bad cold and she'd told him there was no need to worry. Now the strange rattle in his chest sounded more like croup, or rather she *thought* it sounded like croup. She knew the disease was the scourge of babies in the tenements, but she'd never seen a child in the throes of it.

A long rasping, rattling breath sounded in Eamon's throat and he seemed unable to get enough air into his small body. The effort made up her mind for her. Scooping up the baby, Con ran to her next-door neighbor and asked her to keep an eye on sleeping Tahg. Then she threw a shawl around herself and the struggling child and sped out into the darkened street. She felt in her purse for money, relieved to find some there, and turned in the direction of the Jervis Street Hospital, grateful that it was only a few hundred yards away.

The hospital corridor was filled with people when she arrived, all poorly dressed as she, all waiting for the doctor's attention. She hurried past them to the nurse, trying not to hear the awful rattling breathing of the baby in her arms. His color had changed for the worse, and he seemed sicker than when she'd left the house.

"Please, Nurse," she said to the attendant, "I think my baby has the croup, can we see the doctor quickly?"

The nurse looked startled by the woman's voice; speech of such refinement didn't mesh with clothes like those. Imagine the likes of her putting on airs. "You'll wait your turn," she replied in her best clipped speech.

"But you don't understand," persisted Con. "My baby can't breathe! I don't think he can wait."

The nurse looked dispassionately at the little coughing bundle in Con's arms. "Nobody's here because they're healthy, missus. Every one of these patients thinks he should be first." She waved her hand at the waiting faces. "You'll just have to wait your turn!" And she bustled off down the corridor.

Uncertain what to do, Con walked back and forth for a few minutes, crooning to the baby. Was it her imagination or did his skin have a bluish tinge to it now that it hadn't had before? She shifted the laboring child to a position up over her shoulder, and a terrible coughing fit seized it that sent terror to her heart. She had to get help for him.

Ignoring the stares of people around her, Con ran down the corridor to where the nurse had disappeared. No one was in sight in the quiet white hallway. Taking a deep breath—and thinking how frightened and diffident poverty made a person—she summoned up courage to open doors, and finally behind one of them she found a doctor examining a patient and a nurse assisting.

"Please," she said in a distraught whisper, "my baby needs help!"

The doctor looked at the shabbily dressed young woman and

motioned to the nurse to remove her from the room. The nurse grabbed Con's arm and tried to propel her into the corridor, but a fury seized Con as she did so. She clutched the baby tightly to her breast with one hand and pushed the nurse fiercely away with the other.

"Don't you people understand?" she shouted. "My baby needs a doctor. He can't breathe! I can pay for your services. I'm not a poor woman."

The doctor and nurse exchanged glances at that; it was obvious that the woman was poor by the look of her. It was also obvious from her voice that she took on airs. Perhaps the best thing to do was to pacify her. "I shall look at your baby next, madam," said the doctor stentoriously, as if bestowing a great and undeserved favor. "But you must wait until we've finished with this patient." With that he returned to his work. The nurse reached for Con's arm, but the distraught mother shot her a glance that said touching her again would be a risky business.

Con moved back into the corridor distractedly. There was no time to run to Tierney, no time to try to reach a friend who might know a doctor. No way to get faster medical help than here. She must wait . . . must try to be patient. The doctor said they would be next.

She opened the blanket to look at Eamon. Dear God, his face was blue! His tiny arms and hands had a grayish tinge. Each time he coughed, a rattle of phlegm choked off his breath. She stared at the baby in her arms, and as she did so, she saw it open both eyes and mouth in a desperate effort; its small fists opened and closed convulsively, then a strange small sound escaped its open lips, a shudder passed through the body. She knew he was lost.

"No!" she cried to the baby and to God. "No!" and the door opened again. The doctor walked briskly into the corridor and peered into the blanket that housed the little body. He placed his fingers expertly on its neck.

"I'm afraid he's gone," he said. "Like as not we couldn't have saved him."

Still clutching the baby in her left arm, Con swung her right hand up and hit the doctor a resounding slap with her right.

"Precious little you did to try!" she said between clenched teeth. "If both my hands were free, I'd kill you myself!" The doctor, stunned by the woman's vehemence, stood staring at her. The nurse ran for the guard and Con turned and walked blindly, but with immense dignity, to the hospital's door.

"See here, madam!" called the doctor, moving after her. "You can't leave here with the body. You must leave the child in the dead house."

With that, she turned on him such a fierce look that he recoiled from it.

"I'll take my son home and, so help me God, I'll kill the first one who tries to stop me!"

At that the guard ran up to her with the nurse at his heels, but the doctor held up his hand to stay them, and Con continued her departure.

Blindly, she walked to the bottom of the stone steps, blindly wandered home, blindly stumbled into their flat with her terrible burden in her arms.

She did not know what to do with the little body. She straightened out the limbs and brushed the fluff of hair back from his loved little face. She held her hand for a long while on his tiny breast, hoping against hope for a flutter of life there. But the body was growing cold already and it was easy to see that no life remained.

Finally, she dressed the baby in his nightshirt—oh, how long a sleep will it be for you, my son, my son, she said as she touched him—and wrapping him in a blanket, lay down beside him on the bed, where, hours later, Tierney found them when he came home from work.

✍ It took my sister a very long time to get over the death of her son—if, indeed, it can be said of any of us that we get over the loss of a child. But I had learned that we do go beyond it, somehow; it took Con a very long while to do so. We buried Eamon at Glasnevin in a tiny grave, for Con was not well enough to make the journey home—heartsick and weak from sorrow as she was. Although now he lies with the rest of our family, so many of whom died too soon, in the FitzGibbon graveyard.

Tierney, too, was heartbroken. He blamed himself for not being with them the night the baby died. . . . More than anything he blamed himself for being poor. Had there been money for a family doctor, I heard him say despairingly . . . things would have been different. It was a sad and desolate time for both of them, although they clung to each other and to Tahg throughout.

Con seemed ravaged when I saw her for the funeral. I told Edmond I intended to stay with her until she no longer needed me. Unlike Con, who was constrained by poverty, I had the advantage of money and servants. My children would be well cared for by Nanny, so I could be free to try to woo my sister back to life as she had once done for me.

I wonder sometimes why so little has been written of the profound love that can exist between sisters . . . it is such an abiding trust. We two had, by the time of this visit, both suffered much in our effort toward maturity. No longer were we the simple comrades of our childhood days who shared a common history and geography and parentage. Rather were we battle-hardened veterans of life's peculiar wars. We had known much of love and loss—we each had buried a child. And we were changed by it all, changed irrevocably. Yet we were the same confidantes and trusted allies. No friendship can be as deep as that of two from the same womb, I sometimes think . . . no bond as trusted and powerful.

We saw the sorrow in each other and understood, as others could not understand. The loss of the baby had made Con somber and introspective. The misery of my marriage had purged me somehow of hope in the future. We sensed in each other a terrible need . . . and we felt a curious conviction that it was up to each of us to save the other.

I have no way of knowing if my confidences over the ensuing months helped my sister, as I so sincerely hoped they would; she told me that they saved her life, and I hope it's so. But I do know that she precipitated me into the most momentous experience of my own, for she pushed me in the direction of Seaneen O'Sullivan . . . a path I had most surely intended not to tread.

I was curious about the meetings Con and Tierney attended so religiously. I wanted to learn—I craved the comfort of the familial friendship that this secret community of rebels afforded. And I was wildly attracted to Seaneen.

Con knew full well, I think, where my spending time with him would lead—she also knew how desperately I needed to love and to be loved. Where years before she had warned me to beware, now she urged me to take what he could give, so far had life propelled us from the innocence of our girlhoods. God bless her sweet soul for so eminently well-meaning a manipulation.

It didn't take long for the strength and power of the man—and the gentleness, too—to stir feelings in me that were hard to deny. I was confused by what I had begun to feel, but I was alive again. Alive as I hadn't been in a long, long time. ∽

Seaneen's laugh, when it sounded, was a hearty, merry one—younger than the man seemed by years. There was humor much of the time behind his eyes—buried somewhere near the hundreds of quotations that rose readily to his lips. He had read so much of Shakespeare while in prison that he quoted him easily, as if he were an old friend. Indeed all the classics besprinkled his speech. But the laughter was a rarer thing, and when it happened, everyone marked its advent.

"Why so light-hearted this morning, might I ask?" Tommy McGowan inquired of the tough Fenian of bygone days.

"I've not a clue, Tommy," he replied. "I woke up feeling grand entirely this morning. Like a young lad. ' 'Tis the mind that makes the body rich,' you know. My mind is rich this morning."

Several of the men in the room looked knowingly at each other. There'd been an obvious change in Seaneen since the Manningham woman had come to Dublin. No one knew for sure if there was more than a flirtation to it yet—but if there wasn't, there would be. It amused them that Seaneen thought them all ignorant of what was going on under their noses.

Tierney smiled with the rest of them, but with more complication to his thoughts on the subject. He and Con had discussed the growing friendship between Beth and Seaneen with differing concerns.

"He'll be too much a will-o'-the-wisp for her, Con," he'd warned her the day before.

"Seaneen, a will-o'-the-wisp? Are you mad, man? He's as substantial as they come."

"Aye, but his substance is committed to another mistress, Beauty. He's for the movement, heart, body and soul."

"And he's a man and a human one at that, Tierney. Not some perfect marble god as you men seem to think him. My instinct tells me that every time he looks at Beth he remembers he has a body that's his own."

Tierney had smiled at that; he knew she was right. But he also knew that whatever there could be between Beth and Seaneen would be transitory and he wondered with deep concern how well each would fare when it was done.

Seaneen busied himself with the maps and ordnance reports, but his mind was not on them. The thought of the Manningham woman kept infringing on his concentration, insinuating itself into his orderly life. Orderly, *lonely* life . . . he corrected the thought even as it came to him; he laid down the papers with finality and poured himself a whiskey that he didn't particularly want.

Instead of drinking it, Seaneen placed the glass on the table and laid his spectacles beside it. He needed them for reading small print now, and they annoyed him, sure sign of the infirmity of aging that they were.

He rubbed the bridge of his nose where the glasses had been, trying to banish the unwanted thoughts that lurked behind his tired eyes, but they were persistent.

She was so vulnerable and so lovely. There was an innocence about her, too, "as if she feared no danger, for she knew no sin." And she was lonely. It was a hunger he could recognize, for he was hungry, too . . . for friendship and understanding of a deeper sort. And she was so very lovely.

Not with the statuesque perfection of Maud Gonne, or the patrician elegance of the Countess, or the robust, vital beauty of her sister. But rather she was possessed of a gentle womanly warmth that promised depths to be fathomed.

Seaneen rested his head in his big hands for a moment and tried to shake off the wanting. It was not like him to *want* this much—he'd long ago purged himself of the need for love. Not since his wife's death had he ever allowed a woman to penetrate the armor plating that protected his emotions. There'd been women to bed, of course, over the years. Not great numbers of them, but enough for his needs.

But nothing like this . . . this ridiculous schoolboy infatuation he struggled with. She must be twenty years younger than he, and another man's wife. And her husband was just the kind of man he'd been on the run from all his life . . . an arrogant know-it-all Anglo aristocrat, with all the education and privilege and money he would never have. All the civilized accouterments of life that a lady like Elizabeth Manningham *should* have.

He tried to purge the memory of her face from his mind. She had long auburn hair that she wore piled onto her head in a soft halo from which loose strands tended to free themselves. He let himself imagine for a moment loosing the rest of it, letting it fall around naked shoulders, touching, exploring . . .

Seaneen slammed his fist down on the table so hard that the shot glass spilled half its contents and the eyeglasses rose and fell.

He'd have to get a hold of himself, he said, as he downed what was left of the fiery liquid. He'd be damned if he'd go mooning around like a half-arsed adolescent over another man's wife.

Deliberately, he mopped up the whiskey with his handkerchief and laid out the maps he had just put away. He would force himself to concentrate. He would forget that she was beautiful and lonely. He would forget that he was hungry, too.

16 ∽ I paced up and down on the Aubusson carpet, my mind and heart in turmoil. For once, not even Con's sensible advice could help me. This moment of choice was mine alone. Seaneen and I had been leading up to this moment through all the weeks I'd been in Dublin. I had known it the last time we had stood looking into each other's eyes, lost to the world around us. I could not be a coward any longer.

Seaneen would abide by any decision I made about us. I knew that. Rough, lovely Seaneen, with his broad back that bore so many people's burdens. Tough, unrelenting Seaneen, who pushed and pulled at people, bending them to do his will. Deep, unfathomable Seaneen, whose eyes had told me in an instant more than Edmond's would in a lifetime.

Dear God, this confusion was unbearable! The very notion of infidelity repelled me. Unfaithful wives were not women like me . . . good women, good wives who strove to do what was right for their families through a lifetime. Unfaithful wives were wanton, soulless creatures with no breeding and no sense of propriety.

I remember stopping before the oval gilt-framed mirror on the wall and staring at my own reflection. Still young enough, it seemed to say to me. Still young and pretty enough to want to be loved . . . to want to love a man and be loved by him.

Was I never to feel the comfort of a man who truly loved me? I asked myself. Never to feel myself overcome by a lust as mighty as that which seemed to rage within my soul? Never to be *loved?*

I had done my part in my damned-fool marriage. I had kept our bargain, in bed and out. But did that mean that never, never once in all my life would I feel what I longed to feel? I paced up and down the room . . . wanting so much to give in to my own terrible desire.

Scaneen could give me what I longed for. He had the strength and the passion and the understanding for it . . . yes, and maybe even the longing, too. I'd read it in his eyes. He wanted me as much as I wanted him.

It would only be for a little while, of course. There could be no future in it for either of us. But at least there would have been a past.

I dressed hurriedly and took a cab to the Gaelic League meeting where I would see him. I told myself I would not make up my mind until I saw him once again.

I waited, when the meeting was over, for the room to clear. Even the other men who always stayed long past midnight seemed to sense that tonight Seaneen's mind was on other things and they moved out early. I saw him watching me covertly as the room began to clear.

He walked slowly, heavily, to the back of the hall where I waited, and sat down beside me. I saw him search my face for a sign of my decision and, seeing both love and confusion there, he said, " 'Tis a great dilemma I've saddled you with, it seems, My Lady." His face was a network of thousands of fine lines bridged by deeper ones. His eyes seemed old, filled with wisdom and knowledge and sadness and hope. He touched my cheek softly with the backs of his fingers; the scratchy male gesture filled me with yearnings I couldn't begin to describe.

"It seems so dishonorable a thing to do . . . ." I began, needing to be honest with him. "I've never imagined myself in the role of adulteress," I said miserably. He gazed for a moment deep into my eyes after I'd said that and then nodded.

"Nae, My Lady. It isn't the name I'd like to hear on your lips. Perhaps it's best after all not to start something we know we can't finish the right way." I took the hand he offered and held it fast for a moment—he had voiced a fear that was on both our minds.

"What say I walk you home?" he said finally.

"I think it would be best for me to go alone, Seaneen," I replied tentatively, hoping he would argue. But instead he nodded again as if he understood the rebuff. I reached up and kissed him on the cheek and walked out into the darkened night feeling emptied of everything. Desperately empty. The tears in my eyes made it impossible to see. I had done the right thing, I told myself. Why was I in such pain? I remember standing on the street corner, unwilling to go farther away from this man I wanted so very much—unable to go back. I was standing there still, when moments later I felt Seaneen's arms slip around my body.

"I'll not let you go like this, My Lady," he said quietly, as he touched me. "I've little to give you, God knows. But I knew the minute you walked out that door, we're not to part like this. There may be no future for us but, by God, I can't let you go without telling you how much I want there to be a present!"

Till my dying day I'll thank the Lord that he had the wisdom to overrule my well-meaning stupidity.

"I'm such a fool, Seaneen!" I breathed into the old tweed of his jacket as he held me. "Don't you see? I've needed you all my life! Why did I never find you until now, when it seems too late!"

His face, as I looked up at him, was softened from the face I had seen earlier. "Would God we'd met in different times than these," he whispered huskily.

"In different times than these we might never have met at all," I replied.

He smiled a little at that and, holding me tightly in his arms for another minute, said, "Where shall we go then, My Lady? My flat is not what you're used to."

"Any place where I can be alone with you will seem the most beautiful in the world to me tonight."

We walked to his lodging house; it was a poor neighborhood, but the flat was tidy for that of a man alone. I suspected he had cleaned it in hopes that I would visit.

We stood for a moment inside the door, locked in each other's eyes; a shiver of anticipation rocked me. Never in all my years with Edmond had I felt anything like the desire that consumed me.

Finally, slowly, Seaneen reached out to me, undid the fastening of my cloak, letting it fall behind me. I didn't know what I should do in return, so I simply stood there, letting myself feel the incredible, joyous agony of anticipation. My body tingled, my mind soared. I was nervous, frightened, joyous, amazed. I felt more womanly in that moment than ever before. I felt like an innocent child and like a wanton, all at the same time. I wanted him with an urgency there are no words to describe.

"If you but knew how long I've dreamed of doing this, My Lady," he said quietly as he undid the buttons of my dress. Carefully, slowly, as if unsure of the procedure, or as if undue haste might dispel the dream, he loosed my dress and pushed the straps of my chemise down over my shoulders, freeing my breasts. Could it be that he was feeling what I was? I wondered, dazzled by my own emotions. Slowly, wonderingly, he pushed my chemise and pantalets down, down until at last I stood naked before him in the dim light. I was shocked at myself, for instead of feeling self-conscious, I felt very beautiful. And I knew it was his doing.

Then he undid his own clothes, holding me with his eyes as he moved unhurriedly. As if we had all the time in the world.

"You are so beautiful," he said once and I knew that he meant it. Then suddenly, tenderly, he picked me up naked and, crushing my body to his own hard flesh, he buried his head in the crook of my shoulder and sighed a strange long sigh, as if a profound decision had been made or breached. Then he carried me to his bed.

"I knew . . ." I breathed once exultantly as I felt the strength of him fill me. "I knew you would be like this . . ." But he covered my mouth with his own hungrily and I never had the chance to tell him more.

Tender, brutal, wild, soft, frenzied, perfect passion, that night of nights—I thought as I drifted off to sleep in his protective arms. Thank you, Seaneen, for this one perfect night. Thank you, God.

I left for home the following early morning in a haze of happiness. I could barely breathe for it—the joy filling me as if I were a too small vessel. I was bursting with unaccustomed fulfillment.

I was loved . . . I could love back! My body ached with remembered pleasures. My mind was a blur of indelible moments, each one of which sent shivers of remembered joy through my willing body.

So *this* was what I had longed for, unknowing! This wild, animal, passionate, perfect connection that raised you to a place beyond mere mortal experience. Dear God, how could you live without it, having once felt such addictive pleasures? Con's warning of long ago flashed through my mind. "If you had to go back to Edmond after having tasted of a man like Seaneen, you'd live the rest of your life in agony."

Sweet Jesus, how very right she had been, but I wouldn't think of that now. I had another month, perhaps two, before me. A summerful of perfect happiness. Of learning to be a woman as I had always wished to learn. Of giving love and receiving it. Of sharing happiness in the same proportion as I received it. Perhaps there was hope for the future after all.

Seaneen tossed and twisted in the bed. The dream was a violent one . . . a twenty-year-old violence that still smoldered so deep within him that it surfaced only sometimes.

A strange sound, between a strangled cry and an animal growl of fury, wrenched itself from him, and I sat upright in the bed, frightened and disconcerted.

He was quiet again, but his face was pained and his body was covered in sweat, despite the cool night air. I watched him, fascinated, uncertain if I should wake and comfort him or if that would somehow demean the man.

Suddenly he stiffened, boardlike beside me, then opened his eyes and looked covertly around as if to orient himself carefully to his surroundings. Focusing on me staring at him wide-eyed, he tried to smile reassuringly, but there was a haunted expression in his eyes that betrayed the smile.

"I'm sorry, My Lady," he said softly. "I sleep alone most of the time, so I don't have to worry about frightening anyone with my bad dreams. I haven't had that one in a while, thank God . . . but it lurks there still, it seems."

I reached over to touch him and the covers fell away from my body as I did so. I started to pull the blanket up over my breast but he stayed me, grasping my wrist with his hand. "No," he said. "Don't cover yourself. I love your breasts."

He didn't touch them to underline his meaning but the words themselves were unbearably erotic.

"And I, all the parts of you," I replied and he smiled in the dark. I slid down beside him into welcoming arms.

"What do you dream about that's so terrible, then?" I asked, running my fingers over his back lovingly. There were scars on his body everywhere.

"The bad ones are about the time in the jails. Torture does strange things to a man, My Lady. Even if you get through it, you're changed by it. Changed.

"Never do you see other men in the same light of innocence as before. To know one man capable of such studied brutality makes all men suspect. And you doubt yourself, of course."

"Why doubt yourself? Don't you feel pride that you withstood it where others failed?"

"Nae, Lady. For every moment you are being tortured you see yourself for the frail, vulnerable creature that you are. Unmasked, unmanned. A universe filled with pain and no more than a package of bleeding, broken flesh and bones that could give way at any moment.

"You hang on and you pray for oblivion. You beg God not to let you betray your comrades . . . not to let you fail those whose lives depend on you.

"But every instant of that agony you know that you are a hair's breadth from failure. A hair's breadth from the lowest beast that roams the jungle.

"And then it's over, somehow. And you've borne it . . . somehow. But you are never free of the specter that one more day of it, or five more minutes, or one more agony and the outcome might have been different.

"Once you've faced your own frailty, My Lady, you're hard-pressed ever to be proud again."

I turned in his arms and touched his lips with my fingers, wishing I could stay the pain.

"For a woman, it's childbed that bares our own mortality to us," I said. "We are never the same again, after that."

"Aye. We all face our own demons, don't we, lass?" he smiled ruefully. "But, by God, I'm glad they spared us both to have found this. Eh?"

I moved myself into the crook of his body by way of reply.

"You've given me more of joy than I knew the world could hold, Seaneen," I told him honestly. "More of everything."

"How strange that it should be so . . . you who have all that everyone else desires. That you've given *me* the moon and the stars seems much more understandable." He chuckled softly as he said it.

I laughed in his arms and wrapped myself tightly around him. "I wish the gods had given us more time, beloved," I said. It seemed incomprehensible that what we had could only be for a brief moment.

"And I'm grateful that they've given us any at all," he replied as he turned his body toward me, drinking in all that we were feeling, it seemed, as he did so. "But tonight, My Lady . . . ah, tonight, let us pretend we have all the time in the world."

I felt his hands and mouth begin to play the most beautiful patterns on my body, heart and mind. Soft, hard, outside, inside pleasures that astounded me. I struggled to move his powerful body aside to give back, but he held my wrists above my head and pinned me with his weight, and a very, very long time later I felt myself drift tenderly beyond ecstasy and into the untroubled sleep of absolute fulfillment.

"Do you never wish that we were two other people who could simply be in love with each other and marry and have children and live an ordinary life?" I asked the question as we rode the streetcar on our way home from Howth. We had packed a lunch and gone to the seaside to be alone for an entire day—a rare occurrence, and the afternoon had been as lovely as we'd planned it to be.

"Aye, My Lady," Seaneen replied, smiling the contented smile that the happy day had brought. "I fantasize about that a good deal these days, I'm afraid."

"Tell me what you imagine," I asked, and he could hear the contentment of the day in my voice, too, I'm sure.

"Oh, I suppose I see us back in Tipperary where I was born

and grew up. I see myself a farmer—not quite on the scale of your father's farmlands, mind you—but with a bit of land and with fine strapping sons to help me till the fields. And with a little lass or two to hold on my knee." He turned to me smiling and said unexpectedly, "Would it surprise you to hear that I'd like to know your children?"

I felt startled by the thought.

"I love children, you know, and I'm good with them. They like me." He said it with a shy pride and I thought, there are so many things I don't yet know about you, my love. But I only hugged his arm a little tighter in reply.

"We might have had lovely children together," I said.

"We might yet, at the rate we're going," he responded quickly, with a concerned laugh. "I worry for the danger to you, My Lady."

I looked around as if to be certain no one could hear before replying, but the only other person left on the streetcar was an elderly man dozing near the front of the car.

"Don't fear for me," I said, sounding braver than I felt, for the fear of pregnancy had indeed been in my mind since our affair had begun. "Nothing of our love could ever harm me."

Later I had cause to remember my own words. But I never changed my mind about them.

It had been a glorious night with Seaneen—as were they all glorious with him. The bittersweet knowledge that I must leave in a few days intensified our need for each other and every instant of our time together seemed gilded by an almost supernatural beauty. It was more than simple pleasure, although there was much of that, God knows. He'd taught me to live and to feel, to see beyond the ordinary; there was a monumental strength to him that sustained me, like that of a great rock that has been pounded by the sea for centuries, yet remains intact. I both loved and admired him, and in that final week of our time together I think I saw him clearer than I had ever seen anything in my life.

Just as Edmond's cold austerity had left me protectionless and on the outside of life looking in—so Seaneen's warmth and passion made me feel safe at last. It was a terrible irony, as things turned out.

I alighted from the taxi too numbed by joy even to be embarrassed by my overnight's absence from home. Up until then I had made it a point to return home before my children would arise from their beds, so they wouldn't find anything amiss. But this was our last week together and my sorrow about leaving had made me selfish. I would simply tell the servants I had stayed the night with my sister, as I had done once or twice before.

The face of the maid who opened the door shattered me back into reality. It was tear-streaked and swollen.

"What is it?" I asked, instantly alert.

"Little Miss, mum," she managed to say before breaking into sobs. "She couldn't find you this morning when she woke up so she wandered out into the street in her nightdress." She stopped there to renew her sobbing and I did something I'd never done before in my life—I slapped the girl's face.

"Tell me what's happened!" I screamed at the poor simpering housemaid, a powerful guilty apprehension flooding me.

"The driver didn't see her, mum," she sobbed back at me. "He run right over her, but he didn't see her till it was too late!"

Dear Mother of God, it could not be! Not my little Angelica! Four years old is too little to die. I must have said it aloud although I didn't know I had.

"Oh no, mum! She's not dead," said the informer. "Just crippled."

Are there words for what happened in my heart at that moment? My baby looking for me, and I in the arms of Seaneen with no thought for her or the world. My baby searching and not finding me.

"Where is she?" I found I could not breathe.

"We didn't know where you was, mum. We sent Derek round to Mrs. O'Connor's flat and she come round right away. Mr. O'Connor brought the doctor and the ambulance took them all away to hospital."

"Which hospital are they at, Bessie?"

"St. Vincent's, mum," she said, looking at me wide-eyed, as if she expected me to hit her again.

"Forgive me, Bessie," I said as I turned to go. "I shouldn't have hit you."

"That's all right, mum," she called after me as I raced down the steps to find a cab. "We didn't know where to find you!"

The words ricocheted in my horrified brain as the taxi bounced over the cobblestones at top speed.

"We didn't know where to find you."

I spied Tierney first, in the hospital corridor; he held me fast as I tried to push past him.

"You must *wait*, Beth." His voice was urgent, but I tried to pull away from him.

"You can't see her. She's in surgery. Con is with her."

"I should be there!" I shouted, and everyone, nurse, doctors, patients alike, stared at me. "She's my baby!"

A pretty young nurse came toward me, realizing what was happening. "Your little girl is being given every care, Your Ladyship," she said in a kindly voice. "Dr. Langhorn was lecturing here this morning when they brought the child in. He's the best in Europe. If anyone can save her life, he's the one. We're so lucky he was here."

I nodded dumbly, unable to speak. Tierney's hands were still clutching both my arms. I tried to concentrate on the strength of them, watching the whitened knuckles hold me. A violent wave of nausea flooded me and then a cold blackness. I felt myself falling, falling, with only Tierney's hands to hold me back.

When I awoke, I saw Con's frightened face above my own.

"If I had only been there . . ." I spoke the words on all our minds.

"Hush, Sister, hush," she said, her voice heavy with tears. "You cannot think that now. She may yet live."

"She's such a baby . . ." I said helplessly. "Tell me what has happened to her."

Con started to speak, but couldn't; she looked despairingly to Tierney, who said in a terribly strained voice, "She wandered out of the house before anyone knew she was awake. No one realized she could even open the front door by herself . . . but she did, somehow.

"She must have run into the street and the milk-truck driver just didn't see her . . ." He stopped to gather courage.

"Her back and legs were crushed. Dr. Langhorn says he'll try to save her legs, but her life must come first. He's the best there is." ·

"You knew where I was?" I whispered.

"We guessed, when the servants said you hadn't come home. But there was no time to go to Seaneen's. We had to get Angelica here as fast as possible and I couldn't send a servant for you under the circumstances."

"We can still hope there's no need for Edmond to know the full story," Con interjected.

I nodded, feeling dead or, worse than that, feeling alive and responsible. My beautiful, darling little girl, crippled, maybe dying, because of my own selfish folly.

Con put her arms around me and we wept together and waited. Not one of the three of us said another word until the doctor came for us.

For what was there to say?

The moments that change our lives are frozen in perfect bas-relief forever in our minds. Con's face when she told me she was leaving with Tierney . . . Terrance Kiernan holding himself erect as he walked to the workhouse . . . Bethany's casket lowered into the ground . . . my daughter's chalk-white face when they wheeled her by me from the operating room. All are images that will never fade or alter.

Angelica's tiny body barely made a mound in the white sheet that covered the top of her body—a cage had been constructed around her legs. She was still as death.

I felt Con's fingernails dig into my wrist as I began to sway again; the sharp pain brought me back. A tall distinguished-looking man walked behind the rolling stretcher. He was be-whiskered and impeccably dressed.

"I'm Dr. Langhorn," he said in a voice of studied calm. "We did not amputate your daughter's legs, Lady Manningham. But I feel there is little hope that she will ever use them. Her spine was damaged by the carriage wheels and there was only so much that could be repaired by surgery."

"Will she live, Doctor?" I heard the terror in my own voice as I spoke the question.

"I believe there is every reason to hope that . . . she has a remarkably healthy little body to sustain her. But you must understand that she will require almost constant care for a very, very long while. It may be years before she is out of danger and able to care for herself."

I nodded dumbly, guilt twisting at my innards. My beautiful

loving child a cripple, because of me! The thought echoed and reechoed, bouncing back and forth in my consciousness. We stayed at the hospital for days, sleeping in shifts by Angelica's bed, waiting for her to come out of the coma.

Edmond arrived a day later. He could not have known of the circumstances of the accident, yet it was apparent that he blamed my carelessness, as well he should have.

The strangest thing of all was his unexpected devotion to our little girl. Edmond—the distant, the cool, the untouchable— was as devoted at Angelica's bedside as an acolyte at the altar. Gentle, tender, loving words he spoke to her endlessly in her coma. The doctors said she couldn't hear him but he continued nonetheless. Later, when she was better, she was able to tell us how very much those words had meant to her.

Eventually, after many weeks, we were told she was well enough for travel, and in an elaborate caravan we prepared to take her home to Manningham. The servants had long before taken the other children there.

Packed to leave, I called on Con and Tierney one last time before departure. They had been as stricken by our misfortune as I. We kissed and held each other wordlessly, then, as I was about to leave, Tierney came toward me, looking uncomfortable and sheepish.

"Con has said I shouldn't speak of Seaneen to you, Beth. But I must."

I turned white-faced, not knowing how to respond. "I've tried so hard not to think about him," I said.

"I know there's no good way to say this, but for what it's worth, the man's in love with you. He's destroyed by what's happened, Beth. He's given me a note for you. . . ." He reached into his pocket and fished out a well-worn envelope. It appeared that he'd carried it about with him for some time.

I ached to open it; I dared not do so. I held the letter for a long while in my hand, then put it unopened into my purse, kissed them both good-bye and left.

It was a long while—several days after we'd reached Manningham, in fact—before I trusted myself to retrieve the letter and read it.

Dearest My Lady,

For the sorrow that is in my heart, there are no words
—for the agony in yours, there are no comforts.

Yet would I have you know the love I bear you . . .
not as a mitigation of fault in what has happened to us—
we two are surely the most luckless of mortals that our
small moment of joy should have borne such terrible consequences—but because there is strength in love and
surely strength is what you most have need of now.

I would have you know, for whatever it is worth, that
you were no passing fancy for me, beloved Beth. Rather
you were the culmination of so many dreams that I
thought had died . . . the rebirth of hope . . . the re-
kindling of a life that had for too many years lain fallow
of love or hope or dreams.

Nonetheless, if I could have spared you this heartbreak, I surely would have done so. This of course, I
cannot do.

All that is left to me then is to tell you that I cherish
your memory as I do no other, and I pledge you a sacred
trust: if ever you have need of me, no matter where or in
what circumstances, I will come to you, though Satan
himself should bar the way. No idle promise that, My
Lady. Remember it, if ever need arises.

Until then, as for all time, I love you,

                                        Seaneen

I read the letter again and again until each word was committed forever to my memory. Then I burned it in the flame of the
candle near my daughter's bed and settled in to try to cope with
the long years that stretched ahead.

Strange indeed are the ways of the Lord. By my age one has
had time enough to ponder them and certain things are clearer
than they were in youth. . . . Clearest of all is the fact that we
do not understand in the least God's plan for us.

My daughter Angelica was the greatest mystery of my life.
Why this glorious golden child should have been so afflicted
defies all human comprehension. And yet, I have lived to see
the great good she was able to wring from fate, and the good
she did for others, so there is no question as to why she was

saved on that terrible morning—only a question of why she was made to suffer so.

All through the fall and winter of that year she lay near death, sometimes lucid, often not. Always she was in pain. I sat with her by the hour, by the day, by the week, by the month. The other children were kind and solicitous of their injured sister. They would bring her cherries from the grove, and wild flowers in their season. The twins would read to her, in the heady pride of scholarship they now felt at their accomplishments with their tutor. Even Winston, who was growing taller and handsomer than I had ever expected, was patient and kind to the ailing child, when he remembered to visit her.

By summer it was apparent that Angelica would live—crippled and malformed in back and legs—but she would live. Curiously, the long months of pain and illness had not made her fretful, as one would expect of a child of scant five years, but rather she had grown inward and contemplative, and above all sweet-natured, as if having borne more of suffering than was her share, she had grown old beyond her time. Old and wise and full of knowledge, but all the time it seemed she knew it was her own courage and inner strength that were to be relied on.

It seemed to me always that this little girl was older than I.

Edmond was incredibly kind to her. He played with her every day, and when he was with Angelica he was his best self, by far. With Winston he was cool and didactic; he made demands of his son and expected much of him, which worked well enough, since the boy was his own mirror image. With the twins he was kind but relentlessly correct, leaving them to each other's care. But with his small daughter, he was a different man entirely, loving and gentle.

Even toward me he showed forbearance in her presence, although at all other times his loathing was apparent. And not without good reason.

For, eight months after leaving Dublin, I bore my last son and he was not Edmond's. Dark hair and tawny skin, dark eyes and a strong, stocky muscularity that were the embodiment of Seaneen O'Sullivan marked this youngest Manningham. Any who knew both Edmond and Seaneen could never have doubted the child's parentage.

"I had a fierce and dark-haired grandfather on my mother's side," said Edmond within hearing of the servants, the night the child was born. "It is from him the boy has inherited." It was kindly done of him to spare me the humiliation of gossiping servants, but the look of hatred in his eyes when he turned from the cradle chilled me to the soul.

How could so short a happiness have wreaked such damnable destruction? How could one glorious sinful summer have ensnared so many lives in this tangled web? It seemed beyond reason.

I named the child John, not in rebellion against fate for having denied the boy his rightful father, but because it seemed to me, holding him in my arms, that he was so much his father's son that if he could not bear his last name he should at least share his first, in however Anglicized a fashion.

I think I had nearly gone mad with grief in the months that I'd carried him—the burden of this fresh evidence of my sin growing daily within me, even as I sat by the other anguished result of my infidelity. If madness could have spared me some of the pain, I would have welcomed it. And yet, in a bizarre way that I do not fully understand, I never, ever regretted my love for Seaneen or for his child. It was a tiny light that I held sacred in the darkness.

We humans are constructed of sturdy material and we tend to survive whether we wish to or not. By the second fall after the accident, Angelica was able to leave her bed for longer and longer stretches and the new baby was thriving. The curious pattern of our life had reestablished itself, and eventually I came to learn that if I were to care for my five growing children, I must pull myself together and begin again, though it flayed the living flesh from my bone to do so.

To his credit, Edmond never said aloud to me that he knew Johnny not to be his son, although he avoided the child whenever possible. We were married for better or for worse in his mind, and I expect he somehow came to terms with the fact that in me he had gotten the "worse." We had ceased to share a bed long before Dublin, but to the outside world we must have appeared as well wed as any other couple of our class. For my husband there would be other women, and a loveless marriage. For me there would be less.

Such sorrow as that can mitigate even guilt, after a time. Eventually, I made a tentative peace with myself and returned to the task of reestablishing my household. Edmond was becoming rapidly involved in the growing crisis of Home Rule in Parliament and he contrived to be away from home as much as possible. I scarcely blamed him.

I settled down to raise my children and to take from Fate whatever she would allow.

Tahg came to us in the summers, and over the next few years all six surviving children of Con's line and mine comprised the parameters of my universe.

PART TWO

Prologue

◆ I know now that most of the learning in my life was bred from sorrow, and that most of the strength that sustained me in later years was forged in the crucible of desperation. I didn't know either truth then, in the early days of my loveless marriage and my separation from Seaneen.

I railed against fate, I "troubled deaf heaven with my bootless cries." I fought against the unwanted lessons as fate's taskmaster threw each new one in my path. And, like all of us, I endured.

Edmond and I had moved into a period of troubled detente. His presence in the House of Lords was beginning to be talked about, and he spent a good deal of time in London. While he lacked the passion for great oratory, Edmond had a capacity for clear thinking and succinct articulation that made his speeches memorable and provocative. As he was also the soul of probity, he never spoke simply for the pleasure of hearing himself, but only when he had something of consequence to say. In short, he was making a name for himself and he seemed to have submerged his marital failures in other interests.

The children occupied my time, as did the running of my household. My writing had become a daily enterprise, as was the answering of letters from women who had read my book. Women's magazines were being published and my writing met great success in them. I had even begun to travel a bit, when my children's needs allowed. Invitations to lecture were plentiful and I began to find, in the company of other women, support and comfort of a special sort.

It was a curiously activist time, now that I think back— women's rights, laborers' rights, children's rights and Irish rights all mingled somehow in our consciousness as the new century dawned. We were fighting for social justice and for our selfhood—no matter which of the wrongs we changed or in what sequence, eventually we would change them all.

As usual, my sister's hand was in the mix. She had become an important figure in Dublin. She was not known to be the Harper, of course—for only anonymity protected her from the wrath of Dublin Castle—but nonetheless her essays had become essential goads, nudging at the wrongs and injustices that abounded in the people's lives. *She* was one of *them;* she understood. The power of her rhetoric moved people's consciences and, at times, their actions. Make no mistake about it, the Wild Harp, like the Gaelic League and the IRB itself, helped push us inexorably toward our inevitable bid for freedom.

Beyond that, Con had joined Maud Gonne and the Countess Markievicz in all their agitations. She traveled, with and without them, throughout Ireland, standing on soapboxes, inciting people to fight their powerlessness. She became a friend of Jim Connolly and Jim Larkin, the labor leaders, and campaigned tirelessly for the rights of workers. She agitated for women.

More than once we found ourselves on the same platform. More than once we laughed and cried together over the tiny triumph or the fierce futility. We even found ourselves imprisoned together—as I shall recount. We had ventured far from our childhood plans and dreams.

Those years were full and swift and inexorable—but I must let you see for yourself our metamorphosis. ✍

"Dear Dirty Dublin"

Coming events cast their shadows before.

THOMAS CAMPBELL

1 ✍ Con and I were in high spirits as we mounted the platform on that wretched February morning in 1910. The air was wet with the chilling dampness that Irish winters can excel at, but we had gathered a substantial crowd about us, so we felt jubilant

Con was to talk of politics, while I was to champion women's rights and the Countess was to speak of her free lunch plan for the children of the slums. Because of the humanistic character of our rhetoric, we didn't expect the full contingent of police who greeted us. Our publications and our speeches were unquestionably militant, but we were still naive enough to imagine ourselves safe. At any rate, no sooner had we begun to speak than we were told we must move on. Con and the Countess, having the rashest tempers among us, argued with the policemen until finally it became apparent that they would not leave us unmolested. Forced to acquiesce to their demands, we climbed down off our platform, the crowd dispersed and the Peelers finally left us to our own devices.

We were angered by this treatment and cast about impulsively in our minds for a way to make it harder for them to move us. We had been in contact with certain suffragists in London who had chained themselves to the gates of Westminster to make their expulsion impossible. We decided to do the same.

If this seems to you a rash act, I must try to explain the frustration we felt at always being thwarted in our efforts. It was so hard to gather listeners, for women feared their husbands' wrath—and yet, every time that a crowd of brave women gathered around us, the police would harass us to keep our message from being spoken. We were angry and frustrated; our cause was *just,* and our persecution not so. We gathered the tools we needed, and padlocked ourselves to the gates of the

Four Courts. It was a bold choice, as the place was well garrisoned.

A huge crowd gathered about us by the time we began to speak, and within minutes after that a contingent of police arrived. We shouted above their orders to be silent; we cried out that our harassment was one more injustice in a lengthy line.

I heard my own voice raised to fever pitch, decrying the suffering of women and the consummate unfairness of our subjugation. I heard Con shout something about civil rights. I felt rough hands tearing at my body, felt the friction of the hacksaw as the police tore at the chain that bound me to the gate. I heard Con scream then, as a Peeler hit her on the side of the head. I saw her body crumple, held up only by the iron links that bound her to the fence.

I went berserk. I began screaming obscenities I scarcely understood at the men who had hurt her. I kicked and clawed at the ones who held me, and was finally knocked unconscious by a blow that left me senseless until I awoke, aching and bleeding, in a police van on my way to the jail.

The place of our incarceration was dark and dreary. We ladies sat in a bedraggled huddle on a wooden bench in the custody of a wardress who looked as if she meant us no good. We made a pact with each other, that like the ladies in the English Rights Movement we would demand to be treated as political prisoners, not common felons. Before we were forcibly parted, we swore to each other that if need be, we, like they, would resort to the hunger strike to gain our ends.

At my arraignment I had the presence of mind to give my name as Elizabeth FitzGibbon. I thought by so doing to avoid involving Edmond, who was at the time in London, in the scandal of my incarceration.

The indignities of that day will haunt me forever. We were stripped of our clothes; embarrassed and freezing, we were forcibly plunged into a bath so filthy with scum from its previous dozen occupants that I left it with hair and body covered with foul matter.

Our clothes were confiscated and we were given dresses, patched and stained, of the roughest muslin, which scratched our unaccustomed skin raw. The clothes were paradise compared with the shoes, however: heavy brogans, unmatched to each other or to my feet, were given me. They were so large that I had to shuffle them along the ground to walk at all.

We had been told of the severity of prison conditions, but until you have found yourself trapped in a tiny, claustrophobic stone cell, unheated and lit only by a single gas spigot, you cannot really comprehend the horror. Or the sinking feeling of abandonment.

I was sorely distressed by the sobs of other women, a despairing sound of hopelessness and loneliness. And by the foul speech of the hardened criminals. I had not in my wildest imaginings guessed how ghastly are the sleepless agonies of lying night after night on a narrow bed, made from a plank of wood, with cold and dampness of the stone walls and ceiling invading your body and the sounds of women sobbing in your ears. The food was intolerable and lacking in nourishment, the toilets so foul as to defy competent description.

One night I endured the screams of a woman in labor in the next cell—her piteous cries were almost drowned out by the harsh commands of the burly women wardresses who threatened her with being beaten if she didn't cease her noise.

I was desperate for news of Con; she had been sent to the infirmary because of her head wound and reached our cell block only after the second week. She looked very ill.

Shortly after her return to the cells, I was let go. Word had gotten to Edmond in England about my incarceration and he had pulled strings to secure my release. I was livid that I'd been given more lenient treatment because of my husband's position, but I cannot, in conscience, say I wasn't thrilled to escape that hideous place.

From the moment of my release I began to work toward freeing Con and the others. I had been frightened by her appearance and feared for her safety.

Imagine my dismay when word came down from the jail, via Con Markievicz's connections there, that she and the other imprisoned women had declared a hunger strike. Dear God! Can you imagine my terror? Knowing Con's courage and obstinacy, I had no doubt she would not be swayed from her resolve.

What I couldn't anticipate was the extraordinary horror of what they did to her. ∽

* * *

Con O'Connor lay on the hard planks of her cot and stared at the ceiling. She had been fasting now for nearly three weeks. The sharp initial pangs of hunger had subsided to a dull but constant ache; it was bearable, she thought, but there was no way to keep the gnawing from her mind. She had tried exercise when she still had the strength for it, and recitations of remembered verses when her physical strength had ebbed. Finally, reading from the little Bible she'd been given had occupied her, but the constant gnawing in her belly was hard to hold at bay.

Now the disorientation she was experiencing was disconcerting her; she was light-headed, and it was increasingly hard to concentrate. Her vision, too, had been affected and she found it necessary to lecture herself sternly each day about the things she must remember—and the things she must forget. Some memories were too painful to endure.

She missed Tierney with such a visceral sense of loss! And Tahg, and Beth. If she let herself dwell on those she loved, the loneliness overwhelmed her self-control. If she tried to keep them from her mind, the effort exhausted her feeble resources.

Today, she must face the worst ordeal of all. "If you won't eat by yourself, we'll force the food down your throat for you tomorrow," the sadistic wardress had spat at her the night before. She knew from prison scuttlebutt that such things were not unknown.

Con struggled with her resolve, with her fear and with her anger . . . and waited, helpless, for the awful footsteps in the corridor that would make the fear reality.

She heard the rattle of the key in the ancient lock and saw six wardresses and a doctor enter. A great state of agitation shook her body, with heart palpitations and ringing in her ears. She realized how weakened her physical self had become and, staring into the chief wardress' face, she felt the full force of her own vulnerability wash through her like icy swill.

"Will you eat your dinner like a nice little trollop?" said the head wardress in a wheedling singsong voice. Insanely, Con thought of the voice of the witch in *Hansel and Gretel* who came every day to feel the children's bones. I'm going mad, she thought, as she struggled to rise from the cot.

"I am a political prisoner," she managed to say, her throat dry with fear. "You have no right to imprison me or force me to any indignity. I demand my rights. I will take no food until I've been granted political status."

"That's what you think, dearie," said the wardress and, signaling the others, she grabbed Con's arm and pinned it painfully to the bed. All six strong wardresses gathered quickly and, flinging Con's body backward, held her down by shoulders, wrists, ankles and knees. She tried to struggle against their combined strengths, but it was useless.

The doctor endeavored to force her lips apart, pulling the tender skin hurtfully. Failing, he thrust a steel gag between her teeth, cutting the gums and making them start to bleed.

Con tried to wrench her head away, but the wardress held her hair while the doctor wedged a pointed steel instrument into her mouth between her jaws and began to force them apart viciously with the turn of a screw. The pain was excruciating. Panting and heaving, she tried to escape the horrible invasion, but could not. She felt the rubber tube pushed stranglingly down her throat.

She gasped for air she could not draw in; suffocating, she felt a scream rise from some strangled place within her, but the only sound she could make was an obscene gurgling noise.

Barely conscious, she felt the warm broth pumped into her resistant body. As the tube was withdrawn she vomited violently and they left her alone in the mess.

Nearly unconscious, Con lay on the floor of the cell where she had somehow fallen, and tried to find the strength to stay alive.

℘ Tierney, beside himself with fear and rage, had tried to move heaven and earth to get Con set free. But to no avail. He and his friends planned a jailbreak, but the knot of demonstrators outside the prison where the hunger strikers languished made access almost impossible. Each day the crowd grew larger. Hundreds of women, mostly in rags, stood or knelt, rosaries in hand, outside the gates. Daily, the number of guards grew too.

When word reached us of the force feedings, a frenzy broke out spontaneously among the hitherto quiet crowd. We women, fortified by men from the Brotherhood, stormed the doors of the jail; armed only with fists or sticks or rosary beads, we pounded on the doors and demanded admittance, grappled with the police and made as much trouble as we could manage. After a day of incessant lunacy, the outcry from the press forced the police to let the women go.

Tierney and I picked up my sister at the rear gate where prisoners are released. Her throat was so injured she couldn't speak, but there were no words necessary. The haunted look in her eyes was more eloquent than any words I have ever in my life heard spoken.

What is it that drives men and women to a revolution? I have sometimes been asked. It is the conviction that no matter what sacrifice revolution demands, it is not so great as what has already been exacted.

I must endeavor to describe to you my sister's state of mind after the episode in prison, for I believe it lent impetus to many of her later actions. Her emotions were complicated ones, so I must go slowly in my attempt to unravel them.

Con had been brutalized. Her physical being had been savaged and she had felt the fact of her own mortality with dreadful clarity. Yet, it was not death she had come to fear, but loss of self. She was so vulnerable, who had been so indestructible. She was filled with horrendous conflicts: gratitude at being free, rage at her jailers. Yet if she let herself dwell on those emotions, she was all the worse for it!

I ached for her sorrows, as I ached for my own. I tried to comfort her, marveling at the strength beneath the frailty, and the frailty beneath the strength. What complicated creatures we mortals be.

Whatever had been the sorrows of her life before, she told me, she *herself* had remained intact enough to draw from within the needed courage to endure. But the torture in prison had made her feel undone. It would take time to reweave the fabric of herself.

Eventually Con grew whole again. But it was a different whole than she had been before. I learned that we do not escape certain agonies intact. Perhaps the philosophers or priests would tell us that we are better for the suffering, that if life breaks us we become stronger at the broken places. Perhaps we even assuage our own pain with such philosophizing.

Yet did I think, as I listened and watched her, whom I loved so much, should we not be far better off without these terrible learnings? Could we not grow through joys better than through sorrows? Why, God, I asked, have You ordained it so that the lives of the good are as filled with suffering as the lives of the evil? God did not deign to offer me an answer.

All through the early years of the new century, we each continued our struggle against injustice. It is important to remember that all the injustices merged for us. All human rights seemed tied inexorably to Irish freedom. It wasn't quite rational, of course, but revolutions seldom are. None can deny that the true militancy of Con's behavior was forged in that jail cell. From that point on she fought not only for an ideal of freedom, but for a personal score to settle as well.

I must not let you think, however, that our lives held naught but battles . . . those same years held much of home and love and family, too.

Our children were growing up. So, I suppose, were we. ✍

2 "Do you know much about women, Da?" Tahg asked the question of Tierney as they fished from the quay. The father hid the amusement from his voice as he answered. "A wee bit, lad. I'm afraid no man knows very much about them. They're a mysterious lot. Why do you ask?"

The twelve-year-old boy tried to appear nonchalant as he answered.

"No reason in particular. They're just hard to figure, is all."

"Any one in particular?"

"Sort of."

"What's her name?"

"Kitty O'Neill."

"Grand name. What's she like?"

Tahg looked surreptitiously at his father under his dark eyebrows, to see if he appeared overly curious, but the man was casually baiting a hook. He liked to see the way his father did that. Quickly, efficiently. As if he knew exactly what he was doing. His da knew a lot about a lot of things, but it was hard to talk to him about Kitty.

"She's pretty. She has long red hair and she laughs a lot. She's nice, too . . . not stuck up or anything."

"That's good."

"But she's . . . I don't know. Confusing, I guess."

"How's that?"

"I think she likes me, but when I asked her to walk home with me yesterday, she just sort of smiled and said, 'Maybe another day.' Now what's that supposed to mean?"

"Hmm," answered Tierney, thinking how very odd it was to see that his son was old enough to be pondering the mysteries of girls. "That's a thorny question, now, lad, but I've an inkling, if you'd care to hear it."

"What?" The boy looked up from his line, interested.

"Girls are taught to play hard-to-get with boys, lad. The idea is that they're never to let you know how they really feel about you."

"That's pretty stupid."

"It is indeed, but it's the custom. You see, *you're* supposed to pursue her, until she decides to let you catch her."

"Like these fishes, hm?" asked the boy, smiling.

Tierney tousled his son's dark hair and laughed with him.

"Exactly that. But they're a bit more fun when you catch one."

"They do look like they'd be nice."

"Aye, lad. Nice indeed. There's nothing better in the world than the love between a man and a woman . . . although you're a ways off that yet."

The boy nodded sagely and returned to contemplation of the half-submerged fishing line. He loved his father. Reveled in the hours he could spend with him alone. The man could do anything! Sing, play music, write poetry. And there were secret doings with the IRB, too.

The Brotherhood. From his earliest breath Tahg had known those words. From the time he was a wee lad he'd known the names of the heroes . . . O'Leary, O'Donovan Rossa, Wolfe Tone, O'Sullivan . . . it was like the litany in the church, only more heroic. And his father *knew* some of these people, these legends. His mother, too, of course.

He knew it was a great honor for a woman to be in the

councils of the Brotherhood and that his mother, Maud Gonne and the Countess Markievicz were the only ones who had achieved this.

"Tell me about the Countess, Da," he said suddenly, and Tierney smiled, knowing how excited the boy was about joining the Countess' Fianna Boys.

"She's a great lady, Tahg," said his father, casting out his line as he did so. "She was born at a fine old Georgian manor in Sligo, as was your mother. Constance Gore-Booth was her maiden name, and her family home at Lissadell was not far off from where your mother and I grew up. A beautiful old place it is, too, lad. Much like FitzGibbon Hall but without the old keep."

"But how did she get into the Brotherhood?" the boy asked eagerly, and the father smiled at how easily the child spoke the name of the secret group. He knew that unlike most children Tahg understood the need for secrecy and would never breathe knowledge of the IRB to others, but here alone with his father he could ask questions.

"She says she used to see the poor people waiting outside the gates of the Great House to get a glimpse of her and her sister Eva when they'd go out to fancy balls and such; she'd see them in their rags and wonder at their great patience and long-suffering. 'The poor are more patient than Buddha,' she told me. Then one summer she went to the mountains and in an old cottage there she found the Fenian writings of John O'Leary and they caught at her imagination. She went to meet him and it seems that was the beginning for her. I knew O'Leary, lad. There was a selfless fire in the man that could melt a stone with its compassion and common sense."

"But what about the Fianna Boys?"

"The Countess told me she was angered by seeing the Irish Boy Scouts salute the King of England, so she decided to create a boys' group that would be totally Irish . . . based on the Fianna training of young warriors in Finn MacCool's time." He looked at his son's eager face. "But you'll be knowing all about that soon enough yourself."

The boy smiled shyly, but with obvious pleasure. He was looking forward to the Fianna Boys and to meeting the Countess. He'd heard so much about her from the other lads, who adored her. But he wanted to see how she compared with his own mother. He was pretty sure the Countess would come out second best.

The Countess Markievicz strode up and down among the boys in the walled garden of her latest endeavor for Ireland, Belcamp Park. She was resplendent in her soldier's uniform to which she had added an Australian bush hat with an ostrich plume. Besides the rakish military exterior, she positively exuded excitement, forcibly breathing vitality into this new agricultural commune. *This* was the proper place to drill a boys' army! So close to Dublin, yet a thousand miles apart in atmosphere.

"You are here to become part of an elite corps, lads," she began, and every ear was on her, for never had these boys been part of an elite anything. "In the time of Finn MacCool and the Knights of the Red Branch, a boy was trained to be a warrior. He learned the meaning of honor and compassion. He learned the arts of peace and war. He was trained, by great heroes, in how to be a man."

The Countess' Ascendency carriage had not deserted her in her rebelliousness, and her high aristocratic voice sounded sweetly incongruous amid the throng of Dublin street slang that the boys had been babbling to each other before her arrival.

Con, seated near the pink-washed walls of the Georgian mansion that was Madame's headquarters at Belcamp, listened to her friend's stirring speech and watched the enraptured faces of the boys, who with these few rousing words were being elevated out of their poverty and their humdrum lives into heroes. She saw Tahg's face among them, glowing with pride and excitement at the prospect.

She blessed him in her heart, he and all the brave boys, and wondered which among them would be freedom fighters, which among them might someday say to their grandchildren, "Aye, lads, I was with them. Trained by the Fianna I was—and when the Rising came, I was ready!"

She drank in the quiet seclusion of the wooded countryside, silently thankful that it was here Tahg would now train three days a week. She had to remind herself that this was Raheny—a mere stone's throw from Howth, to the east, and teeming Dublin, to the west—not the tranquil demesne of the Sligo FitzGibbons. Here Tahg would surely learn to become part of the old dream. Her son's voice shook her out of her thoughts.

"Mam! Isn't she wonderful?" he said, awed and excited, as he reached her through the crowd.

Con smiled her reply. "She is indeed, Tahg Mor. And you're wonderful, too."

The boy blushed a little at the unexpected compliment, but she could see he was pleased.

"I'm to stay here for a while to find out about the training. Will you be able to get home without me?" He seemed concerned.

"Oh, I think I'll be able to manage, love. You have more important things to be occupying you these days than squiring me about." She laughed her encouragement good-naturedly. "You run along and learn everything. Your father will want to hear it all tonight!"

He smiled happily at the loving dismissal. She could see in his face that he almost leaned over to kiss her good-bye—then remembered himself to be in the company of "men" and thought better of it. He waved as he ran back to the other boys.

Con watched Tahg with the proud wistfulness of motherhood flooding her . . . the love and pride and the terrible tug of the heartstrings that accompanies a child's growing up and away. "And we are put on earth a little space,/That we may learn to bear the beams of love," she thought to herself. Blake's words, they were, on the joy and burden of loving—motherhood had made their meaning clear at last. She smiled inwardly at the notion.

Con watched the Countess giving orders, explaining equipment and supervising the proceedings. Then, comforting herself that Tahg was in good hands, she rounded the corner of the house and began the journey toward home. She chuckled a little at how amused Tierney would be at the notion of a pink HQ!

Their life was settled now, in a curious way. She and Tierney were firmly enmeshed in the intrigues of the IRB, each bringing to it a different passion. Books full of ideas had been bound from the Wild Harp columns. There had been times she'd been forced to stop writing them for long stretches because the Castle had threatened Griffith with closing the paper for sedition. But always she had begun again. Wherever she could be in print . . . pamphlets, letters to the newspapers, leaflets distributed at

Gaelic League meetings, bill stickers on any available brick wall. It was important for the people to know that the Harper was still alive. Somewhere secret. Still alive. Still a gadfly, nipping at the Castle's security.

And Tierney's plays and poems were many. Unproduced and unpublished, still, but there was a comforting immortality in the fact that they existed. One day, people would read them and know of his genius. She hoped they'd live to see it happen.

What irony it was that as their life got better, the danger got worse again. She could feel it in her bones, watching the boys with the Countess. The Rising they had dreamed of vaguely for years was almost upon them.

Despite the apathy of the Dubliners who had so many day-to-day problems in just trying to survive that they had little strength left over for revolution. Despite the Castle's carefully constructed network of informants who managed to subvert so many secret plans at the eleventh hour. Despite the seemingly hopeless odds . . . it would come. And damned soon. She would write an essay about it, today.

It occurred to her that, like the boys, she too should brush up on the skills she would need for the fray. She was a crack shot, but practice wouldn't hurt. And she was a decent-enough nurse. She made a mental note to speak to the Countess about the possibility of infiltrating the hospital so that when the time came there would be access to supplies.

Con shuddered involuntarily at the thought of the hospital. She had never been back inside one since that ghastly night when Eamon had perished.

She thought often of her little son who lay in the plot at Glasnevin. She wondered whether the Rising that was in the air would bring any others of her blood to a resting place before their time.

Shaking off the unsettling thought, Con made her way hurriedly toward home and Tierney.

3

Constance O'Connor
17 Capel Street
Dublin
30 April 1911

My darling sister,

I'm in a strangely melancholy mood tonight—or perhaps it's simply that I am introspective and I don't know how to recognize the symptoms.

It was all occasioned by reading Tierney's newest play, a strange and broody thing it is . . . beautiful but troubled, (And who could expect otherwise in these times, you might ask, eh?) The play set me to thinking about how profoundly life has changed me since we've been in Dublin and it occurred to me that while you and I have skirted the edges of discussing the sea changes of our lives . . . we have not truly done so.

Will you bear with me if I try to "talk" it through in this letter?

Reading the play made me suddenly remember the heartbreak of Seaneen's decree that Tierney's work should not be published. Lord, how I thought my heart would break with that disappointment! It seems to me now that great good has come of it (my inclusion in the group, you know) but at the time anger and sadness quite nearly did me in. I hid my sorrow under the carpet rather than perish in the despair of it . . . I knew you knew the devastation, but as there could be no changing it, there was little you and I could say to each other.

You know, Bethy, for a long while, the place where I had tucked my shattered hopes away was so tender that even I dared not dwell upon it, or probe my own heart's questions. Yet tonight, for some mysterious reason, it has all come gushing through. And so I need to talk to you.

There was such a sense of loss about it, dear sister—almost like a death to be mourned. Loss of hope in the future. . . . I had dreamed such selfish dreams . . . of success and of being vindicated for choosing Tierney as my husband. He would be famous and I would have the last laugh at the scoffers. And we would no longer be poor—good Christ! how I do hate poverty! I hate its indignity and its meanness of spirit. I felt diminished by it —somehow less than I had been—and Tierney's plays were my hope of being more again. I know it must sound foolish to you, Bethy, but it is easy to fall into the trap of taking your whole sense of self from your husband's success or failure, isn't it? For a long while, I was bereft and mourned my losses covertly, sadly, sullenly, fearfully.

Then, too, there was the terror that Tierney would write no more. If there is no goad to push you forward, I reasoned, no goal to reach, no deadline to meet and no prize to be taken, why continue? Even if well intentioned, surely inertia must set in—or so I thought.

Curiously, the result has been quite the opposite. Perhaps *because* there is no pressure to conform to other people's standards, Tierney writes voluminously to his own. What I had not realized until witnessing the performance is that one who is gifted as is my husband *cannot* stay the gift. He writes as he breathes . . . as he moves . . . as he grows. Just as his strange visions come upon him unbidden, so do his poems. His poetry is part of him (he says the best part) and I think he could not dam the flow if he wished to. At least not without grave injury to himself.

So, one fear of mine at least was unfounded—the rest I have learned to live with. Time assuages all deaths, I expect, even that of hope. Or, rather, a new hope springs from the ashes of the old. And so it is with us: I hope now for the future of all we both work toward together, as I used to hope for vindication. And I hope that after Ireland's day is won there will be no deterrent to the publication of all that has been collected.

Which leaves me, of all my complaints, with only poverty! Not that there's much to be said about that which hasn't been. There is absolutely nothing good about it, Bethy, except, perhaps, the learning it has engendered.

The dresses you've sent and the clothes for Tahg are both appreciated and put to good use. Did you know that Des, sweetheart that he is, forever sends me money, which I forever send back to him—so he has taken, instead, to sending gifts to Tahg and corresponding with him from his many ports of call. What a good old thing he is, our errant brother.

If only Des could settle into a real life instead of the fanciful one that occupies his time. What damnable luck that Evelyn was snatched away from him. She would surely have made all the difference.

There now! I feel better already. You always did have the capacity to help me unburden my heart—even at a distance!

But enough of personal problems and on to affairs of state: the growing sense of nationalism is quite palpable now in Dublin. All the young men live for the Gaelic Athletic Association—I sometimes think sporting events will do more to cement the people to our cause than all the impassioned rhetoric of the Harper could! Hurling matches draw crowds to rival a visit from the King—you may imagine how lads like Tahg are caught up in the excitement. The GAA is organized, as you perhaps know, on a parish by-parish basis all over the country. Seaneen says it will have significant political side effects as time goes on.

The Gaelic League, of course, flourishes, God bless it! Encouraging the speaking of Irish, telling the old tales over and over, singing the songs and nurturing those ancient stirrings we Irish feel so deeply.

The theater, too, is alive with a sense of national spirit. There has even been rioting against the work of a playwright whose characters provoked the nationalists. How ahead of his time Tierney was with his first plays, dear heart! Yeats has, of course, carried the torch and created a poetic drama that is nothing if not splendid. The *Countess Cathleen* and *The Shadowy Waters* have moved people deeply and the Abbey Theatre is now dedicated solely to this form of entertainment.

All told, there are nationalist rumblings on every front . . . surely something must come of that, and soon. Meanwhile, Tierney and I pursue our patriotic ploddings, hoping that it will not all have proved in vain. These are intriguing times, my dear sister. I feel a stirring in the atmosphere almost as if the wind has shifted. I'll be anxious to see what it blows our way.

Love to everyone in Sligo, of course, from the Dublin branch of us. I promise a more cheerful missive next time.

> Love as ever,
> Con

∞ I put down Con's letter, wondering if she, like me, had ever mused on the fact that despite her having kicked over the traces and done everything wrong with her life (at least by the standards we grew up with), she had ended up happy, in love with her husband and engaged in work she cared about. While I, who had done everything exactly as was expected of me, was growing old, married to a man who didn't love me and pining for a love that I would never find again. Even in this letter, in which she told of old sorrows, her enormous love for Tierney was evident in every line.

Whatever disappointments and privations she had suffered, at least she had slept every night of the last fourteen years in the arms of one who loved her more than life itself. Could she have had any idea how I longed for that same comfort?

Perversely, as I had grown stronger and more confident, my longings had also grown more insistent. I *wanted* to be loved. At times I longed for what I had experienced so briefly with such intensity that I feared it would overcome my reason. Twice I went so far as to write letters to Seaneen, pouring out my love for him, purging my soul of all its pent-up loneliness and desperation. Both times I burned the letters.

I had fought so hard to heal my wounds and find an outlet for my energies, yet sometimes, in the long lonely nights, I thought I would sell my very soul to feel loved again for a single day.

Perhaps this mood of melancholia Con spoke of was contagious. I tucked her letter into my desk drawer and decided to write to her and to Des. ∽

Desmond FitzGibbon seldom brooded about the future. Or about anything else, for that matter.

He knew it would please his sisters if he settled down to marriage and a family; indeed, he knew he must do so one day soon in order to pass on the FitzGibbon legacy intact.

He had come so very close to marriage just a few years after Con's departure to Dublin—it was easy to imagine how different life might have been had he married as planned. Evelyn FitzMaurice had seemed so perfect a choice of lover and help-mate—how could anyone have foreseen her death at twenty-three? Blood poisoning they had called it, a simple cut on the hand sustained while fox hunting. They had laughed about her clumsiness and he had kissed the hurt away. Five days later she was dead, her arm swollen obscenely, her face as startled by it all in death as his had been, left living.

Then there had been his father's death and his own inheritance—and finally the trip to Europe to forget, with enough money in his account to make forgetting an adventure. Desmond had wandered through the European capitals, gambling here, drinking there, bedding women wherever he alighted—telling himself that grief gave him every right to be dissolute. For nearly a year. Until Paris, where the revolutionary stirrings of the Bohemians had caught his fancy and had given him something to hold on to. He guessed he had always been a revolutionary at heart—or at least a troublemaker. And finally a stint with the Foreign Service that had allowed him to roam under government sanction.

But it was getting to be time to go home. The FitzGibbon estate needed more than an absentee landlord. And it sounded from Beth's letters as if she could use some moral support.

What a ridiculous marriage hers had turned out to be—and with seemingly everything to make it right. At least she had five children to show for her efforts—and her books, of course. Despite the fact that since her imprisonment she had cut down on her rebellious activities for her children's sake, she still had managed to accomplish something important with her life.

He himself had nothing. Nothing at all to show for being nearly forty years of age. And it was high time to change that.

Desmond FitzGibbon
FitzGibbon Hall
Rosskeerough, Co. Sligo
26 June 1911

My dear and much missed Con,

Home is the sailor, home from the sea, old girl, and glad of it, you may be sure.

Not that I haven't had a rollicking good time, mind you, over the years, but even pleasure pales after a while and your brother is glad to be home.

The Hall looked so bloody unlived-in I almost fell to tears in the foyer. Drop cloths covering everything, like so many ghostly specters inhabiting a once lively space. I felt I'd been gone so long that even the furnishings had died and the drop cloths were their spirits left to haunt. But miracle of miracles, the chairs and sofas and tables live—and so, by God, do I!

You and Tierney and Tahg will come, of course, to stay, when chance permits. He's a grand boy, by the way —I loved my visit with you all in Dublin, en route here. I'm proud to have him for a nephew and it set me to thinking. . . . Tahg must be schooled in certain gentlemanly pursuits and one would think this ancestral home of ours a splendid place to do that, wouldn't one? Might he come stay here with his errant uncle, do you suppose —for a year or two? It's lonely in this mausoleum without my gels. [Con smiled indulgently at that—it had been so many years since he'd referred to her and Beth as his "gels" that it seemed another lifetime.]

Before I forget, my conversations with Seaneen O'Sullivan in Dublin did not fall on deaf ears—I haven't a clue what I can do to help your Cause, but I'll be damned if I'll be less the rebel than my darling sisters, so I shall meditate on how to do my part. As you can see, I still like to keep the kettle boiling. Whatever is it in us Fitz-Gibbon creatures that makes us long so for adventure?

No need to answer that, my sweet. Just write of all your own adventures and do let me know about the lad, won't you? I would promise to be a good influence on him, but you'd never believe that—so instead I'll suggest that he might exercise a good influence over me! Keep me on the straight and narrow, or whatever it is uncles are supposed to be on. Do let him come, Con—we'll be good for each other. I feel it in my bones.

Am off to Bethy in the morning. She sounds a bit off her feed in her letters lately, don't you think? Did you know her suffrage books are as popular on the Continent as here?

Will write more as soon as they unearth father's old desk from under its muslin shroud.

Much love and all appropriate
brotherly thoughts,
Desmond

Constance O'Connor
17 Capel Street
Dublin
18 July 1911

My darling Bethy,

Let me know how you feel about Des, will you? He worries me. I do so wish that he and the FitzMaurice girl had been given the chance of a life together. Damnation! Why are the fates so uncompromising with us FitzGibbons?

As you will see, my dear, our brother has returned with a vengeance! Leave it to our family to do nothing other than dramatically—in short he has gone home, he says to stay—and his first stop on the way there was a visit to Tierney and Seaneen. Need I explain what that means about his intention to be in the thick of things while in Ireland?

I'm rejoicing that he's back, of course; he is such a love. But the times are explosive and no one has ever accused Des of prudence.

If I sound confusing, it's only because I feel so about him. Besides all this, he has invited Tahg to stay with him for a bit (to learn the gentlemanly arts, if you don't mind!). I don't know what Tierney and I would do without Tahg, but I think it might be good for both uncle and nephew.

Do let me know what you think. Perhaps I'm just being an old fussbudget about Des—anyone would think he was my son, and not my older brother! But I sense that he's looking for adventure again, and I fear he may find it.

Think about Des and Tahg, my dear, and share your thoughts with me. It's so very tempting to think of his learning to live graciously as we once learned. And I do think Des is lonely.

My love as ever,
Con

Manningham Castle
Taghley, County Sligo
1 August 1911

My darling Con,

Of course Tahg must come to Des and home! I know how much you'll miss him, but you mustn't let that keep you from taking Des up on his offer. Our brother is far lonelier than he lets on and Tahg would give him a reason to cling to his roots again.

And just think what an advantage it would be for Tahg to experience the life of a country squire. Besides all that, Angelica is beside herself at the thought that her beloved Tahg might be close at hand.

To say nothing of his Aunt Beth, who would welcome him with open arms and try to make his stay in Sligo memorable. The children are really all I have of joy and fulfillment, dear Con, and having your son near at hand would add so much to all our lives.

Do say yes! I have a feeling in my heart that such is meant to be.

All love, as ever,
Bethy

4 Win watched his cousin buckle on the old blunt sword and fingered his own. Tahg had come to Manningham Castle at Angelica's request. She was so happy since he was staying at FitzGibbon Hall with their uncle that her whole life seemed to have changed for the better. Her happiness was the only reason that Edmond Manningham tolerated Tahg's coming to the Castle to play.

"I shall be King Arthur and you may be Mordred," Win said impatiently to the other children. "That is, if you ever get yourself put together!"

Tahg looked up, smiling a little. Even though the game was childish, he knew it pleased Angelica and the twins when they play-acted. Johnny was still too small to care what they did, as long as he was permitted to tag along. "I'm afraid you'll have to wait a bit longer, Win," he called back amiably. "I promised a bunch of wild flowers to yon fair maiden." Tahg raised his hand toward Angelica, seated as always in her little rolling chair. Although they were nearly the same age, Tahg was larger and broader than his cousin Winston, and as dark as Win was fair.

"Tahg can't play Mordred," interjected Merry with a dimpled laugh. "He hasn't the disposition for it. Why, you're the only one cranky enough for Mordred, Winston!"

The two girls snickered at that, but Jamie ventured diplomatically, "Why don't we all just play good parts today, Winston? There are plenty to go around. You can be Arthur and Tahg can be Lancelot and I'll be Galahad and the girls can be Guinevere and Elaine." The scholarly-looking boy with the glasses looked pleased with himself at the pacific solution he'd recommended.

"You're such a little twit, Jamie," Winston responded, annoyed. "You always want everything sugar-coated. The game's no fun if there's no fight between good and evil!"

"It's all right, Jamie," laughed Tahg, "I don't mind being Mordred. It's just a game." He finished picking a bunch of daisies and dandelions and, sweeping off the hat of his costume, and bowing gracefully before Angelica's chair, he handed them to her with a flourish.

"Thank you, Sir Knight," she said with great dignity. "You may wear my colors in the tourney," and she untied the ribbon that had held her long blond hair back into braids and tied it onto the hilt of his sword.

"Knights don't wear hair ribbons, ninny!" shouted Winston with exasperation, "they wear scarves."

"Well, she doesn't have a scarf, *ninny,"* snapped back Merry, when she saw the hurt expression on Angelica's face.

"I like the ribbon," said Tahg. "I'm delighted to wear your favor on my sword, milady." He gallantly kissed her hand and she giggled happily. Tahg was her favorite.

"You've got a lot to learn about chivalry!" said Merry disgustedly to her brother Winston. "Tahg and Jamie are gentlemen."

"Jamie may be, but Tahg's not," replied Win hotly. "He's poor!"

"Being a gentleman has nothing to do with being rich!" said Angelica with great dignity. "You're proof of that!"

"You're just too young to know anything about it," said Winston. "I don't even want to play with you babies anyway!" Still clutching his sword, he stomped away from the orchard, where they'd been playing, toward the house.

"We really shouldn't goad him like that," said Jamie, looking after him. "He's got such a bad temper anyway."

"Honestly, Jamie, if you don't grow up to be a diplomat, it will be a terrible waste!" Merry giggled as she said it. She tended to find something amusing in almost everything that happened.

"What Winny said was very ill-bred!" Angelica's voice sounded full of conviction. "Besides, he's not like the rest of us. He may be our brother, but he's too arrogant. It doesn't hurt to remind him."

Tahg laughed aloud at the little girl's vehemence. "Sometimes, Angel, you seem to be the oldest of us all. Do you know that?"

He reached over and tugged at her one remaining braid. "Should I give you back your hair ribbon now that the game seems to be over?" he asked.

"No thank you," she said, smiling magnanimously. "I'd like you to keep it."

"Good," he replied as he untied the little blue ribbon from the sword and tucked it into his pocket. "It'll be my good luck charm from now on."

Angelica smiled happily at her cousin. Her own luck hadn't been very good in life, but she *was* good luck for other people. She didn't know why that should be so, but she knew it was. She twisted her loosened hair around her thin fingers and watched her brother and sister pack up their toys to go home.

She let herself wish for a moment that she could be like them, able to move about freely. Perfectly formed and perfectly beautiful. Then she put away the troublesome thought, as she had so often in the past . . . there was no good to be had in brooding over what could never be. Only working toward what *could be* made any sense at all.

Tahg was glad of the time he could spend with Angelica, now that he was in Sligo, but he felt a curious displacement whenever he found himself at Manningham Castle. Winston had taken pains in the beginning to show that he didn't belong there, with his shabby clothes and his Dublin accent. Of course all that was changing now that Uncle Desmond had taken a hand. Yet there was so much about the place that he loved. Putting up with Winston's snide innuendos with as much good grace as he could muster was a small price to pay for the good parts.

The wide strand that bordered Sligo Bay seemed so like a spiritual home to him. The strange mists that rose and swirled there in the early mornings teased his imagination into feats of storytelling he might never otherwise have achieved, and he did love to tell stories to Angelica. His little cousin delighted so in his tales and in the attention that he lavished on her. Not that the lavishing was a chore for him . . . far from it. She was such a good little person to talk to, so full of wisdom older than her years.

He got on well with Merry and Jamie, too, of course, and he liked Johnny; even though he was the baby, they had always been friends. But Angelica was his favorite among the cousins . . . maybe his favorite friend of all.

Tahg took his place at the dinner table hoping that it would be a peaceful meal. Aunt Beth seemed to go to such pains to keep everyone happy, but Uncle Edmond had an autocratic disposition and Winston echoed it in a smaller version, so one could never be sure of tranquility with the evening meal.

"Father gave a brilliant speech today," volunteered Winston when the smoked salmon had been served. "Everyone said so."

"What was it about, Father?" asked Merry, her pretty, dimpled face interested.

"It had to do with the subject of the third Home Rule Bill, my dear," said her father. "I recounted the fact that it fills the needs of neither the Nationalists nor the Unionists."

"I don't understand exactly what Home Rule means, Father," Merry replied. "But I'm sure you gave a splendid speech, nonetheless," she finished with an emphatic smile.

"If a Home Rule Bill really was passed, Merry," Jamie interjected, "it would mean that Ireland would have its own Parliament and its own laws." He was always interested in politics. "This is the third time such a bill has been presented in the Commons."

"Father said that the bill as it stands 'would give no power over customs or excise, no new opportunity for taxes and no control over the police and therefore it was absurd to even bother with it.'" Winston delivered his nearly letter-perfect quote from Edmond's speech with pride.

"Sir," said Tahg firmly. "My father says it doesn't matter whether the bill is perfect or imperfect, because the House of Lords will turn it down shamelessly, just as they did the others."

"That's very disrespectful, young man. I'll hear none of that kind of nonsense in this house!" Edmond eyed the boy with distaste. He allowed this nephew of his to be a guest at Manningham on occasion because it pleased Angelica, but he'd not allow insolence at his own dinner table.

"Neither I nor the other members of the House of Lords have the slightest interest in what your father has to say, young man," Edmond said and Winston smothered a giggle behind his napkin.

"Perhaps, sir," the boy persisted, "the reason we need our own Irish Parliament is because the members of the House of Lords don't care about the opinions of men like my father."

Jamie and Merry looked at each other, wide-eyed at Tahg's daring.

"Elizabeth," said Edmond sternly. "If we are to entertain your nephew as a guest, I would suggest that you do a more careful job of teaching him how to behave among his betters."

"Edmond!" Beth replied, embarrassed for Tahg and for herself. "If you feel the need to scold me, I would appreciate your doing so in private."

"As you wish," he replied with equanimity, and the children, protective of their mother, turned the conversation to other things.

"What was my mother like when she was young?" Tahg asked his Uncle Desmond; he was seated on the hearth rug in front of the drawing-room fire and feeling very contented about life.

Des smiled indulgently as he put down the copy of Byron he had been reading. It amused and perplexed him that he, the adventurer, had settled so contentedly into domestic life at the Hall with his nephew. The lad was a joy to be with, of course; smart as a whip, intriguingly introspective for one so young, yet full of life and fun and boyishness. He had been shy at first with his uncle, when Des had announced that he was to be trained in the arts necessary to being a country gentleman. "Oh, but I'll never be that, surely," Tahg had said, slightly awed by the notion. But he had responded to every bit of tutelage with unerring instinct. One simply can't deny good breeding, thought Des as he looked at the boy. Even if half of it happened to have been poor.

"You'd best not let your mother hear that you think she's not young anymore, old man," he responded good-humoredly to his nephew's question. "Or you'll see something she was famous for in her youth—her temper."

Both laughed at that, but Tahg persisted. "I really don't think of her as young or old," he said, giving it some judicious thought. "My mother just *is.* You know, Uncle Desmond, like an old tree or a great rock—she's so substantial that you think she must always have *been.*"

Desmond's eyes softened in remembrance. "She was always like that, Tahg. Even as a child. Your Aunt Beth and I used to marvel at her solidity and her conviction. As if she always knew precisely where she was going, and precisely why. God knows, I've wished often enough that Beth and I had shared that trait."

"Was it a big shock to everyone when she ran off with Da?" Tahg asked, pleased as always that Desmond treated him in conversation as if he were an adult.

"Shock, eh? No. Can't say it was a shock to me or Bethy. We knew, you see. Couldn't help but know."

Tahg was amused to hear his uncle's speech become fragmented. The question was an emotional one for him, it seemed.

"Knew she'd do something out of the ordinary. Couldn't help herself, I suppose."

"And Grandfather?"

"That was another story, Tahg. He never got over it, never really forgave. They were alike in some ways, he and Con, except that he always did things by the book, and she never did. Couldn't get over her 'defection,' as he called it."

"That must have made her sad."

"Hmm. Suppose it did, lad. Although to tell the truth, your mother was so mad about your father, I'm not sure anything else really entered in. Never saw anything like those two. Gaga, you know!"

"I think they still are," said Tahg pridefully.

"True enough. I guess the only real disappointment he's handed her was not letting his work be performed."

Tahg's ears perked up.

"What do you mean, sir?"

"Set her heart on it, she had," said Desmond, surprised that the boy didn't know. "Get those poems and plays before the public, she thought, and he'd be rich and famous and she could come back home in triumph. Bitter pill that it wasn't allowed."

"By the Brotherhood, d'you mean?"

"By the Brotherhood, indeed! Nipped his career in the bud, they did. Made him choose, you see."

So *that* was why his mother cataloged his father's works so tenderly. *That* was why she acted as if his was a great unsung genius. *That* was why she always said Tierney O'Connor's work would live when they were all long gone. Tahg had always thought she merely flattered his father in her love for him. Now, her devoted effort made better sense.

"I'm no judge, lad, but if William Butler Yeats thought your father knew what he was doing—and he did!—I suspect he had real talent, eh?"

Tahg nodded wonderingly. He had a feeling that he'd learn about more things than "the gentlemanly arts" while he stayed at FitzGibbon Hall.

And it was so exciting to be here with Uncle Desmond; to live this strange life of self-indulgence and learning. Servants to dress you, servants to feed you, servants to bring your horse around when you wanted to ride. And clothes! Uncle Des had had a wardrobe constructed for him that would have made his friends back in Dublin roar with laughter. All but Kitty, of course.

Kitty would love the clothes and the refinements, the servants and the sense of "having." FitzGibbon Hall was everything her fantasies could conjure. Wouldn't it be grand to be able to bring her here to see what it was like? To pluck her out of her slum, away from her poverty and into her dreams.

He realized Uncle Desmond was staring at him and brought himself back forcibly from his reverie.

"Why do you think my father chose Ireland, instead of the writing, Uncle?"

"Damned hard to figure. Not really a rebellious nature, your father. Not nearly as rebellious as your mother, come to think of it. Loyal though. Full of high principle. I suspect that's it. He'd not betray something he believed in." Des seemed satisfied with his own explanation.

Tahg nodded. How complicated adults seemed to be. His mother giving up the luxurious life at the Hall for love, his father giving up personal ambition for a cause. He wondered whether what they had chosen had brought them happiness enough to make up for the sacrifice.

He wondered what sacrifice his own life would demand of him.

5 "I really wish you didn't ever have to leave here," Angelica said plaintively to Tahg as they sat together under the canopy of heavily laden fruit trees in the late summer sun. "We've had such good times together."

Tahg, seated on the ground beside his cousin's rolling chair, looked up and smiled. "I'll miss you, too, Angel—and I'll write all the time, don't you worry. It's just that I've been here nearly two years now. There's so much for me to do at home—with the Fianna and what's going on in Dublin and all."

"And Kitty, too, I suppose," she said mischievously, thinking of the letters that arrived every week or two at FitzGibbon Hall from Dublin that seemed to make Tahg happy for days after he received one.

He smiled at her as he replied, "And Kitty, too, little cousin."

"It must be nice to be in love," she said wistfully, and the boy's expression darkened.

"Someone will love you, too, Angel," he said with conviction. "Wait and see."

"Not with these legs, Tahg. No boy will ever even look at me. If I were a Catholic they'd just put me into a convent and forget me."

"Pity the poor convent that ever got you, my little pixie. You'd have the abbess apoplectic in a month!"

Angelica giggled at that. Tahg was the only one who understood everything and could still make her laugh at life. He was her special friend and always had been. The one who would take the time to walk slowly with her chair instead of running wildly ahead with the others. The one who would sit and talk with her for hours, of serious things, not just the frivolous fun of parties and such that could have no meaning in her altered life.

Perhaps, if there was one such as Tahg in the world, there might be another, too. A boy for her to love. She tried to push the thought away, but it was getting harder as she grew older.

It had been bad enough to be excluded from games and romps and explorations as a child . . . but it had been bearable. To be excluded from the explorations of adulthood . . . that was a struggle for which she thought she might not be prepared.

"I'm trying to persuade your mother to let you come to Dublin to live for a while," Tahg said; seeing her serious expression, he, too, turned serious.

"It's time you found out about life in the city, Angel. And there's so much I could show you there . . . and so many people I'd like you to meet."

"I intend to live there in a house of my own when I'm grown," she said seriously. Tahg knew how important it was to her to be thought of as an independent person.

"When you do, I intend to be your greatest friend and to take you everywhere," he replied. "You know, I'll never treat you as if you can't do things because of your legs. We'll simply find lots of things you *can* do."

"Oh, Tahg," breathed Angelica, with gratitude. "You are wonderful!"

The boy beamed at the praise. He really did love his little cousin. She was the closest thing to a philosopher he had ever met. And courageous, too. So much of suffering she'd borne over the years, and yet he'd never seen her bitter. Wistful at times, she was. But never bitter.

If he could, he would try to make her life better when they were grown. She was too robust and alive for the entombment of Manningham Castle. Too spirited to sit forever, doomed to a chair and a proper destiny. If he had his way, she'd share in more of life than that. His mother and father would understand. Aunt Beth still felt guilty about the accident, so she wrapped the girl in cotton wool. Uncle Edmond was too engrossed in his own life of politics, and he was too protective. But *he* would not forget his little cousin who shared so many of his innermost thoughts. He would not forget her.

"I want to be a patriot when I grow up, Da," Tahg announced his weighty decision to his father on his way home from the pub, where he had stayed up half the night to hear his father sing. It was a month after his return to Dublin from Sligo.

Tierney felt a tightening in his chest at the words, wondering what in conscience he could say to the inevitable announcement. His son had matured so in the two years he'd been with his uncle. And Tierney was so very glad to have him back.

"Aye, son. 'Tis hard to listen to the old rebel songs and stories without wanting to be part of the struggle."

"No, Da!" replied the boy with seriousness, "that's only part of it. I've been thinking about the time I spent at the Hall. It's so beautiful there that it tends to confuse things a little. It took me a long time to straighten it all out in my own head."

Tierney looked at his son, tall for his age and handsome he was; but there was more to his appeal than that. The boy had an inner strength and a contemplative nature that promised good things of the mind.

"And what conclusion did you come to, son?" asked the father with genuine interest and affection.

"It isn't fair for them to be so rich and so many to be so poor, Da. I wouldn't mind if they'd done some fine deed or invented some great thing that made them rich. But it was only an accident that they were born with so much.

"But they don't treat it that way, Da. Mama's family is honest about it, but Uncle Edmond and Winston and most of their friends are just arrogant and self-important. Do you know how Uncle Edmond despises anyone who's not of his class? I talked with him some and I couldn't believe how he holds the Irish in contempt."

Tierney smiled at his son's intelligent appraisal.

"He's the product of his breeding, Tahg. It's an unusual man who's born to power, and is not corrupted by it."

"But Uncle Desmond isn't like that at all! He and Mama and Aunt Beth all come from the same kind of family and they're honest and good to the people."

"Ah, but they're rare as butterflies in the winter, Tahg Mor. They're not ordinary, at all."

"That's exactly the point, Da," the boy persisted. "What I'm trying to say to you is this—I don't want to be ordinary, either! I want to do something to even things up a bit. I want to help get back Ireland for the Irish. Like it says in your plays."

Tierney took a deep breath before speaking. In his heart he'd always known this day would come.

"Tahg . . . my heart is filled with a lot of conflicting emotions right now. I'm prouder than I can say of you, that you want to help with the Cause. 'Tis a brave and honorable ideal you seek to serve.

"But you're my son, and you mean more to me than all the causes in the world. And so I think I must try to be honest with you about all this, lad. Absolutely honest." Tahg heard the confusion in his father's voice and wondered at it.

They had reached the door of the house in which they lived. Tahg felt let down by his father's response to his important announcement. He'd thought the man would be proud and happy about it, but instead he seemed troubled and concerned.

They tiptoed into the old house and up the stairs to the landing outside their own flat and Tierney motioned Tahg to sit down beside him on the stair.

"Let's sit here awhile, son, so we don't wake your mother. It's a complicated story I want to tell you; or at least the emotions that surround it are complicated, but I think you're up to it." He patted the boy's knee proprietarily.

"When I was a boy, younger than you, I had an Uncle Jack. My father's brother he was, and a rebel born and bred. Dark hair he had, and wild passionate eyes. He was a fine brave man, or so I thought—and he was filled to the brim with rebel songs and stories and poems.

"By the time I was eight or nine, Tahg, he'd taught me the whole blighted history of Ireland. It was Uncle Jack who found I had a gift for the music and he taught me to play the stringed instruments that I've loved ever since.

"When his rebelliousness finally got him killed, he was held to be something of a martyr in our small part of the world."

Tahg watched his father's face carefully, wondering where this story would lead, wondering why he'd never been told of Uncle Jack before.

"I'd loved my uncle greatly and I was devastated by his death, but I was so *proud* of him, son, that in some bizarre way it compensated me.

"You see, we Irish get so steeped in our past, Tahg . . . in our endless troubles and rebellions and our endless quest for freedom. And we learn so early that martyrs are weapons against the enemy, and that death is an honorable offering to lay on the altar of freedom—that after a while I think martyrdom begins to seem almost inevitable to us.

"My Uncle Jack passed the flame to me and I to your mother and now we've passed it on to you, it seems—but it pains me to see the endlessness of it, lad. The father-to-son endlessness of it!"

"You mustn't worry about me, Da," said the boy, awed by his father's honesty. "I'll be all right. Maybe it will end with us; did you ever think of that? Maybe we'll be the last ones to have to fight them."

Tierney smiled ruefully and pulled the boy's shaggy head to his own chest to hug. "I've thought of that. I've thought of that indeed."

There was a movement inside the flat and then the scratchy unlatching of the door, as Con, sleepy-eyed, opened it to see the two on the landing. The sight of her husband and son clasped together in the dim light warmed her. So complete, they looked together; so alike and so very beautiful in their love for each other.

"Would you two care to come in and have a cup of tea to warm you, by any chance?" she called to them, an affectionate smile in her voice. "It's very lonely in here without you."

The man and boy looked at each other, a special knowledge passing between them. Somehow, because of tonight's conversation, a border had been passed. The fact that they had crossed it together was of great importance to them both.

6   James Connolly listened to his daughter Nora read from the newspaper. She was growing toward womanhood but was still a child to be listened to, and played with and praised. He smiled benevolently at the sweet lilting sound of her voice and wondered what kind of young man it would be who would steal her from him. Not that it would happen any time soon, but in a year or two or three, the lads would be noticing his lovely daughter in earnest and then he'd have to cope with the sorrow of that.

"Do you miss America, Da?" she asked suddenly, as if trying to divine his thoughts. She had been watching him while she read, admiring the solid strength of her father. He was squarely built and sturdy, the kind of man who made you feel safe and protected when he took your hand in his own.

"No indeed, child," he replied. "I'm glad we're back in Ireland." He wondered as he said it if that was entirely true. He hadn't come back because he wanted to—only because he was needed.

"I miss it sometimes. I felt safer there," she said sensibly.

He frowned at the wistful note in his daughter's voice. Safe indeed. Was there any place safe in the world for a workingman? he wondered.

"And don't you believe I'll be keeping my own lass safe from harm, now? That's a fine thing to be telling your father." He tried to sound disapproving but she always saw through him.

"Of course you will, Da, as much as you can. But you're in danger, too. Socialism isn't so popular with everyone, you know. It's you I'd worry about before myself, anyway."

The man looked sharply at the child—no, that wasn't right. Perhaps there were no *children* in Ireland anymore. They knew too much, too young, to be thought children. She deserved truth and not platitudes, then.

"Do you know why I do all this, Nora? Why I put myself in danger, which in turn endangers you and your mother and the other children?" The stocky, balding man reached out and pulled his dark-haired daughter close beside him.

"Because you must, I suppose. And because you're pretty famous for your ideas." It was said more matter-of-factly than it was felt.

Connolly smiled at his daughter's kind acceptance of the life he had forged for them. "I do what I do, Nora, because unless we're willing to fight back, lass . . . unless we stand up like men and demand just wages and just conditions, there can never be safety for anyone. Not for me, child, nor for you, nor your sisters and brothers. And not for that young man who will one day come along and try to sweep you away from me to have you all to himself!"

She looked up shyly. Her father had never before acknowledged her approaching womanhood.

"I'd never want to leave you, Da."

"No, lassie, I think you would not. But the day will come when you'll love some young man so much that you'll have no choice but to go off and build a life with him. And when that day comes, lass, he must have a chance at his own manhood. A job, Nora . . . a job and steady wages coming in and the sure knowledge that he can care for you and yours. That's what he'll need. And you'll need it, too. And that's why I fight for labor. And that's why I fight for Irish rights. For that boy's manhood, and for all our manhoods." He shook his head as if it were too complex to explain, and his luxuriant mustache, which the child thought so handsome, shook with the vehemence of the action.

"It's all right, Da." The girl leaned closer to her adored father and kissed the sparse hair of his head. "I wouldn't have you any other way." He patted her as she got up to leave. Her mother, too, understood as unselfishly as that. James Connolly was a man much blessed by the women in his life.

The strike had made all the sense in the world in the beginning, thought Connolly sadly. In the year 1913 Dublin was a tenement town in which 87,000 of the city's 400,000 people lived in houses that beggared description; 22,000 of these people lived in places that even a jaded officialdom had labeled uninhabitable.

It was a city in which the derelict remains of gracious old Georgian houses had been turned into slum dwellings, with a different family occupying each of the rooms that had once rung with the carefree laughter of the rich. It was a city with the highest death rate in Europe . . . and the lowest per capita income. A city in which 2,866,084 pawn tickets had been issued in the previous year of 1912.

So many young children searched the garbage daily for food scraps that a name was needed to describe them, so the "dustbin children" had been christened. And they searched with good reason, for the normal diet of a Dublin slum family was made up of barely enough to sustain life. Both breakfast and supper consisted of tea and bread; dinner brought potatoes, cabbage and onions, with perhaps a bite of bacon or herring added on special occasions.

All these things James Connolly knew firsthand.

But what he knew best of all was the tenuous relationship between worker and employer that made such a life inevitable. The "take it or leave it" mentality that allowed owners to exploit a man to the limits of endurance, knowing that if he dared to rebel a hundred hungry others were lined up to take his place.

That's why he had thrown in his lot with the labor agitator James Larkin and returned to Ireland from New York. He knew that Larkin had begun the Irish Transport and General Workers Union to try to combat the monumental unfairness that the Dublin industrialists were guilty of. He had returned to help make the union work for the workingman. For while Larkin had the rhetoric, the fire-and-brimstone mouth and the intellect to rally the people, it was he, James Connolly, who had the compassion and the understanding of the common man that allowed the workers to trust this new union's intent.

In truth, their union had made all the sense in the world until William Martin Murphy had decided to form a "union" of his own and had founded the Dublin Employer's Federation Limited. What an obscenity that man was, thought Connolly, with his righteousness and his god-awful power over men's lives and deaths.

Murphy had been born into a building contracting business and had, at his father's death, turned it into an empire extending from London to Africa. But the rights of laborers were not high on his list of priorities, and the current troubles had started over his sacking one hundred workers from his tramway company when they tried to unionize.

Connolly sighed to think how simple a beginning the strike had had all those months ago. He and Larkin had agreed that a sympathetic strike was the only means at their disposal of fighting back . . . and so it had begun.

Now, there was a soup kitchen in their headquarters at Liberty Hall because of the hungry thousands of unemployed, and it seemed increasingly clear to the workers that there were really only two alternatives that would exist by Christmas—surrender or starvation.

Connolly pulled his coat collar up around his ears and headed for the Hall. A plan had been proposed by some women to send the children of the strikers to England to sympathetic Irish families there for the duration of the strike. It was a desperate and unpopular move, but it might mean that the men could hold out a little longer, so it had to be considered. The Church had come out against it, of course; the archbishop fearful that Catholic children would come under Protestant influence in England. He'd have his hands full dealing with that.

He and Larkin must decide today if they would sanction the daring plan.

The morning papers were full of the news of Larkin's rhetoric. He'd given another riveting speech that had incensed the strikers to a near-riot frenzy of enthusiasm; not an easy feat when morale was so low.

Con smiled at the man as she passed his desk at the strike headquarters. He was such a large, angular fellow, gangly when seen up close, awkward and ambling. But on a podium or a soapbox or on a street corner speaking for the downtrodden and the weary, he was peerless. An eagle among starlings, able to soar above the crowd and, better still, to help them soar as well.

"I'm off to Lillie Connolly's," she called to him as she put on her coat. "Any messages for himself?"

"None that I can't give him from my own lips, Con," he called back. "James is on his way here within the hour to talk about the question of the children. But thanks anyway."

She nodded and waved as she let herself out of the busy office, noting the long line of frightened, hungry faces in the queue outside. They'd keep coming all day to see Larkin and Connolly. To get help from the union or to seek advice on what to do during the lockout. Increasingly gaunt they were; and increasingly afraid. She wished that William Martin Murphy could change places for a week with any one of them.

She silently thanked God that her family had enough bread for their table. Tommy's business was affected by the hard times of the strike for sure, but Tierney's money came home weekly nonetheless and often leftover food from the pub with it. Tommy loved Tierney like a son and he loved her, too, if the truth were known. She suspected that the offer of partnership Tommy had made to Tierney after Seaneen's decree about his writing had been as much a gift to her as to her husband. Tommy had a gentling way with women, as if he cared for them in a unique and protective fashion. Con knew she was his special friend.

She hurried the few blocks to Lillie's flat, thinking that the small, affectionate woman filled an important gap in her life.

She and Lillie really had little in common, but Mrs. Connolly provided a kind and womanly ear, and was a loving friend.

Lillie Connolly opened the door, a plumpish, small presence with the kindliest of faces. "It's grand to see you, Con," she said cheerily.

"And you too, Lillie," answered Con with a smile.

Lillie hugged the slender woman to her round frame—as she did so, it seemed to Con that her friend was thinner than when she'd last seen her. There were dark circles beneath her eyes as well, sure sign of the privation the strike had wrought for so many of the families.

"The children are in school for the moment and I'm making the week's bread, so I've all the time in the world to talk with you," Lillie said eagerly. There was a merry lilt to her voice that always made Con want to smile. Her hair was heavily streaked with gray and pulled back from her face in an almost-tidy bun.

Con slipped out of her coat and glanced around the apartment as she had done often since the Connollys' arrival from America. She had admired Connolly's writings so much that she had made it a point to meet him when he'd returned to Dublin, asking him to contribute articles to the *Bean na hEireann;* the Countess' magazine; it hadn't taken them long to become friends.

The flat was really no more than two small rooms, barren of any comforts but filled with sunlight and the winsome touches of a loving woman's hand. Five children in such circumstances made it an almost impossible task to keep the place tidy; yet there was not a speck of dust or an unfolded anything to be seen here.

"Sit down, luv," said her hostess, motioning her toward the kitchen table; its ancient enameled surface, marred by black-bottomed chips, was covered with flour and sweet-smelling dough.

"I'll knead with you," said Constance, smiling. A sudden vision from her childhood filled her: she and Beth watching Cook knead bread on the great marble baking table. She could almost hear her own voice, asking for permission to touch the great floury mounds.

"Sure, there's nothing feels as nice in your hands as the new bread, is there now?" Her hostess smiled, pleased by the interruption. Lillie Connolly was not a pretty woman, but something in her smile made you forget that fact. "My mother used to say, 'Into every loaf you can breathe a prayer, Lillie,' but I always think, 'Into every loaf you can knead a bit more love for your family!' " She smiled shyly as she said it and Con laughed as she replied.

"Aye. And I always say, 'You can get rid of all your pent-up hostile thoughts the same way!' " She scooped up a round portion of dough and thumped it down dramatically on the table.

"One punch for King George!" she intoned as she pushed her fist into the mass of dough. "One twist for the Castle and all their bloody laws!" She twisted the dough and thumped it flat again on the table with a resounding thud. "One whack for Mr. William Martin Murphy and his cutthroat scabs!" She folded over the loaf and hit it soundly.

Lillie Connolly looked disconcerted at first, then laughed aloud at her friend's outrageous behavior. "You're so much like my Jim, Con! Would God I had the kind of forceful courage you two have to say such things. I do admire it so." She beamed approval on her guest, who had settled down to kneading the silken dough in a normal fashion.

"I'm the one who admires *you*, Lillie," Con said, meaning it. "You seem to me the perfect wife. Loving and good-hearted . . . and I've no doubt you've never given Jim a moment's trouble because he must leave you and the children so often to go fight his fights.

"God knows I was a bloody terror to Tierney years ago about his neglect of us for the Brotherhood."

Lillie Connolly's eyes widened in disbelief. It would not enter her consciousness that a good wife would harass her husband over anything, least of all a good cause.

"Oh no, dear. You wouldn't do that, to be sure!" she said vigorously, as if to make the offending information disappear. "Why, your Tierney and my Jim are the very best of men. I'm sure you exaggerate."

She finished kneading the lump of dough she was working on and, forming it into a mound, put it into an oiled bowl and covered it with a clean but ragged cloth.

Taking another handful of dough from the huge pot it sat in, she continued.

"Besides, my Jim has told me all about you and how much good work you and the Countess do with the training of the boys and with the strike kitchen, and everyone knows of your speaking tours to help the people."

Con looked up at her friend's pink, nearly unlined face, with its twinkly gray eyes and soft, seemingly boneless cheeks. "It's going badly, Lillie," she said suddenly. "Larkin and your Jim can't hold the men out of work very much longer. Even this scheme about the children will only delay the inevitable. The bastards are going to win and all the suffering will have been for naught. How do you live with that? How does he?"

The older woman stopped the rhythmic kneading for a moment and seemed lost in thought. Finally she said slowly, as if making sure that she said it correctly, "Jim Connolly knows more of the suffering of the men and their families than you could ever dream, luv."

Then, in a seeming non sequitur: "These will be the first loaves of bread I've made in nearly a month." She waved her hand over the bowls of rising dough lined up on the windowsill. "You see, we must never have more than the others—so when they go without, we go without as well. James knows exactly how it fares with the families, Con. But he also knows . . . believes with all his great heart . . . that unless we fight them now, unless we're brave enough to fight and die if we must, it will never change.

"He says that even if we lose now, dear, as it seems we must . . . we will have won *something*. We will have shown them our courage and forbearance. We will have won more people to our side. We will have shown the children that we do not knuckle down to tyrants . . . and that even though we are poor we own our own souls!"

The woman's face was shining as she said it. "One day the whole world will be a safer place for the workingman because of my Jim, and Mr. Larkin. Can you imagine that? People will remember them and bless their names."

Con looked wonderingly at the perfect, unquestioning loyalty of her friend and finally said, "You're right, of course, Lillie. But it can't be easy for you to bear with the danger and the privation. No bread for a month makes a hungry life. I wish to God you'd told me. We could have shared ours with you."

"I don't mind, really," said her friend absently, "as long as Jim can do as he must."

Con watched her, thinking that was probably the profoundest truth of all.

That was where they were different, of course, Con thought. She, too, would serve her husband and his Cause. She, too, would live as she must to make the future a better one. But she did mind that the world was so unfair a place. She minded very much.

It occurred to her suddenly that the days she was putting in at the strike kitchen seemed infinitely longer and more fatiguing now that they knew defeat was inevitable.

Con lay facedown on the bed, near sleep. It had been an endless, hard day working at the Liberty Hall kitchen and on the picket lines. God, would it never end? Four months already and lockouts all over the city. Lockouts and starvation. Fear and violence. Poor old Dublin, what a mess you are; she thought the words as she felt the weariness engulf her and the first soothing wave of forgetful sleep wash in.

A few minutes later she felt a familiar hand trailing gently over her uncovered back. She generally wore a cotton shift to bed, but she had been so tired . . . too tired to undress and dress again in nightclothes, so she had tumbled, naked, between the covers, grateful that this once Tahg was staying the night with a friend. Con felt a momentary uneasiness and annoyance . . . she should respond to that loving touch, turn and let her husband take her in his arms, but she was paralyzed by fatigue and longed only for sleep. Tomorrow could be a terrible day; parting children from their mothers and putting them on boats bound for England sounded sensible in theory, but the awful wrench it would entail! It was heartbreaking even to contemplate.

Tierney smiled at the body of his wife beside him on their bed. She had been indefatigable from before dawn: supervising the strike kitchen, feeding hundreds, encouraging the men at the picket lines. Tommy had left the pub at lunchtime to bring her a bite of food, he'd said. In truth, Tierney knew that Tommy worried for Con's safety and contrived to visit her on the lines whenever he could.

It suddenly seemed to Tierney that he wanted the love he felt for her to flow through his hands to her tired body . . . wanted to give her of his own strength. He began to knead at the tired knot of muscles in her shoulders; strong, patient hands warming and soothing the aching muscles into slumber.

Con lay quiet, feeling the strength of her husband's touch—knowing somehow that the love he wanted to give her at that moment was beyond lust—although lust was seldom far away when they were in their bed together. She smiled to herself to think that after so many years of marriage he could still provoke the stirrings she felt now in her loins . . . still could command her body's responses with a laugh, or a word, or a significant look. What a joy they'd had of each other, all these years. How gracious of God it had been to create this endless quickening bond between men and women who love each other.

She moved languorously beneath her husband's knowing hands and, awake now, turned toward his welcoming arms. There was more than one way it seemed to banish the fears and fatigues of the day . . . and better ways than sleep.

October 1913

The ragged children were bundled as best they could be against the October weather. They stood at Liberty Hall, many barefoot, each with a little bundle of belongings, ready to be marched to the quays for the shipping to England.

Stoic-faced mothers, also in rags, held the little hands and struggled to keep the glistening tears in their eyes from falling. Parting would be hard enough for the babes as it was, without adding more to their burden of fear and loneliness. At least in England they would not starve to death.

An orderly march began, mostly women and children hand in hand. Solemn and eerily quiet, considering the number of babies in the long queue.

Con clutched a little girl's hand as she walked silently with the other mothers, thanking God that Tahg was fifteen years old and that she had not had to make the terrible decision these women had. How damnably unfair this is, she thought angrily as she walked. How ghastly, to force a mother to part with her child just to keep it alive. By God, the Harper would have something to say about this new injustice.

The only sounds were those of the children talking to each other and of their small feet on the cobblestones. Suddenly, Con was aware of the murmur of voices up ahead. She strained to see where the noise was coming from and saw a hostile crowd gathered at the next cross street, blocking their way to the water. As she watched, startled out of her reverie, a babel of shouts and screams and curses erupted from every side as men and women with banners and clubs moved from hiding places in the side streets and from the shadows of buildings. Ahead, near the quay, she could see a huge mob, similarly equipped with weapons.

Con felt a man's hand snatch at the small girl who walked beside her, and she grabbed instinctively for the child, gripping the six-year-old wildly around the waist. A woman appeared from somewhere and began tearing at her clothes, while two men pulled the child savagely from her hands. She began to scream and felt a sharp blow to the head that seemed to come from nowhere. Desperately, she staggered after the child, who was now clutched, screaming, in the arms of a strange man. Con sensed her legs go out from under her and struggled to rise, only to be struck again.

Stunned past movement, Con lay on the cold cobblestones and saw the madness swirling around her. Police with clubs, well-dressed men and women, priests—all were screaming, all violent, all pulling children from their mother's arms . . . shrieking that no Irish child would leave for England!

Con thought she saw Larkin coming toward her and tried to call out to him, but a cold blackness rose up in her and a searing pain shot through her head where it had been struck. She remembered covering her head with her arms, trying not to be trampled by the maddened mob; it was the last thing she remembered as the noise faded crazily around her.

The pain was still with her when she opened her eyes, but the noise had stopped. She felt Tierney's arms holding her and thought she was being lifted from the coldness of the street, but she couldn't be sure if what was happening was real or just another part of the bad dream.

"Get your mother's shawl and purse, son!" she heard her husband's urgent voice say to Tahg; saw blearily the boy canvass the street for her belongings, then, grateful for the safety, close in her husband's arms, Con let herself drift again out of the reach of consciousness.

* * *

"A concussion is what it's called," someone was saying as she began to focus again, this time in her own flat. "You must watch for dizziness or vomiting and keep her in bed for several days at least. I'll look in again before the week is out."

She recognized the voice of the doctor who treated the union men when they were injured in the strike riots. An old friend of Connolly's he was.

"Tierney . . ." Her voice sounded weak even to her. "What's happened to the children?"

He crossed the room to her in two great strides and, sitting on the bed, touched her face gingerly.

"It's all over, I'm afraid, sweetheart. There was no way to get them to the boats. They're home in their own beds for the most part."

She nodded, and felt a sharp pain bisect her head.

"I'd followed you," he continued, eying her worriedly. "Tommy was sure there'd be violence. Tahg and I got there just in time to keep you from being trampled or dragged off to jail."

"I love you," she said, for there seemed nothing else to say. Her voice sounded weak and wan, but the thought was nonetheless comforting.

"Larkin's been arrested," Tierney told her. "I expect this will break the strike once and for all."

"Perhaps it'll be a blessing that the strike's over before winter," she murmured resignedly, her mind still muddled.

"Only if the owners will take back the strikers. But you've no need to worry about that at the moment, Beauty. I'm just grateful to God you're alive. You must rest for a while, so this concussion causes no lasting problems."

Con nodded again, grimacing in anticipation of the pain she knew would accompany the movement of her head.

"I'll lie beside you for a bit," he said, and she could see the worry and fatigue in his eyes. "Tommy'll understand if I'm late for work tonight. I've sent word."

Con felt him lower his large body onto the bed carefully so as not to jostle her; felt his arms encircle her protectively. She tried to force her mind to operate clearly; tried to put the jumble of information and feelings into a semblance of order.

If the owners wouldn't take back the strikers, there'd be wholesale starvation in the city for certain. How long could such agony go on before the people rose up in protest? Didn't the Murphys of the world see that they were bringing about their own downfall? Her head ached too much to think about it now. If only the children were safe . . .

She drifted into sleep with the confusions of the problems still circulating in her brain.

"The great appear great to us because we are on our knees!" Connolly shouted the words to the men, and a cheer went up from their beleaguered ranks. The pugnacious jaw was set in its sternest position. This was a man of the people, a worker who suffered like themselves. What difference if he called himself a socialist, he was a man who understood the plight of other men.

"We have lost this strike, but we will arm ourselves and rise to fight another day. When war comes again, we will not meet it unprepared!"

Connolly slipped down from the platform amid thunderous applause. It was high time they began to train men militarily. In a year or two they would be called upon to bear arms for Ireland and freedom. It was important that the men of the Irish Citizen Army understand the use of weapons and the discipline of the military before that happened.

The Rising Tide
1914–1916

Man can die but once. We owe God a death.

WILLIAM SHAKESPEARE

7

17 Capel Street
Dublin
8 August 1914

My darling Brother,

I never cease to marvel at the changes you have wrought in Tahg. Through this past year of watching his new maturity, I cannot help but wonder if he has caused similar momentous changes in you.

He is every inch the grown-up gentleman in speech, deportment and wardrobe—and yet seems quite unspoiled by your ministrations. Tierney and I feel your instincts as a "parent" must be superb—and to say that the boy worships his Uncle Desmond would be too pallid a description!

I shall never cease to thank you, Des, for giving my son a taste of our heritage. Even though Fate is unlikely to provide such a life for him, the good of it will remain to sustain him—as it has sustained me. You are a lovely brother, my dear, and I pray that you may one day have sons of your own on whom to lavish your good will.

Your suggestion of our sending Tahg to Padraig Pearse's school, St. Enda's (and your generous offer to pay his tuition!) is an intriguing one. The school is a grand place, full of the fierce national pride at which Pearse excels. I agree with you that such knowledge of his Irish heritage would be good for my son. He could not be enrolled until the spring term, but we will see to it that he goes there this autumn for the necessary interviews. A thousand blessings on you for your generosity (not just financial, but emotional) in wanting to provide Tahg with possibilities he might not have without you. No wonder he adores you. I do, myself!

How is Bethy faring, Des? I sometimes think she has the hardest row to hoe of all of us. Seaneen still speaks of "My Lady" in reverential tones and she, no doubt, pines in the same fashion for him. How lonely her life must be, and how haunted by memories. Thank heaven you, at least, are near at hand to give her support.

Her newest book is quite splendid, don't you think? Is it difficult for a man to relate to what she writes? It seems to strike such a universal chord in women. She is already at work on another. I think, perhaps, her writing and lecturing (to say nothing of her occasional bouts with the legal system!) keep her mind off her marriage—although she does seem to be more settled about remaining in Sligo since you are there, too.

Speaking of marriages, my own husband sends his best and encourages you to visit when you can.

Much love from us all,
Con

"Father!" called Winston Manningham breathlessly, as he pulled his horse to an abrupt halt beside the automobile that stood waiting outside Manningham Castle to collect the older man.

"Is it true? Has there really been a war declared with Germany?"

Edmond straightened from the effort of stowing his heavy attaché case into the rear seat of the car. "I'm afraid so, Winston," he replied solemnly. "I've been called to London for emergency discussions."

"How incredibly exciting!" said the boy. "I don't suppose I could go with you, Father?" It was evident from the boy's voice that he would have welcomed an invitation.

Edmond smiled at his eldest son. "Not this trip, I'm afraid, old man," he replied, "what with school and all. But if this thing drags on beyond a few weeks' duration, we might arrange something."

"I'd be really grateful, Father, if you could," Win said with dignity. He didn't want his request to sound childlike.

Edmond reached up to shake his son's hand. "I've said goodbye to your mother and the others, son. I'd like your word that you'll keep things running smoothly in my absence, like a good man. Yes?"

The boy smiled warmly and Edmond patted his leg and the horse's rump simultaneously; then he moved to the car.

"I'll be in touch, of course," he said from its cushioned interior before closing the door.

"You can rely on me, Father," called Win with conviction.

"I'm sure of that, Winston," responded Edmond, satisfied that his son was more than capable of what he'd asked.

Win watched the car disappear down the winding drive with a pang of envy. His father was so extraordinary in every way. Admirable in his career and his personal life—except for his marital difficulties, but that could hardly be held against him. Mother could be so impossible at times. He himself must strive very hard to be exactly like his father. Not that it was so very difficult, really. They were actually awfully alike. Everyone said so.

The last thought gave Win considerable pleasure as he turned his horse's head toward the stable. It was a great comfort to be so very like his perfect father.

8 ❧ Armies seemed to be springing up everywhere by 1914. Con's letters were full of the news of agitation. The Great War we'd all hoped to avoid had been declared, and all the brave boys had begun marching off to fight the Hun. There was even talk of conscription for Ireland. That Edmond and his cronies didn't realize how explosive it would be to try to draft unwilling Irishmen into the English Army seemed incomprehensible to me. The posters said that soldier boys would go off to fight for the freedom of small nations; how could they not have seen that there were plenty of men in Ireland preparing to fight for the freedom of their own small nation! But the sensitiv-

ity of Whitehall to Irish politics had never been exemplary, so I watched the growing turmoil with fascination.

Moreover, for several decades, the English government had skillfully manipulated the social and religious differences between the North of Ireland and the South in order to keep Home Rule from being passed into law. Always on the alert for ways to subvert the notion of Irish independence, Randolph Churchill had decided to fan into flame the religious and social differences between the Protestants in the North and the Catholics in the South. "Play the Orange card!" said Sir Randolph, always known for his sporting instinct, if not his sportsmanship —and England had.

He was referring, of course, to the fraternal orders to which the Protestant working class belonged—the Orange Lodges of Ulster—which were a powerful and vocal protectorate of England's during all these years. Politicians poured oil on the pyre, as did fanatical ministers. Poverty, hopelessness and fear fanned the flames. As did slogans like "Home Rule is Rome Rule!" In short, the English were able to divide the Irish house against itself. By the time the world war broke out, two decades of hate mongering between the poor Catholics who needed employment and the richer Protestants who had it had fueled a conflagration that would be hard to extinguish.

As a result of all the agitation, an Orange leader had emerged in Parliament in 1913. His name was Sir Edward Carson. An articulate and well-homeworked fellow, Carson had risen to prominence, at least in part, through his ability as a relentless cross-examiner. The trial of his Oxford classmate Oscar Wilde had put Carson squarely in the limelight.

It is said that when Wilde heard that Carson was to be the prosecutor at his trial, he told his listeners, "No doubt he will treat me with all the added viciousness of an old friend." Carson decimated Wilde in cross-examination and his reputation as a litigator was assured. Next he turned his hand to the Orange card game and the rest is history.

My husband was a great friend of Carson's, and when the man founded the Ulster Volunteers, Edmond was on his side with a vengeance.

Carson created the Ulster Volunteers to be a citizen army— or so he said—to defend the province of Ulster in the event of Home Rule. And as you might expect, there were rows in Parliament (and on every street corner in the South) over the founding of this paramilitary group. No one could doubt that the pot of the Empire was about to boil over.

Eoin MacNeill, a professor of Irish history, had written a popular editorial in a Dublin paper in response to the announcement of the founding of Carson's Volunteers. "They have shown us the way to defend *ourselves,*" it said. As a result of the overwhelming response to his article, MacNeill was prompted to form an army of his own called the Irish Volunteers. A schoolmaster named Padraig Pearse, popular for his pro-Irish rhetoric, gave a stirring speech at MacNeill's recruitment rally and seven thousand men signed up on opening night alone.

Con's friend, Connolly, had formed an army of his own—the Irish Citizen Army—composed of the workers who had bonded together during the labor strike. My sister and Tierney were in the thick of all this agitation, of course, although I was never sure from her letters—which had to be cryptic for security's sake—precisely what they were up to.

In short, trouble was brewing, with plenty of willing cooks to stir the broth. And leaders were beginning to make themselves known. The fighting force was assembling, and the leaders were emerging from the throng. The chess pieces were being moved into place on fate's game board, and one sensed the coming upheaval with every nerve ending by late 1914.

Edmond spent most of his life at Westminster and Whitehall. He gave brilliant speeches in the House and had become quite a dashing and well-known statesman—at least as far as Parliament and the press were concerned. To be fair, he was most always civil to me and we had evolved a system whereby we could live together with as little rancor as possible. He was a peerless provider; I was a fine mother and hostess. We had survived each other.

Nonetheless it seemed clear to me as the agitation level rose in Ireland that if those I loved were soon to be in danger (and how could one doubt it with all these armies taking the field?) there were steps that I must consider.

All through the year of 1914 I brooded on what was in the air. It was nearly time for me to make some important decisions and I was gathering strength for what it seemed to me that I must do. ☜

* * *

Padraig Pearse, tall and reed-thin, waited for the others to climb the hill to St. Enda's. He knew the O'Connors well through the IRB, but he hadn't yet met their son Tahg, whom they meant to enroll in his school. The boy looked to be about sixteen years old, tall and strapping; an intelligent, handsome lad, he'd been told by his brother Willy, who had interviewed him the week before.

Pearse, waiting, let his eye sweep over the grass-covered mountains behind him and the wide expanse of Dublin Bay before. Howth Head seemed to shimmer majestically in the crisp November air—thoughts of the ninth-century Scandinavian marauders who had founded Dublin rose in his mind's eye unbidden. He smiled inwardly at his own sense of history. . . . Willy had said once that they were both doomed by it, and perhaps he'd been right. If so, it was *his* doom that Willy generously chose to share.

Pearse stood in front of the graceful mansion that was the school, between the stone pillars that held the portico aloft. He could see the newcomers making their way up the long drive from the massive stone gate that marked the school's boundary, its carved lions couchant on the ground, well behind the visitors now.

"So, you've come at last," Pearse said cordially as they reached him. He eyed Tahg with the appraising stare of a schoolmaster, then put out his hand. "My brother had only good to say of you, lad."

Tahg smiled, pleased by the compliment, as was his mother behind him. "Thank you, sir. I'm very grateful to hear that," he replied.

"I've asked some of our young men to show you the playing fields and such," said the proud master of St. Enda's to the new recruit. "The boys in those saffron kilts are off to the hurling field. I don't suppose you'd mind going along with them, would you?"

"I'd be pleased to see it all, sir!" said Tahg with enthusiasm. He bade good-bye to his parents and followed the others happily. He was excited about the opportunity the school offered him . . . and the fact that it was only a tram ride from Dublin meant he could still see Kitty. Con was amused to see her son's immediate response to the schoolmaster and the warmth Padraig had shown toward the boy. Never once in all her dealings with the man in the IRB had she seen the least hint of such pervasive warmth in him. Obviously, his students were the recipients of all he had to give.

"I'm glad you've come," Pearse said to Con and Tierney. "And gladder still you've decided to let Tahg study at St. Enda's. Has he the Irish? He'll need it here you know."

"He speaks well enough," said Tierney. "He should be able to manage."

"Clarke, MacDiarmida and O'Sullivan are in my office," Pearse said as they reached the door, "engaged in a lively discussion of how to correctly mount our rebellion. It seems it's one thing to dream a revolution and quite another to make one work." He said the last with a wry smile.

Tierney laughed shortly at that. "We may all soon find ourselves face to face with that little distinction, Pat," he replied meaningfully.

Pearse nodded agreement and offered a quotation in response. " 'I care not if I live but one day and one night, provided my fame and my deeds live after me.' That was Cuchulain's boyhood motto, you know. It seems to me as appropriate for our time as for his."

Con and Tierney looked at each other, she raising her eyebrow in an expression that had always amused her husband. Pearse was a complicated man and she was looking forward to today's discussion. It was apparent that Pearse intended to take charge; it would remain to be seen just what he intended to take charge of.

There was no need for introductions, as all the people in the paneled study knew each other. Thomas Clarke nodded his greeting. A survivor of fifteen years' penal servitude as a guest of Her Britannic Majesty, he now kept a tobacconist and news agent's shop on North Great Britain Street. Clarke was an unprepossessing man, smallish and wearing glasses; none would have marked him for a patriot, thought Con as she entered the room and returned his nod.

Near Clarke was Sean MacDiarmida, who because of a bout with polio years before kept a cane by the side of his chair; he was at that moment fiddling with the head of it. He and Clarke were the driving forces behind the "new" IRB that had been resurrected from the ashes of nineteenth-century Irish Fenianism. Both men were tough and indefatigable in their devotion to the Brotherhood.

Clarke had for some time been building a secret force of fighting men. From the Gaelic League, the Gaelic Athletic Association and the clubs and literary societies that took an interest in Irish affairs. Con and Tierney had discussed his methods with him often enough over the years. He was not interested in a vast body of recruits, he said, but rather a small and formidable group of disciplined soldiers. No excessive drink would be tolerated in his men, nor the keeping of bad company. Character and intellect he would seek first, and before a man could be approached, he must be sponsored and proposed to a committee.

"So the IRB has elitest tendencies," Tierney had chided him amiably.

"And isn't it a sensible tribal custom to look up to good breeding as a prerequisite for leadership?" the little man had responded.

Seaneen came forward with a chair for Con, then took his place again near the window. Pearse began to speak.

"I've asked you here today, gentlemen . . . and lady," he corrected himself, glancing warmly at Con, "because we all know that the time for us to declare our intentions has come."

"And haven't I been doing precisely that, every day of my life that I've recruited another one of us?" demanded Clarke, sounding feisty.

"Without a doubt," replied Pearse, unruffled. "What I meant to say is that the time is right for a rising. Now . . . while England is at war . . . we must lay the foundation for an uprising in her own backyard!"

"The time may be right," said Seaneen with a wry laugh, "but there are a great many other things that aren't. How exactly do you plan to conjure up guns and ammunition for your little rising, for instance? And which of the several armies that are cropping up do you expect to tap for insurgents?"

"Seaneen's right," said Tierney. "You can't have a rising without guns and a rank and file."

MacDiarmida, as ever on Clarke's side, spoke up with assurance. "Recruitments are going well, O'Connor. The GAA is providing an excellent incubator for Irish nationalism all over the country. We have our fingers on many eligible candidates."

"The only soldiers I'd trust at my back are the IRB boys I'm recruiting myself!" interjected Clarke.

"Aye," said Seaneen, "but we're so bloody elitest with our *crème de la crème* selection, Tom, we'll be lucky to field five hundred men when the time comes. More like a joke than an insurrection."

Clarke looked Seaneen squarely in the eye. "I am quite confident that we will number close to two thousand this time next year," he said in a voice that brooked no rebuttal.

Seaneen grunted, and MacDiarmida quickly spoke up. "Gentlemen, the *numbers* in the IRB are not as important as the strength of our commitment. We must be in accord! Do not forget that the Volunteers are practically at our disposal."

"And Con can get to Connolly," put in Tierney, anxious to avoid a fight, "to feel him out about where he stands with the Citizen Army."

"Jim Connolly is already thinking along the lines of a military rebellion," she said deliberately. "All we need do is convince him to join forces with us. He'll stand wherever it's best for the workers—he'll be in when he sees that our way is the only way."

"I don't trust this 'socialism' that he preaches." MacDiarmida spoke from his position on the settee.

Con turned to him and replied with conviction, "Connolly wants the liberation of Ireland as deeply as any of us in this room! He's a magnetic leader, too. Whatever his politics, his men would follow him to Gehenna, if that was his wish!"

There was silence in the room as Con realized that all eyes had focused on her.

"Gehenna," said Seaneen, breaking the silence with a short chuckle. "Like as not, that's where we're all headed."

Pearse looked up sharply. "If you don't wish to participate in this battle there's no need for you to do so," he said stiffly.

"I've been 'participating' in this bloody battle since I was younger than Tahg O'Connor, Padraig," said Seaneen so quickly no one had a chance to intervene, "so spare me your highfaluting rhetoric about who's needed and who's not!"

"Gentlemen, gentlemen, if you please," said Clarke. "Save your fight for the enemy, if you don't mind."

MacDiarmida quietly brought the conversation back to the subject at hand. "Face facts—MacNeill has over ten thousand

Volunteers who are loyal to him. The Brotherhood will call the shots and the Volunteers will deliver them."

"You're forgetting that MacNeill has committed the Volunteers to absolutely no action *during* this war!" Seaneen reminded them. "He detests physical force! He intends his men to make sure Home Rule is put into effect as promised—nothing more! Do you mean to change his mind overnight?"

Pearse, who had remained verbally unobtrusive since Seaneen's last outburst, stood up and began to pace the room. When he had drawn up opposite Seaneen's position at the window that faced the bay, he halted. The authority in his voice made it clear that he felt he spoke for the majority in the room.

"Mr. O'Sullivan seems to doubt our capabilities," he said archly, and Con could see Seaneen's knuckles go white.

"If there's any man in this room who *doesn't* doubt our capabilities we should take him out and have his head examined!" replied Seaneen contemptuously. "My father used to say it's a valiant flea that dares eat his breakfast on the lip of a lion."

Con heard Tierney expel his breath as he fought back laughter.

"MacNeill will be the sole concern of myself!" Pearse said, struggling to keep his temper in check, "And we'll all handle the 'lion' when the time comes. For now the Brotherhood must increase its numbers and influence. We must acquire arms and we must all work together—"

Clarke interrupted Pearse to finish the sentence. "And the secrets discussed here must remain inviolable!"

Con shuddered involuntarily at his vehemence. There was a lot more brewing at St. Enda's than scholarship.

By the end of the day Tahg had been enrolled at the school for the spring term, and the beginnings of an organized plan for rebellion had been seeded. Con and Tierney O'Connor went home weary and thoughtful. There was much to lose, if consensus refused to root firmly in their little revolutionary bed.

Tierney finished giving Tommy the particulars of the conversation with the leaders.

"Great cry, but little wool, as the devil said when he plucked the pig!" Tommy commented with a wry laugh. "We've got too many cooks, and too many intellectuals, if you'll forgive me saying so. Too fucking many generals and not enough soldiers, if you ask me."

"And too few guns," added Con, looking significantly at Tierney. She knew he and Seaneen were puzzling out a plan to get firearms.

"How the hell do they expect to field an army when all they do is fight amongst themselves anyway?" asked Tommy. "They'll be too busy bloodying each other's noses to fight the English." He snorted disgust at the vicissitudes of the would-be leaders and put down the cup he'd been holding.

"And what exactly does the Harper think of all this?" he asked, turning a benevolent smile on Con. "The Harper's voice has a tendency to be the most intelligent one hereabouts, it seems to me."

Con smiled appreciatively at the compliment and at her friend. Tommy was one of the very few who knew the Harper's identity. She was aware that many in the IRB speculated that Tierney wrote the inflammatory Wild Harp essays, but to the best of her knowledge only Griffith, the Countess and Tommy knew for sure that she was the Harper.

"My Harper self thinks the Rising's inevitable, and long overdue," she responded. "And that it's the only chance we've got. My wife-and-mother self wishes my family lived in a nice safe country, somewhere—if any such there be under God's heaven." She laughed shortly at her own ambivalence.

Tommy chuckled at that and patted Con's hands where they rested on her knee.

"What a sensible old thing you are," he said, and Tierney smiled inwardly at the deep affection that these two had for each other. "Although you're busy exiling your husband and son from the dangers, I noted you didn't suggest a place for yourself on the boat."

"I've been waiting to get my shot at them for a while now," she replied, "but it's nice to know you worry about me. I worry about you, too, Tommy, you know. You must behave yourself for me in the coming days. Ireland has too many dead heroes— she's more in need of living leaders at the moment."

"I would have thought she had more than her quota of those!" Tommy laughed, trying to lighten her mood.

"Well, she has plenty of talkers, that's for sure," Con laughed back. "As to leaders . . . we shall see."

"Don't forget men like Clarke and O'Sullivan, Beauty," said Tierney. "You'd be hard put to call them as other than leaders, I'm thinking."

"Aye," replied Tommy. "I'd trust them two with whatever they set their hands to.

"What've you heard from Beth?" McGowan asked suddenly —then looked sheepish, for each of them realized it was the mention of Seaneen that had called her to mind. "Has she had any brushes with the law of late?"

"Not that I know of, but I've no doubt she would if the opportunity arose." Con smiled as she thought of her sister. "You know, when we were children, Bethy wanted nothing so much as to grow up and fall in love and lead a quietly proper and peaceful life. Now she's fallen into the hornet's nest, like the rest of us." She shook her head wonderingly and her brown curls bounced.

"Life does seem to drag us where we don't wish to go, doesn't it?" asked Tommy with a soft little laugh.

"Well, it hasn't dragged me!" said Con with conviction. "I am exactly where I wish to be. I chose my path and I've never regretted it for an instant."

"Ah," said Tierney with a secret smile, "I seem to remember one night . . ."

She laughed good-naturedly. "One night out of eighteen years isn't a bad average," she retorted, and reached over to ruffle her husband's hair playfully. Tommy watched the response in Tierney's eyes. They had some animal bond, these two; a spirited sexuality that sent sparks flying, even after all their years of marriage. No one who spent as much time with them as he could doubt their fire or their camaraderie.

And she had spoken no more than the truth. Never had he known a woman as sure of her place in life as Con O'Connor.

9   Tahg held Kitty's hand lightly in his own—it felt fragile to him and he held it carefully. He knew she wasn't a fragile girl. Indeed, she had a hearty spirit and was

young and healthy. She didn't seem made of porcelain like some of the girls he'd met; there was a flesh and blood reality to Kitty that was making it harder and harder for him to keep himself in check when they were together. Childhood friends though they were, it was quite apparent that she was a child no longer.

She turned her head toward him, her great, blue, laughing eyes luminous in the moonlight.

"I feel absolutely *wonderful* tonight," she said with happy enthusiasm.

"I always feel wonderful when we're together," he replied, amused by her excitement.

"Oh my, but you are the gallant one!" She laughed, her dazzling red hair bouncing about her face as she moved her head animatedly for emphasis.

"Will you still love me when I'm an actress and I've won my first starring role in a play at the Abbey?"

"I'll be your stage-door Johnny," he laughed as he replied, for her mood was infectious.

"Oh no you won't!" she said with mock disapproval. "There's not a chance that I'd let you anywhere near the theater and all those beautiful girls."

"Then how will I ever see you act?"

"I'll lead you to your seat on the aisle, blindfolded, and then I'll come get you again when the curtain comes down, of course!"

"You really are a funny girl, Kitty," the boy said, as always uncertain as to quite how to behave with her. He'd thought her special from the first time he'd laid eyes on her when they were nine or ten. It had taken him a very long time to get her to allow him to catch her, as his father had recommended. But they'd been great pals now for a long while. And more than that, too.

He put his arm suddenly around her shoulders. She looked quickly into his face.

"Are you going to try to kiss me?" she asked frankly.

"No," he said, startled by the frontal question.

"Damn!" she said vehemently. "I wish you would!"

Tahg looked disconcerted for a few seconds, then, laughing, caught her in his arms and kissed her very willing mouth.

"You don't have to be shy with me, Tahg O'Connor," she whispered into his ear as he held her. "I know you too well."

"I know you, too, Kitty," replied Tahg seriously. "You confuse me a lot of the time, but somewhere deep down inside me, I think I know you better than anyone else in the world."

She eyed the handsome boy she was toying with. He did know her—that was part of the problem.

He hesitated for a moment, then said, "I'm going away, Kitty. I'll be going to St. Enda's come January."

She looked so stricken for a moment that he wanted to reach out to her, but she had already recovered herself before he could do so. He had told her about this possibility when he'd first gone to St. Enda's to be interviewed.

She tried to keep her voice steady when she spoke. "You know, Tahg Mor, if you and I had been born rich—say on neighboring estates like your uncle's—we'd just fall in love with each other and live happily ever after. Provided, of course, you didn't go running off to some secret revolution and get yourself killed." She meant to sound lighthearted, but he heard the small uncertainty beneath the tone.

Tahg leaned toward her and raised his hand to touch her face. She is going to miss me, he thought. She cares more than she lets on.

"Howth isn't all that far away, you know," he said gently, "I'll be home here often enough." She nodded but didn't reply. "Besides, you wouldn't have me even if I stayed home and sat by the fire all the time," he said, trying to lighten her mood.

"That's true, of course," she replied, striving to sound offhand. "It just isn't meant to be, that's all. I'll need to be a great lady and see the world, and you'll need to set Ireland free. We just won't have time for each other."

He grimaced inwardly at how far she'd have to go to fulfill her dream.

Tahg turned her around suddenly to face him, and kissed her long and lovingly.

"We've got plenty of time right now," he breathed into the sweet fragrance of her hair when the kiss was done.

"We do, don't we?" she whispered back as she stretched up toward him to be kissed again.

Seventeen-year-old Winston moved his bishop to the fourth rank and waited expectantly.

Johnny smiled a small half-hidden smile and countermoved.

"Check and mate, brother," the much younger boy said amiably enough, although amiability between the two brothers was hard fought for.

Winston knotted his cool blond forehead with annoyance, then, controlling his anger, said evenly, "So it would appear, Johnny," and with a studiedly elegant gesture he swept the board back on the gaming table, as if dismissing it.

"You won't do as well on Saturday at hounds," he said.

"No," replied his darker, smaller sibling. "I tend to excel more at things of the intellect."

The smirk on Win's face regrouped itself into a tight line and he rose from the table. Why had he even bothered to play with this brother of his, whom he despised just as his father despised him?

Often, often he had observed his father's obvious distaste for Johnny. He knew that his youngest brother had been born in that terrible spring after Angelica's accident. The spring when his parents had stopped loving each other. He knew his father could not forgive his mother the negligence that had caused his sister's tragic injury. He suspected that was somehow tangled up in his father's antagonism toward Johnny. Whatever the reason, there was no question that his father disdained this youngest son's company; the whole family was aware of it. And he himself could certainly understand why.

Not that his brother wasn't smart; he was certainly that. But somehow he didn't belong. And then there was his odd dislike for horses. "He behaves like a city child around them," his father had said with a sneer. "No feel for the beasts whatsoever." It was true, too. His brother could ride well enough now, but he had never liked the animals.

Almost as if he'd heard the thought, Johnny said, "I'll be taking Angelica out in the carriage this afternoon, Win. Do you want to come?"

"And ride in the brougham like a dowager?" replied Winston. "I should think not."

Johnny looked out under his dark brows at the older boy with contempt. He couldn't remember the last time Winston had done a kind act for Angelica. "That's fine, then," he said aloud, emphatically. "We'll have a better time without you."

But Winston was already halfway out the door of the library.

He had better things to do than bandy words about with his brother.

Winston had gone to the political rally to see his father in action. He worshiped the man, never seeing for an instant the self-adoration inherent in his love, for he was a duplicate of his father.

His acerbic intellect was so similar to Edmond's that there was no question in anyone's mind about where his future career would lie when he came down from Oxford. Politics and the earldom would be his destiny, and he would be well prepared for both.

He watched his father chatting comfortably with Edward Carson, who had given the main speech of the day, and the same feeling of admiration surged through him that he always felt when he saw his father in action. The man handled himself with such austere dignity, patrician to the bone. His speech was no less important than Carson's and these were times when there was much need for authoritative voices in government.

This damnable question of Home Rule that had torn the country apart had been tabled because of the war, but it was still undulating beneath the surface. It would soon be time to deal with it, once and for all.

Edward Henry Carson spoke with a judicial asperity—few words, but succinct and pointed ones. It was one of the characteristics Edmond liked best in his friend and colleague.

"There will be an insurrection," Carson said sparingly, "before the war in Europe ends."

"My dear fellow," said Edmond, "how can you think so? These ruffians have no guns, no proper army, and they have a history of fighting more among themselves than with us."

"If I have succeeded in running thirty thousand rifles into Ulster for my Volunteers—as you know I have done, Edmond —they can do the same."

"With all due respect, my dear Edward, you are *you*, and they are *they*. Rather different capacities, both intellectual and practical, wouldn't you say?"

Carson inhaled his cigar deeply before replying. He had an ascetic's face, rather like an ecclesiastic. Thin pockets of flesh marked his under-eye and thin jowls his cheeks.

"I have it on decent authority that your rebels have opened negotiations with the German government."

Edmond glanced sharply at Carson; the man never made statements he couldn't back up with fact.

"If that's so, they will be caught and hanged for treason. Does your 'decent authority' know any names?"

"Not as yet, but he may discover them."

"Will the Germans acquiesce?"

"Wouldn't you, if you had access to an enemy of your enemy's as physically close to that enemy as Ireland is to England?"

"I would, if said enemy could show itself trustworthy and *pay* for the guns."

Both men smiled at that and the conversation turned to lighter topics. But Edmond filed the thought away for future use.

10 "But Desmond," said Con with concern, "isn't it madness to consider dealing with Germany with a war on? It's high treason if you're captured!"

She'd caught Seaneen's pregnant glance at Tierney, as her brother had been apprising them of his plan.

"Con, dear," said her brother solicitously, "you know I spent several years in Germany while in the Foreign Service. I assure you that all Germans are not the ogres they are being pictured. I've already had some preliminary conversations with certain highly placed officials in Germany and I believe it's all quite feasible. They feel our little insurrection will help their war effort."

"I don't like it," said Tierney, frowning. "God knows, I'm all for finding guns for the Rising, but dealing with one tyrant in order to oust another seems immoral to me. Just think how you'd like to have the Germans as your masters, instead of the English! At least the devil you know is better than the devil you don't know."

"I'm afraid I agree with Tierney, Des. I don't like it either.

And what's more, if you're caught dealing with the enemy in wartime you'll be shot as a traitor and there won't be a damned thing any of us can do about it!" She sounded very agitated and her brother put out his hand to cover her own.

"My dear sister," he said in a kindly voice, "if there were any other way, believe me we would take it! The guns from America simply haven't materialized in the numbers we'd hoped. Just think, Con, what a disastrous condition our men will be in if we haven't sufficient weaponry. Why, we've little enough chance of success even *with* the guns. Without them . . ." He let the thought trail off into oblivion.

"It's a relatively simple plan," Des continued in his drawling aristocratic manner. "If I can convince them to send the twenty thousand guns we need, a German sub will deliver them to a fishing trawler—and we'll sail them onto a deserted strand north of here, where lorries will be waiting to distribute them to Volunteers all over Ireland."

"And the money to pay for the guns?" asked Con.

"Less than we had expected, if my German sources are correct. Of course, the weapons aren't perfect, but nonetheless it seems that the Germans are so anxious to help us provoke an incident inside the British Empire, which they can use for propaganda purposes, that they're willing to give us the guns for a pittance."

Seeing Con's still-troubled face, Seaneen interrupted.

"I haven't the scruples you have, Con, about dealing with England's enemy. I've seen too much of their treatment of our own to feel anything but contempt for their bloody Empire. We ask only for freedom, after all. No more than many other small nations are doing. No more than England is supposedly fighting the Germans about!

"Don't you see? England's war is Ireland's opportunity. It may be the *only* one in our lifetime. We *must* grasp it, no matter the personal cost!"

"Ah, Seaneen," she answered quietly in the face of his explosive rhetoric, "I love your passion and your courage . . . but Des is my brother . . . I fear for him. And I can see that you and Tierney are no less tangled up in this scheme than he." She glanced at her husband meaningfully and finished the thought. "I fear for us all."

"If I might interrupt to add a word or two, Con?" The voice

was Desmond's. She knew, looking over at him, why the scheme had possibilities—her brother's own persona made it so. He was a rich man, known in the diplomatic service. His comings and goings would hardly be suspect. Even in wartime, he could travel on the Continent and even seek converse with certain highly placed government officials without anyone thinking it unseemly. Such international impunity was exactly what the IRB needed in order to approach Germany with the scheme of helping the rebellion.

He was just the man the Brotherhood had been looking for. But why in God's name did it have to be Des they'd found? she asked herself with consternation.

His voice sounded calm and clear when he spoke.

"I think I can perhaps speak more knowledgeably about the British colonial mentality than anyone in this room. After all, I've spent the better part of the last fifteen years in the Foreign Service. Been all over Europe, you know . . . and to more than one of those colonial places the sun never sets on.

"If there's one thing I've learned of the English colonial psyche it's this—it simply isn't in their mentality to let go easily. You see, there's a part of them that truly believes the Empire rules by Divine Right . . . that bringing civilization to wild savages is a holy task, a mandate from God Almighty given especially to England. And, in a few places, there may be a bit of truth in it, if you ask me." He smiled disarmingly and Con thought over again that her brother was a dear and special man.

"What I'm getting at, Con, Tierney, is this—if we are serious about setting Ireland free, then we must harden our hearts, as they have hardened theirs. We must be willing to take our opportunities where we find them. And above all we must be willing to strike soon! While some of the old Fenians still live. We owe them that. And we owe ourselves the right to be free men."

Con was startled by the cogency of Des's arguments. He seemed so impassioned about this opportunity that she had feared he'd been tempted to rash action. Hearing him speak so rationally, it was apparent that he'd thought this through . . . yet somehow it still didn't feel right to her.

By the time they all parted, the first streaks of light were already purpling the sky of Dublin and Con watched her brother vanish into the darkened street, feeling very uneasy about his safety.

Before they'd reached home, she had more than Des to worry about. For Seaneen had told her that if Des was successful, Tierney was to captain the boat that collected the guns from the German submarine.

"I have an idea," Kitty said mischievously. "Let's plan out our dreams today. Maybe if we spell them out very carefully, they'll all come true."

Tahg watched her vivacity with absolute fascination. Kitty was the perfect counterpart for his own quiet introspection. Always bubbling over with excess energy and amazing fantasies. Part of what enticed him about her was her ability to fantasize . . . her ability to see herself clearly in a better life. Never had he known anyone with her astonishing determination about the future.

"All right," he said. "You start, because you're so good at it."

She laughed prettily and lay back against the stone stoop of the house, waving her arms expansively.

"Someday," she began, closing her eyes for better clarity of vision, "I shall be a famous actress. Able to move people to tears with a poignant gesture—able to make them laugh at a toss of my head. Men will throw themselves at my feet, but I shall tell them I am spoken for and that, unlike other famous ladies of the theater, I am true to my beloved." She glanced meaningfully at Tahg, to make sure he understood what she was saying, then continued blithely. She was teasing him and he knew it, but he also heard the ring of truth in what she said.

"I shall wear clothes made by a famous couturier, favoring silks and velvets, I think. And lace, of course. I shall travel all over the world . . . to the Vale of Kashmir and Katmandu, to South Sea paradises and the wilds of Australia. Perhaps even to the snow-covered tundra of Imperial Russia to perform before the Tsar."

"And whom will you perform for in the wilds of Australia, might I ask?" said Tahg, getting into the spirit of the game as he watched her.

"For the aborigines, of course! And you'll have to protect me from any unfriendly natives that we may encounter."

"Then I'll be going with you?" he asked, pleased at the idea.

"Well, I should hope so," she said playfully. "A famous actress can't go wandering around the world without an entourage."

"And what if I want to be *more* than just part of your 'entourage'?"

"We'll have to see about that when the time comes," she said offhandedly. "Right now, however, you must tell me *your* fantasy."

"I'm afraid it isn't nearly as good as yours, Kitty. I have a hard time seeing anything for me beyond Ireland and the war that's coming."

"Just because it's your parents' war, does that mean you must get into it?" she said vehemently. "You could do so many other things, Tahg. Be a scholar or a tradesman, or, or . . ."

"A tinker or a tailor?" he laughed as he responded. "Whatever I'm to be, Kitty, I must be one thing first. I must be true to Ireland. Because of my parents, you know . . . and because of all I've seen and heard. But also because of me. I must try to help in my small way.

"Besides," his voice sounded cheerier, "you wouldn't want me to hide behind the door when the action started, would you?"

"I most certainly would, if it could keep you from getting killed or worse!"

"I don't intend to get killed," he said, "but I do intend to do my part."

"Oh, you're going to spoil the game if you can't fantasize better than this!" she said petulantly, tossing her head so that her burnished hair bounced as if electrified.

"Then perhaps we should try a new game," he said as he reached for her, kissing her with such confidence that, for once, flustered and uncertain, Kitty pulled away and said it was time to go home.

I love you, Tahg O'Connor, and I must be very very careful about that, Kitty thought as she bade him good-bye and skipped lightly up the stairs to her family's dingy little tenement flat. It was a lightness she didn't feel in the least, but she'd be damned if she'd ever let anyone know how things got her down.

She could not afford to lose her head over this lovely poetic boy, for she did not have time right now to fall in love. Kitty looked around the tiny airless place where she lived with her father, two sisters and a brother. Bereft of the touches of a mother's hand these seven years since her mother had finally succumbed to the bronchial troubles that had withered her before her time and laid her to rest in a pauper's grave.

With a resolute frown she put the teakettle on the ancient stove to boil.

Picking up a cracked and mottled teacup from the cupboard shelf, Kitty held it up in front of her and spoke to it. "You poor ugly thing," she intoned as if the very condition of the teacup made her resolve all the stronger. "You were cheap and ugly when you were new and now you're cracked and bruised to boot. You're not what I want from life, you poor old vessel! I want porcelain and silver and crystal and linen for my table. Not you. Never you!"

She put the cup down in its equally shabby saucer and poured herself a cup of tea from the battered old crockery pot. Then she walked to the grimy window and looked out onto the gray street that had seemed so sunny a moment ago with Tahg.

"Oh Tahg," she breathed, and her breath made little mist clouds on the window. "How I wish I could just love you and marry you. But I cannot live this linoleum life anymore!"

She had the wherewithal to escape, she was sure of it. She had talent and a rare gift of memory for lines. And she was pretty, far prettier in fact with her wild auburn hair and big blue eyes than anyone in her family had ever admitted to her. But people noticed her on the street . . . the tall graceful girl in the shabby clothes who carried herself like a queen. The girl with the blue-violet eyes and the shaggy mane of hair that was somewhere between chestnut and auburn, that moved when she moved as if it had a life of its own.

And men wanted her . . . why, from the time she'd first shown the barest hint of womanhood men had made leering remarks and lewd comments at every turn.

Oh yes, she thought, looking out the window on the slum that had been her home all her life. I've the wherewithal to escape this, and to have all that I want out of life. But I must be terribly careful not to get sidetracked.

Once I've done what I must do, there'll be time enough for Tahg. Just the thought of him sent a shiver of remembered pleasure through her young body.

If only he were rich, things could be so different for them, she thought wistfully. But to marry him as he was, to live a lifetime trapped in poverty . . . No! She would force that thought from her mind. It was entirely out of the question.

She would correct her speech and learn to behave like a lady. It was easy enough to do; working as she did as a maid for a fine family allowed her plenty of opportunity for mimicry. And every minute that she could, she would haunt the theater. Why, she had almost every nuance of the leading actress' latest part down pat now. In another little while, she would offer herself for an audition and then it would all begin again . . . her life as it was meant to be. As it *would* be!

Kitty put down the teacup and picked up the script she had borrowed from the library. She knew the words perfectly . . . that was the easy part. Now she must breathe life into them. She would have only a few minutes with the man at the Abbey Theatre and her whole life depended on what she could do with those minutes.

11

∝ The Dublin I arrived in, during the late spring of 1915, was a very different place from that of my youth. Not that I hadn't been there often enough over the years, but only when one stays in a city for a long period of time can one really feel its pulse rate.

And an erratic pulse it was in that fateful year. The great labor strike of 1913 had so underscored the plight of the poor that they had substituted militancy for the lethargy I remembered. Hostile stares greeted anyone who appeared rich, and the dustbin children seemed to be everywhere, with their great hungry eyes and their filthy, bare, battered feet.

At the opposite end of the economic spectrum from the dustbin children was the town house we'd bought in Dublin, at No. 32 Waterloo Road, Ballsbridge. It was only a twenty-minute brisk walk from Trinity College, convenient to everything and quite fashionable in those times.

It was a perfect example of the Georgian architectural form and we were happy to have found it. Large gracious windows faced the tree-lined street and the house seemed always full of sunshine. The Georgians decreased window size proportionately by floor, so that the third-floor windows are always one third the height of those on the first floor, and all in all it was a handsome old place.

In such houses the eye is drawn most, I think, to the door; in our case a robust red one, surmounted by a classical lintel and two supporting columns. The transom sported a lovely peacock-tail pattern of glass, and together with the highly polished brass knocker, nameplate and knob, it gave the house a festive and elegant aspect.

I had used my suffrage activities and the publication of my new book as the excuse for an indefinite length of visiting in Dublin, and several of my children had opted to stay behind with Edmond for the duration. I missed Jamie and Merry and Win, who had remained at Manningham, but I had no great concern for their well-being without me. Win was always happiest when with Edmond, and the twins were content as long as they had each other.

For me there was a different rhythm to life with only Johnny and Angelica, and I began to enjoy the contrast. My daughter was so self-possessed a child most of the time that it was marvelous to see the animation that suffused her at the prospect of being near Tahg. He was still at St. Enda's, but could get home easily enough on weekends if we supplied the fare, and of course he would be at home in Dublin all summer long while school was on holiday. She quite hero-worshiped the boy and I suppose with good reason, as he had always taken inordinate pains to be good to her. Johnny, too, loved Tahg and shared his passionate commitment to the idea of rebellion.

Johnny was nearly nine years old when I returned to Dublin. My intention was to stay there for as long as possible. I knew from Con that a rising was imminent. If Seaneen was to be in danger of death, then it seemed to me that he and Johnny must meet, while there was yet time. That conviction had been growing in me for a long while, prompted in great measure by the child himself.

My youngest son was a complex personality. Dark as my others were fair-complected, in family gatherings he seemed a rock among the roses. Where they were tall and lean, he was squarely built and muscular. Johnny was good at his lessons, although not scholarly by nature, and he came to his conclusions by a different route from his siblings. "He has a different turn of mind," said the tutor. "He seeks for different answers." And, so he did. He loved Ireland from his earliest days; from the moment he could read, he pursued her history and anything that smacked of rebellion with unwavering devotion.

Johnny loved his brother Jamie and both his sisters, but he and Winston never saw eye to eye on anything. His cousin Tahg he adored and followed around like a puppy when they were together. I knew they corresponded and that Tahg kept him supplied with Fenian information and the Wild Harp essays, but I never had the heart to interfere, for Johnny took to the Cause like his father's son. Seaneen and I had stolen our few precious moments from the gods . . . but I lived to learn that they are inexorable in claiming what should be theirs.

Perhaps it was because I would not deem it sin, what we had done. Indeed, I clung to the memory of a single summer through all the years as a drowning man to a spar. But I sometimes wonder, if I had been more penitent, would the gods have been less relentless in the payment they demanded? Or perhaps such thoughts are no more than an old woman's foolishness.

For all his good nature, Johnny was restless and rebellious; he brooded over his estrangement from Edmond, chafed by the unfairness of his ostracism, not knowing why such should be so. He carried anger and resentment in him like seeds about to sprout, and while it was understandable, it was also dangerous.

As with all mothers, I loved each child differently according to his or her nature. But Johnny, the child of my heart, I always feared to lose.

Somewhere mixed into all my anxieties about him was the conviction that Seaneen must not die without knowing his son; if there were to be a rising, he would be in grave danger. This was the argument I used to rationalize my trip to Dublin. In truth, perhaps the passage of ten years' time seemed atonement enough—and I was very lonely.

I felt mixed emotions about introducing Johnny to his father —I wanted them to love each other . . . I wanted the acceptance for Johnny from Seaneen that he'd never had from Edmond. But it also terrified me to think of the dangers along that path of knowledge. The seduction of Ireland was awesome enough for a boy, but the seduction of being loved by a hero might prove more than either of us could handle.

Edmond, meanwhile, had his hands full in Parliament. He remained vehemently anti-Home Rule (Edmond was nothing if not consistent) and he'd been in the thick of the Carsonists from the beginning. Of course in 1915 there was the war for him to deal with, too.

To my amazement and his credit, Edmond offered to take our three eldest children, who had stayed with him in Sligo, to London for the coming season. It was time Win observed the workings of Westminster, he said, and since Jamie was becoming quite the little historian, it wouldn't hurt for him to be party to the making of history. It was a great relief to me when he offered, for I'd anticipated a battle over my decision to spend the winter in Dublin. Edmond's announcement made life easier.

We'd been in Dublin for a little over two weeks when I finally screwed up my courage for the fateful introduction. It was my intention to make the moment seem as innocent as possible to Johnny, so I sent word to Seaneen via Tierney asking if he would meet us in St. Stephen's Green as we walked there the following afternoon. I hoped it would seem to the child a casual-enough encounter and I felt that being in so public a place would keep the impropriety of it at a minimum, should anyone see us. I expect I also needed a place that I could bolt from at a moment's notice, if my courage failed me.

How can I tell you what I felt at the prospect of seeing Seaneen once again? Uncertainty . . . elation. The nervousness of a schoolgirl . . . the terrors of a woman. Would he look the same? Would he think me mad to have come now to stir anew ecstasies and agonies best forgotten? How could I see him without weeping? How be near him without throwing myself into his arms? How could I speak of casual things when I carried ten years of desperate longings within my breast?

What if he didn't love me anymore? What . . . God help us both . . . if he did?

I played the scene a thousand times in my head, my agitation increasing with each new enactment.

I dressed and redressed; this suit was too sedate, that dress too fanciful. I tore rings from my fingers and left a trail of discarded garments in my frenzied wake. I finally settled on an elegant day dress with buttons at the collar and cuffs. I was so nervous that I had to have a servant help me fasten them.

And so, at 3:00 P.M. on an ordinary Thursday, Seaneen O'Sullivan and Johnny Manningham stood staring at each other on a quiet pathway in a park that was soon to be a battle-field. I felt as if all motion in the universe had ceased abruptly. The fact that I had intended them to meet for every moment of the previous ten years didn't prepare me in the least for the experience of it.

He was exactly as I remembered him.

"I'm very pleased to meet you, sir," Johnny said clearly in his boyish voice, when I had introduced them.

"And I you, lad," replied Seaneen, his deep voice husky with emotion. He told me later that his heart was pounding so heavily in his chest that he thought we both must surely hear it.

"My mother has told me a great deal about you, Mr. O'Sullivan," Johnny added hastily. "Everyone knows what a patriot you are, sir, so I'm especially glad to have a chance to meet you!" He looked up sheepishly at me, then said, "I'm the bit of a rebel in our family, I believe, sir. I'm the one who's always arguing for Ireland at the dinner table." His eyes were shining at the thought of meeting so heroic a figure. In Johnny and Tahg's hagiography, Seaneen was just this side of sainthood.

I thought I might die of the constriction of heart and throat and lungs that clutched me and the tears that welled. Looking into Seaneen's eyes, I saw the truth understood there, in those deep pools of world-weary knowledge; the truth of all the years we'd spent apart. I closed my eyes for a moment as if to shut out my own knowledge, and when I opened them I saw an immensity of love in the face of the man I'd loved with such strange consequences.

He and Johnny were speaking animatedly, Johnny asking questions, Seaneen looking over at me from time to time as he answered them. I said no word but watched the two, and tried to quiet my own heart in the process. Eventually, Seaneen lifted his eyes to mine again and he said to Johnny, "If your mother will permit it, lad, I'll take you to meet some of the people we've been talking about. But for now, I must speak with her alone. 'Tis a long while since we've seen each other."

The boy looked entranced at the prospect of meeting the legendary men he'd dreamed of since he was old enough to have discovered Irish patriotism through Tahg. "Oh, thank you, sir, I'd like that!" he said, looking up at me for approval.

I smiled at his excitement and somehow managed to say, "Of course, Johnny. You may go with Mr. O'Sullivan whenever you wish. He's a very old and dear friend of mine." My son and I had already discussed the inadvisability of telling Edmond of this meeting. Johnny thought it was because of his father's politics that I had made this stipulation, so it seemed to him a delicious secret we shared. He shook Seaneen's hand in a most manly fashion and ran on ahead to give us our moment of privacy.

When the boy had gone, Seaneen and I stood in an embrace of eyes that erased the intervening years. Can you imagine the poignancy of that moment? Of seeing one whom you have loved and lost, alive again and within your reach? He was older, his face more lined and careworn, but that only made him seem the more beautiful and more real to me. This phantom of my dreams and hopes once again was real.

"Shall we walk for a bit so we can talk?" I suggested, trying hard to control my voice, and he nodded.

"Aye, My Lady," he replied, and my heart beat harder at the old endearment. "It seems we have much to talk about."

"You knew him right away?" I asked.

"Indeed. He's very like my father. And I've dreamt of how he might be, of course, through all the years. Nearly as often as I've dreamt of you."

I stood still for a moment before replying carefully; it was as if the effort of calling forth what I wished to say rendered all other effort impossible. "If it were not for the dreaming, Seaneen, my own love, I never could have survived those first terrible years without you. Your face was always before me, your strong arms round me in the nights. Dear God, how did we live it through?" I saw the heartbreak in his expression and noticed how he clenched and unclenched the gnarled fists at his sides. I longed so to touch him that my hands seemed to have taken on a life of their own. If I was struggling hard for control, I knew he, too, struggled.

"He seems a fine boy," he said steadily, to change the subject. He brushed his hand across his eyes to stay the moisture there.

"He's a wonderful boy! Smart and strong and good-hearted. But he doesn't belong at Manningham, Seaneen. He carries too much of you within him. Often enough I've wished I could just send him to you."

"His relationship to Edmond?"

"They tolerate each other, no more . . . although no word of scandal has ever been spoken."

Seaneen nodded, glancing at Johnny, where he stood several yards away from us. "And now?"

"I've brought him here hoping you would want to get to know him." My words sounded sensible, even to me. I had brought my son to Dublin to meet his father. After that, what happened would be in God's hands.

"And of you and me, My Lady?" he asked uncertainly. "I've carried you in my heart for so long a while you sometimes seem to me a figment of my imagination. Are you to remain only that, now that you're here? I'll abide by your wishes."

I looked down at the clenched hands, the whitened knuckles, and then up again to his face. I saw the terrible strain behind Seaneen's eyes. I wanted very much to make him understand everything that was in my heart. So I spoke very slowly, for it was important that it be only the truth.

"All those years ago, my love, I came very close to dying over what we had done."

He started to protest and I stopped him. "Not because I thought it wrong. I never did! But because of the harm that came to Angelica. And, of course, because I could not have you forever. Yet even in my terrible sorrow, I clung to the memory of our time together. I hated myself for what had happened to my child . . . but I loved you, Seaneen, and I blessed you for what you had given me that I'd been without all my life." I saw that he was watching me as I spoke, as if memorizing me.

"Despite the horror of that first year, I think it was the love I felt for you that kept me alive.

"Angelica was so very damaged, so sick . . . and I so fragmented—and yet, in a bizarre way, the child I carried comforted me. Your child and mine, the one love child of my life."

He smiled the smallest, saddest smile, and I saw in the weariness of his gaze how very much besides a child we had both borne because of our love.

"Then eventually, Johnny was born; Angelica began to heal . . . and I had no choice but to make a life for myself and my children."

"And Edmond?"

"He bears no love for me, but he is a gentleman at the end of it, and we have made our peace."

Seaneen nodded; I could almost hear him speculate what scars had been incurred before the truce was drawn. He cleared his throat audibly. "You don't mind if I spend time with the lad?"

"He's your son, my love," I said as gently as I could. "I hope you will grow to know each other—that's why I've come. He worships you from afar and he thinks of nothing but Ireland and rebellion. I shall stay here with him as long as I can . . . through the winter at least."

There seemed little left to say . . . or rather there seemed so very much to say that it was pointless to say only part of it.

"I think I would give up everything I am," Seaneen said very softly, almost shyly, "everything I've devoted my life to, if I could but hold you in my arms once more, My Lady."

I felt the hot tears burn my lids; I started to speak, not knowing how to voice what I felt.

"It has taken me ten years to find the courage to say this, Seaneen, but I came here intending to be with you, if you'll have me . . . in whatever way I can."

He looked at me, uncomprehendingly.

"I cannot compromise my family nor jeopardize Edmond's career in Parliament with any breath of scandal. He is who he is, but he's done his best with me through the years for propriety's sake, and in conscience I can do no less for him.

"But, if we are discreet and you are willing to have me, I will come to you. Whenever and however often I can."

Seaneen looked at me strangely and I could see the tears glistening in his eyes. "I'll wait for you, then, My Lady," he said softly, and reaching up with his big callused hand, he touched my cheek with the backs of his fingers. "Tierney will know where to find me when you're ready."

So we promised each other everything with our eyes in that one moment, and then he left me. Walking ahead quickly, he caught up to Johnny in a few strides and I saw him tousle the boy's hair as he bade him good-bye.

Johnny came running back to me as I took my handkerchief from my pocket to try to hide my lack of composure behind it.

He looked at me oddly for a moment, as if he would ask me a

question. Then I saw him change his mind and, in a curiously adult gesture, he took my arm and, patting it, said, "Don't worry, Mum. It will be all right. Mr. O'Sullivan is a nice man." As if that explained everything.

"I love you, Johnny," I told him.

"I love you, too," he replied, and we made our way out of the park and hailed a cab for home.

It proved more difficult than I had anticipated for me to be with Seaneen at all. My children were older and more curious. I was better known in Dublin because of my books and the suffrage issue; and, of course, I had to be doubly discreet because Edmond's career was so very visible.

Nonetheless, about a week later I was able to arrange an evening when the children were with Con and the servants were not on call. One glorious night in which to catch up on the dreams of what seemed a lifetime.

I tried hard not to worry that I was more than ten years older now—my body past that first lovely glow of youth that makes all things beautiful—my face beginning to show the lines that, when I was kind to myself, I thought full of character.

What would he think of me after all the years of waiting? Would his memory have so enshrined me that I could no longer measure up? Or would we find that there could be no recapturing the bliss remembered so painstakingly through a decade? I had worried myself nearly into a frenzy by the time I made my way surreptitiously from my house to a hired carriage. I dared not use my own, of course.

Seaneen still lived in the same small flat—two rooms hallowed in my memory so well that I could have reconstructed them nail for nail at any moment over ten years' time.

He opened the door to my knock and I slipped inside, unwilling to stand too long in the hallway, lest I be seen. Once inside, neither of us seemed capable of movement; we stood transfixed. Oh, blessed moment, flooded with love and peace and joy. Somehow I was in his arms and he was squeezing me so hard I couldn't breathe, and we were both speaking and kissing and laughing and crying and holding on as if we'd never again let go.

I felt as if I were falling into him, into his love, into his strength. Oh, remembered strength, that I'd missed so gravely.

And then the laughter and the talking stopped and we were in each other's arms again, but this time with a different fervor. And he was tugging at my clothes and I at his. I felt his hands hard on my skin at last and all fear about my body's inadequacies vanished, for it was what he wanted and perfect in that wanting. Just as he was perfect for me.

We made love with such old exquisite knowledge and such new breathtaking bliss. And I was lost again in this man who was my only love, just as I'd been lost so long ago.

"Do you know how often I've made love to you in my mind over the years?" he asked me as we lay together, exhausted and happy.

"As often as I've wished for you, I wonder?" I replied, awash in contentment and the sense of coming home.

"When I went to you in the park—with Johnny—I was sure you wouldn't come to me."

"Why?"

"I don't know exactly," he said slowly. "You looked so grand, so much the lady. So in control of your life. I suppose I felt I could do naught but disturb your peace of mind."

I laughed at the understatement of the thought. "That indeed you have done, my love. From the first time I laid eyes on you, Seaneen O'Sullivan, you have disturbed my peace of mind."

I looked up into his face then, our bodies touching comfortingly, and nestled in beside him as close as two can be.

"I've made a sort of decision about you," I said.

He smiled, such a lovely sight it had always seemed to me, the young smile in the world-weary face. "And that is . . . ?"

"To spend whatever time is allowed us together. Now. This year. Next year. For all our lives. Whenever and wherever it can be. Never to waste another precious year of our love, as I've wasted so many. Never to struggle over the right or wrong of it, but simply to be grateful that you are in the world and that you love me."

He looked into my face for a long time, as if digesting what I had said, then he folded his body over mine, holding me so firmly that I could barely breathe. He buried his head in the crook of my shoulder and I felt the strangest movement in his back and shoulders. It took me a long moment to realize that he was sobbing silently.

We held each other until morning in a peace I don't think

either of us had ever known. We made vows to each other that night more sacred than any of my life. But in truth we needed none, for the bonds between us had been forged in another time and place and only the strange circumstances of our lives had kept us from fulfilling them.

Johnny finished reading the Wild Harp's latest essay and stared out the window still holding it in his hand. It was *wonderful* to imagine being able to stir people like the Harper did.

To be able to express what was in your own heart and the hearts of so many others was such an amazing gift! Why, he had kept every Wild Harp column that he'd ever gotten from Tahg. He had a stack of them carefully hidden in his closet, far from prying eyes.

It was his secret life. His hope for the future that was embodied in that hidden pile of papers. Someday, he, too, would fight for Ireland. But not as the Harper did . . . with words. He, Johnny Manningham, would fight with guns and fists. He would be a soldier in the rebellion that Tahg said was coming. Johnny had always known that he would participate. Once Angelica had asked him if he loved Ireland so much because he knew it angered his father, and he'd had to ponder that before answering. After all, he had ample reason to want to strike back at his father for all the neglect and disdain that was his portion from the man . . . and Irish freedom was a sore topic, indeed, in their house.

But it wasn't that, he'd finally told her. He always took great pains to be truthful with Angelica, not only because she deserved it, but because she had the uncanny ability to see right through you if you tried to lie.

No, he'd said at last. He loved Ireland . . . because . . . he loved Ireland! It was part of him, like his limbs or brain. Every story he read or song he heard stirred him, made him feel part of something important. He *belonged* with the Irish—just as he did not belong with his father. It was simply the way it was.

Angelica had nodded, accepting the truth of it. She always listened to him . . . when he recited heroic ballads or read her the Harper's essays. When he talked about life and the future . . . when he sought solace about his feelings of displacement. She listened and offered advice or sympathy. She could be relied on.

Merry was great fun to have for a sister and he missed her some, but there was less to their friendship than with Angelica. Merry was adorable and funny and lovable, but she was so sure of her place in the world, so sure of being loved, that she could never fully understand his pain. But Angelica was displaced, too. She had been hurt by life, so she could understand his hurt, his anger.

Mum could be relied on, too, of course. She loved him in a special way. It wasn't that she loved the others less than he, exactly . . . it was that she loved him more.

He looked at the paper in his hand again. There were several things in it he wanted to commit to memory before he put it away with the others. Several things he intended to discuss with Mr. O'Sullivan when he saw him this afternoon.

Johnny smiled at the prospect of seeing Mr. O'Sullivan. Next to Tahg and Angelica, he was the person who best understood what he wished to become. ✑

12

Desmond FitzGibbon
FitzGibbon Hall
Rosskeerough, Co. Sligo
11 July 1915

My adorable sisters (what fun to have you two together in Dublin for a change, so that one letter suffices!),

You will be justifiably startled to hear that I feel obliged to finally answer your many inquiries about the state of my matrimonial prospects. (Oh yes, I know you both attempt to be subtle in your investigations, but nonetheless your efforts are quite transparent.) And, yes again, I *know* you mean only to encourage me toward happiness—and that, my dear gels, is why I have decided to expose to you my innermost thoughts on the subject of marriage and Desmond FitzGibbon.

As you well know, I have spent a lifetime using Evelyn's death as the excuse for my bachelorhood. In all fairness, during the early years, there was reason to do so; doubtless, had she lived, the course of my own life would have been charted differently. Nonetheless, I have had ample opportunity since then to marry, and as I have not done so, there must be more to the story, don't you think? And so I bare my heart. . . .

If the truth be known, I suspect myself of being unsuited to matrimony. I doubt seriously that I could ever love as faithfully and deeply as does Tierney, for example. And while I would be less coldhearted, surely, than Edmond, I've sometimes wondered if I would be any less a failure as a husband. I'm a restless sort, my darlings, and alas, I suspect, a far more shallow one in my loves than either of you. Beside your still waters, I am naught, I fear, but a babbling brook.

When I stay in one place, I long for another . . . when I love one woman, I do not cease to wonder what diversion the rest of womankind might offer me. I'm quite contented by the company of men (not sexually, needless to say!) and sometimes wonder if I should not have made the military my choice of career, as it seems to offer all the criteria I need for happiness: adventure, the gypsy life, a sense of danger and no permanent encumbrances to keep me from my wanderlust.

As to children? *There*, I have missed something precious, and I know it. I suspect I might have done rather a decent job of fathering. The two years Tahg spent with me were among the happiest of my life—and I suppose that in my own heart of hearts, he will always seem to me the son I never had. And, forgive me, never will.

Which brings me, dear hearts, to the reason I am writing this soul-baring epistle to both of you today.

You see, I have drawn a will. (No, no, there is nothing wrong with my health, I assure you, but my solicitor tells me it is a sensible thing to do.) In it, I have left a small bequest to each of you and to Win, Merry, Jamie, Angelica and Johnny. FitzGibbon Hall and the bulk of my fortune, I have left to Tahg. So, it seems only fair that I explain to you why I have done so.

In the first place, I love the lad . . . more than you might imagine. In the second, it has always seemed to me unconscionable that Father cut you, Constance, from his will—so, in part, it seems to me that Tahg will receive no more than would have been his share had your own legacy remained intact. Or, for that matter, had you and Tierney ever allowed Beth and me to give you your fair share, as we tried so diligently to do.

Your children, my dear Beth, are so well provided for —Edmond's estate is vast and your own inheritance and earnings are considerable—that I know I need not fear for their futures. And, too, they have at their backs the security of a lifetime of privilege and a place in society. This safety young Tahg does not share with them. So I am hoping that in your perennial good-heartedness, Bethy, you will understand my gesture and allow me the joy of giving this gift of continuity to my nephew. You see, I have a lovely fantasy that through Tahg's line, a whole new dynasty of FitzGibbons will flourish into the future—what difference if the name O'Connor be the one they bear—it was once the name of kings—and God knows it has been borne always in this generation with honor.

So there it is, my dears. I do so hope that you approve. I'm off shortly on a bit of a journey, as you know, and as I am not certain that I will see you before my departure, I shall trust this to the post.

Be assured now, as forever, of my love,

> Your errant brother,
> Desmond

∾ Con and I read the momentous letter with very mixed emotions. Joy, of course, for this generous and sensible gift to Tahg. But each of us read in the other's eyes the sure knowledge that Desmond had taken this step in case the mission he was undertaking be his last adventure. ∾

Desmond FitzGibbon adjusted the straps of his traveling bag, then straightened his full frame to a standing position, as if satisfied with his work.

He glanced at himself in the full-length, oval mirror, pleased that he looked like any other well-bred gentleman embarking on a European pleasure trip.

"Off to snag yourself one of those Austrian princesses or Italian contessas, eh? You sly young devil," Old Bertie had boomed approvingly when he'd heard the news of Des's trip at the Sligo Harriers Meet the previous Saturday.

"Now, now, Bertie," he'd replied amiably. "I've not the slightest intention of taking a wife. And if I did, you may rest assured I'd find one of our homegrown models more to my liking."

"Who said anything about a wife, lad? Lord, no! I was thinking more of a bit of sport-fucking. I've heard those European ladies can teach you a thing or two."

Desmond laughed at the lecherous grin wrinkling up Sir Bertram's face beneath his monocle. "You have my word, Bertie, that if I learn anything worthwhile from anyone, you'll be the first to know!"

Des smiled in remembrance of the conversation. The best thing that could happen would be for everyone to think him a frivolous, rich young man off to seek an outlet for his high spirits on the Continent.

It would do the Brotherhood no good to have any suspicion fall on him now. No need to let the world know where his sympathies lay.

Fortunately, there was nothing to keep him in Sligo at the moment. No reason at all why he couldn't go to Germany to do his part for Ireland.

Con was in high spirits as she sang; Tommy could see her mood in her eyes as he accompanied her on the guitar. She had a clear, ringing voice, well suited to the old songs. Long ago he had heard her singing to Tahg and encouraged her to sing at the pub with him and Tierney from time to time. Now, when they sang together, her exuberance was contagious:

"A Gypsy rover came over the hill
Down through the valley so shady
He whistled and sang till the green
   woods rang
And he won the heart of a lady.

>   "She left her father's castle gate,
>   She left her own fond lover.
>   She left her servants and her estate
>   To follow her Gypsy lover."

Con smiled at Tierney as she sang; "The Whistling Gypsy" was one of her favorites—it seemed reminiscent of her own love story.

>   "Her father saddled up his fastest steed
>   He roamed the valley all over.
>   He sought his daughter at great speed,
>   And her whistling Gypsy lover."

Of course her own father had never sought her out, she thought sadly as she sang. Not once, before his death, had he relented in his anger at her disobedience. She pushed the old ache from her mind, and thought of the lovely romantic lyric. She, too, had followed her heart, just as the lady of the song had done.

>   "He came at last to a mansion fine,
>   Down by the river Clady.
>   And there was music and there was wine,
>   For the Gypsy and his lady.

>   " 'He is no Gypsy, my father,' she said,
>   'But lord of these lands all over.
>   And I will stay till my dying day
>   With my whistling Gypsy lover.' "

Tierney and Tommy joined in the rollicking chorus:

>   "Ah, dee do, ah dee do da day
>   Ah dee do, ah dee da-dy
>   He whistled and sang till the green
>   woods rang
>   And he won the heart of a lady."

They all laughed happily as the song ended. There was such freedom in singing; such an outlet for joy or sorrow, excitement or frustration.

"I'm sorry I didn't turn out to be a nobleman in disguise, my Beauty, when you ran away with me. It would have made life a touch easier for you," said Tierney, reaching affectionately for his wife. It was uncanny how he always seemed able to read her thoughts.

"Well now, you can't have everything, can you?" she said, smiling cheerfully as she reached for his hand. "And besides, you *are* the noblest man I know."

"You could have had more," he persisted.

"Indeed?" she replied "I might have had a marriage like poor Bethy's, with plenty of money and nothing to sustain my heart." She looked meaningfully at Tierney and he returned the glance.

"On that note, my darlin' boys and girls, I think I'll take my leave of you," said Tommy knowingly. He loved the love between the two of them; it reminded him of his own marriage, as it had been in the good times.

Con and Tierney let their friend out of the flat and, having closed the door behind him, Con turned and found her husband's arms waiting for her.

"I wish I could give you everything," he whispered into her hair as he held her.

"You have given me everything," she breathed back as she lifted her mouth to his to be kissed. The quickening she felt deep inside herself, as his lips found hers, made her realize how completely she meant what she had said to him.

" 'I will stay till my dying day . . .' " she repeated softly from the song, but his eager mouth cut off all possibility of speech, and as she felt herself lifted—oh, how easily he could lift her—and carried to their bed, Con knew that he was life itself to her, as he had been from the first moment. Her Whistling Gypsy, her Minstrel Boy. Her everything.

13

Tierney finished putting away the instruments and began to straighten up the chairs and tables in a signal that the night was over at last. Tommy and he were alone; the last customer had finally straggled out. Tonight he was grateful that the last of them had left early for he was bone weary and he was preoccupied with worry about Con. Tommy, sensing his concern, walked toward him and, pulling out a chair, motioned Tierney to stop working and talk.

"What's eating you?" he asked as Tierney poured himself a pint and sat down.

"I'm worried about Con. The Castle is breathing down the Harper's neck again."

Tommy laughed shortly. "And no wonder after that last bolt she let loose about conscription."

"It was a rare beauty, wasn't it?" Tierney said ruefully. "But you know as well as I there's no deterring her when her mind's made up. She's furious about the idea of drafting Irishmen into England's war and she's not about to keep still on the subject."

"How the hell could they find out her identity, lad? There's but a handful of us who know."

"True enough, but this is wartime and what the Harper's up to is sedition. Whitehall doesn't take kindly to treasonous activity."

"You know what Seaneen quotes about treason, laddie?

'Treason doth never prosper. What's the reason?
For if it prosper, none dare call it Treason.' "

Tierney smiled at his friend's attempt at humor, but he was too concerned to laugh.

"There's no getting her to lay low, I suppose?" asked Tommy.

Tierney's facial expression in response to the question left no doubt about that.

"Then we must take special pains to make sure nobody else gets wind of it."

Tommy looked closely at Tierney, his friend, almost a son, and for several years now his partner in the pub. The man looked worried, and probably with good reason. It wouldn't hurt to try and lighten his spirits.

"What's the word from the lad at St. Enda's?" Tahg was as close to a grandchild as he would ever have.

"He loves the place . . . and Pearse, and Willy and everything about it. From the sound of it, the whole of it is as steeped in mythology as if the faeries built it. Fine stuff, all that, to fill a lad with a sense of destiny about this old island of ours. I heard somebody say the other day that Cuchulain is the most important member of the staff at St. Enda's!"

Tommy roared at that, and they both laughed, the tension broken.

"Well, thank God for that," he said. "We'll need him on our side when the fighting starts."

They finished tidying up the place and walked out together into the crisp night air.

Next morning Tierney left the house early. He felt rested and in better spirits than the night before.

Tierney walked into the pub, grateful that it was empty at this time of day. As he reached Tommy, he was startled to see his friend's eyes full of tears.

"Rob's gone," the man said, his voice hollow as a drum.

"How?" asked Tierney, as monosyllabically.

"They'd been after him since he escaped from prison. Constabulary spotted him, followed him to the house where he was being sheltered by a girl he knew. . . . They shot him as he left at daybreak two days ago."

"What can I say to you, man?" asked Tierney, heartsick at the story. "It's the worst news that could be in the world!" He put his hand on his friend's shoulder and squeezed hard in a gesture of support, remembering his own anguish the night his little son had been taken from them.

Tommy looked past him, tears glistening on his apple cheeks. "You know, I can see him as he used to be when he was just a wee lad," he said, reaching into his apron for his handkerchief. "Always scrappy. Always the first into the fray. Never a fear for himself, mind you, only for his brother Liam, who was smaller. He used to follow Liam at a distance so's the bullies wouldn't bother the lad. When Liam realized what he was up to he was so furious he nearly punched his brother into the next week. But Rob was like that. Good-hearted, you know." He blew his nose as if to punctuate the thought and keep control of himself.

Tierney stood immobilized at his side.

"There's no one left now," Tommy said finally. "I'm the last of us." He hesitated a moment, then said, " 'Tis an unnatural act to bury your sons, lad. An unnatural act for them to go before you."

"I'm so sorry, Tommy," said Tierney, meaning it with all his heart. "What can I do to help you, man?" The thought of his love for Tahg raced through him. Dear God, how does a man cope with such a loss?

Tommy shook his head and rose from the table, standing shakily.

"You can help me pay the bastards back!" he said in answer to the question.

He moved past Tierney unseeing and, pulling off his apron as he went, staggered out of the shop and into the hazy sunlight.

Clarke handed the elegantly dressed man his tobacco and bade him good day amiably. Then, ringing a bell for the boy who ran the shop in his absence, he signaled to him to take over and ambled down the stairs to the cellar.

Three men were there already: Seaneen O'Sullivan, Tierney O'Connor and Tommy McGowan. Since Rob's murder, McGowan had become the most indefatigable worker they had. He was the ideal recruit, in fact, thought Clarke as he assessed the men . . . no ties, no desires beyond vengeance.

"I've asked you to come to discuss the Volunteers," Clarke told them without preamble.

Tierney watched him with fascination. There was no outward semblance of remarkable strength or manliness about the fellow, yet he was made of some impenetrable material. Perhaps it was no wonder, when all that he had suffered had scraped away the hull and left only the tough and stringy husk.

"Aye," Seaneen was the first to speak. "It seems to be growing into a formidable force these days. MacNeill claims to have twenty thousand men at his disposal."

"Just as well," said Tommy, "I've just come back from Antrim. Every man jack of an Orangeman is signed up with Carson's Volunteers to defend the Empire."

Thomas grunted in response. "I think some good will come of MacNeill's crowd."

"Why?" Tierney asked the question.

"They'll all march up and down the streets and distract the Peelers and the IRB will have a better cover than we could have hoped for. But"—he looked pointedly at the faces in the dim light—"we'll have to control MacNeill's Volunteers."

"By getting our own men in there?" offered Seaneen.

"By getting our men on the committee that's running the show."

"MacNeill won't hear of that," said Tommy.

"MacNeill won't need to *know* of it!" answered Clarke as quick as a bullet from a concealed gun. "We've got to get IRB men at the top in the Volunteers."

"We've already got Pearse as director of Military Organization, and Plunkett on Military Operations . . ." offered Tierney.

"Not enough!" said Clarke forcefully. "We'll need a Supreme Council that's primarily IRB. MacDonogh, Ceannt, O'Rahilly —they're the sort we want. Then we can get this bloody thing moving. We'll need you three, of course, where you can influence people."

"Ceannt shouldn't be much of a problem to get around to our way of thinking," said Seaneen, assessing the assignment that had been laid out. "He's a physical force man all the way. MacDonogh, on the other hand—he's a poetic sort, maybe Tierney can reach him."

Tierney nodded. "I'll do my best to feel out O'Rahilly, too," he said. "He's a good man. I'll try to see where he stands on all this."

"What about MacNeill himself?" asked Tommy pointedly. "Why are you so sure he won't be with us when the time comes? He's always been a realist. He'll see it's the only way."

"Ah, but will a realist with a wife and eight children want to go to war?" asked Seaneen pointedly.

"No one's questioning his courage or his willingness!" snapped Clarke. "But we'd be fools not to have IRB men close enough to the man to influence his decision."

"What's the story with FitzGibbon and the guns?" asked Clarke as they got up to leave.

"I've my doubts about the scheme," said Tierney. "Desmond's a damned good human being, but he's taking a terrible chance here. I don't trust the Germans and I don't know that I trust his judgment about the feasibility of this scheme."

"His judgment has never been put to the test before, it's

true," said Seaneen musingly. "But my instinct is to trust the man implicitly. I like him. He's an honorable sort."

"It's hard not to like someone who's volunteering to risk his own money, as well as his neck, for us!" reiterated Clarke. "I've heard from the grapevine that the Clan na Gael in New York is sending a man named Casement to Germany on exactly the same kind of mission. It seems an idea whose time has come, wouldn't you say?"

Tommy and Tierney glanced uneasily at each other. The time seemed to be coming indeed; if the guns came through, there would be bloodshed within the year.

Eoin MacNeill was slightly built. At five feet ten inches and ten and a half stone, no one could call him brawny; but it was his very fair hair and skin that seemed to underline his spareness.

He had never meant to become involved in anything military, it occurred to him, as he laid down the latest dispatch about the Volunteers. A professor of early Irish history at University College had no real business in politics, except that history itself seemed to bear out the fact that those who didn't profit by the mistakes of the past were doomed to repeat them. Now who was it who had said that? he wondered idly.

It almost amused him to think of his pacific life becoming involved in the affairs of empire. Or perhaps it was more amusing that a man with eight children would think his life pacific! MacNeill chuckled a little as he turned toward the window that overlooked the other college buildings. His sense of humor had always been his saving grace; no matter the odds or the circumstances, he seemed always to be able to find something absurd enough to laugh at. An acute sense of absurdity, someone had once accused him of. Well, what could be more absurd than himself as head of an army, he wondered briefly. Unless of course it was Padraig Pearse as head of one; poets seemed no more likely revolutionaries than history professors.

Pearse read again what he had written, satisfied . . . or as satisfied as any poet can ever be with his work, he thought amusedly.

"Oh, wise men, riddle me this: what if the dream come true?

What if the dream come true? and if millions
  unborn shall dwell
In the house that I shaped in my heart, the noble
  house of my spirit?"

He laid the poem aside. He had pulled it out of the pile of his writings in hopes there would be something there to use in the funeral oration he had been asked to prepare. O'Donovan Rossa, the grand old Fenian, had died in America, but he was to be interred at Glasnevin Cemetery in Dublin. A great crowd would gather around the graveside. A superb opportunity to strike a verbal blow for freedom that would be carried by the press, heard by the people, and even, perhaps, be remembered.

It must be a splendid speech. Rossa, God rest him, deserved that it be. He picked up the pen with renewed vigor and began to write what was in his heart.

This speech he was preparing would be one more nail in the coffin of the Empire, he thought, as he began to write. One more lovely nail . . .

"This is a place of peace, sacred to the dead." Pearse's strong voice carried with ease over the heads of the silent mourners at the cemetery. "Where men should speak with all charity and all restraint." Every ear was on him; the people were expectant of an important message.

Con searched through the graveside crowd for Tierney's tall form. He was one of the pallbearers: a great honor, but a dangerous one. She caught a glimpse of him, half hidden by the coffin, and breathed her relief. You could never tell who were the spies; the "ears of the Castle" they were called, and they were everywhere.

"The Defenders of the Realm have worked well in secret and in the open. They think that they have pacified Ireland . . . but the fools, the fools, the *fools!*" [His voice rose in an insistent, rhythmic authority.] "They have left us our Fenian dead, and while Ireland holds these graves, Ireland unfree shall *never* be at peace!"

My God, she thought, there'll be trouble now for sure! It was a breathtaking speech, but there'd be trouble. She began to try to make her way through the agitated crowd but was jostled roughly by the unruly mass of humans, all talking now and gesturing, it seemed. More rebels than mourners here, she thought nervously, wishing she could reach Tierney. And more spies too.

Suddenly she felt a strong arm go around her shoulders.

"Thank God I've found you!" said her son's deep voice. She was grateful to have him home for the school holidays. She heard the concern in his voice as she felt his tall body interposed between herself and the milling crowd. He was big for seventeen, well over six feet already and growing still. So like Tierney in stature and movement, although his face was his own.

"How did you ever find me in this crowd?"

"I was near Father. He spotted you first—as the speech began. It's taken me that long to move through the crowd to you." His voice was strong and sensible and comforting. She leaned against his protective arm for a moment, letting herself realize for the first time how nervous she had been.

Of course, Tierney had seen her. Hadn't he said often enough that he could sense her presence in the dark, at a mile's distance? She smiled at the protective pride she remembered in his manner when he'd said it.

"Thank you for coming for me, son," she said gratefully, thinking how remarkable it is to live long enough to be able to rely upon your child in time of need.

"I couldn't leave you alone in this crowd, Mother. The Castle's men are everywhere. We must get out of here as quickly as we can."

"But your father . . ."

He smiled inscrutably at her concern.

"The men are well armed and there are a hundred IRB marksmen near the coffin in case of emergency."

She nodded. How manly was this son of hers, who had seemed in her mind but a boy until a moment ago. Now, feeling him propel her confidently through the crowd, seeing the looks thrown at him by the young girls and women as they passed, it was very clear to her that he was very nearly grown to be a man.

14 ∾ Angelica was blossoming into young womanhood. I had almost forgotten what a gorgeous experience it is for a young girl from the country to spend time in the city. Although she was denied the parties and pleasures that would have been her due had she been well, she seemed excited and happy most of the time after our arrival in Dublin.

We had dresses made for her in the newest fashion and we took her sightseeing everywhere in the carriage. "When I ride in the carriage, I'm no less agile than any other girl," she said to me once, and it made me understand how tragically my daughter must have missed being well and whole, especially at the age of first flirtations. I saw her flirting quite outrageously from the carriage one day with a handsome young lancer, and it dawned on me that only when she was half hidden did she feel free to be flirtatious.

To Tahg's eternal credit, he was her constant friend. Whenever he could get home from school on weekend or holiday, he contrived means of taking her everywhere in her wheelchair. I later had reason to believe that her great love of the poor and of the Irish people in general probably stemmed from those winter rambles when he took her to what her father would have called "the slums."

She would come home bursting with news of all that she'd seen. In a way it reminded me of that fateful long-ago summer when Seaneen had introduced me to the real world of Ireland. Frequently she would stay with Tahg for a day or two, he carrying her up and down the stairs as if he were a man and she a child. In truth, he was a very manly boy; large like his father and darkly handsome. And Angelica was as light as a small bird.

She had gloriously golden hair that was strangely wavy from crown to end, so it made her look like Raphael's Magdalen when it was unloosed. She had an intelligent and beautiful face, with great searching eyes. . . . For years her eyes had seemed the only animate part of her, and I never ceased to be aware of how intently they prowled her environment, drinking in knowledge. More than knowledge of what they saw, I think, did those eyes drink in; they seemed to have the capacity to see through the exterior of people to their hearts. It was never easy to fool Angelica.

Johnny spent as much time as he could with Seaneen. Sometimes I went along on an outing—more often they went off alone together. I remember watching them strut off down the street one morning, Johnny's small legs struggling to keep time with Seaneen's longer ones. They had the same shape of body, square and stocky. Strong in the shoulders and overall pugnacious, somehow. And they walked with the same assurance; Seaneen's gait had grown a bit more circumspect and stealthy with the years, but I could see in that unguarded moment that he must have had the same confident swagger in his youth that I had noticed in my son.

I loved seeing them together. In fact I was loving everything about my time in Dublin, feeling freer than I had felt in years.

Then I got word that Edmond and the children would be back in Ireland for Christmas 1915.

Edmond arrived with Win, Merry and Jamie a few days before the holiday. Was it my imagination or had they all grown and changed in just a few months' time?

Win was very much the young man, polished and self-assured. He was polite and articulate as a barrister and he carried himself with the dignity of a peer. He was Edmond's shadow, and I used to wonder what those two taciturn males might find to talk about in their continual conversations. God knows, they had little enough to say to me. But in fairness, I must add that Edmond was patient and generous with his older son, teaching him what he would need to know in order to inherit the title and estates. I expect Edmond's relationship with his own father must have been much the same as his with Winston, and it pleased him mightily to have a model son.

Merry and Jamie, soon to be sixteen, also seemed terribly grown up to me. I suppose one doesn't see one's children growing as it's happening, but an absence of any duration provokes seeing them anew. Merry was strikingly beautiful, so much so that I found myself wondering if Angelica would feel jealousy when she saw her. She had black Irish hair and a face from a fairy tale. Her joyous disposition and easy laughter only added to her unstudied charm. There was no question whatsoever but that Merry would be sought after by any young man who laid eyes on her.

Jamie was bursting with knowledge picked up in London. His studious nature had evidently appealed to Edmond's parliamentary cronies, and several rather famous men had expounded to him on their views of history and politics—heady stuff for a scholarly fifteen-year-old. Jamie had matured, it seemed to me, by virtue of having spent so much time with older men.

Edmond and I had reached a decent-enough peace in our marriage, as I expect most men and women of our station did, then. In a strange way we had become relatively amicable companions over the years, sharing experience, if not affection. I was the perfect hostess for his parliamentary career, and he was the gentleman I had been raised to expect. That I had known love, for however brief a time, and therefore knew that such existed in the world, was my own problem, not Edmond's.

It's hard to look back on your own time of innocence and plumb its motives. Though I'm certain that the passion I devoted to my causes was some subversion of the passion I would have wished to spend in love, the complications of my relationship with Edmond always troubled me. I had in my marriage what I'd been bred to anticipate: civility, comfort, and pleasantry . . . and it wasn't nearly enough for me. Could that be deemed Edmond's fault or my own? I wondered. Did Con and I simply come endowed with wilder, more restless spirits than the rest of womankind, so that to fill our enormous and unexpected needs was a task most men were unfitted for?

At any rate, the years had passed for us and all who knew us thought our marriage as acceptable as any, but needless to say, having once again found Seaneen and happiness, I did not look forward to Edmond's arrival.

He was in a curiously good mood; the children had been models of decorum while in London, so it seemed my performance of motherhood had been vindicated. The war, while redolent with terrible news, had nonetheless added a soupçon of excitement to the usually taciturn millings of Parliament, and all in all, Edmond was pleased at the prospect of living in Dublin for a while; he had been sent on a high-ranking diplomatic mission to Dublin Castle so that he might report to the House of Lords on "the Irish Question."

The children were bubbling over with the news of the severe Zeppelin raid they'd experienced in London in October. Even though we'd read about it in their letters, the retelling was an adventure. Even the usually laconic Edmond was filled with news as well.

"Sir Douglas Haig has succeeded General French as commander in chief," he told me over tea the first evening after his arrival.

"I thought French was popular enough," I responded, wondering greatly that Edmond had chosen to discuss his business with me.

John Denton Pinkstone French, First Earl of Cypress, and Field Marshal since 1913, was a controversial soldier; that much I knew. In truth I knew a fair amount about politics, if very little about the military, but French's name was a familiar one in the press.

"He's a rather unstable character," replied Edmond. "Tends toward blacks and whites in his judgments. Spotty war record, too. As many failures as successes, I'm afraid."

"Isn't it rather unorthodox to recall a commander in chief in the middle of a war?" I asked.

"Indeed. The cabinet had no great desire to remove him just now, for fear of talk of instability, but it seems unavoidable."

"What exactly does one do with an old general?"

Edmond smiled at that; he really did appear to be loosening up a bit. I wondered what could possibly have occasioned the change.

"They've raised him to the peerage it seems and made him Commander in Chief of the United Kingdom forces."

"I see. That rather means he'll be the military commander here if any trouble breaks out, doesn't it?" I asked it as ingenuously as I could, for I knew French was both anti-Republican and vehemently anti-Home Rule.

"Are we anticipating a problem here, then?" asked Edmond, raising his eyebrows at me quizzically. I realized in that instant that my husband no longer thought of me as an ignorant woman . . . in fact, I rather imagined he suspected me of being privy to all manner of information.

"There's been considerable activity in our parks and squares. Quite a lot of marching and drilling among the Volunteers."

"Oh, that nonsense! I don't suppose anyone takes them seriously."

"Perhaps not," I replied, amused that he was hoping to get information from me.

"We've been assured that the majority of the Irish people are patriotic enough to wait until the war is over before causing any further agitation. After all, we are an integral part of Great Britain."

"If a reluctant one."

Edmond started to reply, then seemed to change tack.

"I'd like not to argue with you tonight, Elizabeth," he said hesitantly.

This time, I must have looked quizzical, so he went on.

"I've had a smashing time with the children. They're really everything a man could hope for in his progeny. It occurred to me that you've had more of a hand in that than I've ever given you credit for."

"Good Lord, Edmond," I said, startled by the words and the tone. "You'd best not say anything more—it may be too much of a shock for me!"

He smiled oddly at that. "Wherever did we go so wrong?" he asked suddenly, genuinely.

"Nearly everywhere," I answered.

"I expect you're right about that," he responded thoughtfully. "Nonetheless we have raised splendid children together. And I'm rather proud of us for that."

I looked at the man to whom I'd been married for nineteen years. He was so very much a product of his times and class. Not so very different from others who had been bred as he had. But years of unkindness and disappointment are hard to forgive in a single moment. I wondered what in God's name could have prompted such a change of heart toward me. Perhaps his mistress had died and he felt too old to bother pursuing another.

Whatever Edmond's motivations in mellowing toward me, any love I had to give a husband was pledged unalterably to Seaneen O'Sullivan, so I tried to make as light of his overture as possible.

Fate plays such curious tricks on us . . . mating the wrong two so often. I sometimes wonder if the Divine Plan simply cares about getting the right children born into the world, and whatever pairing is necessary to achieve that end, it engineers. I agreed with Edmond about our children, at any rate. They were a lovely brood, each with something special to offer.

As later events proved beyond a doubt.

I was taken to a gathering at the Gaelic League headquarters in Dublin—half meeting, half social interchange—that I feel I should tell you about. They were all there, the ones who would emerge as leaders, and, of course, those soon to be martyrs. I'll do my best to describe them as they seemed to me that evening, for an unjaundiced eye is difficult after all the events that were to come. But that night they were new to me, and I was naught but an interested observer.

When we arrived at the gathering, Padraig Pearse was in heated discussion with James Connolly, who seemed to me all square and stocky as an icebox.

With them was an imposing sort, a rather bombastic man with a luxuriant mustache who, Con whispered to me, was John MacBride, the famous soldier who had led a troop of Irishmen to defend the Boers in the Transvaal. He was also Maud Gonne's estranged husband. It was hard to imagine the regal Maud married to this rough-and-tumble, rather crass soldier, but Con said that Maud had been worshiped so long by languid intellectuals that the first man of action she'd met had quite swept her off her feet. Perhaps she was right.

I was introduced to Joseph Mary Plunkett, a rather delicate and consumptive fellow; a gentle-looking young man with him turned out to be Willy Pearse, Padraig's devoted younger brother.

But the one who caught my eye immediately was Sean O'Casey. He had once been Secretary of the Irish Citizen Army, but had resigned in 1914 because of a dispute about Con Markievicz. He looked every inch the cynic that he was. Red-rimmed eyes squinted out from behind steel-rimmed glasses—eyes with the unfortunate gift of seeing the world as it was, I later learned. He was tall and as wiry as a docker needed to be. He could play the pipes and had done so often in this band or that to make ends meet, Con told me . . . and his sardonic face was a familiar one in both the Gaelic League and the haunts of those who bided their time till rebellion would come, she said.

He was sitting by himself watching the others, a quarrelsome look in his eye. Something about the man interested me and I asked to be introduced.

"I'd best do it, My Lady," said Seaneen, and Con laughed aloud.

"He has it in for Con Markievicz and me," she explained. "Can't abide the idea of women on the Supreme Council. You two run along and I'll find you later."

"So you're the famous lady who tells women how to leave their husbands, eh?" said O'Casey when I'd been introduced.

"You make me sound quite sinister," I replied, amused by the frontal assault.

"No more than your due, I expect," he said, and I couldn't be sure if he was teasing me or being crotchety.

"Crankier than usual tonight, Sean?" cut in Seaneen before I had a chance to defend myself. He squeezed my arm as if to say "Pay this no mind."

"It strikes me there's much to be cranky about, listening to our leaders argue among themselves. At the rate we're going we'll have to mount *two* revolutions so MacNeill and Pearse can each do it his own way."

"So you're surly to ladies in retribution?" asked Seaneen with a twinkle in his voice. "It strikes me we're an odd and convoluted race, Sean, doesn't it you?"

O'Casey laughed at the chiding and put out his hand to me.

"Forgive me, Lady Manningham. Your champion here is no more than correct. But you see we have a tendency toward lost rebellions in Ireland . . . we stage one every fifty years or so. It pains me to be involved with the latest futility."

"You must take heart, Mr. O'Casey," I said. "My friend Emmeline Pankhurst once told me that no one can win a battle unless he *believes* with all his heart that he will win."

"She's right, of course," he replied. "That's why cynics make poor soldiers and why women will eventually rule the world."

"Ah, Mr. O'Casey, we've a long way to go before that happens, I think."

He smiled charmingly and I thought him a curiously complicated fellow.

* * *

Seaneen next introduced me to Michael Joseph O'Rahilly, or "The O'Rahilly," as most called him in deference to both his well-to-do family and ancient lineage. There was something so winsome about the man that when Con told me he was Director of Arms for the Volunteers, I was not surprised. He was, without question, the kind of man others would follow into battle.

It seemed he was not an IRB man, but was acceptable enough to the Brotherhood to have his articles published in their *Irish Freedom* newspaper. His closest friend, Eamonn Ceannt, was IRB, of course, and that may have had something to do with it.

"Has our friend Mr. O'Casey been giving you a hard time?" O'Rahilly asked me with a genuine smile, after we'd been introduced.

"He doesn't seem keen on women in the movement," I replied.

"You must forgive him his trespasses," he said merrily. "The man's a genius—and it puts a burden on his good humor."

"We're a bit of a comic lot, when you get us all together in one room, aren't we?" he asked, as if quite interested in my opinion.

"Better comic than tragic," I replied, warmed by the man's easy charm.

"That is the other possibility, isn't it?" he said with a grin.

"Actually, I find you all quite fascinating and, needless to say, I wish you well," I responded with enthusiasm.

O'Rahilly nodded his sandy-haired head and smiled at that. His handlebar mustache, which was fair and well-kept, gave him a robust look. He seemed a laughing sort of man and yet one whom you would do well to take seriously.

By the end of the evening I had the feeling that I knew most of the players . . . now it would be a question of waiting for the game to begin. ✑

15 "But how in God's name do you think you can pull off a rising without letting MacNeill in on it?" Tommy sounded as angry as he felt.

"We can't let him in on it, because we can't trust him to do it our way," answered Pearse clearly.

"And who the hell says our way is such a bloody good way, might I ask?" Tommy's voice had risen to an unaccustomed pitch.

"I think when you've heard the details of the plan you'll agree that it's more than workable, gentlemen," interjected Connolly, always the sensible one in any argument.

"We intend to immobilize the center of the city and cut off the Castle from reinforcements. We'll control their major buildings, communications and entry and exit routes."

"But for how long?" Tierney asked.

"There are twenty thousand men in some way attached to the military cause of Ireland, if you count the Volunteers, the Citizen Army and the Fianna—that's enough to hold on long enough for world opinion to force them to recognize us as a small nation that wants its freedom."

"And if the twenty thousand don't come, how many of us will there be in Dublin?"

"Between seven hundred and a thousand."

"Against the British Empire!" Tommy's voice was exasperated and derisive.

"No!" said Pearse quickly. "Only against the men at Dublin Castle . . . maybe fifteen hundred of them. Not impossible odds."

"And if they send in ships to shell us?"

"We're counting on the fact that they won't do that. That they won't want to destroy the city any more than we do." Connolly sounded certain of the last of it.

"I still don't see how you can do it without MacNeill. He *is* the Volunteers. He says 'Go,' they go . . . 'Stay' and they stay," Tommy persisted.

"He's right about that," said Seaneen. "The men are loyal to him. I say we'll have to have him in. And The O'Rahilly, too . . ."

"No!" Pearse sounded angry. "The O'Rahilly has made it clear that he thinks we're out of our minds to be doing this at all, at this juncture. If anything, he'll rally the people against us."

"He's a good man," said Tierney. "And a brave one. We'll need him when the times comes."

"I know you feel strongly about it, Pat," Connolly's deep, controlled voice sounded thoughtful. "But I'm with the others on this. We need MacNeill because of the Volunteers and I'd like to have The O'Rahilly because I respect him and he respects the Cause. I must vote that we let them know what's up."

Pearse stared at the others. He was an impassioned man when anything touched his dreams for Ireland, but he heard the sense in what they put forth.

"All right," he said. "We'll give them the chance to come in. But not yet. Not until it's too late for them to stop us. In the meantime, MacDonogh and Plunkett will place announcements in the papers to set up Volunteer maneuvers for Easter Sunday. We'll say the maneuvers are for the purpose of testing the equipment or some such folderol to throw the authorities off the scent."

The other men in the room who had been silent throughout —Willy Pearse, Plunkett, Clarke—now nodded acquiescence to the information. Once the men assembled for their "maneuvers," they'd be told it was a rising they'd been called to.

"Well now, if we're finished with that little business, I've a question to ask," said Clarke pleasantly. "How the bloody hell do you intend to have a revolution without guns?"

"We'll have the guns," said Seaneen authoritatively. "That part's mine to do. Des is already in Germany; O'Connor, Mc-Gowan and I—we'll get the guns."

Tierney placed the plans on the table in the town house's study and looked around at the IRB men who were gathered there with him.

"Desmond FitzGibbon will see to getting the guns across the Channel from Germany," he said. "A German ship will carry the rifles and all the ammunition we need to the appointed spot. The cargo will be transferred to a fishing boat that I will captain.

"The guns will be unloaded the night of 9 April and will be taken in vans inland to stashes in cemeteries. Certain graves will have coffins loaded with guns interred in them, where it's too dangerous to keep them aboveground. Needless to say, the bulk of them will be transported to Dublin, where the Rising will begin."

Tommy listened quietly as his friend and partner spoke of the plan. It sounded flawless, but there were so many places where it could run a cropper. Running guns under the very nose of the Castle was as dangerous a task as any man need set for himself.

But if there was to be a rising there would have to be guns, that was a certainty. He liked Desmond inordinately. It took courage to risk the comforts of an Ascendency life-style for a cause you really had no need to befriend. And the man had opened windows in Tahg's life that might otherwise have remained closed. But Tommy wished he felt more confidence in the outcome of this gunrunning scheme.

Tierney, having finished his part in the evening's proceedings, sat down next to Tommy. Seaneen was speaking now . . . next it would be Pearse and God knows how many others before the night was through. These were high stakes they played for and all the leaders would want to get their two cents in. All he himself wanted was to go home with Con.

He wished this nagging apprehension that kept playing at the back of his brain would dissipate. "The Sight" was acting up again . . . no clear vision yet, but a niggling presentiment of disaster. Not that it mattered much what his vision might show him.

There was no turning back, now that the die was about to be cast. It was far too late for turning back.

"Don't you think it odd, my love, that our revolution is led by a preponderance of poets?" Con and Tierney were making their way home north along Grafton Street from a strategy meeting at which Pearse, Plunkett and MacDonogh had all spoken and it had struck her suddenly as both amusing and dangerous that they were all men of letters, not of guns.

Tierney laughed briefly at her side. "Aye. It's queer enough.

Unless of course you think perhaps poets are able to sense stirrings in the people earlier than most men?"

"Maybe so, but I'd still feel better if there were a military strategist in the crowd, or even a few more like Seaneen and Tom Clarke, who've spent a lifetime fighting with weapons other than words."

"You'd be right, of course, if you're thinking there's any real hope of winning. But I can't help asking myself if that's really their intention, Beauty, or if they all feel the valiant gesture and martyrdom will better serve the Cause."

She shuddered a little in the darkness and held tighter to Tierney's arm.

It was suddenly clear to Con how much she wanted her husband. Wanted his protective arms around her, his body covering her, his mouth pressed all-encompassingly over hers. For the first time it occurred to her that she was glad she had agreed to let Tahg study at Pearse's St. Enda's school for this one year. Much as she loved her son, she and Tierney had grown used to the unaccustomed privacy they'd shared while Tahg had been with Des. Bad times were approaching; dangerous times for both of them. They must make good use of every moment together as a bulwark against the future. Tonight, and in the nights to come, she would very much need to be alone with her husband.

16   Joe Plunkett looked curiously resplendent in his odd regalia. At home he often donned the traditional djellabah of the Bedouins. It was a habit he had adopted while recovering from an illness in North Africa.

Tonight the grim-faced troop of men who met in his stylish drawing room was not the usual scholarly crowd who came there on Tuesdays to discuss politics or agrarian reform. Tonight the men were gathered to hear Plunkett's strategy for the Rising. He had been working on it for more than a year.

"Simply stated, gentlemen," he said in his clipped, decidedly English accent, "the plan is that we take the center of the city by simultaneously overpowering all strategic sectors. We will occupy posts controlling all entrances to the city. We will thereby cut off the men at Dublin Castle from reinforcement by the country garrisons."

The men in the room began to murmur among themselves and he held up his hands for quiet.

"Edward Daly," he said, speaking directly to a man on his right. "You will take the Four Courts. Across the river, you, Sean Heuston, will occupy the Mendicity Institution." As he spoke Plunkett pointed to a large wall map of the city of Dublin on which red X's had been marked to show areas of proposed occupation.

"Eamonn Ceannt, you will hold the South Dublin Union; James Connolly, you will be at the GPO."

"That way you'll be close enough to the Castle to invite the lancers in for tea," volunteered Tommy McGowan with a wry chuckle, and everyone realized he'd done so to ease the mounting tension in the room.

"On the south side, Eamon de Valera, you will occupy Boland's Mill to keep an eye on the roads from Kingstown, just in case His Britannic Majesty decides to send in reinforcements.

"Thomas MacDonogh, it falls to you to occupy Jacob's Biscuit Factory . . ."

"At least your boys won't go hungry, Tom!" Tommy's voice again cut through the tense atmosphere, but Plunkett looked at him with annoyance.

"Michael Mallin, you and your Citizen Army lads and the Fianna Boys will hold St. Stephen's Green.

"Pearse and I will be at the General Post Office with Connolly, where we will set up Command Headquarters."

"Why the GPO?" asked Tierney.

"It's both central and sturdy," was the reply. "And it's visible, too. Pearse here will tack up his proclamation on the door and King George himself can come over and read it if he'd like."

"The last Protestant to tack up a proclamation, Joe, was Martin Luther," said Tommy, amusement in his voice. "Let's hope you end up more popular in Ireland than he is." Everyone in the room exploded at that, their nervousness dissipated for a moment in laughter.

"And what exactly do you think they'll be up to at Dublin

Castle while we're busy occupying every other building in town, might I ask?" Tommy offered the question. "Couldn't we wait till Monday, when half the garrison will be at the Fairyhouse race meet?"

"No," interjected Pearse adamantly. "The religious significance of Easter Sunday is essential to our Rising."

The more practical and less poetic in the room glanced at each other but said nothing.

"Besides," added Pearse, "we're cutting them off from reinforcements while we'll have the Volunteers and Citizen Army men filing in from all over Ireland. More importantly, we must believe the people of Dublin will rise to support us once we declare ourselves."

"Not a chance of that!" snapped McGowan. "They've enough on their minds trying to keep from starvin' to death. They'll think we're all a bloody nuisance if you ask me."

Plunkett stared him disdainfully into silence and continued his briefing. When it was over, Seaneen, Tierney and Tommy left together.

"What do you think?" asked Tommy as they hit the pavement.

"It could work . . . for a while. If we catch them off guard."

"They'll never capitulate," said Tierney. "The English governmental mind will not allow them to knuckle under to this kind of display. They've too many other colonies who might follow suit."

"You may be right, lad," said Seaneen thoughtfully. "But what other choice do we really have? If we don't strike now while England's busy elsewhere with her war, we may never have the chance in our lifetimes to stand up on our hind legs and fight like men."

Tierney nodded, knowing Seaneen was right, but the knowledge didn't make him feel any better.

"Is there any possibility we can win?" Con asked, lying in her husband's arms after the meeting. She had been listening to his description of what had been said; she could feel the tension the question produced in him as he prepared to reply. She knew he would tell her the truth.

"I don't see how," he said finally. "At least not in any traditional sense. There are too many of them and they'll be too well-armed and prepared. At best, we're just a bunch of amateurs fighting for our lives."

"Then why are we doing it? I keep asking myself the question." She had not asked it to plague him, he knew, but rather because they needed to talk it through.

"Because there's a chance if we do, and none if we don't, I suppose. Because we see no other way . . . because it's time to put our money where our mouths have been. You know the answers as well as I, my own love." He wrapped his arms around her as he spoke and held her close.

"Yes. I suppose I do," she said carefully. "You know, it's very strange, Tierney, but now that the time has finally come—the time we've waited for for so long—there's a part of me that wishes we could run away. Anywhere but Ireland. Anyplace where we could just live and grow old together and love each other and see our son marry and bring home grandchildren. Such simple wants they seem to me now. It's as if I can't explain to myself how we've gotten ourselves into this mess! Even though we've spent a lifetime working toward this moment, and part of me wants the chance to pay them back for every unjust deed they've ever done . . . I suppose I'm just afraid." She stopped for a moment to catch her breath.

"And yet . . . I wouldn't turn my back on it! Any more than you would. I want to see it through, this impossible dream of ours. Am I mad, do you think? Are we both mad that we don't just run for it before we're destroyed?"

She pulled herself into a sitting position so that she could see his face as he answered her.

Tierney smiled at his wife, seeing the worry lines in her face, thinking that he seldom noticed the changes in her that their years together had brought. She was twice as old now as when they'd met.

"Do you remember, Beauty, long, long ago," he answered her musingly, "on the strand near your father's estate, when I first told you of Cuchulain and Connla? How they shared the same fate that could not be avoided? I've been thinking lately that in a way that's how it is for you and me. We've a shared fate, I think, all tangled up with Ireland's. In a way it brought us together long ago, and it may destroy us now—yet, I think we must play it out . . . follow it to the end. Almost as if that's the only way to be true to each other." He shook his head to clear it. "That doesn't make any sense, I suppose."

She pulled the covers up over her shoulders and around her and moved closer to him as she replied, "Yes, it does, Tierney. It does and I feel it, too. As if we're caught up in a moment that's bigger than we are—and we're being carried along in it to we-don't-know-where. But we must go with it, to see where it leads us—or else everything we've been, and everything we've lived for, all these years will have been a lie. And we will have sacrificed your writing to a worthless dream."

He reached up to touch her face lovingly. "That still weighs on you, Con, after all these years. Surely no man ever had a more loyal audience for his efforts than that." He sounded very sad as he said it.

She looked into her husband's eyes and, seeing the pain there, she leaned down to his chest so that he might hold her close against him.

"I'm so very, very afraid," she said finally. "So very afraid of the future."

Tierney could think of no appropriate reply, so he held his wife to his heart, stroking her hair and back until he could tell by her even breathing that she had fallen asleep.

Then he lay for a very long time watching her and wondering whether they had a future at all.

"Tommy, old friend," said Tierney amid the debris of the newly emptied pub. "I wish I could get my heart into this Rising, but I've a bad feeling about it."

"I have myself," replied Tommy, wiping a table with a cloth from the bar. "Are we alone, lad?" he asked, glancing uneasily at the bar.

"Aye. The last one left a few minutes ago."

Tommy nodded and sat down at a table.

"What troubles you most?"

"This cloak and dagger atmosphere, I suppose. I think it's wrong not to let The O'Rahilly and MacNeill in on our plans. I respect them both . . . no less than Pearse and Connolly, really. And I feel the people of Dublin aren't with us. I think they'll leave us hung out to dry. Worse yet, I've a bad premonition about my own mission with the guns."

Tommy nodded. "When's it set for?"

"The night of the ninth. We meet the submarine past the twelve-mile limit and bring the guns into Baldoyle by fishing boat. This damned second sight of mine is plaguing me. I have a sure sense it won't work, but no clear vision of what will go wrong."

"Can you abort?"

"No, not without a concrete reason. They need the guns."

From Desmond FitzGibbon's diary—26 March 1916, Berlin:

> In a few days' time I shall be aboard a submarine, party to the maddest and most ill-planned enterprise in the history of mad Irish revolutions.
>
> Honor demands that I carry it through. For that matter to stop it now (even if I could stop it) might bring other men to worse danger.
>
> If it works—how, I can barely imagine—I will go down in history as Ireland's savior. If not, I doubt I shall live out the year. . . .

Desmond laid down his pen and rested his aching head on trembling hands. He had been such a fool to trust the German government, he knew that now. They were using him and his reputation for their own propaganda. *They will give us none of the men and support that they promised . . .* he told himself. *The guns we have purchased are either so old they are ludicrous as fighting weapons or they are Russian and nearly useless to our men . . . and I am virtually a prisoner.*

He picked up the pen again.

"What ghastly folly!" he wrote, thinking how inadequate a statement that was. He wondered if he would even be permitted to leave the country alive.

17

6 April 1916

"You're sure you can handle the boat, Tierney?" Seaneen asked the question with some urgency in his voice.

"Certainly, Seaneen. My legacy as a fisherman." There was a note of rueful amusement in the words. "My da would be proud of me."

Seaneen looked up, annoyed at the levity, but he could see by the strained expressions on the faces of the men in the room that they were simply whistling past the graveyard.

"The boat will be deserted at the dock by one A.M., refueled and ready. You'll go aboard and take her out past Ireland's Eye and well into international waters, where the guns and explosives will be transferred from the sub to the trawler. The trickiest part will be to get her to Baldoyle, then back into Dublin without being spotted. Your men will have to work fast to stash the weapons. They'll unload them as if it was ordinary cargo, onto drays bound for the various cemeteries where our men will be waiting." He glanced around the table at the nervous faces. When he next spoke, it was with determination.

"This load, plus the one that Casement's bringing in, will constitute the major supply of arms for the Rising. It is absolutely essential that it get through. Do you understand?"

Murmurs of assent around the table.

"And if we're stopped by a patrol boat?"

"You'll talk your way out of it," replied Seaneen pointedly.

"Better stop by Blarney Castle to kiss the stone before you go, Tierney," put in McGowan with a laugh. Seaneen frowned.

"Be that as it may, those arms cannot fall into the hands of the enemy."

"How sure are you that there are no informers?"

"Sure enough."

"Well, then, that's it, I guess," said Tierney. "How do I know the boat?"

"She'll have a harp emblem painted on her stern with the name *Countess Cathleen.*"

The men, solemn-faced, filed out of the room, all but Tierney.

"They sense at the Castle that something's up. I'm sure of it," he said evenly when the others had left. "They've tightened security on the water, Seaneen. There's a better than even chance we'll be caught in the harbor."

"There is."

"Then why are we risking it?"

"Because we're pathetically short of weapons, man, and this is a chance to bring in two thousand Mauser rifles and forty thousand rounds of ammunition in a single trip. The council feels the rewards outweigh the risks."

"Bloody easy for the council to think so, snug in their beds!" Seaneen brought his fist down on the table in so quick a gesture that the crash made Tierney jump.

"There's nothing we've asked you to risk that any one of us wouldn't and hadn't! You have the best shot at it because you grew up on a fishing boat, Tierney, but, by God, if you want out, now's the time to say so."

"So I can get myself a bullet in the back when I walk out of here because I know too much?"

Seaneen looked uncomfortable. "There's no one on the council would think you'd turn informer, Tierney." He said the words deliberately and Tierney noted that the man hadn't promised him his life should he leave.

"I've no intention, as it happens, of backing out," he said evenly. "There's none among us can pilot a boat through the shoals but my own fine self, and I'll not have those lads out there at more risk than need be.

"But, I'll tell you this, Seaneen, this plan is ill-conceived and I've an altogether bad feeling about it in my bones. So you'd best hope that Casement makes it through, for I'd lay you money that those cemeteries are more likely to see my men than your bloody guns!" He too brought his fist down onto the table and, leaving it there for emphasis, spoke directly into the older man's eyes.

"I love you like a brother, Seaneen O'Sullivan—but this is a fool's errand."

Then Tierney picked up his cap from the table and, pulling it low onto his forehead, walked out the door without saying good-bye.

18   Tierney raised his collar against the chill air, but to no avail, for the cold was within him.

The street was dark now and nearly deserted. Tierney glanced to right and left as casually as he could, felt gingerly for the gun hidden beneath his jacket and started in the direction of the harbor.

The *Countess Cathleen* lay quietly at anchor, the green-black water lapping at her stern; he could see the harp emblem in the weak light shed by the fledgling moon. There were men already aboard her as Tierney walked uneasily across the gangplank that attached her to the pier.

As he did so a large familiar shape appeared briefly behind the cabin and, startled, he recognized the youthful form as that of his own son.

"Tahg!" he whispered urgently in the darkness and the shape disengaged itself from what it had been doing and moved swiftly to his side.

"What in God's name are you doing here!" Anger flashed behind the father's eyes but the boy stood his ground.

"I've left the school, Da," he said steadily. "I wanted to be here with you in this."

"I won't have you here!" Tierney shot the words back at him. "It's too dangerous . . . too insane."

"I want to go with you, Da," the boy persisted quietly. "I cleared it with Seaneen."

"Oh, you did, did you?" Tierney said angrily. "Well, by God, you didn't clear it with me and I'll have you off this boat or she'll not sail!"

Tahg looked uneasily around him. Several other shadows had ceased their work and were listening.

"Your son's a man, lad," Tommy McGowan's Belfast voice

sounded quietly behind the two men. "You'd not be wanting to take that from him in front of the other lads, now would you?"

Tierney felt Tommy's strong hand reassuringly placed on his shoulder.

He looked sharply into the eyes of his son, and saw there the embarrassment of a young man unmasked before his peers, and hesitated before replying. Tommy was right, of course. He couldn't unman the boy.

"Run along, lad," Tommy said softly to Tahg in the darkness. "Your father was merely concerned for you. We're both glad to have you for a comrade."

Tahg nodded uncertainly . . . waited a moment for his father to speak. When he didn't, the boy moved off in the direction from which he had come, still on the boat.

"He's a man now, lad," Tommy said gently, so that only Tierney could hear him. "And a good one. Like his father."

Tierney nodded, then replied, "I'd rather see him embarrassed than dead." Abruptly he turned and walked into the dark recesses of the boat's wheelhouse.

"And isn't it one and the same thing to a lad that age?" murmured Tommy under his breath, with a rueful movement of the head. "All one and the same, more's the pity." Then he, too, went about his business.

When the boat was readied, and the assembling men were each in their places, Tommy watched from the pier as they slipped the cables from their moorings and the stirring engines propelled the small craft out into the inky water.

"God bless," he whispered to them as they moved from the shoreline, "God bless."

Then he turned and, looking uneasily to right and left, blended with the shadows of the dockside and started back toward the pub.

The transferring of the guns was a simple enough task. The old trawler anchored outside the twelve-mile limit looked innocuous enough, with her age-battered hull and her sturdy bulk in the darkness.

Tierney breathed a sigh of relief as the last of the boxes of guns was loaded on board by the silent crew. So far, so good, he told himself. But the apprehension somehow didn't lessen.

Tierney felt the bulge that housed the gun in his jacket for the hundredth time it seemed and glanced at his watch: 2:38 and right on schedule. At this rate, they'd be finished their work and back in Dublin harbor with the rest of the morning's fishing boats. He glanced uneasily out over the choppy water.

How cold and dark it seemed in the night. Memories of his father standing in the small boat he had fished from floated back with the slap-slap sound of the darkened water against the craft's hull.

What a good man he was, thought Tierney of his father. Good-hearted and willing to let his sons be who they must, no matter what the neighbors might say about it.

Memories of the man floated back, evoked by the eerie essence of the hour. He could see himself, a boy, standing alongside his da in the boat, the night cold chilling his hands and nose, little steam clouds bursting forth from his lips with speech.

"How far does it go down, Da?" he had asked once, when he was very young, and his older brothers had made sport of the question. But his father had answered solemnly, as if it were a worthy inquiry.

"Far enough to keep all the boats afloat and to provide a home for the wee fishies, lad," he had said, puffing contentedly on his pipe that was seldom alight when on the water.

"Far enough to house the graveyard of all the boats that ever sailed and all the men that ever sailed them."

"But not *all* sailors died at sea, did they, Da?" Tierney had asked, aghast.

"Nae, lad. Just those as had that destiny. But 'tisn't a bad place for a man of the sea to rest, you know. Not bad at all, at all."

And little Tierney had looked out over the side of the rocking boat at the great expanse of black angry water and had wondered how his father could say such an implausible thing. That same summer he had gotten his big brothers to teach him to swim, in a protest against the idea of spending eternity at the bottom of the cold, dark sea.

He glanced now at Tahg, who, feeling his father's eyes on him, looked up and smiled, tentatively. The father waved back to reassure him and Tahg went on about his work, relieved of the pressure of parental disapproval.

Tierney smiled to himself in the darkness. He had taught his own son to be a good swimmer, too, in remembrance of his father's conversation. Tahg was a strong swimmer, his body an athlete's. Why, at this strange moment, should that seem to him such a necessary bulwark against danger? "Because you are never so vulnerable as on a boat," Tommy would say . . . had said, in fact, when the question of the gunrunning had first come up. "I'll help you wherever I can, lad," he'd assured Tierney. "But on dry land only, if you don't mind. The singing of the sea chanties is the closest I'd like to come to the big briney."

Tierney watched the German ship weigh anchor and begin to slip away into the distance. The lights of shore should be visible within the hour. He comforted himself with the thought of land.

A whirring sound, far away it seemed, began to insinuate itself into his hearing. Tierney leaned out over the side and listened, all senses alert.

"Ship dead ahead, Captain," said a voice at his back. "Naval cutter, by the speed of her, and heading right for us."

"She may just pass us by," replied Tierney. "We may just be in her normal path. Let's wait it out and see."

"She's signaling us to heave to," a voice called from the bow. "What'll we do, sir?"

"We'll try to talk our way out of it. Secure the caskets in the hold and keep your weapons at the ready!"

"Aye, sir," answered the mate, who in turn shouted orders to the other men.

Instinctively Tierney's eye searched for his son, but the boy was stowing guns already, deep within the boat's small confines.

"Ahoy there!" shouted a clipped voice from the Coast Guard vessel that had pulled alongside. "Identify yourself!"

"Fishing boat, the *Countess Cathleen,*" Tierney shouted back, trying to keep the edge of fear out of his voice.

"What are you doing this far out, at this time of night?" asked the voice, none too amiably.

"Trying to get a jump on the little fishes, sir," replied Tierney with as thick a Dublin accent as he could manage. "And on the competition as well."

"Prepare to be boarded," replied the unimpressed voice over the water.

"We may have to fight for it," whispered Tierney under his

breath to his mate. "We can't outrun them and I don't fancy spending the rest of my life in a British prison."

The man grunted assent and walked quickly back to where the other men were gathered.

A party of three, plus the officer, boarded the small boat.

"We are checking all suspicious vessels for contraband. I have a blanket warrant for search and seizure."

"Contraband, is it?" asked Tierney, playing for time. "And what exactly would you be having in mind, sir?"

The young English officer smiled deprecatingly as he replied, "As a matter of fact, guns are what I had in mind. It might interest you to know that we have just apprehended a German ship traveling in these waters under false identification. And I might remind you that if we do find any weapons aboard your vessel you will all be arrested for treason against the Crown."

"Then we might as well be hanged for a sheep as a goat, wouldn't you say, lad?" replied Tierney as he signaled to the waiting men. Tierney lunged for the lieutenant, but even as he did so his heart sank with the hopelessness of the odds, for there were a dozen more men on the military boat.

Guns rent the silence of the night. Grunts and curses as bodies were launched this way and that on the slippery deck. More men from the Coast Guard vessel prepared to reinforce the men who had boarded.

Tierney grappled with a large man with a gun in his hand as he felt himself struck from behind. He felt his body buckle, falling to the deck; he knew as he did so that he was a dead man. He saw his assailant raise the pistol toward his head—then, miraculously, the man's hand was jerked up and the bullet went wide, giving Tierney time to get to his feet.

"Grab his gun, Da," shouted Tahg's voice urgently in the darkness. It was Tahg's arm pinning the man from behind that had saved him.

He grasped the fallen weapon and hit the struggling man behind the ear with it. As the body slumped noiselessly to the deck, he saw the reinforcements grappling up the side of the boat.

"You must swim for it, lad!" said the father urgently.

"I'll not leave you," said the boy, a terrible strain in his voice.

"Someone must warn them on shore."

"I won't go!" said the boy defiantly.

"There's no time to argue with me, Tahg! No time!"

Tierney looked desperately at the men coming toward them and the inevitability of what was to come made his decision for him.

"Forgive me, son!" he whispered as he tackled the boy with all his weight, sending him toppling over the railing and into the icy water below. He waited only the split second it took to see his son's head break the surface, a look of incredulity on his handsome face; then, saying a prayer under his breath, Tierney raced back into the morass of grunting, cursing, fighting men.

Con paced the floor with a growing sense of apprehension. It was nearly 8 A.M. and no sign of Tierney. The mounting fear was holding her fatigue at bay. He should have been home two hours ago.

Something had gone wrong. No! she argued back at her own apprehension. He is just delayed. He'll be here in another minute. The door will open and he'll tell me how he was caught by the tide, or a drunk in an alley, or by the infernal passing patrols on Sackville Street.

But something *had gone wrong!* Her stomach and her heart knew it and nothing that her head could argue would soothe the growing certainty. She glanced at the clock for the thirtieth time in an hour and made up her mind.

She would find Seaneen. She would put on her coat and shoes and tiptoe down the stairs and sidle into the dangerous darkness and run to Seaneen. He would know what to do.

Con was halfway down the stairs when it struck her that she hadn't left a note for Tierney to tell him where she would be. *Never* did either leave without a note to the other telling of their whereabouts.

She hesitated, ready to retreat and find pen and paper, but something stopped her. It was the knowledge that Tierney wasn't coming home.

The officer stood facing the chair in which Tierney was shackled hand and foot.

"I should not like to be forced to ask you yet again to tell me the names of the others who are involved in this scheme of yours." The menace in his arrogant voice caused the two subalterns to glance at each other. Lieutenant Benchley was well known for his quick dispatch of Fenian agitators.

"There are no others. It was my own doing. No more than that."

The lieutenant's hand shot out at lightning speed and the blow to Tierney's jaw sent his chair sprawling backward. He lay stunned by his own helplessness as much as by the blow, and then felt himself lifted, chair and all, to an upright position.

"I'll accept no lies from scum life like you!" spat the angular man through his teeth. "If I have to beat you or torture you or starve you into the truth, I intend to do so. Do you understand me?" The malicious voice left no room for doubt.

Tierney weighed the wisdom of a reply, and said nothing.

"Do you understand me?" The voice thundered this time and the fist snaked out again, but this time, prepared, Tierney somehow managed to keep his balance.

"Aye," he said as evenly as possible through the pain in his jaw. "I've heard of England's superior civilization. I've no doubt you'll let me taste of it before we're through."

The lieutenant sneered at the rebuke. "We shall see how two days without food affects your cockiness." He waved to the subalterns to remove the prisoner. He'd had plenty of opportunity to deal with recalcitrant prisoners before this one. Irishmen were no different from Boers or Hottentots. He'd found that a little hunger and thirst usually softened them up before progressing to more violent means. There was benefit to be gained by not rushing things unduly.

Tierney lay on the cot in his small cell and tried to assess the situation. Thick stone walls that would brook no assault . . . a pervasive dampness that chilled more than the body. The cold of the Irish climate without warm clothes or blankets. These were the immediate miseries, but bearable enough. And he'd been hungry before; only an officer of the Crown could be insensitive enough to think hunger would frighten an Irishman; hunger was a simple fact of life.

But Con. O dear God, not to see her again . . . or Tahg. He could still see the startled look on his son's face as he'd tackled him. Strong swimmer or not, had he made it to shore? He pushed the thoughts far back in his brain, for they could undo him. Did she know by now? What agonies must she be suffering if she knew? Where would she go? To Seaneen, of course. He'd know what to say. Ah, but the mind is a daft machine, he told himself. What a bloody fake it is to think that *anyone* could say *anything* to her that would make a difference. The internal wrestling match brought an added pain to his throbbing head.

Tierney forced his mind to the immediate danger. He would be tortured. What would they do, whose job it was to wrench things from a man by obscene means? What would he be able to endure? Did any man ever know the answer to that question until the moment came? Had Clarke known that he would survive what they'd done to him . . . or Seaneen? They'd been tortured by experts, both, and they'd borne it. The thought comforted him. It was important to know that it was not beyond a man to endure indignities and torments to protect his friends . . . it was hard, brutal, frightening . . . but not impossible. That was a good thing to remember.

The dim gas light remained on in his cell throughout the night, but Tierney slept fitfully nonetheless and dreamed of his wife.

Two days without food shouldn't weaken a man much, he told himself as he stood in the small interrogation room and waited for whatever would come next, but he was feeling weakened and demoralized and knew that the persistent hunger was part of it.

The two enlisted men snapped suddenly to attention as Lieutenant Benchley entered and swaggered to the wooden table where a full meal had been set out. Instead of making Tierney hungry as it was supposed to do, the intended insult and the arrogance made his gorge rise.

"I'll have the names of your friends and accomplices now, Mr. O'Connor," said the lieutenant as he began to dine.

Tierney remained silent.

Benchley nodded to one of the men, and a fist caught Tierney in the kidney from behind, doubling him. He felt a rib give way with the second punch and, struggling wildly against his handcuffs, realized with sickening finality how vulnerable he was.

"And now, Mr. O'Connor?" The quiet voice was malevolent but interested.

No reply.

The blows began again. Eventually there was little in the

world besides the pain of fists and boots colliding with flesh and bone. When he lost consciousness, they dragged him back to his cell, where he awakened later, stiff from the cold of the stone floor that had seeped into him, and grateful that, for the moment, it was over.

✍ I cannot begin to describe to you Con's state of mind after learning of Tierney's capture. In front of the others she struggled to maintain a semblance of rationality—discussing the feasibility of this plan or that to get him out. Then I would look into her haunted, desperate eyes; reading them, you could make no mistake about the depths of her despair.

She had been in prison. She knew its brutality. And her offense had been minimal compared with his.

By day she tried to get to see him. She begged, pleaded, cajoled and offered bribery, all to no avail. We enlisted Edmond's help, but he was told that the prisoner was held for high treason and would not be permitted visitors who might be involved in his plottings. He responded by asking to see the prisoner himself; surely the Earl of Sligo could not be deemed a security risk. Edmond told us he was sure he would eventually be admitted—but when he returned from his discussions with the Castle about the prisoner, he could not hide from us the gravity of the situation.

I stayed with Con and Tahg during this time. A more loving or stalwart son would have been impossible to find. He was disconsolate about his father and guilty about having escaped capture. But he strove to hide his own sorrows in order to help his mother bear with hers. The bond between my nephew and myself that was forged in those terrible days was one of rare substance.

Several nights after Tierney's capture I was awakened from sleep to hear the stealthy creak of floorboards being carefully traversed. I saw Con's slender body outlined against the window, her arms crossed over her chest as if she hugged away the cold.

I rose from bed and, throwing a shawl around my own shoulders, carried one to her. She didn't turn as I wrapped it around her shoulders, but she spoke in a voice so small and wistful, it remains in my memory.

"I shall never see him alive again . . . ." she whispered.

"You mustn't even think such a thing!" I said, aghast, putting my arms around her shoulders. She did not respond in the least to my touch, but remained stony as a churchyard statue.

"I shall never see him alive again," she repeated, once with a terrible finality, and I knew in that moment that she had ceased to hope. ✎

19   Tierney sat suddenly upright on the small cot in his cell. He shuddered in the darkness, and with good reason. He had seen his own death in a vision. Or perhaps it had been a dream. He shook his head to clear it, aware of the pounding of his heart and the clammy sweat on his body, despite the cold.

He had been watching them from afar in the dream—Con and Tahg together at the side of an open grave. A soft rain was falling and there were other people at the cemetery, gathered in small, huddled groups beneath black umbrellas.

He hadn't been sure at first that it was they, so he had called to them . . . but when they'd turned toward him he had seen their faces and in that awful instant had understood. The grave was his own.

Seaneen had been in the vision and the men from the IRB. And someone, perhaps Pearse, seemed to be speaking to the crowd, for people listened quietly against the rain, expressions of anger and sorrow mingled on their faces. The vision should have faded with waking, but instead he saw it clearly, clearly.

A terrible chilling certainty sat upon him in the darkness. No simple dream had it been, triggered by anxiety or an empty belly. It had been a true dream . . . a dream of prophecy; sweet Jesus, always, always had he known the true dreams when they came to him. From childhood on he'd known there had been things he knew that others did not know . . . things he saw that others did not see.

Oh Con, Con, Con my dearest heart, is this to be the end of us, then? This horror of loneliness and sorrow that I read in your beautiful face? This monstrous agony of longing that I feel, to be all there is left between us?

Never to hold you naked in my arms . . . never to whisper our sweet love words in the night . . . never to know the simple perfection of sleeping beside you till the light of morning?

How lonely to be without you in so long a sleep, my Beauty. How can I bear it?

Tierney put his head forward in his hands and felt strange, unaccustomed tears spill over their rough surface. He sat for a long while unmoving, trying to collect his thoughts, and then he rose from the bed and, wrapping the thin blanket about him for some semblance of warmth, he went to the door and shouted for the guard.

"I'll not be sleeping tonight," he told the man quietly. "Could you be finding me a light for my candle?"

The guard nodded assent and returned momentarily with a lighted candle, which he passed through the bars of his cell. Thanking him, Tierney reached beneath his mattress for the paper he had hidden there, along with the stub of a pencil.

"My dearest girl," he wrote, careful of the size of the words against the hoarded paper.

It has come to me that the end is near (or perhaps only the beginning, if all our metaphysical conjectures or even those of the old Church prove correct), and there is much to say to you. So very much to say.

Nineteen years we've been together—more years than you had been in the world when we met . . . a lifetime, my love. A lifetime of joyous communion for me . . . a lifetime of all a man could dream to find in this world in wife and comrade.

But for you, it seems to me now, there was much to bear with. The terrible fear you've always had of poverty (did you think I never knew, you who sought to keep it from me?) . . . the wish that I would write more and rebel less . . . the terrors you lived with each time the Brotherhood called me to do my part. I knew. I always knew. And yet until this hour it seemed to me that the path I followed was the right one and that in striving to be true to my ideals I was also true to you. Was that no more than a foolish sop to my conscience? I wonder tonight, dear wife.

Looking back on all your patient, long-suffering, courageous years, it seems to me that I have done it all wrong-headedly. I should have flown with you while yet we could—should have wandered over the world's wide rim if need be . . . to some place far enough from Ireland's troubled heart to give us peace. I should have spent my time in writing love songs and sonnets to you, my proud Beauty, my lover, my friend. I'll be damned if I don't think the poems I would have written you might have made us both immortal.

Will you understand when I tell you that in dying I shall have the easier task? To live without what has been for us would be worse by far than death—forgive me, heart of my heart, for leaving you to face the world alone.

I am filled with memories of you tonight, my love. Too sacred to be put on paper where salacious jailers might read and profane them. But you know the memories of which I speak—would that you could know how they sustain me in this awful hour.

How can I tell you how wildly I have loved you from that first moment in my mother's cottage when I saw you and thought you too perfect to be real. How every time I've looked at you or touched you or held you in my arms through all the years, I've marveled at the goodness of God that He could have sent you to me.

You are and always have been, cuisle mo chroidhe, the pulse of my heart. Remember how once we spoke of the Other Side and the place where we would meet there on the broad green bank of the river, beneath the shade tree? I'll go there first to find the way, Con, my Beauty—find me when you can. I will never be far from you, beloved wife.

> Tierney

He began to write furiously, filling the squares of paper with his concise penmanship, pausing infrequently and then beginning again with renewed vigor.

When he was finished, Tierney read through what he had

done. Then, placing the last small scrap of paper atop the bundle, he wrote across the page:

Love Songs for a Wild Harp
12 April 1916

Finally, satisfied, he blew out the candle and went to sleep.

Lord Edmond Manningham stood uncomfortably in the prison commandant's office. It was not his custom to make calls on rebel prisoners and he deeply resented being placed in such a ludicrous position by his brother-in-law's incarceration.

The army captain eyed Manningham with curiosity. Damned odd position the chap was in. Still and all it was sporting of him to visit the prisoner. Or perhaps his wife had forced him into it. That was more likely the case.

"All right then, Lord Edmond," he said in a clipped military diction as he rang for the sergeant. "He's not supposed to have visitors, but the word's come down from the Castle that you're to be an exception."

Edmond looked at him coldly. The man was only doing his duty, of course, but he really had nothing to say to him.

"Thank you for your courtesy," Edmond answered noncommittally to the captain as he followed a sergeant out into the stone corridor.

"Blasted cold down here, Sergeant," he said to the man as they made their way into the dreary interior. The damp chill in the air was bone deep. "Aye, sir," answered the sergeant, with an upland accent. "We find it good for cooling off these Irish hotheads."

He stopped at an iron door with a small aperture cut in it and rattled the key into the ancient lock. When the door swung open the man stepped back, allowing Edmond entry.

"Any trouble, sir, just you sing out. My men are at the end of the corridor."

"There'll be no trouble, Sergeant, I assure you." Edmond tried to see clearly into the darkened cell. He made out Tierney's large figure on the metal cot against the wall. The man tried to rise to greet his guest, but fell back in obvious pain. He smiled embarrassedly at Edmond and pulled the blanket about him closely. Edmond was astounded to see how gaunt the large man had grown since last he'd seen him. He looked sick and hungry.

"Forgive me, Edmond. If I managed to get up at all, I doubt I could stay that way," he said. The boyish quality about Tierney that always irritated Edmond seemed, in this setting, sad and grotesquely out of place.

"What in God's name has happened to you, man?" Edmond's voice betrayed his distress at the only possible explanation for Tierney's condition.

"A bit of colonial justice, Edmond. They put some questions to me," answered Tierney with irony, "and were unhappy with my answers. So they tried to civilize me."

He attempted once more to sit upright; this time the blanket that had covered his body fell away from his chest and shoulders. Edmond stared wide-eyed at the evidence of severe beatings, seen through his opened shirt. Tierney clutched quickly, embarrassedly, at the blanket to cover himself.

"Dear God, man, you've been beaten!" Edmond said it incredulously. "But we've all been assured in Parliament that absolutely nothing like this is happening here!"

"Every day, Edmond. This and far worse. But let's not waste precious time on things we cannot change. Tell me of Con and Tagh. Are they safe?"

Edmond stared at his brother-in-law. Manly and uncomplaining, he seemed in this dreadful situation; like one who has risked all and lost, and is quite willing to bear the consequences. He wondered suddenly if he might have misjudged the man.

"They're well and safe, Tierney," Edmond answered him steadily. "She's moved heaven and earth to get permission to see you."

"Aye. As I knew she would. They've told me, of course, that no one has attempted to see me, but I didn't believe them. 'Tis the only thing I fear, Edmond, that I may not be able to bear me like a man when I see her." The statement was so ingenuous and honest that it needed no reply. Edmond cleared his throat to speak, much moved by the condition of this brother-in-law he had so long detested. He saw Tierney reach up to scratch his head, then lower his hand embarrassedly. It dawned on him that the man was afflicted by lice, a great problem in prisons.

"You must try to let me know how to help you, Tierney," he said huskily, angry at the indignity of what he was seeing. "I've petitioned the Castle and raised hell with the Viceroy and written to Whitehall and God knows what else at Elizabeth's insistence, but I've no doubt it will all fall on deaf ears. You've really stepped into a hornets' nest, I'm afraid, with all the fear of German intervention and the war . . ." He let the thought trail off, feeling impotent fury at the ugliness of the whole situation. "But, by God, O'Connor, I'll do my best to see that you're not molested again. The idea of this torture business is absolutely appalling!"

Tierney smiled and forced his body into an upright position.

"There's more for us to talk of than beatings, Edmond. My worst fears are for Con and Tahg, not for myself. I made my commitment to Ireland long ago and I'll keep it as best I can."

No weakness there, Edmond noted. They'll get little information from this one by torture, I'll wager. There was strength and honor beneath the boyish handsomeness of the man; Edmond wished he had admitted seeing it before.

"If I die here, there's naught I can leave them. A little might come from my poems and plays, if Con can sell them, a little from the pub—but not enough for safety. It pains me to ask charity, man, but I'd not rest easy knowing they were penniless."

"You must know they'll be cared for, O'Connor. You have my word on it."

The younger man smiled somewhat at that, his mouth turning down at the corners in the curious way it had; he seemed greatly relieved.

"Will you take a message to Con, then, and a gift?" he asked, trying to move a little on the cot and wincing as he did so. "A broken rib or two, I think," he said by way of explanation. "I could get worse in a hurling match." But Edmond could see the stoically borne pain behind the man's haggard eyes.

"I've brought paper and pen for you so you can write if you wish," Edmond said, thanking heaven that Beth had reminded him to do so.

He averted his eyes as Tierney struggled to hold himself erect enough to write. The man finished finally, and folded the paper before handing it back to him. Then he reached beneath the mattress with difficulty and, gathering up a sheaf of scraps of paper, handed them to Edmond, who took them wonderingly. "They're for my wife," he said evenly. "It would be safer for

her if no one sees these papers, or knows of their existence,"
and Edmond nodded assent. He noted that the man had not
questioned if he could be trusted, but had assumed he would do
his bidding.

"One more thing," Tierney said softly, and Edmond could
see the effort it was costing him to speak. "Don't let her know
of this." He motioned to his own body, and it was eloquent
enough to make his meaning clear. "She mustn't know, Edmond; she'll suffer enough without this knowledge."

"No," said his brother-in-law, much disturbed by what he
had seen. "She shall not know of it.

"I'll do my best for you, sir," said the older man, indicating
the papers in his hand, and Tierney smiled at the formal address. It had taken years before Edmond would call him other
than O'Connor.

"Only what I've asked."

"God bless you, then." Edmond felt a warm moisture behind
his eyes. This was too much a man to meet his doom ignomini-
ously in a cold, dark cellar. What a ghastly waste it was.

Tierney stood painfully to bid him good-bye. Edmond saw
with horror that his belt and shoelaces had been taken and the
injured man had to struggle to hold up his trousers with one
hand as he extended the other.

Edmond took the offered hand, realizing it was the first time
he had ever done so. He stared for a moment at the unshaven,
uncombed, tattered figure, thinking he seemed curiously, inexplicably, dignified. Then, at a loss for words, he called the jailer
and made his way gratefully toward the warmth of sunlight.

20   The guard pushed Tommy McGowan roughly
into the cell where Tierney lay in a troubled
sleep. The man lurched into the room with the momentum of
the push and landed nearly on top of Tierney's small cot.

Tierney opened his eyes, startled, and moved painfully from
the bed as he realized what had happened.

"Sweet Christ, Tommy! Not you, too." He said it feeling suddenly hopeless as he assisted the older man up from the floor.

"Say nothing!" whispered Tommy urgently. "They've thrown me in here because they're hoping one of us will spill the beans to the other."

"How did they get you?"

"DORA, of course. The Defense of the Realm Act gives them carte blanche for search and seizure. They just waltzed into my place without a by-your-leave and knocked me about some. They said that they had evidence that I know the identity of the Harper—it seems they've been watching both you and me for some time. It may have been an informer—it may have just been damnable bad luck." There was a glint of anger in McGowan's eyes as he said this; he tilted his head toward the door to warn Tierney against saying too much.

"What evidence do they have?"

"They need none, although that blackguard of a Benchley claims to have proof positive about the Harper, of course. They've got no good in mind for either one of us, lad, you may be sure of that."

"Have you seen Con?"

"Aye, and Tahg Mor, as well. Both all right but distracted about your capture. She's been to the prison fifty times trying to see you, but the bastards won't give her the time of day."

Tierney dropped his voice to a whisper. "And the Rising?"

"To go on as scheduled. Casement's shipment of guns is still at sea. The rumor is that FitzGibbon and Casement are being shipped back to Ireland together." Tierney nodded at the news about Des. The man had fulfilled his end of the bargain; it was good that he was getting out of Germany. But if the coast patrol had intercepted his own shipment of guns, what was to keep them from intercepting Casement's too? And perhaps Des, along with the guns.

"Do you think they really know the identity of the Harper?" Tierney asked suddenly, trying to purge the other thoughts from his mind.

Tommy looked steadily at his younger friend for a long moment, then said, "No. I heard them talking when they were bringing me in. They think you're the Harper. They think they've a great prize in you, laddie. A gunrunner *and* a famous dissident. You're a propaganda bonanza. They've only brought me here to try to get to you."

Tierney's gray eyes widened, then he nodded. It made sense, of course. What he wouldn't do to save himself, he might do to save his friend.

"Whatever happens, lad, you must understand where I stand in this." Tommy's voice sounded tense and determined. "Whatever they do to me, you must not endanger yourself. The Harper is important to the Cause, and you, Con and Tahg are the only family I have left."

"Don't be an ass, Tommy! I'll not let them torture you for what we've done."

"Face it, lad! There's little enough chance either one of us has of getting out of here alive. But if it comes to one of us or the other, you've more to live for than I. Remember it!"

They heard the heavy footfall of boots on the stone floor of the corridor; both men looked at each other for a moment, then clasped hands tightly as if in farewell. There was no need for Tierney to argue the point with Tommy, for he already knew that death stood at his own shoulder. There would be no need for Tommy to be injured, and at all costs he must protect the identity of the Harper.

Benchley stood in the doorway, neatly dressed and booted. He spoke to both prisoners.

"How nice that you two are already acquainted," he said amiably, "Quite a catch we've made in your friend here, O'Connor. We have every reason to believe that he is involved closely with the infamous Wild Harp."

"I've never known Tommy to write anything other than ballads," Tierney replied evenly.

"Yes, indeed. And now we are about to see what he has to sing about to us." He motioned to the men with him to remove McGowan from the cell.

"While we're speaking with Mr. McGowan here, perhaps you'll be good enough to think a bit on the questions we've asked you about the guns. We're really quite impatient to have that information, Mr. O'Connor—about who was with you in this gunrunning scheme and what the weapons were to be used for."

Two of the soldiers grabbed Tommy and propelled him into the corridor.

"Your friend is not a young man, Mr. O'Connor. He may not be able to take as much punishment as you. So I'd suggest you do your thinking quickly."

Tierney heard the key turn in the lock and McGowan's voice from the corridor: "Not a word to the bastards on my account, lad. Not one word!" Then he heard a grunt as the man was dragged away.

"Tell us about the Harper." Lieutenant Benchley's voice was cold and amused.

Tommy stood, his hands bound behind his back. He was about Benchley's size and could look him evenly in the eye. He smiled slightly at the man, then threw back his head and began to sing.

> "The minstrel boy to the war is gone.
> In the ranks of death you'll find him . . ."

Benchley signaled the man on the right and his fist caught Tommy in the side.

> "His father's sword he hath girded on,
> And his wild harp slung behind him."

A second man hit him in the jaw and he felt a tooth loosened by the impact of the blow.

Tierney clutched the bars of his cell. He could hear Tommy's voice, as well as the sounds of the beating. The room where they were interrogating him must be close at hand.

Tierney tried to do a rapid inventory of his options. Con had to be protected, at all costs. And Tommy, too. What they wanted from him were the names of the others implicated in the Rising-to-be. Even for Tommy's sake he couldn't tell them that. But he could admit to being the Harper. That, at least, would lead them away from Con. The singing began anew but Tommy's voice sounded weaker.

> "Land of song! sang the warrior bard
> Though all the world betray thee . . ."

Clutching the bars of the tiny window in the door of his cell, Tierney, too, began to sing, as loudly as he could. It was the only support he could give his friend.

"One sword at least thy rights shall guard."

He sang at the top of his lungs:

"One faithful harp shall praise thee."

Then he heard other voices in the corridor of cells take up the song:

"The minstrel fell but the foeman's chains
Couldn't bring his proud soul under . . ."

The voices were not like his and Tommy's, but they were determined voices nonetheless:

"The harp he loved never spoke again.
For he tore its chords asunder.
And said, 'No chain shall sully thee,
Harp of love and bravery.
Thy songs were made for the pure and free
And shall never sound in slavery.' "

The strains of the song echoed and died in the stony corridor. Tierney listened but no sounds could be heard from the interrogation room anymore.

Minutes later, the two guards dragged Tommy McGowan's unconscious form into the cell and left him there.

"I think there was something quare in the food, lad." Tommy said it half an hour or so after the guards had removed their supper pails. "I'm feeling poorly."

Tierney nodded, feeling too nauseated to speak. There'd been something in the food to sicken them, all right, but worse than sick, he was feeling disoriented, dizzy, as if he couldn't quite focus his brain.

"Christ Almighty, do you see that thing on the wall?" Tommy shouted suddenly, and Tierney looked at where the wall had always been. Whatever it was that Tommy had seen wasn't there now . . . but then neither was the wall. Instead, some weird amorphous shape had taken its place, colorful and pulsating.

"Shit, I think they've poisoned us!" Tierney heard Tommy's voice reach him through a veil of cotton.

"No," he managed to shout back, or thought he did. "It's some drug to make us hallucinate." He had been warned of this kind of treatment by one of the Fenians—but who, where, when? His mind was spiraling somewhere out of his control. And Tommy was right—there was some terrible thing on the wall.

Tierney tried to focus his eyes but it was difficult to do. He saw Tommy's shape above him, felt his hand slapping his cheek, but it seemed to be at a distance.

"It sure as hell makes you understand why prisoners go on hunger strikes, doesn't it?" Tommy was saying, his voice clearer now, and a hint of the old mischief in it. "You can't trust the fucking food in His Majesty's hotels!"

Tierney blinked himself back into consciousness with extreme effort. The cell reeked of vomit and his head ached as if it had been beaten, on the inside. His mouth was dry and foul-tasting and he drank gratefully the water from the tin cup in Tommy's hands.

"Not too much now, lad. I came out of it half an hour ago and made the mistake of gulping down too much water." He smiled ruefully at the mess in the cell. "I'm afraid the chambermaid will have her hands full after this little fiasco."

Tierney struggled to sit up. "Christ, I thought I felt bad *before,*" he said, and Tommy chuckled.

"Makes you a bit curious about what other civilizing techniques they have in store for us savages, doesn't it?"

Tierney nodded, grimacing at the pain in his head. There wasn't an inch of him that didn't ache.

"I guess this is meant to soften us up," he said.

"Well, it certainly has done that," said Tommy. "I feel like I'm made out of old rubber bands."

They finally slept but with great trepidation about what the morning might hold in store.

* * *

"You men really should try to do something about your appearances." Lieutenant Benchley smiled from behind the table in his interrogation room. "You do look a bit shabby."

Tierney and Tommy stood across the desk from him, still in the soiled clothes from the night before. "We do what we can, Benchley," said Tommy, "but the valet was late this morning." Tierney said nothing.

"I trust you intend to be a little more communicative with us today, gentlemen. Why, your race is known the world over for its loquaciousness." He smiled unpleasantly.

"But do let me explain to you the rules of the game before we begin again. The information we want is in your possession, Mr. O'Connor. Quite frankly we neither know, nor very much care, about Mr. McGowan here. He just happens to have the misfortune of being your close friend.

"You see, we've come to the conclusion that you were not planning to be very cooperative with us—and since your illustrious brother-in-law is throwing his none-too-paltry muscle into getting you out of here, it behooves us to make you incriminate yourself *before* you are snatched from our grip.

"Thus, Mr. O'Connor, we are forced to use methods we wish we could avoid. I fancy myself something of a judge of human nature, you see. And it is my bet that while you would tell us nothing to save yourself, you might be persuaded to tell us what we wish to know to save your friend.

"So you see, Mr. O'Connor . . . from this moment on, Mr. McGowan's fate is entirely in your hands."

He turned his attention to the two guards who held Tommy between them.

"You may begin," he said, and Tierney turned his head away as the blows began to thud into his friend's body.

"Not a word to them, lad!" he heard Tommy hiss through his clenched teeth. Blow after blow landed on his soft flesh. Finally his body sagged and he sank to the floor despite their efforts to hold him up.

"No answers yet, eh?" said Benchley as the guards threw a pail of water in Tommy's face to revive him. "Then perhaps we must try something more graphic."

He spoke to his two subordinates, who then pulled the now conscious Tommy upright and pinned him to a flogging frame.

Securing his hands, arms and waist in the wooden rack, they tore his shirt from top to bottom.

Christ Almighty, thought Tierney, watching with horror as Tommy's white flesh was exposed to the dark air, he's too old to withstand a flogging.

"All right, Benchley, let him go!" said Tierney clearly. "I'll admit that I'm the Harper."

Benchley smiled. "Very good, Mr. O'Connor. Very good indeed. But I'm afraid that's only part of what we wish to know." The smile died.

"I want the names of your friends in the gunrunning. I want to know where the guns were going and to what purpose."

Tierney looked at him steadily. "I was in it alone. I intended to sell the guns to the highest bidder. I figured somebody would want them."

"Really, Mr. O'Connor," said Benchley with mock sorrow. "Surely a famous writer like the Wild Harp can show more imagination than that in concocting a story." Turning to the guards, Benchley said, "Get a doctor in here on the double."

Tierney knew it was prison regulations that a doctor be present during floggings. A small gray-haired man arrived and examined the prisoner.

"This man is already injured," he said. "He won't live through much of this nastiness."

Benchley nodded and gave an order to the man with the leather lash. Tommy made a strange strangled sound as the first blow raised a welt on his back. Another sound accompanied the second blow; then Tierney realized that Tommy was trying to sing, "Soldiers are we, whose lives are pledged to Ireland . . . Some have come from a land across the sea."

The lash fell again.

A bright red slash appeared on the man's back and blood began to trickle from it.

> "Born to be free, no more our ancient Sireland
> Shall shelter, the despot or the slave . . ."

The sickening sounds of rending flesh interrupted the grotesque sound of the song.

Suddenly Tierney knew what he must do. The only thing he

could do to save Con and Tommy. He himself was a dead man anyway.

"Forgive me, Con," Tierney breathed aloud as he made his move. "I can't let him die like this." He lunged for the soldier in front of him on the left, who stood in silence watching the scene. It was important that he give the man just enough time to get the gun clear of his holster . . .

The shot exploded in the stone confines of the room, the echo ricocheting wildly in the reverberating dimness.

"You fool!" screamed Benchley. "See what he's made you do? You idiot, you've killed him!"

Tierney lay in a circle of blood on the icy floor, a sticky redness spreading across his prison shirt and puddling under him.

"Oh my God, I am heartily sorry for having offended Thee" —it seemed to him that someone was saying the familiar words over him—"and I confess to Almighty God that I have sinned, because I fear the loss of heaven and the pains of hell . . ."

The old words of the Act of Contrition struggled unbidden into his mind in his last moments. He tried to push the disturbing sound away, for he wasn't embarking on a voyage to the Catholic heaven of his boyhood. He was going to the grassy hill beyond the river where Con would come to him. . . . He was going home to Con.

၇ In the days after Tierney's death Con was like one possessed. Exhausting herself daily in training the boys, running messages, dogging Seaneen's footsteps . . . whatever she could find to distract her from the hideous burden of grief she carried. She had even announced to the IRB that she intended to take Tierney's place in the Rising.

For three days after news of Tierney's death had reached us, she had sat in their little flat, the parcel of Tierney's clothing and effects that the Castle had sent her by her side.

"How respectful of property they are . . . they who have no respect for lives," she said to me when we returned from the funeral. It was a day of dark drizzle, the kind Dublin excels at . . . all of us at the graveside gathering had been shrouded in a sea of black umbrellas to ward off the worst of it. She was soaked to the skin, but I couldn't rouse her to even shake off the drenched clothing, so like a sleepwalker she seemed.

The poems Tierney had written in prison seemed to sustain her. She read them over and over—fingering the tattered pages when she was too tired to read them more. Tahg and I sat with her for hours, until it became apparent that what she needed more than anything was to be left alone with her memories.

Tahg took his father's death hard and deep, as I might have expected. He blamed himself for having escaped the boat the night his father was captured, and his usual introspection seemed to have turned in upon itself, so that I feared the agony of his brooding. Then an extraordinary young girl arrived to speak with him.

She was quite dazzlingly beautiful, arresting and unusual—with a theatrical voice that seemed somehow to promise unfathomable mysteries just in passing the time of day. She pulled him physically from the flat . . . hers was a presence not easily denied, I suspect—and when he returned hours later, the terrible intensity of grief seemed to have been transmuted into a more bearable sorrow.

Although we had no way of knowing this at the time it was occurring, during the week of Tierney's imprisonment and the awful week that followed it, Des was going through his own purgatory.

The Germans had proved feckless; they had lured both him and Casement with promises of limitless cooperation, but both men had soon discovered the perfidy of England's enemy. The guns they were offered were nearly worthless, the manpower they had been promised nonexistent, and they themselves were little more than prisoners trotted out on occasion for propagandist purposes.

In their common difficulty Des and Roger Casement—called "Roddie" by his friends—had become confidants and contrived to have themselves returned to Ireland on the same boat. Indeed, had they not been permitted to return on the submarine carrying Casement's shipment of guns, it is doubtful that either would have escaped Germany at all.

It appears that realizing the lack of support from Germany, Des and Roddie had formed a desperate plan to return to Ireland to try to prevent the Rising. On the pretext that they wished to give landing instructions for the arms cargo, they had convinced the Germans to send them to Ireland by submarine.

In truth they hoped to prevent what they now believed to be a futile and disastrous insurrection.

As every schoolchild now knows, their submarine was sunk, the guns lost and the life raft in which Des and Casement attempted to make shore was swamped by high seas. It is difficult to imagine a more disastrous or ill-omened series of events than those that brought my dear Desmond to his final destiny.

On 21 April 1916, Des and Casement made it to shore, only to be picked up by a roving police patrol. The Admiralty had broken the German code and knew of the submarine's mission —as, indeed, they had known of the one that had carried the guns to Tierney.

Mercifully for us, although not for Des, Con and I as yet knew nothing of the escalating terrors that had ensnared our beloved brother.

A few days before Easter, Edmond was called to Sligo for a local emergency of some kind. He expected to be gone a week or so and was apologetic about being away for the holiday, but I must confess I was relieved he would be out of Dublin when the Rising took place. I had been checking on his traveling gear and had just returned to the first-floor hall when I was startled to hear heated voices coming from the drawing room. I stood still at the door and tried to discern who the speakers were.

". . . he got no more than he deserved," was the first fragment that I understood. The voice was Win's.

"He was a hero!" Johnny's voice was next recognizable.

"You have to admit he had courage, Win," Jamie's ever-reasonable voice responded. "He died for what he believed in."

"He was a filthy traitor," Win said contemptuously. "And it's nothing short of disgusting that we must deal with having him in the family."

"Don't be so bloody righteous about this, Winston," said Merry. "Uncle Tierney was never anything but nice to you, and I think it's unspeakable that you are being so cruel about his death. Don't you even feel anything for Mum in this? You know how distraught she is over Aunt Constance."

"Mum?" he said in a derisive tone. "She's not much better than he was. I've heard her talking to Aunt Constance. She's as much a traitor as the rest of them!"

I was so taken aback by the unexpectedness of this statement and by the explosion of young voices, suddenly all talking at once, that I didn't realize Edmond had come up behind me. He, too, had heard the exchange.

He reached past me and opened the door with a sharp tug, startling the children into uneasy silence.

"I have been as guilty as you, Winston, of misjudgment and arrogance where your Uncle Tierney is concerned," he said clearly. "Despite the fact of his being, I believe, misguided in his goals, I now know that he was a good and courageous man, and one of high principle.

"A gentleman admires courage and honor even in his enemies, Winston. That seems to be something you haven't yet learned."

"But, Father . . ." Win began.

"Furthermore," Edmond interrupted him, "if I ever again hear of your treating your mother with disrespect, I will take a stick to your arrogant backside, no matter what age you are at the time. For the moment, you will apologize to her for your consummate rudeness and stupidity."

All eyes turned toward me, standing in the doorway; color rose in Winston's cheeks as if he had been slapped, as, in a way, he had.

"I apologize, Mother," he said in a small voice that threatened to betray him by breaking. "I'm sorry for my rudeness." I nodded my response, too stunned by what had happened—not the least of all by Edmond's defense of me—to speak.

The children left the room as rapidly as they could. Edmond cleared his throat as if to add something, then simply touched my arm in a gesture of support, and he, too, left the drawing room. ༄

21

Good Friday, 21 April 1916
Woodtown Park, Rathfarnham

MacNeill looked more distraught than The O'Rahilly had ever seen him. The usual erudite calm of the man had been badly shaken and his hands trembled slightly as he agitatedly toyed with the papers on his desk.

"I can't let them do it, Michael!" he said with conviction.

"Do what?" asked The O'Rahilly in an effort to keep some sense of order in the conversation. There was, of course, only one thing Eoin could be referring to: Pearse and the others had decided to go ahead with their war.

"They've set it for Easter Sunday. They're calling for the Volunteers and the Citizen Army—the IRB, too, of course—to meet at Liberty Hall. Pearse has lied to me all along!" MacNeill declared angrily. "He swore that no secret plans for an uprising were afoot. We've been betrayed by our own, Michael." He shook his head dejectedly.

O'Rahilly sat himself in the chair opposite MacNeill's desk and tried to sort it out for himself.

"Who's in on it?" he asked; perhaps more information would make the sorting easier.

"At this point, I don't know anything with certainty! I suppose Pearse and Connolly are the ringleaders, but I can't be sure."

"How did you find out?"

"An informer told Bulmer Hobson that Sunday's maneuvers are only a cover for the insurrection." MacNeill looked incredulous as he said, "Last night I confronted Pearse and do you know what he told me? That they—the goddamned IRB—found it fortuitous to use me as a pawn! That paper they showed us from the Castle ordering the Volunteers suppressed may have been a forgery. My God, Michael! Perhaps they've even duped us into calling for a mobilization!"

"You're sure about all this?"

"Oh yes," MacNeill said wearily. "Pearse, MacDonogh and MacDiarmida were here this morning. It seems there is even a supply of arms from Germany expected down in Kerry today."

O'Rahilly rose and walked to MacNeill's side. He placed his hand on his friend's shoulder.

"If things are gone this far, perhaps we must go along with them, Eoin. How did they ever think there would be cohesion among the men if we remained ignorant? The Volunteers follow you, after all, not Pearse!"

"I wish to God I knew that to be true, Michael," he said, despair in his voice. "If the guns are real, this may be our only chance for a rising. If it's not and we act precipitously, it could be a disaster."

"We've got to know more, Eoin, before we make any decisions. I'll let you know what I can find out." The O'Rahilly strode from the room; he seemed in command of the situation and of his own emotions. MacNeill, watching him go, wished to God that he felt more in command, even of himself. The Volunteers would look to him for answers, and he was beginning to feel that he barely knew the questions.

Saturday, 22 April 1916

MacNeill hurried back to the temporary headquarters he had established at Dr. O'Kelly's house in Rathgar Road. Now he knew the worst of it. What O'Rahilly had discovered and passed on to him earlier in the evening had sent him to Pearse at St. Enda's for confirmation. And it was all true. The Castle document was a forgery. No forcible disarmament had been planned. Worse, the *Aud* and her cargo of precious weapons was sunk to the bottom of Queenstown Harbor in Cork. Casement was imprisoned in Tralee, FitzGibbon in Dublin.

Yet, Pearse, with that insulting arrogance, claimed that he, Eoin MacNeill—without whom the Volunteers would still be an intangible concept in the brain of some sitting-room revolutionary—could not stop their mighty plans!

This Rising would be a disaster; it was doomed. Didn't everything point to that end? It was madness, and, by God, he *would* stop it! There had to be a way to let the men know the danger and to keep them from mustering tomorrow.

MacNeill pulled his watch from his pocket. After 11 P.M. already! They would have to work fast to inform the men in the country. He squared his thin shoulders. He was still chief of staff of the Irish Volunteers, and *his* word—not Pearse's, not Plunkett's and not MacDonogh's—was ultimately final.

Sunday, 23 April 1916
1 A.M.

Owing to the very critical position, all orders to Irish Volunteers for today, Easter Sunday, are hereby rescinded, and no parades, marches or other movements of

Irish Volunteers will take place. Each individual Volunteer will obey this order in every particular.

MacNeill held the message in his hands and stared at his own portentous words. It was a desperate move on his part to place this in the newspaper . . . one he might pay for with his life. But there were no choices left now. The Volunteers had been completely deceived by a small group of physical-force men. Pearse and the others were madmen with martyr complexes; leading good men into hopeless battle was unconscionable recklessness.

He read the paper one more time, thankful that he had thought of it— then handed the ad to the girl behind the office counter of the *Sunday Independent,* along with the money to pay for the ad.

"This must run in a prominent spot in the morning's early edition," he said urgently. "I'm willing to pay for that. And I want a large headline so as to be eye-catching. Put this in bold print—'No Parade! Irish Volunteer Marches Canceled. A Sudden Order.' "

"Yes, sir," she said, scribbling furiously, concerned at the worried look in the man's eyes. "I'll see that it does what you want, sir."

He nodded and smiled his thanks, then made his way from the office. Perhaps the advertisement and the messengers making their way across country would save some of the lives of the Volunteers. . . . That was all he could hope for now.

The O'Rahilly stepped into his green Ford touring car and started the engine. He had a long way to go before this night would end. He must get to every man under his command in the Volunteers and warn them that the Rising was off . . . or if not off, that they mustn't join it, for there was no hope of winning; without proper arms, without proper training and, worst of all, without proper leaders, there was no hope at all.

22

Lord Wimborne, the King's Irish lord lieutenant, paced the floor of the Viceregal Lodge in Phoenix Park restlessly, the newspaper advertisement still clutched in his hand. If Eoin MacNeill, the commander in chief of the Irish Volunteers, had taken an advertisement in the *Sunday Independent* to tell people *not* to appear for the action that was to have taken place . . . it was obvious that something important was afoot. Could it be that those ridiculous marches that he'd been witnessing over the past months, up and down Sackville Street, were really a prelude to an armed attack of some kind on lawful authority? It seemed unlikely . . . but these Irish were an unruly, unpredictable lot.

He had asked his under secretary, Nathan, and Neville Chamberlain, head of the RIC, to meet with him to discuss his growing suspicion. Postponement of an action certainly didn't mean that action would never take place: this whole Irish rebel business had gone too far. They had the names of the suspected leaders, and they had DORA, the power to put a stop to them. It was absurd not to round up the instigators and put an end to it once and for all.

It was a pity Birrell was in London. Aside from being an able and witty man, he had a grasp of these Irish goings-on that could be helpful. He was a bit too volatile, perhaps, but well up on what was happening. Birrell stayed in close touch with the Irish Parliamentary Party and he'd held the chief secretary's post for a good deal longer than most of his predecessors. But he was in London at the moment, and that was that.

Wimborne greeted the arrival of Sir Matthew Nathan. Solid, he thought assessingly, as Nathan approached his desk. Serious-minded, too. Nathan was an army man with an engineering background. A political Liberal and a friend of many highly placed officials. Close to both Prime Minister Asquith and Chancellor of the Exchequer Lloyd George, Nathan was a useful man to have around. And the fact that he was a Jew tended to give him a pleasant neutrality in this country so often divided between Catholic and Protestant loyalties.

Chamberlain arrived just as Nathan had entered the room. Wimborne motioned both men to be seated, then rose from his desk and walked around to join them.

"Gentlemen," he began importantly. Wimborne was a somewhat brash, meddling man, not easy to like, and neither of the men visiting held him in great esteem. "I'm convinced that a conspiracy of some sort is evident. You've read MacNeill's advertisement today, I'd imagine."

"Indeed," replied Chamberlain with obvious unconcern. "I would have thought that announcement suggested they've called off whatever it is they'd planned."

"I think the point Lord Wimborne is making," said Nathan, "is that it is most ominous that it had been planned in the first place." He stated this in his quiet, matter-of-fact manner, and Chamberlain seemed annoyed by his response.

"With Casement captured and that German sub sunk with all its cargo of guns and ammunition, I can see no possible way they could stage a rising," responded the RIC man, unchastened.

"Nonetheless," said Wimborne, "I've a hunch that's just what they're up to. No point giving them the chance to regroup. Let's swoop in now and use DORA to put the conspirators behind bars. With the leaders out of the way they'll be impotent enough."

"How certain are we that we know the leaders?" asked Nathan, and Chamberlain responded instantly.

"We obtained a statement this morning from a man named Bailey; he was with Casement. Those German guns were intended for the Volunteers, no doubt about it. Therefore, we have every right to suspect its headquarters staff—MacNeill, O'Rahilly, Hobson, Pearse, Plunkett and MacDonogh. Of course, with Casement in prison, we may already have their number-one man.

"Not a military brain among them," Chamberlain added contemptuously.

"Nonetheless," persisted Wimborne, "I want them disposed of."

"But if we start a wholesale collection of all their leaders, there'll be a terrible hue and cry from the people . . ." Nathan began.

"I'll hear no more about it, gentlemen!" interjected Wimborne impatiently. "Round them up." He was a peppery sort, and neither the under secretary nor the man from the RIC was particularly anxious to provoke a fight with him; certainly not on Easter Sunday. They made their good-byes and left Wimborne back behind his desk. The man spent an inordinate amount of time there, although it was occasionally tittered that one would be hard-pressed to imagine what it was he did during all those hours of conscientiousness.

"This order is going to raise a lot of hell in Dublin when we try to carry it out," said Chamberlain as they reached the stairs at the end of the corridor.

"Then I wouldn't be in any rush to implement it, would you?" said Nathan thoughtfully.

"And just what does that mean?"

"I mean he didn't say 'Do it tonight,' did he? Perhaps it would be judicious to give him a day or two to reconsider before we provoke a major incident where none is needed, eh? At any rate, I want to inform Birrell in London before we take any action; he makes the decisions concerning Ireland, not Wimborne."

The RIC man nodded. Not a bad idea at that, he thought. Tomorrow was a national holiday, after all. Nearly everyone would be at the Fairyhouse race meeting, anyway. He could always use that as his excuse if Wimborne came down on him for insubordination.

Monday, 24 April 1916

Con buckled on her boots, checked her soldier's uniform to see that it was properly done and sighed at her reflection in the mirror. She wore a thick black band around her arm, for she was in mourning.

One of Dev's young soldiers had offered her the uniform. "It'll be easier for you to move around, ma'am," he'd said deferentially, and she'd wondered at the motivation behind this act of acceptance by a man she was to serve with.

"I'd be happy to have Mrs. O'Connor in my command, gentlemen," Eamon de Valera had told the others when Con had asked to take Tierney's place in the Rising. She'd been frankly astonished that it was Dev and not Seaneen who had asked for her services. The tall, intellectual schoolteacher with the great hawk nose had barely passed the time of day with her before that.

"May I ask you why, Eamon?" she'd queried softly, for the other sounds in the room had all but disappeared with Dev's offer.

"Because I admire courage," he had replied with equanimity. "Because I admire it very much indeed." She wondered if, after all that had happened, Tierney would have thought her volunteering courageous or insane.

"Where are you now, my dearest love?" she whispered into the silence of the room. Her heart tightened painfully at the thought of her husband. She wanted to call out to Tierney, as she saw herself reflected in the glass. "Are you waiting for me somewhere, knowing that before this week comes to an end, I may be joining you? Or have you gone from me forever? Christ, but I need you, Tierney," she thought desperately. "Here I am going out to fight for the Cause we've both loved, and the truth is I care about nothing at all since you've gone from me. There seems no meaning in any of this, love, except maybe in fighting the bastards who killed you! That's what the Cause has always been, in truth, isn't it? An agonized retaliation for a long harming. Reprisals for torment of the soul and body.

"I should be a good soldier, love of my heart, for I care not whether I live or die so long as I strike my blow for you."

She smiled suddenly, thinking how mad she would seem to Tahg if he were to see her standing at the mirror talking to his father on the other side of the grave. But dear God, the silence in the little flat was so appalling, even the sound of madness would seem a relief to her.

Con heard the tramp of young feet on the stair and turned to see Tahg's large form fill the doorframe; behind him were several of his friends, all in the makeshift uniform of the Fianna or Volunteers. His face was set and serious.

"But for your hair, Mother, you look like a young boy standing there," he said, and she realized that despite his patriotism it must be hard for a boy to think of his mother preparing to go into battle.

"You look splendid in your uniform, Tahg," she said to lighten the mood. "So much like your father when I first knew him. He'd be so proud of you today, son . . . as I am."

She opened her arms to him, wondering if the presence of his friends would deter him from her embrace, but Tahg came to her willingly and held her. For the briefest of moments, feeling her head on his chest and the strength of his strong body, she felt awash with memories of Tierney—a flash flood of remembered tenderness that would never be again. Wild tears filled her eyes, rising from the deluge of emotions; she squeezed him hard once, then reached up to kiss his cheek.

"God be with you, son," she said. "I love you very much."

"And I you, Mother," said the boy, and there was the strain of unshed tears in his voice.

"Give my best to Connolly," she said finally, for there was no way to say all of what was in her heart.

"Aye, Mother." He hesitated, then said quickly, "I'd feel better if we were to be together where I could watch over you."

She nodded, choked with the simple beauty of the fact that their roles had been reversed now and he craved the chance to care for her safety, as she had watched over his through all the years.

"God grant that by the week's end all Dublin will be ours and we can watch over each other," she replied. But she knew as she said it, seeing the six-foot two-inch young manhood of him, that after this week the boy would be lost to her forever, and a man would stand in his place. Perhaps, already the transformation was complete.

"I'd like to escort you to Liberty Hall, Mother. We're all to gather there."

She nodded, and picking up the pistol from the table, she quickly checked its magazine and clicked the safety into place before tucking it into the holster on her belt.

Seeing the expertise with which she handled the gun somehow sent a shiver of apprehension to Tahg's heart. He pushed the feeling back, telling himself that the better the shot, the more likelihood of survival . . . but something in his mother's calm connection to the weapon had chilled him.

He wondered suddenly if she had any intention at all of surviving this week of Easter 1916.

 We had said good-bye before, Seaneen and I—thinking it would be forever. This strange thought struck me as we saw each other for the last time before the Rising.

I had contrived to get away from home for a few hours; it was even harder for him to escape his duties.

Is it macabre, I wonder, that the greater the danger, the more powerful the urge to make love seems to be? Is it nature's inexorable effort to repopulate, or is it simply the overpowering need to affirm *life* in the face of death?

Whatever the reason, we needed each other that day with so desperate a need that we could barely speak for the wanting.

I felt Seaneen's rough hands scuffle with my clothes the instant we were alone, as I struggled with his. To touch him, hold him, caress him; to feel his filling strength, was my only desire. To be possessed, ravaged, taken; to surrender myself utterly, was my need.

I lay breathless in his arms, exhausted by the shock wave of passion that had washed over us.

Will there ever be another time for us?—the question died on my lips. How could I ask it? What could he tell me that I wanted to hear?

That the Rising would succeed? It was unlikely and I knew it. That they would come marching home victorious and I be there in his bed to welcome the conquering hero, the relief of safety in our hearts? We did not belong to each other.

And what if the Rising succeeded and Seaneen was killed or wounded and I, in my propriety, could not go to him? Or if it succeeded, and the fight be taken to the countryside so that even the comfort of this small and occasional safe harbor would be denied us?

So we lay together, barely breathing, when the flood of urgency had ebbed, and we spoke of unimportant things. Of how the flowers had looked like bits of lace on the hillside over Howth Harbor, of how Johnny had grown an inch over the winter, of how sweet it would be to one day go to church together (an unlikely probability since I was a Protestant and he and all the IRB were under ban of the Catholic bishops—and yet a nice thought, somehow). And he let his fingers troll lightly over my body as he spoke, as if memorizing me with touch.

And I traced with my hand the scars that crisscrossed his side from a long-ago lashing with extreme, special tenderness and tangled my fingers in the black and silver hair that ran in a pattern from chest to loins. And we told each other everything with our silence and our eyes.

"I'd give anything to sleep in your arms a whole night through," I said in a small voice, finally.

"Sleep now, My Lady," he replied tenderly. "I'll hold you in my arms and wake you in a little while to go back." He turned to hold me spoonlike, powerful arms around my breasts, one leg on top of mine in the ultimate protective embrace.

"I couldn't sleep," I said, settling my body back against the encircling strength of his, the perfect peace of our connection flowing through me like balm.

"Nor I, My Lady," I heard him say. But we did. Thank God. We slept for hours in each other's keeping and I realized later that when we parted we'd never said good-bye. ∽

The Easter Rising
Dublin 1916

He who will fight the devil with his own weapons
must not wonder if he finds him an overmatch.

ROBERT SMITH

23

Monday, 24 April 1916

↪ Sunshine warmed Dublin that Easter Monday, an odd happenstance. Odder still was the uneasiness that everyone seemed to feel about the day; rumors of revolution were thick as pea soup in the city, and even those of us who *knew* what was planned felt nervous and uncertain. The statement published in the Sunday paper by Eoin MacNeill, calling off the military action, had created a confusion of monumental proportion.

I knew from Con and Seaneen that the Rising was to go on anyway, but I was not a soldier, so I was left concerned and worried on the sidelines. Con, Tahg and Seaneen would all be in mortal danger, even if all went well. And I was frightened. Frightened enough to decide to take myself to the GPO and watch what would happen there. That way at least I would be close to those I loved when the trouble came.

The forty-foot monument to Daniel O'Connell, the Great Liberator, stood importantly at one end of Sackville Street, and a less imposing statue of Charles Stewart Parnell stood at the other. Halfway between them, Nelson's one-hundred-twenty-foot pillar, a Doric column adorned by England's naval hero, imperiously overlooked the other two. I looked around as I made my way, seeing the wide and pretty avenue in a new light, wondering what it would look like by nightfall.

On the west side of the street, a huge rectangular structure housed the Dublin General Post Office, or GPO. Supporting its front portico were eight columns topped, for some reason, by

Hibernia, Mercury and Fidelity; it was a classical design, although the people who filtered in and out in quest of postal stamps were typically more interested in its convenience than its architecture.

This was the center of Dublin. Within easy walking distance were the beautiful Four Courts, Phoenix Park, the Bank of Ireland, the railway station, the Guinness Brewery, Trinity College and Dublin Castle. It was a quiet place, for the most part, undisturbed by other than commerce. It seemed an unlikely setting for a revolution; perhaps all war zones seem equally unlikely until afterward.

Shortly after twelve o'clock a company of men—perhaps forty strong—two motorcycles, one green Ford touring car, one cab and two trucks began to lumber their way forward down Sackville Street. A few of the men were in gray-green uniform, the majority wore their everyday clothes; they affected a yellow band on their arms in evidence of the fact that this was an army on the march.

No one paid them the slightest attention.

They carried what they could of weapons. Pikes, picks, axes and shovels, as their fathers had for generations; rifles, shotguns, sledgehammers, grenades, as new wars demanded. They also carried first-aid kits, I knew, for this little army had few doctors, and the automobiles carried guns, ammunition, bombs and other explosives. God alone knew what arsenal the other side would have at its disposal. "Everything but the hammers of hell," Tommy had guessed weeks earlier. "And those too if they need them," Seaneen had replied.

"Will these bloody fools never tire of marching up and down the streets?" I heard a police officer mutter to his fellow on the corner as I passed by. The Irish Citizen Army and the Irish Volunteers were hardly to be taken seriously—but the Peelers did consider them a nuisance. I wanted to cry for the little determined band, so unimposing that it occasioned no fear in anyone.

I recognized the three men in officer's green uniforms and swords who headed the column of marching men, of course. Commandant General James Connolly marched with a determined stride out front; beside him were Commandant General Joseph Mary Plunkett and Commandant General Padraig

Pearse, all gazetted with new ranks in their new army. They had mustered the troops at Liberty Hall an hour earlier.

Behind the generals, Thomas Clarke helped Sean MacDiarmida along; crippled by polio, the younger man walked painfully, and with a cane. The O'Rahilly drove the Ford; it was the same car he had driven through the countryside Saturday night, telling people they must not take part in the Rising. He would risk himself, he said, for a just cause, but no one else would he have on his conscience. He was a gallant-looking man who appeared grim enough this day—I had always liked him, and you could not but admire him for having the courage of his convictions to such a marked degree.

In front of the post office, Connolly halted the men. "Left turn," he said, then suddenly shouted, "the GPO. Charge!"

The unexpected order seemed to startle the ragtag company; unused to taking orders, they did not respond. I wanted to cry, watching them.

"Take the post office!" someone shouted, and the troops finally clambered up the steps to do so.

"Smash the windows, barricade the doors," a voice called authoritatively, and they did that, too.

"I came for me stamp and I'll not leave without it!" snapped an old woman on the steps, as others ran past her to escape the beginning mayhem. It might have been funny had the circumstances not been so distressing.

Plunkett, just out of the hospital, had been noticeably weakened by the six-block walk, for he leaned, seeming perilously close to falling, against the building. The surgical bandage on his throat looked woefully uncomfortable, and the wound beneath it must have throbbed from his exertion for he kept fingering it as he stood there. The tuberculosis that was eating at him had left his body considerably weaker than his brain, and it occurred to me that the poor man probably feared he wouldn't have strength enough to see his Rising through to its conclusion. He had labored long on the military strategy for this enterprise and was a passionate patriot in his own way, so I said a silent prayer for him.

Mick Collins, a robust young man with a square jaw and shoulders to match, was speaking on the steps with a Dublin policeman who was pleading not to be shot.

"We don't shoot prisoners," I heard Collins say contemptuously, ordering his Volunteers to take the man away, and judging by the looks of relief on the faces of his own men, they were happy to hear that order. Talking of revolution in isolated meetings was a far different thing from shooting a Peeler in the post office, I suspect.

Men were breaking through the windows and positioning themselves strategically at the ledges to watch the street. An old Shawlie called out from the sidewalk, "Glory be to God, would you look at them smashin' all the lovely windows!" aghast at the waste of it, and the boys inside laughed merrily and called back to her, "Go home now, Mother, or you'll get yourself hurt." It would have made me smile if the whole scene hadn't been so serious.

I saw Winifred Carney, Connolly's secretary, follow him into the GPO. Obviously, she was far too devoted to the man to let him face a revolution without her, so, austere and proper, she carried her enormous Webley typewriter in her arms and followed her general as if the madness around her were a simple distraction to be disregarded.

I edged closer to the foot of the steps just as Pearse and The O'Rahilly came face to face with each other. They displayed no open animosity, but no friendliness either. Pearse had kept The O'Rahilly ignorant of his plans, and O'Rahilly had kept a great many men from joining the fighting ranks. Each man had done his duty as he saw it, God help him.

"You're here?" I heard Pearse say in a controlled voice.

"I helped wind this clock," replied O'Rahilly. "I've come to hear it ring."

"I see," said Pearse noncommittally, and O'Rahilly replied, "It's madness, Padraig. Yet it's a glorious madness and I want to be in on it."

Pearse nodded, saying nothing, and taking the copy of the proclamation from his pocket, he read it through silently, once.

Two policemen ambled past and I heard them speaking.

"The Sinn Feiners have collared the post office," said one to the other with considerable disinterest.

"Bejabers, that's quare work," said the second, and then they moved away, and I found my heart beating wildly, both from the scare of their arrival and the knowledge that they found the proceedings too laughable to be concerned about.

Only a handful of spectators had gathered around me by

now, and none too friendly they seemed to the men in the GPO. Curious and semihostile was more the ticket.

Pearse looked out sadly at the paltry response to his revolution and solemnly began to read the proclamation. He raised his voice as he started, but his usual stylish delivery seemed less magnetic than it had been at O'Donovan's funeral. He cleared his throat and began:

"POBLACHT NA H EIREANN
THE PROVISIONAL GOVERNMENT
OF THE
IRISH REPUBLIC
TO THE PEOPLE OF IRELAND

"Irishmen and Irishwomen—In the name of God and of the dead generations from which she receives her old tradition of nationhood, Ireland, through us, summons her children to her flag and strikes for her freedom."

The people listening in the street around me shuffled uneasily. "What do these fools think they're doing?" said a woman next to me. "They'll no more be able to oust the English than any of the other rebellions were able to do. All it will mean will be reprisals . . . and isn't life hard enough without that?" I struggled to listen to Pearse over her babble.

"We declare the right of the people of Ireland to the ownership of Ireland, and to the unfettered control of Irish destinies, to be sovereign and indefeasible. The long usurpation of that right by a foreign people and government has not extinguished the right, nor can it ever be extinguished except by the destruction of the Irish people. . . ." His voice became more confident as he went along. "Standing on that fundamental right and again asserting it in arms in the face of the world, we hereby proclaim the Irish Republic as a Sovereign Independent State, and we pledge our lives and the lives of our comrades-in-arms to the cause of its freedom, of its welfare, and of its exaltation among the nations.

"The Irish Republic is entitled to, and hereby claims, the allegiance of every Irishman and Irishwoman."

"Not bloody likely that they'll get that!" a man said behind me, and everyone tittered.

"The Republic guarantees religious and civil liberty, equal

rights and equal opportunities to its citizens, and declares its resolve to pursue the happiness and prosperity of the whole nation and of all its parts, cherishing all the children of the nation equally and oblivious of the differences carefully fostered by an alien Government, which have divided a minority from the majority in the past."

"Just like that, they think they're going to fix it all up," the man behind me said derisively, "and I suppose the English are just going to pack their bags and run with their tails between their legs. They're daft, the whole bloody lot of them."

"We place the cause of the Irish Republic under the protection of the Most High God, Whose blessing we invoke upon our arms, and we pray that no one who serves that cause will dishonor it by cowardice, inhumanity, or rapine. In this supreme hour the Irish nation must, by its valor and discipline and by the readiness of its children to sacrifice themselves for the common good, prove itself worthy of the august destiny to which it is called."

"Oh well, 'tis a nice proclamation for all of that, and Pearse is a good speaker," said the little lady beside me. "Did you hear him when he spoke at O'Donovan Rossa's grave? Wasn't that a bit of heaven if you ever heard it?" I nodded, unable to speak for the tears in my eyes. "Now we'd best be on our way, dearie," she said, "before the Castle hears of all this nonsense and sends in the Lancers."

Pearse read the names of the signers—"Thomas J. Clarke, Sean MacDiarmida, Thomas MacDonogh, P. H. Pearse, Eamonn Ceannt, James Connolly, Joseph Plunkett"—then he tacked the proclamation up on the door, eyed the sorry crowd of stragglers and turned to go into the post office.

Seeing that there was little I could do standing on a street corner, I turned and hurried home, tears in my eyes for the probable futility of it all. ✍

De Valera, with Con at his side, marched at the head of his small 3rd Battalion toward their destination, Boland's Flour Mill. It would be his job to keep the inevitable reinforcements the English would send from reaching Dublin. They would land at Kingstown and march into the city, but to get there, they must first pass over the Mount Street Bridge. There he must stop or delay them.

Leaving a dozen men in occupation at Westland Row Station, where the Kingstown-Dublin railway ended, he passed on to Mount Street Bridge. Countess Markievicz and Michael Mallin were to cover the other approach routes from the south, from the vantage point of Stephen's Green.

"We must exercise great economy with the men," he said absently to Con as he carefully selected small handfuls of soldiers—four in one house, three in another, two in a third—and deployed them. The mathematician to the end, she thought, as she watched him decide with intensive calculation.

The seventy or eighty men remaining to his command he marched into Boland's Mill, a great gray limestone edifice with many windows needing to be fortified with sacks of flour from within. The building stood on the canal bank overlooking the Ringsend slums.

"Do you suppose," he said musingly, staring at the area in front of him, "that if we hoisted a flag over that derelict distillery there as a diversion, they might mistake it for our headquarters?"

Con looked at the man with a new light of understanding. He was subtler than he seemed, then.

"It wouldn't hurt to try," she replied, and watched as he gave the order crisply, like one who is used to being in authority.

Pearse and Connolly issued the orders they had planned and waited for the enemy to respond.

Brennan Whitmore was dispatched to knock holes through buildings from the Pillar Café to the Imperial Hotel, in case an indoor escape or reconnaissance route would be needed.

Fergus O'Reilly and a young Abbey actor named Arthur Shields were sent out to establish a wireless setup to communicate with the outside world.

The doctor who had operated on his tubercular throat two weeks before paid a house call on Joe Plunkett at the post office.

A contingent of Cumann na mBan girls arrived to assist with nursing and to take over the commissary.

But where was the goddamned enemy? Pearse and Connolly spent the day wondering.

Other than a troop of Lancers who had ridden directly into the line of fire inadvertently and been killed or wounded for their trouble, there seemed no response at all from the Castle.

The buildings near the GPO had been evacuated, and the occasional sound of sniper fire punctuated the darkness, but beyond the rowdy crowds of looters that had gathered to pillage the local abandoned shops and houses, there was no sign of action whatsoever.

Neither the Irish reinforcements that had been expected nor the British Army was anywhere in evidence.

The leaders at the post office closed the first day of their rebellion in the nervous knowledge that this was the lull before the storm. Tomorrow the British government would have no choice but to respond to their valiant little revolution. No choice at all.

Seaneen O'Sullivan was content not to have his own command. He had wanted to be at the post office with Clarke and MacDiarmida. *They* were the IRB, and this was an IRB enterprise. He would be with them to follow orders, and to help maintain IRB discipline at this makeshift command post, with its makeshift little army. He'd been secretly pleased when Clarke had asked him to forgo the honor of command for the role of helpful subordinate.

Seaneen had been forced by Tierney's death to do some serious soul-searching. The man had been his friend and he mourned him. But he had lost other friends over the long years of his fight for Ireland, yet Tierney's last words to him rang in his head. "A fool's errand," he'd called it, and so it had turned out to be. The guns were lost and good men were lost with them; and now, without the guns, this Rising, too, was a fool's errand.

There was nothing to do but put a brave face on it and do his duty. He'd be damned if he'd do less than Clarke, MacDiarmida and Connolly—or, for that matter, the boys who now sat hunched at their sandbags staring out into hostile streets.

He thought of Beth and of what might have been, but only for a moment. This was no time for melancholy or regrets. This was the time he had labored toward for a lifetime, and besides —he nearly chuckled at the irony of his own thought—in Ireland one martyr was worth a hundred living patriots. Who the hell knew where all this would lead, anyway? None but God— and He didn't seem to be paying much attention.

Seaneen shook himself free of the disquieting internal dialogue and walked toward a small knot of young men who talked together. He was an old hand at rallying the young—tonight it would be an act of kindness to these boys to ply his trade.

24

Monday evening, 24 April 1916
Viceregal Lodge, Phoenix Park

"Bloody idiots!" shouted Wimborne, beside himself with the stupidity of Nathan and Chamberlain for not carrying out his orders.

"Do you imbeciles know exactly what you have allowed to happen by not following my instructions and picking up those Sinn Fein fanatics?"

"I'm afraid we thought it best to wait for advice from Birrell, sir," replied Chamberlain.

"Well, it certainly is a comfort to find out that you *thought* at all!" said the Viceroy between tightly clenched teeth. "One could not have guessed."

"We've declared martial law within the city, sir, and we are doing everything possible to assess the extent of the disturbance," interjected Nathan. "By morning we'll be in a better position to respond, and martial law can be extended to the countryside if it's considered necessary."

"Where the devil is General Lowe when we need him?" Wimborne asked, somewhat mollified. "Wouldn't hurt to hear what the military has to say about all this."

"Lowe is finalizing the mobilization of our troops, sir. Our numbers in Dublin will be greatly increased once reinforcements have come up from the country garrisons."

"Lowe is only a brigadier general," Wimborne said impatiently, as if thinking out loud. "Perhaps we need someone higher up for this job. I think we shall have to put the fear of God into these insurgents. What buildings have they occupied, Chamberlain?"

The RIC chief hastily ran through the list of rebel fortifications, adding almost as an afterthought, "Excuse me, sir, but it appears they've left themselves completely vulnerable to a counterattack. I daresay it shouldn't take long to surround them and force a showdown."

Wimborne stroked his chin slowly and, voicing his thoughts again, said, "Yes. I agree. I believe that with a little help from the army this foolishness can be settled within the week. We'll send for whatever artillery they can spare us from the European front, and if we must shell a few buildings, all the better. We'll give these beggars a damn quick lesson in authority!"

"I hear that Major General Maxwell has been seen around London recently," Nathan volunteered. "He has quite a good reputation, sir. Perhaps he'd be the man for it?"

Wimborne nodded his head, cataloging the information mentally. "When does Lowe get here?" he asked of Chamberlain.

"Tomorrow morning, sir. Maxwell may take a little longer to round up, but I daresay it wouldn't take him long to make short shrift of these Irish."

"Quite so," said Wimborne, reshuffling the papers on his desk. "Just as it should be . . . a military matter and all that. Like to keep our hands as clean as possible."

Sir Matthew Nathan and Sir Neville Chamberlain exchanged glances. This was the first statement from the Viceroy with which they wholeheartedly concurred.

25

Wednesday, 26 April 1916

Tahg watched the young man named Derek O'Hanrahan work with the wounded. He was huskily built, but with sensitive long-fingered hands, an odd combination. He walked with a peculiar gait—not lame exactly—but not quite normal either. His hair was a rusty chestnut shade and his face sported more than its share of freckles.

There was a quiet competency about the man that seemed to cheer the injured even before they were treated. Which was just as well, thought Tahg, as medical supplies were perilously low now and soon all that would be available to these suffering men would be a kind word or medically competent first aid.

"I'll help you with what you're doing," Tahg said to Derek when he saw the man pause for a cup of water. "If you show me what to do, I'll help. I'm off duty for a while."

Derek smiled back, regarding him appraisingly as he did so.

"Be happy to show you what you can do to help," he said amiably in a thick Dublin slum accent, and Tahg wondered how he'd ever gotten to be Dr. Derek O'Hanrahan as he was obviously from a class not usually so well educated. "God knows these poor devils need any help we can give them. And it's probably worse at the other posts that have no doctor at all." The young man shook his head wearily and motioned Tahg to sit down with him for a moment.

"How old are you?" he asked suddenly.

"Eighteen," answered Tahg.

"I'm twenty-five meself," said the other. "Just got me certificate to practice."

"You'll get plenty of practice here," said Tahg, and Derek laughed aloud. He seemed good-natured enough.

"Well, I've always been at odds with the Establishment, you might say—so there's no reason at all for me not to start me medical career in an unorthodox way, I suppose."

"Christ Almighty!" the voice shouted from a nearby window. "That's a warship in the river and she's shelling Liberty Hall!"

Tahg and Derek looked at each other, startled; Tahg jumped up and instinctively grabbed for his rifle.

"They can shell the old Hall all they want," said Derek with a wry laugh. "There's not a soul in there. I heard Connolly say so to O'Rahilly."

A loud boom and crash sounded somewhere in the city, and another fast on its heels.

"If they're shelling the Hall, it means they can shell us, too," said Tahg, an awful apprehension starting in his spine.

As he said it, another crash sounded; it was followed by a blaze of light.

"Jesus, Mary and St. Patrick!" exploded O'Hanrahan.

"They'll have the whole bloody city in flames if they keep that up for long."

"Men to your posts!" Seaneen's voice shouted from the ground floor. "Men to your posts!"

Tahg grasped the rifle, signaled to Derek and ran toward the agitated voice.

"How did you ever get to be a doctor?" Tahg asked O'Hanrahan when the fighting had stopped long enough for him to again volunteer to help with the wounded.

"How did a kid from the slums get to be a doctor, do you mean?"

Tahg nodded.

The young man held up his fine slender hands as if examining them.

"These old mitts did it for me," he said inscrutably. "They seemed to come equipped with knowledge the rest of me didn't have! Anything those old professors wanted done, these hands of mine could do. From day one, they said I could be a surgeon. I got scholarships and such and a famous doctor took me under his wing. Said I had hands like his father—another famous surgeon, mind you. So you see, the hands did it all—the rest of me just went along for the ride."

A curious story, thought Tahg, and a merry sort of man.

"Come on, lad, I'll teach you to change dressings and we'll see how you hold up against the sight of gore."

Before the firing started again the next morning, they had formed a fast friendship born of the extremity of their situation.

Wednesday, April 26
Boland's Mill

"Troops have now been landed at Kingstown. They will have to pass over the Mount Street Bridge in order to reach the center of Dublin." De Valera's voice was calm but penetrating. "We do not know how many there are, but they are said to be in excess of two hundred."

Lieutenant Michael Malone, Dev's aide-de-camp, looked around at the men ranged beside him and cleared his throat.

"We'll keep them from the bridge, sir," he said clearly. The dozen men whose job it would be to do so cried, "Hear, hear!"

British snipers fired continually on Boland's Mill once they had positions on Mount Street.

The British battleship *Helga,* now moored in the Liffey, shelled the distillery, mistaking it for de Valera's headquarters, but a field gun mounted in Percy Place crashed shells through the outer wall of the mill.

Quietly, methodically, Dev moved from man to man inside the bakery giving orders. He was covered from head to foot with flour, and even his unshaven face was white with the snowy substance.

He could see that the whole of Dublin was in flames and messages were sporadic at best from headquarters at the GPO; the news when it got through was bad: the numbers of wounded mounting, communications almost useless, reinforcements non-existent.

He must maintain his cheerfulness to encourage the men. This was not a time to falter.

Thursday, 27 April 1916

"Jesus Christ, Tahg," said Derek under his breath. "Did you see who they've got on that stretcher?"

Tahg looked up from his post at the window ledge where he had been watching Abbey Street burn slowly but surely. He saw a group of men carrying another toward the makeshift infirmary.

"Connolly?" he asked incredulously.

"That's the word."

"How bad?"

"I'll let you know when I've seen him," said Derek as he moved quickly in the direction of the gaggle of stretcher carriers.

When Tahg finished his round of duty he, too, made his way to the infirmary.

"What's the story?" he asked O'Hanrahan, who was bending over the sink washing his hands for what seemed like the thousandth time that day.

"It's bad," he said without looking up. "They've got that captured English doctor to set it, but his ankle's shattered and he's got a bullet hole in his arm. It's the ankle that'll kill him, in my opinion, if they don't get him to a hospital. It's a mess. Bone fragments sticking through the skin. He must be in agony. The chloroform we have didn't do him much good while they tried to set the bone." Derek looked up, and Tahg could see the fatigue in his new friend's face.

"He's a prime candidate for gangrene, if the pain doesn't kill him first."

Tahg nodded, not knowing what to say. Connolly's wounding would be a major demoralizing force for the men. Somehow, the mortality of a leader made them all more mortal and vulnerable than they had been. He shuddered internally at the thought.

Thursday evening, 27 April

Tom Clarke, Sean MacDiarmida and Seaneen O'Sullivan spelled each other at sleeping. While the others slept, Clarke wandered restlessly about the post office, stopping by the younger men to talk for a minute or two before passing on. He knew the end was very near.

Never before tonight had he felt a cathartic need to explain himself. Perhaps it was the specter of death stalking the post office that had made him garrulous, who was usually taciturn.

He made his way to the infirmary, where a light still burned.

"How's it going?" he asked Derek quietly across the bodies that lay in orderly rows now, grim evidence of the week's work.

"As well as can be," replied O'Hanrahan. "We haven't much in the way of supplies. And we could use a doctor with a bit more experience of combat wounds, if you happen to have one handy."

Clarke made a rueful expression with his mouth and ambled into the infirmary room. It seemed obvious to the three young men that he sought company. The usual bellicosity of his bearing had changed and he seemed, for the first time, old and weary.

"Sit down, will you, Mr. Clarke," offered Tahg. "Most of the men are asleep now. We've little enough to do. We were all thinking a cup of tea wouldn't hurt us."

Clarke smiled at the boy's kindness. He seemed a good lad. "Aye, if you wouldn't mind, O'Connor, I could use a cup myself." He pulled up a chair from against the wall and settled in.

"Do you know how many years I've waited for these glorious days?" he asked musingly. "Since I was sixteen. It was 1873 when I joined the Brotherhood. Forty-three years ago, lads. Can you even imagine at your age how long forty-three years can seem?" He looked up suddenly at Tahg.

"How old are you, son?" he asked.

"Eighteen, sir," the boy replied.

Clarke nodded, seeming lost in reverie. Then, unexpectedly, he began to tell them the story of his Fenian years, in a quiet flood of remembrances. Stories of his life on the run in Ireland and New York. Of his assignment by the Brotherhood to go to England as part of a dynamiting team. Stories he seemed to have a terrible need to tell.

"I was sentenced to life imprisonment then, but I ended up spending only fifteen years in British prisons—most of it in solitary."

"How did you stay sane?" asked Tahg, riveted by the story and the haunted tone of the man's voice.

"Oh, laddie, we did everything we could think of to hold on to our sanity. Things you cannot even imagine. I transcribed the Old and New Testaments into shorthand. Twice. And had to steal pen and paper to do it. I had forty days of starvation once in a stone-cold cell with most of my clothes taken from me. I chewed rags to fight the hunger. . . ." He paused for a moment as if considering, then said, "And there were other things I won't even mention." The boys wondered if he would tell them no more.

"Mr. Clarke . . ." Derek began, but the older man interrupted him.

"You'll call me Tom," he said. "There's little need of formality among men who may soon die together." The old man chuckled quietly, sadly.

Derek nodded, as if to acknowledge the common sense of it.

"Tom, then," he said. "We've all been wondering what happened with the countermand order, sir. We might not have won even with reinforcements from the countryside, I know, but it seems a damned shame to have gone through all this with no hope at all."

"Aye, you're right about the last of it. But you see, it's like this. Men—even the best of them—don't always see eye to eye on how to accomplish a great end. There has always been disagreement within the Volunteers over whether there'd be ever a prayer of victory, if we had a rising. There were good men like The O'Rahilly and MacNeill who felt that if we hadn't a hope of defeating the British Empire, we hadn't the right to risk men's lives.

"Then there were others, like myself, and Pearse and Connolly, who felt we had no choice but to strike now. We knew the Castle was onto us and that the World War was our opportunity. If we'd waited much longer, most likely we'd all have been arrested and yet another generation would have gone by without a blow being struck. The longer you sink into slavery, boys, the harder it is to fight back."

The young men exchanged glances, amazed at the candor of Clarke. He was telling them things that only a high-ranking IRB man would be privy to.

"I suppose you're wondering why I'm telling you all this," he said, as if reading their unvoiced question. "It's because two of you are wearing Red Cross armbands—in the final bayonet charge they may spare you. If they do—if you survive—I hope you'll try to make people understand the seven of us who signed the Republican Proclamation. In the days to come it will be important that people not forget our motives."

He turned to Tahg. "And you, lad. I'm telling you because I loved your father. And I'd have you know that he died a hero's death, not that of a failed revolutionary."

"You can't help but admire him," said Derek with awe in his voice when the man had gone. "My God, can you even imagine fifteen years in solitary?"

"My father was his friend . . . he said he was a good man." Tahg's voice sounded distant and sorrowful. They knew his father's death hung heavily about him still. "It makes you feel that no matter what happens here, it's still better that we've finally fought back."

"Aye," replied O'Hanrahan. "I'm with you on that."

They talked a while longer, then, each making a bed on the floor, they slept.

26

Pearse finished his rounds with an increasing agitation. It wasn't right that they had no chaplain here. The men were becoming more and more aware of the danger of death, and when it came there should at least be a priest to attend to their immortal souls.

He beckoned to one of the young girls in civilian dress who had been there all week. She came to him willingly. "We need a priest," he said gently. "You've more chance of bringing one here than any of the men, Kathleen. Will you go to the Pro Cathedral and entreat one of the curates to return here with you?" He raised his eyebrow inquiringly at the girl; he expected unquestioning obedience from the men, but was uncertain of what was fair to ask of the women.

The girl swallowed hard, looked once out the window to the dangerous streets she'd have to traverse to do as she'd been asked, then she nodded affirmatively, and Pearse relaxed a bit.

"There's a brave girl," said the commander in chief, who patted her arm absently and then walked on.

Seeing herself dismissed, she pulled her sweater about her and headed out of the GPO. One block north and one east was all it would take, she told herself, as she peered into the darkness. But there were bloody bodies on the pavement and shots to be heard ricocheting all around her, and two blocks seemed a long way indeed.

She picked her way carefully among the debris on the streets and managed by keeping in the shadows of buildings to make it to the rectory without incident.

Father John Flanagan opened the door to the frightened girl.

"Please, Father," she said in a small voice, trying to quiet her pounding heart. "We've need of a priest at the post office. We've a dying man there."

"I've been to the post office once already this week for confessions," the man replied, annoyed by this unreasonable request. Sackville Street was under siege, and there was a better than even chance they'd never make it to the GPO.

"Surely you cannot deprive a dying man," she persisted in her small determined voice, silently asking God to forgive her the necessary lie.

"A dying man, you say? And why in God's name wasn't he taken to the Jervis Street Hospital?"

"I don't know, Father," said the girl sheepishly, thinking she'd have to make her own confession before the night was over.

Father Flanagan had little feeling for the rebellion; his parishioners had enough travail to cope with, without a war robbing them of the little they had. It was inconceivable that these idiots thought they'd accomplish anything but adding more grief to a city that already had more than its share.

Yet, if a man was in need of the last sacrament, he could not refuse to go. He motioned the girl in and wordlessly, angrily, prepared what he would need. Tucking the little case of viaticum into his bag, he followed the girl into the street.

Quickly the two walked up Thomas Lane to Marlborough Street on the way to Parnell Street—a roundabout route but safer, said the girl. She felt it would tempt fate too much to retraverse the way she'd come, for the shelling had started there with renewed vigor. Bullets bounced off the cobblestones and half a dozen times they had to flatten themselves against the storefronts to stay out of the range of the snipers.

On Henry Street a man cried out to Father Flanagan. The priest looked up, startled to see an old friend running toward him.

"What are you doing here?" he called out. But the man never replied, for a shot rang out, spinning him around, before he slumped to the pavement.

"Dear God, Father!" gasped the girl at his side. "I think they've killed him!"

Horrified, the priest knelt beside his friend. "Can you hear me, John!" he whispered urgently, but there was no reply.

Hurriedly, Father Flanagan kissed his stole, then placed it around his neck. He glanced once right and left as if to dare the soldiers to shoot a person at God's work, then he began the ancient ritual of Extreme Unction.

People began to appear in doorways.

"Is there anyone who can help get this man to Jervis Street?" called the priest when he had administered the last rites. Three boys emerged from a store with a handcart and they helped lift the man into it and moved off with their burden. Kathleen thought the firing had quieted and wondered if it was to let them remove the body.

A young man wearing a Red Cross armband appeared from somewhere and spoke to the priest.

"Where is it you're going, Father?" he asked.

"To the post office."

"Ah well, in that case, you'll want to follow me. I know the safest way."

"You're another of them, then, are you?" said the priest with disgust.

"I am, Father."

"You should be home with your family where you belong," he replied, the fury of the last few minutes bursting through his self-restraint. "A young lad like you! Do you really believe a ragged little handful of you fools with rifles and Red Cross armbands can stand up to the British Army?"

The young man looked carefully at the priest before replying.

"No, Father," he said quietly. "I'm afraid not."

Startled by the boy's sad candor, the priest said nothing; the boy turned abruptly and, motioning them to follow, led the priest and girl across Henry Street to Randall's Boot Factory, and from a vantage point on the second floor he hurried them through holes in the connecting walls of buildings, all the way to the post office.

When they arrived, the priest shook off the debris of the journey and asked to see the dying man. Embarrassed by the lie she'd told to entice him, the girl led him silently to the infirmary.

"And where's this dying man I've been called for?" asked the priest angrily, for he saw no evidence of impending death. "You'd best not let me find out I've been brought here on a fool's errand!"

Tahg and Derek looked at each other for a moment, and then Derek spoke.

"Sure, Father, you've been called for all of us here. Like as not, we're all dying men."

The simple probable truth of the statement stopped the tirade the priest had intended.

"All right, then," he said, the merest hint of a smile appearing for the first time in his voice. "Let's see to the wounded ones first." Rolling up the sleeves of his cassock to show his intent, the young priest settled in beside the first cot and began to speak to the man in a low voice.

27   To attempt to describe the city of Dublin by the end of Easter week would be almost an impossibility.

Everything that could be looted had been scavenged. Everything that was flammable seemed to be ablaze. Fire brigades had formed all over the city, and anyone who could afford to evacuate was already gone.

To venture onto the streets was to risk a sniper bullet from one side or the other. People who hadn't been able to leave their homes early in the week were in terror of doing so later, for fear of being killed in the process.

I had moved, along with all my children, to a house on the outskirts of the city, where at least we were out of range of the firebombing.

Needless to say, wherever my body resided in that ghastly week, my heart was in the center of Dublin with those I loved best. Seaneen was at the Four Courts, Con at Boland's Mill, Tahg at the GPO—all in desperate danger and I unable to communicate with any of them.

Oh, unhappy times! To even recall those weeks when all that was good and beautiful was trodden underfoot and so many that I loved were taken from me! How can I convey the terror of a warship shelling buildings that enclose the ones you love most in all the world? How do you explain the impotent helplessness of running down the street and seeing someone killed beside you as you go? How can I express the sense of irrevocable loss that each new devastation carried in its wake?

I had to get to Con. That was all I could think about as the week grew worse. I had to find a way to get to Con. . . .

Seaneen and I had made our farewells before the battle started. But Con had been so distracted by Tierney's death that I felt we had barely touched in the time preceding the Rising.

I had to get to Con.

Friday, April 28

There was smoke and fire damage everywhere; the air was rife with the eye-stinging, throat-scaring stench of it. Bodies lay on the street: dying bodies, dead bodies, burned or bleeding bodies. I felt the specter of death about me. I had feared ceaselessly for Con since Monday, and now it seemed obvious to me that I, too, would die in this rebellion.

I picked my way rapidly through the carnage with one of Seaneen's men as my guide. He was young and had a kind face. He knew I sought my sister, and, by now, word of her bravery had spread among the ranks, and as she had become a favorite of the men, he had gladly volunteered to take me to her.

We made it to the barricade at noon, no mean feat. The strange sunshine that had persisted perversely all week still clung to us, making the smell of death's hand heavier.

The crude barricades had been constructed of chicken wire and anything that could be meshed in it—chairs, parts of tables, even an errant auto car, along with huge chunks of plaster that had been blasted from houses by the ceaseless bombardment of the past two days.

There was sporadic firing as we approached Boland's Mill, and the danger from the English snipers was considerable. I'd been told this by my guide, Chris, but there was no need for elucidation, for three men were killed before my eyes as we made our way that morning. You can grow old on such a journey—if you make it through at all.

Suddenly I saw my sister, tall and lean behind the barricade. Would it seem strange if I said to you that she was beautiful, despite the circumstances—or perhaps because of the circumstances—she was so in communion with her environment?

I caught a glimpse of her laughing—throwing back her

golden-brown head and laughing in the face of the odds. She shook her fist at some unseen marksman and she laughed. The sound bizarre, but triumphant. A warrior queen she was in that instant. The realization both chilled and heartened me.

She was dressed in soldier's motley—it must have been a young boy's uniform, for it fitted her well except around the bosom. But that tightness was obscured by a bandolier of bullets that was slung across her chest from shoulder to waist and I saw that a bandage was wound under that. On her shoulder, with the casual grace of a minstrel's harp, was slung her rifle. God forgive me, but I think I've never seen so marvelous a sight.

Perhaps it was my relief at reaching her alive—perhaps it was the perfect beauty of seeing a person in complete connection to the moment. Perhaps it was the strength of the love we bore each other. I'll never know. Boadicea, Xenobia, Maeve—they, too, must have looked like this at the head of their legions.

Well, no legion here. The men and boys looked weary, weary. Not as hungry as the troops at other locations, because here at least they had the mill and the flour. As a matter of fact, I'd been told that they'd been baking and feeding the hungry neighbors since taking over the mill.

But they were a handful of men who had held the British Army at bay for five days—and they looked as you might expect them to: triumphant, weary and doomed.

There was a lull in the firing and we ran for it—across the last few yards of street that separated us. And she saw me then. A look of terrible consternation suffusing her face—I knew it was fear for my safety. And then a look of love and relief at seeing me again, with a look of consummate sorrow that this was probably the last time we two who loved each other so should meet on earth.

We embraced wildly, as she pulled me scrambling over the barricade, my long skirt tearing on the wire and debris.

"Dear God," she breathed when she had pulled us to safety. "I thought never to see you again!"

"It would take more than the British Army to keep me from seeing you, my dear," I said, meaning it. We hugged and struggled to brush the debris of the journey from my clothes. "How bad is it?" I asked when I'd caught my breath.

"I could as well ask you that, love," she said with a rueful smile. "We're pretty well cut off here from the world. Our communications people tell us we've sustained some of the worst battles here at the mill. You know we've held back the column of reinforcements from Kingstown fairly successfully . . . so far." She made a meaningful gesture of the eyebrows at the last of it, as if to say she understood the ultimate hopelessness but would rather not speak of it in front of the men.

"How long can you hold out?" I had to ask.

"We've enough food for three weeks, with strict rationing. Ammunition for considerably less, unless our own reinforcements get through." She took a deep breath, then said softly but steadily, "The end is near, Sister. We must not fool ourselves about the final outcome."

"And what then?" I could barely breathe to ask it.

"We'll be shot if we're taken alive. Better than hanging, I suppose. A soldier's death at least. Not a traitor's.

"Have you heard aught of Des?" she asked, trying to keep her voice steady.

"Not a word," I answered. "Although he may have been captured with Casement. Edmond's trying to find out for sure."

She nodded unhappily.

"I've a letter for you from Tahg," I said. "Don't ask how it got to me, or how he knew I'd get it to you; but I've got it." I fumbled in my pocket and brought forth the precious document. She took it gratefully.

"I've one for you as well, Bethy," she said hastily as she produced a crumpled envelope from her jacket. "I wrote it to you last night, in case I was killed or taken, I thought they'd send it to you . . ."

I took it wordlessly, tears welling up in me, enough to drown us all.

"Do you remember, love, when we were little girls?" she asked in a soft voice. "How we used to play in the garden at being ladies . . . how we would fantasize about setting the world to rights and being famous and remembered?"

I nodded, unable to speak for the poignancy of her voice.

"Well, I've tried to fulfill that dream. I've tried to sort it out through these last days . . . did I come here to avenge Tierney or to fight for his Cause . . . or to show my son that it wasn't all idle talk? I've asked myself, and I finally know the answer. It was all those things, love"—she said it looking me full in the eye—"and it was none of them.

"I'm here for myself at the end of it. I'd like you to know that. I'm here because I hate the injustice of what's been done to Ireland and because the people I've loved best, except you and Des, have been of a class that has been beaten and broken and all but vanquished. And I'm here to do my own small part in an immortal deed."

I threw my arms around her wiry body and we held each other.

"The drop of water on the stone of the Empire or to spit in the eye of the tyrant . . . Tierney told me once those were our choices. And you know, Beth, these last few days here, with these brave, brave men fighting and dying for a gesture, I knew that we'd made the better choice."

We held each other and we cried like two little girls—we saw her comrades watching us but we didn't care—and, too, we could see in their faces that they understood. We spoke of childhood and of Father and of the mother Con had never known. It was as if we had put all things in order in our small universe in that one hour's time.

And, finally, it was time to go.

We dried our eyes and tried, for each other's sake, to be brave in our farewells. I didn't know then that we would meet another day, in yet more ghastly circumstances. I didn't know that death was near, but that the place of its rendezvous was not at the barricades.

It took us many hours to get back. The firebombing had all but destroyed Dublin. The sweet archaic charm of the city was little more than a blazing ruin—art, history, literature, architecture, all gentility naught but fuel for an indiscriminate inferno.

I was so heartsore, not even the agony of heat and smoke and ricocheting bullets touched me as we made our way back. Whether I lived or died, it seemed to me, my life was over with hers. And with dear old Dublin's.

When I arrived home, dirty, ragged, smoke-blackened and weary to death, I found Edmond waiting.

The contrast of this elegant and pristine man, slickly booted and still in riding clothes—he had ridden much of the way on horseback from outside of town, for he had been warned that transportation was at a standstill—seemed to me a metaphor for the eternal anguish of Ireland. The rich stayed rich, while, recurrently, the poor destroyed themselves in a ceaseless effort to be free.

"I thought you might have need of me," he said simply.

Too tired to question, too sad for discussion, I sank wearily into a chair and removed my high-buttoned shoes; they were spattered with blood and I viewed them with a detachment that wouldn't have been possible just twenty-four hours before.

"Con is at Boland's Mill with de Valera," I replied. "They expect to be taken shortly. She says she'll be shot with the other leaders."

"Dear God!" he breathed, obviously unnerved by the news. "You FitzGibbon women are beyond any man's understanding." It sounded not unkindly.

"It's my intention to go to the Castle," he said, as if to ward off further news. "I've known Wimborne well enough, and Birrell, of course. I'll see what I can find out for you, Elizabeth." He hesitated, then said, "I'm terribly sorry about your sister."

"Thank you, Edmond," I replied. "I believe you mean that."

He started to leave, then turned and, coming closer to my chair, said quietly, "There is much water over the dam of our marriage, Elizabeth. God knows, I've spent most of the last twenty years loving you or hating you, or both together.

"You have at times so deeply wounded me that I thought I could not bear it. And yet . . . I would have you know that in some strange and convoluted perversity of fate, I both like and admire you. You are not what I wanted in a wife by any means . . . but you might have been a great friend and ally had I been clever enough to let that be between us."

I listened with astonishment. Never once since I'd married him had I heard Edmond speak to me from the heart. There seemed no appropriate reply.

"I've watched you for a lifetime, Elizabeth. Enough older than you, perhaps, to be able to evaluate. Often enough I let emotion cloud my judgment, but always, at the end of it, I knew your worth.

"That's why I've raised another man's son . . . that's why I'll help you now, if I can." Then he was gone.

Despite the profundity of what he had said—and profound

indeed it seemed to me—I could cope with nothing more that day. I sat there and cried silently for a long, long while and finally, still in the chair, I fell to sleep. ∽

28

Con looked up from the wounded man she had been tending and into de Valera's brooding and compassionate eyes. He signaled her to come with him, and she tucked the nearly threadbare blanket in around the young soldier and followed her commandant to a corner of the mill away from the others.

Gunfire was sporadic now that it was so late, but the orange glow over Dublin gave the moment a surreal timelessness. There was the hushed and terrible feeling that perhaps nothing existed anymore outside the place they occupied.

"You look tired, Dev," she said, suddenly aware of her own fatigue.

"Would you think it strange if I said I just want to talk with you for a few minutes?" he asked. "I don't care what we say, I think. Just the sound of a woman's voice will help to put my head in order." He smiled at her, and she thought, once again, what a strange man he was.

Tall and spare and gangly as a heron; a homely mathematician and astronomer, far from his numbers and his stars. She was glad now that it was he who had volunteered to take her into his command. He was a good man and a good leader. She'd had ample time these five days past to learn that.

By way of reply, she motioned to him to be seated beside her on the floor against the wall; the solidity of it seemed safer than the open spaces of the mill's main room.

"I wonder if they'll ever realize it was only twelve men that held the Foresters off all day Wednesday," she asked musingly. "They must have lost two hundred men."

"The world will never know," he said wearily. "I expect Maxwell's dispatches will have it that a handful of *them* overcame an army of our boys." They both smiled a little.

"Have you written to your wife and children?"

He nodded his head Yes. "You know I never told my wife when I left home on Sunday where I was going. It seemed the kinder way at the time. Now, I regret that."

She put her hand on his arm, a maternal gesture. "Perhaps no good-bye will be needed."

He looked at her sharply, hawk's eyes behind round glasses. "You and I both know better than that," he said simply.

"Do you think tomorrow will be the end of it, then?"

"No. I think not. We'll hold them off a while yet."

"You must be less visible tomorrow, Dev. You expose yourself too recklessly. The men need you to stay alive."

"Better men than I have been killed, Con." It was the first time he'd called her other than Mrs. O'Connor. Somehow that frightened her more than anything, for its intimacy said the end was near.

"Ah, Con, if the people had only come out with knives and forks to help us!"

She nodded at that. "It's a hard thing to think we've held our revolution to free a reluctant populace that wishes to God we hadn't, isn't it, Dev? It reminds me of something that Tommy McGowan said to me once . . . 'we the unwilling, led by the unqualified, will perform the unbelievable for the ungrateful.' "

He smiled sadly at the truth of it. "They're just too beaten down, I think," he said, as if trying to work it out as he spoke. "Too poor and too used to being slaves."

"Well, perhaps we've given them a lesson in courage this week."

"Some good will come of it," he said, his voice a little lighter. "Have you heard news of your son?"

"He's at the post office with Connolly and Pearse."

"Good men, those two," he replied, as if that would protect Tahg somehow. "I knew your husband, you know. I admired him greatly."

"I miss him." She said it simply.

"Aye, Con. Some people leave a large space in the world with their passing; Tierney was one. You know, I always wondered if he might be the Harper."

He stood up then, not waiting for her to confirm or deny, and, hands in his pockets, moved to the side of the darkened window—carefully, lest he be seen, and looked out.

"I miss my wife tonight."

"We're a fine pair of revolutionaries, aren't we, Dev?" Con said, laughing softly. "But it's lovely to speak of them, isn't it? Lovely to think of what life was once . . . in the midst of all this."

He smiled at her and she thought his face looked sweet and boyish.

"You've been a good comrade in this, Con. Seaneen was a fool not to ask for you for the GPO; but for our sake here I'm glad he didn't."

"For my sake, too," she said emphatically and smiled back at him. "If there's a bit of tea left, I think this would be the time for it. What do you say?" She pulled herself up to her feet, keeping clear of the window, and they both walked in the direction of the mill's kitchen, feeling somewhat better.

Seaneen O'Sullivan leaned closer to Connolly's face in order to be sure he'd heard the man correctly.

"You've got to get out of here," Connolly repeated, with difficulty. "There's no hope at all unless we can get reinforcements from the countryside."

Seaneen looked at the man's pain-racked expression, feeling wonder at his words. It was obvious that the battle was hopeless; it was similarly hopeless to think that any aid would come from the other counties.

"Even if they would send help, it'd never get here in time," he said to Connolly, who seemed to have aged ten years in a day.

"But at least we would have tried!" replied Connolly with fervor.

Seaneen began to speak, but Connolly grabbed his arm to stop him.

"For me, Seaneen," he said urgently. "Do it for me!"

"An order, then?" asked O'Sullivan.

"No," Connolly said, "a favor to a dying friend."

Seaneen clasped the man's hand in both his own and nodded his head. Only amateurs argued with a man who knew he was dying.

"I'll go tonight, if Clarke will sanction it," he said.

"God bless," replied Connolly.

Seaneen readied himself for escape from the GPO. He had no doubt that he could get out. What he had grave doubts about was whether or not he would ever be able to return here, for surely this hopeless little rebellion would be over before the week ended.

He glanced about him at the carnage. " 'Confusion now hath made his masterpiece!' " he quoted to himself sadly. Seaneen threw one last look at Connolly's prostrate, suffering form, and made his way to Clarke to tell him where he was bound.

Friday, 28 April

Major General Sir John Grenfell Maxwell, DCB, CMG, CVO, DSO, was a man of rigid military principle. On Thursday, 27 April, he had been deputed to Dublin as Commander in Chief of British Forces in Ireland, with plenary powers.

He had spent many years fighting in Egypt and had commanded the reoccupation of Khartoum. He'd been decorated for his service in South Africa, been awarded a knighthood for protecting the Nile Delta against the onslaught of the barbarous Turks. He was a fine military brain, and a political time bomb. Maxwell felt he had been recently done out of his proper command by political maneuvering. He needed an opportunity to vent his spleen.

Immediately upon learning that a military action of unknown scope had begun in Dublin, he had called up all available regiments, issuing orders that they were to be ready to move to Dublin the moment the command was given. Already available in Dublin were the local garrisons, numbering 3,800 men. He was in a fine position to give the Irish a run for their money.

When Maxwell arrived on Friday, it was obvious to his general's eye that the foolish little rebellion would soon be over. Fighting continued in many areas of the city and much of Sackville Street was still engulfed in flames. The rebels were hard-pressed and low on food and ammunition. It would only be a matter of time.

General Maxwell issued an immediate proclamation:

> The most vigorous measures will be taken to stop the loss of life and damage to property caused by certain misguided persons. . . . If necessary we will not hesitate to destroy all buildings within any area occupied by

rebels. . . . All men should surrender themselves unconditionally together with arms and munitions.

While Maxwell was issuing his dispatch, back at the GPO Padraig Pearse was composing a manifesto of his own, for he no less than Maxwell knew the end was near.

Friday, 28 April

The O'Rahilly finished his daily note to his wife and tucked it, along with all the others he had written, into his pocket. He hoped they'd be found on his body and taken to her. He sat thinking wistfully about her for a minute or two. They'd had good devoted years together and five fine children. Would God they'd all be safe when this was over. Never to see them all again was a hard thing indeed.

He left the little room where he'd slept fitfully and ordered all surplus grenades and explosives removed from the roof and top floor. For two days the British had managed to drop shells everywhere around them but only two had hit the GPO. Such luck couldn't last much longer.

O'Rahilly made his way downstairs to see Connolly.

"Would you do me a favor?" the wounded man asked as he saw him. "I've written a message for the men but I've not the strength to read it to them." He held out his text to O'Rahilly and the man saw the withered, blood-drained look of Connolly's hand and knew that he was gravely ill. It was curious, but he had grown fond of him in this bizarre week of failure. He'd come to terms with Pearse, too, and even accepted his conviction now that although the Rising would come to a failed end, the people would rally round its cause and make Ireland free. How strange it was to think that this all had changed for him in the span of a single week.

He walked into the main hall and called the men to him. Tahg moved from his place at the window nearer to the center, to hear. He found himself next to a young man named Michael Collins as he did so.

The O'Rahilly began in a clear voice:

"This is the fifth day of the establishment of the Irish Republic . . ."

Tahg felt Collins nudge his arm, heard the man whisper,

"Today or tomorrow will be the end, O'Connor. I've spoken with The O'Rahilly about it. We'll have to find a way out of here before we're all burned to a cinder."

Tahg looked at the competent young man. He had a square sturdy body and a tough look in his eye, but he was liked by the other men; he was a straight shooter and smart. And something about him made you take him seriously.

"Why are you telling me this?" asked Tahg.

"Because he's asked me to pick six boys to help get the men out. I've been watching you all week. You're okay. It'll be dangerous work but you're a big lad—I think you can hack it."

Tahg liked Collins. He was young but reliable; it was obvious that the older men trusted him.

"I'm for it," answered Tahg. "If you think you can get me sprung from my regular duty."

"Aye," said Collins. "We'll talk when O'Rahilly's finished."

"Fire!" a voice screamed from far away. "Fire on the roof!"

Tahg saw O'Rahilly and Collins snap to attention and run for the stair.

"O'Connor!" shouted Collins as he passed by Tahg, "over here! Come with us." And Tahg ran with them toward the upper floors.

Incendiary bombs were dropping like massive fireflies from the skies. The men were fighting them already with fire pumps and hoses, but the water pressure was inadequate and new fires were exploding everywhere.

O'Rahilly fought his way back through the smoke to the floor below and called up to the man on the roof.

"Come down, O'Shaunessy," he yelled. "I'm ordering you down."

"You know what you can do with your order, sir!" shouted a voice with a smile in it.

"You heard what I said," O'Rahilly shouted back. "We're going to evacuate."

"When I can, sir," shouted the voice. "I'm a mite busy up here now!"

Floor by floor they held the fire back as they moved men away from it. As each floor became unbearable, they retreated to the next. Tahg marveled at the ability The O'Rahilly had to command the men; it seemed a job he'd been born to. Mick Collins, too, had the knack of it, that was easy to see.

Finally, it was clear there was no chance of keeping ahead of the fire. O'Rahilly warned Pearse, MacDiarmida, Clarke, Plunkett, who hastily gathered the men on the ground floor as far from the flames and insufferable heat as possible. Tahg and Mick stood a short distance beyond, listening, as they'd been ordered to do.

"There's a remote possibility some of the men can get to the Williams and Wood Soap and Candy Factory on Parnell Street to set up a new command headquarters," said Pearse.

"Christ, that's a long block through hell itself!" replied Mac-Diarmida.

Beams crashing on floors above had ignited the ground-floor ceiling. Involuntarily, all eyes scanned the ceiling, which was beginning to smoke and scatter sparks.

"Someone will have to lead an advance party up Moore Street to even chance it," said Plunkett.

"That's through the British lines and directly in the face of their guns," said Clarke, always practical.

"I'll give it a try," said The O'Rahilly, and the others stared at the man. There was nothing more to be said.

"We must try to get out the wounded first," said Pearse, finally.

A squad of men began breaking holes through a line of buildings along Henry Street to the Coliseum Theatre. The hospital was a long way off. If the men could move through the shattered buildings part of the way, they might make it.

Pearse and Plunkett gathered the men, gave each a ration of food and said good-bye. Plunkett grabbed hold of Winifred Carney, Connolly's secretary, who had refused to leave him.

"Would you do something for me, Miss Carney?" he asked earnestly.

"I would," she said, looking with concern at the dark purple shadows beneath the failing man's eyes.

"Take this letter to my fiancée, Grace Gifford, dear. It contains my will—I've left her all I have." He pulled a gold bangle from his arm and a large ring from his finger. "I don't think you'll be taken, Miss Carney. Please give Grace these things for me."

She nodded, choking on the smoke around them. Plunkett looked so sickly she doubted he'd live through the next few days. He was a sweet, courageous man, for all his odd ways, she decided, and hugged him once quickly before moving on.

Pearse chose thirty men along with Collins and Tahg from the milling crowd, straining to escape the heat and smoke.

"We are preparing to evacuate headquarters," he shouted to them over the roar of the flames, "but you men will not leave with us! You'll move out as an advance guard under the command of The O'Rahilly. Your task is to secure the Williams and Wood Factory. A difficult assignment. But I'm sure you will succeed."

He raised his voice so all could hear over the roar of the inferno above. "I want all of you," he said in conclusion, "to be ready to go out there and face the machine guns as if you were on parade. If we must surrender, we will do so not to save ourselves, but to save Dublin."

There was dead silence for a moment; the men looked around at each other, their grim faces wet with the intense heat of the fires, the madness and the integrity of the moment somehow both painfully clear.

Then a tentative voice began: "Soldiers are we . . ." it sang as well as it could, "whose souls are pledged to Ireland . . ." Then another, and another joined the song.

Pearse, startled by the response, looked around at Connolly where he lay, and Tahg thought he saw tears glistening in the man's dark eyes.

Soon three hundred more voices rose above the din:

"Some have come from a land beyond the wave,
    Sworn to be free, no more our ancient Sireland
    Shall shelter the despot or the slave."

Tahg heard Mick Collins's rich baritone lend itself to the singing and the deep voice of The O'Rahilly boom out behind him:

"Tonight we man the bearna baoghal*
    In Erin's cause come woe or weal,
    Midst cannon's roar and rifle's peal
    We'll chant the Soldier's Song."

* Gap of danger.

It was the new street anthem that seemed to have been written specially for this rebellion. It had an oddly comforting sound.

Still singing, the men moved out into the carnage of Henry Street and eventual surrender.

Saturday, 29 April

P. H. Pearse: To all Irish Volunteers

In order to prevent the further slaughter of Dublin Citizens, and in the hope of saving the lives of our followers now surrounded and hopelessly outnumbered, the members of the Provisional government present at Headquarters have agreed to an unconditional surrender and the Commandants of the various districts in the City and Country will order their commands to lay down arms.

"The surrender is completed, sir." Maxwell's aide-de-camp brought the pleasing news to his superior.

"The leaders and the men have been incarcerated in Kilmainham and Brixton."

"Very good," replied the general.

"Sir," said the lieutenant, with curiosity in his voice, "might I ask what you intend to do with the leaders?"

"You may," replied Maxwell with equanimity. "We shall court-martial them and execute them, as expeditiously as possible."

"All of them, sir?"

"Old military principle, Wrigley," responded Maxwell expansively. His adjutant really was quite a good chap, worth taking the time for explanations.

"It's a dangerous thing to allow traitors the chance to rally their own kind. Best to purge the rotten apples as quickly as possible before anything else gets spoiled by them."

"Yes, sir," answered Wrigley hesitantly. "Of course, sir. But as they're political prisoners, you see, I'd wondered if that might make some sort of difference under the circumstances."

"Political prisoners?" expostulated Maxwell. "Poppycock! Traitors in wartime, Wrigley. No more, no less. Mark my words, you'll find the Germans at the bottom of all this when we've dug deep enough. I can smell their hand in it.

"Only one thing to do with traitors in wartime, eh, lad?"

"Oh, indeed, sir."

"Best get a good night's sleep, Wrigley. There'll be much to do tomorrow."

Lieutenant Arthur Wrigley left his commanding officer, wondering if the question of what to do with the leaders was really quite that simple. These Irish were an emotional lot. Killing their leaders might have repercussions.

29

Tuesday, 2 May 1916

Padraig Pearse sat on the corner of his prison bed and laid the inkwell on the floor beside him. The scraps of paper that were left to him he juggled on his knee and the pen stood poised above the empty page.

What does one write on the last night of life? He who had been a schoolmaster, poet and commander in chief of the rebel forces asked the question of himself.

Well, now it was over, or would be in the morning. The wise men he had once asked in verse to riddle him answers would be left with the sorting through of it all.

Would it be a different thing to die before a firing squad in the cold reality of an Irish morning than it had been to imagine doing so, as he had done so often in the past? He pondered the thought, but briefly. He had more important issues on his mind.

"Martyrs are our strongest weapon," he had said to his followers, meaning it. "No one, no empire, can withstand the force of a single man willing to die for what he believes in."

People had said often enough that he sought martyrdom. Well, here it was then, the grail of his questing . . . more bitter than he had imagined. Colder, sadder, lonelier. Less noble and less idyllic, less bearable and far less clear cut than he had conjured. Please God, let it be no less useful to the Cause.

Thank God, at least Willy mightn't be executed. Good, loving, loyal Willy, I've led you a merry chase, little brother, haven't I? Blessed God, Willy, was there ever a brother who followed another with more love and loyalty than you? None closer in the world than two brothers if they be friends.

Padraig dipped the pen in the awkwardly placed inkwell and began to write, smaller than usual for there was little paper and little time, and no room for mistakes.

"To my Brother" . . . he wrote the words, then said a silent prayer for the eloquence to say it all as it was in his heart.

> O faithful!
> Molded in one womb,
> We two have stood together all the years,
> All the glad years and all the sorrowful years.
> Own brothers: Through good repute and ill,
> In direst peril true to me
> Leaving all things for me,
> Spending yourself in the hard service that
>   I taught you.
> Of all the men that I have known on earth,
> You only have been my familiar friend.
> Nor needed I another.

He read the poem through once, satisfied. Willy would understand whatever had been left unsaid. Then he inked the pen one last time and signed the poem, P. H. Pearse. He would give the paper to the guard before morning and ask him to deliver it to Willy in his cell. Surely even a guard would honor a dying man's last request.

He picked up the pen again. This time he must leave a message for his mother:

> . . . Lord thou art hard on mothers;
> We suffer in their coming and in their going;
> And tho' I grudge them not, I weary, weary
> Of the long sorrow. And yet I have my joy;
> My sons were faithful, and they fought.
>   P. H. Pearse

Pearse sighed as he signed the poem for his mother. He had written it months ago but these words seemed the most appropriate to send to her now. He hoped to God he wasn't being prophetic when he spoke of two sons going down. There was still hope, after all, that Willy would go free.

The commandant held the offensive papers in his hand. The guard had rightly brought them to him asking directions. The Fenian prisoner Pearse had written it for his brother Willy, another prisoner, he had said; should he deliver it to the man or not? There was also a poem for his mother.

The commandant had thanked the guard for his alert intelligence in having called this to his attention and the man left.

This Pearse chap fancied himself a poet, it seemed, although the commandant could see no great merit in this scrap of unrhymed nonsense. On the other hand, it was just this kind of drivel that caused foment among these native ruffians.

He walked to the fire and raised his hand to toss the papers in, then hesitated. Might be interesting souvenirs at that. Something to show his grandchildren some year hence.

He glanced again at the angular writing and, folding the paper, placed it in his pocket and returned to the work at hand.

Thursday, 11 May 1916

The pain in his leg had spread everywhere. James Connolly bit his lip to keep from crying out in anguish as they carried him, tied to the chair, back to his hospital cell. Condemned to die, they had said. He would have laughed in their faces had he not had to fight so hard to remain conscious against the inroads of the bright white pain.

Of course he was condemned to die, didn't the fools know that! His leg was gangrenous from the shell fragments still resting in the rotted flesh. The whole leg was rotting and in no short order. With or without their bloody court-martial, he'd be dead in a day or so.

They jolted him to the floor, untied the straps that held him upright and his body sagged forward, for he hadn't the strength to sit by himself. The two young soldiers supported him and lifted him into the bed. James gritted his teeth against the groan that such lifting cost him.

The soldiers walked to the door. He heard the men speak to the guard outside in the corridor.

"His wife's to be allowed fifteen minutes tomorrow," the impersonal voice said.

Fifteen minutes in which to end a lifetime of love and trust and devotion, Connolly thought, heartsick. How pitiful was the largesse of so large an empire.

"Can I do anything for you, Connolly?" The voice roused the man from his swooning slumber. He recognized Surgeon Richard Tobin looking down at him and tried to smile. The man had treated him here in the prison before. He was a kind soul in his own way. Connolly tried to speak, but his mouth felt like cotton —dry and thick.

"I want nothing but liberty," he said, and smiled a bit.

"You must go to the sean bhean bocht* for that, I'm afraid, my friend," the doctor replied. "Can I do nothing to make you easier?"

"What do you think will happen to me?" asked Connolly, ignoring the question. It was a sensible query but sounded almost childlike in the awful surroundings.

Tobin cleared his throat before answering.

"You'll be shot."

"Oh, you think that?"

"I'm sure of it."

"Why?"

"They can't do anything else with you, man. Can they buy you?"

"No."

"Can they frighten you?"

"No."

"Will you promise if they let you off with your life to go away and be a good boy for the future?"

"No."

"Then I fear they can do nothing else but shoot you."

"I can see that," said Connolly, and his voice was low and sad.

Tobin shook his head and picked up his surgeon's bag.

"They may not let me see you again until the end, James . . ." He left the thought hanging.

* Literally, a poor, old woman. A metaphor for Ireland.

Connolly nodded. "I'm to see my wife, Doctor. If you could get them to let her bring Nora, my oldest, I'd be grateful."

The doctor nodded a second time.

"I'll do what I can."

Dr. Tobin waited while the sentry fumbled open the iron door. Connolly was dying, that was plain to see. He wondered if God or the English would take him first.

Dublin Castle has a double staircase that is part of the entrance hall, with two wide landings at either side—on every step there was a soldier with a bayonet. Lillie and Nora Connolly walked up the stairs toward the intelligence officer, who had the power to grant them access to the condemned man's room in the Red Cross section of the hospital.

"What are those little square cushions they all have on the landing, Mama?" asked Nora in an attempt to break the deadly silence.

"They're called biscuits, miss," replied the young duty officer who had accompanied them. "The men use them as mattresses when they sleep here."

The young girl nodded, wondering why the soldiers did not leave their posts at night.

Connolly had been moved to the officers' ward, the intelligence officer said. They could see him there in his bed, but an RAMC officer would be with them during their allotted fifteen minutes.

"I'll not be alone with him at all then?" Mrs. Connolly whispered, the heartbreak apparent in her soft voice.

Nora Connolly saw the look of despair in her mother's eyes and, with the new knowledge that she herself was taking on of womanhood, she suddenly understood that her mother and father were lovers as well as husband and wife.

"Certainly not," was the brusque reply. There was nothing to do but nod acceptance.

James Connolly lay—white as the bedclothes—in an army bed, a cage over his feet to keep the covers from his shattered ankle.

"I've been court-martialed, love," he said to Lillie straightaway, and a knowing look passed between them.

The young officer cleared his throat and, glancing at Nora,

turned his face away from the couple and stared pointedly out the window.

Husband and wife spoke in hushed tones for a moment, then Mrs. Connolly motioned Nora to the bed.

"I'm proud as can be of you, lass," her father said, and there were tears in his eyes.

"But I've done nothing, nothing," said Nora, a sob in her voice. She wanted to throw her small body across the man, to hug him, but seeing the look of pain that flitted into his face at the movement of the bed, she pulled back.

"Only for you, child, we couldn't have done anything," he said. "The messages you carried for me were key to making this happen, Nora."

The young girl bit back the words she wished to say: Had there been no messages, perhaps there would be no such horror as this room now held for them.

Connolly glanced toward the man at the window and whispered, "You must take a message to Skeffington, Nora."

Nora glanced quickly at her mother.

"He was murdered, Papa, by an army officer. There's only you and MacDiarmida left. They're all gone, the others!"

A terrible look of desolation flitted across the man's face; his expression told them that he hadn't known.

"Dear God," he said. "All gone?" as if the possibility had not even occurred to him.

"Your fifteen minutes are nearly up," said the officer embarrassedly. Tears were running down Lillie Connolly's face. She had been struggling to keep them back for her husband's sake, but the reality of what was to come overwhelmed her. Nora felt compelled by the anguish in her parents' eyes to pull away from the bed, to allow some semblance of privacy.

"Your life, James," she heard her mother say through her tears. "Not your beautiful life."

"Lillie, Lillie, Lillie . . ." he managed, barely able to speak. "Don't cry so, love. You'll unman me, sweetheart."

The small woman laid her head beside her husband's on the pillow and sought his hands with her own. They said no more words to each other, but clung there till they heard the sounds of the guard in the hall.

James motioned Nora to the bed, took her hand and drew it

under the covers. She felt him press a square of folded paper into it.

"Take this out of here," he whispered urgently. "It's what I said at the court-martial. I was asked what I had to say for myself, but I didn't say it for myself, child, I said it for Ireland. Get it out, Nora, get it out for me!"

The officer approached the bed, but Lillie Connolly stood rooted to the floor like a statue.

"I'll not go, James." Her voice was agonized but steady.

He saw the others in the room come toward her and closed his eyes to keep from seeing the spectacle of the doctor, nurse and officer pulling his wife from his bedside. It was too grotesque, even for this week of grotesqueries.

Nora, in the scuffle, fled back to her father's arms.

"Don't be too disappointed, lass," he murmured quickly into her ear. "We shall rise again!"

"A moment," begged his wife at the door, and turning back, Lillie Connolly looked one last time at the man she'd loved unstintingly for more than twenty years.

"There was more that passed between those two in that instant than most married people say to each other in a lifetime," said the nurse to the doctor as the woman and child moved away down the corridor.

"Indeed," replied the man, and she could see that he was as shaken by the incident as she.

Dawn, Friday, 12 May 1916

Connolly saw the yard where he would be shot through a haze of pain. The chair to which he was once again tied jiggled unmercifully as he was set down on the cobblestones to face the firing squad. The fierce pain made him almost grateful at the prospect of oblivion.

Twelve uniformed Lancers stood at quiet attention. He looked from face to face, unable to help wondering what in God's name a man must say to himself before he participates in shooting another in cold blood. Just workingmen they seemed. Much like the ones he had struggled for all his life. Just plain people changed by a uniform.

The yard was quiet and strained. He wondered if the obvious

tension was made worse by his condition. It must feel odd, indeed, to shoot a man too weak to get out of a chair.

He said his prayers quickly; there had been ample time for praying in his cell. He thought of the strength of Nora's hand in his own the night before and wondered what would become of her now.

He blessed his wife from his heart. Dear valiant Lillie! Was there ever a wife so good and true?

Dr. Tobin was walking toward him with a blindfold in his hand. Well, he'd have none of that now. As Tobin drew nearer, Connolly made a disdainful face at the square of cloth and the doctor told him with embarrassment that he had no choice but to acquiesce.

They spoke for a minute, uncomfortable at prolonging the inevitable. Tobin moved as if to go, then turned briefly and said, "Will you pray for the men who are about to shoot you, Connolly?"

James looked at him curiously, wondering what might have prompted the question. Then he smiled benevolently.

"I pray for all brave men who do their duty according to their lights," he answered, and the doctor tied the blindfold around his head.

Pearse. MacDonogh. Clarke. Plunkett. Daly. O'Hanrahan. Willy Pearse. MacBride. Ceannt. Colbert. Mallin. Heuston. MacDiarmida. Connolly named the names of his own brave comrades in his mind as he waited. He couldn't be sure if they were all dead now.

The Lancers raised their rifles to shoulder level, and a signal was given.

Connolly's bullet-riddled body slumped hard against the bonds that held him to the chair. His shattered ankle had bled through its bandages and blood from the bullet wounds now mingled with it on the cobblestones at his feet.

Was this not a microcosm of the madness of the English/ Irish struggle in one tragic tableau? thought Tobin. Fleetingly, he remembered the story of Cuchulain, lashed standing to a tree in his last agony by his comrade "that he might die a man."

Jim Connolly died a man, he murmured to himself as he watched the orderly cut his friend's body loose from the chair. He had stood taller, sitting in that chair, than most men ever stand.

30 ∽ The morning newspaper on Thursday, 11 May, contained an official statement from Sir John Maxwell issued at Irish Command Headquarters: "In view of the gravity of the Rebellion and its connection with German intrigue and Propaganda," it said, "the General Officer Commander In Chief has found it imperative to inflict the most severe sentences on the organizers of this detestable Rising. . . ." Nearly all of the leaders had already been executed. I took it to mean they intended to execute the remaining prisoners.

"We *must* get her out of there before it's too late!" I said to Edmond, still clutching the paper with the ghastly news. Con, too, had been condemned to death, and although there was talk of commuting the sentences of the women to life imprisonment, it had not happened yet.

"Without question," he replied, to my amazement. "I shall go to Sir Hilary at the Castle myself. This insanity has gone quite far enough."

"And if he won't release her?"

"Then I shall go above him to Whitehall." He seemed genuinely agitated about what was happening. I was surprised and probably looked it.

"You must understand me in this, Elizabeth," he said carefully. "I find what Constance and the others did to have been witless and imprudent in the extreme. But to be scrupulously honest with you, I am no longer certain that there has been no provocation."

I stared at him, disbelieving, and he responded by saying, "I deplore violence, Elizabeth. Theirs and ours. And if there is any way I can contribute to bringing these executions to a halt, you may rest assured that I shall do so." He stood up as if preparing to leave.

"Thank you, Edmond," I said finally. "I don't believe that they will listen to you . . . but I'm very grateful to you for trying." ·

He nodded, accepting my gratitude, and left the room striding briskly.

I had intended to tell him what I planned—if only because I felt I owed him honesty, after all was said and done. But after this surprising conversation, I didn't want to steal his thunder. He wished to help; he still believed in "the System." It seemed to me that we each must try in our own way to save my sister and that there was, after all, no point to my telling Edmond how I would attempt to do so.

I remember walking upstairs to my bedroom and standing in the ornate doorway, staring for a long while at the bed that commanded the center of the room. It had been brought from Manningham Castle when we first bought the Dublin house. I was remembering, remembering: the nights I'd lain in it with my husband, so young and so uncertain, wishing so that he could be what I needed in life . . . and then the long nights I'd lain there alone knowing he would never be . . . and finally the long, lonely years in which it was not he I wanted. The mind plays tricks on you when you feel yourself to be in danger of death. A strange melancholia overtakes you and plays back moments of your life as if they were on film.

Never, I think, in all my life did I feel so strongly the specter of death at my heel as I did that day. A breathing, palpable presence it was . . . so inevitable as to be almost inviting.

Ah well, I told myself. If I am to die, I must settle my affairs. I wrote a note to each of my children—neither maudlin nor full of self-explanation. Rather they were simple notes of my love. Then I came to John's with the realization that if I died, the secret of his parentage would die with me.

Perhaps, after all, that was for the best, I told myself. The past forgotten, old debts canceled.

But something stayed me . . . something in the child himself. Some element in him there was that knew the truth of his displacement. Were he to go a lifetime living the unknown lie, some part of him would always struggle to unveil the truth. I owed him the means to learn who he was.

"My own dear Johnny," I wrote, wondering how in God's name I'd ever find the words to express what was in my heart.

I have a story to tell you . . . one so dear to my heart, so secret . . . that I know not where the secret ends and I begin. It is a story that belongs to you and so I will try, to the best of my ability, to tell it as it should be told. For while it is a story of events and places and people . . . it is far more so a story of a journey of the heart. . . .

When I had finished, I tied all four letters (I had written one to both twins together) into a little bundle, each marked with its owner's name. I left Johnny's on top of the pile with the words "To be opened only in the event of my death" scrawled on its face.

I placed them in the drawer of my desk and left the room thinking it was, perhaps, for the last time.

I stood outside the closed door of Seaneen's makeshift headquarters and tried to gather my wits. Seaneen had escaped capture because of Connolly's having sent him off in search of reinforcements. Now he was the only one of the IRB leaders still at large. He had sent me word of his whereabouts.

I think I had terrified the young officer who'd been left to guard the inner sanctum; it had taken nearly all my accumulated strength to do so. I *would* see Seaneen O'Sullivan, I told him, or, by God, I'd kill him where he stood! I'd drawn a pistol, taken from Edmond's gun room, from my purse then and waved it at the man. What I might have done if he hadn't acquiesced to my demand I wasn't at all certain.

"I'm Constance O'Connor's sister and I *will* see Commandant O'Sullivan!" I'd said it once again very slowly, and the man, agitatedly, fled to the next room, returning a moment later with Seaneen at his side.

"Thank God, you're alive!" Seaneen breathed as he took me into his arms, much to the amazement of the young officer.

"Leave us!" he shouted to the boy, who did so gladly. I let myself be seated in a chair, felt the comfort of his strength flood me with the life-giving warmth it always had for me. Dear God, I'm glad I've loved this man, I said in my heart as I felt his eyes burrow into me.

"They've sentenced Con to death," I told him simply. There was no need for preliminaries between us. "I must try to get her out."

He pulled back from me, obviously startled by the audacity of the idea. I couldn't wait long enough for his reply as I feared it would be "No." "I've come to collect on an old promise," I said evenly, and I think he must have seen the terrible strain of the last days behind my eyes, for his own softened in an instant.

Seaneen leaned toward me and reached up to touch my face with the back of his fingers, a sweet remembered gesture that touched me to the heart. But he said nothing.

"I must get her out of there," I repeated as if he might not have heard. Not only was it a growing obsession that filled me to the exclusion of all else, but the urgency of acting quickly was pushing me as well.

"They say Kilmainham is impregnable, My Lady. Especially now," he said, sensibly enough.

"I can't let her die, Seaneen. Not without trying to save her." He must have heard the absolute conviction mixed with desperation in my voice, for he replied carefully.

"No," he said. "I don't suppose you can."

I leapt on his momentary hesitancy. "I'll need help. A map of the interior of the prison. Two or three good men—uniforms, guns. God knows what I'll need."

"You do know that we're in the middle of a life-and-death struggle, Beth, and that I'm a commanding officer?" he asked steadily, watching me as if to see if I were demented. "You do know that for me to go off on such a harebrained, doomed scheme as this is not only insane, it's not the act of a soldier?"

" '. . . though Satan himself should bar the way,' you said, Seaneen," I answered him.

He glanced sharply at me, knowing I'd committed the note to memory, as had he.

"No idle promise, that, My Lady . . ." he repeated back to me, like the responses of the mass.

I closed my eyes and exhaled audibly—he had not forgotten.

"All right then, my own Beth," he said, making up his mind. "If this is how it is to be, we must hurry. There's talk of commuting the women's sentences, but who knows what the danger is. She could also be shot at any time." He stopped for a moment, looking at me steadily. "But I'll do it without you."

I reached across the table as he started to rise and grasped his arm. "No," I said. "Together." Without me, I would not send him off on a mission that could mean his death.

"You'll slow us down."

"I'll do it with your help or alone!"

He stared at me for a brief moment, assessing my resolve, I think. Then he moved to my side and, putting his arms around me, murmured gently, "My poor brave love. We all must give everything, it seems." Putting his hand gently under my chin, he tipped back my head, and seeing the tears on my cheeks, he brushed them with his hand.

"I love you, My Lady," he whispered as he kissed me once softly on the mouth. "We will do the best we can for her . . . together."

I tried to answer that I loved him, too, and that I always would, but my words were lost in the shoulder of his jacket as he pressed me against him. I felt as if we were in the grip of some force more powerful than we, with no choice but to play out our parts and no sure knowledge of the ending. ∽

31

Friday night, 12 May 1916

Lord Edmond Manningham had to exercise every ounce of restraint he possessed to remain calm outside the Foreign Secretary's office. This business of his wife's sister had simply gone too far. He had made this appointment directly after speaking with Elizabeth, although it had taken all day to cut through red tape and get to Sir Hilary. The afternoon headlines had merely firmed his resolve: TWO MORE REBELS SHOT, the paper had read. JAMES CONNOLLY AND JOHN MACDIARMIDA SENTENCED ON TUESDAY AND EXECUTED/SIGNATORIES TO THE "REPUBLICAN" PROCLAMATION/TODAY'S OFFICIAL STATEMENT.

The ornate door opened and Sir Hilary motioned him inside. He noticed that the man's secretary had discreetly absented himself through the other door.

"My Lord," began the older man, "I've been expecting you

to call, of course. Bit of a sticky wicket we have here, wouldn't you say?"

"It's a damned sight more than that, Sir Hilary, when members of one's own class are being condemned to death for high treason by some kangaroo court held in the bowels of Kilmainham Jail without benefit of proper legal counsel or the respect we might expect to be accorded one of our own."

Sir Hilary raised his furry eyebrows and joined the tips of his fingers together in a fleshy pyramid at the unexpected vehemence.

"The woman did, after all, lead a battalion of dissidents against the King's troops, old man," he replied deliberately. "One can't really put up with that sort of thing, now, can one?"

"They were outnumbered twenty to one, sir; do you really feel the Crown was in serious jeopardy?" The arch tone of Edmond's voice was not lost on Sir Hilary. Edmond Manningham was a popular man in the House of Lords, from a family that had been long respected by the British government. This whole incident of his sister-in-law would have to be handled with extreme delicacy.

"Now really, Edmond, what would you have me do?" he said placatingly. "These damnable rebels have caused no end of mayhem throughout the city and who knows what else those Sinn Fein devils have up their sleeves after all? We really must make an example of their leaders. I'm damned sorry one of them happens to be your wife's sister, but we can't go on playing favorites now, can we?"

Edmond raised an eyebrow contemptuously, as if such specious logic were beneath them both.

"I can't really see why not, Hilary," he replied. "That's been our way of life after all, hasn't it? We favor our own kind over the peasants, we favor the English over the Irish, we favor the will of the Establishment over law or justice and we always have." Seeing that he'd caught Sir Hilary off guard, Edmond pressed his advantage.

"Let me tell you something, Hilary. If you carry out these preposterous sentences you will have given Ireland precisely what she needs and longs for—martyrs! And you will have sullied the name of English justice in the eyes of honest men forever. Those were no trials, man. They were kangaroo courts!

Maxwell overstepped himself. Those people deserve punishment, certainly. But death? Really!

"Anyone who knows a scintilla about Irish history knows that the Crown has much to answer for in this small colony. And anyone who knows one jot about the character of the Irish knows that they worship martyrs.

"Deport these people and the Easter Rebellion will be forgotten in a month. Kill them and there's not a man, woman or child in Ireland who'll rest until the English are hounded out of this land."

Sir Hilary was astounded by the vehemence of Sir Edmond's diatribe. "My dear fellow," he said, the warm oil of diplomacy in his voice, "I had no idea you felt so passionately about this issue. What exactly would you have me do?"

"I'd have you commute those sentences in a show of British compassion and largesse, and I'd have you get Constance Fitz-Gibbon O'Connor released into my custody tonight, until she's deported or sentenced fairly. You must see that you cannot put a woman of her stature into a common prison pesthouse."

"Has it occurred to you that she might not accept your offer of hospitality? She appears quite determined to remain with her coterie of rebel companions."

"I believe my wife might be able to persuade her. She has a son, you know. He's already in custody."

"Yes, I believe I did hear something of that." Sir Hilary appeared agitated beneath his glossy diplomatic exterior.

"I'll tell you what I shall do, Edmond. I can't predict what kind of response I'll get from Whitehall about an offer of clemency for the remaining men, but I believe I can see to it that the women's sentences are commuted to some sort of penal servitude. I'll try to see to it that Mrs. O'Connor is released into your care until sentencing. She has been a bit of an embarrassment to us all, I'm afraid.

"You know young Rodney, the captain who accepted her surrender, offered her a ride back to the prison and she refused. Said she'd prefer to march with her men or some such nonsense. Kissed her sword and bandolier before handing them over, he said. Damned touching gesture, so he told me." Sir Hilary cleared his throat. He'd be glad to get rid of the woman if he could. Perhaps this appeal from Sir Edmond was just the ticket. He'd put in a call to the proper authorities immediately.

32

Friday night, 12 May 1916

I flattened myself against the cold stone wall of Kilmainham and fingered the revolver in the holster at my hip, hoping to God I wouldn't have to use it and wondering wildly if I had been right in forcing Seaneen to take me along. I knew how to shoot and had done so as a child with my father, but I'd never had the knack for it that my sister had, and the notion of actually shooting someone made me physically ill. I prayed to God I wouldn't slow them down or interfere.

I was dressed in the uniform of an English lieutenant, my hair piled under the cap, my breasts bound tightly by a wrapper to flatten them. I knew I'd never pass muster if someone looked closely, but if all went as we'd planned, we'd make it to the cell without close scrutiny. One of Seaneen's own lads, who had been planted two years before in the troops that guarded the jail, had let us in, and if it were not for the absolute terror that was causing my heart to pound uncontrollably, all had gone so far exactly as we had planned. There were a dozen others from the IRB planted expectantly outside the prison walls.

Seaneen was dressed in the uniform of an English captain; he, along with Dennis Flynn and Timmy O'Flaherty, two fine loyal IRB men who had helped plan the escape over the past twenty-four hours, were just ahead of me in the dim stone corridor. I could hear Seaneen's well-rehearsed British diction as he conversed with the guard. He was a new interrogator sent from London to deal with the O'Connor woman, he said. He'd been sent because of the political pressure being brought to bear by her parliamentary brother-in-law. The two subalterns with him were his aides, who would relieve the two sentries for the duration of his interrogation.

I could hear the muffled voices, then a seeming sound of assent, a salute and the two real soldiers, convinced that the two new men and the political emissary were genuine, left their watch and continued down the hall, having been relieved. "Soldiers on the evening watch don't question their relief team," Timmy had told me earlier. "They're just damned glad to get off duty." God, but I hoped he was right. I also hoped no one would find the two soldiers we had left unconscious and trussed up in an alcove farther down the corridor. The two newly relieved guards barely noticed me as I walked, in as manly a fashion as I could, down the flagstones toward my sister's cell.

My heart was pounding so wildly, I thought I might have a coronary seizure before reaching my destination. If I thought I had ever known terror before, I reconsidered. My conversation with Edmond before leaving the house had left me shaken. He had the most damnable habit of being civilized at precisely the moment I expected otherwise of him.

I shuddered in the dark dampness of the foul place and tried to pull myself together.

I heard the old iron of the lock click backward and the door to my sister's cell swing open. Seaneen motioned to me wordlessly and we entered.

The interior was about seven by eight feet, stone-walled and dank. There was a small metal cot with a thin mattress, seemingly straw-filled, against the wall, and a chamber pot visible in the dim light of a single gas lamp's flame. The scene filled me with a sense of unmitigated loathing and fierce anger.

Sitting on the cot, still in the motley she had worn on the previous Friday when I had seen her last, was Con. Her wound seemed freshly bandaged, but there were deep purple shadows under her eyes and her beautiful brown-gold shoulder-length hair had been cut to a short shapelessness. She looked from me to Seaneen, so startled that she said nothing, but her eyes widened in obvious disbelief.

I slipped quickly into the room with my finger to my lips in a gesture of silence. I ran to Con, who had quickly risen, and we threw ourselves into each other's arms and clung there wordlessly for a moment.

Seaneen put his hands on my shoulders and whispered urgently, "There's no time!"

We clung for one instant more, then I opened the briefcase I carried and pulled out the soldier's uniform, shoes and cap it contained. The three men turned their backs and Con stripped off the uniform she wore and pulled on the garb of an English soldier.

"Dear God, let it fit," I prayed as I saw how gaunt my sister had grown. She, who had been so robust and full of life, looked scrawny and weakened. The bones of her rib cage were apparent above the bandage.

Once she was dressed, Seaneen had the men plump up the bed as best they could to make it seem occupied; we locked the cell door and headed for the old kitchen exit that our informant had told them was used only for disposal of garbage. I felt the pressure of Seaneen's hand on my arm as I left the doorway—it seemed oddly reassuring.

The IRB maps, made while one of the IRB men had been a prisoner in Kilmainham, were accurate to the centimeter. Our "inside" man had confirmed that little had changed since the maps were made, but nonetheless we felt relief at the familiarity of the corridors' twists and turns. We made our way quickly past the other cells, across a stairway and through the winding hallways that led to the kitchen. ✑

Sir Hilary Gresham called to his secretary, who appeared without delay, after Edmond Manningham left his office.

"Put in a call to the commandant at Kilmainham," he said brusquely. "Tell him I wish to have Mrs. O'Connor brought to my office immediately."

The secretary placed the call to the commandant, who dispatched a man to the cell of Constance O'Connor—where a plumped-up mattress and a discarded uniform betrayed the fact that an escape was at that moment in progress.

Edmond breathed a sigh of relief. He had been entering his carriage when a young soldier had called him back. It seemed Sir Hilary had reached Whitehall just after he'd left the man's office and they'd agreed to his removing Mrs. O'Connor from the prison until proper disposition could be made of her case. What a piece of good luck.

He hadn't been at all confident, on leaving him, about Sir Hilary's intention. The man was a superior diplomatist and gave little away of his true intent.

Edmond retraced his steps into the elaborate antechamber

with a springier tread than he'd shown coming in an hour before. By God, he hoped those headstrong FitzGibbon women would understand now how diplomacy was able to move more mountains than violence ever could.

Sir Hilary's secretary had asked him to have a seat in the reception room while the proper arrangements were made and the necessary papers prepared for Mrs. O'Connor's temporary release. Edmond must understand, he'd said, that this was quite an irregular act and it would take a few moments to put things in order.

Edmond picked up a copy of the morning newspaper from the mahogany table at his side to pass the time. But the front page was full of the rebel executions and he put it down again hastily, not feeling up to reading about them at this particular moment.

     Con, Seaneen, the two IRB men and I hovered soundlessly in the corridor, waiting for the sound of footsteps in the courtyard to die away. The old iron door that separated us from freedom was no longer in use and had been padlocked for some time.

Timmy O'Flaherty was working diligently at the lock with his locksmith's pick, and even the tiny scratching sounds he made seemed terrifyingly loud to us in the silence of the night.

"My God, Bethy," whispered Con to me in the semidarkness. "What possessed you to attempt this?" It didn't seem by the sound of her voice that she really expected an answer.

"What would Father say if he were here to see any of this?" Con's voice was husky with worry. We spoke in frightened whispers for a moment, then she composed herself. She hugged me one more time and said, "Well, love, if this is how it's to be, let's at least give them a run for their money. If no one has given us away, there's a decent enough chance for making it. There are generally only one or two sentries posted in the courtyard at night, and they'll be on their rounds. They tend to be a bit sleepy-headed there after dark for they think this place is impregnable, so their vigilance is fairly lax in the yard."

I marveled at the calm air of command that was suddenly about her.

Seaneen whispered back, "If we can get out of here without

alerting them, we may be able to make it to the river. Don't lose heart now."

I handed the gun from my holster to Con. "You'll make better use of it than I," I said, meaning it, and she took the weapon wordlessly.

"The men on the outside will have thrown rope ladders over the wall. There'll be damned little time to use them once we get there. Remember it!" Seaneen said, and we nodded.

Timmy O'Flaherty whispered back in the darkness, "I'll take care of the sentries on the west wall."

Seaneen nodded. "Whatever happens, don't turn back. It's only a hundred and fifty yards across the courtyard to the wall. It isn't heavily guarded because its height is a natural fortification. If we make it and jump, they'll have the devil's own time trying to hit us in the dark once we're over. Once outside, Timmy, Dennis and Con head for the river, Beth and I for the canal. Whatever you do, don't lose heart. Nothing's hopeless until you give up!"

Con took a deep breath; I knew Seaneen had added the last just to keep our courage up.

"I love you, Bethy," Con said to me suddenly. "There's never in the world been a sister as good as you."

"I love you, too," I answered, my voice thick with tears and terror.

"Seaneen, men . . . how can I tell you how very grateful I am." She said it gently, and the expression on her face told them she knew the inadequacy of the words.

They nodded acknowledgment.

"Are we ready, then?" Seaneen asked, and we both wondered as he said it if any human could ever be ready for such consummate terror. I thought suddenly of Tierney's death in this same terrible place and knew Con must have been living with that picture ever since she'd come here. Each of us nodded readiness in turn, and Flynn slid the door lock back. The courtyard appeared to be deserted except for the sentries. Neither moon nor stars were visible in the sky's black velvet and a fine mist filled the air with characteristic Irish dampness, but our anxiety made it seem colder than it was.

We let ourselves out one at a time, flattening against the wall as we did so.

"I'll take the sentry on the east wall nearest the river," whispered Seaneen. "If all is clear, I'll signal from the other side of the yard."

He turned a last gaze to me before moving out. We held each other wordlessly for the briefest moment and I could see a garrote in his hands as he slid out soundlessly into the darkness. We waited breathlessly for what seemed like endless moments. Finally, we saw his shadowy figure far across the yard signaling that all was clear.

All four of us gauged the distance across the yard. I saw the two younger men cross themselves as they started out at a silent run across the cobblestones. Both Con and I sped out together after them. Con, swift as a deer, was quickly in the lead. She was nearly across when my foot went out from under me; sliding precariously on the dampened earth, I fell with a sickening thud. Instantaneous knowledge of my own doom flooded me as I hit those god-awful stones. I tried to rise but a terrible shooting pain in my leg made it impossible. I saw that Con had reached the safety of the wall and prayed God she would go up the rope ladder without looking back to see what had happened to me.

Con, always the athlete, reached the wall with a triumphant gesture that somehow said "We're going to make it after all, by God!" I saw her turn to share the joyous knowledge with me—I saw the incredulous expression on her face as she realized I was not at her side. The grotesqueries of the next few seconds are seared forever into my brain, for I could see everything with ghastly clarity from where I lay.

She looked once over her shoulder wistfully at the wall and freedom, then without an instant's hesitation she turned and began to run back toward me, just as the alarm was sounded and lights began to go on all over the courtyard.

I screamed to her to leave me, knowing that she would not; a light glinted off a gun barrel—a shot rang out and I saw Seaneen hit by a bullet as he looked back over his shoulder from the top of the prison wall. With a muffled cry he tumbled over the wall to the ground outside. I tried to rise as I saw a second gun pointed at me, but I could not! I saw Con running wildly toward me, and somehow—somehow, in the hideous split second it took the man to fire, she threw herself into the path of the bullet meant for me. ✍

* * *

The double doors to Sir Hilary's office swung open. The old man himself stood in their center, his face ashen around his gray beard and mustache. He looked so stricken that both Edmond and the secretary ran to his aid at the same instant.

"My dear man," he managed to say in a choked whisper, addressing Edmond, "I'm afraid there's been a dreadful accident."

"Accident?" said Edmond, cold fingers clutching suddenly at his belly from within. "What sort of accident?"

"Your wife, sir, has been shot in an unsuccessful attempt to help her sister escape from Kilmainham. Mrs. O'Connor is dead."

Edmond Manningham's perennial composure permitted him to make the next inquiry in a nearly normal voice, although he felt as if the world had exploded to an end.

"My wife, sir. What is the condition of my wife?"

"That appears to be somewhat uncertain, Edmond. Although she is alive."

The old Foreign Secretary thought the look of anguish on the younger man's face was more than he could bear.

"My dear fellow, allow me to escort you to the prison hospital where they've been taken . . ."

But Edmond Manningham no longer heard him; he was running down the marble corridor like a madman.

"Go after him!" shouted Sir Hilary to his secretary. "They'll shoot him for an assassin before he makes it to the gate!"

The old man slumped into his leather chair and stared down the now emptied corridor, wonderingly.

"I never seen nothin' like it, I'm tellin' yer!" The Cockney soldier standing at the bar of Tommy McGowan's pub took a long swig of his beer before continuing. He knew he had his audience where he wanted them; what he had seen firsthand was the story of the hour.

"The prisoner, she run like a bloomin' gazelle she did; she was all the way to the river wall when she sees that her sister's down. Well, by God, not one second goes by before she doubles back to get the woman. Mind you now, she could of been over that wall and clean away before we could of got our rifles to our shoulders.

"But no, back she goes for her sister, like I said."

Tommy stood transfixed behind the bar. He had been released from Kilmainham after Tierney's death and had spent the weeks since the rebellion being nursed of his injuries by a kindly neighbor. He was still unsteady on his feet.

"Now all the lights go on sudden and the alarm's ringin' bloody murder and people is runnin' this way and that, and this bleedin' sharpshooter puts his gun to his shoulder.

"Now mind you, by some queer trick of fate both women sees him at the same time. And the one on the ground's screamin', 'No, Con, you must save yourself!' and the other one—well, let me tell you she covered that ground so fast, all you saw was a bloomin' blur. And she spots this bloke with the rifle and she screams at him, 'No you don't!' just as plain as that, and she throws herself in this incredible leap—like a bloody gazelle it was—on top of the one on the ground, who's got her arms up by now, to catch her as she comes down!"

Tommy laid down the pint of stout he had been carrying and steadied himself by holding fast to the bar as he listened, aghast.

"Well, doesn't that rifle bullet catch her full in the back, lads, as she hits her sister's arms and the force of it lifts them both like they was dolls; into the air they goes. And then there's another shot from somewhere and then the captain shouts, 'Cease fire, you fools!' and this eerie quiet comes down—and somebody flashes a spotlight on them both where they lay all tangled up on the ground.

"And there they was, lads! The younger one clutched in Her Ladyship's arms—like little girls they was, but all dressed up in their big brother's uniforms! By God, it would've tore the heart out of a bloody stone, it would!"

"What of the men with them?" asked a voice farther down the bar.

"One dead, one shot and most likely drowned in the river . . . that's where his trail ended. One got clean away, he did."

"Who'd have ever thought a ruddy aristocrat'd try a jail break?" asked another of the soldiers at the bar in the silence that followed the story.

"Aye, lad. And who'd of thought a bloody traitor'd throw away a chance at freedom to save somebody else? It gives you pause, it does. Can't say as I holds with this business of shootin' women, whatever they've done," finished up the storyteller with conviction. "Although I'll say this to you. I'd of been proud to have that one as me comrade under fire. She was a brave one, she was, and no two ways about it."

There were several sage grunts of assent at the bar as the listeners ordered another round of beer, and Tommy Mc-Gowan, tears running down his cheeks, staggered away from the sound of the insensitive voices.

33

Saturday morning, 13 May 1916

The Manningham children sat together in their father's study waiting for news. The stunned incomprehension of the first information they'd gotten had given way to weeping, each reacting in a characteristic fashion.

The twins held each other in their grief; Win had already dashed from the house in an effort to find his father. Angelica sat stonily still in her wheelchair and tried to make some sense of what she had heard. Johnny stood tight-faced against his own tears, holding Angelica's hand.

"Tell me again *exactly* what you heard," Angelica said urgently to the weeping twins.

"It was from a newsboy," Jamie managed to say in an unsteady voice; pulling a large handkerchief from his pants, he handed it to Merry, who availed herself of its comforts forthwith.

"I was talking to Captain Aylesworth on the corner when we saw him running down the street crying 'Stop press,' and Captain Aylesworth asked him what had happened. He said that a member of the aristocracy had done an extraordinary act or something like that, and Captain Aylesworth pressed him for news and that's when the boy said it."

"Said *what*, Jamie?" his sister persisted.

"Said that Mother had attempted to rescue Aunt Constance

from Kilmainham and that they'd both been shot and were presumed dead."

"Dear God!" breathed Angelica. "I suppose we can do nothing further until Win finds Father. I don't think any more of us should leave here in case someone calls us."

"We could ring the police," ventured Merry.

"I've done that," said Jamie. "They won't tell me anything at all."

Angelica felt Johnny squeeze her hand and then let it go. There was a fierce look on his face, the kind she always saw there when Father yelled at him unjustly or when he heard something unkind said about the Irish. It was a look that had to do with his passionate hatred for injustice and she knew better than to interfere with him when he was hurting. There was a fierceness in her little brother that wasn't in the rest of them.

She saw him move quietly out of the room and up the stairs; some instinct told her he was headed for his mother's room. Always when he was small, he had gone there in times of trouble. Always he had sought solace with his mother when his father or Win made him feel the outsider.

Johnny Manningham slid the heavy paneled door back and entered the quiet bedchamber. Everything was as he remembered it from yesterday. . . . Could it really be that everything could be changed irrevocably?

He crossed to the bed and touched the coverlet tentatively. So soft and white and ruffled—so like his mother. Even the air here smelled like her—the flowers on the little desk were the ones she liked best.

He crossed to the desk and sat down in the small writing chair he'd seen his mother sit in a thousand times. *She could not be gone!* She was too full of life and comfort and love. Why, since she'd returned to Dublin, she even seemed filled with happiness! Yes, it was true. Never in his whole life had he seen his mother so truly happy.

He fingered the silver pen on the desk top; it was her lucky pen, she'd told him. The one she used to write her books. He picked it up gingerly and it gave him an idea.

He'd write her a letter . . . a letter telling her how much he loved her. And she wouldn't be dead. Hurt perhaps and needing his love—but not dead. Yes. He'd write her a letter and say all the things to her he'd always meant to say.

Johnny opened the desk drawer and reached inside for a piece of paper. His hand closed on a packet of envelopes. Tugging them from the drawer, he saw that they were written in his mother's hand; the top one bore his name.

"To be opened only in the event of my death," it said. Oh God! So she had meant to die . . . known the danger! Somehow the presence of the letter made his mother's fate far more frighteningly certain than the information from the newspaper had.

The ten-year-old boy held the envelope for a long while in his hand, tears spilling down his cheeks and splattering soundlessly onto the escritoire's polished surface.

Finally, painfully, he broke the seal on the envelope that had his name on it. At least there was this one thing left of her . . . this one connection that meant she hadn't forgotten him.

Johnny read the incredible letter with mounting astonishment. *Mr. O'Sullivan,* not Edmond Manningham, *was his father!* So *that* was why his own father had never loved him . . . a thousand episodes flashed through the boy's mind with that one realization. The endless years of trying for acceptance . . . the endless wasted misery of trying to know how it was that he always erred, as if he could do no right.

Seaneen O'Sullivan. His real father! No wonder the easy camaraderie of the man. The understanding heart, the shared ideals, the curious perfect acceptance he had felt from the first moment. As if he could do no wrong.

Johnny Manningham he should never have been at all . . . Sean O'Sullivan should have been his name.

Suddenly the sight of Seaneen and his mother together rose in the boy's mind. She was *in love* with the man . . . of course! He was everything Edmond Manningham was not. No wonder there had been such happiness pouring from her since she'd been in Dublin, the happiness he'd never seen in her before.

A sound on the stair made him start. Quickly, he took the letters and closed the drawer. He would hide them all until he'd had time to think this through.

Dear God, how he needed time to think.

* * *

Edmond Manningham sat staring at the unconscious body of his wife on the hospital bed, an acute awareness of the irretrievable damage done by his well-intentioned act flooding him with desolation.

Had he not petitioned Sir Hilary, the jailbreak would not have been discovered at precisely the worst moment. Beth would be uninjured, Constance alive. How could his well-meant efforts have brought about such destruction? Why was it that every attempt he ever made to win back Beth's affection seemed thwarted by fate?

Well, it was all over now. There would be no forgiveness for this monumental blunder. Just as there had been no forgiveness for what happened when Bethany died, or when he'd sent that god-awful Fenian to the workhouse. She had a long and potent memory, his wife, and her own sense of justice.

There would be no forgiveness now—of that one thing he was certain. And no possibility of mending the tatters of his marriage.

Edmond drew his chair closer to his wife's bed and reached self-consciously for her hand. He felt very old of a sudden, and very alone. Was it possible that the errors of his marriage had been his own and not fate's doing? he wondered absently. Or had the fault been Elizabeth's all along, as he had thought so relentlessly when she was younger? How could any man be expected to deal with such stubbornness and such intransigence? Why the hell had she not just let him handle it!

What difference did it make to place the blame? Truth was that she had come very close to dying tonight . . . and he had realized how very much he didn't want that to happen. Damnation! but life was perverse and happiness a seemingly elusive dream.

Much to his own surprise, Edmond put his head down on his wife's breast and cried like a baby.

Prime Minister Asquith walked agitatedly up and down the Aubusson-carpeted study of No. 10 Downing Street. It was inconceivable that this Irish Rising had gotten so far out of hand.

Damn Maxwell for the arbitrarily harsh path he'd chosen to follow! Why, all he'd accomplished with it was to manufacture a passel of martyrs to add fuel to the Irish conflagration. How typically stupid of the military to have lined the leaders up like common criminals and shot them! Now every humanitarian in Christendom was up in arms.

Even the U.S. government was demanding that they spare the life of de Valera, who, it seemed, retained U.S. citizenship even though he'd lived in Ireland most of his life.

It was absolutely incomprehensible that this stupid little Rising could be causing so much trouble.

Well, there was no help for it but to recall Maxwell as soon as it could be done gracefully, rescind the de Valera death sentence immediately and get the rest of the dissidents into internment camps as quickly as possible.

Then maybe he'd get some peace.

34

Kitty O'Neill made her way through the dank stone corridor, pulling her jacket tightly about her, both to ward off the chill and to defend herself against the insolent stares of the soldiers.

Goddamn you, Tahg O'Connor, for getting yourself into this mess! she fumed as she went. Stupid Rising! Stupid rebels! Stupid country that makes these things happen!

She saw the guard stop at a cell that housed several men. He rattled his key on the bars to get their attention. "O'Connor!" he shouted, and she saw Tahg disengage himself from the knot of men and come forward.

He looked dirty and unshaven, exhausted and sad.

"Well, you've done it this time!" she breathed as he neared the door, but her voice carried more sorrow than complaint.

"What are you doing here, Kitty?" Tahg asked, looking uneasily at the smirking guards.

"I'm here because I love you, of course. I'd not let you go off to prison without seeing you."

"We're to be sent to Frongoch in Wales," he said, as if that made some sort of sense.

"The guard told me."

"What will you do while I'm gone?"

"The same thing I'd do if you were here?" she said defiantly. "Get a job as an actress. Make my own way. Get the hell out of my father's house."

"Will you wait for me?"

"Tahg O'Connor, you are the very limit! I'm not going to spend my life as a camp follower for a lunatic rebel with a lost cause. I've told you that a thousand times. Don't you see," she said with both exasperation and pleading in her voice, "I'm all I've got! I'll never have you as long as there's an Ireland unfree . . ."

"And if you had me, would it be enough?" he asked quietly, gently.

She looked stricken, her eyes wide and trapped in her own needs. "No," she whispered finally. "I must try to have it all, Tahg. Please understand." He saw tears start in her lovely eyes and spoke softly so the others wouldn't hear.

"It's all right, Kitty. I do understand. We each must try it our own way for a while. I know how much you need the security I can't promise you. We'll just wait and see, girl. That's all. Just wait and see."

She smiled at him gratefully, suddenly . . . like the sun peeking out from behind a cloud after a thunderstorm.

He smiled at her, too, wondering if he was the only person in the world who knew she wasn't as tough as she sounded.

"Take care of yourself, Kitty," he whispered. "I love you very much."

She stared at him for a moment, then said, "I love you, too, you big idiot. But that doesn't change a damned thing, does it?"

She turned to go and the young guard with her put his hand on her arm proprietarily. Tahg saw Kitty's eyes kindle; in an instant she seemed a foot taller than she had been.

"Get your hands off me, you Limey bastard!" she spat at the soldier. "The fact that I didn't approve of his revolution doesn't mean I don't despise Englishmen!" And with that she stamped off down the corridor, her red hair flying with the vehemence of her walk.

Tahg and Mick sat beside each other in the lorry that carried them from the military detention barracks at Stafford to the Frongoch internment camp.

"Here's where the chance will be," Mick said under his breath as the lorry jolted over the rock-strewn road.

"For what?" asked Tahg, wondering what chance the debilitating life of a prisoner could offer.

"To organize the men into an army again," replied Collins confidently. "They haven't heard the end of us."

Tahg smiled grimly in the darkness of the van. It would be lovely to think there would be another chance to fight. Lovely to think of revenge. The Cause he'd lived with all his life was no longer a simple abstract of justice and freedom for him now. It was a personal vendetta.

His father shot in a British-run prison . . . his mother murdered in a jailyard . . . his Aunt Beth lingering near death from the same bullet that had killed his mother. He had much to make them answer for.

My brother Desmond had been taken to Dublin after his arrest and put into Arbour Hill Barracks. There he was stripped naked and subjected to severe indignities. He was then moved to Brixton for two days and nights, and finally taken to Scotland Yard for questioning.

Because he had been forced to swim ashore his clothes and shoes were foul and hard with seawater during these early days of his incarceration. Except for the search at Arbour Hill, he had not been out of them. I have been told since that he suffered gravely from the cold and from lice until Edmond was able to get him legal counsel.

I am told that Edmond did all in his power to alleviate Desmond's suffering and to give him moral support. Nonetheless, as every student of Irish history knows, both he and Casement were hanged as traitors—Des in June and Casement in August 1916.

I was mercifully spared witnessing my poor dear brother's ordeal, as I was still too ill from the lung wound I'd received in Kilmainham, and the news was kept from me till the last.

In his final speech from the dock, Desmond made clear his position on being accused of treason. As the son of a barrister, Desmond could have had few doubts of what the outcome of his trial would be, yet, Edmond told me later, few in the courtroom were unmoved by his courage and dignity.

"My Lords," he said, "you have charged me with treason, an

odious crime. And yet a traitor is defined, I believe, as 'one who betrays his country, a cause or an associate.'

"Therefore I must protest to you that I have not betrayed my country. For England is not and never has been my country. *I am an Irishman.*

"As you well know, I was born to privilege and bred to the same arrogance I see surrounding me in this courtroom today. I, like you, was taught that the Irish were a churlish group of savages who must not be consulted in the ruling of their own affairs. I, like you, was taught that we of the ruling class have God-given authority to see to the care and feeding of these savages, as our whim dictates. Yet I lived to learn the injustice of such teachings and it is of these injustices that I must speak with you now.

"For I submit to you, My Lords, that you have done a damned poor job with your God-given authority!

"You have starved and brutalized the Irish; you have laughed at their attempts to free themselves from your destructive rule. You have taken their crops and their labor for your own purposes. You have destroyed their language and their educational system and then ridiculed them for their ignorance!

"You are proud of your system of jurisprudence, you are proud of your mother of parliaments! I ask you, in conscience, can you justifiably take pride in what both have wrought in Ireland?

"Can you be proud of the penal laws that forbade religious, scholastic, political and linguistic freedom? Can you be proud of the potato famine, when you exported the food from Ireland that she needed to feed her starving millions? Can you be proud of your courts that imprison men without trial and your soldiers who shoot on mere suspicion?

"I speak to you as a man who was bred to respect the system which now accuses him—a man who believes your Empire too great to allow itself to stoop so low.

"Get out of Ireland! Now, before an endless bloodbath drives you to do in ignominy what you could have done magnanimously of your own volition.

"For I prophesy that this new century will see an end to your almighty Empire. Before this hundred years has passed, the angry voices of small nations everywhere will have made themselves heard!

"So you see, My Lords, however you dispose of me, or of the thousands more like me who will rise up, *you cannot win in the end!*

"I cannot be a traitor to England. She is not my country.

"I am an Irishman!"

And so, my beloved brother died, with neither of his sisters at his side. Dear, noble, generous, loving man—my heart aches, even now, at the thought of his last lonely hours.

I lay in my bed, when I was finally told of his execution, knowing that only I . . . the least of the three of us . . . was left alive. ∽

35 ∽ I have a clear and terrible remembrance of lying in St. Vincent's Hospital waiting to die.

My sister was gone . . . I'd known it, lying in the dirt of the jailyard with her in my arms. Never more would her laughter warm my heart, nor the touch of her competent hands make everything turn out as it should. Never more would we share the sure knowledge that no matter the perfidy of the world, one other person on this earth felt and thought and understood in perfect harmony.

Scenes blended strangely in my delirium, twisting and turning and merging and fading. Sometimes she was alive again, nursing me after Winston's birth. Young and hale and untrammeled by life's mixed blessings of learning. Sometimes I was at Tierney's grave and her body lay there with his; tangled together they were, in the brown earth . . . entwined in the perfect fit of lovers' bodies, just as I had once come upon them years before lying on the Sligo strand entangled in each other's arms.

Sometimes she was as she had been at the barricade—laughing defiantly at the fate that would be her doom.

Faces appeared and dimmed and then appeared again. Edmond . . . Des . . . my children . . . some that I did not know.

Once I saw myself being ferried across a wide expanse of river. On the other side, Con and Tierney beckoned to me from a grassy knoll. I tried to hurry the ferryman but the current changed perversely and we were washed back to the other shore against our will. I wept and cried out to them to wait for me, and woke up sobbing in my daughter Merry's arms.

I considered it a vision, not a dream—and although no one would have understood if I had voiced the thought aloud, I knew from that moment on that Seaneen was alive somewhere . . . he was not dead. Only she whom I loved so much was gone. Only she.

I knew, too, somehow, that *I* was to live. I, who had caused her death . . . I, who had no wish to live, was doomed to do so.

While I drifted in and out of life, the world around me fell to pieces.

The Rising had not rallied the people to the Cause, but the murders of the Rising's leaders had.

Just as daily, angry crowds had gathered outside Kilmainham, as the fallen leaders were executed one by one— so was the spirit of rebellious anger gathering in the hearts of the Irish people.

By the time I was again well it was all changed, somehow. The Rising that had failed had been resurrected as surely as if the timing of Easter Week had been preordained.

Con was gone . . . Tierney was gone . . . Des was gone . . . Tahg was in prison . . . Seaneen was missing . . . Ireland was embarking on a war of independence.

Sean O'Casey, dear cynic that he was, said it best, I think, in retrospect:

> The castle is alert and confident; files all correct, and dossiers signed and sealed for the last time. Now the Irish may be quiet and quit their moan, for nothing is whole that could be broken.
> But Cathleen, the daughter of Houlihan, walks firm now, a flush on her haughty cheek. She hears the mur-

mur in the people's hearts. Her lovers are gathering around her, for things are changed, changed utterly.

The murmur was in the people's hearts, indeed. And in my own. Oh dear God, there was such a murmur in my aching heart. ∽

PART THREE

History is an account
Mostly false,
of events,
mostly unimportant,
Which are brought about
by rulers,
mostly knaves,
and soldiers,
mostly fools.

AMBROSE BIERCE

Fear is a fine spur. So is rage.

IRISH PROVERB

1 ∽ Ireland after the Rising was a schismatic place: many longed for peace and comfort, others seethed with discontent. A stronger anti-English feeling than had been seen in decades agitated the emotions of the people.

The deaths of the 1916 martyrs had changed public opinion radically: twelve hundred Sinn Fein Clubs had sprouted, and a vigorous new nationalism had taken root. Stepped-up police activity was a constant irritant, and the Sinn Fein political party kept the kettle boiling. A low-level hostility toward the English rankled just beneath the surface.

In short, although there had been relative calm since the 1916 Rising, it was deceptive and uneasy. For many of us it was merely the calm before the storm.

My own life was no less schismatic than that of Ireland. During my long convalescence, I had harbored only two thoughts—to visit Con's and Des's graves, and to find out if Seaneen was still alive somewhere. There was a rumor that he had lived through the horror at Kilmainham, but there was no certain news. Secrecy had grown nearly impenetrable during the months of my recovery: only my irrational conviction that he lived gave me hope.

The leaders I had known were dead; the men, in prisons all over the British Isles. Messages from the prisons were censored —what got through did so only to the secret men in secret places.

Finally, the Christmas after the Rising, the men began to be released from prisons and through one of them I discovered the whereabouts of the small farm where Seaneen's parents had lived. Tahg had connected with a rumor in Frongoch that Seaneen had survived and was organizing men somewhere in Tipperary; as his father's farm was there, it seemed the place to look first.

My long illness and the trauma of Con's death had stripped away the last vestige of my former self. I had only one obsession left: if Seaneen lived, I would go to him. If he would have me, I would stay with him.

In fairness to Edmond, he was kind to me in my recovery, and strangely solicitous. When I announced early in 1917 that I no longer wished to live as his wife, he seemed disproportionately saddened by the news. He told me he would cause me no further pain; if I had decided to live apart from him, he would not try to hold me. I was startled by his acquiescence, but grateful. I was too weak and heartsick for argument and, I think, perhaps he sensed this in me.

As I was preparing to leave on my quest, my son Johnny came to me. He had grown up a good deal during my illness and seemed far older than his eleven years. I thought I noted in him the need for adult conversation as he stood in the doorway to my room and watched me pack.

"I know about Mr. O'Sullivan, Mum," he said gravely. "I read the letter you left, when we thought you'd been killed."

Something in the child's face made me feel more relief than pain at the knowledge; we talked the afternoon away, my son and I, sharing thoughts we had needed to share throughout his lifetime. The end of it was that I took him with me on my pilgrimage to seek his father.

Tipperary is a benevolent country, green fields abounding and tiny cottages dotting the docile hills. Johnny and I made our way, not knowing what we would find there—I brooding all the while about how we would be greeted by Seaneen, if we found him. I carried the carnage of the jailbreak on my conscience; of course, when we set out, I had no knowledge of the exact nature of Seaneen's injuries.

Two young men armed with pistols answered the door of the O'Sullivan cottage at Ballingarry in the gentle Slieveardagh Hills. It was a surprising sight in 1917, although such occurrences would soon be anything but rare. The men seemed belligerent, but I had a pass signed by an IRB man in Dublin, so they let Johnny and me in, motioning us toward the bedroom.

I asked my son to wait with the men while I entered the cottage's other room. I opened the door, feeling nearly ill with anxiety. It was a sunny whitewashed room, poor but sweet, and apparently well cared for. Scaneen sat on the edge of a sway-backed bed. I knew from the moment he turned his head toward the sound of the opening door that he was blind.

I closed the door behind me and moved toward him, terribly shocked by his appearance, terribly shaken by the realization of his sightlessness. He was so much thinner than I remembered; it was obvious that he had been as ill as I. My heart beat violently. He was, at least, alive.

"So you are well, My Lady," he said before I'd even touched him. "I thank God for that." There was naught in his voice but love and kindness.

"My dearest love . . ." I breathed and knelt beside his feet; he put his arms around me. "What have I done to you?" If guilt can be thought of as a physical injury, believe that I was laid low by what I felt for him in that instant.

"Nae, nae, My Lady!" he said quickly, brushing my wet cheek with the back of his hand, as if sensing my tears. "We did what we had to do that night. Those bloody bastards who killed her are the ones who must pay. Not you. Never you."

"What are you doing here, my love?" I asked, trying to control my grief enough to speak.

"We're taking the battle to the countryside, Beth. We'll organize the men all over Ireland and oust the enemy from where they sit so smugly . . . in the country garrisons, in the Royal Irish Constabulary. You'll see. It'll take time and careful planning, but the Rising was the beginning of the end for them."

"But how can you still be involved in it, dearest, with your eyes as they are?"

Seaneen smiled and his leathery face crinkled into those well-remembered lines. "They won't suspect me as I am—my blindness is the perfect disguise. The doctors tell me the injury may not be permanent—so I'd best use it while I can."

"They won't suspect you with armed Volunteers in your house?" I asked incredulously.

"The men are here only until they send me a secretary from Dublin. Someone who can be my eyes."

"Then they've no need to send anyone," I said steadily. "I've no intention of leaving you."

Seaneen's head tilted quizzically at that, his sightless eyes turned to mine. "And what of Edmond and your children?"

"There is nothing between Edmond and me but history. I've already told him I'm leaving. He won't stop me. My children are nearly grown and quite self-sufficient." I was shocked to hear myself saying these heretical things with such conviction. "I think only Johnny still needs his mother . . . and his father."

"He knows, then?"

"He knows."

Seaneen was very still for a long moment. Then he put his arms around me and nearly crushed me to death with the desperate strength of his embrace.

"Sweet Jesus, how I've missed you!" he murmured.

"No more than I've missed you, my heart's love."

"It will be dangerous . . ."

"No more so than living without you." We were both crying now and trying to speak coherently through our tears. We must have made a ludicrous sight.

"I have nothing to give you . . ."

"You have everything I want."

"And Johnny?"

"He loves you more than you can know."

We held each other and said things to each other and comforted each other until a small sound brought us back to ourselves. It was Johnny knocking on the door.

Perhaps there is no need to tell you the travails of separating myself from Edmond and my elder children. Suffice to say that before the month was out I had returned with Johnny to Tipperary to make our home with Seaneen O'Sullivan. In doing so

I left all vestiges of the Beth FitzGibbon of my youth behind me. Henceforward I would be a fugitive, an adulteress and a felon. Henceforward, I would be only myself.

Win was disdainful in his arrogance when he heard the news of my impending departure. It was inconceivable to him that *his* mother could be imperfect enough to bring such disgrace to his father's name. To say that he gave me short shrift in our good-byes would be a kind exaggeration.

Merry and Jamie sat together, seventeen and wide-eyed, as I told them my story and my intentions. He was characteristically generous and went out of his way to excuse me. She, uncharacteristically, asked to speak to me alone.

When Jamie had left us, Merry threw her arms around me and told me that she understood . . . that she had known of my unhappiness as long as she could remember, and that she thought it was the most romantic thing in the world that I intended to run off with the man I loved. She also confided that it was her intention to make her way to Dublin to be an actress. She wanted me to know that she would brook no interference from her father, much as she loved him. She said she would need money to get started in Dublin, and I assured her that I would help her if I could.

Angelica was the last of my children to discuss my departure and the one interview I dreaded most. I loved this daughter in so special a way . . . and, of course, I carried, then as now, considerable guilt about her affliction.

I was in the drawing room when she came to me. It was a pretty room with pale blue moiré taffeta on the walls and a muted flower pattern of blue and rose on the upholstery; for some reason, I can see it clearly now, in my mind, this room in which my daughter and I came of age together.

"I need to speak with you, Mother," she said, in that sensible, patient voice I knew so well.

"And I with you, my dear child," I replied, feeling that was so, but not knowing how to begin.

"I'd like you to know that I'm glad for you, Mother . . . that you love someone who loves you," she said simply. "You deserve that, I think. I know how unhappy Father's coldness has made you." It fascinated me that my children seemed so sanguine in their acceptance of my infidelity. Had I been so transparent in my unhappiness through all the years when I had thought I'd kept up such a brave deception?

I watched Angelica's graceful blond head dip down as she said it, as if she was embarrassed by the womanly intimacy of the statement but determined to voice it nonetheless. She was a child who had great reason to love her father and I knew it pained her to betray him on any level.

"I've figured things out, I think, Mother, after talking with Johnny," she went on slowly. "He has told me the truth, although none of the others know of it. If Johnny is Mr. O'Sullivan's child, then you were in love with him that summer we spent in Dublin, when I was four."

I nodded assent, miserably.

"That night, when I went looking for you and couldn't find you . . . the night that I was hurt . . . were you with him?"

I would have given ten years of my life to avoid that question, but it was a direct and honest one and she had a right to know. I nodded once again, unable to speak.

Angelica hung her head forward once more, as if to compose herself. Her golden hair fanned about her shoulders like a halo and I thought once again how aptly she was named.

"My dear child," I said, tears choking my voice. "If you but knew how much I would give to make it otherwise."

She looked up then, at me . . . the strangest, strongest look in her penetrating eyes. "I forgive you, Mother," she said simply. "I forgave you long ago. That's what I wanted to tell you before you left here."

I looked at her uncomprehendingly.

"I've always known, you see, that there was some terrible secret attached to that night. It's why I've never asked you where you were, I suppose.

"Do you think that I could watch you for a lifetime without knowing the lovelessness of your marriage? I love my father and he's been good to me. But I'm not blind, Mother. I see more than the others do because I've had so much time in which to think!

"I'm a woman, too, Mother. I know the pain of not being loved. If you have the chance of finding with Mr. O'Sullivan what you've never had with my father, then you must take that chance." I felt as she spoke that I was the child, and she the mother.

"And what of you, Angelica?" I asked, moved beyond correct response by what she'd said.

"I'm going to Dublin, Mother. Tahg and I have had plans these many years past. I'll help him and he'll help me. I've told Father I intend to do charity work in Dublin, which is also true. I'm encouraging him to let Merry and me leave shortly; Jamie will be at Oxford. Win and Father should go to London . . . there's much for them to do there and it will take their minds off you."

"You've always been the wisest one of us all, haven't you, child?" I said, meaning it. Wondering at how this tangled web could have ensnared us . . . wondering how she could think so clearly and so generously in her own pain.

"I would like you to come with me, Angelica," I said, and I heard the pleading note in my own voice.

"No, Mother," she replied firmly. "I love you, but I couldn't do that to Father. You must see that. And besides, it's time for me to grow up, now. I must learn to be independent."

I nodded, knowing she was right, as she was right about so many things in life. Much like Con she was, when I think of it . . . stalwart, blade-straight, honorable and true. We made our peace with each other that day, in that quiet blue sanctuary, Angelica and I.

After that I didn't see my daughter again for nearly four years. ✍

2 "The plan is simple, really," Mick had said to Tahg in Frongoch. "Wipe out the informers, get enough guns and ammo for our little war, cripple the RIC, destroy the operation of British government in Ireland and drive them out of here." He'd had the grace to laugh at the impossible scope of what sounded so simple.

"And the British will sit by quietly while we do all this, of course," Tahg had replied.

"Not at all, lad. They'll try to civilize us in their usual fashion, but if we do everything right, 'twill only strengthen the resolve of our people and bring them to our side!"

"A lot of support we've ever gotten from 'our people'!" Tahg snorted derisively.

"Don't knock them, O'Connor. They'll rally when we need them. Remember, all we need is *enough* of them, we don't need them all. 'Handfuls make a full load at last,' my father used to say."

"And after you've crippled the RIC and all that other fine stuff. What then?"

"We make them so bloody miserable in our little emerald gem that they pack up and go home. Discretion being the better part of valor and all that." Mick's amusement was obvious.

"And where exactly will you get your army from?"

"There's ample trained men from the Great War left over, Tahg Mor. And there's plenty of brave lads who never saw a war at all who'll volunteer; not to mention all our comrades from the Frongoch School for the Training and Development of Irish Revolutionaries.

"We'll train them as if they were in His Majesty's Army. Drill, train, discipline, but with a twist or two that'll knock their socks off! There's nothing the English can do, we can't do better."

"I'll drink to that," laughed Tahg, raising his tin water cup in a salute. Mick always thought he had all the answers; yet it wouldn't surprise Tahg if he really did give them a run for their money. On the other hand, the memory of 1916 was still fresh in his mind. Other good men had tried to free Ireland over the long centuries of England's rule . . . and failed.

"It's been tried before, Mick," he said, voicing the uneasy thought. "Never successfully."

"Ah, but never by me, Tahg Mor O'Connor," laughed Collins good-naturedly. "Never by me."

Tahg had replayed the conversation in his mind several times on the train as it rattled over the winter landscape of Wales, bringing the last of the freed political prisoners back to Dublin. The train to Holyhead, then the boat to Dublin and he would be home—what there was of it, now that his parents were gone.

Home. He wondered if FitzGibbon Hall would ever be home to him. He had kept the news of his legacy secret from all but Angelica and Aunt Beth. At first, he had been too saddened by his uncle's death to feel real joy at his bequest. Then, when the initial shock had been dispelled, and he had realized how extraordinary a gift he'd been given, fate had already propelled him into other byways . . . byways that did not lead to manor houses, nor to safety.

Leaving the crowded boat at the Dublin quays, Tahg waved to the men with whom he had held sporadic conversation, turned his collar up against the encroaching cold and headed toward Glasnevin Cemetery.

The cemetery gates swung open, and the orderly rows stretched endlessly before him. He felt disconcerted by the sudden knowledge that without his mother to guide him, he had no sure idea of where, in this city of the dead, his father's grave might be. Now, she lay at his father's side. The not-knowing-where struck him as a physical ache; it seemed somehow a betrayal of their memory.

Tahg made his way to the caretaker's cottage, a tiny stone house at the side of the huge enclosure. The old man pointed silently to a spot on a chart of gravesites and sent him off in the right direction without a word. Tahg wondered if life among the silent dead had made the man mute, or if he had chosen his profession because silence was his preference.

The dusk was beginning to darken almost to night as the young man picked his way among the gravestones to the markers he sought. He made out the engraving on his parents' headstones with tears in his eyes. How very like his aunt to have chosen such words.

Could this really be they? he wondered, looking at the brace of graves . . . these few paltry feet of dirt and grass, his parents? Surely they had been too big, too powerful, too larger-than-lifesize to occupy so small a space.

He knelt beside his mother's grave, which he had never seen before, the finality of it overwhelming him. Always, until now, she had seemed alive to him—separated from him, but alive. Gently, he reached out to touch the turf that grew above it. Half a year she had lain there beside his father in their final sleep. Long enough for the grass to be green and abundant. How he had loved to see his parents hold each other in life, he thought, his father's powerful arms around his mother's tall straight form. Such strength and love there had been between them.

Tahg made the sign of the cross and rose to his feet. He had a promise to make to these two he had loved. A promise of revenge and repayment.

Unbidden, Kitty's words came back: "just because it's their cause, you needn't die for it," she had said. Could it be that he was trapped by love of them into a madness not his own? Could it be that even in death there was no escape from Ireland? He read again the inscription, thought about its significance, then shook his head to clear it.

It had been their cause—but now it was his. After all that had happened there could be no peace without a purging of the terrible anger that fomented within him—no peace without revenge of some kind.

"I love you, Mother," he said softly into the gathering gloom. "I love you, Da. I'll do the best I can for both of you."

Then he put his cap back onto his head and walked briskly from the cemetery in search of Mick Collins and the future.

Tahg watched Michael Collins at the meeting at the Keating Branch of the Gaelic League with fascination. The man was a civil servant and had worked, for a time before the Rising, in an accountant's office. He wrote the precise, small hand of accountants or assassins—or so someone had once quipped. Perhaps both possibilities were valid. How very hard it was to evolve a correct morality for such troubled times, thought Tahg, listening to Collins captivate the men. What is treason and what patriotism? What murder, and what lawful rebellion against tyranny?

Collins's hearty laugh rang through the gathering. It was a merry, male sound, calculated to provoke camaraderie. And Mick was a good comrade as well as a leader.

Mick was also a practical joker, although not a good sport if he found himself the butt of a joke. Too much pride for that. Far too much pride.

And he had much to be proud of: an electric brain that sorted through problems with swift machinelike accuracy . . . an astonishing courage that seemed to brook no interference from seemingly impossible odds. And he possessed a clear, burning patriotism, of the kind that would sanction no opposition. Like an evangelist rooting out sin, he would free Ireland from the rule of England.

Collins's voice calling the meeting to order nudged Tahg from his reverie.

"I intend to create an army the likes of which they've never seen or imagined," he said, his voice powerful in the silent room. "They have the money and the men, so we must counter by having the brains and the ingenuity." The faces of the listeners left no doubt that he had their attention.

"We will harass them, and we will undermine their almighty confidence! We'll steal their guns from their convoys, and burn down their barracks. What's worse, we'll infiltrate their ranks with spies to watch their dirty deeds from the inside out." Collins's voice had risen dramatically as his speech gained momentum.

"Secrecy will be of paramount importance. No man will know more than he needs to know. Few men will know the names of more than a handful of our own."

Tahg smiled at that. Mick was a fanatic for secrecy. Circles in spirals, wheels within wheels. None would ever know his plans, only specific parts of them.

"It is my intention to create an intelligence network among the common people—the farmers, the butcher and baker, the factory workers, the police. A year from now there won't be a mouse that farts in Ireland without our knowing it. A year from now there won't be any corner of this island left where an informer can hide from us. We will start picking them off one by one, as they inform. It shouldn't take the Castle long to get our drift."

Accountants and assassins, Tahg thought concernedly, as he left the meeting. He loved Mick and he knew the man was right about the Castle's eyes. The Royal Irish Constabulary was the lifeline of the English government; a local police force peopled by native Irishmen in the employ of the Castle. Unless the informers were eliminated, there could be no way to win.

But to kill a man in cold blood? Not in the heat of battle, but on the quiet streets of peaceful Dublin? Perhaps that was another story. Or was there any such thing as peaceful Dublin? Had there ever been a time when the heart of Ireland was unsullied by a war not of its own choosing?

He walked down the street wondering what part it was Mick had in mind for him to play. It didn't matter much, he supposed. As long as he had the chance to pay them back for what they'd done to his family. It really hardly mattered at all.

Kitty folded Tahg's latest letter and tucked it away with the rest of them.

Damn him that he could unnerve her so! Damn him for being so relentlessly good-hearted and loving. Damn him that he could so easily bring all her carefully made plans to ruin.

"Into the drawer with you," she said aloud to the notepaper. "And under my stockings and out of my head!" She just wouldn't answer the letters, that was all. If he ever inquired, she would say that she had never received them.

But it was so bloody hard not to wonder about him, she thought perversely. In that awful camp and out. Hard not to fear for him. Hard not to wish things could be different . . . wish him rich and powerful, so that they could have it all together.

Kitty picked up the script she was studying with determination. This play was a rare beauty. This play would give her the break she'd been seeking. She couldn't let a poor man with nothing to offer her interfere with that, no matter how dear he was to her.

She simply couldn't.

Tahg walked by the theater, hands in pockets, cap pulled low over his eyes. Just in case Kitty was anywhere near, he wouldn't want her to notice him. She'd made it plain enough by her silence that she wanted no part of him.

The light gray drizzle felt soft against his skin; "a heavy dew," his father would have said, and laughed. He stood for a moment on the pavement staring at the poster of the women in the play. Kitty was one of several actresses pictured, but to him she was the only one shown. Her laughing, oversized beauty had always moved him strangely. Not just the quickening in the loins that he felt on seeing her, but a deeper connection that she activated within him. A bond that said, "She's part of you, take care of her." A bond beyond his comprehension, or ability to alter.

Her head was thrown back in the poster—her arms extended as if to embrace the world.

He could hear the throaty laughter bubbling up within her as she had posed for it, the older-than-the-world laughter that said, "I've seen it all and I understand who you are." Surely every man who'd ever heard her laugh heard the same beckoning in its siren sound.

He felt happy for her that she had made it this far . . . at least she had begun the long journey toward her dream. Tahg let himself wonder for a moment if she *might* be inside the theater. If somewhere, only yards away, she might be standing and talking . . . or laughing or weeping. Or wondering about him.

No! If she were wondering about him, she would have written back; there had been ample time.

He was only a distraction to her now. A distraction that could keep her from her goals . . . or rather from her *needs*. And they were needs for her, he knew. In the same deeply buried place where the bond between them lived, he had knowledge of her. She was the most needful of them all.

Fame. Money. Power. A chance to *be* someone. All these she needed. And deep down, far, far from the surface— under all the glitter and easy beauty —she needed to be loved. Desperately, wildly, totally. Dangerous thoughts for a man with plans for rebellion and revenge, he chided himself.

He thought for a moment of his legacy. Christ, how Kitty longed for exactly the life that FitzGibbon Hall could provide. How exquisitely perverse the Gods are . . . he thought wryly. They dangle your dreams in front of you and then give you marching orders in another direction. There could be no Fitz-Gibbon Hall for him till the war was over. He had pledged himself to Collins and to Ireland. After that . . . if there was an "after that" . . . he could pursue his dreams.

He looked again at the beautiful face and lush body in the poster. It would be so easy to volunteer to be the one to love her as she needed. How many men will love you for the glitter and the beauty and the talent, and never, never know, or care to know, who you are? he asked the pictured woman silently. How many will sense the need in you and exploit it?

The rain seemed colder somehow and a corner of the poster had been loosened by the wetness: it flapped soundlessly in the wind.

Absently Tahg reached up to push the errant corner back against the wall.

How transitory we all are, he thought sadly. Like the poster falling in the breeze, bringing all the beauty down with it, so could your life be seen, my Kitty. Precarious life as an actress, precarious life seeking to *be* someone. "But then, no more precarious than my own," he said to himself, wondering what it was God had in mind for both of them.

Tahg touched the poster portrait once lingeringly, then, turning his collar up against the rain, he made his way down the deserted street.

Kitty sat alone in the empty theater with the script in her lap. She had no intention of leaving until she had the part down pat. It was the lead she coveted . . . a lead she had no right to imagine for herself. Up to now she had been given only small and decorative ingenue roles to perform. But she *could* play the lead. She knew she could do it. And better than Eileen Shea, who was currently slated for the role.

First, she must learn the lines perfectly. Next, she must give them life. *Then* she must find a way to get the director to let her read for the understudy part.

One break, she told herself in the cold and nearly darkened theater. One break is all you get in this crummy world.

"And all I'll need!" she said aloud, and then looked around hastily to see if anyone had heard the embarrassingly echo-y sound.

What difference if she stayed here all night, every night, learning what she must. Eventually, it would all pay off.

Dear God, it had to. There was no other way out.

Winston Manningham was handsome in an arrogant sort of way. Tall, lean, angular, with dark blond hair and a face that only an ancient and unsullied bloodline could produce; his dignified carriage was as singular as his handsomeness. There was an almost serpentine grace to his movements, a languor that bespoke power and money and the luxury of never having to hurry.

He did well at the study of law. He liked its orderly progression of thoughts, its essential pragmatism, its comforting logic. Most of all he liked the fact that it would prepare him to follow in his father's illustrious footsteps.

Politics. That was the place to make a name for yourself in

these times. After all, there were only three areas of life in which one could wield real power: the military (for which he had no great love), the Church (an absurd idea) and politics. So politics it would be. He would polish his debating skills and hone his agile intellect. It was important to be noticed while still at Oxford. His father would see to it that he met all the right people later, but he must prepare himself now to take advantage of the opportunities to come.

This girl he'd been seeing was simply a distraction. What silly creatures they were, full of protestations of love as soon as you paid them the slightest attention. He would marry, of course, eventually; but only when a proper consort could be found. A girl with the right lineage and the right dowry. And the right docility. He would take no chance of making the mistake his father had made.

There was absolutely no limit to his potential, if he married well. Meanwhile, this absurd girl, and her ridiculous claim of pregnancy, would have to be dealt with. All it would take would be a group of his friends swearing that they, too, had partaken of her easy virtue, and perhaps a bit of money changing hands—then this nasty business would be off his mind. What a sordid distraction it was—best to put it quickly behind him. He wondered absently if any of his father's mistresses had produced any by-blows—any little illegitimate brothers or sisters, here or there. Somehow, he doubted it. His father had made one grave mistake with a woman, in marrying his mother. He doubted that he'd made any others.

Jamie pushed away the leather-bound volume he had been poring over in the university library. It was all so damned unsatisfactory! Nothing that had been written about war really explained it. How curious it was that he had chosen war as his specialty when he abhorred it so.

Perhaps it was the very abhorrence that spurred him on. That, and the feeling that if he read enough, delved deep enough, unearthed the right information . . . *somewhere* he would find the reason why men continued this insanity.

He pulled a scrap of paper from his pocket. He'd copied it from a verse in *The Times*.

All wars are planned by older men,
In council rooms apart,

Who call for greater armament
And map the battle chart.

But out along the shattered field
Where golden dreams turn gray,
How very young the faces were
Where all the dead men lay.

Portly and solemn in their pride,
The elders cast their vote
For this or that, or something else,
That sounds the martial note.

But where their sightless eyes stare out,
Beyond life's vanished joys,
I've noticed nearly all the dead
Were hardly more than boys.

It wasn't poetry, of course, just doggerel. But something about its simple profundity had moved him. If he looked hard enough, perhaps he'd find a way to help the victims of those "vanished joys." That's what he really had in mind to do.

He loved the scholarship of what he was doing . . . loved being lost in his libraries and researches. Loved spending his days in delving and his nights in erudite conversation with the shapers of history, the men who sat in Parliament with his father. What an incredible opportunity it was to be his father's son, especially in these troubled times.

But the more he delved and the more he talked, the more apparent it all became to him. War was naught but a power game to these men. An ego-lifting game for the powerful to play on their imaginary chessboards that encompassed the world. *That* was why the little verse had spoken so eloquently to him—for those friends of his father's were the old men in the council rooms who changed the destinies of the young.

"Close the British Foreign Office for six months," a young radical had said to him the other day in debate, "and you'll have peace in the world for a hundred years!" There was truth in that.

But what part was he himself to play in making a difference? Surely he could not close the Foreign Office, nor change human nature, nor deter the power brokers and those who profited from their exercise of it.

No. He must find some other means of serving mankind. Some means of evening up the score. In the meantime, he would pay very close attention to his studies, he would continue to learn and to grow. Then, one day . . . one day the answer would come to him.

Lady Merrion Manningham
Manningham Castle
Taghly, County Sligo

18 June 1917

Dear Tahg,

Just a small note to keep you posted on the continuing saga of your errant Manningham relatives and their varied travails! One sometimes feels a scorecard would be helpful in keeping track of the comings and goings here at the Castle.

Mum and Johnny are happy with Mr. O'Sullivan (as I'm sure you already know from Johnny, your devoted correspondent). Jamie is doing brilliantly at Oxford—first in his form and all that—and while I miss him dreadfully (never having had to cope with being only half a set of twins before), I am so happy for his successes and his scholarly pleasures that I could burst.

What you don't know yet is that Father has finally consented to letting me go to Dublin to try my hand at acting. He would never have done so except that Angelica took my side and said she, too, plans to go there soon.

As you know, Angelica is the only one in the family whose entreaties Father cannot deny (and I must say she put it all to him terribly well—cogent arguments, no hysteria, etc.). She said, "Merry and I are alone at Manningham, what with Mother, Johnny, Win, Jamie and you away, so whatever difference would it make if we were to be alone at our Dublin town house? We would still be servanted and chaperoned appropriately, of course. And it would make all the sense in the world for a man of your stature to spend more time at his *pied-à-terre* in

Dublin. . . ." As a *pièce de résistance* she announced that she is planning to engage in charity work with the poor, and that Dublin abounds in them!

He was powerless against her sensible arguments. Or rather he was indulgent of her as usual, and I have reaped the rewards of it as well.

Truth is, I'd prefer not to live at the Waterloo Road house for very long—although I shall certainly do so at first. Angelica and I are quite different in temperament and I expect the kind of people I shall be meeting in the theater will be a different sort from the friends she'll choose.

Funnily enough, Tahg, I seem to be more iconoclastic than I'd ever imagined myself. Since Mum's departure, I find myself full of exuberance and a sense of adventure . . . longing to express myself . . . I want to shed my gilded trappings, as it were, and *do* something.

I feel fettered here. There are curious rumblings inside of me that smack of independence.

What a grand adventure it will be when we are all in Dublin. All free and fully grown at last! Each off to a new life full of promise.

Not that I mean to suggest that the old life lacked excitement, but all has been so irrevocably changed in the last year that new beginnings seem the only hope for us.

And I do so want to act, Tahg! God knows, I sometimes feel that, despite my sheltered life, I've seen so much of passionate emotions (our family is nothing, if not passionate) that acting is the only way I can make use of all the images I've stored inside me.

You are in my thoughts often, dear cousin. I well remember the lovely times we had together when you stayed with Uncle Desmond years ago. I know you have always been closest to Johnny and Angelica, but I've taken it upon myself in Mother's absence to keep track of everyone in the family and to make a valiant effort to keep us all from losing touch. To that end, do write me when you can, and I will be sure to keep you on my correspondence schedule!

With love and all good thoughts,
Your cousin Merry

Merry sealed her letter to Tahg into its envelope and began another to Jamie. How very much she missed her twin! She would try to encourage him to return to Trinity instead of remaining at Oxford.

Jamie slipped Merry's letter into the pocket of his oldest and most comfortable tweed jacket and headed out the door. He wondered absently, looking around him, if any other university paid so much attention to flowers as did Oxford. Each college had its garden for scholarly meditation; even the tree-lined pathways looked manicured and loved.

Life had been nearly perfect at Magdalen during the past year. Its ancient tranquility had provided the ideal setting to heal the wounds of the rebellion's aftermath . . . his mother's illness, Aunt Con's and Uncle Desmond's deaths, his parents' separation. The university by comparison was peaceful and un-harmed by such passing fancies as revolutions and personal tragedy. There was a sense of substance, order and continuity here that made Ireland's troubles, and his own, seem distant and chimeric.

His parents' separation had weighed on him far more than he considered rationally that it should. They had never loved each other, after all—and yet, as long as they had continued the charade of union, the family had remained intact. Now it would be scattered; judging from the tone of Merry's letter, she couldn't wait to make her own escape from the cocoon the family had provided.

It was high time they all scattered, of course, high time for them to get about the business of growing up and making lives for themselves. Yet there was a disquiet to the final separation of siblings. Especially of twins.

Nonetheless, it had probably been good for Merry and him to live apart for a bit. Dear loving, nurturing Merry—it had been as hard to part from her as if they had been joined by flesh and bone. Yet there had been things to do and try and see that she could not be a part of.

The thought troubled him. Merry, his alter ego . . . so often his mainstay. Merry . . . the only one who shared his curious duality . . . the gentle surface with the troubled waters turbulent beneath. Neither one of them was as pacific as the world believed. But Merry knew and understood.

It was good that he'd decided to go home to Ireland.

3

THE IRISH INDEPENDENT
12 August 1917

Miss Kitty O'Neill, the young understudy who stepped into Eileen Shea's shoes at the Abbey Theatre last night, gave a stunningly original performance.

The fiery Miss O'Neill added a dimension of passionate energy to the role that sent sparks flying through the audience.

It is creditable enough for an understudy to take over so taxing a role from a veteran performer—but to take it over in such a way as to eclipse the performance of her predecessor is rare indeed. Miss Shea will have a hard time surpassing her stand-in's electric interpretation. . . .

Tahg put down the newspaper review with mixed emotions. He was glad that Kitty was finally on her way. Glad for her triumph . . .

But sad, too. Fame and fortune could only separate them further; neither had any place in the life he had espoused. A furnished room would never be the place for Kitty O'Neill.

He had found, somewhat to his surprise, that he was good at the guerrilla war that Mick was engineering—he had a talent for strategy and a clear head in danger. He'd accomplished each mission he'd been given with an expeditiousness that had surprised even Mick. Perhaps it was not so startling, considering his heritage, but in some ways the evidence of this talent disturbed him.

He shook off the gloomy thoughts and forced his mind to

planning strategy. It was becoming time to spread his wings a little—time to test his instincts. He had a hunch that much would depend on what success the newly forming brigades could manage in the outlying counties. It was all too easy to become so embroiled in the fight in Dublin that you began to think it the world. But the war would spread to the counties now; that's where he'd like to concentrate his efforts for Collins. Mick would have plenty on his hands just coping with Dublin.

Cathal Brugha, as chief of staff, and Collins, as director of organization, were well on their way toward fielding a disciplined little army in these outlying areas. It would take the better part of a year to do it, but once in place the results could be potent. The attack forces that Mick had envisioned in that first meeting after Frongoch would be hard to fight and hard to trace. It would be important to keep a close liaison between the men fighting in the hills and the fighting men in Dublin.

Besides, thought Tahg, a reconnaissance mission to the field would give him an excuse to see Aunt Beth again, and Seaneen.

What an incredible shock it had been to his cousins when Aunt Beth had left Manningham for Tipperary. But to him it had not come as so great a surprise. Tahg had seen Beth and Seaneen together in Dublin before the Rising; not even a young boy, as he had been then, could have been unaware of the love that bound them to each other.

The fleeting remembrance brought with it a pang for his parents. How long ago it seemed since he'd seen them alive and together. He had been only a boy when he'd last talked with them—now he was a man. A man with a job to do. Tahg fought back the memories and let himself out of the quiet house where Mrs. Hanrahan was kind enough to rent him a pleasant room for a pittance because he was Mick Collins's friend.

᷍ "How goes it in Dublin?" Seaneen asked Tahg as soon as he had settled in on his visit to us. What a joy it was for me to see him; Tahg had always been as dear to me as if he had been my own. I remember clinging to his broad form like a child when he arrived. Just the stalwart feel of him reminded me of the old days. Of his mother and father. Of all that had gone, never to return . . . and yet, there in my arms was the continuation . . . their immortality.

"Well enough, Seaneen," he answered. "Mick's a bloody genius at organization. You'd think he was running the War Office in London by the records he keeps and the intelligence network he's putting together. Once it's all in place, he'll go after the spies on their payroll. It's then you can expect all hell to break loose."

"We're making progress here, too, lad," Seaneen responded. "And in the other counties. It'll take a good year to do it, but by the time Collins and Brugha need an army, we'll have one for them.

"It won't be easy or quick to accomplish what we must, but you know what they say. 'The man doesn't dally who stops to sharpen his scythe.'"

"You're right enough about that, Seaneen," said Tahg with a hearty laugh. "This time we must get our ducks in line. The right men, the right munitions, the right strategies. Then, when we take our shot at them, we've a chance of winning."

"We'll win," replied Seaneen with conviction. "If we can interfere with enough of their systems, we can make it too costly for them to stay.

"Eventually, we'll harass them out of here, Tahg Mor. You mark my words. If we play enough havoc with their confidence, if we blow up enough barracks, capture enough munitions, kill enough spies . . . eventually they'll get the hell out of Ireland."

"How exactly do you see that happening?" asked Tahg, interested. It was easy to see the respect he bore Seaneen.

"They'll be forced to negotiate, once we've made *not* negotiating expensive enough."

"But Carson says Ulster will secede if there's even a hint of negotiation. And there's plenty who say the English will never let go of the northern counties; no matter what they do about the south, they'll hold on to the part that makes money. All the railroads and shipping are in Ulster and almost everything else that's lucrative."

"In spite of the fox's cunning, his skin is often sold at market," countered Seaneen with a smile.

"True enough," replied Tahg, "but what if we force them into negotiation and they offer us half a country?"

"Then we'll just have to harass them some more, until they give us back the whole bloody kit and caboodle! Mark my words, lad. It's the English themselves who will win this war for us! They don't understand the mentality of us Irish any more today than they did when they got here seven hundred years ago.

"They think we're a joke, because we've been fighting for centuries and we haven't won yet. What they lose sight of is the salient point—that we've never stopped fighting! And we never will until we've beaten them."

I listened to the two men long into the night. It was apparent that the planned violence didn't sit easily with Tahg, but equally apparent that he was totally committed to what he was doing. He was an introspective young man with a bent toward the intellectual, it seemed. But there was a strength in him that reminded me of Seaneen's own.

There were vestiges of his father in Tahg, too, that were evident as I listened. Tierney had always been reticent of force, a reluctant warrior. While men like Seaneen and Collins believed with their whole soul that force was the only possible road to freedom, the Tierneys and the Tahgs would seek for a more civilized alternative.

Alas, I had lived too long in Ireland to imagine they would find it. ⟋

4

September 1917

The rubber tube was forced down Thomas Ashe's throat that day. By a doctor (God help Hippocrates). His nose, where it had been forced before, and his throat, bled painfully. His eyes watered so he couldn't see. He struggled against the straps that bound his knees and elbows to the chair and gasped for breath while choking rubber clogged his throat on its journey meant to pump two eggs and warm milk into a protesting stomach. A

Fenian stomach that had gone hungry thirty-nine days before the forced feeding had begun.

The eggs never found their way as it happened—for the good doctor had missed his mark.

Ten hours later Thomas Ashe died in agony. Maybe it was just the fact of a ruptured stomach, or maybe it was the fifty hours in the previous week that he'd been deprived of his boots and bed and blanket in a cold cell that had weakened him. Maybe his great heart simply stopped. Maybe we'll never know finally, from the ugliness and the indignity of it, the whole truth.

But we do know a few things, don't we, now? We know that such as this should never be, among civilized men. We know that the men incarcerated at Mountjoy Jail are prisoners of war, not felons, and that as such they should be treated with the common decency generally afforded political prisoners by civilized countries.

And we know that no man embarks upon a hunger strike unless it is the last and only weapon left in his arsenal of human dignity.

We know that we weep for Thomas Ashe and for all that he and others like him have endured.

And that we will remember him.

Do you hear that, Mother England, I ask you now? *We will remember him.*

Tahg laid the pen down carefully, as if the purpose he was engaged in was a sacred trust. The essay was not as good as his mother's would have been in the same circumstances, he told himself, but perhaps it would do. The revulsion he had felt on hearing of Ashe's death had been compounded by the terrible memory of his mother's experience years before.

When Tommy McGowan had suggested that he resurrect the Harper, he had been indignant, even angry. His mother's work had been peerless. Unique and impassioned. No one should tamper with its memory. But Tommy had persisted.

"She was the Harper because she could do good by so being. She could rouse people . . . make them angry . . . goad them into righteous indignation. We've need of that now, Tahg. Do you really think she'd begrudge you the carrying of the torch she lit?"

But he had said "No" to the idea, and had put it all out of his head until he'd heard about Ashe's death. Then the righteous anger he'd felt in his own gut had made him want to cry out for justice.

So he had put pen to paper and this had been the result. He read the essay once more through, to make up his mind—then picking up the pen again, he scrawled "The Harper's Son" across the bottom of the page. That way at least he could pay his respects to what his mother had done, without pretending to be something he was not.

Folding the paper in half, Tahg stuffed it into the pocket of his jacket and headed off to find Mick. He'd let him be the judge.

Michael Collins read the paper twice before looking up. When he did so, Tahg could see tears glistening on his lids. Mick could be as sentimental and soft-hearted as a woman when something moved him.

"So your mother was the Harper," he said, incredulity in his voice. "By God, I always wondered who . . . Some said it was your da, others said The O'Rahilly. What a heritage you've got there, laddie. By God, what a fantastic heritage!" He slammed his fist down on the table, the paper still clutched in it.

"Do you think it's good enough to use?" asked Tahg earnestly, "or do you think I'm a fool to even try to follow in her footsteps?"

"It's good enough to have given me an idea," Collins responded. "We'll stage a funeral the likes of which hasn't been seen since O'Donovan Rossa's. We'll give poor Thomas a send-off that an IRB man can be proud of. All the better now that the Castle has declared that we can't wear uniforms or display weapons. We'll give them a little taste of willful defiance!

"Get that thing printed as a flyer for distribution day after tomorrow, Tahg Mor. September thirty we'll bury Thomas Ashe with every honor a death like his deserves." Mick got up from the table and began to pace up and down with the momentum of his thoughts.

"By Christ, we can use a little of the emotions those Wild Harp essays used to stir up!

"We'll have to get a lot of people moving to make this funeral the spectacle it should be. We'll need the unions and the Volunteers, the clergy, too, if we can get them . . ."

Tahg could see that Collins's brain was already mobilizing—Ashe's death would be a rallying point, a political demonstration and a call to arms.

Tahg knew how incensed Mick was over the reports of Ashe's death. Thomas had been his friend.

He'd see that Thomas Ashe was given a proper farewell.

All Dublin seemed in mourning. Forty thousand people followed the hearse through the streets. Volunteers with rifles reversed, trade unionists, Citizen Army men led by Con Markievicz in full military regalia with a revolver at her belt, all marched in solemn cadence through the hushed streets. The Castle did not dare to stop so many.

A firing party loosed three volleys over the coffin. Michael Collins in Volunteer uniform stepped up to the gravesite; he knew his strong Cork voice would carry easily over the hush of assembled mourners.

"Nothing additional remains to be said," he intoned as the echo of the rifle fire faded under his words. "That volley which we have just heard is the *only* speech which it is proper to make over the grave of a dead Fenian."

Saluting the coffin, he turned abruptly and left the gravesite.

Tahg, behind Collins, marveled at the simple perfection of the words. They would have exactly the desired effect on the crowd, but that wasn't all the reason Mick had chosen them. He'd said what he did because he couldn't trust his voice to keep from breaking in a longer speech.

5   Angelica Manningham closed the account book and pushed her chair away from the desk. She wished there were more money with which to help the poor who came to her so endlessly for aid. The year she had spent in Dublin had given her ample opportunity to learn how the rest of the world lived.

"The poor are as patient as Buddha," Tahg had quoted some-one to her just the other day; he was right, of course. Patient in their rags, patient in their hunger, patient in their endless sor-rows. Ah well, at least she had a chance to do her part. "Her Cause," he'd called it, teasingly. A less violent one than his and Mick's.

She reached up suddenly and pulled the pins from her hair, plaited as it was into thick braids wound into a golden crown on top of her head. Sometimes, when the day was long and tiring, the heaviness of her hair made her head ache. She ran her fingers through the plaiting now; first rubbing her hands against her tired temples, she fanned her hair out into a wavy cascade around her shoulders and back. Her hair was Angelica's only vanity—she would wear it loose tonight when the men from the Organization gathered here for their meeting.

She let her head fall backward, stretching her long neck this way and that, feeling the fatigue drain slowly from brain and body. By day she did what good she could for the people of Dublin . . . the poor, long-suffering, patient people of Dublin, and she carried on her mother's work with women's rights. But by night she had other priorities. What a blessing it was that her father divided his time between London and Sligo these days, so she had the Dublin house to herself.

What a blessing, too, that Tahg had given her entrée to the IRB. Dear, loving Tahg, who had never abandoned her; thanks to him, she, too, could do her part for Ireland, despite her infirmity. And who would ever suspect her? She, the crippled daughter of a famous conservative Member of Parliament, was the last person on earth they'd suspect of running a safe house for the IRB.

It had all happened so quickly, really, and had fallen into place so well. First, the move to the town house they owned on Waterloo Road, then a generous contribution from her father toward her work—a euphemism, she had seen immediately, for a means of making her happier. He knew she had been pining for a change from that lonely old house in Sligo; pining for a project to sink her teeth into, that would make her feel a pro-ductive human being instead of a pampered, handicapped child.

And, as always, her father had acquiesced to her needs. So Angelica had settled into her new life with minimal fuss; had equipped the house with servants and one or two special contrivances to accommodate her chair.

And then Tahg had swooped in to help with everything. Her gallant Tahg had made every new and exciting thing possible in her life, introducing her to his friends and his Cause. In the twelve months since her arrival in Dublin, her whole life had changed radically.

She had hit it off with Mick Collins from the first. She wondered if Tahg had intuited that such would happen before he introduced them. Her cousin might not have "the Sight" as his father had had it, but his intuition was uncannily accurate. Even Collins had remarked on Tahg's inordinate gift of presentiment. He could sense danger with an unerring instinct, Mick said, and he could sense other men's strategies as well.

What in God's name would her life have been like had there been no Tahg in it? she wondered, chilled by the thought. He was her lifeline to the rest of humanity.

"You've been so good to me, Tahg Mor," said Angelica, pouring tea for him from the exquisite silver service he knew had come from her father's house.

"No more than you've been good to me," he replied, smiling. "Giving us a place for the meetings that no one would ever suspect. Making order out of the chaos of the files I've given you. Keeping everything safe here under lock and key."

"There isn't anything I wouldn't do for you, Tahg," she responded. "Or for Mick. You know that."

"Aye, I know you two have become fast friends. I'm glad to see it. You know I was worried you might be lonely here in Dublin. After spending a lifetime around sisters and brothers and servants, it could feel strange to be on your own, with your father away so much of the time."

"It did, a little, at first. So many unsettling things have happened to us. First Mother running off and taking Johnny. Then Win and Jamie going to London. Even docile Merry talking of coming here to be an actress, of all things.

"I think poor Father was so battered by all the changes that by the time I said I was going, he didn't have the strength to fight back." They both laughed at that.

"What a curious group we are, we Manninghams, Tahg. Always keeping the kettle boiling, always fomenting somehow, never peaceful. Even you and I, sensible people that we are, are knee deep in intrigue and revolution."

Tahg looked at his cousin, studying her. She had always been closest to him of all the relatives, their friendship an important stability in his life.

"You are very lovely, Angel," he said, as if to cover the fact that he'd been staring at her. "I sometimes try to decide who you favor. You don't look like either of your parents really."

"Oh, I might have been a looker if it weren't for these old legs of mine." She smiled as she said it, but the smile was empty.

"You're a brave girl about your legs, Angel. Even Mick says you've more courage than the lot of us."

She shrugged off the compliment.

"My life isn't a bad one, now, Tahg. I'm happier here than I've ever been. I love my charities and I love what I'm doing for the Organization. I understand Mick, you know. There's an anger and a dissatisfaction about the disorder of things that drives him. It's what makes him want to tear it all down and build anew. Sometimes I feel the same way, but I keep it contained, just as he does. That's why I work for my charities by day and the Organization by night. It's a chance to change things—even from a wheelchair."

"And you look like butter wouldn't melt in your mouth, my little one," laughed Tahg. "Who would guess what a wild woman you are underneath."

"Oh, Tahg, how I wish there were someone in this world who could guess at it."

He looked at her quizzically, then seeing the sadness beneath the words, said, "One day, lass. There'll be someone."

"Do you think so?"

"I do."

"And what would make a man fall in love with me, exactly?"

He looked at her steadily, his eyebrows knitted together, as if making an important judgment on the spot.

"Your kindness and your intelligence . . . or your gorgeous yellow hair. Your face has possibilities, too, if it weren't for the freckles, of course."

Angelica laid down her teacup, laughing. "You are so good for me, Tahg Mor. Always, always you cheer me."

"And why not? Haven't I worn the lady's colors for damned

near a lifetime?" He reached suddenly into his pocket as he said this and pulled out a battered wallet. Digging into its inner pocket, he drew out a tattered old piece of hair ribbon and handed it to her.

"You haven't kept my ribbon all these years!" she breathed, genuinely astonished.

"It's my good luck charm. Wouldn't part with this for millions."

Angelica reached over impulsively and clasped his big hand.

"No matter what else I don't have in life, Tahg Mor, I'll always be grateful to God that I have you."

He squeezed her hand in return and, reaching into his pocket, gave her his handkerchief, for he could see there were tears shining in her eyes.

"De Valera's been arrested," he said to change the subject. "They've put him into jail again."

"He'll have been in every jail in Ireland before they're through with him," said Angelica. "How much of a loss do you think it is to us?"

"I don't know, to tell the truth. He seems to have what it takes to get the people to follow him. As the only one of the leaders of Easter Week to survive, he's nearly a legend. He's also a sane voice amid all the factions. I think if we get our own Parliament operating, as we're trying to do, we'll need him and Griffith both as elder statesmen."

Angelica nodded. A Parliament in Dublin—a Dail Eireann as they were calling it—was an essential first step toward nationhood. It wouldn't matter how much the physical-force men could achieve, if there were no real government to do the people's bidding at the end of it.

"Who have we got to run the Dail, assuming we can create one?" she asked thoughtfully.

"Cathal Brugha, maybe. Griffith for sure. Dev, if we can get him out. Mick's no politician. He'll be happy enough to leave that to the others."

"Too happy, perhaps," she replied. "You'd best keep an eye on him, Tahg, when it comes to politics. Mick tends to assume that everyone's working as selflessly for Ireland as he is. But history suggests that it's the fighting among our own leaders that usually does us in, as much as our enemies."

Tahg laughed shortly at his cousin's astute appraisal. "I'll do what I can, Angel," he said. "But Mick hasn't a political bone in his body."

They talked till nearly midnight. It eased Tahg's mind to talk to Angelica, she was so sensible a listener. And her ideas were often novel, even daring. What a wife she would have made some man, he thought as he made his way home. What a rotten shame that so few men would ever look beyond her infirmity.

6 "Meticulous organization is what we need here," said Collins, drumming his fingers on the table. "And contacts. We need eyes and ears in the jails . . . friends in low places, you might call them. And we need de Valera out of prison."

Tahg looked alert at the last of it; he, himself, had just spent another eight months of his life at the King's expense. He, like a great many other active nationalists, had been rearrested early in 1918 and only recently released. "You think we can pull it off?"

"Without a doubt," replied Collins as if jailbreaking were something he did daily. "We need him for the Dail. There's no point having a Parliament if we haven't any statesmen to make noise there."

"Fair enough," said Tahg, considering the wisdom of it. "It'd give them fits at the Castle if we could spring Dev and march him up to the Mansion House at the head of a parade."

"A gorgeous idea, that!" replied Collins, who loved the grand gesture. "And after we free Dev, I've a list as long as your arm of men in every prison in Ireland we'll be needing to get out. I want you and O'Reilly to go get them for me."

Tahg smiled a little at how simple Collins always made the impossible sound.

"Has it occurred to you, Mick, that once you've got Dev out and at the head of the Dail there'll be no way in the world to control him?"

Collins eyed his friend with amusement. "It's occurred to me, all right. But the devil you know is better than the devil you don't. Besides that, we need somebody to head the Dail that the English will deign to converse with. They like tall dignified men over in England. Dev looks the part." He chuckled at the idea of how Dev would respond to being thought of as a type-cast actor.

"De Valera is shrewd and political, Mick," Tahg persisted. "And from what I hear, he's no man's fool. We mustn't underestimate him."

"True enough, Tahg Mor. But neither can we fear to put the best man into whatever job we've got. Or we'll never have a government of our own. Besides, it'll make the game all the more adventurous."

"I'll help you get him out," said Tahg. "And anyone else you want, but I've been giving some thought to how I can be the most value to you, Mick. I think I can be of use to you as a sort of liaison between you and the men in country brigades . . . maybe even between you and the politicians in the Dail. When we get Dev out of Lincoln, I'll make it my business to get to know him."

Collins nodded acceptance of the idea, but Tahg could see he had no real sense of danger where the politicians were concerned. Yet, the danger would be there; Tahg could feel it.

It didn't occur to Tahg until he and O'Reilly had laid out the mechanics of the plan to free Dev that it hadn't crossed either of their minds that they might not be able to do it. That's part of Collins's genius, thought Tahg with amusement. He has the gift of making men believe they can touch the stars.

Despite his lanky height and slender angularity, there was a sense of substance about Eamon de Valera. A sturdy, solemn-eyed calm and determination that tended to make men listen to what he had to say.

Dartmoor, Maidstone, Lewes, Pentonville; an odyssey of British prisons had given him ample time in which to study the enemy and to think about the next moves necessary in Ireland's behalf. In order to make changes one must have power; in order to have power, one must have a base of operations. And what better base of operations could there be than to run for election to the Irish parliamentary seat recently vacated in East Clare?

In counties Roscommon and Longford, Volunteers had already been elected to the Dail. Sinn Fein electioneers in uniform had taken to the roads on their bicycles and the people had responded. It was a good omen.

So as soon as he'd been released from prison in June of 1917, Dev had donned his uniform and set out for Clare's little villages. He had no great gift of oratory, but he had lucidity and vigor—and he had a platform: "If elected, I will never set foot in Westminster!" he'd told the people. "The only Parliament the Irish people need ever accept is an Irish Parliament headquartered in Ireland!"

On 23 June 1917 the people of Clare had given him their vote of confidence. After all, Dev was a bona fide hero . . . the only leader to have survived Easter Week.

The Sinn Fein election victories had unnerved the British enough to cause his rearrest in May 1918, but despite his imprisonment he had carried East Mayo and Clare in the November elections.

Now it was time to get de Valera out of prison once again, so that his talents could be put to use.

De Valera looked across the table at the young man who had helped transport him from Lincoln Jail through the dark, alien English countryside to this safe house near Manchester. Tahg O'Connor was rather singularly handsome and quietly confident.

He could see evidence of Con O'Connor in the lad—as she had seemed to him at Boland's Mill during Easter Week—single-minded and fearless in her determination to get the job done. He remembered hearing her speak of the boy who was now grown to be a man. There was much of his father's physical presence in him too; much of the same economy of movement and similar gestures.

Yet, all told, Tahg was different from either of his parents, and it was evident that he kept his own counsel. A good trait in a young man. He had asked incisive questions and listened closely to the answers, sifting out the political hogwash as easily as a cook separating yolks from egg whites.

"I'm very grateful for your help, O'Connor," Dev said finally, to bring the animated conversation to an end. They had talked all the way home from Lincoln and on into the early morning hours. "This breaking out of prison seems a more ex-

hausting business than I'd expected. I need a good night's sleep
in a real bed and I'll be a new man."

O'Connor rose to leave. "I'm glad to have been of help, Dev.
Mick is convinced that if we ever get them to capitulate to
negotiations, you're just the man for the job. After our conversation tonight, I'm inclined to agree with him."

Was there a note of something in Tahg's voice other than just
what the words suggested? Dev wondered; he couldn't be sure.

"You're an interesting fellow, O'Connor," he said, smiling. "I
have no doubt but that we'll see a good deal of one another
before we see Ireland free."

Tahg nodded agreement and, shaking Dev's hand, took his
leave of him. De Valera was everything Mick had led him to
expect, and more.

Every answer had been judiciously thought out and politi-
cally phrased; spontaneity was certainly not de Valera's long
suit. If Mick had any notions of controlling this man's actions
one whit, he had better think again. Dev was a man with a plan
for his own future as well as the country's.

The most encouraging piece of information he'd gleaned tonight was that Dev was determined to go to America to raise
money for the Cause. He hoped that perhaps he'd stay there for
a good long time.

7

Lady Angelica Manningham
32 Waterloo Road
Ballsbridge, Dublin

1 December 1919

My darling Johnny,
    Life in Dublin is the best I've ever known. Tahg takes
me everywhere that I could not go alone. He is well by
the way. Thinner since his second bout with prison, more

introspective than ever, but very solid, I think, and very determined.

My charity work goes well—indeed, in a city so rife with poor, any charity must prosper. Someday I will follow in Mother's footsteps and write a book about it, but not yet.

Needless to say, I miss you dreadfully. It's a terrible thing for an older sister to admit, but you were a joy to me always.

And, of course, I worry about Mother. Although, after the glowing reports in your letters about her and Mr. O'Sullivan, it seems I should be more jealous than worried. What a miracle that they should finally have found each other after all the years they must have pined for each other's love. Well, there's another story in that, isn't there, Scamp?

Are you keeping your terrible temper in tow, now that you no longer have to deal with Father? (Who, by the way, is well and growing more prominent by the day.) I hope so, love; it's the only part of you that scares me.

Tahg has arrived to take me to the theater. His friend, Kitty O'Neill, is fast becoming the heartthrob of Dublin. She is now starring in a revival of Yeats's play *The Countess Cathleen,* and has gotten as extraordinary reviews in this as she had in her first starring role. It's a gorgeous part for her—that of a countess who personifies Ireland and sells her soul to the devil to feed her starving tenants. At any rate, we're off to see her perform and I expect it will be a rare treat for me. For Tahg, who says there is little time in his life for women at the moment, I suspect it may be a bit melancholy as he hasn't spoken to her since his return home.

Life here has opened so many new possibilities to me, Johnny. I'm beginning to think that my handicap will not keep me from leading a meaningful life. And, Tahg, of course, has made me believe that in the process of being "meaningful" I may even have a jolly good time.

I love you, dearest Scamp. If you don't write more often I shall be disconsolate. Love to Mother for me, please, and regards to Mr. O'Sullivan (I don't quite know what else to send, but I mean well).

Angelica

Lady Merrion Manningham
32 Waterloo Road
Ballsbridge, Dublin

15 December 1919

Tahg dear,

May I ask a very large favor of you? I am beginning to make the rounds of the theaters here in hope that I may get a foot in the door of one. If nothing else, I'm honing my auditioning skills, and although my feet are weary, my hopes are high. I do wish I knew someone who could tell me if I'm going about all this the right way. Do you suppose you might introduce me to your friend Kitty O'Neill when the spirit moves you? It really would be an enormous help to me to talk with her.

I do so much appreciate whatever aid and abetment you may be able to give your aspiring-thespian cousin. And, of course, I send my love, as ever.

Merry

Tahg read the note thoughtfully. What a perfect excuse it would be for going to see Kitty, he thought. But did he have the courage to do so and be rejected?

She was famous now. The reviews of her last two plays had made that inevitable. It hadn't taken long at all for the beautiful understudy to find her way into the limelight and into stardom of her own. Judging from what he could glean from the newspapers, she was already the darling of the stage-door Johnnies and well on her way to all she desired.

Nonetheless, Merry's note would be the perfect excuse.

"You're utterly impossible to debate on this subject, Jamie," said Win disgustedly. "You've no perspective on this Irish question whatsoever."

Jamie pushed his glasses back into place on his patrician nose and looked carefully at his elder brother. "Perhaps it would be more accurate to say I have a *different* perspective from yours, Winston."

"As you wish," replied his brother magnanimously, "but you're too soft on those despicable dissidents. Ambushing convoys of military supplies for the constabulary as if they had every right to!"

"In a way they do, Win," said Jamie with a soft chuckle that irritated his brother. "It is their country, you know."

"It is precisely that kind of casuistry that makes you impossible to talk to! It is not their country, in the least. In actual point of fact it is part of the British Empire."

"But not by choice."

"Nonetheless, the law is the law."

"And what a pompous casuistic statement that is, dear brother. In truth the law is only the law when enforced by those in power. We, of the ruling class, have simply had the power to enforce our laws in Ireland for several hundred years now, but that does not mean that the man in the Dublin street accepts them as *his* laws."

"Then he shall be made to do so. In the interest of order."

"Look here, Winston. I'm not in the least trying to provoke a row with you. I simply want you to acknowledge that there are two valid points of view here. Yours and theirs. I personally wish some compromise could be reached between them, but at the rate things are escalating, I can't see much hope of that.

"To be honest, I came back to Dublin because I wanted to see firsthand how wars happen. There's one happening here, you know. As we sit here, there is a war accelerating outside this very drawing room."

"Indeed," said Winston. "And steps are being taken, I assure you, to see that it is quelled quickly."

"Really?" asked Jamie, alert again; his brother did hobnob with the men who caused things to happen.

"New police recruitments from England will be commissioned within the next year. They'll be given enough manpower and equipment to settle this nonsense, once and for all."

Jamie shook his head sadly. "Sending in supplemental troops in an effort to keep the peace always seems to me as sensible as tossing oil on a fire to dampen it."

"You're a hopeless pacifist, Jamie old boy," said Winston affably. "That should be your specialty, you know. Pacifism."

Jamie tilted his head back, as if to keep his errant glasses in place, and smiled.

"Quite astute of you, Winston. That's really, more or less, what I've decided, too."

Both brothers smiled at that and Winston rose from his chair.

"I suppose we'd best dress for dinner, James," he said. "Angelica seems to have arranged all sorts of festivities, now that she's managed to get us all under one roof for a change.

"By the way, is the rumor true about Merry moving in with you?"

Jamie stood up, too, and sounded surprised.

"Merry? Why no, as a matter of fact I believe she's making other plans. Said something about my scholarly life being too dull and boring."

Winston looked at Jamie with disdain and said, "I've no doubt she's right about that, Jamie old boy. You never really did know much about having a good time, did you?"

Jamie let the insult pass. His brother was quite insufferable much of the time, but peace was always preferable to an argument; he had long ago found that the best way to deal with Winston was to ignore him.

8 "Derek!" Tahg called to his friend over the heads of the drinkers and talkers. "Over here!" O'Hanrahan had just entered the pub and was shaking the water from his hat and coat as if he were a drenched puppy.

Derek signaled back and made his way to where Tahg sat. He ordered a whiskey to chase the cold and settled in with a cheerful look on his face. Derek wasn't handsome in the least, but there was a pleasant pugnacity about him that was very male. And as smiles came easily to his lips, there was an aspect of affability about him that tended to attract people. In no way did he resemble a doctor. Were it not for his wardrobe, which was improving as his practice grew, his stocky build and craggy face could have easily caused him to be mistaken for a laborer.

"A man could drown in a single street out there. . . . To your health!" he said, as he picked up the whiskey that had appeared at Tahg's bidding and downed it in a single swallow.

"And to yours!" said Tahg with a good-humored chuckle. He liked Derek O'Hanrahan. Liked his quick wit and street-smart wisdom—his toughness and determination to overcome the odds. They'd remained friends since the GPO, although they saw each other seldom enough now that Tahg's nights and days were occupied with Mick's business.

"Well now, laddie," said Derek as if he were three times Tahg's age, "and how are you keepin'?"

"Well enough, Derek," replied Tahg. "It's getting a bit rough on the streets these days with the reinforcements they're sending in. But I'm holding up."

"How goes your war?" asked Derek.

"Now that you mention it, I was hoping I might be able to entice you into giving us a hand with it. There's more wounded than you could shake a stick at these days, and we've the devil's own time finding doctors who'll go along with us."

"Oh, no you don't!" said Derek with an emphatic gesture of the head. "I've not come here to have you beguile me into trouble. I'd me fill of that stuff at the post office, thank you very much! Sympathetic as I am to what you're up to, Tahg me lad, I'll have none of it!

"I didn't pull myself out of the gutter just to end up back there again, good cause or no. I've the beginnings of a good practice starting up and I've two nice rooms of my own now. And more important, I've peace of mind and a clear conscience. Forgive me for saying it, Tahg Mor, but I'm planning to devote all the energy I've got to making a name for myself, and a nice tidy income, so the specter of poverty takes wing!" He made a wry face as he said it, as if to say that poverty was an odious inconvenience that he never intended to deal with again.

"Ah, Derek," said Tahg, with an amused twinkle in his eye. "You don't know what you're missing, lad. No mayhem nor murder, no sleepless nights, no price on your head . . ."

"Precisely my own thought," his friend replied with a hearty laugh. "I'd much prefer that you have all the good times without me."

"I can't say I don't understand your position, Derek. I just wish you'd change your mind. We need you, man."

Derek's hazel eyes turned serious in the flickering light of the pub. "I know you do, Tahg Mor. And it doesn't make me proud of myself to say no to you. But my mind is made up. I've got to make something of myself, and in my game you can't take time out for Ireland or there'll be no catching up at all."

Tahg nodded. And ordered another whiskey for each of them.

"Mind you. This doesn't apply to your own fine self, laddie. If *you* ever need me, they can drag you into my infirmary under the very noses of the RIC and I'll patch you up. Make no mistake about that."

Tahg smiled at the offer and, lifting his drink toward his friend, he said, "To never having to take you up on your kind offer!"

They both laughed and turned the conversation to other things. But Tahg was disappointed. He had hoped that with all that was happening, Derek would change his mind.

Tahg walked home from the pub after leaving O'Hanrahan behind. He liked the feel of the rain, it was cold and bracing after the heat of the fire in the smoky public house.

But Derek's refusal to help depressed him. It was a mirror of Irish feeling—as if everyone were saying, "I'm with you in spirit, lads, but don't ask any sacrifices of me!" Yet, the time was coming when the sacrifices would have to be made. All over the country flying columns of the Irish Republican Army were being organized and used with increasing success to harass the RIC and the soldiers.

Mick's genius for organization was paying off and his genius for intuiting just where to hit the enemy was uncanny. County garrisons had their guns and ammo stolen in flash attacks. Roadways, where convoys of supplies were to travel, developed gelignite-filled holes in them. Informers met swift and unpleasant ends.

The tables were turning it seemed at last. The hunted were now the hunters. It wouldn't be long before some very large scale retaliation would be put into action and Mick had a major attack of his own in the works.

დ "Now, son, tell me again how you'd go about rousting an RIC barracks if it were up to you?"

Johnny glowed with pride as he responded cogently to his

father's question. Early and late I listened to them talk of military strategy and tactics. For it was now a military war.

Johnny was fourteen and big for his age; smart, too, they all agreed. He was the pride of Seaneen's heart. Like the fervor of a convert to his new religion, Seaneen brought a concentration of effort to fatherhood that no one could fault. And, of course, the boy was starved for a father's love. Johnny lapped it up, like a cat with cream. He listened, questioned, listened, learned. He drilled and practiced, and, to be fair, he seemed to have a talent for all that smacked of war. He was an expert marksman by this time, and he had a gift, it seemed, for explosives. In truth, he had a gift for anything Seaneen told him to set his hand to, with the exception of ruling his rash temper.

Johnny reminded me of Des as a boy, his temper quick to flare. But unlike Des, his anger didn't dissipate after the storm was over, but seemed to smolder afterward, so you were never sure if the danger was past.

He clashed with Seaneen often enough about it, but his temper troubled his father less than it did me. "He's nearly a man, My Lady," Seaneen would say to me. "Men are an unruly lot, especially in hard times. Leave the lad to me." And I would acquiesce to his request, for he and Johnny seemed to share so much I dared not intrude upon. Hero and worshiper, father and son. Long-lost kindred souls, newly together. How could I deem it wrong for them to adore each other, when I, too, was glowing in the happiness that comes like balm after a lifetime of lonely nettles?

Never had I truly believed that Seaneen and I would be privileged to live as man and wife. Not even when we had dreamed aloud of such a miracle, had I believed it might ever happen.

To lie down with the man I loved every night of my life and to awaken beside him every morning . . . to sit reading to him in the evenings, watching his beloved face by the fire. These simple, homely joys seemed to me treasures beyond price. Treasures I had never hoped to attain.

And he was good to me. In ways that I had fantasized, I suppose, but which I had deemed mere fancies. Seaneen, for all his rough, fierce ways with the men, for all his discipline and thunder, with me was always the gentle lover. Indeed he treated me as if I were so precious, it sometimes made me laugh. "Haven't I proved to you what stern stuff I'm made of?" I would ask him. "There's no need to treat me as if I were made of angel wings!" But in truth I reveled in the being cherished, as he reveled in the cherishing.

I was like a bride, feeling young and desirable. All the vanished joys of young womanhood that had been immured with Edmond were fanned into life with Seaneen.

Never was there the barest possibility of our taking each other for granted, we who had pined for each other's touch for a lifetime—and who lived now in such imminent physical danger. We were like young lovers, but with the wisdom of middle age to make us grateful for this second youth.

We made love so wildly and so often that we joked that we had made up the quotient of those missing years. I'm sure we were the butt of amused stories among the men; no one could have missed knowing of our happiness. Of course, they also knew the hardships we had endured and so they were tolerant of our foolishness. Indeed, I think the men took joy in our love for each other. God knows, they treated me with respect and kindness every day I knew them. Then, too, there was such dignity to Seaneen and such respect due him that I'm sure I was accorded grace as his lady, that I would not otherwise have merited.

In such wise we had passed the two years between 1917 and 1919. I used my writing skills to catalog events; I acted as Seaneen's eyes, and as his confidante. Needless to say, I learned a lifetime's worth; I was needed, needed, needed! I gave and was given to in equal measure.

If I was an outcast from the society that had spawned me, I was accepted by one whose opinion I valued more. Dear Con, I used to think, if you could but see me now . . . if you could but share it all with me, this glorious golden gift of life that came from your kind hand.

The only serpent in the garden was a niggling sense I felt of unease about Johnny's warlike nature. He had found a vocation in war and, while it pleased his father, it made me uneasy indeed to see him burdened with so onerous a gift. ↩

9 Tahg watched Mick gleefully distribute all the Christmas presents.

O'Reilly had made the purchases, of course, but all at Collins's instigation. The man loved Christmas with an almost childlike pleasure. No matter his circumstances, Tahg mused, watching the festivities, Mick would somehow contrive to create an almost Dickensian Christmas for himself and his friends. "It's a legacy from my father," Mick had said with great pride when Tahg asked him why Christmas meant so much. "My da knew how to make it an awesome day, God rest him."

Tahg had listened in fascination to the tale of Mick's childhood. It wasn't every man whose father had been sixty years old when he'd wed his mother, a girl of twenty. Mick had been their eighth and last child, born when his father was seventy-five years of age.

Mick had adored the man, and venerated his erudition. Although, like so many peasants of his time, the elder Collins had been educated only in a hedge school—the illegal roadside schools that sprouted when the penal laws outlawed Irish education—the man spoke Irish and French well, and had a decent knowledge of Greek and Latin. And he loved books and learning with a passion that he'd passed on to Mick. Just as, it seemed, he'd passed on a wisdom greater than his years to the boy, and a strict sense of honor.

To say nothing of his inordinate love of Christmas. Tahg saw Mick coming toward him, laughter lighting the man's countenance.

"What say we take ourselves to the Gresham for a bit more Christmas cheer?" he asked, slapping Tahg affectionately on the back.

"Fair enough," O'Connor replied, grabbing his coat from the chair. It was hot in the room with all the Christmas merrymakers. He would welcome a bit of air.

They had barely settled themselves in the Gresham's dining

room when the waiter whispered to Collins urgently, "There's soldiers in the hall, sir."

Tahg saw Mick stiffen at the news, then, with a visible effort of will, become relaxed again and affable.

The soldiers approached the table where Tahg, Collins and O'Reilly sat.

"I'm afraid it will be necessary to search you, gentlemen," said the lieutenant. "We're looking for a man named Michael Collins and you match his description well enough."

"Do I now?" said Collins with a hearty laugh. "You don't say so! Well, that'll be good for a laugh or two with the ladies, I imagine. I've heard they all think this Collins is the cat's whiskers."

Mick stood so that the soldier could empty his pockets; the man pulled out a wallet and flipped it open.

"John Field, is it?" the officer said, looking at the name in the wallet.

"John Field it is," replied Collins easily.

"And what have we here?" The man with the wallet pulled a small piece of paper from it. "By God, that says 'rifles,' sir."

"It does not say anything of the kind!" exploded Collins, as if the victim of a terrible injustice. "It says 'refills,' sure as you're born. You see, I'm an accountant by profession and I require refills for my ledger."

The soldier examined again the photo in his hand, glanced long and hard at Collins, then signaled the sergeant to let him go.

"There's a bit of a resemblance, Mr. Field," he said begrudgingly to Mick. "But your papers are all in order and I don't think you look as much like this picture as you might. The nose is different . . . and the mouth. This Collins fellow has a mean-looking mouth, unlike your own."

Mick looked carefully at the photograph of himself and frowned. "He's an ugly one to be sure," he said judiciously. "Isn't it a great wonder now that the ladies are so fond of him?"

The soldiers grunted acquiescence and began to file out of the room.

"By God, that was a close one." Tahg whistled under his breath as he watched them go.

"Aye. One of my nine lives may have passed over," replied

Mick with a short laugh. But despite the laugh, Tahg could see that he was shaken.

"Get on with you now, Tahg Mor," laughed Mick. "We'll be calling you 'The Conscience' if you're not careful." The two men had been talking about the implementation of Mick's plans now that the intelligence network was in place. And Tahg, as often before, had voiced his concern over the killings.

"Ah well, maybe we could use a 'conscience' at that." Mick finished the thought with a shake of the head.

Tahg had watched in fascination over the past two years as Collins had deftly grouped the men into cells, each with a specified job, each with a small knot of co-workers. Each of the cells was ignorant of the others—none but the most trusted knew the names of the men or the tasks they'd been assigned. Even the assassination team was cloaked in shadow . . . who they were, where or when they would strike were mysteries.

Tahg smiled back at Mick, and at O'Reilly, who stood behind him. Wherever Collins was, O'Reilly wouldn't be far behind. Unless, of course, he was off delivering messages for Collins somewhere else.

"I've a hard time with the killings, Mick," Tahg persisted. "I'll not lie to you."

"And who'd ever believe that?" snapped Collins. "With the hang-dog face on you every time they're mentioned."

"It isn't that I disapprove of your intent at all . . ."

"And aren't you the benevolent one," Mick said with a derisive laugh.

"It's just that walking into a man's bedroom and shooting him in front of his wife could be a mite hard on the stomach."

Mick eyed Tahg calculatingly. He wasn't one to discard a friend or disciple because of a disagreement. Tahg was too intellectual, too questioning to be an ideal soldier; but he was resourceful, and singularly competent once he'd made up his mind about a plan of attack. And he was a good friend.

"The enemy doesn't seem to find it too disagreeable," he replied sharply, then added, "You know damned well they've given us no choice, lad. As long as they've got the informers in the Royal Irish Constabulary to tell them of our every move, we're dead men ourselves.

"Unless we can put out their eyes, Tahg Mor . . . unless we

can kill every bloody louser who's informing on us, we'll never be free. Not from all our patriotic horseshit, or all our patriotic gatherings, or all our patriotic pals in America who dress up in green suits and get drunk on Saint Patrick's Day to sing about the 'auld sod.'

"We've but one chance, laddie! They've *everything* else on their bloody side and you know it."

"Aye. They have that. And I'll be damned if I know why I'm hanging crepe for the bastards. They've sent enough good men of ours to their doom, by God."

Mick's eyes softened. He liked O'Connor and he honored the memory of his parents. A rare pair they'd been.

"It's all right to be 'The Conscience,' lad. Better to have one than not." He laughed suddenly and Tahg thought how like a summer storm Mick's laughter always was . . . refreshing, wild, unexpected.

"Mind you. We don't need more than one. But one won't do us any harm." He reached across and slapped Tahg a playful blow on the shoulder. Those who knew Mick knew enough to be ready for these blows—powerful, surprising, only half playful. He was a man to be respected—and never, ever must you take him for granted in the least way.

The enormous bouquet of roses dwarfed Kitty's dressing table. The lavish cream-colored card bore the engraving of Sir Reginald Milburn and a scrawled note of undying devotion.

So it begins . . . she thought as she put the finishing touch on her lips and dusted pearlized powder over the masterpiece of makeup that was her face. Just as I've dreamed it. Rich, powerful men wanting me, sending me flowers, asking for my favors. Making fools of themselves in writing with protestations of immortal passion.

What difference that Sir Reginald was sixty and looked somewhat like a toad? It was a beginning.

A few more plays like this one and she could have her pick of the men in Dublin.

So it begins.

10 The sweat ran off both their foreheads. Their right arms, locked in combat, strained the muscles and sinews until it seemed they must burst the skin to break free.

Mick's face bore the look of total absorption that always marked encounters like this one. He would challenge a man to an arm-wrestling contest as soon as look at him. And he was strong. Much stronger than his size suggested.

The amused expression that Clancy's florid face had held when the game began had changed to strain. Jesus Christ, but Mick had iron in his arms and shoulders! He was smaller than Clancy by inches, but he was made of iron.

Inch by fraction of inch, Collins forced the younger man's arm backward toward the table.

A roar of triumph from Collins, a wild whoop of childish glee at victory. A quick clap on the back and the game was over, Collins happy again.

Tahg laughed with the rest of them and watched Clancy wipe the sweat from his face gratefully with a handkerchief. Every man who ran with Collins had to be ready for these swift and adolescent rituals. It hardly mattered. Any one of them would die for him, never mind suffer through these games he used to purge the terrible tensions that plagued him.

The meeting over, the men began to wander from the room, each to his own appointed task. Tahg marveled at Collins's organizational ability and wondered where it had come from.

Tahg walked slowly to the table where Mick was still seated and opened two beers, handing one to Collins.

Mick tipped his own glass toward his friend. "Slainte!" he said laughingly; his good nature was always best after winning a wrestling match.

"And what exactly weighs so heavy on your mind that you're walking around here like a zombie, might I inquire?" he asked of Tahg jovially.

"I'm going to go see Kitty, Mick."

"Mother of God, the lad's a glutton for punishment, isn't he now?" he said, but he looked concerned over his friend's decision. He knew Tahg had been wrestling with the idea since his return to Dublin.

"She's the toast of Dublin, laddie," he said gently. " 'Twould seem she's gotten hold of whatever she's been running after. What makes you think there's room for you there?"

"I don't need there to be room for me, Mick. Not now. You of all people know I'm not in a position to give her the kind of life she wants until this bloody war is over. It's just that I've a need to straighten things out with her. To say some things that haven't been said right."

"And you think she'll listen?"

"I think I'll feel better if I try."

"This wouldn't have anything to do with nearly getting caught this afternoon, would it now?" Tahg, Joe O'Reilly and Collins himself had come within inches of being captured at No. 6 Harcourt Street earlier in the day.

Tahg looked up sharply at his friend, then laughed shortly.

"You're an insightful son of a bitch, Collins, I'll say that for you. Yes, it has to do with that!

"When you come within an inch of cashing in, you remember all the unsaid, undone things of your life and you want to set them straight before the next time the old reaper has you on his dance card."

"He'll not reap you, if you listen to what I tell you, O'Connor. No more theatrics like this afternoon or I'll not take responsibility for you, laddie buck."

"You don't need to take responsibility for me, Mick. We're each on our own in this."

"Not while you're under my command, you're not!" There was sudden thunder in Mick's voice.

"All right, all right, I'll watch my step from now on."

"And listen to what I tell you!"

"And listen, too."

"All right, then," said Collins, as if something very important had been cleared up. "I'll go to the theater with you to see her performance tonight."

"We'll never get tickets, man. It's sold out every night."

Collins smiled his cat-that-swallowed-the-canary smile. "I've a man in the theater, Tahg Mor. He'll get the tickets for me."

Tahg shook his head in amusement. That was part of Collins's genius, of course. He had a loyal man in every nook and cranny of Dublin. At the post office and the library. At the train station and in the shops. Even at the police station and in the Castle, he had planted an Organization man, and God alone knew where else.

"You've no need to come with me, Mick."

Collins smiled broadly and clapped his friend heartily on the back.

"No friend of mine goes on a fool's errand like this one without a valiant companion at his back," he laughed. "Besides, I've never set eyes on the lady in question except in the newspapers. I've a mind to find out what all this to-do is about."

Kitty O'Neill bowed regally from the waist and soaked in gratefully the thunderous applause from the audience.

"No demure curtsies for me," she breathed to herself as the adulation filled her with a powerful elation. "Cathleen ni Houlihan is a far cry above curtsies." She smiled benevolently and scattered kisses with a gracious yet imperious gesture of the hand and lips. The audience responded adoringly. It was easy enough for them to confuse the actress and the part, she brought so much to the role.

"How in God's name does she do that?" whispered Mick, rising from his seat for the ovation, as had everyone around him in the theater, which was now thunderous with applause.

"You mean wrap us all around her finger?" Tahg replied with pride in his voice.

"I mean *become* the character, not just play it."

"She says she's never as alive when she's herself as when she's playing someone else. Sometimes I think that's part of the problem." His voice sounded less happy now and Mick looked quickly at the good-looking man at his side. He knew the lad was gaga over the actress . . . had been, in fact, since he was a boy. And that she'd led him a merry chase.

"She's not for the likes of us mere mortals, Tahg Mor," Collins laughed good-naturedly. "You'd be best off leaving her to the gods, or even to one of those fancified English lords she's always photographed with in the newspapers.

"I, on the other hand, happen to know of a pair of more than willing young ladies who'd show us the time of our lives if we'd encourage them in the least, now."

The tall, dark-haired young man smiled at his friend and commandant. His smile turned down just a fraction at the corners as had his father's, but he did not have his father's face. His hair was straight, not wavy, his eyes were the green of his mother's and there was a distance in them, despite the obvious camaraderie of the two men.

"Where do you go when you drift off like that?" Mick had once asked him in exasperation, just as his mother had in other times. For Tahg's eyes had a strange capacity to suddenly become veiled as a monk's, as if their owner was no longer at home to this world, but had traveled to another. Then, as now, the distance served to protect him.

"Thanks, Mick, for worrying about me," Tahg replied good-humoredly, "but I've got to talk to her before I leave the theater. I'll meet you at Delancey's in half an hour." Mick knew better than to argue with a man in love.

"You will not!" he laughed back, his square sturdy body already elbowing its way through the crowd. "I'm off to find a warm bosom to cushion my weary head. Palaver may be enough for you, lad, but I have more active needs in mind."

He waved and then melted invisibly into the crowd; it was a trick he had perfected while on the run. He could be visible one instant and gone the next, swallowed up somehow by his surroundings. The police claimed he used disguises to elude them, but Tahg knew better. Mick Collins simply knew how to disappear into a crowd, and he always had a safe harbor to go to.

"A hundred latchkeys, laddie." He'd laughed at Tahg's inquiry months before. "That's the ticket. The lovely ladies of Ireland take me in and hide me snug as a bug until the bloody Peelers give up on finding me."

Watching till the crowds dissipated, Tahg made his way toward the backstage door. There he marked time again patiently until the crowd of well-wishers dwindled; finally he knocked on the door of Kitty's dressing room.

"Who, now?" called the edgy voice within. He wondered if after the exhilaration of the performance and the praise, there must always be a letdown and exhaustion.

Kitty's eyes, when they turned on him, were at first insincere —the smile on her lips the static one she reserved for fans. Then she realized it was Tahg O'Connor she was seeing and a medley of emotions struggled for first place in her expressive face.

"I *knew* you were out there!" she said emphatically, a vulnerable sound in her voice. "I could *feel* you out there tonight."

He moved swiftly across the dressing room and gathered her into his arms. She had half risen to greet him and he lifted her the rest of the way out of the chair and held her gratefully, hard against his own body.

"A bloody long time it took you to get here . . ." she breathed between kisses, trying to sound angry.

"Aye. They were unpleasant at the camps about letting you go out to the theater."

"You've been out of the camp over two years," she managed to say.

"I wrote you."

"I never got the letters."

He wound his fingers in her hair and pulled her head back from his own to look at her.

"My God, how I've wanted this . . ." he said, and she could see the familiar clouding over in his eyes that always hid his deepest hurts from the world.

"Was it awful there?" she whispered, knowing the answer, unwilling to waste the time they could be kissing in, on speech.

"Not as bad as you'd think. I met a man named Collins. We became friends. We made plans . . ." He looked as if he would say more, then simply crushed her to him, as if afraid she'd be taken away.

Kitty pressed her body against the strength of his. "So much has happened to me since you've been gone, Tahg Mor. Why did it take you so long to come back? We have to talk." Why was she saying these things, feeling these things? she wondered. What room was there between them for love of the kind that always engulfed her when he was near.

"Aye. That we must. Everything's so confused. Right now I just need to hold you."

"And I need to be held," she replied, relieved. There was much to talk about, indeed, but none of it did she know how to say.

"I have my own flat now," she said finally. "We can go there."

He nodded, wonderingly. "I live with another actress, but she's not home tonight," she said quickly.

He nodded again.

Tahg watched while she dressed hurriedly behind the big battered screen, clothes flying to right and left for the wardrobe mistress to cope with. "Neat is something I'll never be, once I've got me a servant!" she'd said laughingly, long ago.

"Will I do?" she asked, emerging from the screen's recesses in a dark green gabardine suit with a tightly fitted jacket and long slender skirt. A peach-colored shirt with a frilly collar picked up the coppery glints of her hair and Tahg felt suddenly uncertain.

"What's the matter?" she asked snappishly, annoyed that the anticipated compliment had not been spoken.

"I don't know," he replied quietly. "You look so grand . . . so different from the little girl with the freckles. I guess you just seemed a little beyond me for a minute there."

"Oh, poppycock!" she responded, mollified that it was awe and not displeasure that had stayed him. "This is just the way successful actresses dress, you ninny!" Kitty stretched up to kiss Tahg on the lips and led him from the dressing room with conviction.

Tahg took off his jacket, loosened his collar and tie and watched as Kitty moved elegantly through the small but pretty flat.

"It belongs to another actress at the Abbey," she called over her shoulder, "but she's getting married in a month. She says I can have it, but I'll have to find another girl to share with me, or I'll never make the rent."

"My cousin Merry might be interested," answered Tahg quickly. "She's trying to get started as an actress and I think she's restless living with her sister."

Kitty stopped moving and came to sit down beside him on the little love seat that seemed far too small for his large frame. She touched his shaggy hair where it fell over his forehead and laughed a little.

"If your cousin lived here, I suppose we'd have to see each other all the time?"

Tahg reached his hand to her face and touched the smooth skin before replying. "If I had my way, I'd see you all the time with or without my cousin." There was a note of sadness in his voice.

"But you aren't staying long?" she prompted, disappointment apparent.

"I'll be in Dublin awhile. But never in one place too long," he said, watching her steadily as if to divine whether it mattered. With Kitty he was never sure.

"And you're involved in things I mustn't ask about . . . is that it?" she asked pointedly.

He nodded.

"Well then!" she said with forced good humor and a toss of her wavy mane. "Let's make the most of tonight. I know a lovely restaurant . . ."

"I haven't much money, Kitty."

"And what a surprise that is!" she responded sharply, then, immediately sorry, said, "It isn't at all expensive, really . . . just sweet and cozy. And the owner has been to my play three times already. We can have a quiet supper and then come back here, Sally won't be home tonight."

Seeing the question marks in his eyes, she said gently, "Three years is a long time, Tahg Mor, and I'm not a virgin, so you needn't worry about compromising me. You've been gone a long while. And I've had things to do . . . places to go. You know that. You've always known that."

Kitty seemed defensive in an unaccustomed way and her nervousness touched him, despite the jealousy that had surfaced at her confession. Of course she was a woman now, he told himself. A beautiful, desirable woman, with plans for herself that might not include an Organization man on the run.

"Ah, Kitty," he said tenderly, holding her eyes with his own. "We each have our own demons, girl, haven't we? You've your ambition and I my revenge. I just hope to God there's something left for us at the end of it. And it's grateful I am for any part of you along the way." It was said so earnestly, she felt tears start behind her eyes. Tahg was a good man, a kind and gentle man . . . perhaps the only one she would ever know.

"We'll make tonight so beautiful, we'll never forget it," she said emphatically, meaning it, and he gratefully took her into his embrace to seal the bargain.

* * *

Kitty lay blissfully happy in Tahg's arms and pondered the perversity of fate. Never, with any other man, had she felt anything as incredibly lovely as what had happened this night between them.

It was as if all the longings and hungers of her life had been sated in one glorious, breathtaking night of lovemaking. Passion she had felt before . . . passion and physical fulfillment. But this was so much more than that! Oh, so very much more.

She turned carefully, trying not to wake the slumbering man. A small smile still played at the corners of his sleeping mouth. Ah, mouth that could evoke such feelings, such desires.

Kitty reached up to touch his lips as if to prove to herself that they were real . . . he real . . . the astounding night gone by, real.

The man smiled as she touched him.

"I thought you were sleeping," she said, voice throaty and considerate.

"I just didn't want the night to end," he replied.

"And what's to happen to us now? You confuse me, always," she said ruefully.

"I know how you feel about the Organization, Kitty. But I'm in it up to my neck and I've got to see it through. They're good lads and they need me."

She nodded. "I'd tell you you're a damned fool if I thought it would do either of us any good, Tahg Mor. But we're star-crossed, you and I. I need so much that you can't give me. So . . . I need to get it for myself. And you, my friend . . . God alone knows what you need."

"I'm hardly in a position to offer you a life until this war is over, Kitty. But when it is, if I'm alive, I'm coming back for you."

"I'm seeing other men, Tahg. I'll not lie to you." She saw his dark brows knit together in a troubled frown.

"I suppose I can hardly ask you to save yourself for someone who may never come home at all," he said sadly.

"Don't say that!" she snapped. "Of course you'll come home. You know that I love you!"

"If you love me, why the other men?" he asked, sounding suddenly angry.

"Because I have to *have* things, Tahg. I have to learn about life! See what it can bring me. I can't act if I've never lived. And I *want* so many things.

"I'll be damned if I'll sit around for a lifetime waiting to see if the Organization will be sending you home in a box . . . while I sit with my poverty-stricken children in my poverty-stricken life and watch everything pass me by!

"Don't you see, Tahg Mor, I can't let myself believe that love is enough for me." She stopped as if she had run out of steam, then added, "And don't you fool yourself, laddie—it's not enough for you either. Or else you'd forget your stupid Organization and ask me to marry you and move away from here."

"And, if I did?"

Eloquently, she didn't reply.

"Ah, love," he said with a faint smile and a sigh. "Then we must be true to one another in our own fashion and see what comes of it, mustn't we?"

He tipped her bent head up to kiss her lips and saw that she was crying.

"Don't cry, little one," he said gently, brushing her loose hair back from her wet cheek. "It may all be all right for us one day."

He turned his body to cover hers on the bed and felt her arms go around him in an intensity of embrace that startled him. She was a strange girl, his Kitty O'Neill. A strange girl. But she was the only one he really wanted, when all was said and done. The only one.

Kitty felt unsteady on her feet after Tahg left. How still the apartment felt without his huge presence filling it. How empty life seemed suddenly, as if all the good had gone with him.

She touched her own body, disbelieving. *This was not like her* . . . not like her to be mooning after a man. It was they who mooned for her!

She touched her breasts and felt the memory of his caress. She felt the ache between her thighs, the deep loving ache of his absence and wanted to cry for it.

"Dear God!" she said aloud. "What am I doing to myself?" Thank heaven she didn't have to go to the theater this morning. As she thought it, she remembered Bridgie. This was Bridgie's day!

Kitty bathed and dressed hurriedly and, picking up the parcel from the table near the door, headed for the orphanage.

Bridgie McDermott had been three years old when her mother had died of poverty and sorrow, among other things. Aileen had been Kitty's best, or maybe only, friend in growing up. Kitty had been too popular with the boys for the girls to seek her out for friendship.

But not so with "Aileen, the gentle," as she had called her. Too gentle, indeed, to live after Jimmy left her and the child; too gentle to survive the poverty and the loneliness. So now all there was to show that gentle Aileen had ever lived at all was Bridgie.

Six years old she was, and made of sterner stuff than her mother had been. Maybe three years in an orphanage toughens you, although the sisters seemed kind enough. And they loved the child.

But then, how could anyone not love Bridgie McDermott? She was tall for her age and dark-haired, with alabaster skin and eyes like blue velvet. She was slender, but with a soft roundness that had always defied her meager diet. What a little beauty she was and how old for her age!

"You could adopt me, Kitty," Bridgie had said the last Saturday they were together. "The sister said so."

"And how could I adopt you, child?" she'd responded, aghast. "I'm not married and I'm not rich and my life at the theater takes up all my time."

"It's all right, Kitty," the child had replied, reading her. "Don't feel bad for me. The sisters are nice and all. I'm just very lonely for a family sometimes and you get lonely, too, so I thought we could be each other's family."

She had hugged the child then, not wanting her to see the tears. Who but Bridgie McDermott would ever think Kitty O'Neill was lonely for a family.

The Anglo-Irish War

Many can brook the weather that love not the wind.

WILLIAM SHAKESPEARE

11 Tahg raised himself warily from the dirt of the roadside. The firing had stopped. He could see a commanding officer in the settling dust ahead. The man appeared to be in his middle twenties, with darkish skin and darker hair. He was stockily built with a short, cocked nose and sharp gray eyes that were, at the moment, searching the debris for signs of resistance. It had to be Dan Breen, the man to whom Seaneen had entrusted the job of organizing the Tipperary Brigade.

Tahg had been on his way to Seaneen's headquarters when he'd gotten caught in the unexpected skirmish with the contingent of British soldiers and their cargo of explosives on their way to the garrison at Hollyford. A destination it would never reach now.

Tahg stood up and shook the dust from his clothes—and the sense of danger from his psyche. The peaceful-looking countryside had deceived him; he'd nearly driven into the ambush like an untrained recruit. It was a good lesson to be learned: never let your guard down for a single moment. Not in these times . . . not in Ireland.

"Tahg O'Connor," he said, introducing himself to Breen. "Out of Dublin headquarters. I'm on my way to see O'Sullivan. And Lady Manningham. She's my mother's sister."

Breen squinted up at him; he was several inches shorter than O'Connor and the dust glinting in the sunlight made sight uneasy. "I've heard about you, O'Connor," he said. "You're one of Collins's boys."

Tahg thought he heard a slight belligerence in the statement, and wondered why.

"Can you tell me the way?" he asked.

"Timmy here is going up there now. You can follow him if you'd like."

Tahg nodded his thanks and followed the boy on the rickety bicycle up the road. This was the first inkling he'd had that Mick might not be as popular with the men under his command in the field as with those in Dublin. It would bear looking into.

☙ "Tahg!" I shouted as I saw my nephew coming up the hill to the house. I'd been on the lookout for Timmy with news of the convoy from Dan, but Tahg's tall form was the one I spotted first.

My God, but he looked handsome; it gave my heart a jolt to see how closely he resembled Tierney in that moment. Only when he'd come close enough for me to see his face clearly was the difference discernible.

"Oh, my dear Tahg," I breathed, to Timmy's extreme embarrassment, as I fairly threw myself into my nephew's arms.

"Quite a welcome you've prepared for me, Aunt Beth," he said, laughing as I hugged him.

I took him by the hand and led him into the cottage.

Seaneen, too, embraced him. And we settled in to tea and talk.

"I happened onto one of your little exercises," said Tahg to Seaneen.

"Aye, I thought as much from the scent of explosives in your clothes. You know, it's amazing how a man learns to rely on his other senses when his sight is gone."

"I take it that little rows like that one are frequent."

"Becoming more so," replied Seaneen with enthusiasm. "We're making our presence known to them. And they, in turn, call everything they do to us a reprisal—whether there's anything to retaliate against or not. The more nervous we make them, the more aggressive they become, lad. They've started storming into cottages, rousting the people from their beds, tearing things up looking for guns. The more of that kind of thing they do, the more the people will come over to our way of thinking. We're only a half step away from a war with them, you know."

"But what's the news from Dublin?" asked Seaneen. It was the question on both our minds.

"The Dail's been declared illegal," Tahg said. "Sinn Fein, the Volunteers, the Gaelic League and the Cumann na mBan have all been suppressed by proclamation."

"Aye," said Seaneen. "It was to be expected in a state of war. What does Brugha say about it, as Defense Minister?"

"You know Brugha. He's a physical-force man all the way. I just hope he and Mick stay out of each other's way. Mick's a brilliant strategist, but he doesn't work well in double harness."

"And Mick's plans—how are they progressing?" asked Seaneen with great interest.

"Like clockwork. His intelligence network is a thing of beauty. You can expect the fur to start to fly any day now. He's turned the tables on them, just as he said he would. I swear to you, Seaneen, we've got a man of our own in every sensitive spot in Ireland. When Mick starts to tighten the noose, they'll feel the squeeze."

Seaneen nodded, understandingly. "It's working well in the brigades, too," he said knowledgeably. "We hit them at the garrisons, or the convoys, then disappear into the landscape. For once we've turned having to fight on our home soil to our own advantage."

Tahg smiled his assent. "That was Mick's plan from the first, Seaneen. Guerrilla warfare . . . no standing army. Hit and run. It's a stroke of genius."

"Hmmm," grunted Seaneen noncommittally, "like all good ideas you'll find plenty of men fighting to take credit for it. Tell Mick to look to his flanks. The men who run the brigades have some genius of their own, you know, and it's hard for a commander in the trenches to give real credit to the one in the armchair."

Tahg looked startled at Seaneen's implication. "Are you saying there's bad feeling in the field toward Mick?" he asked.

"No," replied Seaneen, judiciously. "I'm saying he's in charge of the purse strings as Finance Minister. Which means he's the one who says no to requisitions and such. *And* he's in Dublin, out of the line of fire.

"What I'm giving voice to is an old man's instinct, laddie. Tell him to make sure others are as loyal to him as he is to them."

"I hear you, Seaneen," Tahg responded. "Thanks for the sage advice."

"No charge at all," answered Seaneen with a smile.

We talked the night away about all that was afoot, and Tahg

left early the next morning to check out the other command posts, with some fertile seeds taking root in his brain. ✍

The two women stood in the doorway for a moment, silently sizing each other up. Merry was startled by the remarkable beauty of the girl she had heard so much about over the years from Tahg. She had seen her once onstage, but close up her aura was truly overwhelming. No wonder people all over Dublin were talking about her performances at the Abbey. Her presence was charismatic, startling. If it were not for the woman's obvious earthiness, she would have seemed too lovely to be real.

Kitty stared back at Merry. She saw a young woman possessed by nature of all that she herself had wished to embody. Merry was carelessly elegant, as if no effort went into her perfect poise and dignity. She was stately beyond her years. Obviously aristocratic, and yet there was a softness about her that was not forbidding. Instead she seemed winsome and warm as she held out her hand to Kitty impulsively.

"You are very kind to see me," Merry said. "I feel a little awestruck meeting you after seeing your performance on Monday."

"You were at the theater?"

"Oh, yes! You see I'm desperate to learn what I can. I've wanted to act as long as I can remember, but there's been little chance to learn at home." Merry paused for a moment, then said, "You were absolutely wonderful as the Countess Cathleen. I've always dreamt someone would play her that way."

Kitty felt herself warmed by the compliments. They seemed genuine enough. If there was one thing she didn't want in a roommate it was a know-it-all toff who treated her with condescension. But this girl didn't seem like that at all. If anything, she appeared to be trying to please.

"Come in, come in," Kitty said. "No point our standing in the hall, I suppose."

Merry glided into the flat and Kitty examined the particulars that made up the lovely whole as the girl took off her hat and gloves.

"This isn't exactly what you're used to," Kitty said suddenly, cursing her own belligerent tone when she heard it.

"No," answered Merry, "this seems infinitely more cheery and free."

"I meant, it's hardly a manor house like Manningham Castle."

"I know," said Merry, smiling, "but you see, there's been so little happiness around the Castle these last few years that I think of it as having a great black cloud that hovers over the poor old place."

"Why is that?" asked Kitty warily. She was beginning to like this person despite her determination not to.

Merry sat on the small love seat and thought a moment before replying.

"Do you know how little girls always fantasize about what life would be like if their mum disappeared and they had their father all to themselves?"

Kitty nodded.

"Well, in our case, that really happened. Our mother left us, as I'm sure Tahg has told you—and things were very different from the fantasy, I'm afraid.

"My father became more withdrawn and inaccessible, my brother Winston more self centered, and then Jamie—he's my twin, you see, and we're ever so close—he left to go to school and never really came back. That leaves my sister Angelica, with whom I've been living since I came here, and myself—and we've never really been close.

"Somehow we've just never been a family since Mum left. Not that we were a perfect group before, mind you, but somehow she could always mend things enough so that we felt like part of a loving whole . . ." Merry stopped speaking, as if she'd run out of explanation, but there was a poignancy in the silence, as if she wished she understood better what had happened to them all.

Kitty sat down beside her.

"Funny," she said, "I felt the same way when Mam died. As if the lights had gone out all over the world."

Merry looked up to see that there was moisture in the other girl's eyes. It was odd in one who had seemed so self-assured on stage.

"Perhaps we have more in common than we know," she said softly.

"I don't suppose the rent will be a problem for you?" Kitty ventured, covering her own lapse by changing the subject.

Merry laughed, the contagious bubbly laughter that had assured her of her nickname.

"Lord no," she replied. "Money's one thing I've got in abundance."

"Well," laughed Kitty, infected by the girl's good humor, "that'll be a novel thing around here!"

They made arrangements for the sharing of the flat and each felt more content at the prospect than either had dreamed possible.

12

Lady Merrion Manningham
26 Gardiner Street Upper
Dublin

2 February 1920

My dear Mum,

Life in Dublin is delicious. The theater people are so exciting I feel like a child in a candy store each day that I arrive there.

And I am learning; Kitty has been a grand teacher, reading parts with me, giving me pointers. She's a hard taskmaster, but she is so gifted that you accept that whatever she is demanding makes perfect sense—so you gird your loins and try to measure up.

She is the strangest girl I've ever met—perhaps because I've never known anyone before who has been so poor. Thousands of warring elements seem to make up her persona. Poverty terrifies her so that she spends her entire life in flight from it. I believe she would do anything, give anything, suffer anything for all that I've taken for granted all my life.

Yet I like her—and I can see why Tahg is so damnably attracted to her—moth to flame, it seems, an all the more likely metaphor because of her hair and her astonishing incandescence.

She can be rude, imperious, selfish, snappish and generally beastly—but she can also be patient, loving, helpful and loyal. I couldn't be gladder that she has taken me in —the experience of living with Kitty for a month is as fruitful as living with ten others for a decade.

By the way, there is a small child named Bridgie—the orphan of a childhood friend of Kitty's—whom she frequently visits at the orphanage. Can you imagine? It's all quite like a story. But then so are our lives, dear Mum.

How is Johnny faring with Mr. O'Sullivan? I know I needn't ask about you, as your letters are bubbling over with happiness. I only regret that I never had the chance to see you so happy when we were together. Know that I always wished you joy, so that no matter what anyone says, I applaud you for your courage in grasping life when the chance came.

I am trying to do the same. I shall write and tell you everything, so that you will know all.

Give Johnny a hug for me, and tell him his big sister misses him. I shall send you both tickets for my first good performance.

> All my love, as ever,
> Merry

> 3rd Tipperary Brigade
> Ballingarry, Co. Tipperary
> April 10, 1920

Dearest Merry-O,

Can you believe this poor old country? War on every side: hungry, miserable people asking for no more than to be free.

At least I'm finally able to do my bit. Seaneen says I'm the best shot around here and I'm learning about explosives. Johnny Gelignite, they're calling me. Well at least it's better than Manningham.

Mum is happy here—you wouldn't know her. She walks around singing and humming all the time. Of

course, what woman wouldn't be happy with a hero like
Seaneen O'Sullivan as her man?

Did you know that Aunt Con and Uncle Tierney are
almost legends now? And the Wild Harp essays and poems are like national treasures? I guess I got born into the
right family after all, eh?

Glad to hear that you are getting to be such a glamour
girl at the theater. Who would believe a homely old thing
like you could be a famous actress! Send me a ticket one
of these days and maybe Mum will let me come to Dublin to see you.

Keep on writing to me, Merry-O. You're the only cement that keeps this family holding together. Give my
love to Jamie and ask Angelica if she remembers she has
a little brother. Don't bother to mention me to Win—
he'll be hearing from me soon enough once the war
comes and I've finished my training.

You know I love you.

> Your brother,
> Sean (alias Johnny)

P.S. I'm thinking of calling myself Sean from now on. A
lot of the men are taking Irish names instead of Anglicized ones. What do you think?

Merry put down the letter with tears in her eyes. Johnny
Gelignite—how terrible and how ironic. An explosion waiting
to happen, that's what he was, a tragedy in the making.

"Poor baby," she said aloud. He'd had such a rotten go with
Father, and with Win. Why, oh why had they always treated
him as a stranger? It had never made the least sense to the rest
of them.

At least he seemed happy with Mr. O'Sullivan and Mum. But
Johnny and guns, Johnny and gelignite. What a ghastly combination for destruction.

Merry burned the letter in the hearth as she had been instructed by her brother to do. Every action of his life was that
of the revolutionary. Of course he worshiped Aunt Con and
Uncle Tierney. Hadn't they been martyrs to the cause he
served?

But they hadn't been like Johnny. They had been reluctant to battle, pushed there by fate. Mum had said so. You could read it in their letters to each other.

No. They hadn't been like Johnny. No one was like Johnny.

Gifted, troubled intellect. Anger to fill an ocean; anger that never really dissipated. And dissatisfaction with everything in life, so that nothing but Mum and Mr. O'Sullivan ever measured up to his exacting standard.

None of them had ever blamed him really. How could a child survive rejection of the sort he'd had without damage? That was why he'd been everybody's special pet, she supposed. That, and the fact that he'd been the baby.

How strange it was that this obsession with Ireland had been with him from the cradle. How could that have happened? Could it have been some strange legacy from Con and Tierney and Desmond? Could it be as Father said, that the FitzGibbons were tainted with some Irish curse that sought its victims in every generation? Or could it be that he was not their father's child at all, as she and Jamie had sometimes whispered to each other, not willing to say such a fearsome thing aloud?

Cement he had called her. Well, that wasn't far off the mark. If Jamie was the balm, she was the cement. The one who wrote to all the others, keeping them connected, however tenuously.

Merry watched the ashes of her brother's letter curl and twist into ash. She hated burning them, hated any act of destruction. At heart she was as much a pacifist as her twin.

How could so many extremes exist in one family? she wondered. Winston archly conservative, Jamie a peacemaker, Johnny a revolutionary. Not a moderate among them except for herself and the enigmatic Angelica. No one really knew who *she* might have been had it not been for the accident. Maybe the most adventurous of them all.

Which reminded her that she must see Angelica tomorrow. She hated to let more than a week go by without a visit to her sister. Cement, indeed.

Merry sighed and sat at the small table by the window that faced the street. She used it as a writing table for her endless family correspondence.

Picking up a blank, creamy sheet, she wrote, "Dearest Johnny . . ." then she stopped to wonder if she should call him Sean to please him. "No," she said firmly, aloud, then wrote:

You will always be my little Johnny—call yourself what you will. I have too many memories of you tied up in that name to let you whisk it away on a whim.

Merrion Manningham had the kind of privileged porcelain beauty that interfered with her being taken seriously. Men tended to look into her blue-violet eyes and go no further in their quest for what lay beneath.

She was a good-natured girl who laughed easily and smiled more often than need be. Life had treated her gently in many ways, not least of which was the cushion of love that her twin brother had always provided.

Merry's first year in Dublin had been a coming of age, improved greatly by having Kitty O'Neill to show her the ropes. Kitty, who was so wise and cynical in some ways and so vulnerable in others. Kitty, who could transport you to Elysian fields with her great gifts and her thrilling voice.

Merry missed home and family—the great womb of Manningham, with its quiet-footed servants and its orderly routine of privilege, lurked always somewhere in her mind. She missed her brother's soft, protective love and the safety that her siblings had provided, no matter how diverse and prickly they could be at times.

But there was really no home to go back to now, she supposed. Her mother had been the heart of home; she'd never realized it fully until she wasn't there. She thought she'd write her mother one day and tell her of that realization.

Her father was in England; her sister Angelica and brother Jamie she saw often, of course, in Dublin, but her brother Johnny she hadn't seen since he'd left with Mum. She was actually glad that Win was coming to see her on his Dublin holiday —and he was by far her least favorite among her brothers and sister.

No. There was no home left at Manningham now. Her flat with Kitty was home, and the theater was family. There at least she felt safe and loved. The lights, the music, the plays, the people . . . everything about the theater was like coming home.

Winston and his two chums knocked cheerfully on the dressing-room door. They were in high spirits. The trip to Dublin had been better than good. The accommodations at the Gresham excellent, night life decidedly friendly. The city was even more robust than Winston had remembered. He was looking forward to his new appointment at Dublin Castle; it was a prize plum of an opportunity.

And tonight, going to the theater to see Merry, had been the perfect touch. He'd been damned impressed by his sister's performance; more than competent, she was. Not the equal of that extraordinary redheaded O'Neill girl, of course. But more than competent.

"Come in," said a lively voice from within, and the three young men did so.

"Win, dear," said Merry with pleasure as she rose to greet her brother. "What a delicious surprise!" She hugged him warmly, then waited to be introduced to his friends.

As they all chatted amiably, the door from the next dressing room opened and Kitty burst in, her hair piled high on her willful head, a bathrobe thrown casually over her slip.

"I've quite run out of cold cream, love . . ." she began, then, seeing that Merry was not alone, stopped, composed herself and began again. "I'm so sorry. I had no idea you were entertaining three handsome men in your dressing room, my dear," she offered, her stage voice having replaced the more normal one.

Merry laughed musically.

"Kitty O'Neill, I'd like you to meet my brother, Winston Manningham, and his friends Major Henry Jameson and Christopher Belmont-Chapman, Marquis of Darborough. Gentlemen . . . my esteemed roommate, friend and, of course, the star of our play . . . Kitty O'Neill."

She watched with amusement as Kitty and Winston sized each other up; the expression on Kitty's face one of calculation, on Winston's one of pure pleasure.

"To say that I am delighted would hardly cover my feelings at the moment, Miss O'Neill," said Win in his most courtly manner.

"You are too kind, My Lord," answered Kitty, regally, in the voice she generally reserved for Shakespeare; as she did so she held out her hand in a graceful gesture.

"See here, Manningham," interjected Jameson, "you're not the only one who enjoyed the ladies' performances tonight, you know. Why don't we see if these two charming young ladies would do us the honor of dining with us this evening in celebration."

"Oh, indeed, yes!" put in Christopher Belmont-Chapman, a pleasant-looking young man with fair hair and an elegant self-assurance. "Do consider it. We were quite overwhelmed by your performances and we'd be so pleased to have you join us."

Merry smiled prettily at his invitation. "We'd be delighted to dine with you tonight, My Lord," she replied graciously. "Wouldn't we, Kitty?" She turned to see Kitty and Win still staring at each other, whether because of attraction or some other fascination, she couldn't be sure.

13 ∽ The advertisements began appearing in all the newspapers early in 1920; they were succinct and enticing. Applications were being accepted, they said, for new recruits in the Royal Irish Constabulary. The pay was £3.10.0 a week and previous police experience was unnecessary.

The streets of cities in England and Ireland were teeming with the jobless; so many men had returned from war to find no employment that the ads met with immediate success. Men flocked to the recruitment offices.

Indeed, so many of them appeared on such short notice that it became impossible to clothe them all in proper uniforms; khaki service trousers were mated with constabulary caps and blouses of a green color, so dark it seemed black. These hybrid uniforms recalled for some irreverent wit the name of a pack of famous hunting dogs in Limerick. And thus the new military police force was christened the Black and Tans.

The new troops arrived in Ireland on March 25, 1920. In July they were joined by a contingent of Auxiliaries (or Auxies) who were all ex-officers of the Great 1914 War. Like the enlisted men, many of these officers had found themselves unemployed after the armistice. Although both groups together were to form a military police force, neither was subject to the stern military discipline such a force should have called for.

The hit-and-run guerrilla tactics of the brigades and the

methodical assassination of the Castle's spies had caused wholesale panic among the government leaders in England. They wished to retaliate sternly. The Black and Tans and the Auxies would fulfill their wish.

The summer of 1920 was a strange time for me as a woman. Seaneen, Dan Breen, Seamus Robinson and Sean Treacy were the forces behind the 3rd Tipperary Brigade, which was destined to go down in history as one of the most valiant and important brigades of the war. And, of course, I was there in the midst of their escalating activities.

Tipperary was alive with Black and Tans and Auxiliaries by late June; the sound of gunfire was becoming as ordinary to me as the sounds of birdsong had once been. Because of his sight, Seaneen couldn't participate in the actual fighting. Breen, Treacy and Robinson led the flying columns when they swooped in to do battle. As with all fighting men, it was a great loss to Seaneen that he could only plan the strategies but must leave the glory of achieving the victories to others. Breen, Treacy and Robinson were young men in their twenties, and Seaneen was more than twice their age. To their credit, they listened avidly to his wisdom, but the victories were theirs, not his.

As a "wife" in all but legal name, I watched and listened and helped where I could. But the kind of danger and anxiety that the men around me were able to endure and grow strong on took a great toll of me.

Men find a pleasure in warfare, I discerned; even the desperate danger of it sends their blood racing. Add to this the exhilaration of a noble cause, and they glory in the fray. This perverse pleasure seems to mitigate their suffering, somehow—and suffering there was. Nursing wounded men was a part of my daily routine by summer, and rations were low to nonexistent.

These men of the 3rd Tipp Brigade were not professional soldiers . . . they were farm boys and fishermen, of varied talents and ambitions. They did not *want* to go out and risk their bodies on a fight that had been predestined hundreds of years before they were even conceived, I told myself. And yet, they took to what was asked of them with an instinct that astounded me. Is it genetic, this gift for warfare, in the male? . . . I asked the question a thousand times that summer. Is there some component in their blood that fits them so readily for fighting? Or are they simply so noble by nature that they protect home and hearth and loved ones no matter the cost to themselves?

One thing I know. Men take to war like ducks to a pond; to the camaraderie and the boisterousness, to the tactics and the strategies, to the danger and the mayhem. We women have no such built-in connection.

I loved Seaneen with an almost ludicrous intensity, but to me, always, the war remained an incomprehensible horror. Ruth among the alien corn, I felt myself to be that year; caught in a whirlwind I couldn't change or control.

Had it only been Seaneen and me at stake, perhaps I would have been less introspective. Maybe then I would have been so lost in my love for him, and so happy at the freedom I had finally achieved, that I would have ignored the insanity around me and accepted our personal happiness as a gift from God. But I was also a mother, and watching Johnny grow into a soldier gave me much food for thought that was indigestible.

I could accept the fact that Johnny participated in military actions, despite his age. In truth, he was far from the only fourteen-year-old in Ireland who was doing his part. What troubled me was that he was in his glory; he had come into his own. There were visible changes in my son.

Whereas in the beginning of our stay in Tipperary he had followed Seaneen endlessly, worshipfully—now he struggled to impress his father with his burgeoning manhood. Johnny strove to be *best* at everything he set his hand to—the best shot, the best with explosives. And he had a gift for it. So said Seaneen. So said they all.

Finally, there seemed a place where his combustible temper could find an outlet. Finally, there was an enemy worthy of the anger he had stored so long.

He loved me well enough, this last son of mine, and God knows he followed Seaneen's lead in treating me with courtly courtesy—but his father was his universe. In Seaneen he had a kindred soul; in Seaneen's war, he had found the only peace he'd ever known.

But in my mother's heart I felt a prickle of fear that seemed to grow more persistent as Johnny approached manhood. It is fine to *say* that your child has found his destiny and grown content in it. But if that destiny is a dangerous one, have you done him any favor in helping him find his way there? If your child loved fire, would you give him matches to make him more content?

So I watched with misgivings these two I loved so desperately. Comradely warriors they seemed that summer, Seaneen infusing all his knowledge into a willing vessel, Johnny soaking up each drop of learning as if all life depended on it.

He had grown physically, too, in that year between thirteen and fourteen. It was apparent that he would duplicate his father's stature, as well as everything else about him. He had waxed tough and stocky under the harsh disciplines of soldiering. If the others drilled and trained for five hours, Johnny drilled and trained for six; it was little wonder that his shoulders broadened and his form filled out. He had grown handsome and confident and very manly.

He was liked well enough by the Volunteers. I counted that a positive sign, for they were good and honorable men.

But the danger prickled within me. We were at war now, in no uncertain terms. Houses were being burned, fathers and sons dragged off to jail on mere suspicion of possessing firearms. The Black and Tans had added a new dimension to the battle. They were undisciplined and given to excesses of butchery. The RIC had grown desperate, it seemed, and had issued orders to its commanding officers that they turn a blind eye to the outrages.

It would have been easier to simply hate the RIC en masse. But somehow knowing there were good men and true among them made it harder. What poignantly divided loyalties this war had forced upon everyone in Ireland! In a way, the excesses of the Black and Tans as the year wore on solved this dilemma for me. Between May and the end of July, 556 RIC resignations were handed in; 800 Black and Tans replaced them. About the Black and Tans there could be no question. They were bad, through and through. ✍

14 Mick Collins tucked the small bouquet of flowers behind his back and rang the doorbell. He could hear the rattle of the wheelchair coming down the hallway even as the uniformed servant opened the door.

He gave his cap and scarf to the maid and made his way to Angelica's study.

"And there you are, my proud beauty," he laughed out when he saw her.

"Go on with you, lad," she responded in her best Dublin street accent. "Sure, you're a sight for sore eyes."

He walked briskly up to the chair and kissed her on the cheek, then, kneeling in a mock ceremonial pose before her, pulled the flowers out from their hiding place and showed them to her.

"Oh, Mick," she said in her own voice again. "You are good to me!" She sounded as pleased as a child at the token gift.

Collins smiled at the girl as he rose again to his feet.

"I've missed you," he said seriously.

"And I you," she replied. "How goes it?"

"Well enough. We've put them on notice that we're onto them."

"The hounds and the hare have traded places for a change, eh?"

He nodded, but she saw that something else was on his mind.

"I'm a bit concerned about your cousin, Tahg Mor," he said.

"This Kitty business or the Organization?"

"Both, I suppose. He's off his feed. Not himself. He's daft in love with that redheaded witch, you know."

Angelica smiled at the description. "He's bewitched, all right. But can you really blame him? She's the toast of Dublin. And judging from the accounts in the press, he's not the only man she's bewitched."

"True enough," he said, leaning his broad back comfortably against the corner cushion of the sofa. There was something so relaxed in the gesture that Angelica felt once again a sense of the complications of the man. At one moment he could seem utterly made of steel . . . emotionless, in control. At another he could be a rollicking, gasconading charmer; always, he was heroic and mysterious. Now he seemed simply a pleasant friend, come to call.

"How long do you think the finance offices will be safe from the Tans?" she asked, to change the subject. Tahg's infatuation with Kitty was something no amount of discussion would alter. And they both knew it.

"Mary Street and St. Andrew Street look innocuous enough to be safe from them for a while. You know we've painted fine false names on the doors and taken great pains to look respectable.

"I've a new place, too, on the South Side. Only Tahg and a couple of the others even know it exists. I think of it as my 'war office.' " He laughed shortly as he said it.

"I've moved out of the Munster Hotel, too, you know," he said, sounding rueful. "And it's sorry I am about having to do it. Mrs. McCarthy, God bless her sweet soul, still looks after my laundry for me, so at least I've a change of underwear every Sunday." He laughed good-naturedly. "A man learns to travel light when there's a price on his head."

"How close have they come to finding you, Mick?"

"Since they put the price on my head, they've nearly had me half a dozen times. My guardian angel will be putting in for overtime wages if I'm not careful."

She eyed him thoughtfully. "Is it worth it, my friend? Can you really beat them?"

He leaned forward, his elbows on his knees, a look of excitement on his likable face. "Do you know, lass, it's the strangest thing—the worse it gets, the closer we come to beating them. We've got them on the run now. I feel it in my gut! The Black and Tans and the Auxies are their last colonial gasp.

"We've fixed it so their spies are afraid to spy for them for fear of being shot in their beds. They can't send a shipment of ammunition to a single barracks in Ireland and be certain it'll get through. The men in the brigades have the county garrisons scared of their own shadows. That's why the brutality is escalating! That's why they're letting the Black and Tans pillage with impunity. They're scared, Angelica! Scared witless! A few more months of this and they'll negotiate. You'll see. They'll be forced to give us our day in court!" Mick pounded one fist onto the other palm for emphasis, his dark brows scowling over eyes alive with the force of what he was saying.

"But can you hold out long enough, Mick? Tahg says you're short on money, and these endless skirmishes must be costing a bloody fortune."

"You're right about that, Angelica. In fact, I'm thinking of sending O'Connor out on another reconnaissance mission to the commandants of the brigades to see how they're really faring out there. They all seem to think we've a purse as big as the British Foreign Office, from the looks of what they try to requisition from us. And there are a few of them out there who are none too keen on me as the finance officer.

"I need to know how it lies with them. I can rely on Seaneen for the straight story at least. For the others . . . Tahg will have a chance to test his own diplomatic skills."

"If his diplomacy works on the brigades, maybe it'll work on Kitty O'Neill too, do you suppose?" Angelica mused mischievously.

"We'd best hope not. For if he got her, it would be the worst thing that could happen to him," Mick replied seriously.

"Why ever do you say that?" asked Angelica, surprised by the hostility in Collins's tone. "Do you dislike her so much?"

"Sure, I don't know the woman enough to dislike her. And I think she's the most gorgeous thing I've ever set eyes on—to tell you the truth. My comment had nothing to do with her at all. It has to do with the fact that there's nothing worse for a man on the run than being in love." His intense expression said that he was trying to figure out how to make her understand.

"You see, Angelica Manningham, when you're running, you must be selfish. Eyes in the back of your head . . . ears that hear sounds small dogs would be deaf to. You learn the safe sounds and the ones that bode danger, you know? You learn not to sleep in a place until you know its sounds like you know your own heartbeat.

"You must concentrate on two things only—your mission and staying alive. If your concentration is broken . . . if you're worried about the woman you love . . . and it's damned hard not to worry about one such as Kitty O'Neill, let me tell you—you're a dead man."

"You're worried about Tahg, Mick. Is there a special reason why you're more worried tonight than usual?"

He nodded unhappily. "They're closing in, lass. There are so goddamned many of them. And they're closing in. We're about to hurt them badly, and they'll pay us back in kind. I can feel it coming. There's a powerful explosion in the wind—after that, there's hope of parley.

"I just want to make sure the people I care most about make it through the explosion. I've got word from my man at the Castle that your brother Winston has set himself up as some sort of expert on Mick Collins and his 'team of executioners.' We're going to have to be doubly careful it seems. The word is he's smart and conscienceless." Angelica thought about that description of her brother . . . it was probably no more than true.

Angelica pondered all that Mick had said long after he'd gone. She'd known about Win's new job for less than a day herself. Collins's network of informants was staggering No one knew the situation in Ireland better than he. If he said an explosion was imminent, it was time to put on your protective clothing. She knew the operation scheduled for Sunday would be a dangerous one.

She made a mental note to check with Merry about what was going on between Tahg and Kitty, and with Father to find out about Win. How strange it was that in the midst of war, the rest of life went on nonetheless. Love, hates, personal squabbles and jealousies. She thanked God inwardly that Winston didn't know about Tahg and Kitty. He'd be capable of some grotesque retribution if he knew; he'd always hated Tahg and been jealous of him.

Angelica went to sleep with jumbled images of all their family engaged in some ludicrous gavotte on destiny's dance floor. It was a very disturbing image.

Eleven men were marked for death. Eleven British Army spies who had been responsible for sending good men to death or to torture.

Tahg and each of the others had their orders. The assassinations were to take place simultaneously at 9 A.M. Eleven houses entered, eleven dead men left behind. Tahg checked his revolver and ammunition mechanically; he was an expert in firearms now and did it with an expert's intense concentration.

He knew these men had to die. Just as *they* had probably felt that the men they had condemned were worthy of being sent to their deaths. Queer work for a Sunday, he thought as he heard the church bells toll the seven o'clock mass at the Pro Cathedral. Queer work for any day.

Tahg slipped into the last pew at the back of the Carmelite Church of St. Teresa near Grafton Street and, blessing himself rapidly, knelt with his two hands covering his face.

He felt grief for what he had done. Not remorse, for he believed that the men they'd executed had more than merited that fate. Cowardly men they were, spying and sending others to death or torture from afar, never dirtying their own hands with the deed.

But grief, nonetheless. For the dead men and their families— and for the squad of executioners, too, who would carry the guilt of it with them to the Judgment Seat.

Seeing a priest walk silently up the aisle, Tahg reached out and touched the sleeve of his cassock. "Will you hear my confession, Father?" he asked hesitantly. The priest looked carefully at the young man, then nodded. The hearing of confessions on Sunday was not normal.

"Bless me, Father," said Tahg with difficulty, once inside the confessional. "For I have sinned."

He saw the silhouetted face and shoulders of the priest through the shadowed screen that separated them. He wasn't sure why he'd come here. The IRA was under the church's ban. They'd all been excommunicated en masse by the bishops. Yet today, for some reason, he needed to be here.

Tahg saw the priest's head nod, a signal for him to begin.

"I killed two men today, Father," he began. "I'm not at all sure you should give me absolution, for I'd do it again if I had the same orders. But I needed to come here . . ." He let the thought trail off, not knowing what more there was to say.

He heard the priest move uneasily within the confines of the small confessional booth, heard the bench he was seated on squeak with his movement.

"You were under orders, you say?" the priest finally replied.

"Aye, I was."

"And did you, to the best ability of your conscience, do what you thought was right as an act of war?"

"I did, Father."

"Good man," said the priest unexpectedly. "Say the rosary for the repose of their souls and make a good act of contrition."

Astonished by the priest's response, Tahg began the familiar prayer for forgiveness: "Oh my God, I am heartily sorry for having offended Thee . . ." He had expected threats of hellfire and damnation—would have felt better, in fact, if they had been forthcoming.

". . . and I detest all my sins, because I dread the loss of Heaven and the pains of Hell, but most of all because I have offended Thee, my God . . ."

Tahg heard the little door slide shut and the drone of voices from the other side begin.

Bewildered, shaken, he let himself out of the confessional and the church, walking uncertainly back onto the street. What a strange, unexpected interlude that had been, he thought, making his way toward headquarters. What madness had prompted him to go to confession after so long; what madness had prompted the priest to give him absolution? Could it be that not even God was sure of the right and wrong of what went on in war? He shook loose of the heretical thought and headed for Mick.

Dublin's Croke Park was crowded with Sunday sports enthusiasts. The Gaelic football match between Dublin and Tipperary would be a rouser. The crowd, unaware of the deaths of eleven RIC informers, went happily about their business of enjoying an afternoon's outing.

Kitty and Bridgie had planned a picnic in the park but Kitty had no intention of staying for the game.

"I never saw a football match," cried Bridgie excitedly, as they drew near to the field on their stroll. "Could we watch it? Kitty, please, just for a minute!"

"Just for a minute, love," Kitty responded. She had no interest in football or any other sport, but the child seemed so delighted, it was hard to refuse.

The authorities had intended to search the crowd for IRA gunmen as a precaution. But that was before the events of the morning had taken place. Now eleven men were dead; both

RIC and Auxies were in an ugly mood as they moved in to surround the playing field.

Where the first shot came from, no one knew. The sickening sound of rifle fire and rending flesh is unfamiliar to nonmilitary ears. Even as the woman and child next to her crumpled, and Bridgie began to scream at the bloody mess they had been splattered with, Kitty could barely understand what was happening around her.

Gunshots everywhere. People falling, stampeding, screaming in terror. "Bridgie!" she shrieked as the crush of the crowd pulled the screaming child away from her.

"Kitty! Help me!" the little girl screamed back, caught in a tangle of adult legs and bodies.

Lunging through the insane fleeing crowd, Kitty grabbed for Bridgie and, catching the child against her own body, tried to fight her way out of the mix of dying soldiers and civilians.

Twelve were dead and sixty wounded by the time she clawed their way out of the madness and stood shaking and sobbing on the outskirts of the decimated crowd, Bridgie still grappled to her chest and crying uncontrollably.

Two of Collins's officers, Richard McKee and Peadar Clancy, who had been picked up in a raid twenty-four hours before, and a man named Clune, who had just happened to be in Vaughan's Hotel when they were, looked at each other wonderingly as they were dragged from their cells to the guard room at Dublin Castle.

They had no way of knowing the events of the rest of the day, but the fury on the guards' faces left little room for doubt about what was about to happen to them.

"What are you going to do to us?" asked Clune, fear in his voice.

"You're about to be shot trying to escape," said the sergeant who entered the room behind them. He nodded to the two men with him. Fifteen shots later, the three lay dead at his feet, riddled with enough bullets to have killed three times their number.

Bloody Sunday had come, at last, to an end.

15 Winston Manningham walked pleasantly across Parnell Square and turned the corner into what was sometimes called "Playwright's Territory." He was going to visit his sister Merry. Or rather he was using a visit to Merry as an excuse to see the incredible Kitty O'Neill.

She had caught his fancy that first night at the theater unexpectedly, her haughty auburn head held higher than need be, her mellifluous voice sending a chill of pleasure through his brain; he'd not been able to get her out of his mind. *There* was a girl to lead a man a merry chase, he suspected. What a stroke of good luck it was that his sister had chanced to move in with Kitty.

Winston whistled cheerily as he walked toward his destination. He'd always had inordinately good luck with girls, even without making much effort in that direction. He had no doubt whatsoever that Miss Kitty O'Neill would succumb to his many charms before too long.

Now that he was to be permanently back in Dublin, he'd have time to pursue her. What a stroke of luck it was that he'd been given just the job at the Castle that he'd had in mind for himself. He had studied the possibilities there very carefully and finally come to a conclusion. Michael Collins was the man who was causing more havoc than any other in this damnable war.

By placing himself correctly, he'd be in a perfect position to pursue the man. Not physically, of course. That would be up to the Secret Police.

But someone of intellect and cunning would be needed to track the man down . . . to learn his habits and his weaknesses . . . to become the Castle's authority on the criminal they wanted most. It was a foolproof plan for attracting the attention of the men in high places he'd need to impress.

What a stroke of good fortune it was that his father's reputation, and his own academic record, had opened all the right doors.

* * *

"My colleagues tell me you're doing an impressive job in your new post, Winston," said Edmond, tapping the last remnants of tobacco from his briar pipe. The pipe was an indulgence he allowed himself in middle age that he'd disdained when younger. But now, with his children grown and his marriage ended, his life had taken on a texture of loneliness that had been curiously unexpected. All his life he had resented the lack of orderliness that marriage and children had entailed. Now everything in his life was as orderly as he could wish—and what a bore that had turned out to be! The pipe kept him company, in a funny way. He wondered wryly if such musings were an early sign of senility.

"In such a junior capacity as mine, it's difficult to shine, sir," Winston replied, but Edmond could see it was false modesty and that the young man had been pleased by his compliment.

"Quite the contrary," countered the father pleasantly. "I'm told the report you did on this fellow Collins has been circulated at very high levels. You seem to have chosen precisely the name on everyone's lips as your special province. A young man of your talents can dazzle his superiors by latching on to the right area of expertise, you know.

"This Collins chap is in the eye of the hurricane, Winston. If you can make a show of knowing how to track him, *yours* may become the name on everyone's lips."

"That is my hope, sir. Your footsteps are rather large ones in which to follow."

Edmond smiled at his son's flattery. Winston always went out of his way to show his admiration. He wondered to what extent the boy realized their similarities. It was curious, thought the father watching his son sitting so confidently before him— but in seeing his own mirror image in Winston, Edmond could see his own deficiencies more clearly.

The boy was intellectually gifted—an acerbic intelligence, a precise articulation and a pragmatic attitude had all contributed to his successful career in law school. The same characteristics would doubtless stand him in good stead at the Castle, too. No need to worry about this young man's career potential, that was certain.

But what of his character? Edmond wished he could find more indication of depth in his son—of substance that went beyond the surface amenities. And less of coldness. The boy seemed frostily calculating and somewhat humorless. Edmond wondered if these unattractive traits were also a mirror image of his own.

Perhaps it was unfair to expect deep introspection or philosophizing from a young man of Winston's age, he chided himself. But then he remembered Jamie and smiled. There was no shallowness in his second son, he told himself; in fact, a little less sensitivity might make him the better man.

"You seem preoccupied, Father," Win said, picking up his own pipe and mimicking his father's gestures. "Is something wrong this evening?"

"No, indeed, Winston," Edmond replied, wondering if that were quite the truth. "I was simply musing on the differences between you and your siblings . . ."

"Yes," responded Winston, assuming this to be another compliment. "The others seem far more like Mother, don't they? I seem to be the only one who has inherited most from you."

"Perhaps," said Edmond noncommittally, thinking that if this were true, it might be the most disturbing thought of all.

Jamie put down Merry's weekly letter, a frown on his handsome face. How very like her to write him even when they lived in the same city. He wasn't certain why the news in the note disturbed him so, but it did. Perhaps it was because he'd always had such a hard time trusting Win. Not that he didn't try, but his brother was a complicated fellow and not much to his liking now that they were men.

Not that it was any business of his whom his brother pursued or bedded, but it still made him uncomfortable to think that Winston had set his cap for Kitty O'Neill. Win had a tendency to chase wildly after a girl for a month, then spurn her later as if she had never existed. If he played it that way with Kitty, there was sure to be friction. And Merry was so happy now—living with Kitty, enjoying some small theatrical successes. He didn't want anything to go wrong with the pleasant, protective relationship between the two women.

It was disturbing, too, to think of the potential dynamite in the Win/Tahg/Kitty triangle. With all the eligible women in Dublin it seemed inconceivable that Win and Tahg, who loathed each other, would fall in love with the same one.

What an explosive family they were, he thought with consternation. He and Merry weren't in the least volatile, but the rest of them were like tinder kegs waiting for a spark to ignite them.

Jamie finished dressing and left his house. He was enjoying Dublin immensely. Just as he'd enjoyed his time at Oxford. Not only the intellectual stimulation of the university had pleased him there, but it had been such a boon to be able to spend his spare time in London watching the extraordinary machinations of Parliament. While in England he'd visited with his father as often as his academic schedule permitted—and his father had opened many doors for his scholar son. All in all, there seemed a lovely life stretching ahead for him, if only he could manage to keep the family from erupting again.

"Peacemaker," Merry had always called him teasingly. Well, she'd been right about that. It was something he was obsessed with. Peace. How to achieve it, how to help those deprived of it. Was it because he'd grown up in a country with a war-torn history that had so viscerally touched his own family? Or was it that he, the peaceful one, had always sensed the warlike qualities in his siblings and parents and had grown used to the needs of the conciliator?

Ah well, no great reason to puzzle all this out today, he decided. Today was too peaceful and pretty for so primal a puzzle. But he would say a few words of caution to Merry next time they spoke. Precious Merry. She saw only good in people . . . not that he would wish to change that, of course; but it wouldn't hurt to warn her about the possible destructiveness of the Winston/Kitty affair.

He was really rather sorry he'd promised to play squash with Winston at his club. It was far too nice a day to be stuck inside. And besides, he didn't feel at all well-disposed toward his brother after reading Merry's note.

Winston tapped the paper on the top of his desk with nervous fingers. It was a list of all the places in Dublin that were *not* Michael Collins headquarters.

The man had more holes to hide in than a sewer rat, he thought irritably. That was made painfully obvious by his ability to disappear at will whenever danger threatened. But somewhere there had to be a headquarters . . . or at least a repository for critical papers.

The man was reputed to be a fanatic about orderly paper-work; he was the finance minister in their "government," and finance ministers had papers. Those papers had to be *somewhere*.

Winston called for his secretary, who appeared dutifully carrying his stenographer's pad.

"There you are, Roberts!" he said as the small studious man with rimless glasses appeared in the doorway of the office he'd been given in the Secret Service wing.

"Do you remember that young Auxiliary who was in here the other day? Blond hair, bit of a swagger. Very cocky about his successes in rooting out IRA men? Do you recall his name, Roberts?"

"Doyle, sir," replied the small man deferentially. "Daniel Doyle, I believe. Attached to the Third Regiment, B Company." Win smiled pleasantly at his secretary; the man had an extraordinary memory for detail, almost total recall it seemed. That was why he'd fought so hard to have him assigned as his secretarial assistant.

"See if you can have him come see me, Roberts, will you? I need a man of certain low habits to ferret information for me at a level I can't be conversant with. This Doyle fellow seemed to me to be of the right class for such a task, don't you suppose?"

"I imagine Captain Doyle would frequent the kinds of places you have in mind, sir," Roberts answered phlegmatically.

"And did he also seem to you to be the sort of man who wouldn't balk at getting his hands a bit soiled?"

"Now that you mention it, sir, I'd say he didn't seem the kind that would balk at anything."

"Thank you, Roberts," said Winston, dismissing him. He wasn't in the least sure how he would use Doyle's talents, assuming he had any. But if there was one thing he himself had learned from Collins, it was the importance of accurate intelligence about the enemy. Collins was not the only man in Dublin who could gather clandestine information and then act on it.

One real coup where Michael Collins was concerned and he'd be able to write his own ticket in the diplomatic service. It was becoming an obsession with him. Almost as much of an obsession as Kitty O'Neill.

* * *

Kitty *felt* Win's presence in the hotel dining room as he arrived, more than saw him. There was a strange, physical fascination that he exercised over her that she couldn't quite put her finger on. It wasn't that she liked him exactly—rather that he seemed to ensnare her somehow. With his feral grace and his regal bearing; his ability always to do or say the right thing; his astonishing self-confidence.

And there was that disconcerting family resemblance to Tahg that played some part in it. Not that they looked at all alike . . . yet there was some connection. "Like the dark and the light side of the moon." Merry had laughed when Kitty'd mentioned the resemblance to her. "You'd go a long way to find two less similar men." And she was right, of course. Maybe it was only Kitty's imagination.

But he was so smooth . . . so in control. "You look like Helen of Troy tonight," Win said as he slid deftly into the banquette beside her. "Have you been here long?"

"Not long enough to launch a thousand ships, I'm afraid," she replied, again marveling at how slickly handsome he was, how perfectly groomed and tailored.

"Just as well, I'd say . . . it means I'll have you all to myself tonight."

Kitty stirred uneasily on her seat. "No, Win. I'm afraid that's not the case. I've an early call tomorrow and half a script to learn . . ."

He leaned back in his seat, in a studied gesture, and a small cynical smile played at the edge of his mouth as he answered her.

"We have all the time in the world, Kitty my girl. You may play your cat and mouse game to your heart's content with me."

"Really, Winston," she responded, annoyed that he'd seen through her ruse so easily. "I'm not toying with you. It's simply that you confuse me and everything's going too fast for me. An affair is one thing . . . but actually becoming your official mistress is quite another. I need a bit of time to myself to see how I feel about that suggestion."

"I could set you up in a house of your own and make life very, very pleasant, Kitty," he said languidly. "I can give you everything that you've ever desired, you know."

"That may not be quite so," she replied carefully.

"Come now. I know you find me attractive and I also know you can't possibly disdain the kinds of things my family's money and influence can provide."

"This isn't a business proposition we're discussing, Win. Don't push me."

His expression changed from one of calculation to one of conciliation in seconds. Kitty thought, sensing the change, that he, too, was an excellent actor. Neither he nor she was ready to cut the cord as yet.

"I'm sorry," she said, meaning it. "I'm just out of sorts tonight. I'm having a hard time getting this role down pat, and truth is I'm a bit under the weather. Too much work and too little play, I suspect. It's liable to make me a dull girl."

"Oh no," Win said quietly, moving a strand of hair back from her face tenderly. "Not you. Never you."

The warm oil of his voice and the sensuous touch of his hand sent a shiver of pleasure through Kitty. Why, oh why did she feel such fascination for this man, of all men? Why did his languid, well bred voice evoke such strange tinglings, his gestures represent all that she had sought so diligently? Why, if that was so, did he not make her happy?

"I'm sorry, Winston. About tonight. I would like to see you again."

"And so you shall, Kitty my girl," he responded promptly. "So you shall."

Jamie sat backstage at the theater waiting for Merry to finish dressing.

"I've a mad idea I'd like to tell you about," he said as she worked on the elaborate upswept hairstyle she had newly adopted. There seemed to him to be hairpins like so many croquet hoops sticking out at odd angles from her head.

"Is it about your work?" she asked, still concentrating on the intricate task at hand.

"It is," he said eagerly. "You know I've been working for some time on my history of warfare . . . why men fight so continuously, and so on."

"Yes, love," she replied with a smile. "I know all about it. As a matter of fact I may be the only actress in Dublin who can tell you how Wellington's strategy differed from Napoleon's at Waterloo. You know I have paid attention to every word you've told me over the years."

Jamie laughed aloud and pushed back the shock of hair that had a habit of falling over his forehead.

"No man could have asked for a better person with whom to play soldier, Merry dear. But that isn't exactly what I have in mind at the moment."

"There!" she said, scrutinizing her mirror image with satisfaction. "That's exactly the way it looked in the magazine." She turned to her brother for approval and said with a smile, "If you will buy me dinner I shall listen willingly to the entire campaign at Sebastopol."

"I'll happily take you to dine, my pet, but what I want to talk about is the result of wars, not the wars themselves."

Merry stood, pulling on her gloves, and took Jamie's arm; he'd caught her interest.

As they walked along the quiet street he told her how it had all evolved for him. How his abhorrence of war and his fascination with it had made him brood about the victims. The people who are left behind. The injured. The disenfranchised. The widows and orphans, and all who are imprisoned, tortured, hopeless. He told her that little scholarly work seemed to have been done on the subject, so the field was wide open to him. He said that he envisioned first a book and, ultimately, perhaps even an organization of some sort to help the victims.

Merry listened with growing excitement. Her brother's elation was contagious. He had found a subject that filled him with a sense of destiny.

By the time they parted company, Merry felt better about Jamie than she had since they had been separated.

16   "Where are you taking me today, Kitty?" asked Bridgie animatedly as she let herself be buttoned into her coat. Kitty watched the child lift her dimpled chin automatically, so the top buttons could be done, and noted the gesture with an actress's eye for nuance. How trusting are chil-

dren, she said to herself. Always thinking we'll button them up and take care of them no matter how often we fail them. The child had been unharmed by the events at Croke Park, but somehow the experience had made Kitty feel all the more connected to her—all the more protective.

"We're to meet a friend of mine and go to the park, sweetheart," she said cheerily. "His name is Tahg O'Connor and I've known him a long time. He wants to meet you."

"Is he your beau?" asked Bridgie hopefully, her childish lisp making Kitty smile.

"In a way he is," she replied mysteriously. "And in a way he isn't."

"Why isn't he?"

"Because he doesn't have any money. And I can't love a man without money. And you ask too many questions, spailpin!" She pretended annoyance, but Bridgie knew when Kitty called her a "small potato" she was not angry.

"But I don't have any money and you love me," persisted the child.

Kitty stood up from where she had been kneeling to fasten Bridgie's clothes. She stood back, hands on hips, to admire her handiwork. "I do love you, indeed," she said, "and little girls don't need to have money. But grown-up men who want to woo ladies do need to have some. And he hasn't any. And *you* ask too many questions!"

Bridgie giggled at that and put her hand confidently into Kitty's.

"Will I like him?"

"Oh, probably. I started liking him when I was just a little girl."

"I'd like to have a beau, too," said Bridgie earnestly. "But Mother Superior says thinking too much about boys gives people impure thoughts and sins of the flesh. Do you know what they are?"

Kitty suppressed a giggle and answered seriously. "Indeed I do, and Mother Superior is entirely right. But I don't think you have to worry about that yet. Even if you find a beau."

"That's good," said the child contentedly. "Because I'd like to have somebody of my own."

Kitty squeezed Bridgie's hand. "I can't say I blame you for that, love. Sometimes I think I would, too."

Bridgie wondered at the wistful note in Kitty's voice. She made up her mind to investigate this potential "beau" of Kitty's very carefully. If Kitty had a beau she might get married. If Kitty got married, she might take Bridgie out of the orphanage. At least it was a possibility; whenever she asked Kitty to adopt her, she always said, "But how could I do that? I'm not even married!"

So marriage was definitely the key. Bridgie marched along at Kitty O'Neill's side very anxious to meet this Tahg O'Connor.

Kitty leaned her naked body across Tahg's chest.

"Bridgie was mad for you," she said, nuzzling her chin into the hollow space between his neck and shoulder. God! but it was good to be alone with him. Alone and naked.

"Sure, the women can't help themselves when they meet me," he answered. "All ages. All shapes and sizes." He laughed softly as he said it and, taking hold of both her shoulders with his hands, he deftly moved his body and hers until he was on top.

"I hope you're not going to be the exception that proves the rule," he said playfully, as he moved his head down to hers to catch her mouth with his own.

Kitty returned the kiss, feeling her spirit merge with his magically as she did so. She felt so pleasantly exhilarated by the lovely day they'd spent together. Bridgie's affinity for Tahg had been instantaneous; he'd carried the child about on his shoulders till she thought he must be ready to drop. But he'd enjoyed the day as much as she.

Kitty felt the hard, hot weight of him on top of her, calling her back from her reverie. She wanted to *feel everything* tonight, she thought as she twined her arms and legs around his naked body. The crushing force of his chest against her breasts, then the light teasing touch of his mouth on her nipples. Every touch would drive her wild tonight, she thought as she responded. She felt so inordinately happy.

Kitty felt Tahg's leg move confidently between her own, parting them; felt the long slow hardness of him entering her teasingly, lingeringly, knowingly. Felt the tingling urgency of her own need, as she strove to hurry him—happy that he had no intention of being hurried.

This is what love is, she thought absently, before all thinking was blotted out by feeling. That's why it's all so different with Tahg. So powerfully different.

"Say you love me, Kitty," she heard him whisper fiercely, as the feelings began to surge through her like internal waves. "Tell me!"

"I love you," she heard herself say swiftly in reply. "I love you. I love you. Damn it! I love you!"

The worst of it was that she meant it, and he knew she did. Meant it with all her heart.

How goddamned awkward it was that just when everything was falling into place in her life, her own heart should betray her. To say nothing of her body, she thought wryly, as she felt the warm afterglow of Tahg's lovemaking.

She'd had more than one offer of starring roles since her success as Cathleen. And from really good playwrights . . . the kind of playwrights who wouldn't have given her the time of day a year ago.

She had more rich suitors than she knew what to do with. And none so rich or exciting as Winston Manningham. What irony that he, of all the men in the world, should be pursuing her so avidly. Thank God Tahg hadn't an inkling. Thank God, for that matter, that neither of them knew of the other's existence in her life. She made a mental note to caution Merry not to mention anything to anyone about the two men being her suitors.

At least she didn't have to make any decisions right now. Tahg's time with her was limited and her own career demanded precedence over all else.

She could keep Winston at bay for a while at least. Kitty sighed deeply at the confusion she was feeling. Tahg, dozing at her side, sensed her need and, turning, took her in his arms. With another sigh, she settled back to be loved some more.

Merry examined herself in the mirror and smiled happily at her own reflection. Her new bonnet was darling—bright blue velvet with a pouf of patterned veiling. She noticed that the matching velvet collar of her snugly fitted suit seemed to add intensity to the deep blue-violet of her eyes.

"I wonder if His Lordship likes blue," she asked her reflection amiably, then giggled merrily as she let herself out the door of her flat.

Christopher Belmont-Chapman was quite the most interesting man she'd ever dated—he might even be just right for her, she thought genially as she stepped outside on her way to the restaurant on Nassau Street. Not that she'd been looking for a serious beau when Win introduced them, but they'd had such fun every time they'd been out together that she felt herself drifting toward something quite surprisingly adventurous.

Christopher had offered to have his driver collect her at the rehearsal hall, but she had demurred, preferring to run home quickly to change into her favorite suit and hat before meeting him for lunch.

As the eldest son of a marquis, Christopher had inherited his father's title on the man's death several years before. Not that she cared a fig about titles, as Kitty did, but it was still great fun to picture herself as Lady Belmont-Chapman.

"How silly!" Merry chided herself as she walked along. "We've only been out with each other a handful of times and already I'm thinking about marriage. What utter nonsense!"

But it wasn't nonsense at all, and she knew it. Christopher had made it very clear from the first that he was taken with her and that his intentions were honorable. Now that he'd invited her to visit his family at Darborough, there was little doubt of where his mind was heading.

Christopher Belmont-Chapman, Marquis of Darborough, stood quickly as Merry approached his table at Jammet's. He was awfully pleasant-looking, she told herself, even if he wasn't exactly handsome. His fair hair somehow always managed to look boyish, and his face, which was long and lean, was patrician and distinctive.

"I do hope I'm not late," Merry bubbled as he helped her with her chair.

"Perfectly punctual, as it happens," he said in the casual drawl she found so attractive. "And besides that, my dear, I'm so delighted by your arrival that tardiness could be of only secondary consequence." He smiled as if to put her at ease. "You look perfectly enchanting, Merrion. That pert little hat of yours is precisely the color of your eyes."

"Is it really?" she asked ingenuously. "I hadn't noticed. You're looking splendid yourself, Christopher."

He smiled lazily at the compliment. He tended to be both relaxed and reserved in his gestures and was amused by Merry's effervescence. He wondered, however, if his mother would be equally so.

"Have you considered my invitation to Darborough?" he asked, thinking the weekend he'd suggested would be a lark, whether his mother approved or not.

"I have, indeed," answered Merry. "And I accept with great pleasure. But there is one thing I wondered, Christopher. Do you suppose Kitty might come along with us? It would seem quite appropriate to your mother, I'm sure, that I not travel alone, and Kitty would so love to see Darborough. You know how enamored she is of the great houses."

Merry saw Christopher's gaze cloud over and a small duet of frown lines appear in his forehead; the expression made him look older and terribly important, she thought.

"I'm afraid that wouldn't be an awfully good idea," he said slowly. "Mama would never understand anyone as . . . ah, flamboyant . . . as Kitty. And she's not all that keen on actresses, really." Realizing that Merry, too, was an actress, he tried to recover from the faux pas. "Of course, that doesn't apply in your case at all, Merrion, because of your family background and such."

"Why, Christopher," said Merry, slightly taken aback. "You are a bit of a snob, aren't you?"

"I'm afraid I am, a bit," he replied easily. "But not terribly much, you know. Just a little. And not nearly in a class with my mother. Besides, isn't it no more than honest for those of our kind to be snobs, my dear? I mean, after all, there is an awfully long tradition to uphold. And it is ever so much more fun to be rich than poor, don't you think?"

Merry felt a momentary urge to make a fuss, but decided against it. She suspected that Christopher's feelings would be shared by nearly everyone of their class. She herself had even been guilty of similar condescensions before she'd met the theater people and learned to love them.

"It doesn't sound as if your mother will be predisposed to like me very much," she said unhappily.

"Now don't take on about this, Merrion. Mother is a perfectly splendid creature, she just isn't used to the ways in which modern young women go about leading their lives. She'll adore *you*, however." He paused for a moment and signaled the waiter.

"I rather adore you myself," he said mischievously; then, without waiting for her to reply, he began ordering for both of them very efficiently.

Lunch was heavenly, she told herself when it was done. And it was lovely to be driven back to the theater in Christopher's new roadster. What fun to have such a deliciously attractive beau.

She wondered, however, about his peculiar reaction to her having wanted to invite Kitty to Darborough. Perhaps he hadn't wanted Kitty along for fear she'd spoil their fun. Kitty did tend to make all other women seem pale by comparison.

Well, it didn't seem that Christopher found Merry Manningham in the least pale, she thought cheerfully as she replayed the lunch in her mind. And it would be fun to see Darborough . . . the gardens there were reputedly the grandest in Ireland.

17   Merry finished tidily putting away her clothes and picked up the hairbrush to give her hair the obligatory one hundred strokes it required to remain healthy and lustrous.

Kitty looked up from the script she was studying and eyed her roommate critically. "Are you going out with Christopher again this week?"

Merry laughed at her response. "He's really quite spectacular, you know. And who could resist a visit to Darborough?" She tried to make it sound casual. "And you?" Merry asked, smiling engagingly at her beautiful friend. "Which duke or count or prince do you propose to honor with your favors this weekend?"

Kitty put down the script irritably. The countless suitors who now besieged her were becoming a sore point lately.

"I'm going out with Winston, if you must know," she said peevishly.

Merry stopped smiling. "When you have all the men in Christendom to choose from, I wish I knew why you'd choose my brother! I mean, I don't want to be disloyal to him, Kitty, but you two are so unlike each other." She hesitated, then blurted, "Besides, it'll kill Tahg if you choose Win at the end of your merry romps."

Kitty ignored the last of it. "Your brother," she said, icy and miffed, "as it happens, is a fabulous escort. He's handsome and charming. He knows everyone in the world and takes me to the most fabulous parties and places." She stopped for a moment, then said petulantly, "He's actually suggested setting me up as his mistress. With all the trappings."

Merry looked up, her eyes wide with surprise.

"But surely you wouldn't consider such a mad thing! What a cad he is to even suggest it." Merry looked embarrassed and angry for her friend. "Besides," she said emphatically. "You do not love Winston."

"I don't know if I love him or not!" Kitty snapped back. Then in a quieter tone she added, "He fascinates me, Merry. It's like watching a snake charmer when I'm with him. I can't take my eyes from the man. He's not like the others. And you know very well he can give me everything I've wanted for so long."

Kitty's voice at the end of it sounded so plaintive. Merry merely shook her head concernedly. Her friend was really such a good person. Kitty helped the other actors and actresses with their lines, she had infinite patience when she practiced scenes and she worked harder than any of them. She was really such a softy inside; it was a pity she persisted in showing such porcupine armor to the world.

"But it's Tahg you love, Kitty," Merry said very gently, feeling sorry for her.

"Yes," answered Kitty defiantly. "And a lot of good that'll do either one of us! Oh, Merry, he'll always be on the run with this damned war of his . . . and he'll never *have* anything."

"Maybe *things* aren't all that important, if you love someone."

"That's easy enough for you to say, Merry Manningham—you who have everything!"

"Kitty, dear," said Merry, carefully. "You've been very good to me. You've helped me learn what I wanted to know, and you've given me breaks at the theater I could have worked years for without you. So I'm going to say something to you I've never said to a living soul. Not even to Jamie."

Kitty looked up, surprised at that; there was little, if anything, Merry didn't share with her twin.

"There is a terrible coldness in my brother Winston, Kitty. For all his charm and pleasantries, he's deadly cold. And he's full of guile, too. He'd do anything to get what he wants from you, whether it's to sleep with you or to marry you. But once he's gotten it, the cold could do you in! He's so very like my father in that, Kitty. I've watched my mother for a lifetime being frozen to death by my father. I couldn't bear to see it happen to you." She stopped, looking very disturbed by what she was saying, then continued resolutely.

"I know you need *things,* Kitty. But I also know you mustn't sell yourself for a mess of pottage. You are too rare and special for that.

"Tahg's special, too, you see. There's poetry and passion in him that matches yours. And you need to find a match, Kitty, not just a husband."

Merry reached agitatedly for the package of cigarettes on the table, but Kitty put her own hand over them to stay her friend. "Don't do that," she said softly. "You only smoke when you're upset and I didn't mean to upset you." Merry let the cigarette pack go, reluctantly, and Kitty continued speaking perturbedly.

"The truth is, I'm all torn up inside over this Tahg business, Merry." Kitty shook her head emphatically as she spoke. "I keep trying not to *care* what happens to him. I try not to read about Collins and his men in the papers. And God knows, I've tried to fall in love with someone who has all the things I want. But it always comes back to Tahg. From the time I was a child and he used to follow me home from school, I've been mad for him! Every time I lie in his arms I feel a fulfillment I've never known before and may never find again.

"Suddenly, all I want is to be his wife, have his babies, live to be a hundred with him. Do you know how *that* frightens me, Merry? Can you even imagine how that threatens *everything* I've planned?" She folded up her legs onto the sofa so that her knees nearly touched her chest. Wrapping her arms around them, she rested her chin on one knee.

"I don't know what would happen to me if I gave up my dreams, Merry. They've sustained me for so long."

"Perhaps you just shouldn't make any decisions right now, love," her friend responded gently. "Just don't do anything irrevocable until you've figured it all out. Besides, this stupid war can't last forever."

Kitty looked up at Merry almost shyly. "I've been thinking lately that I'd like to find out more about 'this stupid war.' Ever since Bridgie and I witnessed that abomination at Croke Park, it's been eating at me. I've made such a point of staying out of it —of being angry with those who were caught up in it. But all these god-awful things the Black and Tans are doing have really made me angry. Killings and lootings, dragging people out of their homes. Eighteen thousand people arrested. I just can't keep out of it anymore, damn them!"

Merry wondered at that. Kitty had always made such a show of her neutrality.

"I'll take you to a meeting, if you want, love. At Angelica's. I feel just the same way you do and she's said she'll teach me. Perhaps she'll teach you, too."

"All right," replied Kitty. "Maybe if I can understand it all better, I'll be able to sort this Tahg thing out for myself."

The two girls finished doing their chores and finally went to bed, but Merry lay awake for a long while thinking about all that had been said.

18 The majestic beauty of Darborough took Merry's breath away. Even used to luxury as she was, the staggering proportions of the Great House made her blink in the hazy sunlight as they drove under the massive Palladian arch that heralded the entrance to the demesne. The winding drive, lined with silvered beech trees, had genteelly hidden the magnificent proportions of the house's facade from sight, until suddenly Merry and Christopher had rounded a bend and the house, resplendent against the skyline, had risen into view.

The great granite edifice rose above its legendary gardens to overwhelm even the wild landscape of Wicklow, which was visible in every direction. Its shape was long and low, its gracious varied wings somehow not at odds with the eight-foot-thick castle walls that comprised part of its facade. Classical busts in marble niches, too, seemed to blend with the whole miraculously, as if the unutterable magnificence of the house made individual peculiarities mere eccentricities rather than flaws.

Christopher watched Merry's face with amusement and affection. It was impossible for a visitor not to be awestruck—even as sophisticated a visitor as Merrion.

"It is rather lovely, isn't it?" he said gently.

"Lovely!" she replied breathlessly. "It is without doubt the most beautiful spot I've ever laid eyes on."

He was secretly pleased that she'd included mention of God's handiwork in her compliment. The other women he'd brought here had been too overcome by the size of the house to even notice its setting.

"I'll take you for a walk in the gardens after you've met Mother," Christopher said, his spirits in high gear. This girl would do, he felt certain. Finally, one would pass muster with his implausible mother.

Lady Alice Belmont-Chapman, dowager Marchioness of Darborough, was formidable by any man's standards. She had grown up at Castletown, an estate of only slightly smaller dimensions than Darborough, in a house designed by Ducort and constructed of unpolished Kilkenny marble.

She had grown up in an aura of unmitigated luxury, had toured Europe after her debut and been sought after by numerous dukes and princes, only to return home and choose for her consort the man who owned the finest estate in Ireland, Henry Belmont-Chapman. It was a decision she had never regretted.

Especially so, since Henry had had the grace to die young, leaving her richer and more powerful than even she had imagined. Lady Darborough had never remarried—nor had she ever forgotten for a moment the importance of making the right marital choice as a means of assuring a happy life. With that in mind, she had so far selected carefully the mate for each of her children. But none with such concern as she would that for her eldest son, Christopher, for to him had gone the estate and title at his father's passing. It would be of paramount importance to make certain that anyone he chose as wife would not only have impeccable credentials and dowry, but that she would also pose no threat to her own comfort in ruling her august roost.

* * *

Lady Darborough was taller than Merry by several inches. Even if she weren't, thought Merry with amusement, she would seem to be.

Power emanated from the woman, power and total control of her environment.

"Won't you sit down, Lady Manningham," she was saying. The Marchioness of Darborough managed to imbue the simple question with enough pretentiousness for an invitation to dine with the Queen. "Christopher has told me so much about you."

Merry smiled dazzlingly, and not to be outdone by an autocratic dowager, said sweetly, "You are too kind, Lady Darborough. Whatever few tidbits he might have told of me, they can be as nothing compared with the glowing reports I've had of you. Your son admires you so very much."

Christopher's mother inclined her head a bit at the articulate response, but didn't reply.

"How is Lord Edmond, my dear? I haven't seen him since the past season in London."

"Quite well, thank you, Madam. I'm certain he would wish me to convey his regards to you."

"Quite so," replied Lady Darborough. "And does one speak of your mother, since her rather . . . spontaneous . . . departure, shall we say?"

Merry controlled her urge to empty her teacup into the woman's lap.

"We who love her speak of her often," she replied sweetly. "I'm told she is both well and happy. How very kind of you to ask."

A burst of laughter from Christopher punctuated the interchange. "Now, Mama, you quite deserved that!" he laughed affectionately, and Lady Darborough had the good grace, Merry noted, to smile indulgently at her son.

"She has possibilities," pronounced the mother to her son later on the same evening.

"Lord knows you've scrutinized her closely enough to know," he said amusedly.

"One can't be too careful where one's son is concerned, can one?" she replied enigmatically.

"Oh I know you are keeping an eye on me for my own good,

Mama, but do try to like this one for me, won't you? Otherwise I may be entirely too old to breed before you find someone you deem satisfactory."

"Don't be coarse, Christopher," Lady Darborough chided automatically, but he could tell by the benevolent look in her eye that Merrion Manningham was passing muster. After all, it wouldn't do to have an unmarried son forever. It tended to make one's friends suspect some aberration.

"This one is a cut above the others, dear," she pronounced pleasantly. "She just may do. I shall let you know."

Christopher Belmont-Chapman patted his mother's perfectly groomed hand, trying to avoid the many rings it wore so conspicuously. He felt inordinately content with the way things were going this weekend on all scores.

"You know, I've always mistrusted marriage, Jamie," said Merry, walking with her brother in the park. "And yet I long for it, too. Mum and Father frightened me off a bit, you know. Marriage seems to last a god-awful long time if it's an unhappy one."

"But surely it's of no shorter duration if it's a happy marriage, my pet," said Jamie affectionately. "I think the problem doesn't lie with the institution but with the individuals."

"Of course, you're right," she answered, smiling at her brother's common sense. "But how does one ever know if the *individual* is the right one . . . until it's too late?"

"Getting cold feet about Christopher?" asked Jamie, thinking that it might not be such a bad thing if that happened. "Are you really very sure you're in love with this chap, Merry?"

She looked at him sharply. "Does that question suggest that you think I shouldn't be?"

Jamie looked uncomfortable, but answered, "Christopher doesn't seem to have enough substance to him, Merry. Just a lot of credentials, without the wherewithal to back them up, if you know what I mean."

"Oh, Jamie, I'm so sorry you feel that way! He makes me feel so loved and wanted, and Darborough seems such a setting for an idyllic romance . . ."

"You're marrying the man, my dear, not the house."

"I know, I know," she replied. "But I've felt so awfully

happy since I've been with him." She hesitated before continuing.

"You know, I've been rather lonely since the family drifted apart." Merry sounded so wistful that her brother wanted to take her in his arms and comfort her.

"I miss you, you know," she said simply.

"But I'm right here in Dublin now."

"No, Jamie. It isn't the same as it was."

Merry turned to face her brother; he looked so handsome and sensitive in the dappled light filtering through the trees.

"We have such separate lives as adults, Jamie dear . . . when we were children, no such separation existed for us.

"Perhaps I'm still longing for that sense of completion I always felt with you, Jamie. I've never had it since you left. Perhaps I never will."

"I understand," he said gently. "Being a twin is more like being half than being whole, isn't it?"

She nodded. "I suppose there isn't much we can do about it but muddle through, is there?"

"No, dear," replied Jamie. "Not very much at all."

They spoke of many other things before they parted company, but none that troubled them as much as this.

19 The old building seemed to explode from within. Plaster clattered from the ancient ceiling in a cloud of dirty white dust. Wall boards splintered. Furniture upended itself or skittered recklessly across the room. Startled, Bridgie felt herself thrown hard against *something*. A blinding flash of lightning seared her head, a sharp agony seemed to split her back in two. She felt the heat of fire somewhere near at hand, heard the screams of other children and the shouts of the sisters.

"The door, Sister Mary!" one of them screamed to another. "Can we still get out the door?" Bridgie thought she'd never heard such terror in a human voice and wondered vaguely, in her deepening darkness, what had happened to them all.

* * *

"Sweet Jesus, what have they done to her?" Bridgie heard Kitty's horrified question through the haze she drifted in; she tried to answer her, but found that her words made no sound.

"It was an accident. Just a terrible accident," a nervous voice was saying, somewhere. "They never meant it to happen at all, Miss O'Neill. You see, the house next to the orphanage was a storage place for guns. The Tans had searched it, but couldn't find the weapons. It seems they were so incensed that they set fire to the place and that touched off the ammunition.

"It's what caused the explosion, you see," the voice said sensibly. "The ammunition."

Bridgie could tell that Kitty wasn't listening anymore because she could feel her arms encircling her own small body, hear her voice cooing softly like the sound of a dove. Kitty's tears were warm and wet against her face; every place she touched her hurt, but it didn't matter as long as Kitty was there.

"Bridgie, love," she heard Kitty's voice whisper urgently to her. "I'm so sorry, sweetheart! It'll be all right. Don't you worry. Kitty will make it all right!"

Bridgie tried to answer her friend that everything was better now that she was here, but it was much too tiring to try to talk. Instead she drifted back further into the haze, hoping that Kitty would still be there when she returned.

Captain Daniel Doyle straightened his tunic automatically as he left the barracks. It felt good to be back in uniform. His time in France during the Great War had been the best time of his life.

Should have stayed in the army after it was over, he reflected. But then he'd had no idea how tough it would be to find work when back home. And what work there was to find wasn't up to the standards of a man like himself.

The ad in the newspaper had been just the ticket. Back in uniform, with a captain's rank and none of the constraints he'd had to put up with in the war. Far from it. This war seemed to be a free-for-all. Few rules and fewer scruples.

Which was just as well for Daniel Doyle. Rules and regulations had never been his strong point.

* * *

Winston Manningham resumed his seat in the mammoth conference room, warmed by the admiration he saw in the eyes of the assembled audience. His speech had rocked them—startled the older diplomatists with its articulate sagacity, fired the younger ones with its spirited call to action. He had worked hard and long on the speech, honing its nuances, intuiting what each segment of the audience wanted to hear. Then riveting them with the amount of information he'd been able to gather. Raiding one of Collins's offices had been the coup that precipitated him into presenting his views to such an august audience. With the papers he'd captured as exhibits, he'd have no difficulty in getting them to increase his budget now. The papers themselves weren't all that damning, but they proved he had his quarry in sight. And the fact that he'd been able to do more in a few months than the Secret Police had in a year would increase his prestige considerably.

Win smiled at the responsive expressions on the faces of powerful men. His father would be so pleased with him, so very, very pleased.

Ireland and Collins would be his ticket to prominence, he'd always known it.

Not merely because of his heritage, but because of his inclinations; his special gift for clear thinking about this muddled Irish question would help them steer a straight course through these murky waters. And with his father's friends at Court, his efforts would not go unrewarded.

"You've information for me, Doyle?" Winston asked, the distaste he felt for the man barely under wraps. The information he provided was invaluable, but his unsavoriness was really quite offensive.

"We got an address yesterday from a boy we shot. One of five IRA in the same family."

"What happened exactly?"

"We arrived to find the mother and daughter and the old man holding the fort. We knew the boys were on Collins's team, so I decided to see if I could sweat some information out of the old geezer."

"And did you?"

"Better than that! We roughed up the old boy a bit, and when the women went wild and started screaming, we dragged him out on the back steps and said we'd shoot him if they didn't tell us where to find Collins.

"Well, lo and behold, what comes running out at us but the youngest son. It seems he was sick in bed because of tuberculosis, and they'd hidden him in a cupboard when they heard us coming.

"So out he jumps and says, 'Get your filthy hands off me father!' or some such rot. At any rate, we took the address off the kid's body."

"You shot the boy?" asked Winston, the distaste he felt at the story evident.

"You're damned right we shot him! And what else would we do with him—have him stuffed and put on display? You don't make omelets without broken eggs, Manningham. If you're so bloody squeamish about all this, how the hell do you expect to get Collins? And what will you do with him if we find him? Invite him to tea?" Doyle laughed uproariously at his own wit.

"You forget yourself, Captain," said Winston in an icy voice. "You work for me at a wage that supplements your RIC pay very nicely. I have placed you in the happy position of being able to do your regular police work under the sanction of the Castle, and be paid twice for what you do.

"Do not—for one moment—think that gives you the slightest hint of privilege with me. Nor should it suggest to you that you are indispensable. I assure you, Captain Doyle, there are a great many other officers in the Auxiliaries who would welcome the same arrangement I've made with you."

"Don't get so touchy now," replied Doyle easily. "I like my work. I don't intend to screw it up by forgetting my place. And I am good at what I do. So don't you forget that, Your Lordship, Mr. Manningham, *sir!*" He smiled amiably and stood up. "The information I have for you this morning may be of considerable interest to you . . ." he said, tantalizingly. "I've got the name of another of Collins's boys—one of the inner circle crowd."

"Yes?" said Win, trying not to sound anxious.

"O'Connor," said Doyle. "Tahg O'Connor. I believe he's a relative of yours." The smirk on his face made it obvious that he'd been saving this particular piece of information for just such a moment. "He's been seen visiting your sister Angelica's house."

Winston made no reply.

"With your permission to leave," said Doyle with mock deference, "I'll be about my work."

"You may go," said Winston imperiously. Damn it all! he thought morosely as he watched the man's arrogant swagger. Doyle's right. He is too good at the dirty work he does for me to replace him easily.

So Tahg was part of Collins's elite corps! What a fascinating piece of information that was. Wouldn't it be fortuitous if they managed to capture Tahg O'Connor as well as Collins. It would be a lovely bonus to get rid of that pretentious peasant once and for all.

20 "I don't suppose there's any point in telling you this, Angelica, but my informants have given me reason to believe that our cousin Tahg is thick as thieves with this Collins chap." Win thought he had slipped that announcement into his visit to his sister rather deftly. He waited placidly for her reply.

Angelica patted her lips with her napkin and made an elaborate gesture of ringing the bell for the table to be cleared.

"I'm not at all certain what you mean by that, Winston," she responded, covering her surprise with a smile. "It's a bit difficult for me to picture Tahg in anything clandestine, he's such an honorable sort. Of course, I don't see all that much of him these days, I'm afraid. I've been so busy with my charities that we've more or less had to go our separate ways since I've been here in Dublin."

That, of course, is a lie, thought Winston as he allowed his dinner plate to be removed from in front of him. O'Connor had been followed to this very house on more than one occasion, and very recently. She was a cool one, however—how easily the lie had come to her lips. But then Angelica had always kept her own council; there'd never been a way to pry anything out of her that she did not wish to part with.

"You do know that if it's true and he's caught, he'll most likely be shot."

"What a ghastly thought, Winston! I can't imagine anything more ill bred of you than suggesting such a thing about our cousin at my dinner table."

"I appreciate your sensibilities, Angelica, *and* your fondness for the man. I'm only mentioning this for your own good. If my information is correct, and you are spending time with him, you could be implicated when he's arrested—or shot—however innocent you are of wrongdoing."

He smiled pointedly at the word "innocent," and Angelica didn't miss his implication.

"Kindly done of you, Winston, to be sure," she rejoined sweetly. "But as you well know I've never had a particle of interest in political embroilments. I'm quite content to leave that to you and Father.

"I am, however, fond of Tahg, and will most certainly welcome him here should he choose to visit. And while I appreciate your concern, I'd be hard pressed to imagine anyone interpreting a visit between cousins as a danger to the Crown, can you?"

"Just a word to the wise, Angelica," he replied amiably. It wasn't easy to read his sister, but he felt sure the barb had found its mark.

"Do tell me what you've learned of this Collins creature, Winston, won't you? Father informs me you're fast becoming the Castle's leading authority on the man."

"I like to think that Collins and I are involved in an elaborate phantom chess game, my dear. Never having met each other—but intuiting each other's moves. He's an excellent strategist, but he lacks a certain amount of finesse."

"Do you really have as much influence as Father believes, Winston? Are people really following your direction in pursuing this Collins fellow? I should have thought he'd be the province of the Secret Police."

Winston breathed expansively before replying. It had always amused Angelica that her brother could be manipulated so easily by flattery. He wasn't the least bit stupid, just susceptible.

"You might say that the intelligence network I've created has proven to be infinitely useful to the Secret Police. I've quite a spectacular dossier on the man by now, and a number of arrests have already been made because of the material I've provided them.

"On that basis, I suppose it might be fair to say that I've a substantial amount of power in all this."

"That must please you," said Angelica.

"Whatever I do, I try to do well," her brother replied, miffed that she was misunderstanding his good intentions toward her. She was a damned fool if she didn't realize the danger Tahg carried with him. "And don't be so disdainful of power, my dear sister. Those who wield it have significantly more interesting lives than those who don't."

"I'm sure you're right, Winston. But how burdensome it must be to avoid the corruption that power so often engenders."

"One could hardly think it corrupt to arrest a traitor like Collins," he said tightly.

"One could easily think it corrupt to shoot one's own cousin, however," she replied, and without waiting for a rejoinder, suggested that they adjourn to the drawing room for their tea.

🙟 "You're a hothead, Johnny!" I heard Seaneen shout at our son, as I watched from the cottage window. "And hotheads get themselves killed. And whoever's with them!"

I saw the anger flare in Johnny's eyes, but he held his tongue. Whatever he had done or said had upset Seaneen greatly. I could see the father's anger in the set of his shoulders, the clench of his fists, the angry stamp of his feet on the earth as he turned away from our son.

"I got the job done!" Johnny shouted to Seaneen's retreating back. His father kept on walking, his cane tapping the ground ahead of him; he did not turn or reply.

When Seaneen reached the cottage, I asked him what had happened.

"A man who can't control his temper," he said evenly, trying to keep his own in check, "is like a defective weapon—liable to blow up in your face at the very moment you need him most. Johnny's a good, smart lad, but that temper of his could be the death of him. He damned near sacrificed three lives this afternoon, attacking an arms truck without enough men, and without waiting for orders." He looked broodingly at me. "There's violence in that boy, Beth. Violence that has nothing to do with a just cause or a fair fight. If he doesn't control it, it will control him."

"Perhaps he's just anxious to show you what he can do, my love," I offered placatingly. "You know how he adores you."

"No, My Lady. It's gone beyond that now. I've seen it in other men. The need to hurt, the need to destroy. Bad needs in a man, Beth. And dangerous ones in a soldier."

I nodded, unable to speak past the lump in my throat. I loved my son, but I knew Seaneen was right about him. It was as if Johnny had saved up all his hurts for the day when he could pay them back . . . as if they had grown in captivity, until the payment would be indiscriminate, random.

Seaneen knew how to handle men, everyone said so. I prayed that perhaps he would know how to handle our son. ✍

Edmond made his way up the stairs to his bedroom in the house on Waterloo Road. The dinner with his children had been a pleasant enough affair, but he had not been feeling himself of late, and he had looked forward to being able to retire early.

He closed the paneled door behind him and, sitting down heavily on the bed, bent to remove his shoes. The dizziness he felt on raising his head again made him think, ruefully, that there was nothing good about growing old. No matter how philosophical one tried to be, and how dignified . . . there was simply nothing good about it.

How very hard it was never to curse the eyes that were failing and the hearing none so keen as it had been, the lusterless flesh and the creeping sense of debility. Lately it had all seemed worse than usual.

He felt such mixed emotions about this house where he had lost Beth so completely. It was lovely, of course, to see his children grown so competent and independent here. Even Angelica, about whom he worried so, seemed quite the lady of the manor since she had come to Dublin. And Merry was so happy with her theatrical struggles, it would hardly be appropriate to let her know how unseemly a career on the stage appeared to him.

Win was doing well, of course. As was expected. And Jamie, too, seemed to have found a comfortable niche. The contemplative life of a historian would suit his quiet nature. Yet, what an anomaly it was that war should be the chosen subject for one of such gentle temperament.

Edmond finished undressing. Putting on the dressing gown that had been laid out for him, he reached for the volume of Browning he'd left on the nightstand the evening before. Opening to the passage he had previously marked, he read:

> Grow old along with me,
> The best is yet to be,
> The last of life
> For which the first was made.

Perhaps, if he were growing old with Beth it would all seem different to him now. He wondered for an instant what her life might be like—then blotted out the painful vision.

It was good to have this house in Dublin, he mused as he drifted off to sleep. Good for the children, good for continuity. But he thought perhaps he wouldn't stay here any oftener than was strictly necessary. Too many memories resided at 32 Waterloo Road. Too many memories he was growing too old to fend off.

21 Eamon de Valera stared into the street and sorted through his memories. It was hard to stand here on Christmas Eve 1920, more than four years after Easter Week, and not see its specter. Fire, looting, fractured buildings, dying men. Do such images ever fade, he wondered, or do they remain imprinted on a kind of psychic celluloid that can impose itself over one's current reality forever?

His current reality was Collins. Dev dragged himself out of his reverie and listened to the forceful voice that spoke behind him. He had tuned out at the pleasantries; the "good to have you back in Ireland" part. The sentiment was probably true enough, but it also contained a hint of reproach—"How can you know the situation correctly when you've been in America for eighteen months!"—lurked just beneath the surface of the words.

De Valera turned to face the voice with the strong Cork accent and Collins returned his appraising stare. By God he looks every inch the president of the Dail Eireann, thought Mick, every inch the lord-high president of something or other! Inordinately tall, lean as a scarecrow, and yet possessed of a commanding presence that Collins couldn't explain for the life of him.

Studying de Valera, a fragment of a quote of Seaneen's came to Collins's mind—"I do not like a tall general, nor a long-shanked one." Some old Greek had said it, and they had all laughed when Seaneen had quoted the thought.

"You've done a brilliant job with this 'guerrilla war' of yours, Collins," Dev said with sincerity, interrupting the irreverent memory. "But I feel very strongly that it's time to take a larger political view of things. The minor ambushing of soldiers may not be worth the reprisals we're suffering."

Collins looked calculatingly at the man all Ireland was looking to for leadership. "The Long Fellow" they were calling Dev on the Dublin streets and in the villages. Just as they called Collins "The Big Fellow." At the moment, de Valera seemed longer on words than anything else. "He'll die of wind sooner than of wisdom," Seaneen had once said of him. The memory almost made Mick smile. They'd been at the same impasse for over an hour.

"That's all well and good to say, Dev, but without 'the minor ambushing' of soldiers, as you call it, we'd be right back where you left us when you went off to America nearly two years ago. Which is exactly nowhere!

"What the hell do you think has made them sit up and take notice of us, if not the 'minor ambushing' of soldiers?"

"You persist in misunderstanding me, it seems," said de Valera with quiet exasperation. "No one is belittling your contribution, Collins. But the time has come for pitched battles, not sniper attacks. If we are ever going to have them accept this as a war, rather than a police action, we need battles and victories to show them."

"For Christ's sake, Dev," shouted Collins, "do you have any idea what it costs to outfit twelve men for a flying column, never mind an entire regiment for a pitched battle? We're fighting a war on pennies and hand-me-downs here. Half the time the men eat only because the farmers feed them. It's their *mothers* who mend their uniforms for them, and wash their dirty drawers.

"Use your head, man, for something besides a hat rack, will you? Our brigades use minimal manpower for maximal results. It's economic. And it's the only feasible way for us to fight this war. We've proved it time and again."

De Valera shook his narrow head vigorously as if to dismiss what Collins was saying. "It has also caused them to think of us as a band of unwashed ruffians who sneak around corners to do our dirty work and then disappear into ignominious rabbit holes. They are snobs, Collins! The whole bloody lot of them at Whitehall are snobs. They will never take us seriously if we don't fight a more dignified war."

"Holy Mother of God!" expostulated Collins. "Now it's a dignified war you want from us!" He rolled his eyes to heaven and pushed his hands down farther into his pockets in mock despair. "I'll pass the word to Seaneen O'Sullivan and Sean Treacy, and the rest of them out in their sodden trenches by the side of the road, to tidy themselves up for you."

"There is absolutely nothing to be gained here by sarcasm, Mick," replied Dev dispassionately. "It is childish and self-indulgent. You know as well as I do that the skirmishes—be they tidy or not—are only half the battle. The rest will be in London.

"And you mark my words—the best we can hope to achieve with the fighting is to force them into a corner where they'll have to negotiate. And once we get to that negotiation, a great deal will depend on whether they think of us as their intellectual and moral and political equals—or as idiot ruffians to be ridden over roughshod."

Collins stared at his President for a long moment, then exhaled audibly the breath he had been holding all through Dev's soliloquy.

"You're one hundred percent right," he said, finally, surprisingly. The sincerity was as apparent in his voice at that moment as had been the derision a minute before. "I'll do all I can to get you to Whitehall, Dev. After that, we soldiers will gladly step aside and you statesmen can carry the day." He had been tempted to say "politicians" instead of "statesmen," but there was no point in being petty. They were on the same team, he and Dev. If they played it right, each would use his best efforts to bring them to victory.

"I'll be in touch," said Collins.

As simple as that, thought Dev. He says his piece, makes his judgments, then goes about his business. It would be a fool's move to underestimate this man.

De Valera stood at the window, his long-fingered hands folded behind his back. He watched Collins walk rapidly down the street.

A formidable fellow, without a doubt, he said to himself. Capable of passionate resolves . . . and flash changes of mood. He would have to be used very, very carefully.

Edmond left the posh office of Dr. Linton Fenwick with a good deal on his mind.

The doctor hadn't minced words about his illness; it would be unpleasant, but not inordinately lengthy. In a way he felt relieved that the man hadn't offered hope of cure through surgery or endless medication. He didn't think he wanted his death to be a long and losing battle.

Perhaps it was best to simply face the inevitability, and to use the time left to put his house in order. That would take a good deal of doing, he suspected, but it was an honorable task after all.

He was luckier than some. . . . He, at least, would be given the time to assess and to alter, where the fences needed mending.

Edmond squared his shoulders and looked around him before starting down the familiar street. It seemed curiously alien now that he knew he was a dying man. My God, he thought, startled, how can all perspective be altered so totally in the span of a single hour.

He would rather die at Manningham Castle, where he'd been born, than in Dublin, he told himself—too many unsettling thoughts about Beth were here. But the doctor had told him he must be in Dublin toward the end. His children were all in Dublin now, and he had a house here, after all. So Dublin it would be. But not quite yet. First, he would return to Manningham to put his affairs in order.

Edmond mentally began to make a list of what he must do once he arrived there. There would be much to reckon with to assure an orderly and civilized passing. For all his failings, he'd tried consistently to live by the rules of the game.

Now the last challenge would be to see if he could die by them as well.

22   ∽ The cottage had grown quiet for the night, a condition that was becoming less and less frequent since the war had escalated so sharply over the previous six months. The sounds of battle echoed in my mind. Male sounds filled my life now . . . male voices shouting orders, cursing, laughing . . . male stories recounted by the fire at night . . . male maps and reports and ordnance records overrunning the chairs and tables of our tiny world. I tried to put the news of the men's latest encounter from my mind.

Somehow memories of Con and Desmond filtered in, then; not as they were toward the end, but rather as they'd been as children. I saw in my reverie a certain day in spring at the Hall, oh so very long ago.

The air was fragrant with new blossoms and with fresh-cut clover grass. Con, Des and I had been riding, newly freed from the confines of the wintertime house. It was one of those "God's in his heaven, all's right with the world" days and we had ridden miles, it seemed, giggling and shouting to each other as we went.

We had stopped to rest the horses and I had been struck by how lovely my brother and sister looked, all flushed with the wind and handsomely astride. I had a habit of storing memories for some future moment when I would need them—a fledgling writer's trick, I suspect—and I tucked this scene in among the others gratefully, as I called out to them.

"Do you think life will always be this lovely?" I asked them ingenuously, over the mane of my chestnut mare.

"Don't be silly," said Des. "It'll probably rain again tomorrow!"

"No, no!" I shouted back, feeling acutely the joy of the mo-

ment. "That's not what I meant at all! What I mean is, do you
think we'll always be together like this, even when we're old?"

They had looked at each other then, as if to say "She's daft,
but we love her, so let's indulge her in her folly."

"We shall never grow old!" Con had shouted, laughing, her
clear ringing voice carrying on the wind like a silver bell.

"At least Con and I won't ever grow old, Bethy," Des had
joined in merrily. "I'm not so sure about you, however. You
sometimes seem to be old already!" And they had pulled up
their horses' reins and trotted off, beckoning me to follow.

I remember sitting there watching them, my feelings hurt by
how carelessly they'd rained on my parade. But I loved them,
and they loved me—so I simply trotted after, forgiving them
. . . thinking they were probably right.

"Con and I will never grow old!" The words echoed in my
head. Dear God! Could we have known how prophetic they
would be?

I began to cry . . . there in the darkness, lost in a moment
from thirty-five years before, I began to cry.

I felt Seaneen turn and reach for me in the darkness.

"What's wrong, My Lady?" he whispered softly. "Is it
Johnny?"

"I'm growing old," I sobbed into his shoulder, unable to explain.

"Nae, nae, Beth," he said soothingly. "You can never grow
old." He thought it was vanity that had prompted my tears.
"Don't you understand, My Lady? As you were the last moment I saw you, so shall you be to me forever. I'll never see a
single furrow, if they come. For me you'll always be young and
beautiful."

It was said so gallantly, so lovingly, I couldn't contradict him
to explain.

"I would happily have you see me decrepit with age," I told
him, sniffling, "if it would restore your sight."

He passed his hand over my face tenderly, as if to see it, and
kissed my cheek.

"Did you know that I used to rail against my blindness?" he
said unexpectedly. "When I first realized what had happened, I
felt no gratitude that I wasn't dead. The blackness that engulfed
me wasn't just sightlessness—it was the hopelessness of what I
felt.

"It seemed to me as if my long war was over, and they had finally beaten me! You were gone . . . my son would never know his father. I wanted to be dead." He laughed, a sharp wry sound in the darkness.

"Yet now, my lovely lady, I lie here in your arms—a privilege, God willing, I will have for the remainder of my time on this earth. I have a son who loves me, even if he is a handful . . . and I'm still able to strike the bastards a blow or two, despite my eyes." He laughed softly and stroked my cheek with callused fingers.

"In truth, the greatest happiness I've ever had is *now*. Here. With you. So in return for what was taken, great gifts have been given me, it seems. 'The Lord never closeth one door, but He openeth another,' as they say." He had been touching my face and hair all the while that he spoke. Suddenly, he stopped.

"I've been seeing light as well as darkness, these past few weeks," Seaneen said quietly.

Was it possible? I wondered, marveling that he could say such a thing so matter-of-factly. "Do you mean that you can see?" I asked.

"Not exactly," he replied carefully. "Not objects. But fuzzy shapes and colors . . . as if through a curtain of heavy gauze or a wall of water. But it's better than it was."

The doctor had said that with an injury such as Seaneen's some sight might return, but neither of us had believed it possible. We hugged and kissed; I was so happy with the news. But I sensed in him no elation.

"Why aren't you ecstatic over this?" I asked incredulously.

"Because these gifts I spoke of—you and Johnny—are too important for me to be able to live without them," he said, with a catch in his voice. "I have learned to live without sight."

"But how silly!" I responded stupidly, insensitive in my happiness to what he was really saying. "Now there's a chance that you will have it all! Me. Johnny. Sight. *Everything!*"

He was silent for a moment, then turned to lie on his back, his arms raised above his head in a "thinking" posture.

"The fates never permit us to have everything we want," he said simply.

"Con and I will never grow old!" . . . "The fates never permit us to have everything we want." Both truths reverberated in my brain, somehow connected.

I leaned my body across his and pulled his arms around me to ward off the finality of such truths. "I love you, Seaneen O'Sullivan," I breathed, meaning it with all my heart. "Whatever else there ever is for us in this life, we have each other now."

We made love so sweetly that night that for those moments, at least, it didn't matter if we would ever grow old. ✺

23 ✺ Dublin, by summer 1921, was an armed camp in the midst of war. Curfews banished people from the streets before 5 A.M. and after 8 P.M. The military was ubiquitous and obvious. Armored cars raced through deserted streets; lorries and tanks assaulted private houses, pulling people from their beds, searching for supposed weaponry. Plundering, pillaging, killing randomly. It was a lawless and horrifying moment in time. The six counties in Ulster had been officially separated in December 1920 and had become Northern Ireland. Within another month's time martial law had been declared for eight of the southern counties.

The stretch from Cowder Street to George's Place was called the "Dardanelles," so many attacks took place within its boundaries. The "Igoe Gang" of secret policemen from Dublin Castle patrolled the city to point out wanted men. Ambushes took place daily. Auxies sat in cafes with revolvers at the ready on the tables beside them.

Seaneen and I had been to Dublin in the spring for an important meeting with Collins. To say I was shocked by the appearance of the dear old city would be understatement indeed.

I had been so content to remain in Tipperary during the years of my exile with Seaneen. So content to be needed as never before . . . needed and loved. What more could I have wanted? I sometimes asked myself. But of course I wanted my sister and brother alive again and the war ended. I wanted no danger for my beloved Seaneen and for my son. And I wanted Johnny's terrible temper to be held in check by something more than Seaneen's hand, for he was now fifteen years old and I knew that a father's admonitions can command a boy only until he becomes a man.

Nonetheless, I was happy. My other children, with the exception of Win, had stayed in touch with me. The Dublin trip had enabled me to see again Merry, Jamie and Angelica—and, of course, Tahg.

Tahg arranged a special meeting for Seaneen with Collins—in fact we all had dinner together. Despite the devastation I sensed in the city, Collins seemed exhilarated. "There'll be a truce before the summer's out," he said. "My job will be over and Dev's will begin." He was right about the truce, at least.

On 11 July 1921, at noon, a truce was called. The Angelus bells were rung all over Dublin, men took off their hats and prayed that this would be the beginning of a lasting peace. They had no way of knowing that the worst was yet to come.

On 14 July, de Valera met for the first time with the British Prime Minister, Lloyd George, a formidable character, well known for his debating skills. Their talks dragged on through the long summer months while the people at home rejoiced.

Although the truce had settled nothing, the people's elation could not be contained. They could walk the streets unmolested, sing rebel songs, fly the Irish flag, plan for the future. The black cloud had lifted and there was hope of peace and victory.

Unfortunately, the treaty talks were not nearly so optimistic. Lloyd George offered Ireland dominion status, but with several restrictions that Dev would not accept.

"Negotiating with de Valera is like trying to pick up mercury with a fork," said George.

"Why doesn't he use a spoon?" quipped Dev. In short, little or no progress was made.

When the Dail met on 16 August to consider Lloyd George's terms, Dev delivered a lucid speech to outline what was being offered by the Prime Minister, and he called for a rejection. Meeting in private sessions, the Dail rejected the proposal on 23 August, amid many dire threats in the British press about the ghastly things that would happen if the war was resumed.

In truth, nothing cataclysmic happened after the Dail's rejection, and a lively correspondence ensued between Lloyd George and de Valera, who seemed suddenly to have been recognized by the Prime Minister as a national leader.

The correspondence resulted in an invitation to new treaty negotiations slated for October. Everyone expected Dev to lead the Irish delegation, but such was not to be the case.

Eamon de Valera was a cautious man. He had had ample time to study the cut of his adversaries during his talks in London.

The Prime Minister was a devious man. And he was not above misrepresenting the motives of those who opposed him.

Lloyd George was a superb orator and a brilliant practitioner of repartee, a fact which afforded him few friends. There was a seductive quality about him, too, and he was entertaining, but no less deadly for it. He was well versed in the New Testament and sprinkled his conversations liberally with biblical phrases, although no one, to the best of Dev's knowledge, had ever accused him of an excess of Christian charity in dealing with the Irish.

It was apparent to de Valera that the English intended to enter into serious negotiation, but equally apparent that they intended to make the process and the result as painful as possible.

He had been mildly amused on meeting the Prime Minister to see that the man had had a huge map placed on his wall, with the areas of the British Empire outlined in red. George referred to the map often, as if to make clear how small and insignificant Ireland was in comparison to the whole.

But Dev's schoolmaster eye had noted the map to be a Mercator projection.

"Don't you feel that the immense *distortion* of the size of the land masses on a Mercator gives you a false sense of security?" he had asked ingenuously, tired of George's constant references to the map. He'd done it to serve notice on the man that he was not dealing with a fool. The observation had not gone unrewarded; the map had been removed.

Dev had no intention of going back. Any treaty they'd be offered would be seriously flawed and it would be suicidal to be associated with it. Lloyd George, Birkenhead, Churchill. None of them were fools either.

"Mr. Lloyd George is conveniently elsewhere when it comes to the rights of the Irish Nation," Dev wrote in his diary. "He is the incarnation of the British Empire, which was created in a moment of world absentmindedness."

The Prime Minister had called him "the Spanish onion in the Irish stew," and the thought had rankled. Dev picked up the pen again. "Trying to argue with the Prime Minister is like going for a walk with a grasshopper," he wrote, and smiled at his own irreverent thought.

It was easy to see that these negotiations scheduled for October would be lengthy and delicate. If the treaty reached at the end of them was imperfect—and it was almost sure to be—public sentiment could go hard against the negotiators. It seemed very clear that it would be best not to take part in the upcoming talks.

De Valera tore a sheet of paper from the desk pad and began to make a list of possible candidates for the job of negotiator.

The Treaty

24 Tahg had never before seen Mick look uncertain, yet the man standing behind the desk was almost boyish in his uncertainty.

"They're sending me to London to visit the King," he said with a sardonic laugh.

Tahg frowned darkly; he had feared that de Valera would pull some rabbit out of the hat to keep from going back himself.

"You can't go, man," he said steadily to his friend. "There's no way to win there. Lloyd George and Birkenhead will run rings around you. You're trained for combat, not for verbal gymnastics and politics."

"I've got to go." Mick's voice sounded lost and troubled, like a child facing something he fears.

"You can't go! They'll never give us a Republic and they'll never give us Ulster. They'll batter you into a pudding and then they'll offer you some tidbit with an implied threat, and you'll have no choice but to take it. No fucking choice! Man, don't you see that's why Dev won't go? He knows it's a suicide mission."

"Of course I see, you bloody fool!" Mick's voice thundered. "I know what the louser's up to."

"Then why?"

"De Valera pressed me. I'm a soldier under orders, O'Connor. There are no choices."

"You're the bloody fool if you think that! You've never listened to his orders before."

"No choices," Mick repeated strangely, turning from Tahg and walking to the window.

Tahg watched him, heartbroken by the news. There was no starch in the man, no spring. His shoulders bent in an unaccustomed way and he seemed consumed by an inner sorrow.

"Who else gets screwed?"

"Griffith, Barton for economics, Duggan and Duffy for legal advice, Childers as secretary."

"Christ, man! That tears it. He doesn't mean you to win at all. There'll be so much bloody fighting in your own delegation, the English won't have to waste their energies on you. They can just scrape up the leavings."

Mick made no answer. Tahg could see there was no point in tormenting him. The man was too good a strategist not to have figured it all out the instant he knew.

"Can I do anything for you, Mick?" he asked quietly. But there was no reply.

25 Winston watched the retreating servant, waiting impatiently for her footsteps to fade in the distance. He had purposely chosen an awkward hour for his duty call on Angelica in hopes that his sister would not be ready to receive him. It took her extra time to dress because of her infirmity; if he'd timed the visit correctly, he'd have some minutes to search her study before she appeared. For the first time it pleased him that there were so few servants in the house. It was inconceivable, of course, that both his sisters were content to live like working-class women. Come to think of it, his mother was currently living like a peasant . . . perhaps they'd inherited from her side. Nonetheless, this once, the fact of there being few servants would serve his purpose well enough.

Win walked out of the small drawing room where he'd been left to sit and made his way soundlessly to the study. Charity account books littered the desk, letters from supplicants and stacks of papers cluttered every inch of surface.

Quickly, Win rifled a handful of them. Pleas for help, pleas for money, pleas for understanding were there in abundance, but nothing in the least incriminating. Feeling the minutes tick by, he scoured the desk drawers, the bookshelves and filing cabinets. Dammit! he said under his breath, the anxiety of discovery making him angry. There must be something here we can use! What was it Doyle had told him to look for? Secret caches of paper. Under floorboards, behind bookcases. The small bookcase directly behind the desk caught his eye. Hastily he pushed it aside and felt the boards behind it. By God! One of the planks wasn't doweled down as were the others.

Win tore at the edge of the board, raising it an inch or two; the hole within was filled with papers. He felt the clammy sweat on his forehead and swiped at it absently with his hand, pulling a handful of papers free of their hiding place. On top was a notebook. *Tahg and Mick,* it said on the foolscap *8:00, 25/9.* . . . It had to mean Collins! And the twenty-fifth was the day after tomorrow.

Quickly, Win jotted down the two addresses. One in a decent section of Dublin and another across town in the slums. Winston stared at the paper for a long moment then, taking a pen from the desk, copied the information hastily onto his pocket notepad. There'd be no time to copy everything, and if he removed the notebook Angelica might discover the theft and move all these papers before he could have a proper search mounted. Best to just copy what he could, and leave the rest for later.

Could these two addresses be the IRA safe houses that Doyle and he had sought so diligently? Could it be that the answer to his quest and his future were right here in his sister's house? What classic irony!

This would take some careful thought . . . his father would never forgive him if he implicated Angelica. He'd have to make it appear that Doyle had made the blunder. It might even be worth sacrificing Doyle for this kind of a haul.

Winston settled into rifling the rest of the papers in earnest when he heard the metal clickety-click of Angelica's chair in the hallway.

Quickly, he let himself out the door to the study and met her in the hall beyond; he wondered if the agitation that pounded in his chest was visible to the eye.

"What were you doing in my study?" snapped Angelica, her eyes hard and calculating. "For that matter, what are you doing in my house at this hour of the morning?"

"Is that any way to greet a brother who has stopped by to see you on his way to work, Angelica?" Win responded, trying to sound hurt. "Truth is, I was contrite over our dinner conversation and I wanted to make amends."

"I know who you are, Win Manningham," said Angelica very, very steadily, ignoring his explanation completely. "I know you to the bone!"

Winston looked sharply at his sister's face to see Angelica's penetrating eyes studying him as if he were an insect under a microscope. "Just what is that supposed to mean, dear sister?"

"Spare me the 'dear sister' if you will, Winston; we have never been close. What I mean to tell you is that I am watching you and I know who you are! You can fool Merry and Jamie because they see everyone in the light of kindness . . . you can fool Father because you are the perfect heir . . . and Mother because she can cope no better with you than she ever could with him. You could even fool Johnny at times, withering him with your potent disdain. . . .

"But me, Winston Manningham, you cannot fool! All these long years in my chair have brought me a clarity of insight about human frailty. People do not take the trouble to hide themselves behind facades with me, for they don't crave my approval as they would if I were whole. I have the patience, Winston, to watch, while other people act.

"And I have watched you build your clever, arrogant, self-important stairway to the stars, with Ireland's agony as the mortar. Now you are plotting to trample Tahg and me and the rest of the family by association in your indiscriminate scramble to the top. Well let me tell you this one thing, Winston—if you try to injure Tahg, you'll do it over my dead bones. You may be a match for the Castle, and for the family. You may even be a match for Collins, although I doubt it sincerely. But you are not a match for me, Winston Manningham. I'm putting you on notice!"

"I don't know *what* you are talking about," he said unconvincingly, quite shaken by the violence of her speech.

But Angelica had already turned her chair about and was making her way down the marble corridor, the chair's metal wheels making an eerie sound in the deserted hallway.

Angelica carefully checked the room after Winston had gone. Perhaps she'd been a fool to confront him with his perfidy, but the whole episode had enraged her. Coming into her home, rifling her private papers, seeking to incriminate her friends!

Worst of all, he'd compromised the safety of those she loved and of the tidy life she'd established. Now there was no way of knowing what he'd found!

She checked the wall safe behind the armoire's secret panel, the loose floorboard and the cache behind the bookcase. They seemed intact. He couldn't have had more than a few minutes to search. But still . . .

Damn him! She breathed, looking around her at what had been her sanctuary for so long now.

Violated! That's what she felt. He had violated her privacy and her sense of safety. That same sense of safety she had taken years to establish . . . years of mental striving against the vulnerability of being a woman, unable to defend herself, unable even to run away if danger threatened. Christ! how that awful vulnerability pervades all your senses and robs you of strength and dignity, she thought, angry and agitated.

She'd have to get in touch with Tahg and Mick, tell them what had happened, have them change their plans.

For the first time, the danger of what she was engaged in hit her fully. This was no game they played.

Win left Kitty's flat feeling hurt, perplexed. And more than a little angry.

She had said that she wouldn't marry him—he'd been a besotted fool even to ask her. But it had irked him that she'd refused to be his mistress. It was her privilege to refuse him, he supposed—absurd as it was that a little twit of an actress should turn down a man of his stature. But she had lied about the reason and that really infuriated him.

There was another man. That had to be the answer. All this nonsense about her career and her relationship with some ragamuffin orphan . . . all absurd poppycock. There was another man in this, by God, and he'd make it his business to find out who.

Not that she was such a great loss, after all, he consoled himself. No breeding or background. Perhaps he'd been a fool even to want her.

But he did want her! Damn it to hell! Breeding or no, she'd made him the envy of every man in Dublin. Just to walk into a restaurant with Kitty O'Neill on your arm was exhilarating. And she was more fun to be with than any woman he'd ever met.

Good God, but it rankled to think of being turned down! It would have been bad enough had she been of his own class; but to be turned down by a girl practically from the streets . . . that was really intolerable.

Winston shook his head at his own stupid ambivalence. Either he wanted to marry her, and she was worthy of that place in his life or she was *not!* Either she made him happy enough to brave the gossip of his peers, should he make her his wife—or he should damned well stop thinking about her! Either he wanted her badly enough to fight for her, to find out who this other chap was, and beat him to the prize—or he should forget the blasted girl and find someone new. There's no cure for an old love like a new one, he'd heard it said. Maybe all this aggravation was just a damnable waste of time. Win felt angry, hurt, vindictive and empty. He'd seen the symptoms in other men; it just had never occurred to him that it could happen to Win Manningham. He rifled his memory of his friends in similar straits. Win glanced at his watch. Surely it wasn't too late to roust one of his cohorts out of bed for a bit of pub-induced oblivion. Commiseration and drink were what he needed now.

Winston lowered the pint jar to the table and called for another.

"I say, old man, don't you suppose you'll regret that tomorrow?" Christopher asked the question with a slight speech impediment, owing to his own consumption of alcohol over the past hour. Winston was an ugly drunk and his friends all knew it.

"I'll drink as much as I damn well please, you fool!" Win spat back at him as the barmaid handed him yet another whiskey. Christopher raised an amused eyebrow. Manningham wouldn't feel so uppity if he knew the truth.

"Stupid bitch wouldn't marry me," said Winston for the fourth time. "Can you imagine that, Chrissy? What woman in her right mind would turn me down?"

"Really can't say, old man," replied his friend sensibly, savoring the information he wanted to impart for the right moment. "Maybe you're better off this way, don't you know."

"Why do you say that?" asked Win with a sneer.

"Well, rumor has it she's up to her upturned nose in this IRA business. Might even be involved with this Collins chap . . . or rather with one of his cronies. Man named O'Connor, I believe. Something-or-other O'Connor."

"She can't be!" said Win, suddenly sobered. "I'd have heard about it if it were true."

"Quite the contrary, old boy. It's a well-guarded secret, it seems. The only reason I know the fact is that Merry let it slip one evening. Seems she's terribly concerned about her room-mate's heart in all this. I was sworn to secrecy of course, but your predicament does seem to call for extraordinary measures on the part of your friends, don't you think? Surely Merry will forgive me my indiscretion when her own brother's reputation is at stake."

"How long have you known?" asked Win incredulously, the dizzying information swirling in his brain. How could Merry not have told him? . . . Angelica hated him, but surely not Merry. Did everyone in his accursed family care more for O'Connor than they did for their own brother?

"I've known about it for some weeks now, Winston, but couldn't bring myself to tell you while you were still so sweet on her, you know. But now . . . well, I just think you've the right to know . . ." Christopher let the thought trail off in another swallow of whiskey. There now, he thought as he put down his glass, that will kill two birds with one stone. It wouldn't do to have the taint of rebellion connected even casually with the girl he planned to make mistress of Darborough. It would be best for all concerned if this O'Connor chap were put away some-where. Manningham had the power to attend to that.

So it was true! thought Win, pushing aside the alcoholic numbness he'd been cultivating. There was another man in this equation! How bizarre that it should be his own cousin Tahg— loathsome peasant that he was. Winston pushed back the table suddenly and, without a word, stormed from the pub in a some-what zigzag line. Well, by God, that bastard would never have her. If he had his way, Tahg would never even live long enough to see her again!

Winston made his way to the telephone exchange. Fumbling in his pocket, he pulled out a coin, dropped it, cursing, into the street, then retrieved it and managed to get it into the toll phone.

"Hello, Doyle?" he tried to make his voice as steady as possible once the call connected.

"Yes? Hello. Who is this?" a sleepy voice sounded in the instrument.

"It's Winston Manningham, you dolt! Pay attention. I think we've got him."

"Got who? What are you talking about? Oh Christ! You don't mean Collins?" Winston could hear the excitement on the other end of the phone line.

"I've got two addresses. Less than a day old, so they may still be valid. Someone will be with him. . . . O'Connor."

"Tahg O'Connor? The intellectual assassin," said Doyle, whistling softly under his breath. "Collins's men call him 'The Conscience.' "

"I want him dead, do you understand?"

The line was silent for a moment. "Where did you get those addresses?" Doyle asked, suddenly wide awake.

"I stole them from a damned good source, Doyle, and there's more where this came from. You'd best get on it right away, man, if you know what's good for you. Or better yet, come to my office first thing in the morning so we can get moving on this. These bastards flit from place to place . . . don't know how long they'll be there." Winston rattled off the addresses. "Don't forget. I want O'Connor dead. That's your payment to me for the prize that will make you famous."

"Good as done, Manningham," said the avaricious voice; a click followed and then a dial tone. Winston stood with the phone in his hand for one long moment, then hung up the receiver, a grim look of satisfied vengeance on his handsome face.

Danny Doyle held the piece of paper with the addresses written on it in his hand and closed the door to Manningham's office behind him.

A third address had been added this morning to the two he'd been given over the phone the night before. Now the blighter wanted his own sister's house raided, as well as the other two. The Auxie captain weighed the whole conversation with Manningham in his mind uneasily.

Danny Doyle smelled a rat.

It was all well and good for his almighty lordship to say there'd be no danger to himself in raiding Angelica Manningham's house in search of incriminating papers, but it just didn't sit right. She was the daughter of a very prominent man in the government. And she was a cripple, unable to defend herself—that's what people would say.

And what if the information Winston had was inaccurate? What if Danny Doyle marched in there all blood and thunder and scared that poor sick creature out of her wits, only to find out there were no incriminating papers? It just didn't feel right to him. She was the daughter of a Member of Parliament. And she was a cripple.

The other two addresses seemed safer. But if Manningham was setting him up for a fall—and every instinct said that was a possibility—he couldn't trust those two houses either.

Satisfied that his self-protective intuition was correct, Doyle folded the paper and put it into his pocket. He'd have to play this one out carefully . . . dispatch just the right men to do the dirty work. Roughnecks would do for the two addresses where Collins might be captured, but someone with a bit more class would be needed for the Manningham girl's house. Someone whose motives wouldn't be questioned if there was trouble. Someone like Percy; that tight-assed son of a bitch would do just fine.

Doyle would have to run the operation himself, of course—in case it paid off, he'd want the credit. But if it didn't, there was no way he was stupid enough to get caught in the middle. Daniel Doyle hadn't gotten to be a captain in the Auxies by being a fool, after all.

Manningham might be a toff, but he didn't know the first fucking thing about how to outfox a man whose life had been spent on the streets of Liverpool.

Doyle straightened his shoulders in a military fashion and walked off down the corridor in search of his prey, whistling softly under his breath as he went.

26   The IRA men finished their work quickly and left the house in Ranelagh one at a time. All except for the two who had stayed to see the women home and Tim Byrne, whose house it was where the meeting had taken place.

Angelica, Merry and Kitty were putting on their coats when the loud clanging of the doorbell disconcerted them.

"Open up in there! We know you're in there! Open up or we'll come in shooting." There was no mistaking the hostility in the military voice.

All six people stood riveted for the briefest of seconds as the sound of splintering glass and wood sounded from the front hallway.

"Jesus, Mary and Joseph—it's the Tans!" shouted Byrne, already reaching for his revolver.

Ryan and Murphy pushed the three women into a corner as the soldiers burst into the hallway, guns at the ready.

"We've women here, you bloody bastards! We won't fire," shouted Byrne as the Tans filled the hallway.

"Where is he?" demanded the leader, ignoring the statement.

"Where's who?" asked Murphy defiantly, and the captain replied by shooting him in the leg. As the man crumpled, Merry screamed and ran to the injured man.

"We're after Collins, you idiot!" shouted the Tan officer. "Where is he?"

"He's not here, Captain," said Kitty, using her best stage voice on him; she must think of this as a part she was playing, she told herself . . . she must stay very calm to survive. This was only the third meeting she and Merry had attended. If she kept her wits about her, they might be safe.

"See here, sir," said one of the subordinates with an unpleasant sneer. "Will you look at what we've got here! What say we have a little fun with these Irish girls? They say they're wild in the kip. Maybe watching us have our fun will inspire these boys to tell us what we want to know!"

Tommy Ryan lunged at the man before he'd finished the sentence. Pulling a hidden gun from behind his back, he fired as he went. Shots rang out in the small hallway. The women screamed as Ryan fell, a bullet in his chest; the leering officer crumpled, too, a deadly red hole in his forehead. Byrne was down before his gun cleared his trousers.

Merry knelt on the floor sobbing and Kitty stood, her back to the wall, eyes wide with horror, trying very hard not to scream at the top of her voice. Out of the corner of her eye she saw that Angelica had been knocked from her chair in the wild rush of the bodies.

"Murderers!" screamed Kitty as she looked at the bodies of the young men who had volunteered to take them home. "You bloody murderers! He wasn't even here! There was no need for any of this!"

"I'll tell you what there's need for, lady," hissed one of the Tans, tucking his pistol into his belt. "I'll tell you what there's need for." As he said it he grabbed her blouse and ripped it from neck to waist. Kitty gasped and tried to cover herself.

Merry, roused from tending the man on the floor by what was happening, leapt to her feet and started to run for the door. A man tackled her before she'd gone ten feet; he brought her hurtling to the ground.

"Hurry up," yelled the one remaining soldier. "The crippled one's unconscious. I want the redhead after you're through with her!"

Kitty fought and kicked and bit and screamed. She felt a hand on her mouth and bit so hard she felt the salty taste of the man's blood fill her mouth. She felt a blow to the side of her head that dazed her, heard the voices through a haze of pain and hatred. Felt the man enter her forcibly, hurtfully, heard herself screaming, screaming, screaming as the other man took his place between her thighs.

Merry lay like one dead as the sweating soldier grunted and groaned above her. Eyes tightly shut, one arm thrown over them, she tried to pretend it was all very far away, and that this terrible thing was not happening to her. This ghastly, ugly, sordid, hurtful thing was *not* happening to her. She felt the man slump above her, felt another man take his place. She would not, could not, take her hand away from her eyes to see his face.

Angelica pretended unconsciousness at first, praying wildly

that they wouldn't remember her. When it seemed they'd forgotten her existence, she slithered silently across the floor, pulling herself an inch at a time toward the unused gun in Tim Byrne's dying hand. Give me strength for it, Lord, she prayed as she pushed herself along the cold linoleum. Don't let them notice me. With intense repulsion she watched the violence of the men above the two prostrate women. Dear God, could this violence be what sex was? She, who had longed so to know, shut her mind to the sight of it.

Angelica's fingers tightened around the gun. She pried it loose from Tim's entangling fingers and, raising herself into an upright position with immense difficulty, she aimed the gun at the man who was raping her sister and pulled the trigger. She knew how to shoot; her father had taught her long ago.

She didn't wait to see him crumple as Ryan had, but turned the gun to the man on top of Kitty and pulled the trigger a second time. As she did so she felt a horrid white pain strike her chest like lightning. She tried to see what had happened, but a curious darkness hid her own body from her.

"Christ! You've shot the cripple!" she heard someone shout in the darkness.

"That bloody bitch shot Paul and Jim. What'd you expect me to do?"

"Get the hell out of here, if you know what's good for you! We can get away with a lot, but not shooting a crippled woman!"

"Get your pants on, you fucking idiot," another voice shouted. "I'm getting out of here! That fool Manningham sent us on a wild goose chase. I told Doyle that Collins wouldn't be here when he gave us these orders."

"What are you worried about? You heard what the captain said. A little rape and murder never hurt these Irish bastards."

Sweet Jesus, it was Winston who had done this to them! The thought hurt Angelica as painfully as the bullet had. Manningham, he'd said. It had to be Win! He had found her secret cubby, after all, when she'd caught him in her study. That had to be the answer!

Angelica was filled with revulsion at the knowledge; she felt filled by the sounds of sobbing, too, but they seemed to be drifting away from her. In fact, everything seemed to be fading mercifully now.

* * *

Tahg's body filled the doorframe as he burst into the Byrne house with two other men close behind him.

What instinct was it that had sent him there? He'd known before he'd gone a dozen blocks that he had to go back. Mick had teased him that he couldn't leave Kitty alone for an hour, but it had been more than that.

He took in the scene as he stood in the doorway, horror welling up in him. "Sweet Christ Almighty!" breathed the man behind him, but Tahg was already in motion. Merry's quiet body was nearest the door, Angelica's wheelchair overturned in the hall. He ran first to his cousin Merry, who lay sobbing silently where she had been thrown. She stared up wildly at him as he neared her and tugged frantically at her torn dress to cover herself. Tahg tried to take her in his arms, but she kicked and screamed with a terror he had never heard before. She obviously didn't know him.

"Bastards! Bloody, fucking bastards!" The explosive words came from the direction of the kitchen. Kitty's voice. Oh, sweet Jesus! She was at least alive!

He ran in the direction of the sound. Kitty sat on the floor, her always perfect hair damp and matted, her dress in tatters, tears streaming down her swollen face. She was pressing a cloth with all her strength against Angelica's chest. He could see it was a piece of her own dress she was using to staunch the flow of bright blood from the girl who lay unconscious on the floor. Kitty looked up at him as he entered, as if to question with her eyes if the effort of what she was doing was hopeless.

Tahg knelt quickly beside her and tried to take her in his arms, but she pushed him away roughly.

"No time!" she said incomprehensibly. "Those bloody bastards may have killed her. They've killed everybody!" She turned her head to look into his face and, seeing the love and compassion there, she turned harder. "Men!" she spat at him. "You're all animals. Killing, raping, hurting people! I hate you all!" And with that she started sobbing afresh as she turned all her attentions back to the wounded girl beside her. Kitty sniffled back a great sob and seemed to him, just in that moment, so like a little girl that it sent a fresh stab of anguish to his already overburdened heart.

Tahg pushed her hands gently from Angelica's wound and

felt expertly for a pulse in his cousin's neck. She wasn't dead! The wound was halfway between breast and shoulder—if it had missed her lung, she might be all right. He'd picked up a lot of knowledge about war wounds in the last few years, he thought ruefully. He listened to her breathing just as Derek had taught him to do at the post office, to see if anything vital had been punctured, but he couldn't tell for sure.

He looked agonizingly at Angelica. So frail and white she looked, lying there at that strange angle, covered with her torn, blood-soaked dress. Kitty was right; it was men and their fucking bloodlust that had led to this insanity. What kind of monsters were they that they could wreak such violence on the innocent?

He picked up the unconscious girl quickly and carried her to the stairs, glancing at Merry as he went. His cousin seemed to be in shock; he'd have to deal with that next.

"Mack!" he called to one of the two men with him as he went. "Find bandages. Anything that's clean! Willie, you stay with the girls till I get Angelica into bed." The men nodded back; they looked sick to their stomachs at the carnage.

Tahg found a bedroom and, pulling down the covers with difficulty because of the burden in his arms, he laid his cousin gently on the mattress. She was beginning to come around; the wound was still bleeding, although it seemed less than before. A small moan escaped her as he pulled up the covers.

Angelica looked so small and delicate lying there, this girl who had seen so much of suffering in her lifetime. Tahg stood for a moment watching her, his mind in a turmoil of fury and sorrow. *He* was the reason she was injured, *he* was the reason they all were here.

"She's the one who shot them," Kitty's voice, coming from behind, startled him. "Those pigs had Merry and me on the floor, raping us, and Angelica shot them." The anguish in Kitty's voice was so palpable that Tahg felt an angry nausea rise in his throat.

"I'll make them pay for what they've done to you . . . to all of you," he said, hoarse with anger and a need for vengeance.

"More revenge for you to carry," she said bitterly. "More revenge to destroy your life." She sounded on the edge of hysteria.

Tahg got up from the bed and moved swiftly to Kitty's side.

Taking both her shoulders in his big hands, he squeezed them tightly as he spoke, as if to impart warmth and sanity with his own strength. "You must let me help you, Kitty," he said evenly. "You must let the anger out now, girl. Cry, scream, punch me, if you will. Whatever you need to do. But do it *now!* I've seen what happens to people when they hold it in!" She just stared back at him defiantly.

"Oh, you'd like that, wouldn't you!" she spat at him. "You men are all alike. You'd like to see me grovel and tell you what they did to me. Those ugly, sweating bastards! How they spread my legs and pushed their way into me like bulls! How when one bastard finished with me the other took his turn . . ." Her voice had risen to a hysterical pitch.

Tahg put his arms around her suddenly in so protective an embrace that she couldn't escape.

"They hurt me, Tahg Mor," she said finally, in a defeated whisper. "They hurt us all very much," and she began to cry into the shoulder of his jacket; softly and with infinite sadness, she began to cry.

Mack appeared in the doorway and Kitty pulled herself out of Tahg's arms and tried to compose herself. "Here's the best I could find," the man said huskily, and Tahg could see the fury in his eyes. "They're all dead down there," he said. "The two Tans and three of ours."

Tahg nodded. "I've got to get a doctor for my cousin," he said, keeping his voice steady. "I'll see if I can rouse Derek. But first I've got to get the women out of here before the authorities come. I think Angelica's house is the safest one we've got. They'll never break into Edmond Manningham's home . . ."

Angelica heard Tahg's voice and that of Kitty; the room around swam almost into focus as she heard the urgent whispers.

"I'm getting you out of here, Angel," she heard him say. "We've got to get you all out of here before the police arrive. The boys have a car outside. I'll meet you at Waterloo Road with the doctor."

"Merry?" Angelica managed to mumble, wondering dazedly if it was the pain in her shoulder that was making her speech come out wrong.

"She's in a bad way, Angel—Kitty, too. I'll tell you everything when I get you home." With that she felt herself lifted in his capable arms. She felt safe despite the pain and slipped back into unconsciousness.

"You've got to come with us," Tahg said to Kitty. "Merry, too."

Kitty nodded and sniffed. "Take my hanky from my pocket, Kitty," he said with a sad smile, and she did as he said. "You've never had a handkerchief in your whole life when you've needed one." Without waiting for a reply, he left for the floor below, carrying Angelica as tenderly as if she were a baby.

Willie had carried Merry to the couch and covered her with a blanket. The man was sitting next to her and Tahg could hear him talking soothingly, gently, to her as if she were a lost child. Ah, sweet Jesus, weren't they all lost children, he thought, as he had the man wrap another blanket around the girl in his arms. The whole of Ireland was full of lost, hurt children.

27   Tahg signaled silently to Derek O'Hanrahan in the alleyway. The latter carried a doctor's black bag awkwardly, as if trying to make it seem insignificant to the eyes of any passerby.

Silently, the two made their careful way through back alleys and any thoroughfare not likely to be filled with soldiers or Peelers. Finally, Tahg nodded toward a quiet, elegant house on the other side of the street.

"We'd best go in the back way," he whispered urgently and Derek nodded. Even now the quiet calm of the smaller man was apparent and Tahg thanked God silently that he had a friend like the tough young doctor. He wouldn't have come, Tahg knew, if it had been the men who were hurt. "I didn't sweat my way through medical school to throw my life away on a war we'll never win," he'd said, and somehow Tahg had understood. But this was different. This was family.

When they opened the door, a single light illuminated the hallway. Kitty had gone to the kitchen to make tea; he could hear her familiar movements at the end of the hall. On the second floor, on her own bed under an array of blankets, they found Angelica, her blond hair fanned out on the pillow, her fair skin and big eyes ethereal in the soft glow of the lamp.

Derek looked back at Tahg sharply, as if to say accusingly "You never told me your cousin was beautiful." And Tahg realized that until that moment he hadn't focused clearly on how attractive a woman she was. Always in his mind's eye he'd seen her as the small suffering child who needed his love and was his friend.

Derek was over to the bed in an instant.

"I'm a doctor, Lady Manningham," he said in his calming voice with its thick brogue. "Your cousin has told me about you. You needn't be afraid."

The girl looked up wide-eyed—she seemed quite conscious now—and Tahg could see that she didn't speak because she held back tears. As Derek deftly moved the covers aside, he saw that the left side of her body was gory with blood and a bullet wound was visible between her chest and her shoulder. Angelica's shirtwaist had been removed, but she still wore her bloodsoaked undergarments.

Tahg watched the skilled gentleness with which Derek's fingers probed the area of the wound. The stocky doctor seemed peasant to the bone, thick-limbed and -necked, strong and sturdy, as he worked. Yet there was a delicacy of movement in his hands in touching Angelica that Tahg marveled at.

"You're a lucky little lady," breathed Derek as he carefully worked at the wound. "Another few inches and your lung would have been destroyed.

"Would you leave us for a moment, Tahg," Derek said finally in an official way. "I must examine my patient. You could see to getting some boiling water and bandages while you're at it, man. Bed sheets, cloths. Anything clean will do. Your cousin's lost a good deal of blood."

Tahg nodded in the doorway uncertainly. A stricken look had crossed Angelica's face at Derek's words, and it occurred to him that what she feared was not the pain of an examination but Derek's coming face to face with her infirmity. Jesus, but his intuitions were in high gear tonight. He felt almost as if he could read her mind. He cursed himself silently for not having told the man of Angelica's accident, but everything had happened so fast tonight and there'd been no possibility of speech on their silent journey across town. He'd had all he could do to get Derek to involve himself in anything that smacked of the IRA.

Derek looked assessingly at the small fair face on the pillow. She was brave enough, this slip of a girl. She hadn't flinched when he'd probed around the bullet wound, which must have given her considerable pain. And from the few sentences he'd had from Tahg, she'd been through hell tonight already. Yet there were now great shining tears in the corners of her eyes.

"What is it, girl?" he asked softly. "Are you afraid because we're both young that it's unseemly for me to see you undressed? I've no control over this damnable baby face of mine, I'm afraid, but I've been a doctor for a while now, and you've no need to be embarrassed." As he spoke Derek moved the covers aside gently. For the first time he saw Angelica's frail and withered legs; beneath her cotton petticoat his trained eye could see the odd angle of her hips.

Derek looked quickly at Angelica's face and saw that she'd closed her own eyes as if to blot out what he was seeing.

"So there's the reason why you bear pain so stoically, lass, is it?" he said with a sharp intake of breath. "You've borne it all before now, haven't you?"

Angelica somehow expected him to cover her legs again, but instead Derek grasped one leg firmly and squeezed it. "We'll see to your wound first, girl, and then when we've less urgency, we'll have a look at these."

"No one can help them," she said evenly; not quite bitter, not quite resigned.

"Perhaps . . . perhaps not," he replied. "But who's to say we shouldn't try?"

Tahg was back by then with boiling water and the promise of bandages close behind. He had found Kitty in the parlor with Merry; she was now putting the girl to bed in a room down the hall. Merry's face had looked so ravaged as she passed him on the stair, he'd felt the terrible rage rise again in him.

Derek washed his hands, and cutting Angelica's camisole away from the wound deftly, he bared her shoulder and arm and just a trace of the top of her breast, then he set to work to extract the bullet. Although her face contorted several times as he probed, she did not whimper or cry out. She has seen much of suffering in her life, Derek told himself, the vision of the distorted legs on the beautiful young body angering him.

Tahg noted, as he helped, that Derek talked ceaselessly to Angelica as he worked. The competency of both voice and hands seeming to comfort the girl. When the surgery was done Derek turned to Tahg and said, "If you'll leave us for a moment, Tahg, I want to examine her legs and back."

"Not now! Please . . ." The girl's strained voice sounded frightened and, suddenly, very young.

"Now, Angelica," said the gentle voice, turned firm. "Your legs don't repel me. I'm a doctor as well as a man."

Tahg was startled by the interchange, but left the room nonetheless.

Derek moved the covers aside and, beginning at the soles of her feet, touched, probed, massaged each muscle and tendon of the thin and woefully frail legs. Expertly he tested for pain and movement; meticulously he manipulated each limb.

"Your back as well," he said firmly, as if unwilling to brook an argument, and Angelica turned obediently, but with difficulty, onto her stomach. Her shoulder wound made movement excruciating. She let him lift her petticoat up over her hips, uncovering her cotton pantalets. She felt him "listening" with his fingers as he touched her, moving her back this way and that in an educated rhythm of probing for imperfections. She felt him hesitate at the top of her pantalets, then push them down around her hips with conviction, so he could examine further.

Finally, Angelica knew by the touch of Derek's hands that he was done. She expected him to pull down her clothing as an official act of completion, but instead she felt his hands go gently around her waist for a moment, holding her as if imparting warmth and strength from an overfull reservoir, then reluctantly she felt him let her go.

She turned with difficulty onto her back and he glimpsed a patch of soft white belly as she tugged down her underclothes awkwardly because of the wound in her shoulder. She saw him smile a little as he moved her hands away and straightened the garments for her himself.

" 'Twas a wicked injury, lass. No doubt of that. How did it happen? How long ago?"

"When I was four. A carriage ran me down in the street. I would have died but for Dr. Langhorn's surgery."

He nodded sagely. "He was a great surgeon in his time," he said. "But we know more now than they did then."

"You could help me walk?" she asked incredulously.

"Nae, lass. It may be too late for that now. But I could bring some life back into those legs of yours so they were less alien to you. I could ease the pain you feel. And . . . who knows what could happen, if I could make you hate that part of yourself less." He smiled at her, a most boyish and disarming smile.

"You're a beautiful girl and a brave one. I'll try to help you, if you'll let me."

"Do you believe in miracles, then, Doctor?"

He smiled again. "Sure, I was born to a chimney sweep and now I'm a doctor. Of course, I believe in miracles." She laughed, a small soft sound, and he stood up from the bed.

"It would be good if you could manage not to go around getting shot at, however. For a while, at least."

"I'll try," she said, the vision of the evening suddenly in her head again. She fought it back. What a strange young man this was.

"If I make it back to my infirmary in this mad city, I'll come by to see you tomorrow," he said.

"Is it that bad out there, then?"

"It isn't good."

"Then please be careful," she said quietly. "I won't be getting many visitors."

Derek laughed at that and, calling Tahg to say good-bye to his cousin, he started to go. He stopped in the doorway, then turned one last time and said, "I will come back, you know." Then he was gone.

Tahg and Derek stood for a few minutes in the kitchen, each with a cup of steaming coffee in his hands. It had been so many hours since Tahg had eaten or drunk anything that the coffee hit his stomach with the punch of a whiskey. He needed something to keep him going for the next few hours.

"Angelica's a beautiful girl, Tahg. It's a damned shame to think what she's suffered," said Derek. "I'd like to see her again."

Tahg looked carefully at his friend, wondering at his motivation. As if reading his thoughts in his face, Derek said, "When I was five, the tenement I lived in collapsed. One fine day, as we lay in our beds, the place began to fall apart. Many were killed, but my family lived on the ground floor and my father scrambled us all out of the place as it crumbled, but not before a beam had fallen on me, fracturing my legs and injuring my spine. For three years I couldn't walk at all. Much of that time I spent in a charity ward at the Jervis Street Hospital. That's when I decided to be a doctor when I grew up . . . when I knew I had an affinity for both suffering and medicine.

"When I got home, I was a cripple—but my mother wouldn't have it so. She was a washwoman, but wiser than the doctors. She knew nothing of medicine or anatomy, but she was practical and determined, so every day for hours and hours she would massage my legs and feet and back, after she'd finished at the scrub board. Her hands were rough as sandpaper, but by God they were strong and full of an iron will. Every day she'd tell me I would walk again. A year later I did."

Tahg looked with fascination at his friend. The story explained a great deal: how a child from the slums had decided to become a doctor . . . the man's strange, halting gait . . . his obvious attraction to Angelica.

"She's had a hard time of it," Tahg replied in a non sequitur to Derek's story. "I don't want to see her hurt."

"You're afraid she'll fall in love with me because I'm the first man who has been kind to her?" Derek asked directly.

"Yes."

"And would that be so terrible a thing to happen to a girl?"

"It would if there were no future in it."

"And how could we ever know if there's a future unless there were a present or a past to it?" asked Derek, smiling.

"You're right, of course. No one of us ever knows where love will lead us," said Tahg, the bitterness in his friend's voice obvious to Derek.

"You see, Tahg, there's more wrong with Angelica than a bullet hole in her shoulder or her crippled legs. She hates part of herself; I could see it in her eyes. For all her courage and her intellect, she hates the part of her that's caused such grief. Just as I hated myself until my mother made me hope again.

"I can give her that . . . freedom from self-hatred. And maybe hope to go along with it. I can do that better than other men could because I know what's eating at her. As to the rest of it . . . who knows?"

Tahg nodded, then drained the last of the coffee from his mug. "I didn't tell you all of it," he said steadily. "The Tans who shot her tonight also raped her sister and Kitty. She saw it all."

Tahg saw Derek shut his eyes and grimace with disgust at the ugliness of the story. "Jesus Christ, O'Connor, she must be dying inside!"

Tahg nodded again. There seemed nothing left to say. There was something important to do, but nothing at all to say. The two men, without further words, let themselves out into the alleyway.

28 Win's suite at the Shelbourne was large and elegant. He had not yet established a permanent residence in Dublin and was quite content to live at the hotel, where all his needs were nicely attended to. He liked to entertain and did so with considerable flourish and the hotel suited his purposes for that. But it was late now and the last of his cronies had drifted away.

The knock at the door was unexpected, but he assumed that it must be the room-service people come to clear away the debris. He did not expect to see the apparition of his cousin Tahg, disheveled, angry, blocking the rococo doorway.

"You filthy bastard!" the visitor said, before Win had a chance to compose himself. "Do you know what those bloody lousers you sent after me tonight did when they got there?" The voice was steady and incalculably hostile.

"Don't really much care what they did, if they didn't get you and that scum Collins you play about with."

Tahg was at his cousin's side in an instant; grabbing the collar of his jacket, he pulled the blond man's face close to his own.

"Your pals raped Kitty and Merry," he spat at him. "And shot Angelica!"

Tahg saw Winston turn ashen at that. Then he saw an animal-like instinct for self-protection surface. "I had nothing to do with such things. I don't know what you're talking about," said Winston, trying to keep his self-control. "What are you planning to do?"

"The first thing I'm going to do is to beat the shit out of you, you arrogant, slimy son of a bitch," came the harsh reply as Tahg let fly a hard right to the jaw.

Winston staggered backward, recovered himself quickly, then launched himself at his cousin. They were of equal height, Tahg more muscular but Winston possessed of more pronounced athletic agility.

They grappled furiously, knocking over furniture and lamps, sending the remains of dinner flying all over the apartment. Win landed a blow to Tahg's chin, as Tahg's clenched fist connected with his stomach. Win was propelled across the room, crashing into an ormolu side table and knocking its contents clattering to the floor. Tahg saw a moment too late that the table had held a gun. He lunged for his cousin, whose hand was already closing on the weapon.

"I'll kill you for this!" shouted Winston as he connected with the gun, but Tahg had already leaped across the space between them.

The cold black barrel of the weapon forced its way toward Tahg. It took all the acid energy of the righteous anger that filled him to be able to move the desperate iron strength with which Win held the gun. Slowly, slowly Tahg was able to turn the angle of the weapon away from his own head, twisting the gun to break Win's desperate grip. Slamming his cousin's gun hand savagely into the parqueted floor, he wrested the weapon from his grasp.

Pinning Win with the weight of his own body, Tahg raised himself up on one knee and pointed the weapon at his cousin's head.

"Do you know what you've done to them, you conscienceless bastard? Do you have the smallest inkling of what they've suffered tonight at your hands? To say nothing of the men you had killed, you cowardly son of a bitch. Sending other men to do your dirty work!"

"I never meant to harm the girls," gasped Win. "That was a mistake! A terrible mistake. You must understand that."

Bloodlust rose in Tahg's body like lava as the vision of the scene he'd left came flooding back: Merry nearly comatose, Angelica wounded, Kitty beyond his reach.

He pulled back the safety catch on the gun with a metallic clicking sound.

"You can't do this!" screamed Win in terror. "You can't! You know you can't. We're *family*, Tahg, whatever's happened. I beg of you for my mother's sake, don't shoot me! It would kill my mother." Winston's usual arrogance had subsided into a childlike terror. Cowardice, appalling cowardice, showed in every nerve ending of the man.

Tahg felt as if he were watching the scene from far away. Revulsion filled him like the cold wash of nausea. Seeing Winston, who had done such hideous damage to those he loved, with no cognizance of his crime, no hint of remorse. Just a childlike, terrified cowardice that made him want to retch. He could kill this man and feel righteous in the killing. Suddenly the thought of himself enraged enough to kill this helpless, groveling cretin who was Aunt Beth's son repelled him.

With infinite effort of will, Tahg slid the safety back into place and pulled himself up. Standing over his cousin, he said roughly, "You filthy scum. You're not enough of a man for me to shoot." He turned abruptly and, shoving the gun into his pocket, made for the door.

Winston was on his feet in an instant and over to the night table. Pulling a small revolver from the drawer, he fired point-blank at his cousin's retreating back.

Tahg's large body slumped to the ground, an incredulous look on his face as he half turned toward his attacker. Winston, his hands trembling violently, placed the gun back into the drawer where he stood, and quickly moved past his cousin's body to the door.

As Winston headed for the hotel lobby, Mick Collins and Eddie Joyce slipped unobtrusively into the hotel room. Expertly, Collins examined Tahg and pronounced him living.

"We've less than three minutes to get him out of here. The bloody fool, coming here alone!" he said angrily to no one in particular, as he and Joyce hoisted the unconscious man to a standing position between them.

Looking furtively to right and left in the hallway, they dragged Tahg's sagging body toward the service elevator, where a man in a chef's uniform nervously awaited them.

"Good work, O'Toole," said Collins as they entered. "You're sure the kitchen's deserted at this time of night?"

"Aye, sir. Nary a soul but me and Nellie. Both of us, Organization."

Collins nodded. A car would be waiting beyond the kitchen to take them to a safe house. If O'Connor could last that long. He looked again at the unconscious face of his friend and cursed him that he hadn't waited for a proper revenge.

Thank Christ, Mack Devlin had had the presence of mind to let him know what had transpired this bloody night. Mick sorted quickly through the possibilities at his disposal now. Angelica's house was the safest bet for tonight. Her brother couldn't risk a scandal there.

Mick gave the driver the Waterloo Road address and rode the whole way with Tahg O'Connor's head on his own lap. As soon as he was safe inside the Manningham house, he himself would go for Derek O'Hanrahan, and, by God, the louser better not tell Mick Collins he wouldn't come to save his friend!

Collins said a hasty but sincere prayer of thanks as he rode along silently. If this had happened a month from now, he would already have been gone to the London negotiations. Thank God he'd been here to pick up the pieces.

Kitty O'Neill stood poised above the bedside of Tahg O'Connor. She felt as if she were watching her own life drain away before her. Images flashed like scenes in a play before her eyes. Tahg at eleven following her home from school, bewildered by her refusal to walk with him . . . Tahg at fifteen tentatively planning their future, a future that always included her. Tahg in the Rising, Tahg in prison, Tahg locked in her inmost embrace, in a moment of bliss she would carry with her to the grave.

She thanked God silently that Collins had brought him back here to her and to Derek before he had again melted mysteriously into the black night. She could only imagine the look on Derek's face when the men had come to rouse him for a second time tonight.

She had watched Collins take charge of all of them with astonished admiration. Once he was certain the doctor had come, he'd taken the men and headed off again. There'd be reprisals for this night, she felt sure, from the look of the avenging angel on Collins's face. She looked at poor Derek, who had never wanted to get involved; he was in it for fair now!

"We'll have to get the bullet out of his lung or he's a dead man." O'Hanrahan's voice was deep and deadly serious as he stared into her face.

"Can we get him to a hospital?" she asked, knowing the answer.

"No time. He'll die if we move him."

"Can you do it here?"

"If you can help me."

"Good God, Derek, I'm not a nurse! I don't know if I could even watch."

"You may not be a nurse, girl, but you're the best damned actress in Dublin. Play the fucking part if you must, but help me keep him alive!"

Kitty nodded and swallowed hard; her fear and bile from her stomach seemed to be rising simultaneously in her throat. She steadied herself against the cold metal of the brass headboard and dug her nails into the palms of her hands to keep from fainting.

"What do I do?"

"We'll need sterile water, alcohol for my instruments, sheets for bandages, tape — you'll have to find them all. We'll need better light than this . . . bring the brightest lamps you can find." He stopped to think, great agitation in his demeanor.

"And Kitty . . ."

"Yes!"

"If you know any prayers, now's the time for them."

She smiled wryly at him, thinking that she'd done her share of praying in her life, but she wasn't sure how many of them had ever been answered by other than a No.

Kitty willed herself to be a *nurse* . . . not to faint at what she was seeing . . . not to think of the living lung beneath Derek's scalpel as belonging to the body of the man she loved.

She wiped Derek's brow of sweat when he told her to; she memorized the instruments so she could place the right one in his hand; she helped hold back the gaping edges of the blood-red incision as he extracted the bullet and repaired the damage. She watched the red and white tissue moving, moving, rising and falling, desperately vulnerable without its cover of flesh and bone. Finally she helped him sew the living tissue back together into the semblance of a whole.

Derek stripped the gloves from his hands, hooked the stethoscope into his ears and listened . . . listened. Finally, he

looked up into her anxious face and his lips moved into a determined smile. A small smile, but an encouragement. She thought
she saw tears in his eyes as they met her own.

"Now we must keep him warm and watch him, Kitty. It's up
to God and his own constitution from here on in."

"His chances?"

"Better than they were when they dragged him in here, but
we must keep him absolutely still. And pray to God that the
Tans don't choose this block for a raid tonight."

Kitty nodded and lowered herself gratefully into a chair; she
moved slowly and methodically. She felt as if she had forgotten
how to sit in the long hours of the surgery. A weariness such as
she had never experienced drained her totally.

Derek, exhausted as he was, sensed her weakness and walked
to the chair she sat on. Unexpectedly, he picked up her hand
and brought it to his lips in a courtly gesture.

"You were a great lady tonight, my girl," he said gently. "It
was a grand performance."

She leaned her head against his stocky body by way of reply,
grateful for the hard strength of it, and they both stood for a
moment without the energy for further movement.

Suddenly, a clamor arose from the direction of the living
room. A loud hammering on the door, then the crash of a rifle
butt through the glass panel above the lock.

Kitty was on her feet in an instant. She had heard that sound
once before tonight.

"The Tans!" she gasped incredulously, with such a medley of
emotions in the one word that Derek was stunned by it. They
had all assured her that no one would knowingly raid Angelica
Manningham's house. But what if it were unknowing? What if
it were just some hideous accident of fate?

"If they make it up here, Kitty, he's a dead man," said
Derek, his voice terrifying in its urgency.

Kitty's eyes met Derek's, a look of consummate understanding passing between them; she nodded once and moved toward
the stairs. The doctor saw her collect herself for an instant at
the top of the staircase, then start down. He heard her clear,
exquisite voice ring out as she descended the steps. He couldn't
count the emotions Kitty managed to include in a single sentence.

"Gentlemen, gentlemen! What in heaven's name are you up to?" he heard her call out.

From the top of the stair, Derek, poised and unwilling to breathe, saw the Auxie lieutenant stop short at the sight of her.

"We've had word that there's a Sinn Fein criminal somewhere in this neighborhood, ma'am. We have orders to search this row of houses," he replied courteously, awed by her bearing and unexpected beauty.

"Haven't those reprehensible dolts from the IRA caused us enough trouble already in this area? I'm telling you, Lieutenant, if it weren't for you and your men, a decent woman couldn't sleep nights in Dublin!"

The Auxie looked uncertain and Kitty leaped into his hesitation.

"Lieutenant, what is your name, sir?"

"Percy, miss. Lieutenant James Percy."

"Yes, of course, Lieutenant Percy," she replied, worlds of promise in her words and tone. "Do you know who I am by any chance, or whose house this is?" The Auxie looked sheepish in reply and a young soldier prompted him.

"The lady is Miss Kitty O'Neill, sir. The famous actress."

Kitty bestowed on the man her most dazzling smile. "He's quite right, you know. And the house belongs to Lord Edmond Manningham. I'm simply a house guest of the Manningham family while they're away." Derek, listening above, knew she was so near exhaustion, he marveled at the amount of energy she seemed suddenly able to generate.

"I'm most delighted to have the pleasure of meeting you, ma'am," said the lieutenant, impressed, and somewhat unnerved by the Manningham connection. It might not do his career much good to embarrass a famous member of the House of Lords. Doyle had mentioned no such thing. "I'm afraid we'll have to search your house, nonetheless . . ." he began, but he sounded more hesitant than before.

"Of course you will, my dear sir," replied Kitty magnanimously. "But I'd like to beg a favor of you first, if I may?"

The young officer looked quizzical.

"You see, I've been admiring soldiers like yourself and these lovely men who risk your lives daily to keep the people of Dublin safe from those Sinn Fein ruffians. And for the very longest time I've wanted to do something in return. A gesture of gratitude . . ." She let the thought drift off, so each man could devise a repayment of his own.

By this point all the men in the hallway had relaxed their rifles and were standing by, curiously watching the scene unfold. Kitty continued.

"Would you, Lieutenant, out of the goodness of your heart, allow me to put on a small performance right here and now for you? My insignificant way of paying you back for your gallantry and all? It would mean *so* very much. I wouldn't take but a moment and I'm sure I'll never have such an opportunity to express my heartfelt thanks again, you see . . ." She fastened her expressive eyes pleadingly on the leader, and he melted visibly. That bastard, Doyle! he thought. He knew whose house this was and set me up.

"Well, I suppose, a moment or two, for such an extraordinary honor wouldn't do any harm, ma'am," he allowed gallantly, playing for time to make up his mind about what to do.

Kitty graciously smiled her heartfelt thanks and made her way to the piano that stood in the parlor, thanking God that she'd noticed its existence on the way in.

Seating herself on the bench, the lamplight behind her head giving a halo of brilliance to her dazzling hair, she motioned the men to be at ease and began to sing.

She sang of home and family. She sang of England in the spring. She sang of girls who had been left behind and men who bravely did their duty before going home to them. She sang rollicking, naughty songs from the music halls to make them chuckle. But most of all she reminded them that they were men and that she was a woman . . . the loveliest woman they had ever laid eyes on.

When the strains of the music had died and the men's applause and praise had subsided, she saw the lieutenant rise, as if remembering that he must be about his work. He looked shaken and nervous; before he could give an order, she interjected plaintively:

"Lieutenant Percy? I wonder if I might have a word with you in private?" He nodded, uncertainly, and she led him into the next room.

Sweet Mother Mary, she prayed as they went, this must be the single greatest performance of my life. Please let me make him believe. If I never, ever act again, please make this man believe what I tell him.

She lowered her eyes demurely, as if embarrassed by what she had to say.

"Lieutenant, this is very difficult for me . . ."

Percy cleared his throat, uncomfortable and wary.

"I have a confession to make and it is most embarrassing . . ."

"Miss O'Neill, I'm sure there's nothing in the world about you that is embarrassing."

"Oh, but Lieutenant, dear, there is." She raised her tear-filled eyes to his with an expression that could have melted stone.

"You see, I . . . I wasn't alone here tonight. There's a man, a member of the military as it happens, who was with me when you arrived. I'm afraid we were in rather a compromising situation." She lowered her eyes demurely.

Percy watched the obviously mortified young woman and wanted terribly to reassure her. "Now, now, miss, there's no need for you to tell me all this, surely."

"Oh, but there is, Lieutenant! Don't you see, if you search this house the general will be found and by morning both he and I will have our names dragged through every barracks in Dublin." She moved her hair back from her face and he could see great silver tears collect in her eyes.

Percy hesitated for a moment, wondering what the penalty for finding a general with his pants down might be. Especially in the borrowed home of a Member of Parliament.

"You'll give me your word then that there is no rebel here?" he asked, desperate to escape this difficulty.

"My dear Lieutenant," she breathed meaningfully. "I give you my word on that unequivocally, and I also give you my word that if you save my honor, there will be two tickets waiting for you on opening night of every performance I shall ever give."

The look of gratitude in her eyes left no room for anything but gallantry.

"I shall look forward to seeing you in all those performances, then," said Percy, clearing his throat, anxious for escape.

"You can have no idea, Lieutenant, how grateful I am to you." Kitty breathed her relief and, standing on tiptoe, reached up and kissed him tenderly on the mouth.

Covered with embarrassment, Percy cleared his throat again and, returning to his men, said briskly, "I have Miss O'Neill's personal assurance that there is no reason for us to harass her further."

Within a minute after that, they were gone.

Kitty, visibly shaken, managed to make her way back up the stairs. Her bone-deep exhaustion and the narrowness of their escape swept over her in nauseating waves. Like a somnambulist, she collapsed into Derek's arms and sobbed so pitifully and so long that he was sure she would be ill. Instead, when all her tears were spent, she kissed him once on the cheek and, lying down gently on the bed beside Tahg, she fell into a dreamless slumber.

"D'you think she was on the up-and-up, sir?" asked Percy's subaltern as they rounded the corner.

"Not one chance in a thousand."

"Then why . . ."

Percy smiled enigmatically. "If by some unlikely stretch she was telling the truth, we'd have felt damned foolish catching a general with his trousers down. And . . . if she wasn't . . . why, let's just say we have been privileged to be present at one of the greatest theatrical performances of our time." He chuckled a little.

"One must bow to genius, Henton, mustn't one?" asked the lieutenant, smiling.

The two men rounded the corner chuckling to themselves, Percy making mental notes on the physical injury he would inflict on Doyle for this fiasco.

Angelica lay in the bed somewhere between waking and sleeping. Strange images battled each other, rising like mist, then being replaced by other phantoms. She saw herself running, whole and fleet of foot, running in a dark and unaccustomed landscape, chasing something. She couldn't tell what it was that eluded her pursuit, nor could she feel her legs beneath her, although she knew that they were torn by brambles and briars as she ran.

In the next image she was on the ground, and yet she still felt herself falling, falling—as if the ground were impermanent and she was slipping through it to eternity.

Then *his* hands were clasping her waist, holding on for dear life, wrestling her back from the unknown. And they were strong and hot and hard. They would not let her go.

Next, the ground was solid beneath them again. The man was holding her in his arms, his hands searching her face, her breasts, her belly, in turn. She knew he would make love to her; she reached up to clasp him to her as his hand reached down to caress her most intimate parts. *But they weren't there.* Stricken, she looked down at her own body and saw that it had disappeared below the waist. There was *nothing* there!

She screamed and screamed and screamed and screamed and the dream vanished. Angelica tried to sit upright in the darkened bed, but the terrible pain in her chest stayed her. Surreptitiously, she moved the covers back from her lower body and felt her legs, as if to reassure herself that they were still there.

In the cold darkness she could see the outline of her crooked legs and she began to cry. Crying for what was lost and what would never be. For the love and the children and the life that could not be hers. For her sister and for Kitty and for Ryan, Murphy, Byrne and the others . . . all the others. Finally, sobbing quietly into the pillow, she willed herself back to sleep as the only escape from her terrible thoughts.

29 "Of course, you cannot marry the girl under the circumstances, Christopher! It would be absolutely unheard of. The fact that she was unable to prevent the attack notwithstanding—and who knows if that is true?—she placed herself in jeopardy by being in that house with those ruffians and she is no longer acceptable material for a wife." Lady Darborough had chosen to confront her son in the morning room directly after breakfast.

"Have you considered that she might even be pregnant by one of those creatures who molested her? Dear God! The very idea that you would even consider bringing her here ever again is too appalling for me to contemplate."

Christopher pursed his lips thoughtfully, before responding.

He was shaken, both by the realization of what had happened and by his mother's wrath. He felt he needed time to sort things through. He wished he had never told his mother of the rape, but knowing her resources, he'd felt she might learn of it sooner or later and had decided to face the worst of it now.

"I'm afraid I must make up my own mind about this, Mother," Christopher replied. "I have quite mixed emotions on the subject. Needless to say, I had no idea Merrion had Republican leanings, but nonetheless I do care for the girl . . ."

"You may care for her all you wish," said his mother. "Simply do not marry her!" She fingered the bridge deck she held in her hand expertly. "I cannot keep you from your father's inheritance, as you know, Christopher, but I can keep you from mine. Kindly consider *that* while you are contemplating your mixed emotions."

Hostility gleamed behind the insolent look Christopher lavished on his mother before leaving the morning room. He had a lot of thinking to do about this, indeed.

How could Merrion have done such a witless thing as to have been in that IRA refuge? How utterly reprehensible to have left herself open to such an appalling event. At first, when he'd learned of the attack, his heart had gone out to her—she had seemed like a broken bird or a wounded child as she'd sobbed out the story to him afterward.

But dammit! She had brought it on herself with her consummate stupidity in hanging about with such people! What did that say about her character, after all? Perhaps his mother's warning about Lady Elizabeth Manningham's influence on the girl shouldn't have been treated so cavalierly.

Damnation! How could she have spoiled things so thoroughly for him! Christopher Belmont-Chapman intended to marry only once in his life. That left very little room for mistakes.

"You can't mean what you're saying, Christopher," said Merry, appalled by the heartbreak in her own voice.

Christopher lowered his elegant head for a moment, then looked up quickly. He found it very difficult to look at Merrion and say what he had to say.

"I'm afraid I do, my dear," he ventured finally, clearing his throat in an effort to make his voice sound more certain. "You must understand my position in this. I have to consider my good name and Mother's. I don't mean to suggest that what happened to you was in any way your fault, you understand . . . but damn it all, Merrion, it did happen! We can't change that."

"But no one really knows about it, Christopher. It's been kept as quiet as could be," Merry ventured, trying to stay in control of her voice.

"Such things never remain a secret, Merrion. You know that as well as I. There's always someone who knows, who knows someone else, who tells someone . . ." He put up his hands in a gesture of ultimate exasperation.

She started to speak again, but he stayed her with a gesture.

"Worse yet, Merrion," he said, "*I* know about it. You see, I'm afraid I just couldn't live with the knowledge of all those other men . . ." He let the thought trail off impotently.

Merry opened her mouth to speak, but no sound came. What could she say to refute the awful truth? She was damaged goods. Even to herself.

Hadn't she lain sleepless every night since it had happened wondering if, even now, she might be carrying within her womb some monstrous evidence of what had been done to her? Christopher couldn't possibly feel more revulsion toward her than she felt herself.

Oh, Christ! If she could only root it out! This horror that seemed to lurk within her now . . . this stigma that she carried like a burrowing maggot. This feeling of uncleanliness . . . of being sullied somewhere deep inside, where soap and water could not wash away the stain.

Merry tried to gather enough of her own resources to at least bring this ghastly conversation to an end. "I think you'd best leave, Christopher," she said with as much dignity as she could muster. "Perhaps you should consider marrying your mother. You and she are so well suited."

In other times she might have laughed at the dumbfounded expression on Christopher's face. But at this moment she felt it doubtful that she would ever laugh again.

Merry closed the door behind Christopher's retreating form and walked back into the room as carefully as if the floor had dissolved beneath her feet.

She felt light-headed and sick to her stomach. The world seemed to be closing in around her ominously. She wondered if she might be losing her mind.

30   Angelica lay in bed and struggled with her desire for vengeance. Her pain she could somehow manage to bear with; she had known pain before. But Merry's desolation was something Win must pay for. And Tahg's hideously damaged lung, which had nearly cost him his life—that he must pay for, too.

Cold-blooded bastard that he was . . . she had always known Win's arrogant selfishness would hurt them in some way. Always, she had known how jealous he was of Tahg and how she wished him ill.

She had put her brother on notice that if he hurt the ones she loved she would not let him get away with it. An eye for an eye and a tooth for a tooth. Old Testament justice was what was needed here.

Angelica had thought of going to her father with the story of Win's perfidy. God alone knows what Edmond Manningham would do to his son if he learned that Winston had caused Merry's rape and her own injury.

But she loved her father, and he was very ill—ill enough to be confined to bed in this very house for the last five days. It would be wrong for her to leave the meting out of justice to him in his current condition. Besides that, too much had been said over the years about Win's likeness to his father. Too many wrong conclusions had been drawn. Win was not like Edmond, only a shoddy imitation.

No. She must do this deed herself. And the punishment must fit the crime. Three dead, one nearly dead, one seriously wounded, two raped. All under the pretext of capturing Mick Collins. And a pretext is what it had been, all right. Winston had been after Tahg O'Connor. It was Tahg he'd intended to have killed. The rest of them were bystanders.

She had considered going to Mick and asking him to deal

with Winston. But Mick was occupied with preparation for the Treaty talks in London. More than that, her sense of fair play had stayed her. Win was a Manningham—she would give him a sporting chance.

She would set a trap for him, as he had set one for Tahg—only if he chose to hurt again would the trap be sprung. And it would be sprung by his own hand.

That way the outcome would be his to choose . . . that way Winston himself would decide his own fate.

31   "We must summon Mother, Winston." Angelica's voice was determined. She was able to sit up in her chair now, but with difficulty, and her shoulder was still relentlessly painful. She had seen her brother only one other time since her injury.

"No," Win replied without taking time to consider the request.

"Father is very ill; he may be dying," she persisted. "He wishes to see her."

"I'll not have that woman in this house."

Angelica shook her head disgustedly at her brother. "This is my home," she said, "not yours. It may interest you to know it is not part of Father's estate. He has put it in my name. And I shall invite my mother into my home whenever I choose. Father is old and needy, Winston. Surely even your monumental selfishness cannot encompass denying your father his last wish."

Winston looked at his sister with considerable hostility.

"Very well," he said with a small false smile. "Have it your own way. But so help me, Angelica, if she upsets him in any way, I'll have the authorities on her before she's any older. She is a fugitive from justice, you may recall."

"I don't doubt for a moment that you are capable of betraying your own mother to the police, Winston. She is, after all, the only woman in the family that you have left unmolested." Win looked wonderingly at Angelica. She had never mentioned his connection to the night of the shooting and rape.

"However," she continued without pausing to see the effect of her statement, "I doubt seriously that you would brook the scandal it would provoke in all the newspapers if you were to have Elizabeth Manningham arrested in her husband's house."

Win smiled again, in an effort to cover his discomfort. "You really are very bright for a woman, Angelica. What a pity your handicap will keep you from ever being more than a poor soul." Winston waited to see the damage he had produced with that, then turned on his heel and started to walk away.

Angelica sat still for a moment to recover herself. Then she called after him in a tone he had seldom heard, "You unmitigated bastard! Do you think I don't know what you did to us and to Tahg?"

Win stopped still in his tracks. He'd wondered if Angelica knew more about the incident than she'd let on. At first he had lived in fear that his complicity was known by her. Then it had occurred to him that Tahg was the only one who knew the truth of it, and he was dead or dying. If Angelica knew the full story, it meant Tahg wasn't dead and that was dangerous. Without question, that was a very dangerous circumstance.

"Is he alive, then?" Win asked as casually as he dared.

"He's alive, Winston, but too ill to deal with the likes of a cowardly wretch like you. But just you wait until he is well . . ."

"*If* he ever lives to get well, Angelica." Win threw the words back at her. "Now that I know he's alive, rest assured I'll have men into every rat hole in Dublin before suppertime."

"You'll never find him," she said definitively. "I'm the only one who knows where he is. And I will never lead you to him!"

"We shall see about that!" said her brother as he stormed from her room.

Angelica watched his departure with a mixture of anger, contempt and hurt. He was so goddamned vicious when provoked! *I must not let his cruelty cloud the issue,* she said sensibly inside her head. *The only important thing that has happened between us today is that I have let him know that Tahg is alive and that I know where.*

Resolutely, she turned her chair and moved with a metallic sound down the quiet hallway toward her writing desk.

* * *

Carefully Angelica noted the events of the week of 25 September in her diary. It was ghastly to relive what had happened by recording it, but her plan left no choice at all.

"*Never* will he find the house at 14 Upper Dorset Street!" she wrote, emphatically underlining the "Never." "*Never* will he find the rented room where my poor Tahg lies near death, with none to attend him but an elderly charwoman. It would break your heart to see someone you love in that little ground-floor room he occupies at the back of the house. The only comfort it affords at all is in the fact that it opens onto the small patch of yard beyond. But, of course, that can be of no use to Tahg now, when he's so deathly ill. God curse my infirmity that I cannot go to my cousin when he needs me.

"At least Mick has promised me that when he returns from London on the weekend he will see to moving Tahg to a proper place, where proper care can be given him."

Resolutely she turned her chair and moved with a metallic noise down the quiet hallway. A servant appeared at the sound and moved toward her chair.

"Shall I help you, Miss Angelica?" he asked politely.

"No," she said hastily. "No thank you, William. I should like to be alone for a bit, I believe." She kept on moving as she spoke, hoping that the man did not see the bright tears glistening on her cheeks.

Winston left Angelica in a state of intense agitation. He could not leave Tahg alive, that was a certainty. Not only could Tahg accuse him before his father of having been responsible for harming the girls, but the man would most likely seek his own vengeance as soon as he was well.

No. He must be dealt with now, while he was still disabled.

Damn Angelica, with her almighty righteous indignation! He mustn't let his anger with her interfere with his clear thinking. There had to be clues to Tahg's whereabouts in her house. Somewhere in her personal papers there must be an answer! But where? He couldn't trust Doyle to do the dirty work this time—the little bastard had turned out to be smarter than he'd anticipated. He'd have to do it himself. At least there'd be no problem about seeking access to Angelica's house now that Father was staying there because of his growing illness. Starting tomorrow he would make daily filial visits until he could find some evidence of Tahg's whereabouts.

Winston had already reached home when he remembered his sister's diary. By God! She'd been toying with it this very morning, as they spoke. That book was her constant companion . . . had been ever since her childhood.

"When you cannot do things others can," she had told him years before, "you content yourself with living through the pages of your diary, where all your most intimate and sacrosanct thoughts reside."

That's where he would find it! In the diary. Without a doubt it was the only place to which she might entrust the address.

But how to get the damned thing away from her? She'd always guarded it like Cerberus at the gates of Hades.

Mother! That was the ticket. Mother would be brought there to see Father. Surely Angelica's attention would be diverted by that. He would have to contrive to get the diary while mother and daughter engaged each other's attention.

If only Angelica didn't keep it locked in the safe. No! That was ridiculous. She was a cripple. She couldn't move freely. It would have to be kept close at hand, in her bedroom or her study.

Satisfied that he had puzzled out the worst of it, Win let himself back into his suite at the hotel. He'd have to eat humble pie with Mother, of course, to make his visits appear sincere ones. But that was little enough to pay for the information he needed.

Win took the revolver from the drawer in his night table and inspected it carefully. There would be no room this time for mistakes.

༄ When Angelica asked me to come to see Edmond, I had no way of knowing that his illness was only one of the dramas being played out beneath that roof. I was already in Dublin for a meeting Collins had called, so I arrived the morning following her invitation.

Edmond Manningham lay white upon the pillows of the great bed that had been shipped to Dublin years before, when we'd purchased the Waterloo Road house; it seemed less formidable to me now, as did he. Edmond looked frail and bony, the patrician length of him somehow fragile beneath the covers.

Although Angelica had prepared me for the worst, I was still unsettled by his appearance.

Edmond seemed nervous when he saw me, as was I. But he composed himself admirably and lifted a hand to me. I clasped it, and was painfully aware of the sharp white bones beneath the blue-white skin.

"Good of you to come," he said, as if the invitation had been to tea.

"The children told me you were ill," I replied. "I hadn't realized . . ."

"There was no reason that you should," he said; his voice seemed to demand much effort of him.

"Is there something that I can do to help you, Edmond?" I asked, feeling strangely moved by his condition. It is unsettling to see one who has always been powerful when he is bereft of power.

And, too, after all the intervention of the years, he seemed, irrationally, an old friend from the long ago who was somehow unexpectedly needy.

"Yes, Elizabeth, there is indeed a boon I would ask of you," Edmond said with difficulty. "I wish to settle our affairs before I die . . . I wish to make peace between us if that is possible." There was no mistaking his sincerity. I was quite taken aback by the notion that he would think of me as he lay dying.

"There is no need, Edmond," I told him, meaning it. "Our battles are far behind us. And, in truth, I have much to be grateful to you for."

He smiled sadly at that. "You were not what I'd bargained for, Elizabeth," he told me in a low, determined voice. "Too rebellious, too vulnerable. I'd lived so long a bachelor that I'd fancied the addition of a wife would simply add to my pleasures. A glorified extra servant, you might say, but with breeding potential." He laughed, but the sound was hollow.

"Edmond, there is no need . . ."

"But there is, there is, there is! Don't you see? Elizabeth, I was not so different from the other men of my class in all that. We were never taught to be other than selfish with our wives . . . never taught that a woman had a heart and a soul as well as a body.

"You were so loving and so very open when you came to me. I hadn't the faintest idea how to respond to all that. And you had a mind of your own under all that gentleness. I wanted to break you to harness, but I hadn't the sense to know that a light snaffle would have done.

"I saw it all as a consummate nuisance, a demand I wasn't up to. Yes, that's it, you see! That's what I wanted to say to you. It was *my* lack, *my* deficiency and I told you it was yours! What a cruel hoax to play on one so young and defenseless." He seemed very agitated. I tried to interrupt, but he wanted to continue speaking.

"I recall it all, now that I'm dying . . . I remember everything with such great clarity.

"You would come to my bed so tentatively and yet with such desire. And I—fool that I was—serviced you as if you were a mare in heat. No love, no kindness. None of the gentling you deserved.

"I wouldn't let you in, would I, Elizabeth? Wouldn't let you near enough to possess me. I couldn't, you see. Too afraid of intimacy. Too afraid of sharing or loving. Too afraid of my own inadequacy. Not as a lover, you understand; I fancied myself good at that. But as a *beloved*—I somehow knew I didn't have the stuff for that role.

"There's a cold streak in us Manningham men, Elizabeth. Deadly cold.

"I see it in Winston. Dear God, I've learned so much about myself from seeing my reflection in that boy." He sounded anguished and my heart went out to him. There was no doubt in my mind that he was dying. And there was a curious cleansing in his words. A balm for ancient hurts, although I know not why it should have been so. I strove to soothe him in return.

"You tried to behave honorably toward me, Edmond, despite the trials I put you through. I've always been grateful." I wanted to console him, wanted to bridge the gap of the years. We were too old and knowledgeable of each other to be enemies. "You accepted Johnny when you knew he wasn't yours."

"Only because I knew your agony would be all the greater if I did." The cruelty of that took me aback. I had to wait a moment until the pain of remembrance subsided. Why had this man still the power to hurt me after all this time? It struck me suddenly how much of hurt he, too, had known.

"Then you must have loved me once," I replied, "to have hated me enough to be so cruel."

"I have loved you, Elizabeth, ever since the moment you stopped loving me," he said resignedly, the awful irony hanging in the air between us. There was nothing I could say to that. Does God laugh or weep at such follies as ours?

"We have fine children," I said after a time. "They are the good that came of us." The act of dying leaves little need for recrimination.

"All but the one who is most like me," he said bitterly.

"He is like you only on the surface, Edmond. Win has never had your character, nor your integrity. Besides, I have felt guilty enough over the years about our eldest; no need for you to add to the tally."

"You, guilty? And, why, might I ask?"

"It cannot be easy for a boy of Winston's rectitude to have a notorious scarlet woman as his mother."

Edmond laughed aloud at that, suddenly, and for the first time. A little of his youth came back with the laugh, and I remembered how handsome I had thought him once.

"You were no scarlet woman, Beth! Only one who needed to be loved. If you'd had other than a fool for a husband, it would all have been different." Never in all our lives together had he called me Beth.

"I've always wondered, you know . . . wanted to ask you, but it seemed indelicate . . ." He averted his eyes from mine. "Did this rebel of yours make you happy?" He asked it soberly, the laughter gone.

"Beyond all earthly expectations."

"Then perhaps I did you a good turn after all in driving you into his bed." The sorrow in Edmond's voice made me want to weep.

"You're a strange man, Edmond," I said. "But I would have you know I bear you none but kind thoughts." I laid his cold hand back upon the coverlet. But he reached for mine again.

"It was the folly of my life to let you get away," he said urgently. "Please believe me that I am grateful that you found happiness. Would God it might have been with me."

I held his hand for a long time after that; tears of remembrance and forgiveness take a long time to shed. In all the years that we had been separated, it had never occurred to me that Edmond might be lonely. The effort of talking had exhausted him and he seemed to be asleep. I stayed because there was so much more to say and I didn't know the words. So I held his hand and thought long silent thoughts about what might have been.

Had Edmond loved me, I would never have worked for Ireland . . . nor would I have understood the plight of women enough to write about it. . . . There would have been no Seaneen O'Sullivan for me to love and learn from. . . . Angelica would not be crippled, nor Johnny Manningham ever born. My darling Constance might be with me still.

Circles within spirals, wheels within wheels. God's great intricate tapestry of our lives. Tangled skeins, tangled skeins.

I forgive you, Edmond. Forgive me, too.

God forgive us both. ✎

32   Winston Manningham hovered soundlessly outside the rear window of No. 14 Upper Dorset Street. The place seemed quiet enough; there was no discernible movement within the corner room that, he deduced from Angelica's description, must be the one.

Stealthily, he made his way to the casement window, which by some stroke of fortune was open wide to the night air. He could make out the still form of a man in the bed within; his back was to the window and the covers were pulled up high, to thwart the breeze from the opened window. There was a smell of disinfectant and medication in the air. It was the right room.

Nervously, Win pulled himself up and over the window ledge. His shoes scraped the exterior wall as he did so, a small sound in the darkness, but unnerving. He stopped, waited to see if Tahg had heard or moved, then, seeing his quarry undisturbed, he sidled over the sill and let himself into the room.

Winston stood poised for a moment, to accustom his eyes to the interior darkness, and withdrew the revolver soundlessly from his pocket.

He thanked his stars that he had been present some weeks before at a demonstration of the new pistol silencing devices that had been invented a few years earlier in Europe but had only recently come to Ireland. The "silencer," as it was called, would muffle his shots enough so that he could make his escape before anyone discovered the body.

Winston, eyes now accustomed to the gloom, saw two photographs in inexpensive frames on the nightstand near the bed. One was of Kitty O'Neill, one of Angelica Manningham. He felt the detestation he'd harbored for his cousin for a lifetime rise within him. Tahg had been a thorn in his side as long as he could remember. Always the others had preferred him to their own brother. And Kitty . . . he was well rid of any woman who would give herself to the likes of Tahg O'Connor.

Winston raised his gun, aimed carefully and remorselessly fired two shots into the sleeping man. They thudded strangely in the quiet, causing the form on the bed to move ever so slightly.

Anxious to be sure he had done the job right this time, Win moved to the bed and pulled aside the coverlet. Beneath it, there was no body. Only bunched-up blankets and pillows where a body should have been.

Horrified, Win saw that a note was pinned to one of the pillows. Straining to read it in the moonlight from the window, his heart beating so insanely he thought he might faint, he tore it from its place beside the bullet holes.

"Think of this as checkmate in your little game with Fate, Winston," the note said in Angelica's large and forceful scrawl. "And think of me as your Avenging Angel."

Two figures moved swiftly from the shadows; despite his struggles, they overpowered the terrified man and dragged him from the room.

Several days later, the Dublin papers carried banner headlines about the execution by the IRA of the one man at Dublin Castle who had come so close to capturing Michael Collins.

○ October will evermore seem to me the month of funerals. Dead leaves. Final reckonings.

Winston was buried with every honor that could be lavished on a member of the aristocracy murdered by dissidents. Edmond, too ill to attend his son's funeral, died the following day.

The two services blend together now in my memory. There was a sorrow in my living children as they stood by the graves of their brother and their father that went beyond the loss of death. I did not yet know as I stood beside them in the cemetery how life had betrayed them.

Merry and Jamie stood together. Their hands entwined as ever. Merry's face was pale as a marble angel on a tomb. She seemed disoriented and far, far away. Angelica, usually stoical, wept unrestrainedly in her chair. Johnny, stony-faced, stood beside me—what his thoughts must have been, I would not wish to know.

Where is Tahg? I had demanded. What has happened to Merry? Why will no one speak Winston's name aloud? What in God's name had happened to my children! Finally, the night of Edmond's funeral, Angelica relented and told me what had happened to them all. It was neither confession nor apologia, but rather some final reparation to the truth. I held her in my arms—my golden child, so tarnished by the world. Shocked. Horrified. Heartsick, I was. The ghosts of all the hopes and dreams I'd cherished for my children danced insanely before me.

Images rose and dissipated, like waves of illness. The ghastly night when Winston was born . . . Angelica being wheeled from surgery, Con's stricken face behind her . . . Edmond turning from the cradle after seeing Johnny for the first time.

And other phantoms, too. Con, Des and I planning what life would render to us; laughing, dreaming . . . expecting only joy of the years.

How could we know it would be our children who would make the final payments? ✍

33

Michael Collins
Cadogan Square
London, England
3 November 1921

Dear Tahg,
 I've a heavy heart tonight—the talks go badly. Chur-

chill despises the Irish, that's a certainty. But I did manage to have my fun with him today.

He came to the meeting with a great long list in his pudgy hand—it turned out to be an itemized tally of all the places where our boys have breached the Truce.

I scribbled a note to Dalton asking if we had any answer to the allegations—he said no. What can I do? I asked myself. We've put ourselves in the worst possible light.

So I listened for a few more minutes (the list was a long one). Then I banged my fist as hard as I could on the table and shouted, "For Christ's sake, come to the point!"

I thought Dalton's hair would leave his head, it stood so on end waiting for the wrath to come. So I gave a bloody great shout of laughter at the whole ridiculous scene, and by God, didn't Churchill laugh, too!

All the steam was gone out of him after that—but, of course, it was a small victory in the face of so damned many defeats.

I'm not a statesman, Tahg Mor. I've been sent here to do what must be done—but it should have been done by others. If they'd had as much moral courage as they had wind, we'd all be better off. Whoever heard of a soldier who fought the enemy in the field being sent to negotiate the peace? I'll do my best with God's help, but it's rough work, Tahg. And little light do I see at the end of the shaft.

> Your friend,
> Mick

Angelica fussed with her hair for the hundredth time and waited for Derek's arrival.

Her chest wound was nearly healed now, so his visits were not as frequent as they had been in the beginning, but they were far more personal. And today was the day he'd said they would talk about her legs. She smiled ruefully at the frail appendages that had caused her so much pain and anxiety for a lifetime and thought that for once she was grateful to them . . . they were the reason that Derek O'Hanrahan was coming back.

When he arrived, she let him in gracefully and he wheeled her chair to the drawing room. After she had rung for tea,

Derek took her hands in both of his and said, "Angelica, I've been thinking about you a very great deal, girl. And I've decided that the only way for me to attempt to help you is if we are absolutely honest with each other."

She smiled quizzically at the strange beginning. "I'm always honest, Derek."

He shook his head as if to dismiss that fact as irrelevant.

"No, no. I don't mean *that* kind of honesty, lass. I know you're an honorable person. I mean that there are games that men and women play with each other . . . flirtations and inexactitudes. You tell me I'm brilliant, I tell you you're beautiful—which by the way, you are—and suddenly the honesty has deteriorated into something less."

"Why are you saying these things to me, Derek?"

The stocky young man stood up suddenly and began to pace up and down in front of her chair. His red-brown hair fell down over his forehead and he had a habit of tossing his head to send it back where it belonged. He was too male for it to seem a vain gesture.

"Because I'm confused about how I feel about you, I suppose," he answered earnestly. "I'm attracted to you. There's no doubt about that. But I can't sort out what's personal and what's professional interest in your case. Which, by the way, I believe I can help."

She laughed suddenly and said, "Do you always do that? Interrupt yourself with pronouncements?"

"Yes, I do," he said seriously, and continued to gaze at her steadily.

"You see, I know things about what you're feeling that most men wouldn't. So I want to help you."

He came and sat down beside her abruptly.

"I've also been warned by your cousin that if I play you false, he'll have my hide for it."

Angelica burst out laughing, a lovely, honest sound, and Derek laughed, too.

"There now," she said, "that's better. Now I'll be candid with you! I'm just as confused as you are—perhaps more so. I look forward to your visits as if you were Father Christmas. I'm afraid to hope that you can help my legs and yet I *do* hope.

"More than that, I think you are so attractive a man, I'm

quite startled that you've even bothered to take an interest in me . . ."

At that he turned to look her full in the face. "How cruel it is that your injury has made you feel less beautiful than you are," he said, sounding so earnest that it made her blush.

"You must think me a perfect fool to be babbling on like this, Angelica, when we barely know each other."

"No," she said, meaning it. "I'm grateful for your candor, Derek O'Hanrahan. People are so relentlessly polite to you when you're handicapped that you must spend half your life just sorting out the truth."

The tea tray arrived and Angelica poured for both. Derek watched the grace of her movements. The to-the-manner-born stylishness and ease with which she did the things he'd had to learn by rote, and often forgot.

She watched the sturdy peasant maleness of the man, the direct unpretentiousness and simple competence of him, and was entranced. Could it be that he could really help her? Could it be that he might ever be more to her than a doctor?

"I think I know what we must do," she said thoughtfully.

"And that is?"

"We must simply become friends and let the rest of it take care of itself." She smiled as she said it, an open, warmly honest smile, and he grinned back.

Derek's face was too irregular to be thought handsome. His nose was fine and straight but it tipped up slightly at the end. His eyes were keen and merry and there seemed always to be a smile hiding just behind his mouth—except when he was troubled or very serious. Then his auburn brows knitted together over sober eyes and two lines gathered in his forehead that had not been there before. She thought he had the most interesting face she'd ever seen.

They spoke of his childhood and of hers. Of the injury that had separated her from other folk. He told her of his part in the Rising and how he'd decided, despite Tahg's entreaties, not to become embroiled in the later troubles.

They talked and laughed, and she watched his curious habit of suddenly leaping up and pacing back and forth as he spoke, as if the momentum of his words forced his body into motion.

Finally, almost embarrassedly, he asked to examine her legs and back, and she realized by the force of her own response that such intimacy was far more awkward now because they had already become friends. But it was welcome, nonetheless.

She felt the competent touch of his hands as they lingered on her legs and back. She lay propped up on the bed as he began to massage the long-dormant muscles with strokes so firm they seemed to impart a life-force of their own to parts of her that had seemed long dead.

"You must learn not to hate your legs," he told her seriously. "Not to fear them. They are not in charge of your life any longer, Angelica. From this day on, we are in charge of them, you and I!"

He told her how his mother had massaged life back into him and, more than that, had given him hope.

"You must reestablish the connection in your mind between you and your legs, girl. You must make them yours again."

He taught her exercises that she must do and prescribed warm baths and rubs. More than anything, he made her believe that change was possible.

"I must go now, lassie," he said finally, after several hours had flown by. "But I'll be back, you may count on that."

He helped her into her chair and she wheeled herself to the door to say good-bye. He turned to leave, then suddenly, impulsively, turned and kissed her on the lips. He smiled and was gone, and Angelica sat still as a stone in her chair, wondering . . .

> Michael Collins
> Cadogan Square
> London, England
> 20 November 1921

Dear Tahg,

The party's getting rough over here—there's damned near as much fighting among the members of our own delegation as there is with the other side.

Duffy and Barton insist that Lloyd George is only bluffing. They think we can keep ourselves out of the Empire entirely if we just hold our ground. Griffith and I are convinced that's a daydream.

We must be practical above all else. They'll never let us out of the Empire, but they may give us enough autonomy within it to run our own show. If we go off chasing moonbeams, we haven't a prayer of getting what we need.

Meanwhile, can you beat the fiasco of Brugha sending men to London to raid barracks here while we're sitting right in their laps? Does he mean to sink this ship before it sails? To say we looked like jackasses, when they told us what those fools had done, would barely cover it. How can we convince them we can run a country when we can't even control our own people?

Take care of yourself and of Angelica. She has more courage than the lot of us.

Mick

Angelica raised her legs from the bed with an enormous effort. So far, everything had been exactly as Derek had said. Pain. Exercise. Striving. Pain. One more inch off the bed. One more moment of movement than before. One more inch into the future.

The strain of the morning's exercise session had covered her body in sweat, and now she lay savoring the small victory, feeling life in her legs—not a lot, but enough to open possibilities. She felt a cold draft from the window touch her exhausted, happy form and reveled in the feeling. As she seemed to be reveling in so many feelings these days.

He was *so wonderful!* He had made everything new again. New and full of hope. Focusing inwardly, Angelica played again the memory of the first day that he had kissed her, really kissed her. It was still her favorite memory of him; alive with sexual promise, unexpected, glorious, hers.

Derek had been massaging her legs, as he had done a dozen times before . . . coming to her house after closing his little infirmary, or early in the day before opening its doors. It had been late at night and he had seemed weary and strangely quiet. Usually Derek talked incessantly while rubbing her legs, instructing her about her dormant muscles, telling her how to will them individually into life.

Lord, how she had looked forward to the strength of those hard, knowledgeable hands kneading life into lifeless limbs. Touching parts of her that were far beyond the parts that he touched physically.

She had watched him concentrating on his usual effort, seen him stop, still silent, letting his fingers trail gently, lingeringly over her skin.

"Angelica . . ." he began huskily, keeping his gaze riveted on her knees, it seemed. And then, suddenly, it wasn't her legs at all that he wanted to touch, but all of her. She saw the agony of indecision on his rugged face as he reached up to take her in his arms. Oh, strong, brawny arms that yet seemed gentle in their passion, and uncertain, warm, seeking lips that taught her mouth to kiss.

"I'm sorry," he had stammered when it was done, but she knew he wasn't sorry, and that was the most wonderful part of all.

Angelica stretched herself, catlike, and reaching for her right leg, pulled it into a pyramid. She didn't hate her legs now . . . she even thought they *looked* better. Healthier, rosier, plumper . . . more like other people's legs. It had taken two months of patient, painful effort, but it was working.

Derek had said she might even stand on them one day, up-right, firm. She thought if she could once see herself in a mirror, standing up, looking whole, she could die content.

Angelica giggled a little at the thought, loving the fact of her own hope.

"Oh, Derek," she said aloud. "Can you even imagine how much I love you?"

When the maid came in with her breakfast tray, she found her mistress already sitting up in bed brushing her hair and humming.

"I'm falling in love with your cousin," Derek said bluntly as he finished examining Tahg's back. The healing wound had left an ugly scar, but it had healed solidly nonetheless.

Tahg attempted to turn his head to see his friend, the good news putting a grin on his face.

"Hold still, dammit," said Derek. "You'll undo my brilliant handiwork."

"That's great news, Derek," said Tahg, ignoring the admonition. "She told me as much about your own fine self, as well."

"Did she, now?" asked Derek, trying to sound casual. "And who would believe it?"

"Have you thought any further than being in love?"

"You mean marriage or some such?"

"Of course I mean marriage, you dumb cluck. That hurts, by the way!" Tahg grimaced as Derek's hands prodded the area of his back around the healing wound.

"Do you mean marriage would hurt?" asked Derek with mock seriousness, slapping his friend's shoulder, a gesture which generally meant the examination was over.

"No, I didn't mean marriage," laughed Tahg, "I meant my back." He moved down from the examining table and stood in front of Derek, trying to get into his shirt unaided, not an easy task.

Derek watched his patient's movements. Tahg was painfully thin for a man his size, the weight loss especially apparent around the ribs. But he was better than either of them had a right to expect, considering what a close brush he'd had with death. It would be a while yet before he would be well.

"I don't suppose it does any good to give you sound medical advice, Tahg Mor, but I'll do it just to keep myself in practice.

"You've been a very sick man. The grim reaper damn near reaped you right before my very eyes . . . and Kitty's, I might add. And you're very far from well. Just because you can paddle around under your own steam a bit, instead of lying in the bed like you did for damned near two months, doesn't mean you're well."

"I'm much better, Derek," Tahg began.

"But not *well*, do you hear me? You haven't your strength back. You'll start out fine in the morning, and be out of steam by noon! You must take care of yourself or I won't be responsible for the consequences."

"Funny," answered Tahg, "Mick once said the same to me."

"How is he?"

"All right, all things considered. He's taking it very hard that there's no way to get what he wants for Ireland."

Derek raised an eyebrow. "Mick won his war, it seems, but he's in for a royal screwing before he wins the peace. Is that it?"

Tahg nodded and tried painfully to put his arm into the sleeve of his jacket before he replied. Derek watched the effort with concern. Tahg's was a strong body, but it had been through a terrible ordeal.

"Dev seems to have stepped out of the way of the bullet in this. The delegation gets little useful advice from the man and plenty of grief. He was one smart politician not to have gone with them."

Derek chuckled. "And what a surprise that is, now, isn't it?" He took off his white coat as he spoke and hung it on the hook behind the door of the shabby little infirmary he was so proud of.

"Your doctor prescribes a couple of stiff drinks at the local public house, laddie. How would that sit with you?"

"I thought doctors never prescribed alcohol for their patients," Tahg laughed.

"Sure, I'm not prescribing it for you, at all," replied Derek. "I'm prescribing it for meself! Truth is, I need to talk to you about this Angelica business. It's got me scared out of my mind."

Tahg smiled a little at that. Derek was always so cocky, so self-possessed, but then he'd never been in love before.

"Come on, O'Hanrahan," he said, pushing his friend toward the door, "I think it's you who need a doctor tonight."

Collins slipped into the pew at 6:02 A.M. and blessed himself. Few of his friends knew that he attended daily mass . . . almost no one knew how profoundly religious he really was.

Mick let the scent and sound of the quiet church fill his soul with balm. The incense and the burning candle wax . . . the rustle of ladies' dresses as they knelt or stood . . . the drone of Latin phrases . . . so beautiful in their composite mystery.

"Sweet Jesus," he prayed silently, "I've tried so hard. Please give me strength to see this through. Please give me the wisdom to deal with them, and the grace to control my temper."

He saw the priest turn and raise the chalice toward the praying parishioners, and heard the tinkle of the Offertory bell.

"Your sacrifice was so great, Lord, and mine so small," he said in his heart. "Please help me do my part as You would see it done."

Bending his head to his weary hands, Mick Collins said a prayer for guidance. They'd never let all of Ireland go; he knew that now. If he signed the Treaty as it stood, his own might kill him for it. And yet, was there any other way to do what was best for Ireland?

Is that the sacrifice You want from me, Lord? he asked suddenly, staring hard at the raised ciborium in the priest's hand.

Sweet Jesus, help me to know!

Michael Collins
Cadogan Square
London, England
1 December 1921

Dear Tahg,

How goes the healing? Angelica writes me that you're a lousy patient. No patience at all, to let nature take its course. You're a lucky man to even be alive, so I hope you'll take her advice, which comes straight from the young doctor she seems so taken with. Is he really good enough for the likes of her, do you think? She's a rare bird, your wee cousin, and not to be wasted on an unworthy man. I think we'd best take her love life under advisement when you are well and I am back in Ireland.

If ever I get there alive, of course.

We fight with His Pomposity (LG), His Pain-in-the-Arse (Birkenhead) and His Imperial Bulldog (Churchill) endlessly. We fight among ourselves as much. No instructions are forthcoming from our illustrious Dail Eireann.

They have us by the short hairs and they know it. We can't go on with the war—our people are dead tired of it and the money's low to nonexistent. Whatever they offer us, we'll have to take it in the end—all we can hope for is that we can dredge out of them enough so there's a shot at peace and unification.

It has become apparent in the last few days that they'll never let go of the North. They're in it for the money and that's where the money lies—the rails, the shipping, the factories are in Ulster, as well as the bulk of the Protestants. I can see no way in hell to pry it all loose from their greedy fingers.

And, oh laddie, they are good at what they do! These old boys have been trained from infancy to do their dirty work in an elegant and civilized manner. Sometimes I feel we're the worst country bumpkins by comparison. Other days I think our integrity puts them to shame, despite their fancy rhetoric.

So here we sit, with a half-arsed compromise on the one hand and the threat of war on the other. It reminds me that my father used to say "It's damned difficult to choose between two blind goats!"

Take care of yourself and don't let me hear of your running around before the doctor gives you leave or you'll have to contend with me.

> Your friend,
> Mick

34 Winston Churchill sat in his study, a glass of brandy in one hand, a cigar in the other. His plumpish body was comfortably housed in a velvet-collared smoking jacket and his small feet were raised on a tufted leather hassock.

"You know, Clementine," he said, expansively gesturing with the hand that held the cigar, "in all my life, I have never seen so much passion and suffering in restraint as that man Collins displayed today when it became apparent that they'd have to sign the Treaty, like it or not."

"Really, dear?" answered Clementine Churchill, politely interested. "I should have thought you detested the man."

Churchill raised an eyebrow significantly in his wife's direction.

"I've thought the entire delegation fairly contemptible from the first," he responded promptly and with good humor, "but there was something quite heroic about the man today. Something quite tragically Greek, I should think."

"Aeschylus or Euripides?" she asked, intrigued by his change of heart.

"No," replied Churchill thoughtfully, "Herodotus, perhaps. 'This is the bitterest pain among men, to have much knowledge but no power.'"

Clementine smiled indulgently at her husband. "I had more in mind, 'Yet I do hold that mortal foolish who strives against the stress of necessity.'"

Churchill chuckled appreciatively. "Well said, my dear. Since you are so enamored of Euripides this evening, perhaps you may recall that he also said, 'Man's best possession is a sympathetic wife.' "

Both Churchills smiled at that, and went about the business of being pleasantly married.

Michael Collins
London, England
3:00 A.M.
5 December 1921

Dear Tahg,

Well, it's done now. "Signature or war?" That was the choice Lloyd George gave us today. Griffith told him on the spot, "I will give the answer from the Irish delegation tonight, Mr. Prime Minister," he said, "but I personally will agree to sign this document and recommend it to my countrymen." The poor man looked like the wrath of God, sickly and dark under the eyes, when he said it. All the fights I've had with him notwithstanding, Griffith's a good and honorable man.

The battle raged all day and much of the night—Duggan, with us for the signing, Barton and Duffy holding out against it. At 2:00 A.M. we did the deed, God help us all.

When you have sweated, toiled, had mad dreams, hopeless nightmares—you find yourself in the London streets, cold and dank in the night air, thinking what have I got for Ireland? Something she has wanted these past seven hundred years? Will anyone be satisfied with the bargain? Will anyone?

I tell you this—this early morning I signed my death warrant. I thought at the time, how odd, how ridiculous, a bullet might just as well have done the job five years ago.

Say a prayer for me, Tahg Mor O'Connor. I'm a lonely man tonight.

Mick

Mick folded the letter and put it into an envelope. Tucking it into his breast pocket, he walked slowly to the window and stared out. Soon it would be dawn.

In the night the snow had sifted itself onto every branch and twig. It had filtered onto window ledges and piled itself in corners.

Powder drifts marshmallowed the sidewalks and soft indentations dimpled the way where feet had gone, and been covered again by nature's inexorable blanket of whiteness.

Michael Collins stared at nature's bounty almost listlessly. For the first time since his battles for Ireland had begun, he knew he was a dead man.

This time his hundred latchkeys wouldn't save him; his ability to disappear in a crowd wouldn't save him; his fearlessness nor his brain.

This time he had been betrayed by his own—and that is the one karmic doom that no Irishman ever outruns.

35   ∽ Seaneen and Johnny faced each other like two bulls who pawed the earth in readiness for mortal combat.

"Collins was right to sign the Treaty!" shouted Seaneen at his son. "Dev's a dirty coward to pull his support out from under him when he knows damned well there wasn't a fucking thing the man could do but sign the goddamned thing!"

"Collins's the coward!" Johnny spat out contemptuously. "The bloody traitor, sold us out to the Brits! By God, he deserves to die for it."

"I'll hear none of that kind of talk!" thundered Seaneen. "Who the hell do you think you are to take the measure of a man like Collins? He's spent his whole bloody life fighting for Ireland. If it weren't for Mick there'd have been no negotiation, no possibility of peace." Seaneen's face was red with the force of his anger.

"Do you think any one of us really thought he could make them give up the whole of Ireland? We did not! Do you think they don't know they've got us by the throat? No food, no money. A country ravaged by their bloody butchers—and by our own! Do you think they wouldn't step on our delegation and then scrape them off their shoes if it wasn't for the stature of Mick Collins and Arthur Griffith?

"You think because you can pull a trigger and kill a man you can have everything you want? Well, it damned well isn't so!" Seaneen's face was fierce with fury, his lips a tight line, a vein pulsed at his temple.

I looked from one to the other, the horror keeping me in my place, just out of sight within the shadow of the bedroom door. I watched the colors come and go in Johnny's face as his father berated him. Damaged pride, fury, passion, hatred, love. Christ, it was like watching someone flayed alive.

"You're wrong," he managed to say finally between tightly clenched teeth. "You're my father and I love you, but you're wrong about this! Collins has screwed us and we won't let him get away with it. We can win, don't you see? We've got them on the run! If we have to murder every fucking one of them, to drive them out of Ireland, we can do it!

"And we will. By God we will! There's talk among the men. There's plenty in the IRA who're willing to fight this bloody Treaty. We'll break off on our own and leave Collins and his lily-livered pro-Treaty cowards to fend for themselves."

"You're talking civil war," shouted Seaneen.

"You're damned right, I am," my son shouted back at him.

"You're a young fool, Johnny," said Seaneen.

"And you're an old one! Too old to be making decisions for young men like me and Breen and Treacy!" The words were said in rage, of course, but they should never have been spoken. Too late to unsay them, Johnny realized what he had done.

Seaneen stood still as granite, hurt to the bone. Johnny, unable to undo what he had done, shook his head, once quickly, like a troubled lion, then turned from his father's sightless stare and slammed out the door.

Neither man knew that I had been standing in the doorway, blessedly hidden by the doorframe. I pulled back even farther into the darkness; it had been a scene that neither wife nor mother should have witnessed.

Seaneen stared at the closed door for a long time after Johnny slammed it; it seemed almost as if he could see it, he stared so intensely. I was afraid to move at all lest he hear and remember me. God, how I wanted to put my arms around his drooping shoulders.

Finally, he walked to the chair he liked best by the fire, groping his way along. For the first time since I had known him, Seaneen looked his age, as if the years had come upon him by some instantaneous fairy spell.

I sat down on the edge of the bed, a sinking feeling in my stomach. Trouble, it said. Coming events cast their shadows before them. ∽

The fight at the Dail in the Mansion House had gone on for hours without losing momentum. Bitter, angry, hateful words were strewn deliberately by both sides.

Dev had proposed the formal rejection of the Treaty.

Speech after speech argued the points, endlessly. Tahg and Mick finally strode from the room, worn down by the futility of all that was being said there.

After the meeting de Valera issued a statement calculated to whip up the arguments into a whirlwind throughout the countryside.

"They called me a traitor," Mick whispered to Tahg as they walked back home through the darkened streets of the city. "Can you beat that? They actually called me a traitor." The anguish in Mick's voice was so palpable that Tahg couldn't answer him. For what was there to say?

6 January 1922

Sixty people crowded one end of the hall where the Dail had been called for yet another emergency session.

De Valera had made his proposition clear: "Stand by me as President and I'll get rid of Collins and go to the English with a separate recommendation, instead of the Treaty."

Griffith, haggard but statesmanlike, rose in desperation to speak his mind and to defend Collins, who was under attack, it seemed, by nearly everyone. A lifetime of journalism in Ireland's behalf rose in his conscientious, humorless mind. A lifetime of service to a cause that seemed about to be lost in a storm of self-interested rhetoric.

Griffith's conscience would not allow him to keep silent now. He rose and spoke of Mick. He told them that Collins was a man who had worked from six in the morning, until two the next, for years in Ireland's behalf. It was Collins's indomitable will and matchless energy and genius that had carried Ireland through the crisis years, he said. "And though I have not now and never have had ambitions about either political affairs or history," he told them with more emotion in his voice than any had previously heard there, "if my name is to go down in history, I want it to be associated with the name of Michael Collins."

He wondered when he sat down if anyone had listened to a word he'd said.

After weeks of vicious debate in the Dail and out of it, the vote was finally taken.

"Let the Irish nation judge us now and for future years!" cried Collins. When they did, the vote was sixty-four for, fifty-seven against the Treaty as it had been signed by the delegation. The peace Treaty was ratified and the war was officially over.

Collins was beside himself—he offered his hand to Dev, but "the Long Fellow" refused it. Instead, de Valera resigned as President and proposed himself for the position of President of a new Republic.

Another chess piece had been moved into place on fate's inexorable game board.

36   Derek clenched and unclenched his hands behind his back. If Angelica had been less heartsick, she might have been amused at the curious figure he made pacing up and down in her small drawing room.

"Don't you think you'd best say whatever it is that's on your mind?" she asked finally.

He stopped at that, and turned to face her.

"I don't know how to say it."

"Surely you don't expect me to say it for you," she replied bitterly, knowing full well what was to come.

The unhappy man moved toward her then, a look of loving compassion in his face. He dropped down beside her chair as he had a thousand times before and took her hand in his own.

"It isn't that I don't love you, Angelica," he began, looking sorrowfully into her fathomless eyes. "It's that I'm not up to what it would mean to be married to you."

"Because I'm a cripple?" she asked straightforwardly, and he winced at the word.

"'Tis only your body that's damaged, my friend . . ." he began, as he had in the past.

"It appears that is enough to deter you."

Derek sat back on his haunches, as if defeated by her bitter voice.

"I'll try hard to be honest with you, girl. But you must let me say it all. Up until now, I've loved you so much that I thought we could overcome everything. But then the question of marriage came up. And suddenly I knew how scared I am of it. Scared of having a wife who can't do with me all I've dreamed of doing, scared that we might not have children . . ."

"But you said I could conceive."

"Yes, that's entirely true, but could you give birth with your impaired pelvis, without killing yourself . . . that I don't know. I don't want that responsibility. It isn't even that I don't want it, so much as that I can't bear it!

"I'm afraid of it all, Angelica. Afraid of people saying I married you for your money. Afraid that I'm rushing into something I can't handle . . ."

"Enough!" she practically shouted the word at him. "Do you think I have no heart to break? Do you think because my legs are damaged, the rest of me is indestructible?"

Angelica tried to regain possession of herself. "You have given me hope, Derek . . . and you have given me love. I will try very hard to remember these things so that I needn't hate you!" She said the words in a small and deadly cold voice that unnerved him, then turned her chair around abruptly and left the room.

Angelica sat as still as death for a very long while after Derek had left her. Hurt and anger swept through her in alternating waves, pushing and pulling at her stomach and brain.

She had sensed the change in their relationship ever since the question of marriage had been raised.

So it would never be as she had dreamed. Never the comfort of Derek's arms to shelter her . . . never the fulfillment of his children at her breast. Alone, she would be as she had always been. Alone, and less than whole.

Absently, she began to pull at the pins that held her hair. Oh, the ache of it! The terrible bursting sorrow that seemed to have settled poundingly in her head.

The loosened hair fell carelessly from its braided prison and surrounded her shoulders in a sheltering yellow veil. She wished she could hide behind its concealing comfort forever.

Suddenly Angelica grabbed the windowsill and determinedly pulled herself from her wheelchair with monumental effort. She had never in all her life stood alone. The pain of being upright for even a moment was nearly overwhelming; a staggering nausea accompanied the pain. Angelica grabbed for the chair, but it skidded away from her. Desperately, she held the window ledge, straining for balance. Slowly, heartbrokenly, she lowered herself to the floor, a feeling of consummate helplessness washing over her.

I will not let this destroy me, she said over and over in her head. I will not let this break me down.

Tears. Tears. Tears to fill an ocean, she thought. I will not let this break me down!

Derek sat in the park outside the hospital with his head in his hands. What had he done? He had hurt the person he loved most in the world. He had said all the things he'd wanted to say . . . needed to say. All the terrible hurtful things that had been growing in him over the past month. But he didn't feel better for having said them. And he didn't feel free.

Instead he felt empty. A great sense of loss weighed on him. Empty of love, empty of promise, empty of hope for the future. What did it matter if they couldn't have everything, if they had so much? And didn't every husband who loved his wife worry about her prospects in childbed. . . . Should he who was a doctor have less faith in God than the simplest layman? Disgustedly, he rose from the bench and, jamming his hands deep into his pockets, began to walk.

Derek moved quietly about the room in his infirmary, where Tahg had agreed to meet him. He felt his friend's eyes watch his nervous movements. He busied himself in putting away the in-

struments and straightening his desk, until it was too absurd to
continue the irrelevant tasks.

"What's happened?" he heard Tahg say. "You look like
you've been kicked by a horse."

"I didn't know it was my looks that had attracted you,"
Derek responded, but there was no mirth in his voice.

"What's happened?" Tahg repeated the question pointedly.
"Why did you ask me to meet you here?"

"I've broken off with Angelica, if you must know."

There was silence for a moment, then Tahg spoke.

"Coward," he said.

"Just a minute, there!" Derek began angrily, then, thinking
better of it, said, "You're right, of course."

"I'm sorry, Derek," replied the man in the chair opposite his
desk. "You're the loser in this."

Derek's eyes raised themselves to Tahg's for a moment, then
he looked away, paying strict attention to the floor in front of
him as he began to speak.

"I couldn't face the whole thing, Tahg. It seemed too much.
. . . Now I think I've made a terrible mistake. I thought I
might try to see her, to talk it over."

Tahg's eyes were full of contempt.

"Don't do her any favors, O'Hanrahan. Angelica deserves
better in a man than one who isn't sure he wants her."

Derek started to reply, but stopped himself; he watched without speaking as Tahg rose and left the room.

Hat in hand, Derek stood in the drawing room where he and
Angelica had met so often over the last months. Our whole
courtship in a single room, he mused, as he waited for her to
appear. The familiar sound of her chair told him she was coming. He twisted the cloth cap nervously as he waited for the
paneled doors to open.

"Good morning, Derek," Angelica said, her voice even. "I
didn't expect to see you again."

He walked quickly toward her.

"I didn't expect to be here, Angelica. I've not slept all night. I
must have walked a thousand miles."

"A comfort that is denied me," she said; he couldn't tell if
her voice was bitter or simply weary.

"I've come to ask you to marry me," he said quickly. "I've

been a fool with my stupid fears. A terrible fool. I want you to be my wife, Angelica. Please forgive me for yesterday."

Angelica held one long blond tress tightly in her fingers. He noticed for the first time that her hair was loose, an unusual style for her in the day. She looked very beautiful despite the darkened circles beneath her eyes, which examined him searchingly before speaking. Her voice was low, but distinct, when she finally replied.

"I do forgive you, Derek. It took me most of the night to do so, but I do forgive you."

"Then . . ."

She held up her hand to keep him from speaking.

"But, I cannot marry you."

The dumbstruck look on the man's face almost made her smile.

"You see, my friend—and you have been my friend, indeed— you simply do not love me enough for me to give myself to you."

"Angelica. You can't mean this! I've worked it all out, my fears I can deal with . . ."

"You misunderstand me, Derek. Your fears are not in question now. Mine are.

"You see, for the first few hours after you left me yesterday I thought I would die from the grief of losing you. I even considered suicide for a brief moment—although it finally struck me as insane that someone who has fought as hard for life as I could contemplate throwing it away. But, you see, I thought I couldn't live without your love." Her voice faltered and she stopped for a moment to compose herself.

"Then, somehow, I began to pull the pieces of myself together again. When I decided to live, not to die, I had to take inventory of myself." She took a deep breath, then said, "That's when I forgave you."

Derek sat down clumsily on the settee. Never had he imagined that she, too, could say no to their future.

"I don't understand what has changed," he said, bewildered. "I thought you wanted to marry me."

Angelica wheeled her chair closer, a deliberate intimacy. Her eyes seemed softer when she replied.

"I did, Derek, my love. I did and I do. But when you said

those awful words to me, I realized that you were not the man I'd dreamed of.

"You see, my friend, of all the gifts you've given me, the most important was a sense of my own worth. As a woman, as a person. There may not be any man in this whole wide world who has the courage to love me as I am—really love me! And it will take courage, Derek. Nothing will ever be easy for a man who takes me for his wife.

"But one thing I know for sure. I can never settle for less than such. I could see in your eyes yesterday that always, always you would see your sacrifice in marrying me. You would think it your due that I be grateful, and you would feel that you had done me the greatest of favors.

"I just can't settle for that, Derek. You've made me a whole person despite my handicap. If ever a man loves me enough to count himself lucky to have me, I shall marry him and spend the rest of my life convincing him that he was right. If there never is such a person for me . . . well, I'm a rich woman. I have my home and my servants, my work and my friends. It will have to suffice."

Derek O'Hanrahan sat, head bent, hands clasped together, elbows on knees; he was the picture of dejection. Neither he nor Angelica spoke for what seemed a very long time.

"You're right, of course," he said finally, miserably. "I just assumed like a fool that the choices were all mine . . . only mine. I don't know what to say to you, Angelica. I do love you as you wish to be loved. I could be that man."

He raised his eyes to hers.

"If you'll have me, Angelica, I can be that man."

"I must think about all this," she said softly, seeing his sincerity. "I've been thinking only with my heart for so long where you're concerned, Derek. Then yesterday I realized that I must think with my head as well. Don't you see the great gift you've given me . . . the gift of *choice?* A year ago I would have been so grateful that a man wanted me, I'd have leaped at the chance, and most likely lived to regret it.

"I do love you, Derek—but I didn't love the man you were yesterday. I must think through what you've said to me. You've given me back myself—such a great gift. I think perhaps I'd rather leave it at that, and be grateful to you for a lifetime, than marry you and find out you haven't the courage I need."

Derek shook his head wonderingly.

"You're a remarkable woman, Angelica Manningham. I would be proud to have you as my wife. I feel honored, I think, to have you as my friend." He stood up uncertainly, walking the two steps to her chair and bending to her level.

"After all that's been said, I wouldn't ask you to marry me if I didn't believe I could handle what comes of it. I'd count myself the luckiest man on earth if you'd say yes."

With that he kissed her gently on the cheek; then Derek let himself out of the room and out of the house.

Angelica wheeled herself to the window and watched thoughtfully as she saw him walk down the street; his hands were in his pockets and he looked deeply troubled. She watched until he was out of sight and then sat staring at the nearly empty street for a very long while.

37

"Take it down from the Mast, Irish Traitors,
It's the Flag we Republicans claim,
It can never belong to Free Staters,
For you've brought on it nothing but shame.

Why not leave it to those who are willing,
To uphold it in War and in Peace,
To the men who intend to do killing,
Until England's tyrannies cease."

꩜ I listened to the young men singing the obscene lyric, sick at heart. To call men like Michael Collins and Seaneen O'Sullivan traitors was beyond all reason.

The ferocity of the fight between the moderate IRA men like Seaneen and the fanatical ones like Johnny was sapping the last pitiful reserves of strength we all had.

Dev was dead wrong to repudiate the Treaty and to claim it

was in opposition to the will of the people. In truth, the people were weary to death of the devastation of battle. They wanted freedom from British misrule, and a chance to rebuild Ireland, but by no means did they feel that the Treaty was a blunder. To have seen the rejoicing in the streets, as men and women realized they could once again walk without fear of being shot in their tracks, would have been to understand the true tenor of the people after the Treaty was ratified. The Irish Free State created by the Treaty had dominion status, like that of Canada. It seemed a perfectly acceptable condition to the majority of Irishmen.

Yet the extremists, with Dev to egg them on, seemed not to want freedom at all, but only the endless struggle to achieve it. Seaneen, who had spent a lifetime fighting for Ireland, saw, as did Collins, that wars that do not end in treaties end in disaster and destruction.

Rory O'Connor, Liam Mellows, Ernie O'Malley and others like them headed the anti-Treaty forces. They called themselves Republicans, and their opponents, Free Staters. From March of 1922 on, they splintered the IRA into warring factions and plunged the whole of Ireland into bloody civil war.

Mick Collins was, without a doubt, devastated by the turn things had taken. Tahg's letters were full of his efforts to mend the broken fences within the Organization. The Treaty had been the only sane option for the beleaguered country; but Dev and the other hotheads would have none of it.

And it wasn't only the Republicans that Mick had at his throat during that awful time. The English, too, did their best to bury him. They called for the strictest possible interpretation of the Treaty, leaving no latitude for those trying to keep the peace. And the men in Ulster felt Collins had abandoned them to England's rule, so they, too, turned against him. By summer 1922, Michael Collins was besieged on all fronts.

He attempted to restore discipline, but every day, it seemed, men changed sides. Seaneen and Johnny were not the only father and son to find themselves on opposing sides of this war.

Anti-Treaty forces took over the Four Courts and held it until 30 June. Republicans and Free Staters who had once been comrades under fire attacked each other vengefully during the battles there, screaming vilifications at each other from both sides of the barricades.

It was inconceivable to Collins that men who had been his loyal comrades-in-arms—men he had called "friend"—could turn against him and call him traitor. He spent the summer going from brigade outpost to outpost trying to accomplish with lucidity what obviously could not be done with arms.

When he and Tahg stopped in Tipperary on their way to Cork in August, Collins seemed still to believe that he could win the dissidents there back to the fold. They were some of his oldest friends (and at that moment among his most hostile foes), so we were surprised and concerned at his optimism, for it seemed to have no valid basis.

Mick was bitter and appeared on the verge of illness from the terrible strain. The stress of the months in London, the trauma of being castigated by men he loved, the anxiety of trying to hold together, by sheer force of will, a warring nation—all these had become distressingly apparent in his deterioration. Mick Collins seemed a haunted man.

"Where exactly are you headed?" Seaneen asked him as we all sat down to dinner.

"On a tour of the local outposts in Cork," Mick replied. "I'll meet with as many of the officers as I can, and try to reason with them. I believe we can get them to come over to our way of thinking yet. There's nothing to be gained now by civil war, Seaneen. I've got to make them see that."

"What concessions are you prepared to make them?" asked Seaneen astutely.

"There's little or none I can give," Collins answered sadly. "It's a crying shame we're any of us in this position at all, but it won't be made better by diluting the truth. Lynch, Deasy, the others I'm going to see . . . they're good men at heart. This cursed conflict is worse than Cain and Abel's." He seemed terribly agitated and I saw Tahg watching his friend with grave concern.

"De Valera stirred up the pot against you, lad," said Seaneen, but Collins waved off the thought with a gesture of his hand.

"It isn't only Dev," he said, poignantly magnanimous. "There's many a man I counted my friend who's turned on me and called me traitor."

"Are you sure it's safe to travel in Cork with tempers running so high?" asked Seaneen.

"Sure, they'll not shoot me in my own county," replied Collins with a hollow laugh.

I had reason later to remember the conversation. ∽

The little convoy lumbered its way along the road from Bandon to Beal na mBlath. An armored car rolled behind the yellow Leyland tourer in which Collins and Sean O'Connell sat. A Crossley Tender moved along in front of the touring car, and a motorcycle scouted ahead. Tahg O'Connor was not with the party; Mick had sent him on ahead to start the negotiations and loosen up the leaders before Collins's arrival. "Let them blow off steam, Tahg, without me in the room," he'd said. "They'll be all the more rational for it, later."

As they entered the valley of Beal na mBlath, a bleak place made bleaker by the wreckage of the recent fighting that had made most of the roadways there impassable, Collins picked up his rifle from the floor of the car and placed it carefully across his knees. There was an evil feel to the valley.

The men of the Cork No. 3 Brigade who lay in ambush could see the winding road for mile after curving mile. They had been in wait since morning and it was nearly sunset. A section of their party had already departed in disgust, thinking it too late for an encounter that day. Only a skeleton force was left behind on the barren hillside.

Lieutenant Smith on his motorcycle, riding fifty yards ahead of Collins and the others, spotted the overturned dray that blocked their passage around the bend in the road and turned to warn the others.

Shots rang out as the trap was sprung. "Drive like hell!" Dalton shouted as he realized what was happening.

"No!" shouted Collins, countermanding him. "We'll stand and fight them."

A burst of fire shattered the windscreen of the Leyland.

Bullets cracked from the hillside. Commandant O'Connell ran back to Collins's side; Dalton and Joe Dolan bolted from the armored car and lay breathless beside them.

The Republicans in the ambush party directed their main firepower at the men in the Crossley Tender. It was Collins they were after, but they might have to kill the others to get to him. The members of the ambush team who had left minutes before heard the shots and, startled, ran back down the road to help their comrades.

Collins looked around him, his blood pounding with the danger. They were in a vulnerable spot. Flat on their bellies, some distance from the armored car's protection, he and his men were pinned to the ground with no hope of reinforcements.

To their right the ground climbed steeply, cutting them off from escape. To the left open marshland and a stream made retreat unlikely. Behind them lay the ridge where the ambush party waited.

For nearly thirty minutes they held their own with no advantage taken on either side; then came a lull in the firing. Collins, knowing the hopelessness of their position if they could not gain more advantageous ground, got cautiously to his feet in hopes of moving to a better position. Using the armored car for protection, and firing to cover his own dash from relative safety, he began his move. Shots followed him from the hillside.

" 'The Big Fellow's' down!" someone shouted. Shocked beyond action, Collins's men ceased firing. Realizing something important had happened, but not knowing what, the Republicans intensified their attack.

Sean O'Connell crawled through the hail of bullets to Mick's side and whispered a desperate Act of Contrition in the dying man's ear.

Dalton screamed to his men to increase their fire. O'Connell, dragging Collins's body with him, crawled for the protection of the armored car.

Firing slackened. Then stopped. The ambush party melted into the terrain and were gone.

"It's a desperate, deadly-looking place, isn't it?" whispered O'Connell hoarsely to no one in particular as he knelt beside Collins's body in the gloom of the battle's debris.

It was nearly dark. To the little group of desolate men huddled in the Beal na mBlath roadside, it seemed even darker.

The message from Seaneen had been short and to the point. The courier had overtaken Tahg on the road toward Macroom. "There's talk of killing 'the Big Fellow,' " it said. "West Cork. Beware."

Tahg raced the car as fast as it would go along the dusty, pockmarked road. No wonder his hackles had been bristling all day. Something ominous and oppressive had been gnawing at his gut ever since the strange nightmare had awakened him the night before.

A great bird of prey, there had been in the dream; a raven black as pitch with blood-red drops on his beak. It had alighted on a golden harp and dripped red gore on its ancient strings.

"There's blood on the harp!" someone had gasped in the dream, a woman's voice, clear as an angel's it had been, but disembodied.

"Ah, no!" another voice had cried piteously. "Not blood on the harp. Not again." And then there had been a great whoosh of wings, and a raven a thousand times the size of the first had swooped down and snatched the bleeding harp in its talons and carried it off. A terrible eerie keening sound, high-pitched and not of this sphere, had been ringing still in Tahg's ears when he'd awakened.

It had been a warning. If only he was not too late to get Mick to turn back.

He careened around the desolate turns in the valley of Beal na mBlath, finally finding the spot where the Crossley Tender sat like a disabled animal, across the road, the men standing around it or kneeling beside someone on the road.

Tahg screeched his car to a halt and, leaping out, ran to the knot of men.

Spotting O'Connell, he shouted, "Where's the Big Fellow?" as he ran. The others looked away and O'Connell pointed wordlessly to the ground. Then he saw him, crumpled and lifeless. One arm was bent at an obscene angle and his legs were spread out like a child's in sleep.

Heartbroken, Tahg knelt beside his friend. There was a gaping hole near Mick's left ear; blood and brain matter were scattered on the ground beneath him. Collins's eyes were wide and staring, glazed with the astonishment of death.

With infinite tenderness, Tahg closed the lids over the accusing eyes and touched his friend's cheek reverently before he drew away his hand. The cheek was still warm to the touch, but it was a lifeless warmth.

"Has anyone said the Act of Contrition for him?" he asked, his voice ragged with rage and tears.

"I did," said O'Connell. Seeing the anguish in Tahg's face, he started to explain.

"It was an ambush. We told him to stay down, but you know the general. He kept moving around, taking chances . . ."

"Enough!" shouted Tahg in a thunderous voice that stopped the man. "I know what happened," he said. "I know what the murdering bastards did to him!"

Oh, Mick, Mick, Mick! Tahg cried out inside himself. Why did you let them do it? Why did you let the lousers win?

Gently he unfolded Collins's hands from the crumpled position into which they had fallen. For a long time he knelt beside him silently. Finally he took out his handkerchief to cover the oozing wound and, putting one hand beneath the man's knees and another under his shoulders, he struggled to lift him off the ground. The dead weight of a two-hundred-pound man is not an easy burden to raise.

"Here, let me help you move him," cried Dalton.

"No!" Tahg spat the word gruffly. "I'll carry him."

Lifting his fallen comrade in his arms, Tahg carried him to the armored car and, placing him reverently on the seat, sat with Mick's damaged head on his lap all the way back to Cork, oblivious of the blood and ruin.

"They'll never shoot me in my own county!" Collins had joked with him at Seaneen's cottage. "We should have known better than that, Mick," Tahg murmured to the corpse in his arms. "Put an Irishman on a spit and you'll find two more to turn him," Seaneen had said cynically. "We have a damnable tendency to destroy our own." And Tahg had thought it too harsh an appraisal.

"Oh, Mick, Mick, Mick! We owed you so much better than this." Tahg said the words aloud, and the driver of the car, glancing self-consciously into the rearview mirror, saw O'Connor, with his arms wrapped round his ravaged friend, crying unashamedly.

Tahg cast about in his mind for some token of his to leave with Collins before they laid him to his final rest. He wished there were something symbolic and personal . . . some part of himself that Mick would have appreciated.

He had so little of his own, Tahg thought absently. No jewelry but his father's watch—it didn't seem right to part with that. But neither did it seem right to let Mick be buried without some token of their friendship.

The corpse lay in its Volunteer uniform in the coffin, still on the catafalque, where it had lain in state. The wounded head had been repaired, so that Sir John Lavery could paint a last portrait; the big body was in repose. There were combat ribbons on his chest, befitting a general killed in the line of duty. He looked both the fallen chief and a handsome young warrior dead too soon, thought Tahg sadly. The other mourners had left and he was once again alone with Mick. This time would be the last.

Staring at the medals, the idea came to him. Tahg reached into his wallet and withdrew the tattered blue ribbon Angelica had given him so many years before.

Walking to the side of the coffin, he unfastened the pocket over Collins's left breast, intending to tuck the tiny ribbon into its depths—then changed his mind.

"She'd want you to carry her colors, Mick," he said aloud to his friend. "She'd want you to carry her love with you, wherever you're bound." He patted the cold hands and tucked the frayed ribbon in between them. "Mine, too, old friend."

Then he turned and walked quickly from the room. Somehow, he didn't want to be there when they closed the coffin lid; he didn't think he could bear it.

The Final Hosting

In a quiet watered land, a land of roses,
Stands Saint Kiernan's city fair;
And the warriors of Erin, in their famous
generations
Slumber there.

There they laid to rest the seven Kings
of Tara,
There the sons of Cairbre sleep—
Battle banners of the Gael, that on
Kiernan's plain of crosses
Now their final hosting keep . . .

ANGUS O'GRIEVE
(translated by T. W. Rolleston)

38   ∞ "They've killed Mick." Tahg said the awful words raspingly, as if they stuck in his throat. "The bloody bastards ambushed him."

Seaneen's head came up slowly, a look of curious recognition in his expression. "There's not so much danger in a known foe as in a suspected friend," he replied bitterly. "He was a dead man the day he signed the Treaty, Tahg. He was a fool to let Dev give him the dirty end of the stick . . . but he was a damned fine soldier, in his own way."

"He was my friend," said Tahg, and Seaneen recognized the note in his voice that said "Tread lightly."

He nodded, understanding. "There'll be no stopping the bitterness of the civil war now, lad," he said, his voice kind and weary.

"And which side will you be on?" Tahg sounded angry.

"Ireland's side, Tahg, as I've always been. You can't do business with Englishmen—but the people are weary of war. I'm not sure the land can take a further battering. We may have to be satisfied with the scraps from their table," Seaneen replied, and Tahg saw suddenly how worn he looked. Old, and tired of the long fight.

"And you?"

"I don't like either side, if you must know," answered Tahg bitterly. "I wouldn't follow Dev to a dogfight, and I also know there was no way to get more than Collins got for us. If Mick hadn't signed, they'd have declared all-out war. He had no choice at all."

Seaneen nodded. "The old war-horses like me will have our work cut out for us in the days to come, Tahg. I'll try to convince them that 'the doing of evil, to avoid an evil, cannot be good.' "

"Maybe history will show us the right and wrong of it," Tahg said bitterly.

"Ah, laddie," replied Seaneen. "And what are the histories of the world but lies?"

"How could they have done it to him, Seaneen?" asked Tahg suddenly, his voice anguished.

"I read a verse once, long ago, Tahg Mor," replied Seaneen. "I can't remember where it came from, but it stuck with me. It said:

> 'For those who fain would teach the world,
> The world holds hate and fee . . .
> For Socrates the hemlock cup
> For Christ, Gethsemane.' "

Tahg looked once eloquently at Seaneen, admiration, sorrow, heartsickness in the glance. He shook his head, as if to say he couldn't speak more of it without being betrayed by his own emotions. He cleared his throat in an effort at control and spoke again.

"And Johnny? What of him?"

"Oh, the lad would pay money to get into a fight, wouldn't he? Wherever the worst of it is, he'll be. No talent for peace, that one. None at all. He'll be on the other side from his father this time."

It was what we had both feared for our son, I thought, listening to the two men. There would be no holding Johnny's vengeful nature now.

"I want out, Seaneen." Tahg said the words soberly, and

Seaneen cocked his head to one side, as if listening to more than had been said.

"How far out?" he asked.

"Totally," Tahg answered firmly. "Out of the killing. Out of the politics. Out of Ireland, if need be. At least for a while. Mick was the war for me, Seaneen. His death has shown me the futility of it all.

"There's no end to the sorrows of this blighted place, man! I don't want to devote my whole life to Ireland, only to be shot in the head for it by a man who was once my friend.

"I'm no coward, Seaneen. I've killed my share. But it's over for me. I'm getting out while there's still the hope for life and love in the world. I'm sick to death over what they did to Mick, and what they'll do to Ireland now."

"You've got a plan?"

"I'd like safe passage to go home to FitzGibbon Hall, long enough to make what arrangements I can for its safety. It'll probably be burned down by my friends, if not by my enemies, and a lot of people's livelihoods depend on the old place." He took a deep breath, then said, "I'm going to ask Kitty to marry me, although I've little hope she'll say yes."

"You're a dead man if you stay in Ireland." Seaneen said the words in such a way that there was no question of their accuracy.

"I know. I thought I'd go to New York and lie low for a while; this madness must come to an end sooner or later."

"They'll call you a coward and worse," said Seaneen evenly.

"Aye, that they will."

Seaneen nodded. "I can get you safe passage for a week, no more. After that you're on your own keeping."

Tahg clapped a hand on Seaneen's shoulder gratefully.

"You're the only one whose respect I care about, Seaneen," he said, his voice full of emotion. "Do you think me a coward, too?"

Seaneen pursed his lips, as he sometimes did when weighing an important decision. Finally, he spoke.

"We have a lousy habit in Ireland of sending our best into banishment and betraying the ones who stay.

"I'm an old man, Tahg Mor. Grown old in the service of Ireland. But I've lived long enough to know it sometimes takes more courage to live than to die. 'It's better to turn back from the middle of the ford than be drowned in the flood,' my father used to say to me, and when I was younger I didn't understand. Now I'm old enough to know that no matter who succeeds or fails, the peacemaker always gets fucked." He shook his head regretfully at the thought, and then continued:

"Scattering is easier than gathering, lad. We'll need men like you alive when this is over, to help with the gathering, if there's ever to be an Ireland free.

"You know, I've been thinking lately about what Horace said about freedom. Oh, but those old Greeks were wise to all our human follies, weren't they? He said, 'Who then is free? Who but the man who commands himself.' You can go command yourself, Tahg Mor O'Connor, and you can take my blessing with you . . . and my respect."

I stood with tears of gratitude in my eyes, near to the man I loved. I think I have never been prouder of him than in that one moment.

Tahg and we took our leave of each other. The next time I saw him was on one of the saddest days of my life. ✑

39 Tahg reread the letter from the solicitor outlining his inheritance. FitzGibbon Hall, the tenant farms, the fishing rights, the strand, the fens. He had spoken of it to no one but Aunt Beth and Angelica since Desmond's death five years before.

How ludicrous it would have been for an IRA man to own just the kind of estate the men of the Brotherhood were burning down all over Ireland. Provided, of course, that they hadn't already been burned by the other side in reprisal for some attacked garrison.

Aunt Beth had seen to everything at the Hall for him as an interim measure. Well, the interim would soon be over for him now.

If things went the way he hoped when he asked Kitty to marry him, there'd be reason to put down roots in such a place as FitzGibbon Hall. If not . . . there'd be no need for permanency anywhere.

Tahg knocked on the dressing-room door and waited for admittance. He hoped she'd be alone.

Kitty opened the door and stared at him, disbelieving. She had thought him on the run, somewhere near Cork.

"My God!" she said, pulling him hastily into the room and shutting the door. "What if anyone sees you? Man, you're *wanted* by them! There's a price on your head."

"I've come to ask you to marry me," Tahg said simply, and she began to speak but he put his fingers to her lips to stop her.

"Hear me out, Kitty, before you answer me. Mick's dead. They've killed him."

"Oh my God! Who?" she gasped.

"The IRA, his own friends probably, before the bloody Treaty played its havoc with them. It's all over for me, Kitty. I'm getting out."

She stared at him incredulously; then, realizing that they were both still standing at the doorway, she took his hand and led him to the tiny love seat that was strewn, as always, with discarded clothes. Pushing the debris aside absently, she pulled him down beside her.

"You'd really leave the Organization?"

"Aye," he said, his voice deadly serious. "Mick was the Organization for me. If they could do this to him, I want no part of them. No part of the interminable bloodshed, either. We're in it for fair now—if the civil war we've had so far wasn't bad enough, now we'll have worse.

"I've come to ask you, Kitty . . . if I give it up, will you come away with me and be my wife?"

"Where would we go?"

"Somewhere saner. America, maybe. Eventually Sligo, if this bloody mess ever comes to an end. Somewhere to build a life. To live and love each other and have children. To somehow escape this bloody sacrificial insanity I've been caught up in all my life. Kitty, will you come with me?"

Kitty's mind was in a turmoil—how could she possibly go? How could she leave the theater and all her hopes? How could she abandon her dream?

On the other hand, some voice seemed to argue back, how could she live without this man? This strong, kind man who would give her enough love to fill the ocean of need in her. But would it be enough to keep the need for "things" at bay? Could she really marry someone other than Tahg, just to be rich? Could she really sell herself for a mess of pottage, as Merry had warned her?

"My God, Tahg! I'm so confused. I never expected this . . ."

"I told you when it was over, I was coming back for you."

"But it isn't over, not now. You never said when . . . I never thought you'd really do it."

He stood up wearily and said, "I'm leaving tomorrow, Kitty. With or without you. I hope to God you come with me. And Bridgie, too, if you like. We'll take her, too. I have more than enough love for both of you. I'm going back to the Hall on the twelve-thirty train tomorrow. I've got to see the old place once more before I go. After that, there'll be no way to find me." He turned and headed toward the door.

"And, Kitty, my own love . . ." he said without turning around as he reached it. "Whatever you decide, I want you to know . . . I'll understand."

Kitty stood rooted where she had risen from the love seat. Her hand moved involuntarily to her mouth, where it remained as if a deterrent to speech. She nodded dumbly at Tahg's retreating back, not knowing what to say, not sure her voice could say anything at all without breaking.

For minutes after he had gone, she stood in the same position, the weight of her heart having turned her to stone.

"But why on earth didn't you tell her about your inheritance, Tahg?" asked Angelica agitatedly, looking at her dejected and heartsore cousin as he sat in the drawing room of her house. It was long past midnight; the late-night stillness in the street outside seemed to underscore the unseemliness of the hour when he had come knocking at her door.

"Because of you," he said simply.

"And what exactly does that mean?" she asked with exasperation. "I'll be damned if I'll let you share the blame for this folly with me!"

"You had the courage not to marry Derek because he didn't love you *enough!* I must find the courage to let go of Kitty if she doesn't love me enough. FitzGibbon Hall and the inheritance are only accidents, Angel. They might sway her, but they don't have to do with *me* and what she feels for me. I must *know* what she feels. Don't you see? Finally, after all the years, I must know."

Defeated, Angelica nodded, understanding it all too well.

"Agonizing, isn't it?" she said, more than asked. "You wish so much that they'd be their better selves and come through for you, don't you?" He nodded glumly, and she could see the misery so plainly in his hunched-up shoulders that she wanted to cry.

"On the other hand," she said quickly, while still sure of her voice, "in this case, I don't know that you've made the right decision. You know she loves you, Tahg—there's never been a question about that. You know she has this obsessive need to escape poverty. And who in God's name could blame her for that? Thus far, I haven't seen one damned thing poverty has to recommend it, to be honest with you. And who can say Kitty isn't within her rights to use all her resources to better her lot? More power to her that she knows what she wants, and has tried so hard to get it.

"Now here you are with the wherewithal to offer her everything she's ever dreamed of, and you won't even tell her you've got it! You know there aren't many men who wouldn't use what they can provide for a girl as a cogent argument on their own behalf." She smiled indulgently at her cousin. "I think you've been unduly influenced by that song your mother always sang about the Whistling Gypsy!"

Tahg laughed aloud at that, just as she'd meant him to.

"You're absolutely right, as always, Angel," he said, "but nonetheless I do need to know how she feels about *me*, not about my inheritance. I've seen too much of life and death in the last few years to have any illusions about what fate can provide in the way of happiness. And I've seen Aunt Beth and Seaneen's love for each other in a cottage that the gatekeeper at Manningham Castle would disdain to inhabit. I *want* that, Angel! I want that kind of love or . . . I guess I'll settle for not having any. The disappointment would be too terrible if we married and she bolted at the first sign of rough weather. I've seen how it is with men and women who love each other. They can survive anything because of it."

"I have the horrid thought that you and I may take our high-flown principles into a lonely old age, my dear Tahg Mor," Angelica replied with a short laugh, but it had a rueful sound.

"And then on the other hand," she amended her thought before he could reply, "we may live to find the unicorns we seek —and wouldn't we have the last laugh then, my friend?"

He walked to her chair and, bending, put his arms around her. They held each other wordlessly for a moment, then Tahg left her, to return to his flat to pack his few belongings for the journey home.

Kitty sat, stunned by Tahg's words, incapable of movement. So the moment of truth had come at last for them. In a way it was a relief.

Hastily she finished taking off her makeup. She dressed distractedly, ran a brush feverishly through her hair and left the theater.

The cold air felt bracing, life-giving, after the closeness of the old hall. She had to think, had to go home. This would be the most important decision of her life. Sweet Jesus, why didn't she know what to do?

Kitty stood back for a moment and stared at the old theater —she could see the poster with her own face glittering in the lights under the marquee. Could she really give it up? Was that what Tahg wanted her to do? Give up everything she'd dreamed of, hoped for, struggled to get and finally gotten? Or was it just the peripheral appendages of what she'd gotten that he wanted her to leave behind—the fawning men and their proposals of marriage.

He'd said he was giving up the Organization. Would he really do it? Would he even be allowed to do so and live? They couldn't stay in Ireland, that was certain—not until this bloody mess was over, anyway.

Kitty pulled her fur-trimmed wrap closer to her throat and face. This was one moment when she didn't want to be recognized. She just wanted to go home and think. About the haunted look in the man's eyes as he had made her his offer— about the strong dark shape of him filling the doorframe, asking her to be his wife . . . about what she could lose if she said no.

All her life Tahg had been there, somewhere near or far, but he had been there for her. When friends had rejected her or poverty had weighed her down, he had buoyed her spirits and kept her going. She had always known that his love could be relied on. Even when she'd pushed him away and gone to other men's beds to search for what she needed, she'd known that he understood and would forgive.

She had not planned to marry him . . . had not planned to have his children, nurse his wounds, listen to his problems, hold him in the dark times. And yet somewhere deep within her those images slumbered—as if some miracle would free the two of them from the bondage that kept them separate. Somehow he would be free of the Organization's terrors and rich enough to give them the comforts she craved, and then . . . then it would be time for the slumbering images to become reality.

"No!" she said aloud to herself as she fumbled for her latchkey. "No, Kitty, my girl! Those are childish fantasies. He will never be rich and may never be safe. What you must decide today is whether you want him just the way he is—that's what he finally wants to know—and isn't it about time that he asked you the question? Do you love him enough to go with him, just the way he is? Or are you willing to let go of him? Forever."

She let herself into the darkened flat hoping Merry might be there. Dear, gentle, sensible Merry always knew how to help her sort things through.

Poor Merry, so shattered by the rape. No easy laughter bubbled to her lips these days. God curse the rotten bastards who had hurt them so! God curse the whole stupid mess of a country that let such things happen to people.

She tried never to think of the rape . . . tried hard to contain those hated visions that would rise up like bile at unexpected moments to undermine her confidence. Tahg had understood her horror. He had held her through the nights when she would wake screaming, choking, gasping for breath. He had cajoled her into his waiting arms; gentling, kissing, wiping away the hurtful tears.

"Cry, sweetheart," he had said over and over to her, in the bad times. "Cry it all out, my love. It's right for you to cry over what was done to you."

So she had cried in his arms and he had supplied an endless stream of handkerchiefs. He had stayed with her when he was well enough to come to her, despite Mick's many summonses, despite the war, despite everything; and each time he'd said he wouldn't leave her until she could handle his going.

How could she ever repay that tenderness? How could she live without that kind of love, once having known it? Would all the money and social position in the world make any difference if she married someone else who would not hold her through the bad times? For there would be bad times. Life let no one off scot free.

Kitty lay on her bed fully dressed and began to cry. "Cry it out, sweetheart," Tahg had said to her a thousand times, holding her in the protective circle of his strength. Wishing he were there to hold her now, Kitty curled herself into a miserable ball and cried herself to sleep.

Tahg's eyes searched the crowd at the station, not daring to let himself hope: 12:26, it said on his watch. Only minutes left before the train would leave.

He would have to be on the alert. Who could say at this point if his own comrades were already after him?

Seaneen had promised him the time to go home to the Hall, to see if any damage had been done there during the recent local raids; after that, if he decided not to go back to the IRA, he'd be marked for death.

Red hair glinting in the sunlight caught his eye. He strained to see if it could be Kitty. Jesus, Mary and Joseph, there they were! Despite the green velvet beret that kept it partially from view, that hair could be no one's but Kitty's. She was hurrying toward him, dodging the passengers, Bridgie's small legs nearly flying over the platform in an effort to keep pace.

"Thank you, God," he whispered under his breath as he pushed his way toward them through the train station crowd. "Thank you, God!"

"As you can see, I've made up my mind," she said breathlessly as they reached him. "You've got us for better or for worse. And believe me, Tahg O'Connor, I can't guarantee that it's not the worse you'll get! I'm confused and scared to death and I don't want to give up the theater . . ."

"You don't need to," he interjected hurriedly, but she didn't stop.

"And I'm going to hate being poor and I'll probably complain all the time . . ."

"You won't need to be poor either," he said, smiling.

"Do you hear that, Bridgie?" said Kitty to the child. "The

man's daft, absolutely daft; are you sure we should throw in our lot with him?"

"I'm sure," said the child with conviction, and Kitty finally stopped talking because Tahg had scooped them both up in his arms and was hugging them, crushing them, kissing them, loving them all at once. People all around them on the train platform were staring or pointing.

"I love you, Kitty O'Neill," Tahg was saying over and over. "You'll not regret this, girl!"

"By God, I hope not," she answered back. "But we're making a spectacle of ourselves at the moment, so if you don't mind, let's get on the train before they have us arrested." She tried to sound exasperated, but Tahg could hear the laughter in her throaty voice.

Tahg bundled them aboard the train. He had taken a first-class compartment in the hopes that they would appear; there was so much to say, and all of it private. He had rationalized the act by telling himself that if they didn't come it would be a safeguard against being seen.

"What are you doing wasting money on a compartment?" asked Kitty wonderingly as they settled themselves for the ride.

"It's all right, Kitty my love," Tahg replied joyously. "Everything in life is perfectly all right!" The elation in his voice made her want to hug him. Whatever happened next, it was glorious to be loved so much.

"What did you mean, I won't have to give up the theater?" she asked suspiciously as she helped Bridgie out of her little coat and settled the child happily at the window.

"I've no quarrel with your acting, Kitty. It's a part of you and I love all the parts. Once we're married you can act to your heart's content. If you're not too busy with other things, of course," he said mischievously.

"And what other things, might I ask?" Kitty looked at him queerly.

"Things like being the mistress of a great house . . . you know it isn't easy to keep an estate like ours in shipshape. And there are social obligations of all sorts to contend with . . ."

"What in God's name are you talking about, Tahg Mor? Have you gone mad?" she said, this time with real exasperation.

Tahg leaned across the seat and took Kitty's hand in his own before he replied.

"Will you marry me, Kitty?" he said very solemnly.

"You know I will or I wouldn't have come, you idiot!" she said fiercely. "But what *are* you talking about?"

"My Uncle Desmond, whom I loved very much, as you know, left me FitzGibbon Hall and the rest of his inheritance when he was executed.

"I never told you because I wasn't sure I'd live to enjoy it . . . and I didn't want you to marry me because I had the estate." He looked determined but sheepish as he said it. "I promised myself that if you turned me down, I'd sell the damned thing and go to America."

Kitty looked so incredulous that it almost made the man laugh. "You're telling me the truth?" she whispered.

"Aye, lass. I'm telling you the truth."

"What's FitzGibbon Hall?" asked Bridgie. But Kitty and Tahg were in each other's arms, engaged in the kind of kiss that makes speech quite impossible, so the little girl turned back to the window, smiling, and watched the city buildings whiz by.

They were going to be a family now. Just as she'd always dreamed they would. She could tell.

40   As everyone knows, the remainder of the civil war was a bloodbath of epic proportion. The people had voted pro-Treaty—they wanted peace. Yet the dissidents had strength enough to cause a full-scale war that lasted well into 1923. Brother against brother, it was—father against son, former comrades murdering each other as if under righteous dispensation from God Almighty to do so.

Johnny, called Sean by his comrades, joined the dissidents, splitting openly with his father. The fact that we'd seen it coming didn't mitigate the pain of the parting. My son remained with the most violent wing of the IRA for the balance of the war; we heard tales of his escapades, violence heaped upon violence.

Seaneen's moderate voice won him as many enemies in the last months of 1922 as he'd had friends before. Although we didn't know it at the time, a group of Republican leaders took it into their heads to issue a death order for the most influential of the moderate leaders.

Seaneen's name was on the assassination list. ✍

Johnny pushed his foot to the floorboard and felt the battered automobile leap forward. There might still be time to warn Seaneen! The execution order had gone out only hours before. Christ Almighty, how could they order the death of a man like his father? Was the whole world gone insane?

His parents were at their cottage in Tipperary; it shouldn't take more than an hour to reach there if he wasn't stopped. There were men around them most times, he knew. Except at night when they wanted privacy; there was only one man on duty outside the cottage at night. The assassin would know that. And one man's protection can be breached.

Cursing the arbitrary order to execute the Free State leaders, Johnny careened around the last corner and saw the familiar whitewashed cottage in the distance, with an audible sigh of relief. What memories that place held for him! It was the only happy home he'd ever known. It looked peaceful enough, he thought as he pulled the Ford to a halt.

With habit, born of a life in danger, Johnny parked the car in the trees at the foot of the hill and began to pick his way cautiously up the road. Strange, he thought, the sentry should have spotted him by now. Instinct made him reach stealthily for his gun.

"Don't try it, Manningham," a voice behind him cut the darkness.

"The name's O'Sullivan," he replied, forcing his own heartbeat to quiet.

"Manningham or O'Sullivan," replied the voice, "I can't let you warn them. There's still time to leave, Sean—this isn't your affair."

"That's my father you're after, Stephen," Sean replied, having placed the voice. "I'll not let you kill him."

"And how are you planning to stop me?" asked Stephen, but too late. Sean spun around and hurled himself in the direction of the assassin, pulling his gun from its place as he went. He knew the inevitable shots would rouse the sleepers. There was no other way.

* * *

⟡ Seaneen and I were wakened by the sharp crack of gunfire. Seaneen automatically groped for his gun, years of sleeping on the run momentarily outweighing his sightlessness. It had seemed we heard two shots and then silence.

I threw a shawl over my nightgown and moved cautiously to the window. As there had been no further gunfire after the first shots, it seemed safe enough to do so.

"What do you see?" Seaneen whispered urgently.

"Two bodies—not twenty feet from the house," I whispered back, puzzled. Where was our sentry, and whose bodies could they be?

I heard men running, then recognized the voices of our own men startled from nearby houses by the gunfire.

It was some minutes before we knew the terrible truth.

By some benevolent stroke of perverse fate, Tahg appeared at our door the following morning. He and Kitty had returned from America a few days before, he told me; as the newspaper he worked for in New York was convinced that the war in Ireland was ending, they had sent him home to cover the story.

He had left Kitty at FitzGibbon Hall to see to the damage there; but he'd had a firm conviction that something was wrong with Seaneen and me—so, true to his instincts, he'd gotten into a car and headed for Tipperary.

Thus it was that by the grace of God my sister's son was with me at the moment of Johnny's final journey home.

I remember standing by the body of my son as if I had been turned to granite, Tahg's hand strong in mine, the undertaker's voice reverberating in my ear.

"What is the boy's name, madame?" he asked me for a second time, or perhaps a third, by the sound of his exasperation. "I must have his name for the headstone."

My heart stood still in some suspension of all life and thought. "What *was* his name?" I asked myself like a sleepwalker waked too early. Dear God, what was the name of this last child of my body and heart? Johnny or Sean? Manningham or O'Sullivan? How could I have robbed my son of his very name, who was now robbed of his life? Or . . . had I anything to do with his strange destiny at all?

"I'm not sure," I answered, barely recognizing my own voice, and I saw the man look closely at me to see if I were mad.

"Her Ladyship has had a terrible shock," I heard Tahg say. "Let me speak to her alone for a moment."

The undertaker nodded and left, shaking his head as if to say never, never in his long life had he spoken with a bereaved mother who knew not the name of her son.

"You must sit down, Aunt." Tahg's deep voice was gentle, and he led me to a chair as if I were a child.

"You understand?" I asked, knowing that he did. He nodded.

"He was Sean to all his comrades, Aunt. Sean O'Sullivan . . . like his father."

"I know," I replied, still confused in my heartsickness. "He loved his father more than life, Tahg. . . . But if he's buried with a different name from the one he was born with, it will be as if he never existed. He was born John Manningham . . ." I heard the anguish in my own voice and could not say more.

"An accident only, dear Aunt," Tahg answered gently, and I marveled at his ability to think rationally after all he, too, had endured. "It was naught but fate's accident that you and Seaneen weren't man and wife."

I nodded, blinking back my tears. How could it be that there were still tears in me, after all that had been shed? How could it be that this child of my heart could be gone forever? And that the little boy, Tahg, whom I'd cradled in my arms so short a time ago, should be grown so wise and gracious? But then again, I told myself as he left to find the undertaker, how could he not be so . . . for wasn't he Con and Tierney's son?

Thus the child who was born John Manningham was buried Sean O'Sullivan, in the FitzGibbon family plot, with all the others of my line who had died too soon. "May he be our last sacrifice for Ireland," I prayed, as I stood at his gravesite. And, indeed, he was.

Seaneen and I lived many happy years together after the war, but we never forgot our son or ceased to mourn him. In truth, his passing was an inconsolable sorrow for his father, who had taught him the arts of war that finally brought him down. I tried to comfort Seaneen, when I was strong enough, by telling him that the seeds of destruction in Johnny had been sown long before that final moment—that the only real happiness the boy had ever known in his life was in the love he'd shared with his father. Yet, I would find Seaneen often at the boy's grave in later years, when we had moved back to Sligo. He could not see the words cut on the stone clearly, but he knew them nonetheless:

> And the King was much moved, and went up to the chamber over the gate and wept, and as he went, this he said, "O my son Absalom, my son, my son, Absalom! Would God I had died for thee, O Absalom my son, my son!"

Epilogue

∾ There are those who will say that what I've written here does a disservice to Edmond Manningham's memory and to my own honor. There are those who may even say I've invaded my sister's privacy in telling so intimately her story and Tierney's to a world that perhaps need not have known so much. So I feel I must in fairness try to explain to you my motivations.

Life, it seems to me from the vantage point of my advanced age, is no more than a series of lessons to be learned or taught. A strange and remarkable adventure . . . and a love story, if we are among the favored of the gods. Thus, it appears no more than right to pass on the lessons we learn and the tale of our loves to the next generation, in whose hands I will leave this document. If any beyond our family should become privy to its tale, you may assume that our progeny, Con's and mine, chose to share the legacy they have inherited.

I am, today, seventy-six years of age—long past the agonies and questionings, the loves and lusts, of my youth . . . and yet, by God, I swear to you that what stands out from all of what I've chronicled here, and all of what I've learned, is the importance of the love stories. Con's and Tierney's, Seaneen's and mine, Tahg's and Kitty's, the others, too. And the fruits of those loves—the children and the poetry—are all that matters when the wheat is finally winnowed from the chaff.

I have no doubt that Con and Tierney would have agreed to share the story of their love, as did Seaneen before he died. For, in these latter curious days, the young have need to know that such can be.

As to Edmond—he was a good man at the end of it, and an accomplished one. Strangely enough, I believe he would not have quarreled with the way I have portrayed him.

Make no mistake about it, I know that in my infidelity I did my husband a great wrong. But as God is my witness, I know not how I could have done otherwise and fulfilled my own destiny. I do not seek to mitigate my blame in saying this, but rather to explain that as the years run on and you are able to look back on an expanse of them, you begin to see patterns and designs to the fabric of your life that you did not notice in the living. Another hand than ours weaves the pattern from the tangled threads, I believe . . . to what end I am not certain. The only purpose I am able to imagine is that of love and learning and the eventual acquisition of wisdom.

Is this enough in return for all that we suffer, you may ask? And I would reply that I think it is enough.

For Edmond, whom I did not love, I was the instrument of his learning to be human. For Seaneen, whom I loved with every fiber of my heart, I was the instrument of both his doom and his salvation. Riddle me that one, O wise men, if you can, as Padraig Pearse would have said. Riddle me that.

You have every right to wonder what became of all of us after the war was done, as eventually it was. So I will tell you:

Angelica married an American. A robust laughing man, who somehow took her infirmity in stride, as if it were no more than a minor inconvenience. He was very tall and strong, from an astonishing family that having been poor had become rich, and now had turned its hand to politics. He carried her about with him as easily as if she were a sparrow with an injured wing.

She taught him statesmanship and he taught her how to laugh. It was a lovely, love-filled marriage and produced three children, who are grown now, of course, whom I see only on the occasion of their rare trips to Manningham Castle for a holiday.

Merry married a peer, but not so happily. She was so damaged by the rape and her rejection by Christopher that I believe she married the first man after that who asked her. It may be fancy on my part, but I think she never felt a whole person after her separation from Jamie. They adored each other always, of course, but their lives took them in differing directions, as adult lives tend to do—and for her, I believe that was an insurmountable loss.

She divorced her first husband, after bitter litigation, and pursued her career for some years before finally marrying a playwright who has since become quite famous. They've lived contentedly, it seems, in London for the better part of a lifetime.

Owing to Winston's death, Jamie, of course, inherited the earldom when Edmond died. He led a scholarly life, and many of his ideas came to fruition in an organization called Amnesty International, which was founded long after his death. He never married, but seemed to me always more than content with his lot and, for the most part, happy. Although he, like Merry, seemed to miss the close bond of twinship they had once shared. Perhaps neither ever found true happiness apart from the other.

Tahg and Kitty's marriage has been something to behold! Each got precisely what he or she wanted . . . she became a great lady and he got the woman he'd loved so long, to wife.

It appears to all that she's led him a merry chase—I've never seen anyone enjoy the fruits of being rich with as much gusto as Kitty O'Connor. She travels, she entertains, she is always followed by the press. She raised her children as if they lived at Buckingham Palace, and has played the role of mistress of Fitz-Gibbon Hall with all the zestful talent she displayed on the stage.

Tahg settled in to being a country gentleman, as if to the manner born. He became a writer, or course, as one might have expected from the son of such parents; and he is accepted by many as the leading chronicler of Ireland's rebellious history and as a journalist of note.

I've heard others titter about how Kitty runs rings around her quiet husband, doing as she pleases with never a thought for his wishes, but that is quite untrue. Anyone who knows them well knows that unlike as they are, they have that special *something* that keeps two people lovers for a lifetime. He has given her all she ever wanted . . . she has given him herself. It is enough for each, and more than enough.

Tahg and Kitty lived in America for the first year of their marriage, to escape the civil war. Kitty did well on the stage in New York, and Tahg worked quite happily for the *New York World*.

FitzGibbon Hall was partially destroyed by fire in their absence, but they restored it on their return. They also moved the bodies of our beloved dead from Glasnevin to the FitzGibbon churchyard, where now they all await my tardy arrival.

Although I set out to tell you the story of my beloved sister, I see that I have gone beyond that task.

Or perhaps there was no way to untangle us each from the other, and from our children. When one reaches my age, in fact, no one person seems entirely independent of the rest. It is not merely the sins of the fathers that continue from generation to generation, but the virtues as well. And the connections.

I see myself and Con now, immortal in our progeny. Which brings me full circle to where and how I began this history.

Why, you might ask yourself, having waited nearly four decades, did I set pen to paper now, to tell my tale? God knows there have been biographers and historians enough who have already done their best or worst for my sister, attributing to her motivations that she never had (you see, Dr. Freud has given everyone license to determine other people's motivations), recounting words she never spoke, painting her as everything from a fanatic or reprobate to a saint—any one of which would do her complex character an injustice.

There have been biographies of Con, of course. I read the first few, abandoned the rest in distaste and disappointment. I've always intended to set the record straight before I died, but the pain of reliving those ancient agonies deterred me. And having escaped death so inadvertently on that terrible long-ago night, I always expected that fate would somehow doom me to a ripe old age. So I felt that there was time.

Then came the conversation with the children—teenagers, they are called now, a sobriquet that allows children the latitude to relinquish membership in the human race for eight years before becoming adults.

I caught Jenny and David in the library discussing Con; their great-aunt she would have been, of course.

"She was some kind of a twitty martyr," said the boy.

"Probably a masochist," agreed the girl knowledgeably.

"I guess you're right. Probably had some kind of a death wish. You know, my teacher says the whole bloody lot of them in Easter Week wanted to die. They were only looking for some kinky way to get their brains blown out."

I stood terribly still for a long breathless moment, listening. Could we have fallen so low in only three generations? Could these arrogant, know-it-all children be of her seed and mine? Could they know so little of nobility? Suddenly all the world's ills seemed embodied in these two ignorant babies, and I was forced to speak.

"She was the noblest person I've ever known," I said, trying to keep my voice steady. "In a time of heroes, she found a very special place in history."

They looked at each other sheepishly, then David, the bolder, rebutted.

"My teacher says there are no such things as heroes. Just attention-seekers who use a cause to get their names in the papers."

"Then your teacher is wrong!" I said, meaning it. "He is so wrong that the world may come to an end because of people like him."

"What do you mean?" asked Jen, always impressed by vehemence.

"Ideals! Noble ideals, child, are the best of what we mortals can be! Striving to be better than we are is what separates us from the jungle cats. Heroism is a thing of the heart, not of the head. That's why your teacher doesn't know of it, I suspect.

" 'The only thing necessary for the triumph of evil is that good men do nothing.' A great man said that once and my sister understood it when she wasn't as old as you are now. Why, she ran off with Tierney when she was eighteen and he wrote the famous Wild Harp poems for her when she was in her thirties."

"They are beautiful," said Jen wistfully. "I read two of them in school."

"My teacher says they're sentimental and old-fashioned," offered David.

"Your teacher seems to have quite a lot to say about life, David. Do you ever question what he says?"

"Sure I do. I don't just accept stuff. I decide for myself."

I walked to the bookshelf nearest the window and tugged an old portfolio from its recesses. It contained the originals of the poems Tierney had written for Con in prison, which had made him famous. There were tears in my eyes when I handed them to Jen, and I saw that she was startled by that.

"Then read these," I told the children, "and judge for yourself what kind of woman might have inspired them . . . and what kind of man might have written them. And while you are doing so, ask yourself why one piece of work lives on and others settle into well-deserved obscurity. Ask yourself why people still read Tierney O'Connor's poetry and Con's Wild Harp essays, and what your teacher will leave behind him for history to remember."

I left the children and went to my room. About an hour later, Jenny stood in the doorway, obviously chastened, and said, "I'd like to know more about her, Grandmere. Would you tell me her story?"

And so I have. Her story, God rest her gently . . . and his and theirs . . . all gone now to wait the final hosting or to new bodies one and all.

I call to mind the words that are on her gravestone; I've loved them always, for they speak so optimistically of resurrection.

> Take your revenge now, O Empire!
> Wreck bodies you could not chain,
> Rip hearts you could not buy
> But the souls—Oh, you damn fools!
> The souls escape you and new bodies claim them.
> And, even, already their tramp is on the hills.

An Explanation

I've endeavored in my storytelling to be painstakingly accurate about the momentous historical events which form the background for my tale (with the possible exception of making William Butler Yeats's meeting with MacGregor Mathers several years later than it could actually have happened, and basing the episode of Con's being force-fed on a London incident of the time rather than a Dublin one for the sake of my story's sequence). But inasmuch as "events" are but a small part of the truth of what happens in any given time, I feel an explanation is in order.

My story is a biased one—written entirely from the point of view of the Irish, in a time of high passions and terrible struggle. It is not a history book and therefore does not explore both sides of a very complex problem which has repercussions even today.

Much has changed since the time I've chronicled and much remains the same. I would therefore like to suggest the books listed here to any reader interested in learning more about the people and the times.

Because of the appearance of Sean O'Casey, Eamon de Valera, Michael Collins, Padraig Pearse, James Connolly, etc., in *An Excess of Love,* along with the fictional characters, I have had to take the liberty of putting words into some very articulate historical mouths. I have tried to remain true to their personalities and characters in doing so, but where I have failed I wish the responsibility to be mine, not theirs. It is an awesome task to imagine what Sean O'Casey might have said to William Butler Yeats on a particular morning, I assure you.

Many who read this work will find a similarity in Constance FitzGibbon O'Connor to the real-life character of the Countess Markievicz (née Constance Gore-Booth), who is so well known to those who remember the story of Ireland's Troubles. Therefore I believe a few words of explanation are in order.

The Con in my story has a sister who is a writer, as did the Countess. My Con is a member of the Anglo-Irish Ascendency class, as was the Countess. My character is a leading figure in the Easter Rising. So has Con Markievicz gone down in history. There, I think those who know the Countess' history will say the resemblance ends.

My heroine's character and person are more similar to those of my own sister, Connacht Cash, than to anyone I've ever found in literature or in life. Indeed, much of my motivation for writing this story came from my desire to express in writing the extraordinary bond that can exist between sisters. An important truth that seems to have gotten lost in this age of sibling rivalry and other Freudian-permitted silly-business, is the knowledge that sisters can share a rare connection and friendship. I have sought, in my story, to say aloud that this is so.

I have been fascinated since childhood with the characters of the Gore-Booth sisters, whom Yeats immortalized in *Lissadell:* two wealthy young women who, each in her own way, chose a revolution rather than a life of Castle Seasons and luxurious insulation that was her birthright. I've wondered about their relationship with each other and about their curious place as activist women in a time when women, to be thought women, had to be passive and lacking in opinion. So I've used the fact that they existed as a jumping-off place for the invention of my own players.

If you are wondering why, then, I did not simply write a history of the times, the reason is this: I wanted to let certain characters live—against the backdrop of a turbulent time and the last poetic revolution—I wanted Con and Tierney and Beth and Seaneen and Edmond to play out their love stories. A rebel, a poet, a wife/mother, a revolutionary and an autocrat. All caught up in a moment in time that will never come again.

Thus, I hope that once you have taken into account that my characters have borrowed for the duration of this story the place of some others in history, you will see that the story is otherwise mine.

And, of course, theirs.

Cathy Cash Spellman

☐ **AN EXCESS OF LOVE**
  12394-1 .... $3.95

☐ **SO MANY PARTINGS**
  18066-X $4.95

☐ **PAINT THE WIND**
  20813-0 .... $5.95